ALSO BY DAVID L. GOLEMON

THE
MOUNTAIN

An Event Group Thriller

DAVID L. GOLEMON

St. Martin's Paperbacks

This is a work of fiction. All of the characters, organizations, and events portrayed in this novel are either produc-ts of the author's imagination or are used fictitiously.

THE MOUNTAIN

Copyright © 2015 by David L. Golemon.
Excerpt from *The Traveler* copyright © 2016 by David L. Golemon.

All rights reserved.

For information address St. Martin's Press, 175 Fifth Avenue, New York, NY 10010.

ISBN: 978-1-250-05765-5

Printed in the United States of America

St. Martin's Press hardcover edition / August 2015
St. Martin's Paperbacks edition / April 2016

St. Martin's Paperbacks are published by St. Martin's Press, 175 Fifth Avenue, New York, NY 10010.

10 9 8 7 6 5 4 3 2 1

For Valisa, Eunice, Steve, and Buck—
The members of my first EVENT . . .
I miss them beyond measure.

ACKNOWLEDGMENTS

To the extensive libraries of H. G. Wells and Edgar Rice Burroughs, so helpful to an author with some very strange questions.

Also, for Albert Einstein, someday they will prove that you were one of them all along!

PROLOGUE

History is a guide to navigation in perilous times. History is who we are and why we are the way we are.

—**David McCullough**

MESOPOTAMIA, THE TIGRESS AND EUPHRATES RIVERS (FIRST AGE OF MAN) 13,056 BCE

The family gathered as the sun broke free of the black, roiling clouds for the last time. All forty-two men, women, and children sat silently on bedding of wool and goatskin. The evening meal was a heavy one. A virtual feast compared to normal building days, for the great father had warned all who would listen that there would be many days of hunger ahead. Three goats and twenty fat, roasted goslings sat before the group untouched as the darkness and an uncommon cold reclaimed the world after their brief taste of sunshine. For many in the group that darkness brought on horrid visions of what was to come. The family of men grew silent as each one heard the same sounds emanating from the closed-off world outside.

It was a three-year-old great-granddaughter who broke the spell of silence when she began to cry. Her mother, only fourteen years of summers herself, was feeling the fear just like her daughter and all of those gathered around the meal that night. The young woman began to remove the child from the supper circle as others of the family averted their eyes.

"No, bring me the child," the great-grandfather ordered

moments before the young girl could slink out with her crying daughter clutched tightly to her chest. "She is only feeling and saying what the rest of my children are thinking and
hiding. Everyone at our circle of family wants to do nothing
less than the child is doing, even unto myself, so how can I
fault the child?" His granddaughter reluctantly handed over
her baby.

The large family watched as the old man held the girl to
his face so he could see her better in the tallow-fueled illumination of the lamp bowl.

"I shame myself, granddaughter, but I cannot remember
the child's name," he said, not so much in embarrassment but
as a way of reminding his extensive family that he had been
rather busy the past fifty-six years. Or was it simply because
the elder was ashamed that over those same years he had
completely ignored the trappings of a normal father—he
failed to know and therefore love his own kin.

The girl-child stopped crying and started hitching her
breath when the old man's long and graying beard caught her
attention. She slowly reached out and took a small fistful of
whiskers and tugged. The move elicited the first smiles
around the meal fire in what seemed like many years—ever
since their father had ordered the family away from their an-
cestral home to this makeshift tent village deep inside the
last forest near the confluence of the two great rivers.

"Her name is Leah," his granddaughter said as she looked
apprehensively to her husband when the baby took hold of
the great-grandfather's beard. He was smiling at the baby and
so she relaxed. Finally there was a great belly laugh from the
man most of the older children had not seen jest in their entire lifetimes.

"You have named her after my sister?" the old man asked
as he finally managed to control his laughter.

His wife of sixty-five years laughed also, happy to see her
husband finally view them as his family and not the slaves
they had been for the past half-century. All thoughts of the
darkness and shadows were absent from the old man's mind
for the first time in years. The angels of the Lord may have

been God-sent, but the old man knew exactly what they were—the deliverers of death. He despised the orders of the Lord to allow the destruction of so many innocents, and he was not allowed to help them. God was allowing children, such as the girl-child he was now holding, to be destroyed by his edict. His enemy was now those very same blackened angels of death that haunted his world. The old man and his God had come to a crossroads and the split was evident.

He again saw the eyes of the child as she laughed and continued to tug at his beard. His eyes softened and he allowed the thoughts of darkness and angels to slip out of his mind as his great-granddaughter convinced him he had done right by his family.

The design and building of his life's ambition had been given to him in thought and dream by the Lord God. It had also come to him in dream that his was the only family of man that would survive God's wrath. The shadows punished him every time he attempted to convince his onetime friends and neighbors of their true plight. The old man went against the decision of God himself.

His wife reached for a wooden bowl and started filling it with meat and herbs for her husband. She ladled thick brown gravy over the meat. The old man handed the child back to her mother and then nodded his head in thanks when his wife held before him the steaming bowl.

The mood was soon broken and the smiles died away as surely as the sun setting behind the darkening storm clouds to the south and west. The elder was the first to see the shadows near the animal pens move. He knew *they* were there with his family. He had been warned in dream and nightmare many years before that the shadows would be with them in the days leading up to this night of nights. He averted his eyes so that the children would not notice what had joined the family this evening in the midst of the last days.

"Father, I saw a long line of soldiers today. They marched to the south. The gossip near the two rivers reports that the war you predicted began two years ago in the great southern sea and the ringed island at its center."

The old man, grateful to turn away from the hovering shadows of *them*, placed a piece of bread into his mouth and looked at his second-eldest son.

"And how does my son Shem know this when he was to be harvesting the bounty of hay and barley our livestock will need upon our great journey?"

"Because it is now impossible to travel anywhere without crossing the paths of many soldiers gathering to fight the evil in the south. Your son Shem has learned that there are even strangers from a distant land calling themselves Greeks among the rebels that are joining forces."

The old man continued to chew his bread and look at his son. His eyes moved to the darkest corner of the enclosure and saw a large shadow break free of the wooden side of the Ark and then disappear through the unpitched crack in the large loading ramp. That shadow was soon followed by four others.

"Father, if what you have said is true, we are out of time. The war has been raging for two years now and from rumor we hear that the final blow to the evil ones on their island fortress has commenced. They say the combined barbarian army will win."

"My son Shem has always been the thinker, and now we learn that he is a war general also." The old man smiled for the briefest of moments. "You are so sure of this great military campaign that you are predicting outcomes, both victor and vanquished?" He tossed the remains of his bread into the fire. "Tell me, Shem the thinker, the family's master general; do the barbarians have the essence or the sheer power to end our world with their bone-edged swords and wooden ships?"

"How would I know this? We here in this valley know nothing of war, nor even the people fighting it. The barbarians like ourselves wear nothing but skins, hides, and roughly woven homespun, when the false gods on their island kingdom wear finery the likes of which we have never before seen. They have science, we have goats. They have riches and slaves while we have nothing but mouths to feed. No, father, the barbarians cannot end this world. As you have said to us as many times as there are stars in the heavens—only God can end the time of men."

The old man knew the shadows, although departed from the interior, could still hear and feel what was being said in their absence; *they* always had. He again tried to ignore the thoughts of shadows. "You think, but you do not take the path that will allow you to think it through without cloudiness, Shem. The barbarians are no better than those they see as evil. They want the power and knowledge of the island people, and if they had this power of knowing God's sciences they would be no gentler a taskmaster than the Titans on the ringed island. This is why the world ends. All of this"—he gestured at his family who watched him now with their frightened eyes—"will be gone and that is the way it was meant to be. The great ringed island has brought the very power of God's elements to bear upon the world—a power only the Lord our God was ever meant to wield, and thus our world will come to an end, and only the righteous"—he smirked at his gathered clan—"or the stubborn will live to start anew."

"Grandfather, will our family be the only ones left upon the face of the world?"

The old man smiled in all sincerity and then reached over and placed his hand on his great-grandson's cheek.

"No, there will be thousands, hundreds of thousands who will join us for the second coming of man. It will be a time and a place where we can live and grow together and not seek the ways and riches of those civilizations before us. No, we will see and come to know many different peoples on our path back to our home."

The great-grandson was about to speak again when the first rumblings from the earth were felt through the furs and homespun cloth upon which they sat.

The father slowly stood with the help of Shem and looked at his large family as the shaking earth gradually settled.

"The time of the end is upon us." He looked at his three sons, their wives, and many, many grandchildren, and using the strength of his convictions the old one remained calm.

"We must set our minds to what is to be done in this, the beginning of end times. You must harden your hearts, for the next two days will be the most horrible of your lives. You will all, every one of you, see friends and yes, even family, perish as the world shakes off the evil that has dominated it for over five thousand years."

At the end of his words his family started to rise as one. He looked at each and prayed that his path had been the right branch in the road to take. A barren road he had been placed upon at birth was now coming to an end as once more the world started to shake. This time the earth moved in a deeper and more pronounced motion.

The war between the barbarians of the combined world and the false gods of the south—the Atlanteans—had begun in earnest and the false gods were losing.

The known world of the first age of man would end in less than two days.

As Hamm traded the last of their hoarded gold for the remaining three shoats left in their neighbor's pen, he grimaced as he heard the laughter behind him from his shameless old friends. He ignored them as best he could as his five sons maneuvered the three small pigs from their pen and started them along the path to the once-thick forest that grew between the two rivers.

As the laughter at his family's lifelong endeavor continued, Hamm looked up and saw the giant trees ahead of him, and it was then that he realized how much the forest had vanished in the thirty-two years they had been building their father's hopeless folly. The deforesting had caused many a hardship for his kin and even more so for their neighbors, who had come to hate the family of Noah.

As they cleared the screening line of giant trees, leaving the mocking laughter behind them, Hamm had to stop and look upon the false deity they had built. The Ark had taken thirty-seven years to design and construct and had cost the family everything they had in life, and even that of their children's and grandchildren's lives. From the gold riches of his father's family to the many hundreds of pounds of precious coin made by his sons, all had gone into the construction of the monstrosity towering to the top of the few trees remaining, which were tasked with holding the great vessel anchored into place. The once-great and very powerful family was now close to destitute, and with everything they owned aboard the Ark, they had nothing but the clothes on their backs and the laughter of old friends in their ears.

As he was about to turn away he saw a shadow peel away from the highest point of the Ark and then vanish beyond the curvature of the bow. This was not the first strange darkness he had seen. For the past forty years the shadows that acted as if by magic came and went and their father, who Hamm knew had seen the strange shadows, never spoke of them. Even when one of his many offspring asked him about the darkness that seemed to have an intelligence, he would just shrug his aging shoulders, smile, and then say he had not seen a thing. The subject of the shadows was rarely brought up any longer.

The trees held the enormous Ark taut to the earth in the ever-increasing winds. The giant, ages-old trees and their vines were intentionally entangled among the wood of the great vessel anchored to the earth. The Ark stretched four hundred and fifty-five feet from arched end to arched end. The spire-like bow of the ship rose to a hundred feet above the ground and it was there that Hamm saw his father perched, looking to the far-off southern borders of the two rivers. The skies there were glowing red and black. White and gray ash had started to fall only an hour before, falling ever thicker, like sickly snow from a dying sky.

Hamm could see and hear the near panic in familial faces and voices as they herded the last of their farm animals over the thick, strong ramp and then aboard the Ark. They had bought as many animals and beasts of burden as they could before the end days, making them the butt of even more laughter and mockery by their neighbors, extended family, and former friends who counted the money offered for their animals and grain even as they laughed at the foolish family of Noah.

"Hamm, you and Shem commence to raising and moving the ramp into place. The Atlanteans have unleashed Hell to the south. It is now time!"

Hamm heard the words of his father and wondered as always how he knew these things, but did not ask. All the same he felt his blood go cold as the skies started to darken even more than the previous two days. The earth once again lurched under his feet and he stumbled as the ground seemingly came out from beneath his sandals.

The world started to break apart from the power being unleashed by the warlords to the south.

The known world of the first age of man had actually ended two hours earlier in the Poseidon Sea. The large body of water, which would eventually become known as the Mediterranean, exploded with the power of ten thousand nuclear weapons as the seabed cracked and split from the power of the Atlantean sciences of earth and sea, along with the necromancy of tectonic earth movement. The combined strength of the allied barbarian states that had suffered through the reign of terror for five thousand years at the hands of the inhabitants of the circular-ringed island was now devastatingly close to their homeland.

The attack started in earnest on the morning of the end of days. The strength of the Greek fleet under the command of Jason of Thessaly, coupled with a ground attack under the command of another Greek, Heracles the Barbarian, had pushed the Atlanteans to use the one thing they thought could save their island empire—the total destruction of the combined Greek and Egyptian fleets. This would be accomplished through the use of sound-inducing bells arrayed on the sea floor. The audio assault would fracture a localized section of tectonic plate, and that localized fracture would in turn create massive tsunamis that would swallow the entire thousand-ship fleet of their barbaric enemies.

As the great machines were put into motion the world erupted. The Atlanteans' map of the tectonic plates had not taken into account the spiderweb makeup of the earth's crust. The grinding of one plate would cause a domino effect of the audible attack on the planet and spread far beyond the defensive area desired in the middle of the Mediterranean. Each was linked one with the other, which meant that the advanced race of Atlantis had set off a worldwide chain reaction that would change the face of the earth for all time.

The earth continued to rumble and roll beneath their feet. As Hamm looked to the sky, lightning wrenched the darkness and brought fire to the night, affording him a look at what it had taken him a lifetime to build. The Ark stood strong against the increasing winds and the constant shaking of the world. The ground beneath his sandaled feet lurched and the Ark rolled. The father heard the screams of the children inside as the wooden vessel rolled to the right and the old man feared it would continue to tumble until it tipped on its keel and was crushed beneath its own weight. Just as it hit the optimum point where it had to roll over, the restraining ropes still attached to the strongest of the remaining trees snagged and held firm as the Ark stopped its roll. The towering trees continued supporting the Ark but swayed as the smaller trees were uprooted and thrown into the hurricane-force winds shaking the world. Then the rains started in earnest. Viscous mud and stone struck the wooden ship at the same time as the first dirt-infused drops of rain started to fall. Enormous fireballs arched across the night sky as mountain-sized boulders and spits of land were hurled into the air from the horrendous explosions of the earth to the south.

The father watched as Shem sent the last of the goat herd aboard. He knew they had lost a good ten percent of their animals because the firestorm had started without notice of quake or wind. The water was now broaching the banks of both the Lira and Mud rivers, or as they are now known, the Tigress and the Euphrates, sending freshwater to mix with the sea falling from the sky. As the old man looked around he saw the waters rise to the base of the ramp, and he felt the first true fear he had felt since he had been a child when the nightmares of water and of drowning had started—the sea was coming and nothing in God's world would stop it.

He felt the first sensation through the thick leather soles of his sandals and then the night sky started to shimmer and shake as the vibratory effects of the incoming sea distorted the perception of all living things. The father stumbled, trying desperately to gain his feet.

"Now!" he screamed into the blowing wind and falling mud and rain. "Raise the ramp!"

"Father, we need to cut down the remaining trees!" Shem called as he took his father by the arm to stop him from gaining the sloping ramp, which now had a quarter of its length under water.

"There is no time, the sea comes now! Do you not feel it?"

Shem did. The black clouds above started swirling as the distant waters came on so powerfully that they actually changed the direction of the winds, causing so much static electricity in the air that the trees around them were terrifyingly illuminated with what would eventually become known as St. Elmo's fire.

"Go, my son, the Lord's night of nights is upon us!"

Noah stood by as he watched his sons and grandsons fight to raise the ramp. Ropes were taut and the men were screaming in terror as the weight of the large wooden ramp slowly started to rise from the gathering waters. As the men struggled to shut out the horror of the night, Noah wiped water from his eyes, fighting to see the outside world for the last time as the ramp was slowly raised. He saw several dozen women, children, and men claw through the rising waters and beg for entrance. Several men even managed to take hold of the rising ramp as it cleared the swirling waters. Noah so wanted to assist the men who only hours before had laughed and ridiculed his salvation, but as he started to reach out for the hand that was pleading for help, a shadow shot past the old man and as Noah watched in abject horror, the shadowy figure seemed to reach for the struggling man's hand and pry it loose from the ramp, brutally snapping the man's fingers as if they were nothing but dried twigs. The shadowy entity flew from the death of the first to a second set of hands that had managed to grab the ramp, prying them off even as Noah reached to help. The shadow turned on the old man and he felt its force as it slammed into him, clearly revealing the face of darkness for the first time. The mouth extended and Noah felt as well as heard the roar of an otherworldly animal. The large blackened teeth were transparent, but lethal looking. Noah jumped away, truly frightened for the first time after seeing the angels for what they were—not angels, but God's killers of men.

The ramp closed for the last time. The screams of the lost were clearly heard above the wrath of the storm. Noah was in shock at seeing the shadows send his neighbors to their deaths.

He felt his chest where the shadow had slammed into him as he had attempted to help the men he had known his entire life. It was ice cold to his touch and he knew then that whatever was watching out for his family was as merciless as the Lord God that had sent them.

Before the initial wall of water struck the land side of what is now modern-day Iraq, the rivers themselves had exploded from their shallow banks to drown or crush most of the inhabitants of the two-rivers region. Men, women, and children, who had spent the bulk of their adult and young lives ridiculing the family that had foolishly built the Ark on dry land many miles from any body of water deep enough to carry her weight, were dying a death they had been warned was coming.

The old man was struggling with six oxen as the wide-eyed animals fought panic. They too had the instinct to know the world was breaking apart. All two thousand seven hundred animals of the family of Noah were close to panic as the great Ark rocked on its ten-foot-wide keel.

The trees holding the giant ship in place swayed in the

increasing hurricane-force winds that now gripped the entire Middle East. Shem and Hamm with their sons at their sides were battling ever-changing forces in an attempt at placing the last of the thick pitch around the ramp's strong frame. But still, water forced itself through the small areas where the builders were off on their measurements, and no amount of pitch in the world would seal the doorway completely.

Noah watched as the women finally tied the last of the livestock down in the animal hold where water was falling rapidly as each and every flaw in the Ark's design was now under relentless attack. Noah knew his life's work would only last so long in the disaster. The design that had come to him in a series of dreams that had lasted the whole of his first twenty years of life was now close to falling apart.

Women, men, and their children were in the water outside the Ark pounding and pleading to be allowed inside. Hundreds of their neighbors were screaming for help as they pounded on the thick wooden hull of the only structure left standing within a hundred miles. The old man saw the shadows return, and then several broke free of the wooden wall of the Ark and vanished between the minuscule cracks in the framing. Then the sounds of screams were heard over the roar of the storm. It sounded as if the men and women outside were being attacked by something unseen. Noah, grateful his family was now too busy to see and hear what was happening outside, placed his hands over his ears in an attempt to close out the horrible misery on the other side of the thick hull.

"Father, we can still get a few of those men and women inside before—"

Hamm's words were cut short as every member of the family of Noah felt it at the same time. The sound of wind, rain, and thunder was silenced by the deep bass rumble now coming from the south. Everyone with the exception of Noah froze as the terror of what was coming stilled their hearts. The old man knew he had been meant to see the killer of their world. He was to bear witness to the death of the first age of mankind.

The paralysis of his sons and family broke as they screamed for their father to come down. The old man was climbing through the crisscrossed beams securing and strengthening the thick members that made up the massive hull. As the Ark announced the arrival of the sea and its preceding waves by rolling once again, Noah breached the top deck and slammed his hands into the small wooden doorway that led out onto the long, sloping deck. He gained the slick, wet, and mud-covered beams and immediately looked toward the south over the chest-high side wall.

He turned away from the death below and tried desperately to pierce the frightening storm and the darkness that fought to hide their unseen killer. Then he saw it as well as felt it. A brief flash of chain lightning illuminated the sky to the south and that was when the wave became visible.

Noah's eyes widened and he took hold of the Ark as he searched for the peak of the giant tsunami but was failing to see it. Then he finally realized why—he was looking for the wave at several hundred feet and not high into the sky. His eyes roamed to the heavens and then he saw it. The deliverer of death. The wall of water was forty miles away and closing fast on the two-rivers region, and as far as he could tell the wave was over a mile in height.

"God protect us," Noah screamed as he now hurriedly entered into the dark as the sound became unbearable. The wave was destroying everything man had accomplished in his first age and the world would soon be changed forever as they fought to start again. Finally the tsunami crested at thirty miles out and was over a mile into the sky. The white foam of its roll was self-illuminating because of its lightning-white brightness against the blackened night sky.

The sea struck the land with the force of two worlds colliding. The water hit and then rebounded into the sky and then hit again. The water of three differing seas scrubbed the land clean of all features as it took tree, shrub, and beast in its rush north. Noah looked far below at his drowning neighbors as they went under. The strange shadows below ceased their killing and then vanished inside the Ark just before the final verdict of man was handed down.

Noah felt his legs pulled out from under him as his sons finally broke their paralysis and attempted to get their father under control as he fought the door against the hellish winds. As they pulled him inside they latched the doorway and Shem quickly started slamming pitch into the seal, and then they made their way back to what they hoped was the strongest section of the Ark—its exact center. The animals were screaming and trying to break free of their restraints as the ship rocked sharply to the side as the first of the advancing waves struck. The trees securing the Ark stopped the roll of the four-hundred-foot behemoth but could not stop the whiplash that came when the trees snapped back against the onrush of advancing water.

The roar of the wave was deafening. Children added their screams to those of the animals as the sound was seemingly coming from the heavens far above them. It was almost as if the planet itself was crying out in pain and anguish. Noah prayed that the crest of the tsunami was now low enough not to engulf the Ark and crush it under its incalculable weight.

The wave struck the giant ship and all heard the sound and feel of the trees securing the Ark to the earth being torn out like turnips. This time the Ark had nothing to stop its roll and it went over onto its side, throwing men, women, children, and their thousands of animals into the leaking walls.

The wave snatched the Ark as if it were a feather in a windstorm. The force of the blow coupled with the spin of the ship sent Noah and his family against the sides and held them in place by sheer centrifugal force alone as the ship spun in a circle. Still the sea rose as the great oceans to the south, east, and west finally met at the junction of the two rivers. The Ark was taken almost a half mile into the sky by the roll of the largest tsunami ever to hit the planet, and still the earth moved from the disaster brought upon their home by the advanced race of Atlanteans.

The Ark was traveling northward at a speed approaching one hundred miles per hour and the ancient home they left behind was now nothing but an inland sea.

The known world and the first age of man ended at exactly 7:35 in the evening of October seventeenth, in the year 13,002 BCE.

TRABZON, TURKEY (THE OTTOMAN EMPIRE) SEPTEMBER 18, 1859

With aching legs and pounding hearts ready to burst from their chests, the four men stopped and tried to hear the sounds of the night around them. The rain was making it impossible to know how many of the devils were nearby. Real shadows blended perfectly with the darkness that had seemed to engulf their world since leaving the mountain. An hour earlier they had lost professors Beckley and Thorsten, and student assistant Harold Iverson, at the small boat where they had attempted to rendezvous with their ship, which awaited the return of the expedition in the choppy bay.

The three men had fallen to the silent and very deadly shadows that had come at them from hiding. They had reached for the men and then drew them screaming into the blackness beyond this life. The devilish shadows had even brought down a burly Turkish policeman who was assisting them with their equipment. Now the citizens of the small port town had been alerted to the research team's presence and the remaining four were on the run from not only the shadowy killers of the mountain, but also the much-angered Turkish townsfolk.

"Look, let us face facts, gentlemen. Not all of us are going to make it," Professor Kensington said in a staccato, out-of-breath voice as he pressed his back to a wet and age-worn brick wall. He looked at the oilcloth in his right hand and then thrust the parcel into Ollafson's shaking fingers. "It's your show, old boy, your theory, your discovery. Get this to whoever will listen." He held the cloth to the chest of the older Scandinavian professor until he accepted the charge hesitantly. "The three of us will cause a commotion. You get to the boat and then to the ship," the younger man said, smiling briefly, "and to place a dramatic point on this conversation, old man, don't look back."

The professor took the bundled artifacts and then looked to his colleague. "I can't do that. I cannot leave you behind!" Lars Ollafson shook his head as he looked from frightened face to frightened face. "How will you explain a dead policeman to the authorities without explaining why he had to die and what it was that killed him? They will think you mad!"

"The authorities will be the least of our worries, Professor," Kensington answered and again smiled sadly. "Now, when we move, wait a moment and then get to that boat. Don't ever stop, no matter what you hear. This find must make it back to the States at all costs."

"But . . ."

"Believe me, Lars, I'll accept being caught by the Turks, but those others from the mountain I would just as soon not deal with. Now, you have to—"

Kensington was stopped in midsentence when suddenly the oil lamp bolted to the side of the brick wall flared and then slowly died. As they nervously watched they saw the shadow cast by the wall start to expand, as if the darkness was drawing an awakening breath.

"Damn, they've found us again!" Kensington said harshly as he reached out and took Ollafson by his coat collar. "Please, old boy, that thing cost the lives of everyone except you on this expedition." He patted the older professor on his shoulder as he looked around him through the relentlessly falling rain. "Good luck, Professor. Get someone, anyone, to listen to our story. Make them understand that it is up there, waiting for man to reclaim it! Now, off with you, sir!" he said and then sprinted from the safety of the small alley followed by the two remaining men from the shattered expedition.

Lars Ollafson saw the three men, his last remaining friends in the world, leave him alone in this hostile, far-off empire. He heard the shouts and the angry voices of the villagers as they gave pursuit. He thought to himself, and not for the first time, that it would be far luckier if his friends and colleagues were caught by the Turks rather than the darkness that had already claimed more than eighty-two lives. He knew the townsfolk, angry after finding their dead policeman, were preferable to facing the shadow creatures. Hanging would be a far better fate than being dragged into the shadows and lost forever to God only knew what evil dwelled on that cursed mountain. Yes, he thought, hanging by the Turks was a far better alternative than the damnable shadows.

He waited as long as his nerves would allow. The old man looked down at his small package and closed his eyes against the raindrops. He shook his head and then without thinking another moment he ran from his hiding place. He heard a scream fill the night above the din of falling rain and shouting men. He squeezed his eyes closed and fought his way to the dock. He saw the boat before him. One of his companions was still half in and half out of the boat, having fallen where he had died a half hour before when a shadow lurking under the old, rickety pier had reached for the man's throat and taken his life as the others cowered in fear only feet away. The sailor's skin had turned an icy white under the touch of the darkness and then it seemed the life had drained from his eyes with a suddenness that explained to the educated men in no uncertain terms that they were dealing with a part of nature that no man had ever seen before.

Ollafson quickly shoved the dead man's feet over the side and let the body slip beneath the dark waters of the bay. Professor Ollafson swallowed and allowed a whimper of sadness and fear to slip through his bearded features as he watched the body of the young man vanish from view.

He quickly untied the boat from the wooden cleat and then hastily sat on the wet bench and started rowing blindly from the dock. He chanced a look back at the small village. He was confused, as instead of seeing candles and lanterns alight from the noise interrupting their sleep, it seemed the villagers were actually extinguishing the lights of their homes, not wanting anything to do with the strange calls and screams of the night around them. He spied many of the angry men of the small town returning quickly to their homes as something had quelled their anger over the murder of their local constable. It was as if the men thought the darkness around them was a far greater threat than the foreign devils they pursued. As he watched, the shadows seemed to engulf the small seaside village. He saw shadows lengthen and then roll slowly through alleys and streets looking for the men who had invaded the mountain.

He tried to breathe through his sobs of terror and sadness as he rowed toward the awaiting vessel that would take him from this nightmare land. He chanced a look forward and hoped the *Agatha Anne*, the ship that had brought the ill-fated expedition to the Ottoman Empire, was still there.

As he rowed he saw the oilcloth-wrapped bundle awash in seawater on the bottom of the small skiff and he couldn't help but think it was something they were never meant to take from the accursed summit.

The lives of eighty-two men had been lost on the black slopes and the pass leading to the flatlands after their running battle from the summit. The fortunes of six American and three British families lost for the simple cost of discovery. Now he alone had the task of persuasion ahead of him. Ollafson knew he had little time to act as the world was near the point of tipping into darkness more fearful than even the shadow demons of the mountains. He knew trying to get those in American power even to listen to his fantastic story would be a battle as fierce as the one they had just fought on that blackest of mountains. He would now return home to a country that was about to rip its own guts out in an internal conflict that would change the face of the world forever just as a flood had almost fifteen thousand years before.

The year was 1859, and in America, brothers would soon be killing brothers by the thousands.

RAPPAHANNOCK RIVER, EASTERN VIRGINIA
JULY 28, 1863
The small detachment of cavalry was hidden behind a stand of trees that lined the southern bank of the Rappahannock

River. The rainstorm hid the small unit well from the eyes they knew were upon them across that small ribbon of swollen water. Men and horses had been through many years of war and were disciplined not to utter a sound even in the driving rain. Horses didn't whinny or snort and men sat stock-still in their saddles. The experienced cavalrymen knew the art of war and how to achieve their ends.

All eyes were on the lone rider in rain gear who sat upon his horse just at the edge of the southern side of the Rappahannock. The rebel officer was on a large roan with a gold-trimmed Union saddle blanket, something he'd had since his earlier days as an officer and a gentleman for the enemy he was now facing—the U.S. Army. The man silently continued to watch and wait.

On the northern side of the river a singular figure on horseback lightly laid spur to his mount and the horse and rider moved easily out of the cover of trees. He eased his horse toward the water's edge and then lightly placed pressure on his knees, telling his mount that was far enough. The horse stopped and pawed at the swollen, swiftly running river.

The rider's men watched silently. Most had hands on pistols just beneath their foul-weather slickers, as the meeting taking place was not something they could have ever imagined since the whole bloody mess had started in 1861. The man at the edge of the river moved his head only slightly and looked at his men. He knew they were as anxious as he to receive their guest, but unlike his men his apprehension came in the form of knowing just who it was that had braved the storm and several miles of Confederate pickets to attend the meeting. This man was either the biggest fool in the world or the bravest, because the army he was here to see had suffered its first humiliating defeat just twenty-one days earlier in a small valley whose name would forever haunt the men who fought there those long, lost days—Gettysburg.

The man turned back to face his opposite on the far bank. He then looked toward the dark sky and wondered if God would ever allow his army to see the clear moonlit sky again.

It was as if the Lord had forsaken their cause in the span of three days of hard fighting that left General Robert E. Lee's Army of Northern Virginia hurt and on the run. The man with the feathered, plumed hat then fixed the man across from him with his dark eyes.

Major General James Ewell Brown Stuart, Confederate States of America, waited on the United States to make the next move. Stuart, Jeb to those who knew him best, felt the rainwater running through his thick beard but fought the temptation to wipe it clean, deciding if the rain did not bother his adversary across the river he wouldn't allow it to bother himself. He waited.

The soldier across the river seemed to break the statuesque spell he had been under and then turned his horse away and bounded up the muddy bank of the Rappahannock. Jeb Stuart could see the gold piping running the length of the man's uniform pants. He knew then that the visitor was a Union cavalry officer. Horse and rider vanished into the trees on the far side. He knew without turning around in his saddle that his small unit of men were now preparing for any nasty surprises that might arise from this highly unusual and clandestine meeting.

The rain seemed to diminish as the rider returned, this time in advance of an ornate carriage with oil lamps illuminated on each side of the driver who sat atop it. The officer upon the mount took hold of the lead horse of the six that drew the carriage and eased them and their charge into the fast-moving waters of the Rappahannock. The horses flinched at first but Stuart could see that the rider had a calming effect on the team as they eased into the river and made the crossing. The horse and rider then allowed the carriage to cross as they made the far side. The cavalry officer easily approached Jeb Stuart when the carriage finally battled its way up the bank.

Stuart waited. What they were doing this dark night was far beyond the pale of Stuart's understanding. General Robert E. Lee had ordered that he meet and safely escort the envoy directly into the camp of the Army of Northern Virginia. Stuart had the feeling that President Lincoln was asking for a truce so Lee could consider the surrender of the army to General Meade, who had failed to destroy Lee at Gettysburg. This was the reason Jeb Stuart was tempted to end this little meeting right now. He kept his hands on his saddle as the Union officer approached until their two horses were nose to nose. The man raised his right hand into the air and brought it to the brim of his dripping hat.

"Lieutenant Colonel Hines Jorgensen, First Division of General Buford's Corps, at your service, sir."

Stuart was hesitant in returning the military respect accorded by this officer, but in the end Stuart's West Point training kicked in as if he had never left the service of the United States Army. The salute was returned.

"General J. E. B. Stuart, at yours, sir," he said, and then bowed and amazingly his horse did also, allowing its right foreleg to stretch out and its left to bend. The Union officer was impressed, but then the man had seen this Confederate general do some amazing things on the field of battle, as he was a rebel that every cavalry officer in the United States knew on a level they wished they didn't. Horse and rider straightened and then Stuart gestured toward the trees behind him as his small unit of cavalrymen made their presence known. Jeb Stuart turned back to the Union officer and held the man's eyes.

"You were supposed to have only you and one other," the Union man Jorgensen said, "not an entire unit."

Stuart smiled for the first time in what seemed like months. "These men are not a unit, sir, they are my personal guard. It would be somewhat of a personal embarrassment if Mr. Lincoln's mysterious envoy turned out to be an assassin, now wouldn't it?"

"Mr. Lincoln is far above such intrigues and you of all soldiers should know that, General. He wants this foolishness to end and end soon."

"That, sir, is not up to me."

"Then may I suggest that you take us to the man that it is up to?"

Stuart didn't say anything in return but instead spurred his large horse and made his way to the carriage where he stopped and looked up at the carriage driver. The man had a set of three stripes up and three down, and the single star in the middle told Stuart all he wanted to know. His eyes roamed to the man's face and then recognition struck his memory like a hammer slamming home upon a nail.

"Sergeant Major Wilkes, it has been a long time. I think it was on the Cimarron I saw you last." Stuart smiled at the memory. "I think a wild Comanche was attempting to fill your hindquarters with arrows. How have you been, Sergeant Major?"

The bearded soldier sitting atop the carriage kept his eyes straight ahead. Stuart felt his horse move as he waited for his old Indian-fighting comrade to respond.

"Sergeant Major? It's me, Captain Stuart," he said, refreshing the sergeant major's memory with the rank he had at the time they served together in Texas.

"I know who you are, sir, and I wish to gather no memory wool with you." The sergeant major finally looked down at the general. "Nor do I wish to recall our past service together, sir. The captain I served with was a United States cavalry officer. The man who stands before me here on this dark night is a traitor"—the sergeant major looked away—"to not only his country, but also to the men we buried along those dry riverbeds in Texas."

Stuart lowered his eyes and his head and moved his horse to the carriage door and then leaned over and pulled the door's handle. He looked down and inside the dry compartment and his eyes widened, and he hated himself for allowing the man to see his surprised expression.

"Young man, you are allowing rainwater to enter my carriage, so if you would not have me drown, may I suggest you close the door and get me to the man I came here to see. I'm rather chilled to the bone and my whiskey flask is running dangerously low."

Jeb Stuart closed the carriage door and then straightened in his saddle. He turned to his second-in-command and nodded his head. The captain eased his horse up to face the carriage driver but the sergeant major kept his eyes straight ahead. Stuart watched the exchange.

"You will follow these men closely. Any variation in our route that is not initiated by my men, and you will be shot as spies. Do I make myself clear, Sergeant Major?"

"The sergeant major knows how to follow orders," Stuart said as he sadly turned away from his old friend, knowing that no matter the outcome of this war, it would take years to heal the wounds of the country. Stuart guided his horse back to the driver of the carriage.

"I'm glad you've survived thus far in this insanity, Sergeant Major. So few of us have," he said and then eased his horse into the trees and vanished.

The small but stout sergeant major watched his old commanding officer leave the clearing and then he lowered his eyes.

"He's tired. The war is finally getting to his conscience, I believe," the captain said by way of explaining Stuart's behavior.

Finally the bearded sergeant major broke his spell after the shock of seeing the one-time U.S. Cavalry officer in the garish gray uniform of a Confederate general, and slowly glanced down at the captain and, with rainwater flooding from the leather bill of his cap, cleared his throat.

"That man was born to fight and he won't give a good goddamn for his conscience until one side or the other wins. No, Captain, that is a soldier," he said and then took the reins and whipped them upon the team, drawing the carriage forward to follow his old friend who was now his bitter enemy.

The Confederate captain watched the carriage vanish into the line of trees with his men closely following. He was amazed to hear the sergeant major describe Stuart as a traitor complete with hate-filled eyes, and then to hear the same man turn around and praise his old commanding officer as a friend would have.

The war was taking a toll on the very fabric that made the country great—the division of brother against brother and friend against friend would be the death of the dream.

The war had to stop and stop soon.

HEADQUARTERS, ARMY OF NORTHERN VIRGINIA

The old man saw the wagons overflowing with wounded as they slogged their way through the rain-soaked, tree-trunk corduroy road the engineers had laid down just a few weeks before when the intact Army of Northern Virginia headed headlong into the disaster that had become Robert E. Lee's only blemish on his Confederate war record—Gettysburg. The lone passenger inside the dry interior of the ornate carriage saw the misery that had become the new face of Lee's undefeatable army. He leaned back in his seat and knew that the South would never smile again after Pennsylvania. He tipped the open flask of whiskey to his lips and drained the contents that eased his mind at seeing this great travesty first-hand.

The faces that stared back at him and the sergeant major were not in the least hostile, but rather offered expressions of utter disbelief at what had happened just two weeks past in that small college town across the river. The men did not have the look of defeat on their tired, muddy faces; instead, those faces held the belief that Lee would see them through. No, the man thought, this army was far from defeated and he knew that was why he had been sent—for that day when this madness would finally end.

The carriage was brought to a stop, but not before the man inside saw the armed guards just outside his window. He braced himself as the door opened.

"Sir, I trust you will comport yourself as a gentleman during this meeting. I do not believe I have to offer any dire warnings if you do not," Jeb Stuart said as he took a quick step back and then nodded for an aide to take his place as an umbrella was held out for the occupant of the carriage.

As the guest of the Army of Northern Virginia exited the carriage to curious looks from every man in view, Stuart tipped his hat and then turned to leave, his knee-high boots splashing through the water.

"General, sir," the sergeant major called out as he tied off the carriage's reins on the seat and then expertly hopped down from the bench in a graceful leap. He adjusted his blue and gold cape and his uniform tunic as he waited for Stuart to approach.

"How may I be of service, Sergeant Major Wilkes?" Stuart asked, slowly pulling off his gauntlets as he waited for the bearded sergeant to state his business. He was shocked when his old comrade came to attention in the driving rain.

"You have my apologies, General Stuart, for acting the boor, and for not conducting myself properly as a noncommissioned officer in the United States Army. I must state that our past association was . . . *is* . . . far more relevant than I led you to believe earlier." The sergeant major half-bowed and then returned to attention. The soldiers who witnessed this man, who only weeks before was more than likely trying to kill the very man he was saluting, were mindful of what was really happening inside the camp of Robert E. Lee.

The reputation of J. E. B. Stuart was that of a southern gentleman, and even back in his cavalry days in Texas he held firm that you always conducted yourself as such even when faced with adversity, and even defeat. All eyes widened when Stuart removed his famous hat with the ostrich feather cocked at the side.

"Apology accepted, Sergeant Major," was all he said, and then turned to leave, replacing his hat. It had been as if he had no response to his old friend.

"Jeb?" the sergeant major said before Stuart could get too far in the rain.

"Sergeant Major Wilkes?" he said as he slowly turned back to face the Union noncom.

"You watch yourself and get through this, you hear?"

"Always bossing me around and never knowing who outranks who," Stuart said, but with a smile. He then straightened to the posture of a ramrod and brought his hand up to his hat to salute his old friend. "When this is over I'll continue to teach you those etiquette lessons I started on the Rio Grande a million years ago."

The sergeant major slowly lowered his hand and watched his old friend walk into the rain-soaked world and into American history.

As he turned, Sergeant Major Wilkes was confronted by three men. He came to an abrupt stop and then relaxed when he saw one of the men with as many stripes as himself holding out a tin cup of steaming liquid.

"T'ain't no South American coffee, only chicory," the sergeant with the graying beard said as he held out the cup.

"It would curl your hair to know what Captain Stuart and I had to drink hunkered down fighting the Comanche in North Texas, I ought to tell ya," Wilkes said as he accepted the hot tin cup with a nod.

"Why do I get the feeling you're a' goin' to tell us anyway, Billy Yank?"

The Union civilian was hunched over with his cloak protecting him from the downpour of rain that had Lee's camp swimming. The fires were built high and then he realized why—the Army of Northern Virginia was getting ready to move and the high campfires would tell the Union sentries across the river that they were hunkering down for the night. The old man's eyes saw the wagons being hitched and the wounded being loaded. Yes, the army was making a run for Richmond and the embrace of Jefferson Davis and his Confederacy.

Two well-appointed guards stood on either side of the door fronting a modest home. An old woman sat in a rocking chair darning as the two sentries kept their rifles straight. When the guest stepped onto the porch, the one on the right eased the door open as the guest removed his hat and sloughed off some of the rain.

"Thank you, young man," the guest said as he stepped into the warm house where he was greeted by a dark-haired major with a beard that was thin enough for a lad of fifteen.

"Sir, I am Major Walter Taylor, steward to General Lee. May I take your cloak and your hat, sir?" the man with the sparkling uniform asked as he half-bowed to the much older man.

"You can do more than that, young man. You may offer me some libation to warm these old bones, as I have seemed to run out of my own supply while wading across that damnable river."

The major seemed uncomfortable as his reach for the hat and cloak faltered momentarily.

"Sir, we carry no such refreshment at headquarters. I'm afraid the general—"

"—will have to assign the major another dangerous mission to find our guest his whiskey. After all, his reputation very much precedes him and thus we should have been far more prepared."

The old man turned and saw a somber soldier with white hair and even whiter beard step from the back of the small house. The eyes were dark and they looked as if they had not closed in the days since the common massacre in Pennsylvania. The man looked as if he was no longer invincible—just the way the visitor wanted him.

"Perhaps our host, Mrs. Gandy, has a supply of medicinal whiskey in the house that you haven't found and destroyed, Major."

The old man nodded his thanks at General Robert E. Lee, who stood with his hands behind his back. Lee's right hand felt for the rocking chair and then his body seemed to stabilize as he nodded a greeting to his guest. Lee was dressed in a clean uniform that looked as if it had been recently pressed. His gold sash was wound perfectly around his waist and his boots were recently polished.

Major Taylor finally accepted the soaked hat and cloak, nodded at his commanding officer, and then quickly vanished.

General Robert E. Lee stood his ground next to the fire and the welcoming embrace of the rocking chair but made no move to sit. His gaze held the man before him, and a silent standoff ensued. It was Lee, ever the perfectionist, who broke the spell.

"It is an honor to see you once again, Mr.—"

A door in the back of the house opened and Lee was interrupted by a small man impeccably dressed in the battle-red blouse of Her Majesty's government. The man glared at Lee's guest as if the politico carried the plague.

"Many apologies, Colonel. I'm afraid my guest has arrived and I have to attend to urgent matters. May we continue our meeting in the morning?" Lee said to the British army man, who looked from the uneasy guest to his host and then bowed to the general.

"As you wish, General," the British colonel said as he retrieved his coat from a hook on the wall and then bowed once more on his way through the door, but not before giving the visitor a stern look as if it had been distasteful even being in the same room with him. The door closed and Lee's guest turned back to face the general who was finally moving forward to greet him properly.

"Excuse me for not introducing you to the colonel, but I quickly assessed that your mission to my encampment may be more covert than I was led to believe. After all, it's not every secretary of state for the Union who would brave the wilds and enter the camp of his mortal enemy."

"Then how about accepting it at face value as one American speaking with another; that way you may be able to maneuver around it."

Lee smiled. It was a sad and lonely-looking effort but he finally held his right hand out. At that moment his aide returned holding a clear bottle filled with clearer liquid.

"Colonel Freemantle didn't look at all happy," the major said as he removed his rain slicker and watched his commander with his very unusual guest.

William H. Seward, the United States secretary of state, took Lee's hand and lightly shook it.

"Yes, Colonel Freemantle was against me taking an envoy from Mr. Lincoln into my camp. He seems overly worried about something and I suspect it has to do with the flurry

of message activity between the colonel and his queen." Lee
released the hand of Seward and then gestured for his aide to
assist his guest to a chair in front of the fire. "And I must admit
to finally having something in common with our friend from
the Empire, as I am just as curious to know why Mr. Lincoln is
reaching out to me at this particular time."

"General, after the savagery of the past three weeks, the
president believes it is time we start talking."

Lee sat in the old and rickety rocking chair and gestured
to Taylor that he should tend to his guest's request for a drink.
As Taylor brought Seward a teacup with apologies for it not
being a glass, Lee fixed the secretary of state with his intense
eyes.

"Any communication pertaining to the continuance of the
war should properly be directed south toward Richmond, sir,
not here. The civilian leadership has control of this insanity,
not I."

Seward accepted the small teacup with a nod of thanks.
The long gray hair of the radical Republican shook with
nerves as his head bobbed to drink from the small cup. He
took a sharp intake of breath before placing the cup back into
the saucer as he managed to swallow the burning liquid.

"Many apologies, sir, but since the Confederacy is being
starved by your blockade our normal supply of whiskey has
vanished, we are thus left with what the boys can make on
the run."

"That is quite enough, Major Taylor. I'm sure Mr. Seward
does not need to be educated on the supply and logistics problems of our new nation, especially since he probably knows
our troubles even better than ourselves."

The major bowed and then, with an apologetic nod to
Seward, left the room.

"Tempers are rather short these days and nights,
Mr. Seward."

Secretary Seward placed the cup and saucer on the small
table to his right and fixed Lee with his own look that had
frightened many a senator before this insanity had begun two
years before.

"Yes, the president is also not in a jovial mood. Not only for the Union boys lost, but southern youth also. He's sick of this war. The man has not slept a full night since Fort Sumter."

"As much as I would like to please Mr. Lincoln, his sleepless nights are somewhat out of my area of expertise or control, sir."

"General, I must say that the mission the president has seen fit to send me on goes against everything I stand for. I believe this war should be brought to its inevitable conclusion and what comes after that war should be hardship for your people to make up for the countless deaths in this war. I am not of the same mind as the president. I and many others believe the South needs to be punished." He deflated somewhat. "But as I said, the president has chosen another path."

Lee stopped the slow movement of the rocker as the true feelings of the secretary of state were made crystal clear. He sat motionless waiting for the small secretary of state to get to his point.

"However, I was not sent to conduct an investigation as to the cause and effect of the war and what will come after for your people."

"If the outcome of the war will be as you say, Mr. Seward, won't they be Mr. Lincoln's people, not mine, nor Mr. Davis's, but his?"

"Just semantics, General Lee—nothing but semantics. It's obvious through the sheer force of President Lincoln's will your people will see far more leniency than either American political parties would ever be willing to accede to on a natural basis. Too many have died."

"Then thank the Lord for Mr. Lincoln's clear vision of what's right and what's wrong."

Instead of continuing the debate, Seward reached into his greatcoat and brought out a sealed envelope. As he held the letter out to Lee, the general saw the simple scrawled words on its front. It was addressed to General Lee in a flowing handwritten style that spoke of education. He accepted the

letter as Seward leaned back and retrieved the teacup filled
with the harsh moonshine, which in his opinion proved the
southern soldier far superior in at least that area of war—
drinking. Seward watched Lee turn the envelope over and
examine the red wax seal securing it. The image of the American bald eagle was embedded in the wax with the nation's
motto—"*E Pluribus Unum*," Latin for "Out of many, One."

The general looked at Seward as the old man sipped the
harsh brew and continued to watch and gauge Lee's reaction.

"The battle we have just endured does not spell the end of
this army, Mr. Seward. Before I open this letter from your
president, I want that made perfectly clear. Until the leadership decides otherwise, I will continue to fight and the Army
of Northern Virginia will do the same."

Seward placed the cup in the saucer and then fixed Lee
with his dark eyes.

"That is the president's belief also, General, so perhaps
you should read the letter first before you declare war all over
again."

Lee's eyes held those of the secretary of state for the longest time. He had always heard about Seward's sharp tongue
and now he realized just why Lincoln had chosen him as the
secretary of state—the man was not made to end this war,
he was appointed to see it through, and his harsh rhetoric
would make that happen sooner than would have been possible with a more soft-spoken man. Seward was, Lee realized,
here to ask something the secretary of state personally
didn't agree with, which intrigued Lee to no end. He knew
Mr. Lincoln had ideas that were well in advance of the rest of
the nation, so the message made him as curious as a schoolchild waiting for his marks. Lee broke the seal and slowly
rocked as he read.

The secretary of state noticed with raised brows when
Lee's chair suddenly stopped moving.

William Seward accepted a refill of the burning liquid
from Lee's aide as the general read and then reread the letter. He examined the signature at the bottom and then gestured for the major to join him as he stood slowly and tiredly

from the rocking chair and moved toward the back of the room. He folded the message so only the bottom portion showed and held it for Major Taylor's perusal of the document.

"Major, you more than anyone on my staff has seen captured communiqués from Washington, and you know the signatures of most who give orders in that mosquito-plagued city."

"Yes, sir, I believe I am comfortable with your assessment."

Lee gave him the note, being sure that only the signature was visible. The major examined the name—A. Lincoln. The flowing tilt lent credence to Lee's assessment of an educated hand. Taylor looked up at his commander-in-chief and slowly nodded his head.

"You are sure this is Mr. Lincoln's signature? There is no doubt?"

"General, either the president signed that or they have a forger in their government that could falsify my own signature in my presence."

"Thank you, Major. Would you excuse us, please?"

Major Taylor bowed and left the room. The rain was still falling and Seward could hear it drumming off the roof of the farmhouse. General Lee slowly sank into his rocker, folded the letter, and started to place it in his tunic, but Seward quickly placed the cup and saucer down and held out his hand, which had finally stopped shaking since the warm homemade whiskey was flowing steadily through his old and tired system.

"Yes, I would presuppose the president would not like the contents of that letter getting out to the press, as it would surely mean the end of his political career and more than likely the beginnings of a long stay in a sanitarium."

Seward took the letter and without a word tossed it into the large fireplace. He watched the last of the note go up in flames and the red wax seal melt into the flaming wood. In just a few seconds the message was nothing but ashes. Seward then took the poker and smashed the ashes until there was nothing left. He leaned back in his chair and took a deep breath as he reached for the fortifying home-brewed whiskey once more. He held the cup in the air in a mock toast.

"To the president of the United States, for as insane as he is, he has managed to surprise even myself." Seward finished the cup as Lee watched him in silence.

The general finally ceased rocking and looked toward the fire. In the flames he could see the burning of southern cities. He could smell the lives of many a family going up in smoke just like the firewood he was watching. After reading the letter he knew that the world had finally gone insane.

"General Lee, would you please put pen to paper telling the president that his wild plan is not acceptable to you at any cost or in any form? That you, Robert E. Lee, agree with the many of us in his own cabinet that this . . . this . . . proposition is pure folly." Seward closed his eyes momentarily and then they opened once again as he tried to control his passion. "Getting more boys killed for something as foolish as this makes both sides in this loathsome conflict seem desperate and insane to the rest of the world and would generate a contempt among civilized nations as to our childish ways. All to bind wounds at the end of this conflict. Believe me, General Lee, there is no salve in the world that we as a nation can apply to our wounds that will ever allow either side to forget this madness. Far too many an American boy has died to just forget."

Lee stood and walked to a large table where the battle maps of his campaign had been covered with a bedsheet in anticipation of Seward's arrival. He took up a pen, dipped the tip into an ornate inkwell, and started writing. He finished by placing his own seal on the envelope and then paced back to Seward, who was now standing and donning his coat, holding his hat in his hand. General Lee handed the American secretary of state the sealed envelope with his own crest on the seal.

"Then the world will believe both Mr. Lincoln and myself insane, Mr. Seward. Tell the president I have given him reluctant permission to use volunteers only"—he lowered his eyes—"as I figure my boys would rather go to their deaths that way than dying off in a northern prison camp."

Seward looked at Lee with astonishment written across his lined and tired face. "You are acquiescing to the president's request?"

Lee turned away from the stricken secretary of state. "I have explained my actions in my response to Mr. Lincoln." He turned back to face Seward. "The president is right, Mr. Secretary. The nation will be devastated after this conflict has played out to its final passion play, and something will desperately be needed as a balm to every American's soul."

"The president is a fool, and I expected you to tell him so in not so many written words, to deny him permission to use your men in this folly that will only see embarrassment and death to those boys."

Lee smiled, a sad and forlorn gesture that did not sit well with Seward, and then the general walked twenty feet and opened the door for his guest.

"Tell me what your interpretation of insanity is, Mr. Seward. Mine is killing each other by the thousands just because we're Americans and slaves to our outdated causes—on both sides. No, Mr. Secretary, I believe the president's insanity and my own walk hand in hand down this mad trail to our own individual hells that await us." He held the door for the northern secretary of state.

Seward placed the return answer for his president in his coat and then angrily put his top hat on his head. He reached out and took the clear bottle of whiskey from the table and then turned to leave. After this meeting he wanted nothing more than to get drunk on his long ride back to Washington.

"I beg your pardon for one moment, Mr. Secretary," Lee said as Seward stopped at the bottom step and turned.

Both men failed to notice Colonel Freemantle of Her Majesty's Coldstream Guards, there in the capacity of an observer to the American Civil War, as he watched and listened beneath the shelter of the front porch. He was beyond curious as to the politician's business in the headquarters of the Confederacy.

"I believe you gave me all I needed to know, General, that both sides are so maddened by bloodlust that they will send American boys off to die in a foreign land that they only read about in Sunday school."

Lee ignored Seward's anger. "I am obviously curious, Mr. Secretary—what Union officer has the president chosen to lead this impossible sortie into the unknown?"

Seward looked up at the dwindling rain and then back at Lee. "I believe he is an officer you may know very well, General."

Lee stepped out onto the porch and waited. Colonel Freemantle pretended as though he were wool-gathering by looking away.

"He's an officer that fell out of favor with General McClellan after the Peninsula campaign when this officer accused the general of cowardice. The president ordered Secretary of War Stanton to hide this man away from McClellan by sending him out west to count red savages or something to that effect."

"His name and rank, sir?" Lee persisted.

"Lieutenant Colonel John Henry Thomas." Seward turned and made his way back to the carriage.

At that same moment Colonel Freemantle, the British observer, slipped away off the porch and into the rainy night. The colonel had his own communiqués to write to Her Majesty, Queen Victoria regarding the most unusual meeting in the annals of modern warfare. He was sure to remember the name that he overheard on this rainy night in Virginia. That would be the starting point where Her Majesty's government would start to unravel this strange development in the American destiny.

General Lee turned and entered the house. He walked to the rocker and then eased himself down. His aide came in and placed a blanket over his legs and then waited for the general to speak. Lee only sat and stared at the fire.

"I wish I were going with them," Lee mumbled under his breath.

"Sir?" Taylor asked.

"It is nothing, Major, just gathering wool." Lee seemed to come awake as he forced the strange meeting from his thoughts and quickly returned them to where they desperately needed to be—the conduct of what remained of the war and how he could make the Army of Northern Virginia hang on long enough to get peace negotiations started.

The aide was about to ask the general his meaning, but Lee stopped him with his quiet voice.

"Send for General Longstreet. We move the army south before midnight."

With the most unusual meeting of the Civil War concluded, the United States of America was about to embark on the most dangerous international excursion in its short history— the invasion of the Ottoman Empire.

BUCKINGHAM PALACE, LONDON, ENGLAND
JULY 30, 1863

The dawn skies broke open with bright sunshine only a few hours after the heavy rains had washed the British capital clean with their fury. The palace was all bustle this morning in preparation for the queen to meet with the French ambassador. All who worked within the confines of the palace knew only too well that if Victoria was anything she was a stern hater of French politics. Today she would harangue the French representative about their massive ship-building program that had begun to worry the queen's admirals.

The prime minister of the United Kingdom sat patiently in the long and richly appointed hallway awaiting the call that would see him into the queen's drawing room, where she sat eating a hastily prepared breakfast. As servants hustled from one end of the hallway to the other he watched the faces of those who worked closely with the queen and he could tell they were all on edge. Hushed whispers that would represent shouts in other parts of the country were heard coming from the head butler to all of his minions.

The telegram from Portsmouth had arrived at his offices at three thirty that morning and the prime minister had informed the palace that he needed an immediate audience with the queen as soon as humanly possible. He had been granted the time and now he sat waiting on Her Majesty to finish her toast and tea.

Prime Minister Henry John Temple, the third Viscount Palmerston, or as the queen herself liked to call him, Pam, was a humorless man who found the shortcomings of others far more irritating than a man in his position was allowed to feel, or, voice.

"Excuse me, sir, but Her Majesty will see you now," the queen's attendant said, clearing his throat as an interruption of the thoughts of the sour man.

Lord Palmerston nodded once and then reached for the leather satchel at his side, which contained the information he had received from Portsmouth that morning. He stood, fussed with his coat, and then followed the assistant into the queen's private quarters.

The news would soon be delivered to Her Majesty that the Americans were once more raising their ugly heads.

The queen of Great Britain and her colonies turned her head and faced the prime minister as he began the established procedure for greeting the queen. She wore an intricate woven bathrobe and her thinning hair was hidden under a white nightcap. She said nothing but swished her hand through the air toward the small table at which she sat. Palmerston finished his bow anyway and then came forward.

Victoria an the aura about her that she was destined to be the leader of the most powerful nation on earth, and she knew it—current state of dress notwithstanding.

"Pam, what brings you out of that little hovel of an office at this hour?"

"Your Majesty, I have received a communiqué wired from Portsmouth this morning. The message was relayed from HMS *Slaughter* as soon as she docked."

Victoria sat stoically and with her delicate right hand shoved a small piece of leftover bread from one end of her empty plate to the other as Palmerston opened his case.

"It seems I remember that my ship *Slaughter* was attempting to run the American blockade outside of Charleston. Am I correct in this or is my memory failing?"

"Your memory is as sharp as ever, Your Majesty. She was indeed, and she did manage to break into the harbor and deliver the war materiel we promised the Confederacy."

"Not that it will do our American southern friends any good at this point. It seems their setback in Pennsylvania early last month may have written the final chapter in their rather short history," Victoria said as she sadly shook her head.

"From the reports I received, their General Lee is quite capable of reversing the current trend of defeat."

"A flood is a flood, Pam, you know that. Once the waters of defeat gain a sloping ground there is no stopping it from inundating your house, and the southern house is taking on water at an alarming rate, wouldn't you say?"

"Yes, Majesty," Lord Palmerston said as he nodded and then held forth the cable from Portsmouth. "It took some time for HMS *Slaughter* to sneak out of Charleston, but she finally managed to get past the Union blockade in a thick bank of fog. She carried back far more than cotton mercantile on the return trip." He handed Victoria the yellow paper. She took the offered telegram and then held up a small pair of reading glasses to her gray eyes as she read.

"Our Colonel Freemantle has spied more than war in America. What do you make of this meeting between Secretary of State Seward and General Lee? I would think that any surrender request would have been forwarded through to Richmond and President Davis."

"Normally yes, but my people suspect it is more than that." Palmerston again reached into the satchel and brought out another flimsy telegram delivered by ship. "Our man at the White House has passed along a report of a seemingly benign meeting between President Lincoln and Professor Lars Ollafson. He's a theology professor at Harvard University. A rather brilliant scholar, so much so that he had accompanied our own Professor James Kensington, of Oxford, and three other Englishmen and four American scholars on a field expedition."

"Pam, why exactly are you telling me this?" Victoria asked as she stood from the small table and gestured to her ladies in waiting that she was ready to get dressed.

Palmerston averted his eyes as the queen maneuvered to a large silk screen.

"I'll refresh your memory," he said as he placed the satchel down. "Professor James Kensington was the man who had an audience with you more than four years ago to ask for funding for an expedition."

Queen Victoria stuck her head around the screen and looked at the prime minister. "Not that silly old wives' tale again?"

"It seems our esteemed Professor Kensington received outside assistance after you curtly dismissed his expedition as"—he lowered his head—"folly."

"So I did," she said as she again vanished behind the screen. "So, what have we, Pam?"

"Professor Kensington is dead, along with six others, and the entirety of the expedition's personnel have vanished with the exception of one man—Professor Ollafson. He escaped Turkey with a large parcel and then made his way back to the United States where he took the meeting with Mr. Lincoln and most of his cabinet, and after this meeting there was great dissention, as reported by our man in the White House. After that the professor vanished. Where? We do not yet know."

Victoria reappeared from behind the dressing screen still wearing her robe. Her hair was now exposed and brushed, but the prime minister could see her aging was progressing quickly with the strain of her rule.

"Mr. Lincoln is reputed to be an extremely smart man. You are not telling me he will choose to go after this rather dubious prize that has exactly zero percent of a return on investment?"

"Evidently, Your Majesty, Mr. Lincoln was shown something from Ollafson's venture to Turkey that may have changed his mind."

Queen Victoria closed her eyes and then stepped back to continue dressing. "Right now we have our own troubles with the French, and now we receive word that hostilities could break out at any time in Africa. The Province of Natal's a little nervous about the Zulus across the Buffalo River. And here we are, using resources we cannot afford to be wasting, to examine if the American president has gone completely insane. With the problems he faces, even if the war is truly coming to a close, he has no time for foolishness such as this. So, from this point forward, Lord Palmerston, we take a wait-and-see attitude toward this preposterous theory that seems to have taken hold of every theologian in all of Europe. We wait, we see what our very puzzling Mr. Lincoln will do. Instruct your man at the White House that his queen is curious as to the details of the plan"—she again stuck her head out from behind the dressing screen—"if there is a plan. If there is, then we will deal with the Americans accordingly. If they make a run for the Aegean Sea and the Strait of Constantinople beyond, we will know Mr. Lincoln has fallen for this rather dubious fairy tale. If the Americans think they can get into Europe, we'll be there to remind them who rules the world's oceans."

Palmerston gathered his satchel and bowed even though the queen couldn't see him. He stopped and faced the dressing screen again.

"Your Majesty, if this is a fairy tale, as you believe—"

"You did not hear that from me, Pam," she said as she stuck her head out again. "My beliefs in that regard wouldn't go over too well with my subjects."

"But, if you believe that, why would we worry about Lincoln and what he believes may be there?"

Finally the queen emerged from behind the screen fully dressed. Her gown was rigid, but sparkling. She looked well, and now a far better match for the French ambassador.

"Because, Mr. Prime Minister, Mr. Lincoln is as much an

agnostic as myself. However, if the president of the United States sponsors this expedition, then whatever this Professor Ollafson passed on to the president makes the British Empire somewhat nervous. Thus"—she looked into the mirror that was held in front of her—"if Mr. Lincoln sees advantage in this foray then we must show just as much enthusiasm and fortitude. Clear?"

"Not at all, Majesty."

"Good, then I have not lost my ambiguous touch."

As Prime Minister Palmerston left the palace he suspected that he might soon be witness to a confused race to find out what the real truth was in eastern Turkey.

PART ONE

GHOSTS OF DAYS
GONE BY

Thou shalt be killed if thee can't find
the demon lurking in thou mind.
So off I ventured, to quench my thirst
of corpses piled with hearts-a-burst.
And on that quest what did I see?
The Wicked Path of Destiny.

—Joseph Clifford

1

The eight members of the Senate Oversight Committee were stunned to silence. The same could be said for the press seated inside the crowded room. Even military officers were visibly shocked at the comment uttered moments before by the United States Army officer seated before the panel. As the room burst into chatter, several of the higher-ranking military men, mostly army officers, glared at the man seated at the table with his JAG attorneys and then angrily left the chamber. The U.S. Army lawyers were all still shaking their heads at his statement as the men implicated in the cover-up stormed out. After all, it wasn't every day that one of the official wunderkinds of the U.S. military so readily committed career suicide in front of the entire nation.

Senator James Kellum, head of the Joint Armed Services Committee, hammered the gavel several times to quiet the observers and guests.

"Ladies and gentlemen, I will clear this chamber if there is one more outburst like that. This is not a soap opera with good guys and bad guys. This is an investigation into the charges of misconduct by supreme command authority in a combat area. People's lives and careers are on the line here and I will not let these proceedings devolve into anarchy."

The C-SPAN cameras seemed to be locked on the tired and scarred face of the young army major sitting beside his JAG counsel at the table. The man didn't seem to hear the commotion that his last statement had unleashed. The major pursed his lips and shook his head as he must have been feeling his career slipping out from underneath the polished chair he was sitting in.

He calmly poured himself a glass of water from the decanter before him. He sipped from the glass and waited for the senator to regain control. On the television screens of millions of viewers nationwide the C-SPAN cameras had zeroed in first on the green beret that sat upon the tabletop and then the rows of ribbons on the left breast of his green uniform jacket. The camera's sharp eye focused on the first ribbon on the top row. It didn't look like much, but the powder-blue ribbon with five stars represented the Congressional Medal of Honor. The camera's lens lingered and then slowly moved to the heavily tanned face of the army major who wore it. Although he appeared unfazed, the few men and women who knew him also knew the major was dying moment by moment. The chamber finally became still as the last of the high-ranking officers left the room.

Major Jack Collins calmly waited for the hearing to continue.

The senator from Missouri broke in before the head of the committee could continue his line of questioning, which drew the ire of the representative from New York. "Major Collins, to clarify your last, rather harsh statement that the decision to alter the highly detailed plans of the assault were ordered from CENTCOM," he demanded as again the raised voices of questions sprang from the onlookers inside the chamber. "Can you explain why someone would override a battle plan that had already been approved by the commander of Central Command?"

The young major thought before he answered. He knew that the question was a loaded one that had been specially

prepared by the only man on the committee whom Major
Collins trusted, the senator from Missouri who had asked the
question now so it could not be shunted aside by the oversight committee chair, Senator Charles Fennel of New York.
Collins, without glancing at his fidgeting JAG representatives, leaned forward, as did half of the nation toward their
television screens as he prepared to end not only his career
but possibly many others in and out of uniform.

"The answer to your question, Senator, is not an easy one.
It took me seven months to get to the truth after my assignment in Iraq was completed. By then the people responsible
thought it would have been put to bed, or as they hoped, forgotten."

"From my understanding, the investigation into the
debacle had been completed eight months before, soon after
the events had taken place," the senator from Missouri noted.
"Which was a little faster than I thought it should have been,
but the results of that investigation did not sit well with you,
am I correct in saying that, Major?"

"You are correct. When you're speaking about the lives
of twenty-seven men—men who I trained, worked, and lived
with, no sir, the investigation in my eyes fell far short of the
truth."

The head of the armed services committee, James Kellum,
was staring at his colleague from Missouri, as were the
C-SPAN cameras. Everyone in the country could see that the
senior man from New York was as angry as anyone had ever
seen him.

"I'll ask you directly, Major, were numbers of Apache
Longbow gunships and Blackhawk helicopters allowed for in
the planning of Operation Morning Glory adequate for the
mission to succeed?"

"In my original operational plan there were more than
enough evac and support ships to cover all aspects of the mission in Afghanistan. Every soldier on that raid should have
been lifted out safely from the area after the operation was
complete."

"Yet almost two full squads of Special Forces personnel,

including twelve Army Rangers, were"—the senator from Missouri looked down at his notes momentarily for emphasis to his question—"in your words, Major Collins, 'left on the deck' because of inadequate evac response. Is this more or less correct?"

"The plan called for all personnel to be evacuated at the same time. The Taliban insurgents have a bad habit of waiting for the initial first wave to lift off and then striking at those troops left uncovered in the LZ, or landing zone. That was why the extra Apache Longbows were allotted, the added firepower to assist those left on the ground until the second wave of evacuation Blackhawks lifted off the last of the rear guard. The second attack group of gunships never arrived. The Apaches that were there had RTB because of fuel concerns. My men were left out there with no air cover whatsoever with over three thousand Taliban insurgents in the mountains surrounding them."

"How many of the twenty-seven American boys made it off of that mountain, Major?" the senator asked as the chamber fell silent.

"None."

"Major, what happened to those men?" the senator continued.

"Six were taken alive into the mountains. We found their bodies three weeks after my return to Afghanistan."

"The rest?"

"The description of their condition the next morning is not something I will go into here. Suffice it to say these men were massacred."

"During your personal investigation what was it you uncovered in regard to the missing element of air cover on April 6, 2005?"

"That three Apache and six Blackhawks had been reassigned in my absence for escort duty by CENTCOM, not in Afghanistan but in Florida through MacDill Air Force Base."

Again the gavel silenced most of the shocked and angry people watching inside the chamber.

"The decision was not made in theater, but at MacDill? Is that unusual, Major Collins?"

"Highly. Someone at CENTCOM changed the orders on the logistics of Operation Morning Glory to provide security in another area of responsibility."

"And what area of responsibility is more important than the lives of twenty-seven American soldiers?"

Collins stayed silent as the head of the armed services committee grew red and he began to fume as he awaited the fall of the guillotine blade. Thinking now that this committee should never have been formed, and wouldn't have if that bastard from Missouri hadn't taken it to the press, Kellum slammed the gavel down again as he angrily silenced the room. The major looked from the tabletop to the man glaring at him from the center of the podium.

"The commanding general at MacDill changed the orders to provide security for a fact-finding inquiry from Washington on the conduct of operations in the Kabul area. This committee was escorted by the six Blackhawks and my three missing Apache Longbows. The area commander in Kabul ordered the helicopters to leave the investigative committee at a secure location and proceed on mission for dust-off of my men. The order was overridden from Kabul after the senators and committee complained about staying over in a small village. Because of their comfort concerns, twenty-seven men won't be coming home."

It had been the former CENTCOM commander who had angrily left the chamber a few moments before when he realized Collins was not going to play the game. The threats to Collins and his career had not had the desired effect on the obstinate major.

"Major Collins, according to your investigation, what civilian personnel were involved in the fact-finding mission to Afghanistan that month?"

Collins looked straight at the head of the senate oversight committee. "Senator James Kellum and several civilian contractors from various corporations."

The gavel slammed on the table again as the room erupted. The senator from New York shot to his feet as the wooden gavel fought for order. "I pray you have proof of that statement, especially after the commanding general of CENT-COM cleared my committee of all of these rumors."

Collins smiled, reached down and retrieved his briefcase, and placed it on the table before him. The room hushed as Collins removed a plastic-covered sheet of paper. "Yes, Senator Kellum, I do have proof." Jack held up the paper and placed it on the desk before him. His JAG lawyers frowned as they all knew Collins had just officially ended his military career. "The order was issued by the commander of CENTCOM and countersigned by yourself, Senator."

That was it. The statement was out and entered into the official record. The first soldier to turn on a four-star general and the civilian senator who controlled the purse strings of the military. As the words and career of Jack Collins faded, the eruption inside the senate hearing chamber exploded into a cacophony of shouts and gasps. The major easily slid the memo over to the front of the table where a senate aid removed it for the committee as the room continued to erupt and Senator Kellum kept slamming down his gavel.

EVENT GROUP COMPLEX, NELLIS AIR FORCE
BASE, NEVADA

Almost a full mile beneath the sands of the abandoned World War II target range was an ancient underground sea that had vanished more than six million years before. All that remained was the largest cave system in the continental United States. While dwarfing the Carlsbad system of caves in New Mexico, the Nellis system was not a park or recreational site. The cave system was never placed in any registry of geological wonders like its sister in neighboring New Mexico's desert, but had been kept secret since its discovery in 1922. The reason for this silence was rumored to have been built in 1943–1945 by the same men and women who had designed the new Pentagon building in Washington. Their fi-

nal architectural drawings would never see the light of day
in any public or federal planning office in the nation, though.

The cave system was home to the darkest organization in
American governmental history. Department 5656 was officially a part of the U.S. National Archives and was more
obscure than most aspects of the National Security Administration. The department, unofficially named the Event
Group, was assigned the task of discovering the truth behind
world history. To investigate how and why we got to where
we were. To avoid mistakes of history so they could never
be repeated. The head of this group now sat inside of his office on the seventh level of the complex that was situated
above seventy-five more levels of archives, specimen vaults,
and engineering and science laboratories.

The small, balding man looked over at the former head of
the agency who was sitting across from his large desk. The
tall man had a black eye patch over his right eye and his cane
was propped against the director's desk. The bald man shook
his head sadly as he watched the developments on C-SPAN.
He looked across at the six-foot-six silver-haired man who
had stayed on long after his official retirement four years before to assist in the daunting task of assisting the new director
in navigating his way through the ins and outs of keeping the
facility, its duty, and its personnel secret above all government
agencies.

"So, I wonder who assisted Major Collins in obtaining that
top-secret memo?" He smiled at his former boss and the man
who had recruited him fifteen years before. "I suspect it had
to have been someone who knows where to find such things
inside the Washington trash heap."

Former United Sates Senator Garrison Lee of Maine
smiled and shook his head in the negative.

"Nah, my days on the Hill, absconding with the secrets
of others, have long been over."

"How about the old OSS days? You still know how to get
things others don't."

"The Office of Strategic Services would have resented that

statement. We were as honest as the day was long, Director Compton."

"Uh-huh, just like its little bastard offspring the CIA?"

Garrison Lee laughed as the double doors to the office opened and a woman with silver hair and gold-rimmed glasses hanging from a chain entered. Alice Hamilton, assistant to the director of the Event Group, came toward the desk and placed a file on the top.

"There you go. The major's orders have been cut and the president has signed off on them."

Garrison Lee reached out and picked up the flimsy set of papers. "You don't know how many favors I had to give up to get that signature. The president is not real happy with our Major Collins."

"I wonder why," Alice said, never afraid to speak her mind, especially after serving with the Group almost as long as Lee himself. In fact, speaking her mind was just why she was retained by the newest director of Department 5656, Dr. Niles Compton.

"Well, the president's and the army's sad demeanor toward one of its own means that we get the man we wanted all along." Lee stood and with the assistance of his cane walked toward the far wall to pour himself a cup of coffee. "Did you put in the correct date of Major Collins's arrival in Nevada?"

"Yes, as you requested. He has the needed time off—two weeks to think about what a mess his career's in should allow the major to at least listen to your pitch to join our underground ship of fools," Alice Hamilton said as she headed for the double doors, but she stopped before opening them and turned to both men. "But you better be careful just what it is you wish for, gentlemen, because this Major Collins is unlike any soldier you have ever met. I mean, what other officer would throw it all away out of principle and dedication to his fallen men? I would think that would make him dangerous to bureaucrats like yourselves."

Alice smiled, batted her eyelashes as was her irritating trait, and then left the large office. She hoped that they understood that they were about to deal with a career officer who was shockingly, to the army's dismay, a man of deep convictions on the right and wrong of things. It was what they were looking for, and the two men in the office knew they were just like Major Jack Collins; therefore they were comfortable with their choice.

"That damn woman is as irritating now as when she worked for me," Garrison Lee said as he sat back down into his chair facing the director. "But she's right as always about one thing," Lee finished as he sipped his coffee.

"What is that?" Compton asked, really not wanting to know.

Lee smiled and placed his cup on the desktop. "Men like Major Jack Collins have a very low tolerance for people like us."

"You really mean people like me, don't you?" Compton asked.

"Not at all. But one thing I do know, if we hadn't interfered, Colonel Collins would have had this shit pile land right back on the president's desk as being ultimately responsible for the fiasco in Afghanistan. I'm just glad my old friend from Missouri changed his avenue of attack and left the president out of it."

"Your point?" Niles asked, getting a little nervous.

"Just the same as Alice's point, I guess. If the man was willing to bring down the president of the United States, do you think he would hesitate to do the right thing in this agency if we let him or his men down?"

"Well, you took a lot of years of research to find out just what kind of man he is. Now you know. With this new insight into the major's character, do you still want him to lead the security department?" Niles asked with a smirk.

"Absolutely."

EVENT GROUP COMPLEX, NELLIS AIR FORCE
BASE, NEVADA
JULY 2006

The Event Group Complex was relatively quiet at 3:40 a.m. on Sunday. Director Niles Compton moved through the deserted serving line inside the vast dining hall. The on-duty chef was wiping his hands on a white towel as he came from the kitchen after hearing the director was in the dining area. He, along with the entire mess crew, knew that Dr. Compton often toured the facility at the oddest hours, but this stop-in was unprecedented, as the director usually just called and had coffee or a meal delivered to his office on level seven. Compton's presence in the serving line at this hour woke the sleepy-eyed mess personnel like no alarm ever could. As he approached the serving line the director was pouring a cup of coffee and perusing the pastry selection.

The chef looked over the interior of the cafeteria and saw only one other person at the far end of the room, sitting alone and staring at a cup of coffee. It was the new head of Group security, Major Collins. The man had not moved since coming in an hour before. The entire complex was in a mood because of the extreme losses the Group and the 101st Airborne had sustained in the desert event last week. It was well known that the new major was not taking lightly the deaths of so many, and it was now rumored that as a result, Collins was going to turn down the offer of permanently staying with the Group. The man looked as if he'd had enough of fatalities in any form.

"Dr. Compton, can I get you some breakfast, or maybe a late dinner?" the tall, very thin chef asked. The military rank displayed on his chef's whites was that of a United States Navy chief petty officer.

Compton stifled a yawn and then turned to face the navy cook. "No thank you, Chief, just trying to stay awake for the most part," Niles Compton said as he nodded at the taller man.

With one last look toward the major, the chef moved back to his kitchen and Niles Compton steeled himself for what was to come. He turned with his cup and saucer and saw with relief that Garrison Lee had come in early as promised to go over the situation with Jack Collins. Lee was fresh off a heart attack brought on by the events in the Arizona desert. It had been extremely hard to keep him isolated long enough to get the heart condition under control because Garrison wanted to be in on the extensive debrief of the small green alien, the Matchstick Man, the lone surviving extraterrestrial crewman from Chato's Crawl, Arizona. Lee had undoubtedly used that excuse to get out of the house he shared with Alice Hamilton in Las Vegas. The main objective of this morning's meeting was to conclude Major Jack Collins's introduction to a federal agency in which he had already taken life, and ended it. It was rumored that Collins was about to leave the Group and fall into an uneasy retirement from the U.S. Army.

Niles waited for Lee to get himself a cup of coffee and then they both moved through the deserted cafeteria to confront Jack Collins about his upcoming decision. As they approached, they saw that Jack was perusing the personnel files of the Event Group personnel who had been killed in action last week. His face was stone as he read the names to himself. He was so absorbed in his task that he did not even glance up when Niles and Lee joined him.

"I was wondering when you were going to corner me, but I suspected with the senator's health problems I would have had the time to formally commit my answer to paper."

Niles reflected that Collins was not your ordinary military officer. Jack was a thorough, analytical thinker and that was what he and Lee were after.

"We figured the ambush technique was best for the situation," Lee said as he placed his cup and saucer down without waiting to be asked. "I suppose you wouldn't mind the company of an old fart and super nerd long enough to bend your ear a while?" Lee finished as he sat, placing his cane against the table as he gestured for Niles to do the same. "Besides, with my retirement, Alice has me doing some very strange things around the house, like fixing things, or cutting this, or trimming that. I would rather be here bothering you than turn into Mr. Fixit at home."

"I take it Alice doesn't know you left home?" Jack inquired.

Lee pointed to the double doors of the cafeteria and Jack

saw Lee's assistant Alice standing there with her left brow raised and shaking her head.

"Don't be foolish. It would be easier to escape a Russian gulag than to escape her scrutiny. She drove me here, which means I have very little time to conduct business, so I will get started."

"I've pretty much decided what I'm going to do," Collins said as he pushed his cold cup of coffee away.

Niles stirred sugar into his own cup and then looked at Collins. He removed his glasses, a frequent move that Jack had learned meant Niles was about to get serious.

"Last week when Alice and Lieutenant McIntire gave you the grand tour of the vault levels, we never got a chance to ask what you thought of our finds and artifacts," Niles said as he placed his glasses on the tabletop and slowly raised his coffee to his lips.

"The tour was cut quite short, as you well know, when you called about the event in the desert."

"Well, the senator and I would like to finish up that tour before you make your final decision on your appointment to this Group." Niles placed his cup down and looked at Collins, who still hadn't committed to anything. The deaths in the desert had really affected him.

"Major, you have to understand what we do here far better than we have been able to explain thus far," Lee said as he joined Compton in trying to persuade the major to give them a chance to show him why they needed his expertise so badly. If the fight in Arizona hadn't explained it, they knew exactly what would. They were about to pull out the ace they had up their sleeves.

Jack glanced up and saw that Alice was still watching them. He knew then that Alice was also a part of this plot, not just Compton and Lee.

"I'm afraid young McIntire doesn't know the full story. There are only three people in the world that have all the puzzle pieces, Major, and that is what we wish to finish up tonight. The right tour, the right artifact that will tie this whole thing together for you," Lee said as he too looked back at Alice and then slowly stood with the aid of his cane. "Mind joining us, Major Collins?"

"Okay, where to?" Jack stood along with Compton and started a journey into the past that he never would have dreamed about.

"The largest, most secure depository in the United States. Level sixty-one, vault one," Niles said as he led the way out of the cafeteria.

Lee placed a hand on Alice's shoulder and then turned to face Niles and Jack. "It's story time, Major Collins, and you are about to get wowed."

Collins raised his eyebrows but followed them out the door, only pausing long enough to receive a knowing smile and wink from Alice Hamilton.

"Wowed is just about right," she said as she fell into line heading for the elevators.

The tube elevator operated on air-cushioned propellant and traveled close to fifty miles per hour. The four stepped off and went to the security arch, where one of Jack's people accepted IDs and proceeded to send them through the eye-scan check, clearing them all for entrance into the vault level. Jack followed the three inside an enormous hallway that had the dreamlike facade of several hundred bank vaults—the most secure location outside of Fort Knox and the NSA building. Each vault contained an artifact from the history of the world, and Jack had not returned to the vault level since his mission to Arizona, simply because he never wanted the wonders of the vault levels to sway his decision about staying or leaving the Group. The magnificent finds had the ability to cloud the mind and could make the process of deciding his destiny far more difficult.

Lee and Alice stopped at a familiar spot, the first vault Jack had seen at the Group. Lee had pointed it out to him the day of his arrival. He knew by the size of the reinforced steel door what artifact lay beyond—the Ark. The last time he'd seen it he hadn't had time to explain to Lee and Compton that he was far from being a believer in the fantastical story of

Noah and his Ark. Collins found it hard to believe in anything other than his own ability and keeping men under his command as safe as he could.

"I suppose you need no explanation of what's behind this door?" Lee said as Niles Compton scanned his ID into the reader and stepped back as a smaller access door opened beside the larger, impenetrable stainless-steel door.

"I know what you claim it to be, but I've yet to be convinced, and to tell you the truth, gentlemen"—he nodded at Alice—"and lady, I am at least skeptical, and unbelieving at the most."

"That's exactly how you should feel, Jack," Niles said as he stepped aside to allow the three to precede him into the giant vault area.

Collins saw it in person for the first time and he had to admit the monitors inside Niles's office did the artifact no justice. No matter what this object truly was, Jack knew it to be impressive. The Ark was a broken wreck, but its age could be summed up in just one word—ancient. It was the oldest thing Collins had ever laid eyes on. He didn't need too many impressive degrees to see that. The ship, if that was what it really was, was only a quarter of its former tonnage. The object ended in a jagged and twisted wreck. The beams and what remained of its wooden decking had long since turned to petrified stone. You could see the grain in the wood and know what it was immediately. The bow of the vessel soared into the heights of the giant vault. Spotlights illuminated the scaffolding placed around the artifact where many a teacher, professor, and student had crawled over its exterior searching for clues as to its real identity.

It had been explained to Collins that the Ark had been officially carbon-dated to more than thirteen thousand years old. That was still a bone of contention inside the Group because the theology department espoused the accepted theory that the Noah civilization was only five thousand years old. The Event Group and its personnel never argued between departments but everyone knew it was an accepted fact that Virginia Pollock and her Nuclear Sciences Division were never, ever, wrong in their time and age calculations, and if you knew Virginia Pollock you'd better not begin to question the science. She was a firm and adamant believer in dating material and had never been proven wrong on any established date.

Jack followed Niles, Lee, and Alice up the staircase of the closest scaffold. Their footsteps made loud clanging sounds as they moved across the steel. Collins saw amazement in everyone's eyes. They must have already taken in the sight of the artifact many, many times before this morning, but clearly the viewing never failed to induce awe. Collins didn't feel that way. It wasn't because he was a cold military analyst, or that he didn't have a great imagination. It was the fact that something described as divine providence ordered this vessel constructed under the direct supervision of God, which Jack considered ridiculous. A romantic would always love to believe that God had mercy on man and saved them with the Ark of wood, but Jack was a realist and knew that God had long abandoned mankind, including men from antiquity.

"Fairy tales, right?" Lee asked, penetrating Jack's inner thoughts. Lee placed his cane on the railing overlooking the ancient vessel.

The wooden construction on the centerline main deck looked as precise as many a painting proclaimed. Collins could see the hairline fractures where the Ark had either been dismantled or damaged. The reverse-engineering to reconstruct the Ark must have been a massive undertaking. There was a house-like structure on the upper deck, and about eighty-five feet of the pitched roof and frame remained intact and looked as if this was where the supposed family of Noah would have lived high above their animal pens. Collins moved his eyes from the sight below to the single piercing eye of Lee.

"Excuse me?" Jack said as he failed to get the point even though he had been thinking about the same word only moments before.

"Just fairy tales. Stories that make for good Sunday school lesson plans. Good versus evil, the fight of man against nature, the determination of the human soul. Yes, many a good lesson is derived from such a story, wouldn't you say?" Lee said as he moved to the major's side and then gestured with his free hand as the other stabilized his weak frame against the railing. "But a fairy tale nonetheless," he said when Collins remained silent. He patted Jack on the back and then held out his hand for Alice to continue.

"The Ark, if that's what it is—and you will have to decide for yourself if that's the case—is not the only artifact we have here at the Group that substantiates the data we have collected." She took out a large aluminum box, which she opened and held out to Lee. Garrison Lee reached inside and gently, as if he were handling crystal, removed a leather-bound book. It was as though Lee were touching divinity itself. "The real treasure here, Jack," he said as he felt the warmth of the leather beneath his fingers, "is not that petrified jumble of wooden beams, but this."

Collins looked at what Lee was holding and was satisfied that he was looking at a journal, surely not as old as the object below in the vault, but old; within a hundred or two hundred years would be his estimate.

"Major, you are a student of your family lineage, correct?" Niles asked as he placed his hands behind his back, which he did every time he went into teaching mode.

"Yes, my mother and sister have concluded we started somewhere in Ireland and came to the colonies in 1678; nothing before that, though. On my father's side, they arrived even earlier."

"Military men—I must admit I never felt the calling, Major," Niles said, almost apologizing for that fact. "Special people I have come to admire." Niles turned and nodded at the book Lee held in his aged hand. "How many in your family have given the ultimate sacrifice, Major?"

"Three, at least as far as my mother and sister's limited history tells of both my father's and my mom's side."

"Yes, your file says Civil War, cause of death unknown. The Spanish American war, I believe you lost your great-uncle in Santiago, Cuba. And then finally your father in 1972, somewhere in Southeast Asia."

Jack remained silent, as he never spoke about his father to anyone. That area of his life was off-limits to anyone and everyone. He just continued to eye Niles Compton as he spoke.

"This journal is from 1864 through 1865. It covers the event that brought the artifact before you back to these shores. It was written by a man much like you, Jack. A person such as yourself will be able to determine its value, its very validity. You'll know after you study this what to think about that down there." He waved at the Ark below them.

"I have learned in life, gentlemen, that the same people who wrote stories about things like this"—Jack also gestured toward the ravaged vessel—"also wrote in journals, and they both usually have the same failing. If it was written by men, be it the Bible, the Koran, or anything else, it's fallible. Men love to embellish. Stories told about things like this"—he nodded at the journal and then the Ark—"or that, are sometimes made more readable, more exciting if they just add this, or add that. No, I'm not a big believer in journals or the writings of ancient scribes who told tales of the power of God or the foresight of a single man."

Alice smiled and it was almost as loud as a shout. Jack looked at her and she stepped up to him and patted him on the shoulder.

"I told them they would have to allow you to read the journal to make you a believer."

Lee held out the leather-bound journal.

"What do you say, Major, a little light reading and then we'll meet again to discuss your future with Department 5656. Fair enough?" Niles asked as Lee continued to hold the journal out for Jack to take, or leave it and the Group behind.

Collins nodded and took the offered book, and before he could change his mind the trio left the major and exited the largest vault ever constructed.

Collins watched them go and then slowly paced toward the

viewing stand that served students when they were being taught in one of the varying tasks that the faculty had arranged for them. He sat and looked at the Ark below him, and then at the leather journal. He read the words in the lower right-hand corner that used to be inlaid with gold but were now just a discolored indentation.

"John Henry Thomas, Colonel, United States Army, August 1864–April 1865."

Jack ran his fingers across the broken and cracked leather where the gold lettering used to be, and then again looked away and wondered why Lee, Alice, and Niles believed this would have any bearing on his decision. He took a deep breath and momentarily thought of the men and women he had lost just this past month in the desert. He closed his eyes, so desperately tired of writing letters to his dead soldiers' parents, wives, or husbands. Collins was sorely tempted to leave the journal on the seat beside him and deliver his resignation to Compton. Instead he held onto the old book and decided that he would give the Group this one shot to sway his choice—to stay, or retire into a bleak future without the career he had chosen.

He opened the one-hundred-and-fifty-year-old journal and started to read.

PART TWO

LOST SOULS OF THE POTOMAC

.... They banish our anger forever when they laurel the graves of our dead! Under the sod and the dew, waiting the judgment-day, love and tears for the Blue, tears and love for the Gray.

—**Francis Miles Finch**
(1827–1907)

2

The small man had been waiting every day for the past three years. Like clockwork he would arrive at 6:00 a.m., except on Sundays, and sit in the same chair patiently awaiting his name to be called. For three years it had not. The staff, including the president's personal secretary, John Hay, even called the goofy professor by name, his form and figure had become so familiar.

Professor Lars Ollafson had met with Abraham Lincoln the second week into his term as president. Every day since that meeting, the former professor from Harvard College had returned, hoping for the answers to his questions of three years before. The man had been patient.

It was now past seven in the evening and most everyone had left the hallway where visitors and office seekers piled in to see the president. Ollafson sat alone, his old and battered leather case at his feet. His beard was growing long and looked as if it had not been trimmed in over a year. His clothes were looking ragged and unkempt. Ollafson was polishing his glasses when the door to the president's office opened and John Hay emerged. He was reading a document when he looked up and frowned. The young secretary was saddened to see the old man still waiting to see the man who had tried to ignore him for the past three years. He grimaced and then approached the sorrowful soul sitting alone.

"Professor," Hay said as he stepped up to the old man and sat beside him. "The president sends his regards, but with the action happening in Virginia and with the festivities of the anniversary of our independence, the president just hasn't the time to meet. I'm sure you can understand."

Ollafson replaced the old and bent wire-framed glasses on his small nose and inspected the youthful face of John Hay.

"The victory of General Mead in Pennsylvania, was it as resounding a defeat for the southern forces as the newspapers claim?"

Hay was taken aback by the inquiry. He sat back in his chair and looked the old professor over. He replaced the letter he was reading into his small case and then smiled.

"Well, Professor, yes, it was a resounding victory for our boys and the president is absorbed in continuing the fight even as we speak." He continued looking at the man who was now an outcast among his own kind. "However, Mr. Lincoln is quite adamant that General Mead follow up and destroy what's left of General Lee's army. There is some hesitation, I'm afraid, and we just may lose the advantage. So, that's the main reason the president has very little time for other matters."

Ollafson squirmed in his chair but still made no move to gather his case and once more leave the White House without seeing the man he'd come to see. He pursed his lips and looked at the far younger secretary.

"The president, he said . . . I would know the time. I believe now is that time."

"Perhaps it is not the exact victory the president once referred to, as many things have changed during these hard years."

"He said I will know the time," he repeated.

Hay exhaled and then slowly stood. "I know you've waited

many years for this to happen, Professor, but the war has changed the president."

"That is why I must remind him. Now is that time he spoke of three years ago. It has to be now or others will see to it that it is too late to act. The history will be lost to others who will not share in the glory of the find. We must act and act now." He stared straight ahead as he spoke, not focusing on anything other than the point he was attempting to make.

John Hay looked down upon the professor. "I'm sorry." He started to walk away as the features of the old man drained of color. Hay made a show of clasping his small case as he paused on his way out.

"I would say that the best chance you might have to see the president is when he sneaks out at eleven o'clock to visit the soldiers' home on the outskirts of Washington City. Seeing his boys and asking if they needed anything calms him." John Hay half-turned as he placed his case under his arm and adjusted his suit jacket. "But being Mr. Lincoln's secretary, as I am, I would be remiss in saying that." He started walking away from the silent and stunned professor, who watched the secretary's retreating form. "Good evening, Professor Ollafson."

Ollafson just nodded his silent thanks and then reached for his leather case. He pulled out his pocketwatch, which had also seen better days, and noted the time. He had a long wait and he knew he couldn't do it on the White House grounds.

Professor Lars Ollafson knew where he had to be at eleven o'clock.

The professor had paid his cab fare and the carriage had left him at the dirt road leading to the soldiers' home. The festivities of the Fourth had dwindled down to only a few shots being fired into the air by rowdies across the river. Every time a loud report sounded Ollafson would duck his head as the noise reminded him of the running fight with the dark forces four years before. Every night he had been visited since returning from the mountain, and his memories of those days and nights refused to fade from his old and tired mind. He would swear he could hear the screams of his friends and colleagues who died on the slopes and roads of that black place.

The sound was so light that the professor almost missed it among the gunshots across the river. The horse's falling hooves came to his ear and he forcibly tried to remove the memory of those days from his thoughts. He gathered himself and looked out upon the road, spotting a large brown roan approaching. The figure on the mount was clearly recognizable. His pant leg was hitched up far past his ankle, allowing Ollafson a good view of a white leg and beyond that, cotton long-johns.

Abraham Lincoln rode easily and without movement as he made his way along the road to the old soldiers' home. The tall hat he was known for was not on his head but was held in his left hand. The dark hair was tousled and his face was lowered as his thoughts carried the president to another place, another time. This nightly sojourn was the only time Lincoln had all to himself. His sneaking out was a secret he thought was shared with no one.

Ollafson swallowed and then stepped out into the darkened road. Before he could utter his greeting another rider came springing out of the line of trees. Ollafson's eyes widened behind his thick glasses as the second rider came charging toward him with a drawn weapon. The professor threw his hands into the air and stepped back as the rider thrust his mount past the president's and came between him and the man in the roadway.

"Stop or you will be fired upon!" the man said loudly as his horse slid to a halt.

"Whoa, whoa," Lincoln called out.

"No, no, do not shoot, it is Professor Lars Ollafson, of Harvard Yard!" The professor actually hopped up and down several times in his anxiety over the thought of being accidentally shot.

"Mr. Pinkerton, are you going to shoot a distinguished man of learning, especially when you are not even supposed to be here?" Lincoln said as he placed his tall stovepipe hat on his mangled hair.

The heavyset man on the horse looked from the professor to the president. He un-cocked the double-shot derringer he held in his right hand as his own bowler hat came flying free of his bulbous head.

"I had to see it for myself. You have gone against all advice; all of my warnings have thus far been treated like folly. You cannot do this, Mr. President. This sneaking out without escort has to stop!" Allan Pinkerton spun his horse around and then slid his small pistol into a shoulder holster he had secured under his black coat.

"I see that my secret isn't quite the secret I thought it was. What tipped you off, sir?" Lincoln asked in mocking kindness even though he was furious deep inside.

"Mrs. Lincoln isn't as preoccupied as you may believe, sir. She informed me of your clandestine activities several weeks ago and I have been following you every time you leave the White House."

"So, my own wife is the spy. I should have known."

"Now, for you, sir, who are you and why are you here?" Pinkerton sprang from his horse and roughly searched Ollafson for any weapons. Allan Pinkerton's eyebrows rose when he pulled a brand-new navy Colt revolver from Ollafson's coat. Even Lincoln raised a brow when the weapon was shown to him. But still the president remained silent. "And what was the plan for this?" he asked the much smaller man. Ollafson was still too shocked at Pinkerton's sudden arrival to answer without stuttering. "Well, man, speak, will you?"

"I . . . I . . . I . . . am afraid of . . ." Ollafson lowered his head in shame.

"Come on, man," Pinkerton said as he lightly shook the professor.

"From what I've heard, the professor here has an inordinate fear of dark places. Does my memory fail me?" Lincoln asked as he clumsily stepped down from his horse with one leg momentarily getting caught in a stirrup. He straightened and then walked up to the pair. The moonlight allowed him to see the professor's frightened face. Lincoln reached out and patted Pinkerton on the arm until he released the old man's suit collar. The president reached out and took the Colt revolver from the security man, looked it over, and then handed it back to Ollafson, who was just as stunned as Pinkerton.

"Mr. President, you cannot—"

"Far be it from me to remove an item that makes a man feel more secure. After all, Mr. Pinkerton, I have you."

Ollafson took the offered weapon and then placed it back into his coat pocket.

Pinkerton reached down, retrieved his bowler hat, and angrily placed it on his head. He turned to face the president.

"All right, I did not want to do this, but I'm going to inform Mrs. Lincoln about this . . . this . . . security debacle, and let me say, sir, she will not be pleased." Pinkerton started to turn away and move toward his horse.

Lincoln smiled down upon the much smaller Ollafson.

"That woman has not outwardly been pleased for the past three years, especially with me."

Pinkerton ignored the remark and then pulled himself onto his horse. He spun the animal around and faced the two men.

"Don't come-a-hollering when those Johnny Rebs lie in wait and ambush you both. I guarantee you won't be laughin' and foolin' around then, will you?" he said as he spurred his horse and sped away.

Lincoln closed his eyes and then paced toward his horse and took up his reins once again. He was getting ready to step into the saddle when Ollafson spoke.

"You promised. It is time, Mr. President."

Abraham Lincoln lowered his head and wrapped the leather reins around the pommel of the McClellan saddle. He took a deep breath.

"Your expedition has already been approved by my office, Professor," Lincoln said as he finally pulled himself up into the saddle.

Ollafson was stunned at the quiet announcement. He didn't know how to proceed. He didn't know if it was worse when he thought the president was ignoring him or the fact that the decision had already been made and he was to be left out.

"And . . . and you were not going to inform me?" Ollafson said, his heart sinking.

Lincoln placed both hands on the saddle's pommel and then gently patted the horse on his thick neck. "It was thought that with your current . . . your current ties at the university, it may not be in good security conscience to allow you to go. I am sorry, Professor. My secretary of war says he will not support me in this if you are included on the expedition. Your foreign ties are what stand in the way of his trust."

"But, but I am an American. I have my papers proclaiming this! Why am I not included? I am loyal to the Union."

"It's not your loyalty as an American, Professor, it is your former acquaintances and colleagues that scare Mr. Stanton. It was hard enough to get that old war dog to see things my way, Professor. If I lose his support, we lose the expedition."

"Mr. President, the expedition needs me. I am a loyal American and I no longer have those friends, those acquaintances, nor the colleagues. Why am I being left behind?"

Lincoln lowered his head. "I'm afraid our little secret is not the secret it once was, my good professor. It seems there have been loose tongues wagging about." Lincoln shook his head sadly. "But when are there not wagging tongues in this bullet-hole-riddled vessel we call Washington?"

"Mr. President, I—"

"Professor Ollafson, the British government has somehow received word that we may be interested in a region of the eastern Ottoman Empire, and you and I both know they will go to untoward lengths to see us embarrassed. And if this information leaks to our very opinionated press corps, I am afraid I will not only be laughed out of office before my task is complete, but we will also lose all national credibility after this madness ends. If you are involved, the British will know exactly what it is we are trying for, and we just cannot have that. I promised certain people, north and south, that this would not be the case. I am truly sorry. You will be in on the final drafting of the orders but will not participate. I have to think about the young boys I am sending on this voyage. I will answer to them and them only."

"Mr. President, if I could only—" Ollafson pleaded.

"Ride with me for a spell, Professor. It's been so long since I spoke to a man with so many letters after his name that wasn't seeking a posting, or this office or that one."

Ollafson looked up at the thin man on the horse and then saw the tiredness written on every line of the man's face. Since 1860, when the professor first met the president, Abraham Lincoln had aged. One hundred years' worth of worry and pain were etched in those deep-cut wrinkles.

Lars Ollafson nodded his head and slowly walked beside the president as if the men were only on a nightly constitutional as they continued Lincoln's journey to see the wounded.

An hour later Lars Ollafson stumbled from the front doors of the old soldiers' home. He held his hat in his hand as he leaned from the porch railing. He swallowed as he tried in vain to get his emotions and stomach under control. He finally lost his late supper into the bare earth of the garden. Abraham Lincoln stepped from the hospital and hesitated as he took in the night air and sky. He half-turned back to peer inside the home for his wounded soldiers and shook his head as he raised his tall hat. Down below a black private held the reins of the president's horse and another that had been delivered for Ollafson.

"It appears we may see some rain before dawn." The president momentarily placed his hand on the smaller professor's shoulder, looking into the roadway beyond as if he were searching for something in the darkness. "It's never an easy thing. The first few times visiting this place shook me to my very soul, Professor. I told myself as I gazed upon those boys in there that what I was doing was the right thing." The president squeezed Ollafson's shoulder and then quickly patted it as he broke contact and moved off the porch. "But I lose my convictions most times when I look into some mother's son's eyes as he lies dying." He accepted the reins from the private and mounted his horse awkwardly. He adjusted his long legs into the stirrups and took in a deep breath of the night air. "Healing."

Ollafson wiped his mouth with his pocket handkerchief and glanced up to see the president just sitting there. "Sir?" he asked, not understanding the one-word comment. The professor kept envisioning the young boy inside who had no lower jaw, and he became aware of his stomach trying to come back up to invade his throat once more.

"I must find a way to heal this bloody wound I have inflicted upon the nation." Lincoln looked over at Ollafson and tipped his hat to the smaller man. "You have given me an opportunity, my good professor, and a chance at bringing back together an entire people. Even if we find absolutely nothing in that faraway place, just the attempt should do nicely. The rejoining of two peoples into one would be a salve to the nation."

Ollafson saw the sadness, the deep-seated agony that the president was experiencing, and for the first time thought he understood. Mr. Lincoln cared little for what was supposedly buried on that mountain; he was far more concerned about the men being sent to retrieve it. If he could see them return as one, then the voyage would prove that wounds could be bound and a healing could take place. Not for treasure, not for discovery . . . this was for his country.

"Professor, please understand, I have to give those boys the best chance possible at returning. Otherwise what is this all about?"

Lars Ollafson only half-nodded his head.

"I ride alone back to the White House, Professor." The president turned his horse as Ollafson stood rooted to the porch. "My company is not warm after my visits to this place, you understand," he said softly as his horse ambled down the dirt road. "You'll be contacted soon."

The professor watched the president leave and he became saddened for the man who was leading the nation. He placed his hat on his head as he turned back toward the open door of the hospital in time to hear a boy cry out for his mother. The cry was void of hope.

With determination Ollafson bounded down the steps and took the offered reins from the private. He knew now that bringing back the artifact was the only thing he could do to assist this man. He had come to admire him even though he now knew that the president was wrong. It did matter that they find it. The nation needed the guidance, the inspiration. He mounted the horse and spurred it forward. Lars Ollafson rode hard.

They needed to know that God was on the American side and there was only one place in the world where that could be accomplished—the Ottoman Empire.

The president slowly moved into the grand hallway and then paused as his eyes looked toward his office. He placed his hat on the small table as he turned toward the window, deep in thought.

"You should be well asleep by now, young man," he said without turning from the window.

John Hay stood silently behind the president. He never knew how his boss was always keenly aware when he attempted to come upon him with stealth. He shook his head in wonder.

"I have secrets also. I always wait up until you return from the soldiers' home."

Lincoln turned with a small smile on his lined face. "I knew that too."

Hay held out a telegram for the president, who looked from his secretary to the yellow paper and then turned back to the window and the brief flash of lightning in the distance. The illumination only caused him to think about General George Meade and his failure to pursue Robert E. Lee into Virginia fast enough to end this damnable war. It was as if the lightning had illuminated the future for his thoughts. He knew Meade would fail.

"You read it, Johnny, my eyes have beheld enough misery for one night. I can't see anymore."

Hay grimaced as he watched the president's shoulders sag. The young secretary knew that another change in command was forthcoming. Which would mean Mr. Lincoln would soon bring back a general the president despised—George McClellan was the only man capable of getting the grand army back in the war after their victory at Gettysburg. He decided that now was the most opportune time to deliver the message from the War Department and Secretary of War Stanton. Hay read the telegram.

"War Department to A. Lincoln. Be advised that orders have been transmitted to Fort Dodge, Kansas. Expect delay as subject is not currently assigned to post. Signed Stanton, Secretary of War."

Lincoln said nothing as his thoughts were in ten places at once, per his usual mode of mind games.

"What if the colonel is not found in time? Do we attempt to bring in another commanding officer to lead the expedition?"

"No," Lincoln said as he watched another bolt of lightning streak across the sky on the far side of the Potomac. "There is only one man who can do what we are asking."

"If you are thinking about relieving General Meade with your old enemy George McClellan, the odds are pretty good that our colonel, if he arrives intact from the west, will meet Little Napoleon here in the capital, and then you know all hell will break loose."

Lincoln finally turned away from the approaching storm and smiled broadly at Hay when the secretary used the derogatory moniker for McClellan.

"Are you saying the two may kill each other?"

"Possibly."

"Well, they always say there is a bright side to all things."

"Yes, sir."

"Inform me when the colonel acknowledges receipt of his new orders."

"Yes, sir." Hay turned to leave.

Lincoln rocked on his heels momentarily as he thought about his old acquaintance, Thomas. He would love to see the face of the man when he received the orders recalling him to Washington. He would more than likely think he was being recalled to finally be hung for his transgression against his old commander—one George B. McClellan. He smiled.

"Colonel John Henry Thomas, it's time to come home."

3

There was no decent water, no shade, and no protection from the unrelenting winds of the plains. The sparse trees were windworn and scraggly. The branch of the small creek, dubbed Sandy Creek by an obviously gifted mapmaker ten years before, was nothing more than a ribbon of water in the spring runoff at its height and a muddy wallow for buffalo in the summer months. The site was unappealing to the two men dressed in filthy clothing and even filthier hats, which they used to shade their eyes—eyes that had long felt as if they had half of the Sahara desert embedded in them.

The larger of the two men took in a deep breath of the stagnant summer air as he gazed upon the site the experts had chosen from their comfortable offices at Fort Dodge and Washington. The location had either changed dramatically in the past six years since it had been surveyed or someone had outright lied on their field report as to the possible location of a new fort. This was not the place the two men had hoped it would be. The large man with black hair removed his brimmed hat and wiped sweat from his face. The smaller man with the graying beard kicked at the sandy dune from which they spied the small barren valley.

"You wanna know what I think, boyo," the smaller of the two said as he too managed to wipe sweat away that immediately reappeared as if the filthy shirtsleeve had never been used. "I think if the buffalo have bypassed this place, we need to look somewhere else."

The big man replaced his dirty white hat, glanced at his companion, and slowly mounted his horse. As he adjusted his sore hindquarters into the saddle he finally spared the man the only few words he had uttered that morning.

"No, this is not the place. No covering trees, no fresh water within three miles, and the winds here would drive your average trooper mad within a month. We'll go farther north and hopefully find what others may have missed." He slowly turned his large roan and lightly encouraged the big mount with the taste of his spurs. "And, Sergeant Major, at least add a 'Colonel' when you call me 'boyo.'"

The smaller man smiled as he too mounted his horse. He laid spurs to the animal and shot forward to catch up.

"Aye, Colonel Darlin', that I can do, at least from time to time."

United States Army Colonel John Henry Thomas didn't respond as he kept riding at a slow gait. He was about to pull the old territorial map from his shirt when the third member of their party rode up, pack mule in tow. Thomas nodded to the Indian, who had been waiting for them on the side of the small rise.

Gray Dog was a Comanche who had been with Thomas for many years when he had found himself in either Texas or New Mexico territories, and long before the start of the madness in the east. They had been separated since 1861 and had no contact until his reassignment to Fort Dodge to assist the war department in locating desirable areas for future army accommodations. Thomas knew the brass in Washington were possibly gearing up for a major push into Indian Territory after brother stopped slaughtering brother in the civilized east.

Gray Dog was all of twenty summers, and Colonel John Henry Thomas had known him since the boy was fifteen years old. The Comanche had been orphaned after hostile Kiowa killed his entire family near the Brazos River in Texas on the very same day that Colonel Thomas had lost his wife, Mary, to the same band of Kiowa. Now Gray Dog once more joined him on his reassignment to Kansas. After all those years Gray Dog had refused to wear the white man's clothes and had remained full Comanche, to many a Texan's discomfort.

"Is it too soon to say I told you so?" Gray Dog asked in almost perfect, unbroken English as he joined the two men. The coyote-skin cap he wore bobbed up and down as he maneuvered his mount and pack mule in beside Thomas as the sergeant major gave the Comanche a dirty look.

"Would it stop you if I said it would be?" Thomas said as he pulled the map from his shirt.

"Yes it would, especially since I already said what was meant to be said," Gray Dog said with a smirk.

"Goddamn Indian speaks better English than me," the sergeant major muttered under his breath. "And in words I never understand."

Thomas opened the map to survey rugged terrain ahead. "You'll have to excuse Sergeant Major Dugan. He's just thrilled at the prospect of riding farther north."

"And why don't you take that damn dog off your head? It's starting to get to me."

Thomas looked up from the map to eye the filthy bowler hat that Dugan wore. The small Irishman was always mad at the world, and Gray Dog was a frequent target for his frustrations. He had also known the boy from his days with Thomas while riding with the fifth cavalry in Texas.

"And he's a jealous sort of Irishman because you wear better headgear than he. You get a coyote, he gets a dirty and very much dead skunk."

Sergeant Major Giles Dugan quickly removed the stinky bowler and looked it over. He was happy to be wearing a hat of his choosing over the blue cap of a cavalryman. He sniffed, recoiled, and then angrily placed the hat back on his head. He snorted and cast Gray Dog another withering look. He was about to comment when a shot rang out across the prairie. It was quickly followed by another, and then another.

"What the bloody hell?" Dugan pulled on the reins of his horse. Thomas and Gray Dog had already stopped and were listening intently.

"Northeast," Gray Dog said as he spied the sloping land ahead, which afforded no view of the area in front of them. More and more gunfire erupted, and to Thomas gunfire meant white men. These were the first sounds of gunfire he had heard since the battle of Antietam in 1862.

"I believe that is the sound of Spencers, Colonel boyo," Dugan said as he turned in the saddle to face the colonel. "Lord knows we heard enough to know."

Without a word Thomas reached over and relieved Gray Dog of the mule's reins and then nodded the Comanche forward. The Indian without command to his small horse shot away as Thomas dismounted and tied off his horse and the pack mule on a scrub brush. He quickly removed his Henry repeating rifle from its scabbard. Dugan, seeing this, did likewise.

"Come out here in the godforsaken wasteland only to walk head-on into a firefight. Who in the world wants to shoot each other in this heat?" he mumbled as he pulled an older-model Spencer carbine from his saddle. He quickly followed Thomas as he made his way forward in the wake of Gray Dog, who had silently gone ahead to spy the happenings in the valley.

The two men had only gone a hundred yards when Gray Dog returned and brought his Appaloosa to a brutal stop as he hopped from the old cavalry blanket covering the horse's back. He immediately caught the extra-heavy Spencer carbine Thomas tossed to him.

"What do you have?" Thomas asked as he kept moving forward.

"Soldiers. They are attacking a family of Sioux."

"A family, you say?" Dugan asked as he hustled to keep up with the two younger men.

Gray Dog didn't respond but only led the way to the ridge ahead. He ducked low and then crawled to the edge. Thomas and then Dugan joined him as the gunfire ceased below. The colonel quickly assessed the scene. Below at about two hundred yards, ten U.S. cavalrymen had dismounted and were checking the bodies of what looked like eight Sioux Indians. Thomas quickly noted the small children and women lying among the dead. He gritted his teeth as he heard a few of the men laughing at the sport of killing the family.

"Stupid sons of bitches! What did they have to go and do that for?" Dugan asked as he saw that at least the family had gotten off a few defensive shots before dying at the hands of the troopers from Fort Dodge. At least three of the ten men had taken arrows and were being attended to by their comrades.

"Look," Gray Dog said, pointing to the three circled buffalo-hide tepees and the meat still roasting on a spit over the undisturbed fire. "The family of Sioux had stopped for a meal by the small, muddy creek. They were doing nothing but eating a meal, John Henry."

Thomas remained silent as he scanned the horrid scene below. He was about to comment when a scream sounded in the preternatural silence that always falls after a gun battle. He looked to the left and saw a large man with the three stripes of a sergeant pulling a Sioux woman by the hair and laughing. Thomas became furious as he knew what was going to befall the young woman next.

"Sergeant Major, disable that trooper . . . now!"

"T'would be a pleasure, Colonel Darlin'."

Dugan aimed his Spencer. The act of shooting was natural for the man from Belfast, the best shot Thomas had ever seen. He had learned his trade while a guard for the Knights of the Vatican before joining the U.S. Army as a lad of twenty.

The man was still laughing as the bullet hit before the sound of the blast could echo down to the other men. The large round caught the sergeant just left of the groin. The man looked shocked and immediately released the woman's hair. He screamed after his hand went to the wounded area of his leg and he fell to his knees. The other troopers looked stunned until they realized they were under attack. They drew their weapons, aiming in all directions around the small Indian encampment. Thomas spied the man in command as he ordered several of his men to relocate their positions. As the young officer reached for his own pistol in its holster, Dugan's second shot exploded a geyser of sand and dirt only inches from his feet.

"Hold your fire!" Thomas yelled, dropping to his knees in case the troopers below became brave enough to fire on an armed and wary attacker, unlike the small group of familial Indians they had just slaughtered.

The men in the valley looked around in fear as they swung Spencer carbines in all directions.

"Stupid bastards. If we leave 'em alone, they'll just shoot each other. Look, they don't know what to do with someone shooting back at 'em."

Thomas finally stood and presented his filthy form to the men below. Gray Dog followed suit and then Dugan, with the still-smoking carbine aimed below.

"Who are you and why are you interfering with United States Army business?" the young officer called out. Thomas noticed that the man had holstered his revolver.

"It doesn't matter who we are, you stupid son of a whore!" Dugan yelled out while still aiming his weapon.

"Sergeant Major," Thomas said in rebuke to Dugan.

"This is the one time I agree with Hair Face," Gray Dog said. "I think we should shoot them all down like they did that Sioux family."

Thomas gave withering looks to both Gray Dog and Dugan.

"Colonel Thomas, is that you?"

John Henry Thomas started down the slope, disregarding the frightened troopers below, who were shaking and still aiming their weapons at the three men approaching. As the colonel entered the killing field he felt his stomach roil in his gut. Two of the male Sioux had already been scalped, the hair and skin discarded by the soldiers. Three small children lay within an arm's reach of the mother who fallen to protect them. Thomas glanced at Dugan and nodded his head in the direction of the woman who had been about to be scalped, which to Thomas would have almost been preferable to being manhandled by the pig of a man moaning and writhing on the ground in front of him, cursing that he needed help.

"Colonel Thomas, I'm Lieutenant Biddle, C Company, Fort Dodge. We were sent to find you, sir."

Thomas tossed his Henry rifle to Gray Dog, who was staring at the man on the ground with hatred in his eyes, and then he confronted the young, fresh-looking lieutenant who stood at least seven inches shorter than the colonel.

"But you decide to stop off for some sport instead," John Henry said as he took the man by the tunic collar and shook him. The colonel had been ashamed of army blue since the battle of Bull Run in 1861. He caught himself before his famous temper became apparent.

"Colonel," the boy stammered as Thomas released his uniform collar. "We thought they were a band of hostiles that raided into Kansas last week. We thought—"

"Enough, Lieutenant."

"She's dead, Colonel, shot before this animal started dragging her away," Dugan said, rising from the body of the young woman.

"May I attend to my wounded man, sir?" Biddle asked, afraid to look the large man in the eyes. The wounded sergeant had stopped screaming and was mumbling as the blood flowed heavily from his wound. Soon he stopped moving completely and the lips stiffened into a tight line of death.

"That man fell to enemy fire from the hostiles, and that is what your report will read, Mister, is that clear? If it isn't, consider yourself under arrest for the illegal killing of an aboriginal family."

The lieutenant swallowed hard against the bile rising in his belly. Thomas glared at the new officer until he could bring his boiling blood back down to normal. He was sorely tempted to give the boy a hard whack across the face, but past experience—and the reason for him being out west in the first place—stayed his gauntleted hand.

"Tend to your other wounded and get these bodies buried."

"No, John Henry, leave them," said Gray Dog as he continued to check for any form of life from the eight Sioux. "They will be found and the death rites performed by their own. More Sioux will come." Gray Dog looked up after checking for a pulse from a small boy of only six or seven. "More will come."

Thomas nodded but didn't like leaving this innocent family for the wolves. He finally turned to the lieutenant with a scowl. "Now, what in the hell are you doing this far away from Dodge?" he asked as he took a menacing step toward the young man who was reaching into his tunic as quickly as he could. He pulled out a telegram and passed it to Thomas, who was finally joined by Sergeant Major Dugan. The officer appraised the bearded sergeant and his filthy bowler hat and wondered just what sort of soldiers these men were who traveled with a savage and were as arrogant as any two men he had ever seen before.

"Major Cummings received this telegram from Washington City."

John Henry opened the folded paper and read. Dugan, ever curious, held his patience while Thomas finished reading.

"Well, boyo, has the brass in Washington found a new and better way to have us killed than being stuck out here in Indian territory"—he looked over at the lieutenant—"where it seems young fools have the right to shoot and kill whoever they want?"

"Who are you?" Biddle asked Dugan.

"He's the second name mentioned in this telegram, and he is a sergeant major, in every way your superior, is that also clear, Lieutenant?"

"Yes, sir!"

Dugan raised a brow and snickered at the boy's naiveté.

"Well, since it mentions your old sergeant major, what in the bloody hell does it say?"

Thomas turned and walked a few steps away and then addressed Gray Dog, who was looking at him, afraid that he would again lose his friend to the war in the east. John Henry winked at him.

"Feel like traveling?" he asked the young Comanche. He turned back to Dugan. "We've been recalled to Washington."

"Now, Colonel Darlin', don't tell me we're going to drag dog-head boy with us?"

"I'm not leaving him again. He comes with us and the Army can go straight to hell if they don't like it."

"Well, we're probably being recalled just to be put in front of a firing squad anyway." Dugan smiled at Gray Dog. "Yeah, maybe old dog-head should come along."

Gray Dog only watched the two men, who always seemed to be at odds. He knew Dugan was close to the colonel, almost as close as himself, but the man was rougher than a corncob and he took a lot of getting used to.

"I guess old George B. McClellan finally got his way and reached out and grabbed us."

Thomas quickly and briefly smiled for the first time.

"Oh, no, McClellan isn't in command any longer. We received word that General Grant turned the Rebs back in Tennessee and George Meade whooped Lee in Pennsylvania . . . somewhere called Gettysburg."

"Then who in the hell recalled us?" Dugan asked, perplexed, as he was expecting to be either court-martialed or designated to the west for the rest of his career. Thomas handed Dugan the telegram.

The sergeant major opened it, observing the colonel's smile. He lowered his eyes and read the words slowly. He wasn't as accomplished as Gray Dog at reading, but he managed. It was the one name at the bottom of the telegram that gave him chills. He folded the telegram and then walked away a few paces, still seeing that name—Stanton.

"The secretary of war?"

"Yes, but he would never have sent that without authorization," Thomas said as he accepted the telegram back from Dugan.

"Who, then, Colonel?"

"I imagine the order came from the president."

"President? You mean President Lincoln?" Dugan said as the color drained from his face.

"Yes, at least he was president before our little trip to the western climes."

The young lieutenant just stared at the filthy men before him. Just who in the hell were these two that they received personal messages from not only Secretary of War Stanton, but also from Abraham Lincoln?

Two hours later Gray Dog, Sergeant Major Dugan, and Colonel John Henry Thomas were riding east toward Fort Dodge and closer to the madness that had overtaken the nation.

They assumed they were heading back to war against their brothers in the south.

4

The fort was built on a small rock island lying in the Narrows between the lower end of Staten Island and Long Island, opposite Fort Hamilton. Hamilton was designed and built by Robert E. Lee, then a major in the United States Army, and overlooked the older post that housed the rebellious men of the Confederacy. The crowded conditions would have shocked most northerners, who complained so bitterly about the treatment of Union soldiers in camps such as Andersonville. If the truth had been known, Fort Lafayette was almost as bad. There was no funding to keep prisoners fed and clothed with the massive slaughter still continuing in the south. Lafayette held mostly commissioned and noncommissioned officers the Union would never exchange back to the South for Union officers. The men here were considered much too valuable to the Confederate war effort and would remain interned for the duration.

The man stood six-foot-three. Most of the weight he had been able to maintain through the early years of the war had long since departed. Confederate Lieutenant Colonel Jessup Taylor stood over Lieutenant Giles Pentecost, a boy of only twenty, who stared up at him from the ragged cot where he lay dying. It had been six days since the four nurses and the constantly drunk country doctor had been to the camp to treat the sick. That left most of the care and healing to the other prisoners of the camp, and they were losing a battle with the elements, the food, the lack of cold-weather clothing, and the biggest killer of all, typhoid fever. This was what young Pentecost and over a thousand other prisoners were dying from. The rest were sick with malnutrition, trench foot, and the filth of living in such close quarters.

"We tried, didn't we, Colonel?" the boy said as his eyes stared at a spot to his right where Jessy Taylor wasn't standing. Taylor stepped to the side, hoping the boy could see him better. He didn't. The eyes were covered in white film and the face was drawn. Taylor reached down and took the boy's hand. He had to pry the filthy blanket from his fingers to do so.

"We gave them hell, Giles, old boy."

The young lieutenant went into a fit of shivers as another prisoner stepped to the cot and handed Colonel Taylor a wet cloth. He nodded to the other thin prisoner, who was starting to suffer the chills of the early onset of the same illness. Taylor used his free hand to apply the cloth to the boy's forehead. Thankfully Pentecost closed his milky eyes as the coolness touched his burning skin.

Suddenly the young lieutenant's eyes opened and seemed to fix on Taylor.

"Why didn't General Stuart come back for us?"

Taylor didn't know how to answer. They had performed a rearguard action to stall and make time for Jeb Stuart's cavalry to escape from the Virginia countryside more than a year past. The action had caused the surrender of Taylor's regiment, which never received orders to fall back after Jeb Stuart's escape. They had been in a series of camps since their capture and had finally arrived in New York and Fort Lafayette last fall. Since that time Taylor had lost more than three hundred men to disease and starvation.

Taylor recalled that dark, rainy night on the outskirts of

Antietam. General Robert E. Lee had praised Taylor in the Richmond newspapers, saying it was a classic textbook example of a rearguard action. Taylor thought differently. The heroic James Ewell Brown "Jeb" Stuart had escaped the trap but had never sent word back to Taylor to break off the action and return to the Army of Northern Virginia. Taylor knew Stuart to be a brilliant commander, but that night he had fallen far short of his reputation, just as he had at Gettysburg in July the previous year when he became a missing element in Lee's attack in Pennsylvania.

He finally looked back at the boy with his customary answer to that infernal question. The boy was staring at nothing. He had died. Taylor gazed at the face of the young man who had been barely old enough to shave, and then angrily tossed the now-dry cloth into a corner.

"We'll take care of the lieutenant."

Taylor finally stood on shaky legs and faced the man he had been with since the start. Sergeant Major Ezekiel McCandless nodded that he too was saddened at the loss of the brave boy. Taylor brushed a hand through his dirty brown hair. He felt the lice crawling on his fingers when he lowered his hand but made no move to shake off the pests.

"That's eight just this morning. We have to plant them now; the heat's going to turn them fast, I reckon."

Jessy Taylor angrily pushed past his sergeant major and stepped outside into the hot sun. His gray undershirt was already soaked through with sweat and it was only eight in the morning. He looked toward the high fence and the guards who patrolled it. One was eating an apple and staring at him, and was soon joined by the commandant of the camp, Major Nelson Freeman, a Boston abolitionist's son who held no love for the Confederacy or the men who fought for her. Taylor saw a cruel smile cross the major's features. He actually nodded his head in greeting at Taylor and then moved off with his hands behind his back as if he was pleased another Rebel was on his way to hell. Colonel Taylor knew he would kill that man someday for his cruelty at Lafayette.

McCandless ordered two men to carry the body away to

join the others who had died that morning and the previous night. The sergeant major used the tattered remnants of his uniform jacket to wipe sweat from the sides of his thickly bearded face.

"We have to get the men out of here, Colonel. Anything is better than dying like pigs in a filthy pen."

Taylor glanced back up at the smiling guard on the wall, who tossed his half-eaten apple down into the muddy yard where six men immediately started fighting for it.

"The last that I heard, Ezra, most people feed their pigs." Taylor's eyes never left the corporal, who was now laughing at the winner of the fight for the apple core. The man was covered in mud, as was his trophy, yet he ate the apple without concern for the filth.

"And yes, it is time for us to take what's left of our boys and get the hell out of here."

"'Bout damn time too."

Taylor looked at the sergeant major, who had lost more than seventy pounds himself, and nodded. "I want officers' call at sixteen hundred; all noncoms will attend. We have to start gathering information, as much as we can get. I need to know what harbor is the closest. We'll never be able to get anywhere overland; we have to make our escape by sea. That means the Yank guards who are known to be loose-tongued have to be handled right to get what information we need."

While Taylor spoke he continued to spy the retreating form of the camp commandant as he made his way around the stone battlements.

The most renowned Confederate cavalry officer outside of Jeb Stuart, a classmate at West Point, had made up his mind to get his men out of Lafayette or die trying.

CENTRAL PARK, NEW YORK CITY

Professor Lars Ollafson waited patiently, tossing bread crumbs to the pigeons that walked around his bench. He held the satchel between his feet as his eyes scanned the area around him. The people of the city avoided the park for the most part, since the army had taken it over for training.

Several Union soldiers walked past, laughing as they made their way from the Sheep Meadow at the center of Central Park. Ollafson watched the soldiers leave, and then as his eyes moved he spied the man he had been waiting for. The young student walked to the bench and sat. He unfolded a *New York Herald* and started to read.

"I have the lockbox secured, Professor. The artifacts will be well guarded."

Ollafson didn't respond as he tossed the last of the bread onto the ground. He carefully used his shoe to slide the satchel toward his student.

"Is that everything, Professor?"

"All except for the two planks. I still need them for the president's meeting with the war department."

"I thought you were not to be included on the expedition. I was under the impression the president refused to let you go."

Ollafson stood. "With the ace I have up my sleeve, young man, I don't see how Mr. Lincoln can leave me out of it." He finally looked down and spared the boy a brief smile. "I mean, he does not know what is really there, does he? The expedition has taken far too long to plan and coordinate. If the president's chosen officer does not arrive from the west soon, all will be lost."

"I don't understand," the boy said as he finally lowered the newspaper to look at his former Harvard professor.

"It has taken me more than a year to get the expert translation of the symbols, and now I will explain the real reasons we must get to our find before anyone else." The smile grew on Ollafson's face as he turned and started to walk away. "The president cannot refuse me when he's informed. There is too much at stake."

"What, Professor? What is more important than the artifact?"

"God, young Simon. God."

Fifteen minutes later the student carried the heavy satchel toward the New York Bank and Trust Company in Times Square. There he would deposit the satchel in a safe where no one could access the material except Ollafson himself. He smiled as the doorman opened the glass door for him.

"Deposit vaults?" he asked.

"Second floor, sir," the doorman said. The former student in Ollafson's Harvard religious studies course nodded and moved toward the stairs.

Just as he stepped onto the marble-tiled second-floor landing, he was confronted by two uniformed New York City policemen. They deftly grabbed the young man by the arms and steered him toward a room where another man in civilian attire was waiting with the door opened. The student started to say something, but that was when the club silenced him and he went limp in the two men's hands. The satchel fell to the floor and the man holding the door smiled and retrieved it, following the three inside the empty office.

The two men dumped the boy unceremoniously on the wooden floor. The one on the left knelt over the young student.

"Ah, we must have hit him too damn hard. He's not breathing."

The civilian looked unconcerned as he stepped over the boy's dead body, removed an envelope from his jacket pocket, and handed it over to the corrupt policeman. He opened it, saw the bills inside, and then nodded and the two policemen left the room. The man waited until their footsteps retreated, and then he dropped to a knee and opened the satchel.

He was shocked to discover it filled with papers. Old paper, new paper, a few rocks, but no artifacts. He angrily emptied the bag and then tossed the satchel as he searched in vain for the material he had been hired to retrieve. Frustrated, he pushed at the gathered papers, knowing he had just wasted a thousand dollars and would have to face the people who had hired him for the job, and they were far more unforgiving of failure than even himself.

He cursed his luck, realizing that Professor Ollafson had removed all evidence of the artifact from his satchel before handing it over. As he was about to stand, something caught his eye. He reached out and turned over a large and very thick paper and studied the design upon it. His brow furrowed and he reached up and removed his top hat, then took the paper to a window so he could see in the dim lighting of the room. He held the paper up as the light revealed strange designs on its surface. It looked to be copied from something. A rubbing, perhaps—he wasn't sure. He decided that maybe he wasn't left empty-handed after all.

When the well-dressed man with satchel in hand stepped from the bank building, ignoring the pleasantries of the doorman, he could not help but see the strange drawings and writings on the pages he had recovered. They were burned into his retinas and he could not shake them free from his brain.

An hour later the man with the satchel crossed over Seventh Avenue and headed for the Knickerbocker Hotel. Throughout the long city blocks, he had not noticed the other passersby, or even the women's temperance group as they serenaded him against the evils of drink. He roughly pushed past them without hesitation.

As the doorman opened the hotel's front door, two men immediately fell in beside him as they approached the staircase. There were no words exchanged as the three made their way to the sixth floor and into room 602. The man gave his top hat and coat over to one of the men who had escorted him up, who carefully placed it on the coat rack in the fancy suite. The man removed a set of handcuffs and then placed the satchel on a large table in the center of the living area. He stared at the old beaten-leather case for a full minute. He took a deep breath and then held out a hand to the gruff-looking gentleman in an ill-fitting suit, who laid a padlock into his palm and then stepped back just as a knock sounded on the door. The man nodded his head toward the door. The second withdrew a revolver and this action elicited a frown from their boss. He quickly holstered the weapon underneath his coat.

"We do not have gunfights in the Knickerbocker Hotel," the man said with a heavy French accent.

The second brute opened the door and stepped back as a woman in an elegant violet dress with matching hat walked briskly into the suite. The man with the satchel and handcuffs did not turn to see who it was; he already knew. The man who had opened the door returned to the table as the woman nodded her head and then sat quietly on the love seat as she daintily removed her light gloves.

"Was there any trouble?" the woman asked as the man padlocked the satchel. He finally acknowledged the woman as he turned to face her.

"No, not after the foolish constabulary accidentally killed the courier, no trouble at all." The man raised his left brow, waiting for his employer to say something about his methods. It didn't take long.

"That was just a boy," she said, her accented English also hinting at the South of France.

"One that will never become a man. Sometimes, Madame Richelieu, bad things have to happen to innocents, as I am sure you are aware in your business."

"Murder can become quite expensive in our line of employment, Mr. Renaud. You should have taken the satchel and made it look as if he was robbed by one of these American thugs roaming New York."

The tall man shrugged and then used his left hand to indicate the man who had opened the door should raise his right hand. When he did, Renaud placed the handcuff on his wrist and then snapped the other cuff through the leather-and-steel-wire handle of the large satchel.

"If you arrive without the satchel, your hand had better be missing also. Is that most clear?" Renaud said as his brown eyes glared at the courier.

"Yes, sir, very clear."

"When at sea, you are to deposit the satchel in the captain's safe and leave it until you arrive in France. Is that also clear?"

"Clear, sir."

"Good. Madame Richelieu has your passage voucher."

The woman rose and handed the man two tickets purchased that very morning. "I'm afraid you have very little time. I suggest you and your partner leave this minute. American merchant ships do not dally leaving the harbor."

The man took the tickets and then he and his associate left the room.

Renaud removed a white kerchief from his breast pocket and slowly wiped his hands clean. He never understood how working men could live with constantly filthy hands. He shook his head in disgust and threw the monogrammed kerchief into the wastebasket. He spared the woman a withering look.

"Do you think they will allow a woman to berth on one of the expedition vessels?"

"If my dear friend Professor Ollafson goes along, how could he ever leave his Aramaic and ancient-text expert behind?"

"If you are so trusted, Madame, how is it you failed to know about the little surprise that awaited me inside of the satchel?"

The woman stared at Renaud. She pulled a long hatpin from her wide-brimmed hat and removed her dark veil so she could see the man Paris had assigned her two years before. She angrily stuck the long pin back in the hat and then turned on him.

"The artifact was not inside?"

"No, it was not. But there was something quite interesting that the good professor did not share with his ancient-languages expert."

"What was it?" she asked. "And why did you let it leave here without allowing me to examine it?"

"That will be determined by others in our government, not you. It seems Paris has lost faith in your efforts to uncover the real reason for the professor's interest in fairy tales."

"I have done my job. Perhaps you should also. Why the big push from Paris?"

Renaud smiled and walked toward the credenza where a silver service had been set up. He poured himself a glass of port while offering the woman none. He drank deeply from the crystal glass and then sat in the chair Madame Richelieu had vacated.

"Once certain people in power found out the Americans were involved in this ridiculous pursuit of myths and legends, naturally we had to become more aggressive in the quest to find out what it was they were going after and why."

"You fail to realize that—"

"Enough." The man stood and poured himself another drink. "Are you aware of what happened at Hampton Roads last year?"

"I fail to see—"

"That, Madame, is exactly why I was attached to you— because you fail to see." He returned to his seat and relaxed, stretching his long legs out and fixing her with a kindhearted, poor-little-girl-doesn't-know-anything smile. He shook his head. "The United States and the Confederate navies in one day made every wooden warship on the high seas obsolete."

A look of dawning understanding came to the beautiful woman's face.

"You refer to the battle of Hampton Roads between the Union *Monitor* and the Rebel vessel *Merrimack*?"

"Yes, now I see that you may be on the verge of understanding."

"A little, perhaps. But I am no military strategist."

The man chuckled. "No, Madame, you are not. But I and my department are experts. With the Americans on both sides of the Mason-Dixon Line coming up with naval sciences such as the world witnessed in Carolina between two advanced warships, do you think we would allow an American expedition to go unnoticed? Will we let them recover something that may even place them further ahead of the world? Whether it be military or philosophical in nature is no matter. We must curtail this American arrogance. Whatever is there, we will recover it. If they think this artifact is important, who are we to allow them to get to it first? This is not the way the real world plays, and the Americans and their barbaric president must learn this."

The woman remained silent as she realized once again that she had been used by ruthless men in Paris.

"Now our intelligence sources say that the British have become aware of Professor Ollafson's discovery. They even had men ensconced in the last expedition to the area in 1859."

"Then why did they not steal the artifact then?" she asked, becoming curious as to this man's real intentions.

The tall man lost the look of arrogance for the first time. "Because, Madame, for reasons about which we still are in the dark, Ollafson was the only one to return from the expedition alive."

"The professor never mentioned anything like that."

"Because he knew how important this find was and he knows how to keep a secret, a secret your prowess as a spy failed to uncover, foolish woman."

"And now?" she asked a little nervously, as Madame Richelieu knew she was in over her head.

He stood, placed the empty glass on the table, and turned on the woman as his arrogant smile returned.

"Simple. You had better be sure we are included on the roster of that expedition."

"You? How am I to justify your presence when we are not even sure if President Lincoln will allow the professor to go?"

"I and your superiors have every confidence in your abilities—of persuasion at least."

"And if I do, you expect to just take whatever is there away from the Americans?"

"Not us. We are only to observe and report. Others will take what we need. Paris has prepared far better than the Americans."

"The fools are willing to go to war for what you believe is a fairy tale?"

"There will be no war. Paris believes the Americans will never make this public knowledge, not after the deaths of so many in their little familial squabble. To waste time and precious money on an expedition? No, whatever happens on the high seas will remain there. No one will witness the death of any wayward warships that get in our way. Whether they be American, British, or German, no one will ever know."

Paul Renaud of the French Army looked at the novice spy like a new life-form that he had just discovered, and then laughed at the expression on her face.

"If the Americans want to play, we will play."

Madame Richelieu knew at that moment that the Americans were not the only nation to have gone insane—it was the entire world.

BRITISH EMBASSY, WASHINGTON, D.C.

The courier from Her Majesty's government droned on as First Viscount Richard Bickerton Pemell Lyons, Her Britannic Majesty's Ambassador Extraordinary and Plenipotentiary to the United States, stood silently listening at the open window as he tried to catch the afternoon breeze that broke some of the summer swelter in Washington. The portly, mustachioed man listened, and when the courier was finished, he stood waiting for the ambassador's answer.

"Her Majesty and Lord Palmerston know my feelings and opinion on interfering in internal matters concerning the bloody Union. If they think the United States will take that interference lightly, they are not thinking very clearly in London." Lyons went to his desk and sat heavily in the large chair. The captain remained at attention, and that was just the way Lyons wanted him. He did not trust the military and never would. That prejudice was starting to show more and more as this American Civil War continued. Finally he placed the message from Victoria and Lord Palmerston on the desk, rubbed his tired eyes, and nodded at the captain. "Please sit, Captain. The heat has me out of sorts this afternoon and this message of yours has not made my day any easier."

"Apologies, My Lord."

Lyons waved off the false apology and reached for the crumpled message once more.

"And how are we supposed to infiltrate this . . . this . . . expedition?"

"I am to inform Lord Lyons that the army has already taken that step."

The ambassador was shocked as he looked from the message to the courier. "Excuse me?"

"Her Majesty's armed forces will have not one, but two personages onboard any American naval vessel leaving for Europe. One of these individuals will be in the inner circle of command."

"If they are found out, the Americans may very well turn all of this advanced weaponry you're so frightened of our way. Do they realize that at the palace?"

"Whatever happens over there, or on the high seas, will remain secret. No one the wiser. They cannot go to the press with this. Their President Lincoln would be committing political suicide if they did."

"When are the Crown and the army ever going to realize that they cannot analyze the Americans in such broad strokes?" Lord Lyons stood from behind his desk and leaned forward to look the captain in the eyes. "The army underestimated American ability twice before, if I'm not mistaken, and here we are doing it again. Lincoln is unpredictable; the Crown must realize this." He slammed the message on his desk. "Now, who are these infiltrators?"

"I am afraid I do not have that information available to give you, My Lord."

The glare was famous. He held the man's eyes, searching for the lie. It was there in the way the captain raised both brows.

"Does the Crown know why the Americans are doing this?"

"Again, My Lord, I have very little information to pass along. The P.M. and Her Majesty thought the less you know, the better for all . . . on an official basis, that is."

"Do not play word games with me, Captain. If this thing goes public it will be a disaster. Our upper classes may favor a Confederate America, but our people are adamantly against the South. Slavery is distasteful, Captain, and if we are caught hindering an American reconstruction we could all feel the heat. Revolutions are not just an American and French invention; they have been going on for quite some time in the world.

"What happens if the Americans get what they go after? What then?" Lord Lyons walked around his desk and confronted the Captain, who didn't know whether to stand or remain seated. "Go to war?"

"Her Majesty's navy may have a surprise or two in store for the Yanks if they do succeed in their mission. A rather nasty surprise." He smirked as if he were privy to the navy's plans. "Do you have a return message for Her Majesty?" the captain asked as he finally stood with his black cap under his arm.

"None. Dismissed, Captain."

The red-coated army captain clicked his polished heels together, bowed, and then left the well-appointed office. Lyons watched him leave and returned to the window. He watched more soldiers and civilians move along the street and then closed his eyes in silent prayer.

"Just what are you after, Mr. Lincoln?"

WASHINGTON, D.C.
AUGUST 1, 1864

The two men were sore from their long journey from Kansas. The train was full and everyone was looking out at a city that had very nearly been taken by Robert E. Lee a year before.

Colonel John Henry Thomas was not interested in the view as the train started to slow as it entered the station. Sergeant Major Dugan was also not looking out the window but making faces at the boy who kept popping his head up now and again from the seat in front of them. He would stick out his tongue and the boy would laugh and dip back below eye level. He finally tired of the game and looked over at Thomas, who lay half-reclined on the wooden seat with his dirty white hat tenting his eyes. Neither man had bothered to shave since their time on the plains. Their orders were clear—return to the capital at the fastest possible speed with no delay.

"We're coming into the capital, Colonel," Dugan said as

he looked out of the filthy window to see the old wooden platform as the train slowed.

Before Thomas could remove the hat and answer Dugan, there were several screams of horror from the front of their car. Thomas heard the car's conductor stutter as he shouted and women screeched.

"Hey, you can't be in here! Get back to the baggage car where you're supposed to be."

"Oh, Lord," said Dugan as he nudged Thomas with a sharp elbow. "Old dog-boy's makin' an appearance."

John Henry Thomas finally removed the hat from his eyes and looked toward the front of the car where the shouts of fear and loathing could be heard. He immediately recognized four soldiers he had seen earlier and the train's conductor holding a very angry-looking Gray Dog as he attempted to get by the roadblock.

"Damn it," Thomas muttered as the mother of the small boy turned with a gasp at the colonel's language. Thomas was about to apologize but decided he had better save Gray Dog from hanging first. He stood and tipped his hat at the woman and then made his way up the aisle as the train came to a stop at Harrisburg Station.

"Goddamn Indians and darkies are taking over the damn country, thinkin' they can do anything they want," said a gruff sergeant with a bandage around his head. Agreement was mumbled by the other three soldiers and conductor holding Gray Dog at bay.

The Comanche was dressed as he always was in a shirt of purple material that had been purchased for him at Fort Dodge for his trip east, and Gray Dog had thought at the time that Thomas's gift was a wonderful joy to wear. The boy had been proud. But it wasn't the shirt that was so frightening to the unenlightened—it was the breechcloth over the leather leggings and that infernal coyote head on his black top-knotted hair. All the passengers were leaning as far away from the Indian as they could get without jumping from one of the open windows. One middle-aged woman had already swooned and her outraged husband was tending to her.

The wounded sergeant and his friends held Gray Dog, who was struggling to escape the filthy hands holding him. Finally the sergeant drew a revolver and was raising it above his head to strike at the Comanche. As he brought it down a powerful hand grabbed the sergeant's wrist and twisted.

"What the hell do you—"

The sergeant stopped abruptly when he realized a big man was about to break his wrist, and his eyes widened when he saw that the man had two embroidered silver eagles on his shoulder boards. The other three soldiers saw the same thing and immediately released the angry Indian. Thomas again twisted the sergeant's hand until the pistol fell free, where he caught it and without wasted motion tossed it backward to Dugan, who was standing right behind the colonel. Thomas released the sergeant's hand as the four soldiers came to an abrupt attention.

"At ease," Thomas said as he reached in between the four troopers and the conductor and pulled Gray Dog free of the mass of men.

The sergeant didn't know if he should salute or again reach for the Indian.

"This man is with me, and if anyone touches him again I'll throw that man"—he looked at the people staring at him from their seats—"or woman through the nearest goddamn window. Is that clear?"

"But, Colonel, he's an Indian," the sergeant said.

"And he was supposed to stay in the baggage car," the conductor said with all of the mustered indignity he could spew.

"We'll soon be off your train, Mister. As for you four, I would think we have our hands full enough without picking fights with Indians"—he looked at the five soldiers one at a time—"or darkies."

"Yes—"

"Now get away from me."

All five of the men saw the killer eyes of the man in front of them, and not being used to seeing an officer in such worn and dirty attire, it was frightening at the very least.

"You should have waited until the sergeant major came for

you," Thomas said as he and Gray Dog made their way back to their seats. Several women and a few of the male passengers leaned as far away from the Indian and crazy colonel as they could.

"I wanted to see Washington City."

"You could have waited. We'll be seeing plenty of it before too long."

"Wanted to see now," Gray Dog argued.

Thomas knew that Gray Dog was not a servant of his nor an employee. Gray Dog thought himself free and not tied to anyone. He tolerated the orders given to him by John Henry, but he wasn't forced to follow them if he did not want to.

"If I ever get the chance, I'm going back to the Brazos to hang Reverend Percival for teaching English to this boyo," Dugan said as he reached up for the colonel's bag. He angrily tossed it to Gray Dog, but it bounced off the small Comanche's chest and hit the floor. Gray Dog looked at Dugan and his eyes told him the tolerance and respect that he showed John Henry in no way related to his feelings about Dugan. The prejudice of the man came out of every pore. John Henry knew the truth of the matter. Sergeant Major Dugan saw the exact same prejudice that he'd faced in Ireland by Englishmen, now being thrown at Gray Dog, and he was angry but didn't know how to say it.

John Henry Thomas reached down to retrieve his valise but Gray Dog beat him to it. The Comanche just didn't want Dugan to hand it to him. *Principle,* Thomas thought.

"Let's go see what this is all about, shall we?" Thomas said, eyeing both Gray Dog and Dugan as he moved down the aisle.

"After you, dog-boy," Dugan said as he half-bowed to Gray Dog.

"Old and ignorant fools always go first, hair-face," Gray Dog said as he halfbowed in return.

" 'Hair-face'? Why you coyote-wearing son of a—"

"Oh, this was a good idea," John Henry said as he shook his head and moved off, to all the passengers' relief.

The man who would command the strangest expedition in the brief history of the United States had arrived.

The patrons of the Willard Hotel were aghast at the sight in the main lobby—two soldiers in filthy frontier uniforms, who still carried most of the dirt and grime of the prairies clinging to their skin and their clothing, from the dual suspenders of the officer to the grimy yellow kerchief of the sergeant major next to him. However, even more shocking was the savage Indian in their company. Although completely dressed, his bird-bone chest piece and the coyote hide on his head shocked most and angered the rest. This was the position the hotel's manager was attempting to point out.

"Sir, your rooms are ready, but I'm afraid our bylaws will not allow your . . . your . . . guest to stay in the hotel. I am sorry."

John Henry Thomas looked around him at the well-dressed men and women. He saw the brass in the lobby—the officers were either on leave or were the professional types Thomas despised. They all looked at him in his sand-encrusted blue cavalry uniform as if he had just crawled out of their kitchen cabinet. He glanced at Gray Dog, who was busying himself staring at a feathered plume rising from a lady's large hat. She finally noticed when his fingers reached out and touched a feather the likes of which he had never seen before. Sergeant Major Dugan slapped his hand away, eliciting an angry glare from the Comanche.

"Look, you are supposed to confirm my party, no matter what or who it consists of," Thomas voiced, knowing that it was falling on deaf ears, especially after the second attempt of Gray Dog trying to snatch the long purple feather from the lady's hat. She screamed and quickly moved off as Dugan again held the Indian at bay. Thomas rolled his eyes and then angrily slapped his white, wide-brimmed hat on his striped pant leg, creating a small cloud of dust that elicited gasps.

"Having a problem checking in?" a voice sounded from behind Thomas, who knew something was wrong when he saw Dugan stop his angry rebuke of Gray Dog.

Thomas turned and he then he knew why Dugan was so angry. Standing before him was an army officer. His mustache and small beard were expertly trimmed and his double-breasted dress uniform immaculate. The officer stood before him, holding a cigar at chest level and looking up and into the eyes of the much larger John Henry Thomas. The man who had attempted to have himself and Dugan court-martialed two years prior stood before him. Major General George Brinton McClellan, "Little Mac" as he was called, was standing arrogantly before him as if he was the exterminator sent to destroy a household pest.

"Perhaps it's the company you keep, Colonel," McClellan said as he examined both Dugan and Gray Dog. "I see nothing much has changed in two years, except for one or two items," he finished with a note of disgust as he eyed Gray Dog up and down.

"General," was all Thomas said as he immediately held out a restraining hand to Dugan's ample chest as he turned his attention to Little Mac instead of Gray Dog. With a slight shove he sent the sergeant major reeling away.

"I see you still have that little wart of a man at your side. I was quite hoping he would have been scalped by now." McClellan looked at Gray Dog as he wheeled Dugan about and walked a few paces away. "But I see you made friends with the hostiles out west. Very good way to keep your hair, Colonel."

"What can I help you with, General, or is it candidate McClellan?" Thomas said, throwing his twin saddlebags over his shoulder as he looked down upon the small two-star general.

Mac rolled up on the heels of his shoes and then flicked his cigar ash. He smiled. "Correct, it may not be 'General' for very much longer, Thomas, old man. It seems I still may be able to hang you and that mutinous little bastard Dugan after all, only this time I will not be signing off on the order as commander of United States forces, but as commander-in-chief."

Thomas remained silent and as neutral as his features

would allow, although he did feel some of the empty-stomach bile rise in his throat at the thought of this man as president.

"I wish you luck in that . . . endeavor," Thomas finally managed to say as his fingertips rose to his black hair in mock salute. "On both the presidency, and hanging us."

"Miserable son of a—"

"At ease, Sergeant Major!" Thomas said.

"I will someday see to it, Colonel, that you are stripped of the popularity you have with men in power, most assuredly that great baboon that sits in the White House at this very moment."

Thomas couldn't help it. He took a menacing step forward, having almost the same angered reaction as at the battle of Antietam that started this whole mess for him and Dugan. Several other army officers and a few naval officers started to take interest in the standoff in the lobby—until another presence entered the room.

"Well, until such a time as we call you commander-in-chief, perhaps you can let these men bathe and shave for their meeting with the real president?"

McClellan turned and he immediately lost his good humor. A man he hated almost as much as Thomas or Lincoln was standing before him. Of equal size to Little Mac, the man in the immaculate three-piece suit stood with an even larger cigar than McClellan's.

"Mr. Secretary," McClellan said as he half-bowed, his sword jutting out far enough that Dugan wanted to kick it.

Secretary of State William H. Seward stood with an immensely satisfied smile on his face. One arm was behind his back and one was holding the cigar—meaning he was not about to shake the general's hand.

"Yes, with Mr. Lincoln and Mr. Seward here in your corner, I suspect you'll go a long way, Colonel, at least until the election."

Little Mac turned abruptly on his heel and returned to the table he'd been sitting at, where the curious eyes of financial backers were watching the spectacle at the front desk.

"Now," Seward said as he turned to the front-desk clerk,

"these men need rooms, and I am here to secure them, or to close this hotel down for harboring suspicious activity."

"Suspicious activity?" the manager said with all of the dignity he could muster.

"If I wished to do so I could surround this hotel and bring out at least six spies for the Confederacy that I know of. Should I start picking them out for you, sir?" Seward said as his gray, wiry brows rose.

The hotel's manager knew the power that Seward wielded and immediately turned and lifted two sets of keys off the hook. "I'm afraid only two rooms were reserved. We are currently full."

Seward reached out and took the room keys and then tossed them haphazardly to Thomas. "I'm sure they'll figure out the sleeping arrangements on their own."

Thomas nodded at Seward, whom he knew from the night the president had pardoned him and Dugan and then clandestinely sent them on their way out west to count Indians and survey for new fort locations.

"Colonel," Seward said with a distasteful glance at Little Mac, who was looking their way and laughing with his well-appointed friends. "You and you alone will meet with the president at exactly twelve midnight. A carriage will be out in front of the hotel at eleven thirty. Be there."

Seward turned away and started to walk toward the large bar for a quick pick-me-up before returning to the hot and dusty streets of the capital.

"Mr. Secretary, what is this about?" Thomas asked as he tossed Dugan one of the keys.

Seward stopped and then his smile grew as he turned to face the weary man they had dragged from the plains. "I could tell you now, Colonel Thomas, but I think this should come from the president," he said as he started to turn away, then he stopped and faced John Henry once more with an even larger smile. "I would never deprive Mr. Lincoln of the look you will give him when he informs you of your mission. I assume it will be as priceless as mine was." He laughed, shaking his head as he finally walked away.

"Don't tell me I have to share a room with—"

Thomas closed his eyes as Dugan voiced his concerns about the sleeping arrangements.

"Not one, but all of my favorite people are showing up. This is going to be wonderful," he mumbled in resignation as he moved toward the stairs.

5

An hour later John Henry returned from the bath and spa area, clean for the first time in what he thought was a full year. Gone was his beard that had been in place since the last stages of the battle of Antietam. The mustache that curled at the corners of his mouth and the small patch of beard below his lip were the only facial hair that remained. A new uniform had been delivered to him from the war department, and he even sported new shoes.

Thomas entered the room on the third floor of the Willard and immediately saw Sergeant Major Dugan leaning out of the window. By the shaking of the Irishman's hindquarters, Thomas could see he was angry.

"Are you such a son of a bitch that you're now screaming at pigeons?" the colonel asked as he tossed his old, dirty uniform on the floor. "And why are you doing it in my room and not your own?" he asked as he went to the dresser and poured himself a small glass of whiskey.

"It's that goddamn Indian, boyo, he's out on the damn ledge and will not come down!" Dugan said as he ducked his head back in the window. "And the only reason I am in your room, Colonel, sir, is that this coyote-wearing bastard is just sitting there on the ledge. Causin' quite a spectacle down on the street." Just at that moment a knock sounded on the door. Thomas shook his head and pulled the door open to see the hotel's night manager.

John Henry immediately held up a hand to stay the manager's disapproval of Gray Dog's nocturnal activities.

"We will bring our friend in. He . . . he . . . likes to sit in high places, not so unusual for Washington I would think," Thomas said as a small joke. The night manager just stared at the colonel.

"He is scaring people down on the street, sir."

Thomas only nodded and then unceremoniously closed the door on the small, prissy man's face. He downed the liquor and then went to the window where he grabbed Sergeant Major Dugan by the suspenders and pulled him away from the window. He ducked his freshly combed hair out of the window and saw that Gray Dog was sitting calmly on the ledge with his moccasins hanging idly over the side. The ledge itself was only nine inches wide but the Comanche didn't seem to have a problem with either the narrow dimensions or the height at which he risked his life. Thomas shook his head when he realized that Gray Dog was talking to his ancestors. He sat looking up at the full moon. Thomas cleared his throat.

Gray Dog didn't respond at first and then his nose wrinkled and his head slowly turned. He saw Thomas and his new haircut and the clean-shaven face and his eyes betrayed his amazement. Much to John Henry's shock and horror, Gray Dog leaped to his feet. The colonel's eyes widened when he realized that Gray Dog would fall right over and go crashing down to the street far below. There was a gasp from the few onlookers that had camped outside on the walkway to see the strange Indian fall. Then came an audible moan from the crowd as the Comanche did not fall but balanced gracefully on the nine-inch ledge and made his way to John Henry.

"Don't suppose it's asking too much for you to come inside the hotel?"

Gray Dog didn't respond as he dropped to one knee with John Henry cringing in fear the Indian's equilibrium would give way. It didn't. Gray Dog brought his hand to John Henry's face and touched the freshly shaven and perfumed skin of his cheek. Thomas allowed him to feel the difference.

"Stupid bastard," Dugan mumbled from behind. Thomas used his hand to signal for Dugan to hush.

"Now, come inside," he said as he eased back through the open window. Gray Dog easily ducked inside and then gave Dugan a withering look.

"Now, can you two get along long enough for me to find out why in the hell we are here?"

"Ah, Colonel, I can't turn my back on this savage for one minute without him getting into some kind of mischief."

"Deal with it," Thomas said as he reached for the new hat box on the end of his bed. This was also delivered over from the war department. He opened the round box and withdrew a new hat. It was turned up on the side and had his silver eagle planted on the front. A bright red feather adorning the side made John Henry wince.

"Ah, that is an adorable chapeau, Colonel Darlin'."

John Henry shot as angry a look at Dugan as Gray Dog had delivered only a moment before. Thomas ripped the long red plume from the blue hat and tossed it on the wooden floor. Gray Dog immediately sprang forward and retrieved the feather and stared at it.

"That may keep him occupied for a while." He turned to face an astonished Dugan. "Now, go to your room and lock yourselves in so he doesn't head down to the theater district or something. Can you do that, Sergeant Major?"

Dugan just glared at Thomas. "Come all this way to babysit a coyote-wearing savage, why I ought to—"

"That's enough. Just follow orders without question, for once in your miserable career."

Dugan saw that Thomas was not in the right mood for any

bantering or complaining. He just nodded his head and then looked at Gray Dog, who was now blowing on the red feather, amazed at its softness.

Thomas shook his head, opened the door, and quickly left.

"Tonight John Henry learns his destiny as written by the Great Spirit."

Dugan poured himself some of the colonel's whiskey and then turned to face Gray Dog, who was still staring at the brightly colored feather and blowing lightly to see it fluff and wiggle.

"Great Spirit my Irish ass, boyo." He swallowed the glass of whiskey whole and then reached for the bottle once more.

"This is why I am going with John Henry. The spirit that lives on mountain far away is calling me, as it is you, and I will go to see this great thing." Again he blew on the feather. "Where does this big red bird live?" he asked as he blew on the feather again.

"Red bird?" Dugan then saw the feather and realized that Gray Dog had changed subjects on him. "Oh, no, that is from a peacock, a strange bird that lives down south, I think. Now what in the hell do you mean, 'great thing'?"

"John Henry will know. We will both go into the darkness to find what calls us."

Dugan stared at Gray Dog and shook his head before downing the second glass of whiskey.

"Darkness, Great Spirit, mountains, you talk like a bleedin' officer, boyo. And don't think I ain't noticed your English gets better around John Henry."

The carriage was out front of the Willard at precisely thirty minutes to midnight. The coach was empty, occupied only by the driver sitting on his high seat. The corporal saluted as he opened the door for the colonel. Once in, the coach sped off into the humid Washington night.

The road they traveled was a familiar one that led northward from the capital. John Henry felt as though he was heading into court to find out his execution date. After the debacle of Antietam, Thomas had decided to resign his commission after the last shot of the war was fired. His career was over in the army and he knew it. Even though most general officers knew he had been right to challenge the orders of Little Mac, he was never to be fully trusted again because of that challenge to command. He wouldn't fight Indians after the war and he wouldn't be garrisoned in some far-off European posting. He would return to Texas and live a quiet life raising his cattle. The life he always intended to live with Mary.

The coach soon arrived at a small farmhouse just three miles outside the city. The corporal opened the door for Thomas with a tip of his cap. John Henry stepped out and saw the small but very well-kept house with a picket fence surrounding a patchy lawn. He pulled open the gate and made his way up the walk. The house seemed dark but the lantern on the front porch illuminated the front of the yellow house in crystal clarity.

"My staff thinks my mind is gone. foregoing their security and meeting out here," came a familiar voice from the porch.

John Henry stopped as he reached the front steps of the house. He looked to his left and saw two long legs with one pant leg showing a bony, white ankle. His eyes swept over to the man who was stretched out on the porch swing. John Henry immediately snapped to attention.

"We've come far too many miles for that nonsense," came the soft, very tired voice. "Come sit for a moment before we join the others."

The man John Henry Thomas had known for more than fifteen years sat with his trademark stovepipe hat upon his lap. His black hair was now graying and was in its traditional scattered state. The beard was thinning and the man's eyes were as drawn as his face. He had aged fifty years since he'd last seen his friend.

"And don't you dare say anything about how tired I look. I get enough of that from Mrs. Lincoln, and that damn Seward."

"Never, Mr. President," John Henry responded without

much conviction as he eyed the president of the United States. He eased in beside Abraham Lincoln and then also stared out into the yard. The president reached out and patted John Henry on the knee.

"I am happy to see you, my boy." For the first time Lincoln looked over and took in the colonel. "Glad the wild Indian tribes didn't get your hair."

"They may not be as wild as everyone has been led to believe, sir."

"I suspect they are not. But some angry politician will claim they are eventually." Lincoln took in a deep, long, and very sad breath. "I would like to protect them, but alas that task may have to fall to another." Again the tap on the leg. "Life used to be a lot simpler. How long has it been since you escorted me around when I was an attorney for the railroads?"

"Fifteen years, Mr. President."

"You were what was known as a young shavetail, Lieutenant, if I recall correctly."

"You do, and I *was* a shavetail."

Again Lincoln patted Thomas on the knee as he drew up his own legs and placed the hat on his head. "I wish we had more time, my boy, to reminisce about better days, but we have some surly gentlemen awaiting us inside." Lincoln stood slowly. John Henry heard his joints popping audibly as the president stretched his long frame.

John Henry rose as the president turned toward the front door. "Sir," he said as he gripped the ridiculous Union officer's hat in his hands. Lincoln stopped and turned. His sad smile was in place as he waited for Thomas to say what was on his mind. "I never had a chance to thank you for what you did for me and Sergeant Major Dugan after Antietam."

Abraham Lincoln allowed his smile to grow and for the first time Thomas saw a little of the old log splitter there. He shook his head as he turned away for the door once more.

"After all of this time I thought you would have hanged that ill-tempered Irishman by now. How is the old coot?"

"The same, only worse. But one thing he is, sir, is grateful."

"I think maybe you both ought to hold off on your praise of your savior until you have heard why I brought you back from the wilds of Indian Territory. You may not be too grateful afterward."

The door was opened for the president as he stopped and turned to John Henry with a sad look on his wrinkled and drawn face. "Shall we?" He gestured for Thomas to follow.

The living room of the small farmhouse was darkened as they were escorted in by a private from the Washington barracks. A door opened and Thomas heard the cessation of talking in a smoke-filled room. As the president entered many of the men around a large table stood, but Lincoln waved them down with a flash of his hat.

"Gentlemen, Colonel John Henry Thomas," Lincoln said as he placed his hat on the table and then sat at its head.

John Henry looked around the room to see many a familiar face. Sitting next to Lincoln was the sour and long-bearded face of Secretary of War Stanton. His rotund size took up a lot of space as he was glaring at the new arrival. Stanton, it was presumed, had not been in favor of saving him nor Dugan after Antietam, but relented when he found out the order saving them would go against General McClellan's wishes. He hated Little Mac as much as the president himself. Thomas nodded his head at the secretary. Next to him was the man he had seen that very afternoon, Secretary of State William Seward, his ever-present cigar lit as he looked at Thomas with raised brows. On the far side of the president was a man Thomas had only seen pictures of, and those images did not come close to revealing the stern presence of the secretary of the navy, Gideon Welles. Next were several men and a woman Thomas did not know.

"We'll save the formal introductions and make them as we go, shall we?" Lincoln said and then cut off Secretary Seward before he could say something. Lincoln patted the man's arm, trying to get his former antagonist, turned close friend, to relax.

"To begin, I would like placed into the formal record that

I am in serious doubt as to the reasoning behind this action. It's foolhardy and ill advised." Edwin Stanton puffed out his chest and waited for the president to give him a rebuke.

As John Henry took his seat he made eye contact with the woman, whose expression told him he was just another despicable military officer to her.

"Yes, we know your position, oh mighty Hermes. Besides, wise one, there is no formal record of these particular proceedings," Lincoln said, eliciting snickers around the smoke-filled room. "Colonel Thomas, the gentleman to your right is Professor Lars Ollafson, most recently a professor of biblical studies at Harvard University. My son vouched for him over three years ago when I was introduced to him." Ollafson nodded his gray head at Thomas. "Next to him is an assistant to his former department, Miss Claire Richelieu, an interpreter of ancient tongues and written language— quite an accomplishment for a young lady."

The woman who was known in other circles as Madame Richelieu didn't nod or smile; she just looked at the colonel without greeting.

"Professor?" Lincoln said as he gestured for the small man to take over the meeting.

"In the spring of 1859, I and many close colleagues from differing nations funded and mounted an expedition to eastern Turkey. We gather tonight to discuss that journey and what we are to do next."

"I guess that's already been determined by God, without my approval I may add," Stanton cried as Lincoln frowned at him, silencing the irritable man.

"As I was saying, after this meeting concludes, we should come to the logical deduction by all parties"—he looked at Stanton with raised brow waiting for another interruption, but Stanton only mumbled and grumbled—"that the new expedition must proceed at all cost and speed." Ollafson looked at the president, visibly angry. "After all, this was supposed to happen last year immediately after the Battle of Gettysburg, but it is only now we prepare."

"Professor, once more may I explain that an expedition

this size and this complex takes planning, safeguards—that's time, sir," Lincoln said. "Now continue, please."

John Henry looked from the white-haired professor and glanced at the president.

Ollafson cleared his throat. "The question Mr. Stanton needs to ask himself, and anyone else with any doubts, is why was it that so many knowledgeable men in the fields of not only religious studies, but also archaeology, lost languages, and human history, were so interested in eastern Turkey?" Ollafson stood from his chair and then through the cloud of hazy cigar smoke lifted a small wrapped article and placed it on the table. He stared at the oilcloth-wrapped parcel for the longest moment and then he placed a hand on the shoulder of the pretty woman sitting next to him. "My assistant in ancient languages will explain." The professor returned to his chair but kept his eyes on President Lincoln.

The lady stood and then without ceremony tossed the oilcloth away from the parcel. Lincoln watched the eyes of the men around the table. Only he, Stanton, and Seward had ever seen the artifact before. John Henry noted that Richelieu had a peculiar strength about her and automatically knew her to be the type that hated men for their preconceived notions on the subject of women in any profession. Thomas didn't hold with that since he had seen plenty of women take a hospital element with all its death and horrors and make it their own. Yes, Thomas had grown to respect the women of the world.

"We have here two prime examples of what is known as Angelic Script, or what is being taught at universities worldwide as the Enochian language."

"Which, I must confess from my limited reading skills, is known as a language thought up by two men in the 1500s, and that this Angelic Script you proclaim is the basis of this theory of yours, was and still is a fraud," Lincoln said as he challenged the woman for the benefit of the men around the table. Lincoln never led anyone anywhere unless he knew his subject would benefit from it.

"Precisely." The woman returned the challenge with her

green eyes. She then placed a white glove on her right hand and lifted the blackened stone to the weak lantern light. "These symbols here are a warning, described in that very same Angelic Script alphabet. A warning, or a curse if you prefer." She showed the line of strange circles and glyphs to the men in the room. "I have an alphabetic key for those who wish to double-check my facts." Her gaze went to Stanton and then to Seward. Both men only looked on with mild interest.

"This, gentlemen, is wood," Ollafson said. "We cannot know its age. We only estimate that it has to be at least five thousand to ten thousand years of age."

Seward snorted and Stanton closed his eyes while shaking his head. Gideon Welles, the secretary of the navy, seemed keenly interested.

"How can you come up with that estimate of its age?" Welles asked, looking like a stern teacher at a boy's school with his white beard and hair.

"Excellent point, mighty Poseidon," Lincoln said, comparing Welles to the Greek god of the seas.

"Two reasons," Claire said as she again lifted the first of the heavy slices of thick, petrified wood. "One, this particular piece of wood came from a specific area of the globe. Two, the name inscribed in Angelic Script found on this smaller piece." She touched the second.

"You're dancing around the question, woman," Stanton said in his no-nonsense voice.

"Yes, I guess I am. It's the theater coming out in me. This first one was recovered by a Turkish explorer in 1827. This second was discovered in 1842."

"The point, woman!" Stanton said as Lincoln again scolded him for interrupting.

"They were both found on the mountain in eastern Turkey called Ararat."

Silence met her disclosure and it confused her momentarily. She turned her attention to the new man in the room, John Henry Thomas.

"It's the mountain mentioned in the—"

"—Bible, as the resting place of the Ark described in

Genesis," Thomas answered for her. "Most of us went to Sunday school, ma'am."

She nodded to Thomas and then with a stern look at Stanton she said, "Yes, but maybe more than a few around the table needed to be reminded. Now, the second reason is this." She held up the second piece. "Placed side by side we have a story. The first states that whoever disturbs the resting place of God's gift to man will suffer the wrath of heaven and all of its archangels." Claire Richelieu dabbed her gloved fingertip at each symbol as she explained. "This one is the bridge that completed the theory. It's a name. You see here where the broken end of the wood cuts off after the dire warning of a curse?" Most leaned forward in their chairs, all except Stanton and Lincoln, to see better. "The name is simple and was the easiest to decipher. The word inscribed on the wood, or stone if you prefer, is the name Noah. Coupled with where these were discovered, the name gives us the true identity of these artifacts. Noah's Ark is real and can be located just where the Bible said it would be, Mount Ararat. The evidence is right here on this table. It's a fact the Ark is where I say it is."

Stanton snorted; Seward turned his head angrily, which he did every time he heard the theory; Gideon Welles laughed aloud but clapped his hands in delight; and Lincoln only smiled. As for John Henry Thomas, he was beginning to feel ill. Claire Richelieu nodded at the professor and then sat as she peeled the white glove from her right hand. Her eyes went to John Henry, who sat stoically silent at the far end of the table.

President Lincoln stood and walked to the cold fireplace and placed his arms on the mantel as if deep in thought. Thomas knew different; it was Lincoln's famous pause before he told everyone his plan, which he had formulated a full year before sending for Thomas. The president turned and walked back to the table, reached down and took a small book from the tabletop, and slid it down the table to John Henry.

"It's time to call in favors, John Henry. I figure you owe your president one. That, sir, is a journal. Two years' worth of entry space. You will take that with you and recover or gather proof of whatever it is upon that mountaintop. You will make it an American discovery."

Thomas made no move to retrieve the leather-bound journal. He looked from it to the president. Then a look toward Ollafson and then finally Claire Richelieu.

"This, in the middle of a war we may very well still lose?" Thomas was looking at Lincoln as if he had lost his mind.

"As my old war horse here will attest"—Lincoln placed his hand on the thick shoulder of the long-bearded Stanton—"the war will be over in a year. The forces in rebellion have never fully recovered from their Pennsylvania adventure. It's cut and dried. General Sherman is down south at this very moment explaining it to them."

"I cannot accede to your order, Mr. President, out of good conscience. I could never do this while men are fighting and dying on both sides of the Mason-Dixon Line. I request a combat assignment."

"Denied," Lincoln said, almost angered at Thomas's response. "You will do what is asked, and I have my reasons, Colonel."

John Henry noticed Lincoln used his rank instead of "my boy" or "John Henry."

"The war was the simple part of this equation. The peace is what will be hard fought. Imagine yourselves, Americans all, how you would feel after losing a war, which Americans have never done before. We have beaten back the world's most deadly power not once, but twice. The thought of losing is inconceivable to most Americans, north or south. Hatred will rule the land for three hundred years. Unjust sanctions will be placed on the South—sanctions I want to avoid at all cost. This"—he pointed at the two pieces of petrified stone—"can save precious time in our endeavor to bring true peace to the nation. You, Colonel Thomas, will bring back that prize on the mountain for the nation or proof that it truly exists, and the men that will assist you in doing this will help solve that reconstruction problem I have referred to."

"You have lost me, sir," John Henry said as his jaw muscles clenched.

"I imagine I have." Lincoln nodded at Stanton.

Edwin Stanton slid a thick piece of paper down the table and it landed in front of Claire Richelieu, who picked it up and handed it to Thomas.

"That is a roster of Confederate prisoners of war. The war department has selected one hundred and twenty individuals under the command of an officer you may know. These prisoners will be given the opportunity to participate in this . . . this . . . miscarriage of military spending. These men are offered as a goodwill gesture by their commanding officer, General Robert E. Lee. You will be in overall command." Stanton sniffed and snorted as Lincoln watched Thomas for reaction.

"Lee signed off on this?" Thomas asked.

"Yes, he knows as well as we that the war for the South was essentially lost at Gettysburg."

John Henry Thomas knew he had to delve back into his history and current events of world politics.

"You do realize that this amounts to no less than an invasion of the Ottoman Empire? And the last I knew they were busy forging alliances with England and France. They are nervous as they watch their empire being reduced by thousands of miles each and every year. And we're just going to sneak in and steal what amounts to their property? We'll be ending one war just to enter a world war soon after."

Lincoln, instead of disparaging Thomas and his argument, laughed for the first time. "You see, gentlemen, this is the right man for the job at hand. He understands what's at stake for this country."

"I wasn't agreeing with you, sir, I was warning you of what will happen."

"Yes, and we do have a way around that. The Ottoman Empire, or in this case a little closer to home, Turkey, is trying to push itself into modern times. They have begun a massive railroad buildup and infrastructure construction inside their nation. The United States, ever a friend to the Empire, has made a gift of a thousand miles of railroad, which will connect their eastern provinces with Constantinople and the northern Black Sea. This gift is from the people of the United States on the anniversary of the birth of their leader, Sultan Abdülaziz. He has gratefully accepted this gift."

"Your force will pose as civilian engineers that will lay out the route of said railroad, one east from the capital and the other south from the sea," Seward said proudly, as it was he who had thought up the ruse. "While you and your second-in-command will be official Union Army engineers, the president thinks enough of his railroad years soaked into your head to pass muster on that account."

"Force?" Thomas enquired.

"With the Rebel prisoners, you will be in command of two hundred army, marines, and naval personnel," Stanton finished for Seward. "Much more if you count the crews of the vessels involved."

"Colonel, this will have a most healing effect on this country. The nation, together, will bring back the grandest prize in the history of the world. I cannot stress enough that a successful expedition by two warring sides will show that no matter the differences between us, we are one, and forever will remain so."

"Hear, hear," said Gideon Welles as he rapped his knuckles on the tabletop. This elicited sour looks from both Stanton and Seward.

John Henry felt as if he were a rat trapped in a maze of confusion. He suspected that everyone, including his old friend Abraham Lincoln, had lost their minds in taking resources from a war that in his opinion was far from over. These people were underestimating the war prowess of Robert E. Lee. Thomas knew the man personally and also knew that even if the war was eventually lost due to his setback at Gettysburg, Lee would fight a war of attrition, which was what they were all taught at the Point . . . fight until the other side tires of war.

"Along with this dubious command, who else is a part of this expedition?" Thomas asked, avoiding the subject of everyone being absolutely insane. "These two?" He gestured at Ollafson and Madame Richelieu. "Why not ask Jeff Davis to join also? That should add even more credibility to this mission."

"That's about enough, Colonel," Stanton said angrily. "I may not back this plan as well as maybe I should, but listening to serving line officers fighting the legitimate chain-of-command has come to be quite tiring."

John Henry knew he had possibly gone too far. He nodded with a resigned feeling of being ambushed. He was more afraid of being labeled a shirker of presidential orders like his enemy, Little Mac.

"And the good professor will sit this expedition out, my boy," Lincoln said with a kind nod toward the man who had found the artifacts.

"On the contrary." Ollafson looked as if he were a big-game hunter and his quarry had just entered his killing field. "I beg to disagree with you, Mr. President. I and my assistant will be coming along. You need us." He nodded toward Claire. "Both of us."

"You'll do as you are told, sir." Seward glared at the Scandinavian professor as he flipped a long ash from his ever-present cigar. "And be pleased that we have acceded to your wishes about this whole endeavor."

The professor didn't respond; he only leaned over and brought up another parcel. Even his young assistant was surprised as she eyed the oilcloth as it was laid upon the table.

"What in the Sam hell is that?" Seward asked. Lincoln raised his scraggly brow and watched as the professor played out his hand.

"The final piece of the puzzle, gentlemen, and the reason you have no choice but to include my assistant and myself passage on this voyage."

"We do not like surprises, sir!" Stanton said as he slapped his hand down upon the tabletop.

"Which is exactly what Colonel Thomas will get if you allow this expedition to commence without us."

"Okay, Professor, show us your hole card," Lincoln said.

"Without me, everyone going to that mountain will die, just as my colleagues died five years ago." Professor Ollafson unwrapped the last parcel and everyone, with the exception of Claire Richelieu, leaned forward.

"My God," was all she said when she saw the writing.

Ollafson smiled. "No, but maybe God's executioner."

The only person in the room who understood what she was looking at was Claire Richelieu. She was flabbergasted to say the least. For a spy with her credentials to be fooled by the old professor stunned her. He had held out from her the most important information imaginable. The symbols that were etched into the stone made her weak in the knees. Could Ollafson be putting one over on not only her but the learned men around the room? Was he running the bluff of all bluffs?

"I was notified this evening that a student of mine was murdered for this." He waved his hand over the petrified wood. "This is the artifact that we recovered on the expedition of 1859. Many men died to get this out. Yes, we two are going, only because without us you will not be able to decipher the old tongue of the angels. We"—he placed a hand on the suddenly shaken Claire—"will go, and you must allow it to give the colonel here every advantage."

"Please, Professor, explain the ace that you have just presented the game. We are most curious, I assure you," the president said as he kept his dark eyes on the man from Harvard rather than the artifact he had just presented.

"The assassins of my student presumed I had passed this on for safekeeping. They were wrong and my dear student paid horribly for my bluff." His eyes went to Lincoln. "It is now obvious I had been watched without knowing."

Madame Richelieu felt the twinge of guilt in the pit of her stomach for the young man's death at the hands of her colleague from the French army. If she couldn't keep her calm she felt that everyone in the room would know her complicity in the unseemly matter. As she looked at the scripture on the ancient wood she shuddered and prayed it was a hoax by the old man.

"The symbols depicted upon the wood reveal that you may be dealing with far more than you realize inside the glacier where the Ark is entombed. I said that on the last expedition, we had been attacked—well, not only attacked, decimated. Forty-seven men. From the summit of that black forbidden rock to the lower valleys, we were assaulted at every elevation until our assailant weakened as we came closer to the sea."

"All right, my good professor, I'm sure you have Colonel Thomas's attention. You sure have mine. So tell us, sir, what does this particular artifact tell you?" Lincoln asked, hoping to call Ollafson's bluff on the validity of the plank and its feigned or real significance.

"It only adds a name to the entity giving the curse its power and backing according to the wishes of the Lord God himself." Ollafson glanced at the stunned Claire Richelieu. "Please, Claire, since this is also new to you, and by the look upon your face, just as shocking, perhaps you can explain to them the symbols I have kept from everyone, including my closest advisors and colleagues."

The woman cleared her throat and stood on shaky feet. She nervously looked at John Henry, who watched silently. She couldn't help it—for some reason she felt the colonel could see directly through her ruse. Not only Thomas's suspicious gaze, but Ollafson's duplicity also gave her doubts.

Never before had she seen the symbols, but she knew them to be as devastating as the professor claimed. She started to explain.

"This first symbol here." She pointed, immediately regretting not putting her white gloves back on. The touch of the petrified wood under her finger sent a wave of nausea through her stomach until it threatened to tighten her throat, making speech difficult at best. "It's rough and burned very deeply into the ancient wood." Her finger moved away as she found she could not touch the symbol.

"According to the ancient Hebrew texts I've studied, it symbolizes the names of all of God's archangels as one entity, a very rare symbol, and one I have never seen depicted in any form outside of mere guesswork by scholars. But these other two next to it symbolize one particular archangel rarely mentioned at all in the Bible. Usually when God has to kill, he will call upon the angel Gabriel, a chap we have learned throughout biblical history to be very adept at killing. But when the Lord has a task that is devastating in nature, he could never trust one archangel to perform it. He needed all. Michael, Rafael, Gabriel, Simon, and the rest. According to Hebrew scripture, when they are called, a piece of each is used to create this one archangel to finish the untasteful job, and that is this name here." Her fingers came close, but she could not bring herself to touch the stone. She pointed at the second symbol.

"This is the name that is never to be used or said aloud. A name synonymous with death. Not like the children's tales made to frighten them into behaving. It is the name of the angel of death, and it is his job to see the curse through. God wanted this mountaintop protected, and he's sent his best soldier to do it."

"Every schoolchild knows about the specter of the angel of death, Madame. The scythe, the hooded robe, very frightening indeed." Stanton snorted, even though looking at the symbols left him with an uneasy feeling. And in these times the subject of death had numbed the secretary of war.

"Every schoolchild has been lied to," Ollafson said, breaking in. "The angel of death is so much more than a scary image. He is sent when the killing is on a mass scale. I have seen how this darkness works."

"The last symbol?" Lincoln asked as his eyes took in an unbelieving John Henry who had remained silent since the rebuke from the president.

"The name of the Angel of Death?"

"Yes," Seward asked with almost childish curiosity.

"Azrael," Claire said almost as a whisper.

"Yes, Azrael," Ollafson repeated. "And I have seen him."

"Yes? I would be most interested to know what he looks like. We may have seen him in Washington," Seward half-joked. Ollafson wasn't.

"Just step out into the night, Mr. Secretary. You will see his image."

"And that is?" Seward pushed.

"Blackness. The dark, the night killed my colleagues, and that blackness has teeth, gentlemen."

The looks around the table were cold but remained neutral. Lincoln looked at Thomas.

"Colonel Thomas, it looks like your expedition's roster has grown by two names."

Thomas looked from Lincoln to Ollafson, and then his eyes found the woman. She sat silently looking at the plank of petrified wood. She finally looked up and that was when John Henry knew this woman wasn't bluffing. She was truly frightened.

"Now, one last bit of business," Seward said as he pulled out two envelopes. "Your second-in-command—it's about time you know who it is and where you can go to find him. He may be a familiar of yours."

FEDERAL CONFEDERATE PRISONER OF WAR CAMP, FORT LAFAYETTE, NEW YORK

Colonel Jessup Taylor looked at the moon as the first of the dark clouds started to move past. He knew there would be rain soon and that was nothing but good news for he and the men he planned to lead out of the camp that very morning. He lay on the louse-infested bunk and turned his head.

"Time, Sergeant Major?"

The gruff old soldier rolled onto his side and looked at the colonel in the darkness of the wooden barracks.

"Sorry, Colonel, I left my pocketwatch in my other suit." He snorted.

"I meant the time of the guard's last walk-through," Taylor hissed.

"Ten minutes."

Taylor slowly rose from his bunk and then lightly tapped on the cot's wooden frame three times. Silently several men rose in the darkness and made their way to the shuttered windows. All but the one through which Taylor observed the moon were secured. Five of his healthiest men waited by the large double doors of the barrack. Their dress was in a state that guaranteed they could not walk the streets of Brooklyn without immediate discovery, so at this juncture of his plan the men started to strip their tattered uniform coats and shirts. Jessop Taylor nodded at the youngest of his men, Private Wilcoxin, a devout boy of seventeen from Wheeling. The boy produced a wrapped brown-paper package and snapped the white string that held the large bundle together. Taylor nodded when he saw the freshly cleaned wash that had just been returned from Fort Hamilton across the way. They were Union enlisted men's uniforms.

"Not exactly my favorite color, Colonel," a ragged corporal said as he held up the Union-blue jacket of a private.

"Hell, I'll take anything that doesn't house the entire louse population of the north," another said as he quickly donned his jacket.

Taylor accepted his absconded uniform jacket from the private. He winked, acknowledging the boy had done well in stealing the laundry that afternoon.

"Guard," hissed one of the men at the doorway.

Taylor finished with the last brass button and then nodded at the largest of his men, Anse Poteet, a sergeant from Georgia. The giant stood at six-foot-six and had worn out more cavalry horses than an entire troop during the three years of war his men had seen.

Poteet opened the rickety wooden door an inch and then waited. When the boot falls came close he opened the door with a quickness that would only be expected from a much smaller man. The ham-sized fingers quickly closed around the guard's neck and without a sound pulled the man inside. With eyes wide in terror, the guard looked around frantically when the giant hand closed around his mouth. Poteet looked up at Taylor, a knife in his free hand, but Taylor only shook his head. Poteet nodded and then brought the knife's hilt up and then down upon the young man's head with a thump. He immediately went limp.

"We're not going to get too far if we allow mercy to come

between us and that gate, Colonel," the sergeant major said quietly as he glanced out the open doorway.

"We only kill those that need killing, Ezra." Taylor nudged the unconscious guard with his worn boot toe. "This isn't who I want," he said with finality.

"Wait a minute. You're not comin', are ya?"

"Your job now is to get as many as you can to the harbor. Corporal Yulee can handle most anything with a sail. That's all, Sergeant Major. Get my men out of here."

"And what is your grand design?" the small sergeant asked angrily, as the colonel had not bothered to share this part of the plan with him.

Taylor looked at his men gathered at the door.

"I have a man to talk to for a while. I'm going to hold that cowardly bastard while you get those boys free. As long as I have Major Freeman, the rest won't be able to blow their own noses."

"No!" the sergeant major said as loudly as he dared and even reached for the colonel's sleeve as he slipped out the door and into the rapidly developing storm.

"Goddamn him," the sergeant major hissed. "Well, you heard him, let's get to the stables, Private." He turned to look for the young man who had delivered the uniforms. "Get the other boys together and wait by the doors until we signal. Hey, where did Private Wilcoxin go?"

The sergeant major cursed as he glanced around for the boy, but he was nowhere to be seen. "Well, hell, we can't wait. Hope he catches up." Sergeant Major McCandless left the protection of the barracks and started through the rain toward their goal.

Colonel Jessy Taylor watched the southern guard tower and saw no movement. The soldier normally manning the post must have been hunkered down as far away from the rain-washed edges of the covered box as he could get. Taylor knew the soldier was an old man by the name of Jennings, a left-over from the Mexican war and one not very affable to discomfort. Taylor had specifically picked this night because of the rainstorm and the fact that they had all the right Union staff on duty. Lazy men, volunteers for the prisoner of war camps that allowed them to serve but not to fight. Cruelty was the order of the day and these men, roughs and toughs from the boroughs of New York for the most part, loved their duty and followed Major Nelson Freeman's orders to the letter.

Taylor signaled to the barracks and the sergeant major moved the first of the men toward the fenced section of the compound where the stables and the armory were located. The four-man guard unit was huddling under the eave of the roof's overhang. Taylor saw they were laughing and slapping rainwater onto each other. They figured, and rightly so, that the men inside Lafayette were so weakened by disease and malnutrition they couldn't even walk, much less escape.

Taylor watched the first sixteen men, in their newly cleaned Union jackets and a few borrowed Billy Yank caps, move toward the four men, who didn't notice their approach. He grimaced when the men were jumped. He didn't want the guards killed. That was a point he had made with McCandless—they would not lower themselves to the Union camp commander's level and kill for no reason if the guards gave up, which he suspected they would when faced with the angry men they had been abusing for over a year.

More men moved forward from the barracks when the sergeant major gave them the all-clear. They would place as many men as possible inside the four wagons allotted the post and then simply escort them out with a small unit of riders. That was the plan, anyway.

Taylor looked up and saw the dim light coming from the commandant's office and private quarters. With a look back at his men who were now moving into the stables and the large stone barn, he saw the first flash of lightning. He quickly used the white light to view the parade grounds now filled with windblown waves of mud and water. It was clear. He moved to the stairs and ducked underneath. He knew an orderly would be on duty, but Taylor suspected the man had his boots up on the desk and was napping, as was his habit at night.

He waited for the signal from the barn. He knew he had not been able to get as many men to escape as originally thought. He would only move out thirty-six. These were the healthiest. He would remain behind with the others—if he survived Freeman's wrath. His duty on this dark night was clear. He would remain and hold Major Freeman, and then stand trial for it and the escape. He would do this to protect those that came after him, to draw attention to the conditions at Lafayette. The man in charge of the camp was insane and he had to end this.

He moved out from under the wooden stairs and then crept silently upward. Another streak of lightning and the view changed as his eyes moved to the barn below. The rumble of thunder shook and rattled the windows around him, and then the nightmarish reality became clear. The thunder had not been the only sound heard. Gunfire had erupted inside the barn. He quickly turned and burst through the commandant's door. He immediately saw that the orderly was not at the desk and he most assuredly was not sleeping. He was standing next to Freeman's private quarters with a shotgun pointed his way. The dreamlike sequence was made real when Taylor saw the Union corporal smile. He raised the weapon and took aim at Taylor's chest as more gunfire erupted from below. Taylor closed his eyes and listened to the falling rain, knowing his chest would soon be exploding out through his back. That was when the door opened and Major Freeman stepped out with six men behind him. Another soldier went to the wall and sent the brightness of the lamp to full.

The gunfire outside dwindled to nothing. Taylor eyed Freeman and then shook out of the wet Union-blue coat. He let it slide to the wet floor.

"Caught with a Union uniform in an escape attempt." Major Freeman looked around first at his men and then the tidy office. He walked to an old file cabinet and tilted the five-foot box until it capsized. Drawers popped free and papers spilled. "Or was the colonel using the stolen uniform for spying purposes?" He looked around him, a look of mock disgust on his mustachioed face.

"He's a spy, Major. Hell, as far as I can tell, there ain't been no escape attempt. He was here to gather information and wasn't wearing his proper uniform. Yep, a spy."

"Which means, Colonel Taylor, I can legally shoot you." The smile grew on Freeman's face.

Taylor deflated when he realized they had all been set up to be murdered by the ingenious Freeman.

"I can see that Boston College education is paying off, Major," the haggard Confederate colonel said as two men took up station on either side him.

"Actually, it wasn't all that difficult to figure out what was happening. As you know, I keep my ear pretty close to the ground," Freeman said as he walked to the main door, pulled it open, and allowed the wash of the rain to cool the room. He stepped back as a corporal entered the office portion of the quarters. "Report?"

"Thirteen dead, fifteen wounded." The corporal smiled and looked at Taylor. "Them boys tried to put up a fight, Major. We had to subdue the escape attempt in the harshest terms."

Before the corporal could react, and with the smile still on his face, Taylor reached out and grabbed the man's well-maintained sideburns and brought his face down into his right knee. He felt the corporal's nose break under the on-slaught and the man screamed in pain. Taylor was about to bring his knee up again when Major Freeman brought his pistol down on Taylor's head, dropping him to his knees.

"Colonel Jessup Taylor, you are under arrest, sir, for spying inside a federal installation. You are hereby ordered to face camp punishment. This is to be carried out at noon tomorrow. These men will witness on an official basis, not that we will need their testimony."

Jessy heard the words as they were spoken but the world had become a spinning, blurred view that made his stomach give up the watery celery soup he had eaten earlier. He went to his hands and vomited as blood coursed down his head and onto the wet floor. He was grabbed and brought to his feet. He wobbled and one of the men holding him slapped him hard on his bearded face. Then as the corporal straightened he pulled his hand away from his destroyed nose and delivered a punch to the colonel's face, making him go limp as he was held. His eyes remained closed until the pistol barrel of Freeman's weapon raised his chin. When his eyes opened he saw a man enter the room.

"No one does anything in my camp without me knowing about it, you traitorous scum." Freeman laughed as the image of the man came into Taylor's view.

Taylor let out a moan that was quickly covered by the Union guard's laughter. Standing before him, twisting the Union cap he had stolen and still wearing the Union-blue jacket, was Private Johnny Wilcoxin, the same lad who had provided the stolen laundry for the escape.

"I . . . I . . . just didn't want to hurt no more, Colonel."

Taylor tried to raise his head and speak to the boy but Freeman stepped forward and brought the barrel of his Colt revolver down once more. This time Jessy Taylor went out for good.

"Rebel force, turned back." Freeman looked at his men. "That'll look good in the papers, huh boys? Maybe get me a personal write-up for that baboon in the White House to read?"

As the major's men laughed, Lieutenant Colonel Taylor was taken away to face his execution the next afternoon.

STATEN ISLAND FERRY, NEW YORK CITY

The silence had been palpable since the train ride north from the capital. It had continued in New Jersey and even now as they looked out at the early afternoon sun from the deck of the paddle steamer, S.S. *Westfield II*. The rainstorm of the night before had made the afternoon clean, the smell of the city having been washed away.

Sergeant Major Dugan watched John Henry Thomas for a long moment and then glanced at Gray Dog. The Comanche was wearing his bright purple shirt and was currently touching a small redheaded child. He had never seen such majestic, bright red hair before. Just as Dugan was about to slap Gray Dog's hand, he heard a gasp and a rotund woman in a black dress pulled the boy away in terror. The child was still smiling at Gray Dog as his mother admonished him for being so close to the savage.

"Don't touch people, you . . . you . . . damn Indian! This here is not the plains, boyo, it's civilization."

The look on Gray Dog's face was incredulous. From what he had observed thus far in the east, these people were anything but civilized. Not like his own, where anyone's property in camp was shared by all. He would never understand John Henry's people.

"Now, are you going to tell me what has you so riled up?" Dugan asked, turning his attention to the colonel, who had his hat off and was looking toward the docks of the city as the ferry made its way across the sound.

John Henry remained silent as he took in the skyline of a city he had visited many times in his youth. When on holiday leave from West Point he couldn't rightly just hop on a train and return to Texas, so he would come to the city with other displaced classmates. This was the city where he had met his wife. A small cotillion had been put on by the Gentlemen's Club of Astor Place. He wanted to smile at the memory but knew it to be too painful. John Henry had lost his young bride Mary five years earlier near the Brazos and his family's ranch. She had been killed in a Kiowa raid when he had been deployed into southern Kansas chasing Gray Dog's people. He always blamed himself for her loss.

He finally turned to face the sergeant major. Gray Dog even moved closer to the two soldiers when he thought the colonel was finally going to speak for the first time since he had awakened them at three in the morning and then placed them all on a semi-deserted train north.

"Sergeant Major, this afternoon I want you and Gray Dog to return to Washington. I will have transportation orders for your return to posting in Kansas. You two will not be traveling with me after today."

The Irishman laughed and nudged Gray Dog, who took

the shot to the ribs with annoyance as he didn't understand the white man's humor.

"That is one thing we won't be doin', Colonel Darlin'. You know better. Now, just tell me what those madmen in Washington has us doing."

Thomas was about to explain when an old deckhand approached the three men. "Gentlemen, please step back. We are about to dock, and the crazy son of a bitch driving this damn thing has a tendency to smash the bow into the wharf every now and again."

Thomas saw the ferry coming in at breakneck speed so he decided he would have to delay explaining until later.

"Secretary Stanton telegraphed Fort Hamilton to send over three mounts and a small detachment of marines to escort us to Fort Lafayette. Evidently the camp commander is one of those Boston bluebloods and a hard-nose when it comes to his prisoners."

"Another war-avoiding rich man, you mean, and just what do we need a detachment of marines for?" Dugan asked while looking suspiciously at Gray Dog.

"We are heading into hostile territory to see an old friend of mine." He looked back at Dugan. "And as far as the detachment of marines is concerned, that will become obvious when I've had time to explain."

Dugan and John Henry watched as the ferry was tied to number-three dock. As for Gray Dog, he was busy looking at a few of the Union warships that had gathered in the harbor. The Comanche had never laid eyes on anything larger than a shallow-draft river barge in his life. He gaped at sailors scrambling up and down the ships' rigging and was in amazement at the sheer size of the frigates and cruisers. It wasn't until Dugan nudged him that he came out of his trance.

Many men, women, and children walked past the three men with wary eyes upon the Indian. Dressed as he was in leather leggings, the coyote head on his top-knotted hair, his bone chestplate, and the brightly colored gift from John Henry, the purple shirt, he was a sight among the working men and civilized women. His black hair was hanging loose, and two large eagle feathers dangled from the back. Children were amazed and men and women horrified at the sight. Sergeant Major Dugan dipped his head at the ladies and nodded at the men but made a horrid face at the children as they walked past.

"There's our men," John Henry said as he spied twelve blue-clad United States Marines with three extra horses arriving just beneath the dock area. The three men walked down the gangway and were greeted by a young lieutenant who saluted as he stepped forward.

"Second Lieutenant Jenson Parnell," he said as he saluted John Henry. The salute was returned but the young clean-shaven lieutenant, a recent graduate from the U.S. Naval Academy at Annapolis, kept the salute in the air as he examined the Comanche, who was staring at his turned-up hat with a red feather pinned to the side.

"At ease, Lieutenant. He's not exactly officer material," John Henry said just as Dugan slapped Gray Dog's hand away from the marine's hat.

"Uh, uh, yes, sir," Parnell said as his hand slowly came down and his head bobbed to avoid having the feather garment taken from him by the Comanche.

John Henry didn't hesitate as he climbed aboard one of the horses, realizing just how much he missed it when he wasn't in the saddle. Dugan followed suit but stopped short when the enlisted marines in the group shouted at Gray Dog. Thomas and Dugan watched as the Comanche fulfilled a ritual that most white men could not fathom. Gray Dog had unbridled his horse and tossed the McClellan saddle from its back, leaving only the blue blanket. Then he grabbed the animal's mane and pulled himself up onto the creature's back. He looked at the men staring at him and realized that he was the center of attention.

"Excuse my friend, Lieutenant. He's a little more at home feeling what his mount will do. That's a Comanche way of feeling the animal's back muscles and the leg tendons. He knows in advance what a horse will do. That's their way."

Parnell looked from a curious Gray Dog to the colonel,

quickly gathered up the discarded saddle and handed it to the unit's corporal, and then mounted himself.

"Just never seen no Indian before, sir," he said as he took up station next to Thomas.

Thomas pulled the reins of his mount and started forward. "Don't worry, Lieutenant. His people are probably the greatest light cavalry on the planet. Now, shall we go meet my new second-in-command, sir?"

Lieutenant Colonel Jessy Taylor was chained and shackled to the wall inside the barn. The blow to his head delivered by Major Freeman had concussed him enough so that Freeman was actually sorry the Rebel colonel would more than likely expire before he had a chance to hang him. Taylor felt the pain in his wrists and hands long before the pounding of his head as his eyes fluttered open. He blinked against the bright sunshine that reached his eyes through a hole in the old barn's roof. The colonel tried to get his bare feet to move to take some of the strain from his shackled wrists. He finally managed to relieve the pressure by standing as best he could. He tried to open his eyes once more.

"Excellent! You're not going to die after all—at least not until I say so," said a familiar New England–accented voice. "You had me worried enough that I had my corpsman stitch up your head to stop the blood loss."

Taylor blinked as his blurry vision started to focus. He took in the thin frame and the immaculate uniform of Major Freeman. He stood before him, but when Taylor moved his head he hastily stepped back. The Confederate colonel knew the man to be afraid of his own shadow. Taylor had seen men like Freeman the whole of his military career. From West Point to the Cimarron River in Texas, either wearing Union blue or Confederate butternut, it never mattered. Cowards like Freeman would forever be a blight on the fates of real soldiers.

"My . . . my boys?"

Freeman took a cautious step forward, making sure the guard armed with the Spencer rifle was aware he was doing so. The weapon was cocked, ready to dispatch Taylor at the moment the order was given.

"Excuse me, Colonel? What was that?" Freeman placed a hand to his ear in mocking fashion.

"My men?" The words were barely audible.

"You mean *my* men? You obviously don't take care of them the way you should, Colonel Taylor, so now they are my men."

"Where is Sergeant Major McCandless?" Taylor's head finally moved upward to glare into the dark eyes of the abolitionist's son.

"Ah, the sergeant major." Freeman placed a manicured hand on Taylor's black hair and patted the colonel like a wayward child. "Well, he is a responsible noncommissioned officer, Colonel. He is with your men, watching over them since you sent them off to die in a manner not befitting a real soldier. Yes, he is with the others."

"Don't hang my men. They . . . were following . . . orders."

Freeman stepped back from Taylor in mock shock. "Hang them? I would never do such a thing." To Taylor's horror the major laughed and stepped away, but reached out and took a brutal hold of curly black hair once more and forced the colonel's head up. Taylor's vision focused as he knew immediately what he was looking at.

"No, I won't hang them, but their suffering at your hands and through your orders is over, Colonel Taylor, as you can clearly see."

A moan escaped Taylor's bloody mouth as he saw the bodies on the hay-strewn floor of the barn. They were uncovered and each was caked in thick mud. The blood coating them had dried to a sickening maroon color. His eyes roamed the twenty corpses in front of him. Sergeant Major McCandless was near the center. His bearded face was looking up blindly at the rafters of the roof. The men he had sent with the sergeant major were arrayed to his left and his right. Another moan escaped his lips and his head started to dip once more as he wanted nothing more than to seek shelter from this horror by slipping into the pleasures of unconsciousness. Freeman's hand once again brutally pulled Taylor's head up.

"No, no, no, no, Colonel. This is the result of your arrogance in trying to escape my care." He gestured with his free hand. "This will be what awaits all of you bloody sinners in the South, my friend—death and dirt, that's what awaits the traitors and their kin."

Taylor mumbled something.

"What was that, Colonel?" Freeman said, eager enough to hear that he bravely took a step toward Taylor as he released his hair.

"I said, I am going to kill you." Taylor slowly looked up and then smiled with bloodstained teeth. He spit with all the strength he could muster.

Freeman felt the bloody spit strike his perfectly curled moustache and he immediately stepped back from the chained man. He quickly took a kerchief and wiped the bloody spittle from his face.

"I would normally say that would have cost you dearly, traitor, but my plans for you remain unchanged." He looked at the first guard and then nodded to Taylor. "Unchain the prisoner. His execution will be carried out immediately."

The private glanced at Freeman only momentarily and saw the crazed look in the young officer's eyes. He immediately moved to release Taylor.

"Your sentence of death will be carried out at exactly the hour of noon, Colonel. I am just sorry your men could not join you on the gallows."

Freeman tossed the bloody kerchief to the ground as Taylor was dragged from the barn and then the stable area. He walked out into the sunshine then smiled. He turned to the corporal next to him.

"Assemble the camp's company. I want his men to see what happens when a man thinks he can outwit me."

On the afternoon of August 2, 1864, the war was truly over for Taylor and his men.

Twenty minutes later the riders entered the Fort Hamilton area of Brooklyn and Thomas was taken by the surreal setting of peace and tranquillity of the wooded area. But the preternatural quiet disturbed him. While the activity at Fort Hamilton was brisk, three hundred yards away was a very different picture at Fort Lafayette. The prisoner-of-war camp was silent, and Thomas saw several women holding banners outside of the main gates being confronted by army personnel, who seemed to be angrily addressing the women's group over a sensitive issue.

It was marine lieutenant Parnell who held his hand up, stopping the marine escort mere yards from the gate. He nudged his horse slowly forward and approached the nearest private.

"Clear a path and open the front gates," he ordered, trying to make his schoolboy's voice sound commanding. Thomas and Dugan watched from horseback.

"The camp is closed this morning to all visitors on order of Major Freeman, camp commandant." The private looked nervous as he took in the army officer being escorted by the marines. He stood rigid when he saw the embroidered silver eagles on John Henry's shoulder-boards.

"I guess that double-breasted monkey suit does command attention. Maybe you should wear it more often," Dugan said with a smirk and a spit of tobacco juice. Many of the protesting women saw this and grimaced. Dugan winked at the largest woman he had ever seen standing in the front.

"Sorry, Lieutenant. My orders are explicit."

"Soldier, open that gate," Parnell said as calmly as he could. There had been rumors across the street at Fort Hamilton that the officer running Fort Lafayette was a little on the bizarre side.

John Henry saw another soldier approach. This was a sergeant who was obviously in command of the gate. He was bearded and had an arrogance about him that Thomas immediately disliked.

"Now, Lieutenant, the private has his orders as well as myself. No one gets in today. We had an escape attempt last night and we are in the middle of sorting it all out." The man's beady black eyes went to Thomas, who sat stoically watching the confrontation.

"Why don't you just let me shoot these rear-echelon sons of bitches?" Dugan said, staring at the arrogant sergeant. He was getting so angry he hadn't noticed that his chinstrap had slid up and covered most of his mouth, so John Henry heard nothing but a garbled request.

"Adjust your headgear, Sergeant Major," Thomas said without looking over at him. He easily slid from his saddle but motioned everyone to stay mounted. He adjusted his uncomfortable coat and the sword dangling on its strap at his side, and approached.

Dugan angrily removed the leather chinstrap from his mouth and then turned that anger on Gray Dog. "And you, you think you're impressin' people with that purple shirt the colonel got ya? Well, let me tell you, you don't wear a Comanch' breastplate over it. And what's that, your official dress feather hanging there?"

Gray Dog looked from the scene before him and turned his gaze to the feather hanging from the middle of the bird-bone breastplate over his shirt. He fingered the feather and then looked curiously at Dugan.

"Like talkin' to a rock," Dugan said as he turned and watched the colonel.

Thomas took young Parnell by the shoulder and moved him out of the way as he confronted the sergeant and the private. Through the thickly slatted gate he noticed a lot of activity in the yard of the prison. He turned to one of the women after Parnell angrily stepped aside.

"Ma'am, Colonel John Henry Thomas. What is this all about?" he asked with a tip of his upturned hat.

The woman came close to curtsying but caught herself. She was middle-aged and was wearing mourning black with a veil over her face. She angrily turned to the two guards.

"Sir, this is Wednesday, and our ladies' group has permission from your war department to bring in medicine and extra food for those poor delusional souls inside the prison. These men will not allow us to pass," she said as the other women, many of them older than the first, started to agree, shouting angry epithets at the men at the gate. "We do this because many of these mothers and wives have husbands and sons at places like Andersonville Prison. Perhaps if we feed and take care of their sick, they could possibly do the same for their boys."

John Henry wanted to say that although noble in act, this was not a very realistic proposition, but as he looked at the faces of the many anxious women at the gate, he decided now was not the time to inform these women that the South was on the verge of starvation.

"I'll see what I can do, ma'am," Thomas said as he touched the brim of his hat. He stepped around the woman and then faced the arrogant sergeant. As he stepped up he gestured behind him for Dugan, making a movement with his thumb and index finger. Dugan saw this and immediately removed the string from his flapped holster. Gray Dog immediately moved his horse to the far side of the column and without anyone noticing he dismounted and disappeared into the shadows of the large trees lining the front of the fort.

"Sir, I have my orders," the burly sergeant said.

"Lieutenant Parnell, have your marines dismount, please."

Parnell smiled as he gave the command. The twelve marines did as ordered and lined up behind the lieutenant.

John Henry never looked behind him to see if his order had been obeyed. He simply stared at the well-fed sergeant before him. His blue eyes cut deeply into the man's black ones.

"In thirty seconds, if that gate remains closed I will give the order to open fire on your men. Is that understood, Sergeant?"

The heavyset man looked around at the suddenly anxious marines to his front, who seemed to relish the thought of firing on his men. He knew the marines at Fort Hamilton had been wary of everyone from the camp, simply because of the rumors that floated about Brooklyn concerning cruel punishments and murder inside the prison. He swallowed as he turned and took in the dangerous man before him.

"But, sir!" he protested.

"Lieutenant, deploy two-man fire teams, we will assault

and then enter the prison on my command," Thomas said, still staring at the bearded sergeant. Dugan actually drew his Colt revolver from its holster.

"Sir, I have orders that no one—"

The sergeant felt the knife at his throat. He had failed to notice the Indian who had vanished a moment before. Gray Dog had used the heavy shadows of the thick trees to get close enough that his own guard detail did not see him. The bowie knife had been a gift from John Henry and it was Gray Dog's most prized possession. The knife dug in and Thomas and Dugan both didn't know how Gray Dog could see anything because the bulk of the sergeant obscured everything except the shiny blade. The private standing next to the sergeant stepped back. The women gasped and moved as far away from the gate as they could.

"Open the gate," the sergeant said without moving his head.

The private turned and gestured behind him. The large doors of the gate finally started to crack and then it opened. Thomas smelled the prison before really laying eyes upon it.

John Henry returned to his horse and mounted. He ordered the marines to do the same.

"Gray Dog, leave him be. He's decided to be a soldier again," he said as he spurred his horse forward. He tipped his hat at the women who were watching. "Ma'am, I'll see what I can do about getting you in."

Gray Dog vanished along with the knife. The sergeant spun around, but saw nothing as the Comanche disappeared as fast as he had arrived. As the sergeant gingerly touched the line of blood at his throat he was amazed to see Gray Dog had already mounted and was riding past him without so much as a look.

As the escort rode through the gates, more than one of the marines had pulled a kerchief from their uniform jackets to place over their noses. The mud-caked parade ground was awash in bodies laid out in the afternoon sun. The colonel quickly counted twenty-two.

"Jesus, Colonel, what in the hell went on here?" Dugan

asked as he took in the scene. He kept his pistol free of its holster. Gray Dog was the only one of the command group who wasn't shocked by what he was seeing. After all, he had seen the army's work many times before.

John Henry saw the makeshift and rickety scaffold at the center of the parade ground. Seven men were lined up on the top and they all had ropes around their necks. There were also several Union guards and an officer staring at him from on high.

"What is the meaning of this? The camp is closed to all outside personnel."

"You come down from there, you dirty son of a—"

"Sergeant Major!" Thomas said, not too loud. Dugan looked put out and disgusted.

"Who is in command here?" John Henry asked as he stepped from the saddle once more.

"I am in command, and who, may I ask, are you, sir?"

"Come down here and report, Mister," John Henry said, loud enough that all of the camp heard, even those prisoners lined up to witness the executions. The colonel's eyes roamed over the seven men about to be hanged. One was being supported on shaky feet by a younger man. John Henry immediately recognized who he was looking at and became furious. He waited as the major who was overseeing this punishment descended from the scaffolding. John Henry quickly turned to Parnell. "Lieutenant, send a man to Fort Hamilton. I want two companies of armed marines here immediately."

"Aye, sir," Parnell said as he gave the order to one of his men, who was more than happy to leave the stinking interior of the prison.

The Union officer in immaculate dress came down and stood before Thomas, refusing to salute him.

"Sir, while you are in my prison, I must inform you that there is no higher authority than mine, and this punishment is being carried out in accordance with camp procedure and military law."

John Henry remained looking at the man on the scaffold

being supported by two of his own. He appeared only semi-conscious. "Sergeant Major, check on those bodies, please."

Dugan quickly dismounted and went to the long line of men who were lying in the stinking mud of the camp. He leaned over the first few.

"Shot in the back." He moved the brown and mud-caked hair of a young Confederate soldier. "Also shot once in the back of the head." He straightened. "Over half of these men were murdered, Colonel. Looks like they were shot from behind, and those that didn't die right off were executed," Dugan said as he took in the spit-and-polished officer who was arrogantly staring at Thomas and his men. The sergeant took a menacing step toward the first guard he noticed was standing too close. The man backed away three steps. Dugan smiled and then spit a long stream of tobacco juice from his bearded face. "That's about what I thought, you bunch of heroes."

The marines under the command of Thomas could not believe what they were seeing. The blood from the dead men mixed with the mud produced by the storm the night before, and the sight made them sick to their stomachs.

John Henry handed his reins to the closest marine, and then placed a hand on Major Freeman's shoulder and pushed him brutally away. The major backpedaled and then fell backward into the mud. This brought cheers from the starving men lined up to watch the hanging. As for Freeman, he was stunned to the point he couldn't talk.

"Lieutenant Parnell, this man is to be placed under arrest." Thomas didn't wait. He made his way to the scaffolding. "Relieve all noncommissioned officers of sidearms and keys. They are also under arrest."

With a smile Parnell jumped to attention. "Yes, sir!" he said, giving the army salutation instead of the navy way.

Thomas walked up the stairs slowly. Gray Dog was right behind him. The Comanche didn't understand fully what was happening, but he saw the intense sorrow on John Henry's face and knew that his friend and protector had been deeply saddened.

"Cut these men loose," he said to Gray Dog, and then moved as quickly as he could toward the first man in line, who was being held up by a private in a butternut-colored jacket.

"Those men were wearing Union blue during their escape attempt, and their commanding officer was caught inside the headquarters gathering intelligence. Thus they are being hung as spies, so you have no right to interfere with—"

Dugan lightly rapped the major on the top of his head with his Colt. "Hush now," he said as Freeman grabbed the top of his hat where it was now indented from Dugan's blow.

"Ow," was all he could say.

Gray Dog pushed the first guard away rather brutally, sending the man tumbling down the wooden steps to land in the mud below. Another tired and worn cheer erupted from the gathered prisoners. The Comanche started cutting the ropes and releasing the men.

Thomas looked at the boy holding up the officer. He nodded at the boy as John Henry removed the rope from around the man's neck and then the private's. He allowed the officer to fall forward and Thomas eased him onto the mud-covered decking of the scaffold. The black hair was blood soaked and the eyes nearly swollen shut. Suddenly the green eyes flashed as the man tried to sit up. "No," he said in a barely audible whisper. "Not my men, it was me!" This came out a little louder.

"Easy," John Henry said as he tried in vain to wipe some of the blood away. The green eyes were barely visible through the swelling but John Henry hoped the man could see him nonetheless. The wounded officer raised a hand, took a filthy grip of Thomas's tunic, and pulled him close. "Hang me, not them."

"No one is getting hanged today," he said, as even Gray Dog had stopped to watch the exchange. Thomas removed the grip of the man's hand and then looked at the face and how it had aged since he had last laid eyes on him.

It had been in Texas in 1861. They had served together chasing Kiowa and Comanche who were raiding frontier farms and ranches along the Brazos and the Cimarron. When the war began, like most of the professional officers at the time, they had said farewell as the war divided the army like nothing before. This man had been called home to Virginia, himself to the Army of the Potomac and Washington. From the looks of things they had both taken a bad road and now were here together again.

"Jessy. Jessy," he said as quietly as possible.

The eyes tried to open but the swelling kept them mostly closed. The green eyes, bloodshot through and through, opened as best as they could. They focused on the clean-shaven face before them.

"John . . . Henry . . . Thomas," Taylor whispered, and then the eyes closed.

Thomas laid Taylor's head down and then stood to face the men below.

"This prison is now mine." He saw the arrival of fifty U.S. Marines as they entered the post at a rapid pace and in formation. They split off as if on cue to cover not the prisoners, but their guards, who started to lay down their weapons in the mud. The bayonet points looked very menacing. These were not unarmed and defenseless prisoners—these were marines and they looked the part. Thomas then looked down at the major, who was still holding his head where Dugan had tapped him.

"This action is illegal," was all he said.

"Sergeant Major, place this officer into submission, and you do not have to be gentle about it," he said as his eyes grew with the fire he was feeling in his gut. "Place him in irons and then have the marines escort him to Fort Hamilton. The same for the noncoms. For now, allow that ladies' group in to care for these men, make sure they are fed." Thomas stood and then pulled Dugan in close. He looked at the lined-up bodies of Confederate murdered lying in the mud and grime of the parade ground. "And get one of these marines to get the *New York Herald* over here before officialdom takes charge. People need to know about this."

"Still won't be a lot of sympathy for the Rebs, you know that. Our boys fare far worse down south."

"Do as ordered, and make sure those ladies are forewarned of what they will encounter this side of the gate. Is that clear?"

"It sure is, Colonel Darlin'."

"You don't have that authority," protested Freeman. "I was appointed by General McClellan himself."

John Henry knew the letters tucked inside his tunic at that moment made him the most powerful man outside of the White House. Instead of telling the major the predicament he was in, he watched as Gray Dog with the help of two marines assisted Lieutenant Colonel Taylor from the scaffolding.

Thomas's second-in-command might not see the sun set that day.

WASHINGTON, D.C.

Claire had been sleepless since the meeting the night before had broken up and she and Professor Ollafson were escorted to the Willard Hotel. While lying awake in her room she had heard sounds in the hallway outside her door. When she cracked it open she spied Colonel John Henry Thomas, a gruff little man in sergeant's stripes, and a third man dressed in leather leggings and a purple shirt walking down the empty hall toward the stairs.

Throughout the sleepless night she had deep and disturbing thoughts about the artifacts Ollafson had surprised everyone with that night. The images of the Angelic symbols flew through her mind and each vision gave her uncontrollable chills. It was as her mother used to say about a goose walking on one's grave.

After her futile hours chasing sleep, Claire ended up in the hotel's dining area. She had just finished her morning tea and was about to make her way back to her room when she saw a familiar face staring at her from the corner of the room. The brazenness of the man never ceased to amaze her. The French master spy was sitting in the dining room with no more fear than a man would have at his own breakfast table. Their eyes only met for a moment before Claire left the dining room.

Madame Claire had been in her room less than five minutes before the light knock sounded on the door. She knew the game she played was the most dangerous in the world. She removed her long, sharp hatpin, took a deep breath, and then made her way to the door and cracked it open an inch, making ready her hatpin weapon.

"Are you going to wait until I am discovered lurking in the hallway like a forlorn lover?"

Claire swallowed when the man spoke in his unfettered and unaccented English. She opened the door and stepped back to allow the Frenchman in.

Paul Renaud walked toward the desk and then tossed his hat on its polished surface. "Generals, generals, generals everywhere. They ply the waters of Washington like a grouping of sharks smelling blood." He smiled. "Each one wants to become the next man in charge."

Claire closed and then locked the door. "I suspect that Mr. Lincoln may have found the right man in this General Grant. I believe he may make short work of the South. The president seems to like him very much."

"Speaking of the apple of the president's eye, what have you learned about our colonel from the west?" he asked as he made his way to the sofa and then sat. He touched the material and grimaced as he rubbed his fingers together with a sour face. The Willard was not exactly the Knickerbocker Hotel in Manhattan.

Claire slowly pulled the light blue gloves from her hands and then tossed them on the bed with her unpacked luggage. She took a deep breath and then made her report.

"The man, unlike most military professionals, keeps his private opinions to himself, so that makes him a very hard read. But you can tell the president trusts him like no other, even his closest advisors."

Renaud looked curious. "And why is that, do you think?"

"From what I could learn, this Colonel Thomas has been

associated with Mr. Lincoln for nearly fifteen years. The army and the railroads assigned him to be Lincoln's personal bodyguard during the president's legal days when he represented the railroads in several hard-hitting litigations. From what I hear they are extremely close. So close that Lincoln actually intervened when Thomas faced a general court-martial on charges of dereliction of duty and disobeying a direct order of the commanding general at Antietam."

"Yes, I seem to have read something about that when last in Paris. I understand that caused a rift between General Mc-Clellan and the president."

Claire turned and wanted to smile at the small man but stopped herself. It seemed she knew something he didn't. "No, the rift between McClellan and the president is a little deeper than that. Thomas was on the fast track for a star on his shoulder-boards before the incident. Who knows, maybe even eventual command of the Union forces? Lincoln has that much confidence in John Henry Thomas."

"All right, they have their man and now we have him. Now, you and the professor, are you in on the expedition?"

Claire walked to the credenza and poured herself a glass of water. She feigned taking a drink and then turned to face the most dangerous man she had ever met. That was when the thought struck her. It had come to her only a half hour since she had seen Angelic Script on the petrified wood. She shuddered as the image of the symbols blazed into her mind.

She mentally shook herself and then halfheartedly smiled. "Yes, we are in. From what I understand we will depart without much notice and at the colonel's discretion."

"Excellent. I need the names of all naval vessels involved."

"I don't have that information."

"Obtain it, Madame."

"That you will have to do on your own. I haven't the time."

He laughed as he stood and placed his expensive hat on his head. "I also do not have the time. You see, I must pack because I am now a part of the team." He held a fist halfway up in mocking gesture of a cheer. "I am replacing the student that came up mysteriously dead in New York."

"Is that why you murdered that boy? Just to gain passage?"

"I am just taking advantage of an accidental death," he said, his eyes sparkling as he opened the door and then paused. "It was nothing to get a letter of introduction to Ollafson from Harvard, as you know we have many high-placed officials ensconced there." Again he smiled, and then he left.

Claire turned and faced her unpacked luggage and then went to the door. She had to stop to clear the images of the professor's symbols from her head. She didn't let Renaud know about what she had discovered or what Ollafson had held back from her. She had her reasons, none of which coincided with the fact that Renaud might not be the most proficient killer on this trip after all. She suspected something on that mountain may be even better at it, and Ollafson had actually seen it in action.

Claire went to the hallway and then took the stairs down a flight. She cautiously walked the corridor until she came to the right room and rapped her small knuckles against the door. It opened and she stepped through. The man was wearing his uniform. She thought maybe the arrogant bastard slept in it, but that was as far as she would allow her private thoughts to go when she thought of the man before her.

"Wonderful, you weren't arrested after all." The British Army officer closed the door. "So, the meeting with the president went well, I take it? You and Ollafson will be included?"

Claire appraised the blond Englishman. Captain Steven McDonald, British Army Intelligence, was chipper of mood as he waited for her answer. The man who had couriered Her Majesty's wishes overseas stood and waited with that irritating smile he had.

"Yes, but I am afraid we are not the only ones included on the passenger manifest, Captain."

"And just what does that mean?" he asked as he gestured that she should sit.

She ignored his hospitality and turned to face him.

"Our friend Renaud will also be going. He will be attached to the professor and myself as an assistant."

"A very dangerous game he is playing," McDonald said as he placed a hand to his chin and started pacing.

"It is also a dangerous game I also find myself in, Captain."

McDonald stopped pacing and smiled. The man's Scottish aristocracy came through at these moments of levity, and she hated him even more for it.

"Such is the life of a double agent. But you will also have the company of one who will watch over you." He smiled as he took in her beauty. "I am also included on the crew's manifest."

Claire was shocked. "You?"

The smile remained. "Yes, you are not the only persuasive one. I am to be included as Ollafson's personal secretary. Hired just this morning by your dear employer when he requested a diarist from his old department at Harvard."

Claire watched as the captain turned and opened the door for her. He smiled again. "My dear, it will be reported to Her Majesty that you have done an excellent job of infiltrating the French spy ring here in America. She will be most grateful."

Claire was in shock as she left the room. Was every spy in the western world going on this expedition? For the first time since becoming an agent for both France and England, Madame Richelieu was beginning to think she was as insane as the rest of them.

6

John Henry watched Jessy's eyes as they fluttered open. It had been three hours since he had taken over the prisoner-of-war camp at Lafayette. The U.S. Marines were now in control. The prisoners would get better treatment, at least for the time being.

The colonel knew he didn't have much time to do what needed doing. He looked to the corner of the darkened room and saw Gray Dog praying to his ancestors. John Henry didn't know if the prayers were for them, the Reb colonel, or something else. He never asked Gray Dog about his praying habits.

Thomas removed the wet cloth from Jessy's forehead and then stood and removed his double-breasted tunic. The cottony white shirt was already soaked through in perspiration. He tossed the coat on the floor, adjusted the suspenders, and then leaned over his old friend and classmate.

"I would have sworn old Jeb would have had you shot by now," he mumbled as he applied another cloth to the back of Taylor's head.

Thus far there had not been much of a stir at Fort Hamilton as far as the takeover of the prison was concerned. A simple and very brief telegram from the war department had seen to the quick and thus far quiet transition. The letter from the president bearing his signature had had the desired effect on the marine major manning Fort Hamilton.

"Maybe he didn't have me shot, but he sure as hell . . . left my ass in the bushes a week before Gettysburg."

John Henry smiled as he heard the softly spoken words.

"Yeah, that's the Jeb Stuart I know. Great tactician, terrible friend."

Taylor finally managed to open one eye as he took in Thomas. Then with a curious look he turned his head to the right when he heard the soft humming and chanting coming from the dark corner. He managed to focus momentarily on Gray Dog and then his head fell back.

"I see you still associate . . . with . . . the . . . very best . . . families."

John Henry laughed as Taylor regained some of his old self.

"Actually, you were the one that found his family massacred in '58. He's been with me ever since." He looked at Gray Dog, who had stopped praying and was watching the two old friends.

"Long time ago," Taylor said as he tried to sit up. "My . . . my men?" he asked when he found he couldn't come to a sitting position on the small bed. He lay back down and rubbed the bridge of his nose, where behind the skin and bone there was a little devil hammering his brain to pieces.

John Henry looked at his bearded old comrade. Taylor had aged since leaving Texas four years before. The gray in his beard was testament to the fact that he had seen some hard fighting in Stuart's cavalry. Now he had to tell his friend about his murdered men, which would not sit well with Taylor, especially for what he had to tell him about his immediate future. He reached down and retrieved his coat from the floor. He produced a handwritten letter and then opened it.

"Twenty-two dead, sixteen wounded."

"Ezra?" Taylor asked as his arm immediately covered his battered face.

Thomas looked at the notes he had hand-delivered from Lafayette only thirty minutes before.

"By Ezra, do you mean Sergeant Major McCandless?"

Taylor didn't respond, only waited.

"Dead."

The arm came away as Taylor's eyes glared at his old friend. The one open eye was filled with splotches of blood from the concussion he had sustained at the hands of Major Freeman.

"Sons of bitches," he hissed.

Thomas folded the report and then laid it beside Taylor. He nodded his head. "I suspect that we are. All of us."

Taylor closed his eye. "What in the hell are you doing here?" Taylor asked as his chest heaved silently and his tears soaked into the muddy blue coat he was still wearing.

"The man that did this will never harm anyone again. He may have influential people backing him, but so do I. I suspect he will get off of the murder charges, but his professional career as an officer is over. Secretary Stanton said he would see to it. But to be frank, Jessy, things are only going to get worse for all prisoners, North and South, if this damnable war doesn't end soon."

"He'll get away with it until I catch him and kill him," Taylor said as he finally lowered the arm and took in Thomas.

John Henry watched Taylor closely. Even Gray Dog was interested in what was being said.

"When the time comes, I'll hold him while you use that famous knife of yours to convince him of the errors of his ways."

"Lost that damn knife at Fredericksburg."

"I think we can come up with something, Colonel."

"The rest of my men?" Taylor asked, his voice somewhat stronger than a moment before. He reached over and found the report John Henry had tossed next to him and he fought against the darkness of the room with his one good eye to see the names of the dead.

"Being fed and cleaned as we speak. The ladies' auxiliary for Fair and Ethical Treatment of Prisoners has taken over the care of your men, at least until the army gets over their initial shock at having their little secret out in the open."

"Now," Taylor said as he placed the report to the side and tried to sit up once again. This time with the help of John Henry he managed to come to a sitting position. "Why are you here, just out to enjoy the wonders of prison camp treatment?" Taylor felt the swelling around his head and grimaced when he touched a sensitive spot.

"I have a letter for you."

"You came all the way here to give me a letter?" Taylor laughed out loud and then immediately regretted it. He winced as he grabbed the side of his head. This was immensely funny to Gray Dog, who smiled from his corner. "I know that look, John Henry. It's the same one you were wearing when we filled the commandant's office at West Point with duck feathers as a senior prank."

"Well, while not on that epic scale, it is pretty good. I have been laughing since one o'clock this morning. Laughed all the way from Washington. I would never have believed the creative way both of our high commands have come up with killing us."

The blank look on Taylor's face said in no uncertain terms that Thomas was crazier than when he was but a schoolboy.

A knock sounded on the door and John Henry opened it. A man in a blood-stained white coat with frazzled gray hair was there.

"Doctor Halverson. Are you Colonel Thomas?" he asked as he peeked into the room and saw Gray Dog sitting on the bare wooden floor. He blinked and then his eyes spied Taylor. The doctor pushed past Thomas and went to the wounded man. "I have just come from Lafayette. I am the doctor here at Fort Hamilton and I have been treating the Rebel prisoners. Malnutrition for the most part. But there has been brutality there." He turned and with his eyes looking over his round spectacles he said to Thomas, "That should be looked into." He turned and raised the swollen eye of Taylor and then shook his head. "Boy, they really laid into you."

"They had their fun," Taylor said.

The doctor straightened and then frantically felt around his white coat and the jacket underneath. He took a deep breath when he found what he was looking for. He pulled out a folded telegram and held it out to John Henry.

"A rather boorish and foul-mouthed little sergeant major asked me to relay this to you. It just arrived from the telegraph office."

John Henry unfolded the telegram and read.

```
PROCEED TO THE BROOKLYN NAVY YARD
IMMEDIATELY UPON FINISHING YOUR
TASK AT LAFAYETTE. PIER NINETEEN,
SLIP SEVEN. THERE YOU FIND YOUR
COVER STORY. THIS TASK MUST BE DONE
IN PERSON WITH NO, I REPEAT, NO
ESCORT. IMMEDIATELY AFTERWARD YOUR
TROOP OF VOLUNTEERS IS TO REPORT TO
BALTIMORE FOR SHIP ASSIGNMENT AND
DEPARTURE-STANTON.
```

"Doctor, how many of the prisoners are healthy enough for travel?" he asked as he placed the telegram in his pants pocket and then removed a watch and noted the late hour.

"None. I said they were malnourished, Colonel. If not fed a healthy diet soon they will not be able to walk, much less travel."

"Doctor, if fed properly for three weeks will they regain their strength?"

"Possibly. I can't say for sure. These prisoners are all former cavalrymen. They are strong, but I can make no guarantees."

"Good enough. Please get a complete roster of Colonel Taylor's healthiest soldiers to that foul-mouthed sergeant major you met. Tell him we move out tonight. I also need ten wagons and the marine detail that was assigned to me earlier."

"My men aren't traveling anywhere. What is the meaning of this, John Henry?" Taylor asked as he saw the astonished look on the doctor's red face.

Thomas finally held out the letter he had brought in to show Taylor. He opened and then folded the note until only the bottom portion was showing. He held it close to Taylor so he could see it in the dim lamp.

"Do you recognize this signature and seal?" John Henry smiled. "You should. You probably received enough signed orders from him the last three years."

Jessy Taylor's eyes remained on Thomas's for the longest time. Then his one good eye strayed to the letter and the signature that was verified by the wax seal. The good eye widened. John Henry smiled and then asked the doctor to step from the room. He then unfolded the letter and gave it to Taylor, who read it with suspicion. Thomas pulled another letter out of his uniform jacket. As he watched, Taylor's mouth went slightly ajar. Then he looked at Thomas as if he had lost his mind.

"That's not the only madman's signature, Jessy. Here's another one you know." He held out a second letter but didn't divulge its contents, only the name. The two names would be floating in front of Taylor's eyes even after he closed them fifty years later.

R E Lee

C.G. Army of Northern Virginia

And then on the second letter's lower half was the second signature that completed the madness:

Abraham Lincoln

BROOKLYN NAVY YARD,
BROOKLYN, NEW YORK

The horse-drawn trolley allowed John Henry the time to think. As he stared out at the busy streets of Brooklyn and the bustling activity near the navy yard, he knew that his old friend and West Point classmate Jessup Taylor was near the end. He could see it in his face and hear it in his words. Gone was the prankster, the man who bought every round but never seemed to pay for it at the end of the night. He was not only worried about Taylor, but the men of his command. He still didn't have any idea who was to accompany him other than the few Confederate soldiers deemed healthy enough to withstand the voyage. This was definitely an army plan.

The bell rang as the trolley pulled up to the navy yard. The guard shack was well manned as he stepped from the car. He was saluted by a naval rate and then passed through after showing his card and orders. A two-man navy escort went with him and guided him through the maze of dry docks and buildings until he reached a slip that was covered in a tarpaulin as large as the roof covering the Hippodrome in Manhattan. He looked around and saw civilian workers entering and exiting the dry-dock area.

"This is as far as we can go, sir," the petty officer said as he and his companion spun on their heels and left the area.

"Colonel Thomas?" came the accented English from behind John Henry.

He turned and saw a small man with pure white hair. He was wearing civilian clothes and looked angry. The little man's face seemed familiar.

"Yes, I am Thomas," he answered finally.

"What you see before you is your cover story." The man gestured toward the giant tarpaulin. "It is meant to give the Turks something to see as far as a railway is concerned." They stepped up to a smaller guard shack and saw a rather large marine standing before it with a menacing Spencer carbine at port arms. He didn't look friendly. The small man's accent was strange, and it was one Thomas had heard recently. "It is basically a large barge, capable of seagoing travel. Very stable. It will hold several thousand tons of railway ties and rail. Even for a locomotive, however, looks can be deceiving, Colonel."

John Henry stepped through the tarp's opening and was

stunned at what he was looking at. Yes, there were railroad ties and rails going into the hold of the giant ship-shaped vessel. But it was what the railroad equipment was hiding that made Thomas's eyes widen.

"May I present to you, Colonel Thomas, your ace in the hole if you ever need it. This is the sail barge U.S.S. *Argo.*"

"I see you are a man of the classics, sir," Thomas asked, referring to the name of the ship before him.

"Yes, the *Argo* was the vessel Homer listed in his classic tome about Jason and his amazing Argonauts." He looked at John Henry and his smile widened. "Fitting name, do you not think?"

John Henry didn't answer. Instead he looked from the barge and its amazing contents back to the man who was smiling and rocking on his heels as if he were a proud parent looking at a newborn son. He finally recognized the face with the long sideburns he had seen in the eastern newspapers. The man was famous. And it wasn't the same accent of Professor Ollafson he had heard the night before. It was another, close but not the same. He was hearing a Swedish accent and the name he was searching for was a naval engineer's name: John Ericsson, a name most of the world was familiar with since he'd come on the scene two years before, when a battle that changed the world took place off the Carolina coast. That little fight, if John Henry remembered correctly, was one called the battle of Hampton Roads. The man before him was the designer of the Union ironclad, U.S.S. *Monitor.*

"I wish I were going with you, sir," Ericsson said as he continued to smile and rock on his heels.

"Believe me, sir, you do not."

"Nonetheless, Colonel, an adventure looms in your future and I so wish . . ." The engineer turned toward Thomas and then smiled with mild embarrassment. "Just an old fool planning ways to beat the gods at their own game. Anyway, I will be traveling with you to Baltimore where you will see the other three ships of your armada."

"Armada?"

Ericsson laughed and then closed the tented tarp. "The sail barge will be towed to Cape Hatteras, where the four vessels will rendezvous. From there your journey begins in earnest."

"Mr. Ericsson, do you have any idea what all this work was for?"

"Yes, yes I do, Colonel Thomas." The man's eyes were alight with passion.

"And your belief in—"

"Does it matter what one's beliefs are, Colonel Thomas? What is a worthier goal in life, fulfilling this mission of discovery, even if nothing is discovered, or using my inventions to kill other men?"

Thomas watched the crazed man in whom Lincoln had such a firm belief. By all accounts the mad little Swede was insane at the least and a genius at the most.

"No, Colonel, this mission is the only mission. To die in an attempt is so much more desirable than taking a bullet from a brother, wouldn't you think, sir?"

For the first time John Henry was going to show a hole card in his personality. He raised his dark eyebrows and his blue eyes blazed at the smaller man.

"I have found dying is dying. It doesn't matter to the dead what the cause was, all he knows is that he's dead and would much rather have been alive and bypassed all of this so-called glory."

Ericsson did not take offense. He nodded his head. "I think the world would be a better place to live in, Colonel, if there were more professional soldiers such as yourself. But until that day arrives, I will keep building my little wonders to stop those men who do not think as you and I. Now, shall we go?"

Thomas watched the man walk away with a light step. He closed his eyes and then opened them to see the giant tented tarp and wondered just what in the hell he was to do with Ericsson's gift. He looked up and saw a skeletal locomotive being loaded onto the three-hundred-foot barge.

As Thomas watched the activity at the navy yard he turned away and saw the sun lowering in the eastern sky and wondered what was waiting for his little madcap expedition over that horizon.

As he watched, the cloud formation of billowing fluff made the shape of a huge mountain with its peak rising to the sky. The sun cast an angry glow to the image and then the shape vanished as if he had been seeing things.

Out there the mountain waited.

PART THREE

THE NEW ARGONAUTS

For the moment, let them enjoy a calm sea and a fresh breeze, but for Jason, there are other adventures—I have not finished with Jason . . .

—Zeus, father of the gods

7

FORT HAMILTON, BROOKLYN, NEW YORK

John Henry was escorted to the fort's main orderly office where he was shown a desk he could work at. He removed his tunic and hat, he untied his black tie, and loosened his collar. As he walked to the far corner he was happy to see that the fort's marine major had left him a bottle of whiskey. He shook his head in appreciation and poured himself a drink. Just before he lifted the small glass to his lips he saw dust filtering down from above and he slowly pulled his Colt revolver from its holster. When he stepped back and looked up he cursed as he saw Gray Dog sitting atop the room's rafters. His legs were crossed and he was balanced as he watched John Henry below.

"Damn it, get down from there. What are you doing in here? You're supposed to be with Sergeant Major Dugan."

"I don't like forts. Bad places. The big city across the river smells bad. We will go soon?"

John Henry took one last look up into the rafters, holstered his weapon, and finally took a sip of burning liquid. A knock sounded on the door.

"Come," he said as he placed the glass by the bottle and

then returned to the small desk and seated himself. Thinking quickly, he unbuckled his gun belt and placed it on the desktop.

The door opened and Thomas saw it was Dugan. The man was filthy, evidence that while he had been at the navy yard, the sergeant major had been helping with the prisoners. For a man who had so little love for the South and the men fighting for her, he had even less sympathy for those who committed atrocities like they saw today. A good man, a little bad tempered, but Dugan could usually be counted on to do the right thing . . . eventually.

"Colonel Darlin', that sawbones is out here and wants to report."

"Send him in and then bring Colonel Taylor in after."

"He's getting ready for chow, the first they have had in three days."

"Bring him here, and tell Hamilton's cooks I want one full meal with plenty of vegetables for all of his men. The colonel will eat in here with me. See to it."

"Yes, Colonel." The head remained looking inside the office.

"What?" Thomas asked, annoyed.

"I have to admit it, I have gone and lost old coyote head. Can't find him anywheres."

John Henry just used his thumb and pointed upward. Dugan squinted into the darkness of the room and saw Gray Dog looking at him.

"Why you little—"

"Sergeant Major, the doctor."

With one last glare upward into the room's rafters, Dugan stepped aside for the aging physician.

The doctor, instead of reporting, nodded at a curious Thomas and then walked straight to the whiskey bottle. He poured himself a drink and quickly downed it. Then he poured another and drank that. Thomas didn't bat an eye when a third was poured. Finally with an overflowing glass the doctor walked to the chair in front of the desk and then sat heavily. His white coat was covered in blood and filth. His eyes were red and bloodshot. Thomas could see that the naval physician was a virgin to brutality on this scale; thus he knew the doctor had never seen a battlefield.

"Now that you have had your drink, Doctor, do you have a report for me?"

With a withering look of despair the doctor downed the third drink and placed it on the desktop with an eye toward the bottle a short distance away. John Henry reached out, placed a hand over the mouth of the glass, and pulled it toward him. The doctor looked momentarily offended and then nodded.

"Most of those men won't see the next snowfall, Colonel." The doctor pulled out a filthy kerchief and wiped his brow, then covered his mouth momentarily. He coughed with a threat of losing the whiskey he had just consumed. He got his nausea under control and glanced up and saw the strangest thing. An Indian was looking down upon him. "Does the colonel know he has an Indian in his rafters?"

"How many men can make the trip, Doctor?" he asked, ignoring the physician's observation.

"In my professional opinion, none, Colonel. There is not one man ensconced in that infernal camp that is not malnourished, filled with lice, or has dysentery. Hell, most have bad feet from the mud. We call it immersion foot."

"If fed properly for two to three weeks, would they regain strength?"

"Yes, but until then many would die. It's not just the intake of food, Colonel, it's the intake of vitamins the men have been missing."

"How many, Doctor?" John Henry knew the man to be near shock after treating the wounded and the sick, but he had very little time.

The naval physician looked at his notepad and grimaced. "Out of four hundred and sixty-five, those that made it through the murderous night, that is, I can scrape together one hundred and two semi-healthy bodies."

"Far short of the hundred and fifty required," John Henry mumbled. Then he looked up. "What is the lieutenant colonel's condition and prognosis, Doctor?"

The man looked at the empty glass and then he lowered his head, knowing that avenue of escapism was closed to him at the moment. He flipped through his notes.

"Lieutenant Colonel Jessup Taylor, malnourished and has dysentery. He has also contracted scarlet fever. The man is a walking reference book on illness. I also treated the colonel for an infection from a saber wound he received last year. I can't believe it hasn't killed him after so long. One tough soldier. Yes, he will heal. He is currently suffering from a severe concussion."

John Henry studied the doctor for a good while. The heavyset man was becoming uncomfortable when at last John Henry slid the glass back to him across the desk. With a grateful nod, the doctor immediately went to the corner and poured himself another drink. He hesitated momentarily and then, instead of drinking it, he slammed the full glass down on the tabletop and then made for the door, opened it, and then without asking permission left the office.

Thomas understood. He had seen death in all forms, but this doctor was used to treating ailments no more threatening than the scurvy or intestinal problems the navy encounters. He'd seen for the first time what army surgeons were dealing with on a daily basis while the world around them committed suicide. He was thinking how close in feeling the doctor and he were when the door opened and two guards escorted a very much cleaner Jessy Taylor inside, wearing shackles on his wrists. The two marines looked uncomfortable as they stood on either side of the Rebel.

"Remove the shackles," John Henry said as he kept his eyes on the doctor's report in front of him. They did so. Taylor looked at his onetime friend and then rubbed the spot where the shackles had chafed his wrists.

"Gentlemen, please pass the word, until the army comes to take possession of the prisoners, they are not to be shackled. I want every asset of Fort Hamilton brought to bear.

These men need to be fed, clothed, and have medicine available to them. See to it." Thomas ordered, and the two marines saw the determined look in the man's eyes.

"Aye, aye, sir."

"Excused."

"Sir, there is a large tray of food out here."

"Bring that in."

Taylor remained staring down at Thomas. He looked far better than he had that morning. The swelling had gone down around his eyes enough so that Taylor could at least see. The two men remained quiet while the guards brought in the food and placed it on the colonel's makeshift desk. They left and still the silence continued. John Henry made a note on the doctor's report and then placed pen and paper aside.

"Sit, Jessy. Eat something."

When he didn't react but just stood rooted to the floor in front of the desk, it was Gray Dog who silently hopped down from the rafters, went to the large tray, and lifted the covers off the dishes one at a time. He looked át John Henry and then at Taylor. He grabbed a small game hen and held it in front of the Rebel officer.

"You can have it," Taylor said as he saw the Indian's fingers digging deeply into the greasy meat of the small bird. Gray Dog looked from the colonel to the bird and then started eating. He walked to the corner and sat on the floor.

"You'll have to excuse Gray Dog's manners. Sometimes his etiquette and English vanish at the same time. He likes to revert when the mood suits him."

"I remember Comanche manners, John Henry. He was more than likely hoping I was going to choke on it."

"More than likely. Now, please sit. We have much to talk about."

Taylor looked at the tray of food before him and swallowed. He took an apple from a plate and then with a curious look at Gray Dog, he finally sat. He took a bite of the apple and then closed his eyes as he chewed. He grimaced as the hard fruit hurt his teeth. After so long with a diet of oatmeal and maggoty meat, his teeth had grown soft and almost dysfunctional. Still, the apple tasted better than any he could ever remember eating.

John Henry studied his old classmate. He reached out for the coffeepot and poured two cups. He slid one toward Taylor, who took the cup with the apple still in hand and then drank the hot liquid. He didn't care about the burn to his lips and tongue. The coffee tasted heavenly. Finally Jessup Taylor laid down the empty tin cup and tossed the apple core on the tray. John Henry drank his dark coffee and watched Taylor.

"My men, are they being fed?"

"As we speak."

Taylor placed a hand over his eyes. "It's my fault. I knew what Freeman was capable of, but as always I thought I could outthink the bastard. I gambled with my men and they paid the price."

"You did what a commander does—he looks out for his men. I know you were watching them die slowly and I know what is happening on both sides of the Mason-Dixon Line, and it isn't pretty. The hate is going to continue long after we stop killing each other in droves."

"And this asinine scheme of Lincoln's is going to change that?" Taylor laughed for the first time in what seemed like ages. He scratched his beard and then reached out and took a pecan from the tray and popped it into his mouth. "We are going to chase a child's Sunday-school fairy tale and this will make everything good again? And all along I thought the South had all the arrogance needed to call the entire war effort insane, but I see you northern boys don't do too badly at delusional thinking either. The plan is foolish and we won't find nothing out there except a pile of rocks and dirt. I'm surprised Lincoln was able to talk you into this. And I thought he was your friend."

"If there is only a slight chance that Ollafson is right, we may do some good, Jessy. I have never known that lanky bastard in the White House to be wrong about anything." He fixed Taylor with a withering stare. "Anything."

"And that is where you and I part ways, again," Taylor said

as his green eyes returned the look of mistrust. "That man will not only leave this nation a laughingstock in the world, he'll start a war overseas that this country will never be able to win."

"I disagree. We could win that war. As a matter of fact, if that's the downside to this mission, the president is willing to do it. A war would also bring the nation together as much as this fairy tale you speak of."

Taylor looked from John Henry to the food. He looked back.

"Okay, John. What if I say yes? Do I get to command my men?"

"Yes, I will be in overall command, you will be my adjutant."

Taylor leaned back in his chair. "I want as many men as I can take out of here. I don't care if they die on the way to the docks, as long as they are free of men like Freeman."

"Done."

Taylor reached for a large slice of bread and started eating. "I suppose you have a plan that doesn't include a section where we all die, or are able to avoid a world war?"

"Not yet, but by the time our train arrives at the capital we will."

"We?" he said as he swallowed the bread.

"Yes, *we*. If I go down I am sure as hell blaming you for it." John Henry smiled at his old friend for the first time.

"And what will stop me and my men from escaping at the first opportunity?"

"I will have more than a hundred federal personnel on board to stop you. I will have twenty marines on each ship who will be more than happy to shoot each and every one of you." He smiled wider. "So, nothing is stopping you at the moment. After all, Jessy, you've done so well in the war thus far."

Taylor returned the smile as his eyes went to Gray Dog, who was watching the exchange with interest. "I guess we both may have failed to achieve much, other than running into trouble."

"As usual. From West Point to Indian territory, our luck remains unchanged."

Taylor slid his empty coffee cup toward Thomas. Ignoring it, Thomas stood and retrieved the whiskey bottle and poured that into the cup instead. He poured himself a drink and then held it up to Jessy.

"To insanity at its best," Thomas said in toast.

"May it ever be so humble." Taylor hesitated and then said, "And always alive and prevalent."

The two men drank, Taylor ate, and they made a plan that fit with the crazy mission to which they had been assigned.

Gray Dog watched the two friends as they argued over the parameters of the mission ahead of them. As he studied the two officers he knew what they were missing—a belief in the far-off mountain and the killing powers that dwelled there. But there was also something else the Comanche noticed—the two men had something between them that was unspoken. Gray Dog was sure that these two men were no longer the friends who had once thought of each other as brothers—there might even be hatred there. Underlying, but hate nonetheless. He was silent as the men planned the fate of so many.

The expedition to God's forbidden mountain would begin in less than sixteen hours.

NEWARK, NEW JERSEY

It was one A.M. when the eighteen covered army wagons from the ferry started to unload their unusual cargo. Most of the men had to be assisted from the transports by the U.S. Marine guard detail assigned to Thomas. They would escort the detail to Washington. As Thomas watched from the train platform he was joined by the naval engineer Ericsson, who was brought to John Henry by a subdued and very tired Sergeant Major Dugan. Without a word Dugan walked away to further assist the weakened Rebel soldiers. John Henry watched as Jessy Taylor spoke with each man before he was led to a railroad car. His eyes roamed to the perimeter of the out-of-the-way platform and saw his marine snipers stationed where he had left them. They were there to guarantee no prying eyes. It wouldn't do to have the public learn that more than a hundred prisoners of war vanished overnight.

"I had not been told this part of the plan. I am shocked at their condition." Ericsson, usually brash in thought as well as speech, was wringing his hands. Thomas knew him to be a man who tried not to think about what his marvelous inventions were capable of. The result, while not directly related to his work, was disturbing nonetheless to the engineer.

"We all knew this wasn't going to be a pretty thing when it started." He took his gaze away from the emaciated men below shown in flickering torch light and then fixed Ericsson with his blue eyes. "The president knew going in this was going to be personal. The worst fights are always between brothers, it seems. This is the end result of two hundred years of blind faith that this could never happen, not here. This is what we deserve."

"I sense a bitterness in you far beyond what you are seeing, sir," Ericsson said, almost as disturbed by the colonel's sadness as the vision of the prisoners being loaded like cattle.

"My family were ranchers once, or so we had hoped, a few years ago. One by one they were taken by Indians, sickness, or just plain despair. But that made some sense; it was life. This"—he gestured toward the Confederate prisoners—"is blackness. Hate that has been boiling over for years, and I am so tired of it. Sometimes I think we don't deserve to continue on as a nation."

"Surely you believe in the cause in the North?" Ericsson asked in his heavily accented English.

"That"—he pointed at the last of the starved men were boarded—"is the end result of two causes. If it weren't that or this, it would be him, or them. Yes, Professor Ericsson, I don't give a good damn for causes anymore."

Ericsson did not pursue another question. He could see the man before him now saw the end result of his craft and he hated himself for being a part of it. To his relief, the sergeant major reappeared with the Comanche Indian in tow. Ericsson was frightened of the red man, so he quickly tipped his hat toward the colonel and then left to board the more comfortable car farther up the line.

"Detail is all aboard, Colonel."

Thomas looked at Dugan and nodded. The sergeant major, he knew, was feeling the same sense of horror he was at the sight of the prisoners. Dugan was having a hard time justifying his hatred toward the secessionists the way he had only two days before.

"Are there plenty of blankets and water in those cars?"

"Yes, Colonel. They have rations for the ride to Washington." Dugan was about to turn and walk away when he stopped and, without turning back to face Thomas, said, "Colonel, I can't bring myself to lock them in."

Thomas saw the sergeant major's shoulders slump as he waited for Thomas to blow up over prisoner security.

"Those men have to be protected from themselves for the time being, Sergeant Major. They won't be thinking right until they have their strength back. So until that time comes, lock them in. They would only be committing suicide if they tried to escape like this."

"I didn't see it that way," Dugan said and then slowly walked off. Gray Dog lingered, watching the small man lower his head as he started to place chains through the doors of the boxcars.

"Why keep other white men in cages?"

John Henry started down the platform steps and started to make his way toward the cars in the front of the train.

"Some things aren't so easily explained, Gray Dog. Let's just say the white men are angry and you can thank God they stay that way." He looked at the Comanche as he spied Jessy Taylor waiting by the steps of the passenger car. His old gray coat had been replaced by a private's blue blouse and he was wearing a Union cap. "Because when this madness is done, they only have one way to turn after that."

Gray Dog did not need an explanation of the words of John Henry. He looked at the last of the locks and chains going on the doors and then followed the colonel. He didn't board the train but climbed to its roof instead and then sat. Thomas shook his head as he confronted Taylor.

"Is this the treatment we can expect for the entire journey?" Taylor asked as he placed his arm across the car's opening, stopping Thomas from entering.

"Until I can trust you, yes." Thomas lowered Taylor's arm and stepped up the stairs to the car's interior.

"And when is that? When we're at sea and can't run?"

John Henry stopped and turned. He was backlit by the oil lamps inside the car and Taylor couldn't make out his friend's features. He looked like a Greek god looking down from on high with a heavenly glow.

"No, not even then, Jessy. When we get to Turkey, we'll discuss your men at length and the ways to earn my trust. Now, let me buy you a drink and figure out how we can do what's asked of us and get all of these boys back in one piece." He stepped aside and gestured for Jessy to go ahead.

"Something tells me you won't succeed."

"That's why I was chosen. It's called being expendable."

The locomotive sounded its whistle and the train started to move south.

8

The train with its human cargo was six miles outside of Baltimore. John Henry Thomas and Jessy Taylor paused while going over the map of the Ottoman Empire. Taylor leaned back on the bench and then toyed with the half-full whiskey bottle. He glanced out of the dingy, soot-covered window and then his heart caught in his chest. Was his bad eye giving him that much trouble?

"What is the story on that little fella?" he asked while still staring out the window.

John Henry folded the map and then saw what Taylor was looking at. A surreal vision was staring in at them from an upside-down position. Gray Dog adjusted his feet and then vanished from the window as if he had never been there.

"Long story. But where we're going we may need that Comanche's insight into certain things."

"Well, I surely hope he doesn't go popping his head in with my men until they get used to him," Taylor said, staring at the spot where the Indian had been. "Now," he said as he turned back to Thomas. "Tell me about this Sultan Abdül-aziz."

John Henry pulled out a sheaf of papers and rummaged through them until he came to the page he needed. "From all accounts he's so interested in modernizing his empire that he pays little attention to his subjects. Secretary Seward believes he hasn't but a few years in power left before the people oust him. Sultans do not have a good track record for keeping their subjects happy, and every twenty or thirty years they let the monarchy know in no uncertain terms just how angry they are. Seward's assessment is that he's so weak of mind that we should have very little trouble posing as railroad and army engineers."

"Sounds about as foul a situation as we have here, huh, Yank?"

"Knock that crap off. Yank, Reb, it all amounts to being idiots." John Henry put away the report on the sultan but held his eyes firmly on his old pal from the Point. "From the time we board ship until the time we return, we're neither northerner nor southerner. If we go in separate, they will pick apart our little ruse very quickly."

Taylor smiled with his swollen lips. "That's what your Mr. Lincoln wants anyway, doesn't he? What I mean to say is, he is not known to be overly zealous when it comes to religion. He doesn't think that damn children's tale is even there, does he?"

Thomas had to admit to a degree that Taylor was right. He had never known Lincoln to bend a knee to God or anything else. Lincoln believed in law. The Constitution was his Bible and that was why they were in the war they were in. So, no, he did not believe the president was in awe at Ollafson's tale of wonder. But then, he also knew the president had absolutely nothing to lose but a military officer whose career was in the outhouse and a Reb colonel who had seen far better days. This was not counting the men under his command—at least on the southern side they were as expendable as both colonels leading them. He didn't yet know what army dregs were going to be tossed into this bizarre equation.

Instead of commenting on Taylor's observation on his commander-in-chief, he brought out the Confederate roster.

"You'll need an adjutant. Who do you suggest?" He slid the roster across the table and Taylor, after downing a small glass of whiskey, looked it over. It only took him a moment.

"Corporal Poteet. He served with me in New Mexico territory. He's the only Texan I've ever known that could track those damnable Apaches. Yes, he'll make a fine sergeant major, with your permission of course."

"Permission granted," Thomas said as he underlined the name. His eyes continued to survey the roster of starved men even though his brain had stopped taking in information.

"You don't believe in this mission?" Taylor asked as he poured himself and Thomas another drink.

"Not at all." He took the drink and downed it and then looked up and saw Gray Dog standing next to him in the aisle. He had come upon them without sound or flash of movement.

"Riders, John Henry. Twenty or more."

At that moment the train started to slow. The whistle sounded as Thomas stood. "Gray Dog, alert Sergeant Major Dugan and the marines. This isn't right."

John Henry looked at Taylor and then stood from his chair. Jessy started to do the same but John Henry motioned him back down.

"With that drawl of yours, may I suggest you sit this one out, Colonel?"

"I'll keep this bottle company. It's a better conversationalist anyway," he said as he downed another shot.

John Henry felt the train decelerate rapidly as Dugan entered from another car with two marines next to him.

"What have we got?" Dugan asked as he quickly lowered the window closest to him and looked out, first toward the front of the slowing train and then the rear. "Goddamn Injun is right. We have riders, Colonel Darlin'."

The train came to a screeching stop and as John Henry stepped out of the car he saw why. Fire was blazing on the very rails on which they traveled. "Sergeant Major, take ten marines and filter into these woods. Wait until you see something untoward and then move on the element if you have to."

"And what is untoward, Colonel?"

"Untoward means me being shot for any reason."

"Yes, sir."

John Henry saw the first of the riders approach at a gallop. He could see by the long gold stripe on his pant leg that he was a cavalry officer, and by the looks of his mount he had been riding hard for quite some time. The horse and rider were both lathered with the effort.

"I am looking for Colonel John Henry Thomas," he said as the horse skidded to a stop.

Thomas stepped forward and addressed the young first lieutenant. "I'm Thomas."

The rider removed his gauntlet, reached into his uniform tunic, and pulled out an envelope.

"From the war department, sir."

Thomas took the message and stepped into the light streaming from the car. He opened the envelope and saw the words. As he read, John Henry realized he was dealing with something he had not been briefed on.

"Sergeant Major Dugan," he called out.

The rider and his accompanying men heard the sound of several Spencer carbines as they were cocked and uncocked.

"Sir!" Dugan said as he stepped from the trees.

"Lieutenant, did anyone think to bring me some wagons?" he asked.

"Yes, sir. Twenty army wagons are a mile back."

"Sergeant Major, get the men off the train, quickly. Get them lined up and into the woods. Post the marine pickets. Nothing gets inside the perimeter, and especially nothing out, understand?"

"Not at all," he said angrily as he quickly moved out.

"What have we got?" a voice said from behind.

Taylor's question was a loaded one. As Thomas turned to face him he gestured.

"Some congressman has gotten wind of the shipment from Fort Lafayette and is throwing a fit about the illegal transport of prisoners without authorization from the war department."

"I thought the war department was in on this," Taylor said as he hopped from the train car and started to assist in unlocking his men. "They probably believe they were brought to the woods to be shot and buried."

"They are aware, but they can't get caught up in this because they could never explain it properly. They would rather do this thing covertly until it all blows up royally in their faces."

"The congressman is aware of your destination."

Thomas looked at the young lieutenant and then crumpled the message. "Get the wagons up here immediately. Is there a hospital near the harbor where they treat war wounded?"

The cavalryman looked confused. "We have three doctors standing by at the pier, sir," he answered.

"Lieutenant, is there a hospital near the docks where the casualties from the front are being treated or buried?"

"Yes, sir. Camp Monroe serves as the main hospital."

"Good," he stepped up to the young officer and spoke to him in a whisper. Taylor saw the cavalryman looking shocked at his new orders, and then he suddenly turned his mount and bolted off to the south with the very confused look still on his face.

"What are you up to? I don't believe you can disguise these men. A blind person would be able to tell who they are."

"No, I can't disguise them, so we have to actually turn them into something they are not."

Taylor saw Thomas deep in thought and knew the colonel had a plan. His eyes would always light up when he had thought something through.

"Are you going to let me in on your plan, especially since it's my men with everything to lose?"

"Well," John Henry said as he faced Taylor, "it may well be we have to kill you anyway." He winked and then stepped up to assist in unloading the weakened men.

Taylor was stunned at the wink and smile of Thomas, but he thought he was beginning to see how his men would be allowed into Baltimore.

"Sergeant Major Dugan, Lieutenant Parnell will be in

command, but you take charge of the prisoners and get them into the woods and march them as quietly as possible to the docks." He looked from Dugan to the young marine lieutenant. "Mr. Parnell, your job is to get this command into the dock area without being caught. Can the Marine Corps do that?"

"That and much more, Colonel," Parnell said as he briskly saluted. He jumped on the large roan mount and started guiding the tired and worn men into the roadway alongside the railroad line. The rest of the marine detail was broken into two groups. One would accompany Thomas, the other Dugan and Parnell.

BALTIMORE, MARYLAND

Claire Richelieu and Lars Ollafson stood by the entrance to the U.S. Navy dry-dock area where they had been instructed to wait. Claire nervously looked around, feeling vulnerable as she waited beside the professor and their silent entourage of equipment and luggage. Her eyes often roamed over to the leather case that held the petrified wood with the Angelic curse. She forced back a shiver as she looked up and saw the fog start to roll in off the Chesapeake. Ollafson looked at his watch when they heard the sound of horses coming their way.

"I was beginning to worry we were going to be left behind. It's—"

"Hush, Professor," Claire said as she stepped forward and placed a hand on Ollafson's shoulder to quiet him. "Those are carriages, not a military unit coming," she said as her eyes studied the gateway beyond the front of the dock area. The naval guards at the gate heard the same as they stepped expectantly from their small shack.

"Suddenly you are an expert—"

The professor stopped when he saw two carriages filled with men stop at the gate. An unseen man inside the first carriage spoke some harsh words to the two navy men. Then from behind the twin carriages there was the sound of many footsteps as ten men left the rolling fogbank and stood beside the carriages and the two guards. Claire could hear one of the naval personnel explain that the dock area was closed to all civilians. She heard the angry protest from within the carriage, and then she saw the footman hop from the top seat and quickly open the door for the robust man who stepped from its interior.

"Oh, my God, that's Senator Harriman, I believe. Not a very nice man," Ollafson said, worried that their plans had been leaked.

Claire was well aware who the Democratic leader from Indiana was. The man was a staunch advocate of hanging every southern leader and commander when the war was completed and the South totally destroyed. The man was Lincoln's staunchest enemy when it came to the way the president conducted the running of the war. A complete and utter follower of one general in particular: George McClellan. Claire was beginning to smell a rat, and the smell was familiar to her.

"Inopportune timing, I would say," came the voice from behind them.

Claire and Ollafson turned and saw the speaker. There was another man standing right behind him. Claire knew he had been there all the while and was forever undressing her with his eyes. Captain Paul Renaud of the French army stepped up and dipped his hat and head at them both. The man was expertly dressed in his new traveling clothes.

Claire closed her eyes when she realized who it was. She stepped up to the smaller man and leaned into him. She made sure Ollafson was not in hearing distance.

"This is too bold a move even for you. Are you insane?"

Renaud tossed his half-smoked cigar into the foul waters of the docks and then smiled. "Why? I am a history expert by trade, and my credentials, at least for the moment, are impeccable." The arrogant man smiled and then whispered, "Madame, you did not really believe I would leave this in your hands, did you? My superiors in France were not very impressed with the way that old man kept certain things from you in his research. They thought a more experienced set of eyes should be on hand. So, here I am, ready to do my part as ordered by the U.S. War Department." Renaud brought out a set of forged orders that were perfect in every detail, even countersigned by Stanton himself.

"Those had better be perfect. This Colonel Thomas is no man's fool. The president picked him for this assignment for a reason." She smiled halfheartedly even though the man before her terrified her. "He will smell a rat."

"He would only smell a stupid rat, Madame. I, on the other hand, am a smart rat."

"Excuse me, but who is this man, Claire?" Ollafson asked as he placed the pocketwatch back into his vest.

"Benton Cromwell, Professor Ollafson," Renaud said. "A pleasure to meet you."

Claire turned to Ollafson with a smile. "He says he's been assigned by the war department as their specialist on historic locations."

"I think we should all wait for Colonel Thomas for the introductions. After all, it looks as though we may have a problem brewing here."

Claire again turned to the Frenchman. "Why do I smell your work in this?"

"Not I, dearest Claire, but we did intercept a communiqué from London expressing the desire of Her Royal Majesty Victoria that the expedition be slowed somewhat. I suspect our British friends are behind this little commotion. Now I guess we'll see if your Mr. Lincoln chose the right man for his adventure."

The two naval guards had given up as the large round man burst past them and was joined by other men as he came through the gate. The men with him were the capital police force for this district.

"I'm Senator Marcus Harriman. I want to see the man in charge."

Claire and Professor Ollafson were silent as the large man with the brown beard started wagging a rather large cigar in their faces. It was Renaud who intervened.

"Perhaps you should pester someone with a uniform on, sir. They would more than likely be the person in charge, not a woman and an old man," he said as he confronted the much smaller senator.

"Then I pose my inquiry to you, sir. Who is in charge here?"

Renaud smiled arrogantly. "Why, I assure you I haven't faintest idea, sir."

"Has the entire army gone mad?" The senator bit down on his cigar and then turned and faced the woman and older man. "You I know," he said, jabbing his cigar at Professor Ollafson, who flinched away from it. Claire took a protective step toward the blustery man in the hundred-dollar suit. "Now, tell me where I can find"—he pulled out a paper from his suit jacket and then adjusted it to read in the weak light of the dock area—"Colonel Thomas. The man absconded with over a hundred Confederate prisoners of war from New York this morning and I want to know who authorized this transfer, which took place in the middle of an escape attempt investigation that was being conducted by the camp's commander."

"I assure you, sir, we have no clue as to what it is you speak of," Claire said, for Ollafson was looking quite intimidated. She was beginning to wonder just where Colonel Thomas was. She had a feeling this man was used to getting what he wanted.

"Goddamn army thinks they can do whatever they want!"

Renaud knew immediately that this Senator Harriman was in the well-lined pockets of the British government and that he had been sent to at least slow the start of this curious mission or to stop it completely. The British were always so proper in their methods, never using the head-on approach of men such as himself.

Suddenly the sound of horses and wagon wheels echoed through the fog. Claire bit her lower lip, knowing that it was Thomas and his new acquisitions coming into the dock area. The colonel was walking directly into a trap, and if he was caught with Rebel prisoners of war, and if the reason for it became public knowledge, Lincoln could never survive the scandal and he would most assuredly lose the upcoming election to that pompous little ass, McClellan. Yes, Harriman was going for broke in his attempt to embarrass the president.

"Hah, I knew he would be arrogant enough to come right through the front gate with his escapees. The man will hang for this." Harriman tossed the cigar away and then turned to two of the capitol policemen. "Arrest these three," he said as he started for the wagons that had stopped at the gate.

One of the two policemen moved his rifle to port arms and the other approached the man in the army uniform first. He started to reach for his arm, but Renaud just smiled.

"If you so much as touch me, I will kill you." He glared down at the policeman who was looking at him with apprehension. "And your companion. I would suggest waiting to see how this plays out before you commit yourself to this course of action. It could be beneficial to know if you backed the wrong horse in this race."

Harriman, with the other eight policemen in tow, approached the gate, making his bulk seem as imposing as possible. He puffed out his chest as he spied the big man in the saddle of the lead horse. The colonel stared down upon the senator and his bearing gave Harriman a momentary pause. His office had been tipped off to this unprecedented prisoner movement by an unknown source, but as soon as Colonel John Henry Thomas's name was mentioned, Harriman knew Lincoln was behind whatever was happening. The senator remembered two years before when the president had most illegally saved Thomas from a general court-martial.

"You men spread out and make sure no one exits the rear of those wagons. You, sir. Are you Colonel Thomas?" he asked, hoping his booming voice was as intimidating as it was on the floor of the senate.

John Henry remained silent as he removed his hat and wiped his brow. It had been a harrowing ride for the past hour as he had made his way from the military hospital on the outskirts of Baltimore. His horse was lathered, as well as those of his small command of wagons.

"I believe I asked you a question, sir. Are you Thomas?"

John Henry observed the four people waiting at the entrance to dry-dock seventeen and saw the woman Claire Richelieu looking his way. She seemed worried. He only hoped she and the professor had kept their lips tight thus far so he could get this little ruse to pass muster. He finally stepped down from his horse.

"I'm Thomas," he said simply as he tied the reins of his horse to the small pommel on the saddle. "What can I help you with?"

"I want the men in those wagons. You absconded with them with no legal order from the prisoner-of-war camp in New York. They are to be returned to that camp immediately and you, sir, are to be placed under arrest, as are these three people." He gestured toward Claire, Ollafson, and a last man whom Thomas did not know.

"I have orders to deliver my cargo to the docks. I have done so. If you want what's in those wagons, you are more than welcome to take them off of my hands, Mr. . . . Mr.—?"

"It's Senator, Senator Harriman, and I have a warrant signed by a federal judge giving me the right to take what is in those wagons, and to arrest the man responsible for removing the prisoners from New York."

John Henry slowly removed his gauntlets and then fixed Harriman with his blue-eyed glare. "You want what's in those wagons? They're yours, sir. I gladly turn them over." He mockingly bowed in surrender as Harriman smiled in victory. He would finally hang Lincoln and the out-of-control military that loved him so much.

"Arrest the colonel," he said as he turned to face the first wagon.

John Henry smiled as the senator left with five of the policemen right behind him. Thomas finally placed his gloves in his belt and watched the first policeman hesitantly approach him, holding a set of wrist restraints. John Henry's smile widened.

"Oh, damn! We didn't get too far, did we?" Ollafson said as the first wagon's rear tarp was thrown aside.

Claire was as worried as Ollafson, but Renaud watched John Henry Thomas and smiled as he guessed at what was happening.

"I expect this Senator Harriman is going to get exactly what he came for."

As the covering was thrown back, Harriman was assailed by the smell coming from the bed of the wagon. He stepped back and threw a hand over his mouth and nose. The smell hit the policemen next and the first of these doubled over and vomited.

"What is the meaning of this?" Harriman demanded to no one other than the dead men piled in the back of the wagon. He ran to the next in line and his senses were assaulted once again when he unveiled the contents of Colonel John Henry Thomas's wagons. The senator ran to the next, and then the next. All the while Thomas kept his eyes on the senator and hoped he didn't have the gumption to thoroughly check the dead men in the back. He suspected Harriman wouldn't, as he too leaned over and expelled the expensive dinner he'd had that night at the Willard Hotel. After that dinner was lost, the senator's voice echoed through the dock area.

"I have been tricked!"

John Henry smiled.

ONE MILE OUTSIDE OF BALTIMORE, MARYLAND

The progression of the men was slow. Lieutenant Parnell's marines tried not to push the Reb prisoners too hard, but they were having a difficult time keeping the ragtag group together as some were much stronger than others. It was Parnell who rode up to confront the Confederate colonel about how he was allowing his men to be stretched out in too long a line.

"Colonel, we will have to call a halt. Your men are falling off and we can't keep them together."

"Lieutenant Parnell, while I commiserate with your predicament, I am hardly the man to make the protest to." He looked over at Sergeant Major Dugan, who was walking beside him at Colonel Thomas's request so he could keep a close eye on Taylor.

"Call a halt," Dugan said.

"Now!" Taylor yelled at that very moment.

Before Dugan or Parnell could react, Taylor's men started pulling marines from their saddles. The guard detail was immediately subdued by men who had pretended to be far worse for wear than they truly were. Before Dugan and the young marine knew what was happening, they had their own weapons trained on them.

Taylor shrugged as one of his men tossed him an Army Colt. He cocked it and then smiled at Dugan and Parnell.

"Endless apologies, gentlemen, but this is where my men and I will say good-bye. Our lines are right across the river."

Dugan stepped forward angrily. He knew he had let down John Henry and he had decided he would rather die than face him. Taylor stopped the old sergeant major by shoving the barrel of the Colt into his rib cage.

"John Henry has thus far treated us with respect. Do not make me do anything other than that, now that the situation has reversed itself." He shoved harder until Dugan backed up a step. Then his hands as well as those of Parnell were roughly pulled to their backs and tied. "Sergeant Major, a man very much similar to you in every regard was murdered just last night in New York for following my orders. He was a good man, as I am sure you are, but do not think I will hesitate in killing you and all of these men just as surely as my sergeant major was murdered. Now, gentlemen, we must be off." The smile widened as a horse was brought to Taylor and he mounted.

"The colonel will find you," Dugan said as he and a humiliated Parnell were shoved down to the base of a large tree and then tied to it along with the rest of their command.

"John Henry has been chasing me since West Point, Sergeant Major, and he hasn't caught this old boy yet!" Taylor said loudly as he spurred the black horse he was riding. His mount reared and pawed the air, then shot off into the woods where Taylor's not-so-sick men awaited their colonel.

"I thought he was going to kill us," Parnell said as he took a deep breath.

"When John Henry finds out about this, you'll wish that Reb had pulled the trigger, I can assure you."

The two men heard the silence of the woods around them and then the sound of a Rebel yell came through the fog with a loud whoop.

"He's going to hang us," Dugan complained, shaking his head.

BALTIMORE NAVY YARD, BALTIMORE, MARYLAND

John Henry was still smiling when he arrogantly shoved aside the policeman and his manacles. He approached the senator, who was still wiping vomit from his mouth. The man would taste the oysters he'd had for dinner for more than a year afterward.

"Here is your roster, sir," John Henry said as he held out a piece of paper. "All the casualties of the escape attempt have been documented in my report. They are all yours, Senator," John Henry said with a smirk.

"They're all dead," Harriman said after he caught his breath.

"Yes, bullets to the backs of their heads usually do that."

John Henry watched as the senator actually attempted once more to examine the backs of the first and second wagons. Thomas had emptied out the hospital of every Confederate body he could find and had tossed the poor bastards unceremoniously into the backs of the wagons. It was a close-run ruse, as he had to deal with the astonished looks of the military hospital personnel as he did so. He didn't know how much flak the president would catch over this, but it was the only way he could have pulled this off. After all, he had not been forewarned that Harriman was on the trail of the prisoners. It seemed Major Freeman in New York might have had a little more pull than even the president thought.

The smell emanating from the ten wagons was starting to get to John Henry when the senator abruptly turned and left with the capital police in tow.

"I will get to the bottom of this, I assure you, sir!"

"Yes, I'm sure you will," Thomas said as he removed his gloves and then turned toward the three people waiting inside the gate. He was about to approach when a marine came running through the gate out of breath.

At the same moment, Professor Ericsson stumbled out of the back of the last wagon, and he too was puking up his own dinner after being unceremoniously tossed into the wagon after the clandestine hospital run.

Thomas took the young marine private by the shoulders and shook him.

"The prisoners—they have escaped," the boy finally managed to say.

"Sergeant Major Dugan?" asked Thomas, fearful his old friend had been killed by another old friend.

"They harmed no one, sir. Just tied us up and then skedaddled."

John Henry released the boy. He turned toward the darkness beyond the gate and the thick fog forming through the trees. "Gray Dog!"

Suddenly the fog parted and there was the Comanche appearing like a spectral image. Thomas had not known where he was, but he always showed up when called. He gestured at Gray Dog and nodded his head. It was amazing that he had not had to explain what he wanted the Indian to do. It seemed that the Comanche always knew in advance. He pointed.

Gray Dog didn't respond to the order. He simply took the first horse he found, stripped the saddle, and then deftly hopped onto the large animal's back and vanished into the fog.

"Goddamn it, Jessy," John Henry said, replacing his gauntlets as his horse was brought to him. Trust had never entered into the equation because he thought the men under Taylor's command were too weak to pull anything off. This was the last time John Henry would underestimate his old friend. He took off through the gate hoping to catch Gray Dog and help return Colonel Jessy Taylor to the docks. They had less than two hours left to catch the morning tide.

The mission thus far had been a disaster and they had not even left Baltimore harbor.

Taylor was proud of his men. They had reacted as if they had not spent the past two years locked away in hell. He watched the men struggle through the thick woods, soaked by the bogs they constantly waded into because of the damnable fog. He dismounted and helped one of his older men into the saddle. The private, an old boy from Wheeling, was tired and far weaker than his younger brethren. The man fought against the silent order given by Taylor but finally relented when he realized his pride was keeping their small, desperate column from escaping. He nodded at the colonel and then slowly rode into the fog. Taylor's eyes followed the old man and he hoped he had not led the men into another disaster. He felt better when he thought about John Henry.

Corporal Franklin Loudermilk, a skinny, mean man from Richmond, joined Taylor.

"Think it was right to leave them blue bellies just tied up, Colonel? I mean, the way me and some of the boys look at it, they's *still* the enemy."

Taylor didn't answer right away. He knew the man beside him would be bucking for the sergeant major's responsibility, but the truth of the matter was Loudermilk was a cad of the first order. The man was rumored to prey on the weak. In the prison camp, his own comrades would find food and other supplies missing, and Loudermilk and a few others were suspected. Taylor did not trust a soldier who was so zealous about killing four years into the war. Enough was enough, in his opinion.

"Is that what you think?" Taylor asked without looking at the corporal. He stopped and waited for a few of the stragglers to catch up. With a nod and half-smile he encouraged his boys to move faster. "Well, you go back and tell the boys"—he now looked directly at Loudermilk—"that my order stands. We kill, we get caught. How many weapons do you see, Corporal?" he asked as some of the passing men noticed the anger in his voice.

"Well, none but what we took from the Yanks," was the meek and cautious answer.

"So unless you intend to chuck rocks at our pursuers who *are* armed, don't go makin' the Yanks murderous, because frankly our odds of escaping John Henry Thomas are about the same as the chance of my taking your opinion into account. Now get moving, Corporal."

Taylor watched the man raise his brows and then smirk and move off. Taylor knew that man needed watching.

Jessy stopped, preparing to wait for a few other stragglers, when the night around him fell silent. Suddenly a *whoosh* flew past his right ear. He flinched when the arrow stuck in the tree next to his head. Before Taylor could react he heard a man yell something he couldn't understand and then a gunshot sounded. Jessy cursed as he moved quickly forward. He knew it was John Henry's boy. He hadn't liked the looks of the Comanche. In his opinion, they were the sneakiest of all the tribes.

There were more shouts ahead. Another gunshot.

"Hold your fire," he said as loudly as he dared.

As he pulled up beside a tree he saw the men around him hunkered down with as much cover as they could find. He only hoped the fog would be confusing to not only the Indian but the men he knew were out there. John Henry's men.

As these thoughts crossed his mind, he knew it was over. Hoofbeats sounded through the trees as riders rode in on the group of escaping men at breakneck speed. Only cavalrymen rode as foolhardy as that, and John Henry Thomas was the best cavalryman Taylor had ever known. The man from Texas was a far better tactician than Jeb Stuart and also more keen to enemy responses. John Henry was known in the Indian days as the great liar because the Indians always found him where he wasn't supposed to be. His nose for finding men was legend in the cavalry corps. Thomas eased his horse from the tree line.

"Tell those men to hold their fire, or so help me we'll convince them the easy way," John Henry yelled as his horse came to a sliding stop just in front of Taylor.

"All southern men, hold your fire, lay down your weapons," Taylor said, his eyes never leaving Thomas, who was busy staring down at him with his Colt drawn and aimed right at his head.

In the woods he heard men curse, others shouting profanities as the marines on horseback herded them into a tight circle. The fog wasn't helping much as the men were roughly handled this time in respect to their newly found strength.

John Henry released the hammer on the Colt and then holstered the weapon. "Bugler, sound recall," he said as a young marine rode up next to him. The boy looked confused for a moment as he thought about the army bugle call that had been requested. "Blow something, boy," Thomas said as he approached Taylor.

The bugler decided that maybe the marine recall was the same as the army's. Regardless, it was marines out there anyway. He blew the brief signal to reform with the prisoners.

"If it weren't for that Indian, you would never have found us," Taylor said as John Henry reached out and removed the pistol from the belt of Taylor. The colonel unlocked the cylinder and then removed it, his eyes never leaving Jessy's.

"The next time he won't miss with that arrow. The rest will be shot on my orders. Are we understanding each other, Colonel?" Thomas asked as he glared at his onetime friend. "I have no time for this."

"Well, John Henry, excuse me if I'm not a big enthusiast of chasing horse-crap fairy tales. Even if you find something, you think it will change a damn thing? You're as much of a romantic as your boss, my friend. Telling my men to die for this is laughable."

Thomas took Taylor by the shoulder and pushed him into a solid object. Gray Dog was there and he had no expression as he tied the colonel up with rope.

John Henry stepped up to face Taylor. "You're as blind and stubborn as you ever were, Jessy."

Thomas angrily walked away as Gray Dog easily moved Taylor forward toward his angry men. They were no longer treated as weak men. These were Confederate cavalry once again and they would be treated as such—dangerous.

Claire Richelieu had heard the distant reports of weapons fire, which was also heard by the navy and marine personnel at the dock area. Claire was no expert, but she knew that the random shots had come from the general direction in which Colonel Thomas's Indian had disappeared. She fanned her hot face as Ollafson nervously waited.

"Professor Ollafson?" came a familiar voice from behind them. Claire closed her eyes, for she had been fearful of this moment from the time she had been informed they would have a second person as company on the voyage.

"Yes, I am Ollafson," the professor answered, apprehensive though he was after the excitement of the evening.

The man was in a nice civilian suit with a small bowler hat on his head, which he removed as he held out a letter to the old professor.

"I am Steven McDonald. I am replacing your student Henderson as your personal secretary."

Ollafson opened the letter and moved closer to an oil lamp on the side of the warehouse building. He read its contents. The letter was countersigned by his former chair at Harvard. Ollafson looked the signature over and decided it was authentic.

"I never requested a replacement. Young Henderson knew too much. I doubt you can be as helpful to me."

The thin man with the perfectly curled blond moustache leaned over so the professor could hear him. His eyes locked with Claire's and then came a small wink from the British Army captain.

"Professor, the department was worried after Henderson's body was found. The university asked me to keep a close eye on you and your assistant. I am sorry about that young man in New York, but that should tell you that you need more than just Miss Richelieu to watch over you and this expedition.

I am well armed and can be very helpful in deciphering the difference between Aramaic and the Angelic script you have discovered. That is my specialty, sir."

Ollafson was taken aback by the man's credentials, especially since the professor had never heard this man's name mentioned during his entire time at Harvard Yard.

Even Claire was astonished by what McDonald claimed. If he did understand the historical subject matter he had just mentioned, she realized that she had sorely underestimated London's interest in this mission. France might have been willing to kill to learn what was so interesting in eastern Turkey, but now England was risking having a master spy turned over by the Americans. It seemed the two base powers in Europe were willing to risk what amounted to war with the most powerful military nation on the planet—the United States.

"Very well, Mr. McDonald. As you seem to already be aware, this is my assistant, Claire Richelieu. She will be your immediate superior. Do nothing unless Miss Claire says to do it. And please, stay out of the military's way. Colonel Thomas seems to have his hands full at the moment," Ollafson said as he placed the envelope with the letter into Claire's hand. She looked at it and raised her lovely brow. Before she could place it in her bag McDonald reached out and took it from her, held his index finger to his lips, and said, "Shh." He slipped the forged request into his own suit jacket just as the third member of their small academic team stepped up.

"Mr. McDonald, this is Benton Cromwell. He's a specialist in Angelic Script," Claire lied as she looked from the master spy of France to the British version of the same. The two men appraised each other and both immediately became suspicious.

"I don't know if Colonel Thomas will like this," Ollafson said as he scrutinized the two men he had never laid eyes on before. "But, we have little time to make a case for him."

"Speaking of the colonel, I believe they are back. I pray there was not any bloodshed."

McDonald turned his attention from Claire, who was angrily looking his way, to the front gate as the prisoners were slowly herded through. The men looked worse than they had before, but Claire noticed a radical difference in their demeanor. They looked far more rebellious than Thomas had described them in his telegram earlier that day. All had their wrists tied in front of them, and the mounted marines had weapons out and trained on the line of scraggly men. Thomas was riding in the front, looking angry and tired. He dismounted and gave Sergeant Major Dugan his instructions. He turned and removed his gauntlets and then faced Claire, Ollafson, and two men he had never met before.

"Colonel, this is Mr.—"

John Henry walked past the tall man extending his hand in greeting. He eyed Claire as he strode by and then, without acknowledging the professor or the two newcomers, John Henry walked through the warehouse doors and then vanished.

"Charming man," McDonald said as he watched Thomas disappear.

"And he doesn't grow on you either, so may I suggest, especially for you, stay clear of the man, as his ability to smell a rat may be far more advanced than even you know."

McDonald turned and winked. "Until the time comes, dear Claire, I will be the epitome of proper manners."

Claire could see the coldness in the captain's eyes and felt the same chill she had when she'd spied the petrified samples. She then turned and watched as the prisoners, some bleeding from minor gunshot wounds, walked past them and into the warehouse. The last man through was the Rebel colonel, who looked at Claire and the others as if they were but children being led astray by a magical con man. His eyes lingered a moment longer than necessary on the face of Captain McDonald but they quickly moved off as Gray Dog, the last man in the sad progression, gently pushed Taylor through the door.

John Henry bounded up the steps of the warehouse and entered the semi-darkened office of the manager. The cigar smoke was thick and acrid. John Henry slapped his gantlets together and then slammed them onto the desk where a man was sitting with his feet propped up, his cigar ablaze and his face a mask of anger.

"Not a very auspicious start, would you say?"

John Henry held the beady eyes of Secretary of State Seward for a moment and then he reached out and took the bottle of whiskey from the desk. Before pouring he glanced into the far corner and saw Professor Ericsson sitting there. He nodded his head and then poured the drink.

"Did you expect an officer with West Point training to do something other than what he did?" John Henry didn't wait for the secretary to answer his rhetorical question; he drank instead. "I'm surprised he waited so long. The man I knew before the war would have ended up with the entire train and ridden it all the way back to Richmond."

"I am so pleased you found out your Rebel friend is still capable, but if he tries that in the Ottoman Empire it could get you all killed. The sultan wouldn't be too friendly if he learned the truth about why we are the there. I'm not real sure on the sultan's theological leanings, but I'm pretty much positive he would take offense if we waltzed in and stole a prized biblical artifact right out from under his bulbous nose. What do you think, Colonel?" Seward said as he examined the ash on his cigar and then angrily flicked the tip.

Thomas did not comment. He poured another drink as the door opened and Gray Dog led in Colonel Taylor, and then the Indian left without a word.

"Well, this must be the designer of this madness," Taylor said as he looked at Seward and then over to the corner and the silent Ericsson.

John Henry placed his glass down on the desk and then roughly pulled Taylor to the side, and then to everyone's shock, he pulled a bowie knife from his belt. He held it in front of his old friend for the longest time. Seward watched with interest while Ericsson was convinced he was about to see a man get eviscerated right in front of him. John Henry lowered the knife as Taylor smiled, and then simply cut the restraining rope from his wrists. He then poured Taylor some whiskey and gestured for him to have a chair in front of Secretary Seward. He sat, but not before draining the glass and then holding it out for a refill.

"The next attempt at escape, and the colonel has been instructed to line your men up and shoot them." Seward held a hand up when Taylor started to comment. "You, sir, are under orders, and may I remind you that they are not my orders, nor Mr. Lincoln's orders, nor even the colonel's here. They are orders signed by the commander of all southern forces, Robert E. Lee. His orders, sir, and you will obey them or face the consequences. Your execution would not only be legal north of the Rappahannock, but south of it as well. Am I clear on this point?"

Instead of answering, Taylor turned the glass up once again and drained it. Again he held it up so Thomas could refill it as well as his own glass. Seward drained his own glass and placed his feet on the floor.

"One hundred eight sets of civilian clothes are onboard. Enough food to assist in fattening the prisoners up has been obtained from the stores of the U.S. Army."

"Stop right there," Taylor said as he sipped the glass of whiskey this time. "My men are not going to wear anything other than their own uniforms. After all, Mr. Secretary, we know what happens to soldiers who are caught out of uniform." He downed the whiskey.

"Nonetheless, Colonel, you will wear civilian clothing. What you wear under that clothing is not a concern of mine." Again he angrily flipped the ash from his cigar. "Now." Seward stood and walked to the door and opened it. A young naval officer stepped in and stood at attention.

"Gentlemen, this is Captain Steven Jackson. He'll be in command of your three-ship formation, including Mr. Ericsson's barge. He will also command the marine element onboard the squadron. While on land you will still hold superiority, Colonel Thomas."

The young man nodded as he took in the colonel and the shabbily dressed prisoner smiling at him. This irritated the naval commander to no end.

"We are ready to board the men now, sir. Weapons, food-stuffs, and other supplies have been loaded. We have confirmation that *Argo* is on station at Cape Hatteras and awaiting our tow."

"Thank you, Captain," Seward said, dismissing the exuberant naval officer.

"Sir!" Jackson replied as he turned, with one last curious look at Taylor and his irritating smile, and left the office.

"Eager boy," Taylor said as he placed his glass on the desktop.

"Capable, from my understanding," Seward said as he faced Thomas and Taylor.

"The point our Rebel friend was making, Mr. Secretary, is the fact that he is too young," Thomas said as he stepped to the window and looked out on the line of men being issued their civilian clothing.

"I have worked with that young officer for three years, gentlemen," Ericsson said, speaking for the first time. "He understands my designs and concepts better than your own admiralty. He knows how things work. Use his knowledge. As I said, he may be young, but that boy has the best grasp of naval tactics I have ever heard. Your own secretary of the navy has chosen this man special for what is to happen, and believe me, you will need him."

Thomas shook his head and then ran a hand through his hair. "It seems I read in one of the eastern papers about this boy. Is he the officer that advocates the use of nothing but marines in a naval situation and not the army? That he wants the Marine Corps to expand to a fighting, offensive force?"

"Exactly," Ericsson said. "Jackson by all accounts is as brilliant as yourself, Colonel Thomas, or so I have heard." Ericsson bowed in deference to Thomas and Taylor.

"Brilliant?" Taylor laughed as he stood. "He accepts this assignment about chasing a myth, a mere legend, and you call this man brilliant?" Taylor stepped up to John Henry. "If he was that, Mr. Secretary, Mr. Ericsson, he wouldn't have left his wife at home to be butchered by Indians, instead of taking them to Fort Bowie, would he?" he asked with a murderous look at Thomas, who took a menacing step forward.

"Sore point, I take it?" Seward tilted his head trying to get a read on the Confederate officer. "May I suggest you tread lightly on the subject of his wife, Colonel Taylor?"

"Would you?" Taylor said as he reached for the bottle of whiskey and without waiting for a glass took a long pull as he stood in the doorway. He hissed as the burning liquid made its way down his throat. "If his wife was also *your* sister?" He walked out after corking the bottle and tossing it to Ericsson.

Seward strode to the window and watched Taylor walking down the steps to join his men.

"That, I did not know."

As John Henry stood beside Dugan and Gray Dog they heard a commotion behind them as men were led into the warehouse. There were more than a hundred of the most beautifully uniformed soldiers Dugan or Thomas had ever seen. Crisp and sharp creases were in their pants, and their shoes were shined to perfection. The soldiers looked a little intimidated as they saw the bearded and filthy men awaiting the issuing of civilian clothes.

A second lieutenant broke away from his men, who were now standing at parade rest, and he made his way over to John Henry.

"They have got to be the prettiest troopers I have ever laid my eyes on," Dugan said as he removed a stub of cigar and watched the young officer move toward them.

"Colonel Thomas?" the boy asked as he stepped up and crisply saluted. John Henry returned the salute and then took the offered set of orders from the second lieutenant. "We have been issued orders to join your group, sir." John Henry noticed the boy still had his hand up in salute. He stared at him until the hand finally came down. "We are ordered to complement the marines, sir."

"Is that right?" Dugan said but quickly went silent when John Henry shot him a look.

"Yes, sir, one hundred men. We don't know where we are going, but we are ready for anything." He smiled and then looked at Dugan with pride, but the smile quickly vanished when his eyes fell on Gray Dog. He blinked and then turned to Thomas.

"Your equipment?" John Henry asked. "Lieutenant?"

"Parmentier, Lieutenant Chauncey Parmentier." He was smiling as if he expected John Henry to fall over himself after the introduction. "You'll be happy to know we have worked with the president on more than one occasion, sir."

Thomas's eyes widened as he heard this statement coming from the proud officer.

"Your equipment?" he asked again as he shot a look at Taylor, who had just joined them.

"The navy is already loading our equipment, sir," he said with pride edging his answer.

"Who and what are you?" John Henry asked as he glanced at the lieutenant's orders, looking desperately for an answer to his question to sort through the sick feeling he was starting to get.

"As I said, we have worked with the president many—"

"Lieutenant!"

"The Third Illinois Drum and Bugle detachment, just transferred from I Corps," he said proudly as Thomas became physically ill.

The sounds inside the warehouse were suddenly no opposition to the new sound of laughter coming from Colonel Jessy Taylor as he slapped John Henry on the back before joining his men.

The lieutenant watched the strange officer leave and then turned to John Henry with a smile. "As I said, Colonel, we have worked with the president many times. Mostly at the White House, but I'm sure we can handle anything or play anywhere you want us to perform." The smile was wide as the boy, who looked no more than eighteen, waited for the accolades on how lucky the expedition was to have such qualified men along.

The laughter of Taylor echoed in the emptiness of the warehouse.

"Well, I guess the guest list for this little shindig is now complete. I feel so much more confident that the Army has sent its absolute best to help us." Dugan cursed, spit, and then walked off.

As the laughter of Taylor continued, John Henry was sorely tempted to pull out his revolver and shoot his old friend and brother-in-law in the back to shut him up.

The three warships sat at anchor as the early-morning fog rolled in. Crowded into a whaling boat, the passengers traveling with the expedition sat looking at the three older ships. The first, U.S.S. *Carpenter*, was already moving through the fog as she was off to rendezvous at Cape Hatteras with the U.S.S. *Argo* carrying the bulk of the railroading supplies and Ericsson's gift to the expedition. She glided past and was soon swallowed up by fog. John Henry had met briefly with her young captain, Lieutenant Chauncey Abernathy. The lad had been no older than the young naval officer, Commander Jackson, who was in total command of the naval element of sailors and marines. He understood his orders. He would lay to the *Argo*, tie on, rig her sails, and hopefully by then the other two ships would have joined them.

The second ship was carrying horses, supplies, and cold-weather gear. This ship, the U.S.S. *Chesapeake*, would also carry the armaments intended for the expedition inside her large hull. Thomas had decided early on that only the marine guard would have access to sidearms during the voyage. Thomas knew Taylor, or should now that his old friend had tried to escape, and would never allow him the chance to do so again.

As they approached the third warship they saw her clean lines. It wasn't like Stanton or Secretary of the Navy Gideon Welles to give up a brand-new warship without what must have been immense pressure from Lincoln. So, with two older, thinner-hulled vessels they tossed in a sweetener, the U.S.S. *Yorktown*. She was so new that as the whaleboat tied up to her boarding ramp, her brass fittings sparkled in the weak oil lamps of the deck watch. The prisoners, with the exception of Colonel Taylor, were all aboard and already ensconced below.

First up the ramp to be greeted by the ship's first officer was Claire Richelieu. The lieutenant held her gloved hand and assisted her down from the ramp. He saluted and half-bowed as he gestured for her to step behind him, where she was again greeted by the young man she had seen walking into the warehouse, Lieutenant Commander Jackson. He bowed with no real enthusiasm. Next was the man posing as Ollafson's assistant, Steven McDonald. Claire watched the man vigorously jump the last three steps of the small ladder. He landed and then shook each of the two officers' hands. He nudged up against Claire, who moved easily away from the Englishman. Assisting the professor down from the ladder was the Frenchman Renaud in his guise as student translator Benton Cromwell. To Claire, the man could not have chosen more ridiculous cover name for himself, as if the English name would lend credence to his tale of deceit. Pleasantries were exchanged as Sergeant Major Dugan gruffly made his way past the reception line and went to the railing and watched.

The last three were Gray Dog, Taylor, and finally John Henry Thomas. The two naval officers saluted John Henry and gestured for him to follow. The others all fell in line as they made their way belowdecks.

"Colonel, you will of course take my cabin," Jackson said. "I expect you have ample business to cover during the voyage. The sergeant major and your . . . your"—he stumbled as he turned to look at Gray Dog—"your Indian can bunk next to him."

"Gray Dog will sleep wherever he is comfortable, which may mean five or six places during the night," Dugan said, cutting in abruptly as he and Gray Dog exchanged looks.

"We have a separate berth for Miss Richelieu. I hope she will find it accommodating. It's an old tack room the boys made . . . well, they made it a bit more private," Jackson said with an embarrassed smile. Taylor and John Henry exchanged looks that silently noted how very uncomfortable Jackson was around women, especially a woman onboard his ship. "Professor, we have a work area marked out for you and your assistants. You'll be rather cramped, but it should do fine." The naval officer stopped at the bottom of the stairs and waited for the others. "Now, I have the main cabin set up for you to brief my officers and those of the marine force commander, Lieutenant Parnell."

Jackson waited for his second-in-command to open the door and they proceeded inside. A large table with three maps spread out on its surface greeted them. Each had a chair. Coffee was served by a black steward as they seated themselves. Introductions were made to all. John Henry eyed the two new assistants for the professor with nothing other than mild curiosity as he'd been told the students would be a bit younger. McDonald and Cromwell looked to be well into an academic life rather than mere students.

As the steward placed a china cup in front of Jessy Taylor, the two exchanged looks of curiosity. The large black steward had graying hair and had been in the navy most of his life. He knew a secessionist uniform when he saw one. Taylor winked at the shocked look on the black man's face. He took the coffee without thanks. The steward continued to eye the Rebel colonel long after the others had been served.

John Henry stood over the three maps and looked them over. They showed the seas into which the three ships were headed, their separate dangers made apparent by markings Jackson had placed on them. The man at the middle of the table sipped his coffee and then looked over at Gray Dog, who sat on the deck in a darkened corner of the main cabin. Ollafson saw the Indian look his way and hold eye contact for the longest moment before he turned away. It was as though the colonel's man could see right into Ollafson's soul. To the old man it was quite unnerving to say the least.

Jackson went to the door and then gave the orders to his second-in-command to get the *Yorktown* under way.

"Gentlemen," John Henry started and then stopped and

dipped his black-haired head at Claire. "And lady. This is our route to Turkey. Commander Jackson's latest naval intelligence briefing conducted this morning indicates that we should not encounter any interference from here to Spain. To get past Gibraltar without the British getting their hackles up will be a challenge, but our navy has done that a few times before."

The no-nonsense Jackson bowed his head. "Yes, we run a regular game with the Brits. They look to harass us, we dodge them, and slip from one corner of the world to the next with them always a day late and a dollar short, as it were. The British have not given us any concern."

Thomas was looking at the young and very arrogant Jackson. He understood the boy was steeped in naval history. Could recite Nelson's entire battle plan from Trafalgar, even noting where his lordship made more than just one crucial mistake during the battle that could have finished off the French a full year earlier than they had. His entire family worshipped the sea, and this was why Jackson was so bitter being torn away from a war in which he had yet to contribute anything other than this mission to babysit a professor and his ridiculous theory.

"Good. I'll hold you to that prediction. I don't mind if we get caught going in, it's the getting out that has me concerned. Gibraltar is one hell of a choke point."

"Not only Gibraltar, Colonel," Jackson said as he leaned over the map. "You have the Aegean and then the Bosphorus Strait to contend with. Now those are choke points that will cause us trouble."

Thomas looked at the map as Colonel Taylor joined him. The Rebel's finger went to the map's depiction of the Bosphorus Strait. It was the natural choke point that led from the Dardanelles and into the Black Sea. He knew the plan called for the two warships with the equipment to transit the strait while the third, the *Yorktown*, would anchor at Constantinople to be greeted by the sultan himself.

On deck came the shouts of men as they lowered sails. The loud noise of the ship's anchor sounded through the thick wood. Claire exchanged looks with the two spies she had managed to get onboard. Each seemed pleased with himself after the large deceit to get on the ship. She wanted to tell the others during the briefing that the fools didn't have to dodge the British or the French. The two nations were well represented right here.

John Henry watched Taylor glide his finger along the map as the *Yorktown* slowly started to move toward the mouth of the Chesapeake. Finally the colonel looked up and into the blue eyes of Thomas. "Why, I'd just place a twenty-pounder on either side of the strait at its narrowest point and blast any ship trying to transit. That is, if I were the Turks." The smile widened as Taylor took his seat.

"That is what the *Argo* is for," Thomas said as he quickly moved on.

"All right John Henry, I'll bite. Just what is the *Argo?*" Taylor asked as the other heads, with the exception of Ollafson and Claire, nodded in agreement.

John Henry smiled for the first time. "Since it probably won't make the voyage without sinking straight to the bottom of the Atlantic or the Mediterranean, it really doesn't matter. But if this crazy mission finds something on that little hill of a mountain, and we run into trouble on the high seas, without the *Argo*, we'll be blown out of the water if our friends in Europe wish it so. But as I said, our secret weapon will more than likely sink long before she is needed."

"Well thought out." Taylor grinned facetiously and then slapped Ollafson on the knee. "Now that's a Yankee plan if I ever heard one."

"Gentlemen, we have gone over so much, but we have not touched on what it is we are after," Ollafson said, rubbing his leg where Taylor had slapped it. He stood and located the map of eastern Turkey.

"I thought we would cover that at another briefing, Professor," Thomas said, eyeing the man, who refused to sit.

"In other words, Professor, old John Henry wants to go over it in private first, especially since he doesn't believe in fairy tales, or your God any longer. Why cover something in a briefing the colonel refuses to believe is even there?"

John Henry looked at Taylor. The man was quickly learning the habit of pushing his former brother-in-law to the point of anger, where he knew John Henry became unreasonable. He wasn't going to allow Taylor to get under his skin as he always had.

"Colonel Taylor, during the voyage you will drill your men. Get their weight and strength back. They are going to need it." Thomas held eye contact with Taylor for the longest moment before the Reb nodded his head. The smile was still there.

"Mess Steward Grandee will be in charge of the prisoners' supplementary meals. He has designed a heavy caloric intake for the duration of the voyage. The colonel's men should be healthy for their little hike up a small mountain like Ararat."

Taylor's eyes went from Commander Jackson to the brown ones of the steward, who was in the process of winking at the Confederate colonel. Taylor suspected he should show the black man some respect since he could place anything into their meals. He would have to warn his men to keep social commentary to themselves while dining. He smiled again at the mess steward, who smiled back this time.

"Miss Richelieu, I expect you to keep belowdecks during any exercise time for the prisoners. I don't know how much control Colonel Taylor has over his men after tonight, so we'll just remove temptation from the equation." He looked at Claire, who was not happy with the arrangement but understood the colonel's chauvinistic ways. "And Commander, anytime our lady guest is out and about, she will require a two-man marine guard at all times."

"May I ask when the shackles will be removed from my men?" Taylor asked, the smile no longer in place.

"As soon as we clear into deep water," Thomas said as he looked over at Dugan, who stood beside the door at parade rest. "See to it, Sergeant Major."

"Yes, sir."

"Besides, if they cause trouble after that, they will be weighted down and thrown overboard." He again looked at Taylor. "Is that perfectly clear?"

Jessy nodded. "I find it interesting that you named one of your ships the *Argo*," Jessy said as the others rose to leave and to get some sleep.

"Yes? Why is that?" John Henry asked.

Taylor turned to others around the table as they stood. "John Henry wasn't as astute in the classics as I was at the Point. I was always attentive to my studies while John was steeped in military affairs of studentship. But as you can see by my attire"—he gestured to his gray uniform—"I am a true romantic."

"Your point, Colonel?" Ollafson said, wondering where the Rebel was going with this line of conversation. John Henry only waited with irritation as he retrieved his hat from the steward and walked toward the door. He stopped and turned.

"The point is, I've read Appollonius Rhodius. Have you?"

Ollafson shook his head.

"Well, Rhodius was a Greek poet. His *Argonautica* was required reading at the academy. I absorbed it."

"Colonel, we are all tired," Jackson said to hurry him along.

"What Colonel Taylor is trying to tell you is the fact that we will be traveling the very same route as the main character's voyage in," explained Thomas.

"Fascinating," McDonald said, breaking his silence for the first time. "And who was this brave soul?"

"His name was Jason," Thomas finished.

The others looked at each in turn as they recalled the tale from antiquity.

"Yes, and everyone here is what Rhodius called the Argonauts."

"Imagine that!" said the Frenchman, who looked at Claire with a raised brow.

"Yes, the colonel is correct. We seek the Ark of Noah, although for Jason, it was a search for the Golden Fleece."

They all looked at Claire, who surprised them with her classical knowledge.

Taylor laughed and then finally stood from his chair and made his way to the door where he awaited the sergeant major to open it. He turned.

"Each as fictitious as the next." He smiled, bowed, and then left the cabin.

John Henry watched him leave as the others filed out behind him. Only Claire remained for a moment as she pulled off her gloves.

"Tell me you believe the professor," she asked as John Henry held the door for her.

"I believe in very little, Miss Richelieu, very little."

"A man who can't believe in magic anymore," she said as she moved past him into the companionway, "is really kind of sad."

Thomas watched her go and wondered what she meant by magic. He shook his head and then saw Gray Dog rise from the shadows. He looked at the colonel and then after the lady.

"Not magic, John Henry, but bad medicine waits for you on the black mountain."

With that, Thomas watched him leave and wondered if everyone he knew were living in the same world as himself.

In the world he knew, there was no magic. There was only struggle and death.

9

John Henry stood upon the quarterdeck of the *Yorktown* as
she speedily made her way to the selected rendezvous point
with the *Argo*. He was looking through the leather-bound
journal he had been ordered to keep by the president. As he
reviewed the pages he had written, he came to realize that
absolutely no one other than Professor Ollafson, and possibly his assistants, believed in what they were attempting to
do. He had yet to commit his opinion into the official record
of the voyage. While he firmly believed they would find nothing on the slopes of Ararat, while his written words would
undoubtedly confirm his nonbelief in the tales of the Bible,
he still firmly believed in Lincoln.

He closed the journal after entering the morning's events:
Thus far the prisoners had behaved, although at several points
since departure they'd had to separate several Rebels from
their marine guards and the sailors of the huge warship. The
animosity between North and South belligerents was readily
apparent.

As he watched the men below, the sailors were going about
their business and steering a wide berth around the Confed-

erates, who were washing and mending their old and worn uniforms. John Henry had learned that Taylor and his men were adamant that they would wear their Rebel clothing anytime they thought they would have to fight anyone—that was including John Henry and his men. Until then they would reluctantly wear the civilian clothing given out to them by the war department.

"I have been meaning to ask you, sir, how in the world did the president convince you to go on this wild-goose chase?"

John Henry had not realized that Captain Jackson had strolled up behind him. The young naval officer was smartly uniformed even in the harsh heat of the afternoon sun. Even his two-cornered hat was perfectly adjusted to his head. Thomas looked the officer over and then decided it was time for him and the naval element to talk.

"I don't think about the orders I am given, Captain Jackson."

"I assure you, sir, neither do I, but I am rarely given orders this ambiguous. But then again, maybe the navy explains its orders far more clearly to its officers than the president to you. No offense, of course."

John Henry turned away and continued watching Taylor and his men as they tended to their old uniforms after the backhanded comment by a studious Jackson.

"As I said, I carry out whatever orders I am given."

"Is that what happened at Antietam?"

"So, you are a student of land engagements as well as sea tactics?" John Henry asked without facing the twenty-eight-year-old officer.

"Only in the sense of history. My expertise is in the development of naval tactics in coordination with land forces, as I believe that is the future of America's military."

"So I understand." Thomas finally turned to face the commander of the small flotilla. "In that frame of context, I am sure that is why Secretary Welles selected you to join us. When and if the time comes, I hope the secretary's confidence in your abilities is warranted."

Jackson placed his hands behind his back and rocked on

his heels, expecting the army officer to answer his inquiry about Antietam. He didn't. Jackson was about to ask again, not understanding the colonel's hesitancy to answer a question about which every military man in the country had a personal opinion. The hatred shown by General McClellan toward Thomas was legend. One man never showed up the other in front of witnesses. And most assuredly one did not call out his commanding officer on a charge of cowardice and dereliction of duty. He was about to broach the subject again when a call was heard from high above.

"Ship ahoy!" came the call from the lookout in the crow's nest a hundred feet above. "Ten degrees off the starboard bow!"

John Henry and Jackson both looked. There she was. The U.S.S. *Carpenter* had *Argo* already in tow. Both vessels were rigged for sail and were under way.

"Captain Abernathy is right on schedule," Jackson said as he looked through the telescope in his hands. "I calculate they are at a respectable eight knots. Not bad at all." He lowered the spyglass and then turned to his first officer. "Mr. Harvey, set all sails and let's get moving, shall we?"

The officer saluted and went out to give the order to deploy every sail the *Yorktown* had.

"Did Ericsson design the *Argo* to ride so low in the water?" John Henry asked as he lowered his own field glasses.

Jackson gave out a short laugh. "We learned from the battle of Hampton Roads, Colonel, that Mr. Ericsson is never totally sure about anything. And the *Argo* is one of those things."

"Well, I hope she doesn't founder before we may need her," Thomas continued as he again raised his glasses and studied the two ships. The *Argo* was much wider of beam than her tow, the *Carpenter*. However, she rode in the water well below her high-water mark and it looked like any rough seas would sink their ace in the hole.

"As I see it, Colonel Thomas, she could go to the bottom right now and we would never miss her, simply because there is nothing on that mountain to find, thus, nothing to protect or defend," Jackson said and then moved off to motivate his men to hurry.

John Henry heard the doubt in the captain's statement and he wondered if his own attitude was festering so much that it was starting to spill over into the thoughts of the men under his command.

"All right, you Rebs gather up your washing and your knitting, time to go below. It's noontime and you know that our lady passenger has the deck at noon. Time for chow anyway," Dugan said as he started herding the men down below. Dugan stopped in front of Taylor, who glanced up at John Henry. The sergeant major eventually did the same when he saw Taylor was ignoring his command. John Henry shook his head and then Dugan let out a frustrated but silent curse and then left the colonel on deck. Taylor turned and made his way to the quarterdeck and Thomas.

"You think my men don't have a modicum of decorum, do you? I assure you the boys treat women in the south as well as yours do in the north. Miss Richelieu has no reason to fear them. Besides, John Henry, that woman looks capable of fending off any suitors that may crop up on this little trip."

Thomas turned and faced Taylor. This was the first moment they'd had together since his betrayal the night before. The escape attempt was still fresh in the colonel's mind.

"The order of exclusion stands, Colonel."

"Colonel? Are you that put out at me that you forget we were once friends, and even related?"

"I guess there are too many years and far too many battles to return to old times, Colonel. After last night I realized that. The order stands."

Taylor raised a brow and then turned and saw the object of their conversation step onto the main deck. She was followed by Ollafson and his two assistants, who seemed to irritate the old Swede to no end. Thomas's eyes were on these two odd ducks and not Claire Richelieu.

"She is something, though, isn't she, John Henry?" Taylor asked, thinking Thomas was studying Claire.

Thomas was taken by surprise by Taylor's misinformed assumption. He shook his head and then went to the small set of steps that led to the main deck and offered Miss Richelieu an extended hand.

"Thank you," she said, not allowing Thomas to assist. "If I'm expected to climb a mountain in the early onset of a Turkish winter, I think I can negotiate these ten steps, sir."

Thomas smiled and then stepped out of the way with a fingertip to the brim of his western-style hat. He laughed when the freshening wind of the speeding ship blew the large purple feather garnishing her wide-brimmed hat into her face.

"Don't let my man Gray Dog see that little item. He has a thing for fancy feathers."

"Is that right?" she said as she went to the railing to enjoy the cool air sweeping the deck.

"Yes, he just can't imagine the strange eagle it came from, being purple and all."

Claire turned and for the first time John Henry saw the woman smile.

"So be careful. That coyote hat he wears used to belong to Mrs. Lincoln."

Both Thomas and Claire turned to see Taylor, who had joined them at the railing.

Claire didn't say anything. She only looked at Taylor and saw that there had at one time been something between these two men. She had heard the conversations below from the whispered voices of the crew and some prisoners. She studied the Confederate colonel, half-smiled, and then returned to face the calm seas.

"So, from what I understand, you're the lady who speaks in the language of the angels?"

Claire smiled without turning. "Please, I only speak in the tongues of archangels, Colonel Taylor. Never, ever just an everyday, ordinary kind. That would be quite beneath me."

Taylor laughed and then stepped up beside the woman with the flaming red hair. John Henry silently moved away to join Professor Ollafson, who had his hat off and was also taking in the coolness after so long below going over expedition planning.

"Having any trouble below with the men? I mean, the close quarters and all?"

Ollafson turned and faced the colonel. He smiled and then held out his hand to shake. Thomas hesitated, wondering if the professor even remembered who he was. He knew he was wearing his cavalry uniform and not his dress, but he didn't think it was that much of a difference. He wondered if maybe the professor was on the short side of senility. He shook the old man's hand anyway.

"No, no trouble at all. The crew has been very helpful."

Thomas released his hand and nodded at the two men who had joined them. Neither Cromwell nor McDonald offered a hand in greeting and Thomas was at least thankful for that.

"My meaning was the prisoners, Professor."

"Oh, them." Ollafson looked uncomfortable as he glanced around. He then leaned into John Henry. "Those men scare me, I'm afraid. I have never seen Rebel soldiers up close before. The last two days have been eye-opening, to say the least."

"Well, in the end you will discover that they are only men like you and I, Professor." John Henry looked at the two men next to him. "Gentlemen, will you excuse us for a brief moment so I can have a word with Professor Ollafson?"

Both men dipped their heads and then silently moved away. Only Cromwell turned back momentarily, catching himself before anyone could notice his curiosity. The man next to him, McDonald, had not noticed anything.

"Professor, how well do you know your two new assistants?"

Ollafson removed a handkerchief and then wiped his sweating brow as the sea and wind assisted in cooling him down.

"Not at all, I'm afraid. They seem to be knowledgeable enough on the subject matter at hand, but in answer to your question, Colonel, I have never seen either of them before. But my assistant Claire has, and I trust her implicitly."

"Implicitly enough not to trust her with your interpretation of the petrified wood and its warning before our meeting in the capital?"

Ollafson didn't answer the second inquiry as he stopped wiping his brow and fixed Thomas with his eyes. "That has nothing to do with trust, Colonel, I assure you. It has to do with keeping my friends and my colleagues alive and breathing. In case you weren't informed, my young assistant was murdered in New York just a few days ago. So forgive me for keeping certain facts close to the vest, as they say."

Thomas was now about to explode. He faced the professor and the old man could see Thomas was not a man who liked surprises.

"Why in the hell wasn't I notified about this murder of your student?"

Ollafson was hesitant to answer. He looked out to sea toward home and then decided it was too late for Thomas to turn the ships back to port.

"I . . . I . . . well, Colonel, I was afraid the expedition would have been delayed or that I would not be allowed to participate."

"For God's sake, Professor, you lost a kid to a murder and you're worried that you would not get to go?" Thomas faced the opposite direction and saw that his loud exclamation had grabbed the attention of not only Captain Jackson, but Claire, Taylor, and the others. They watched from afar. John Henry forcibly calmed himself before turning.

"You will never keep anything from me again. If I'm to get everyone home from this I need help. Do not get my men killed because you are afraid to say something. Is that clear, Professor?"

Turning even whiter than he had been, Ollafson nodded his head in silence as he witnessed the wrath of John Henry for the first time. Thomas turned and left.

"Well, I never heard the professor so cowed before. Your Colonel Thomas must be a man of deep thought."

"Well, maybe not deep thought, but he can scare the hell out of people when he wants."

Before Taylor could comment on Thomas's demeanor further, a brown hand reached down seemingly from nowhere and plucked the purple feather from Claire's hat. The hat actually lifted from her head for a brief instant and then settled as the feather was freed. She looked up just in time to see Gray Dog disappear into the ship's rigging above their heads.

"You thieving bastard!" Dugan called as he returned from the lower decks. "You give that back!"

Claire readjusted her hat and then looked from Sergeant Major Dugan to Taylor. "I must say one thing—this little odyssey is going to be interesting."

"I suspect so, even with the warnings on those maps belowdecks."

"What warnings?" Claire asked as she removed the hat for good, exposing her curled and coiffed red hair.

"The ones that describe the legend about the place we are going."

"I don't follow you," she said as she stabbed her hatpin into the hat.

"The warnings that say, here there be dragons."

She watched as Taylor removed his gray hat and then bowed as he left. She tried not to take Colonel Taylor seriously, but then realized she didn't know exactly what to expect out there even with his bad joke. She looked to the east and shuddered.

"Here there be dragons." She took a deep breath. "Maybe not dragons, but something far worse."

The three ships, with the *Argo* in her disguise as a barge in tow, slowly made their way toward the one place on Earth God had placed off limits to mankind—Mount Ararat.

It was one thirty A.M. and the *Yorktown* was battened down for the night. The shipboard watch kept their eyes mostly on the horizon, looking for lights of another vessel in their vicinity, but every now and again they would cast wary eyes on the deck below. Thus far the Confederate prisoners had been well behaved, but a warning from the army colonel persuaded the naval crew to be aware. He suspected their strength gain from a steady diet would tend to make Colonel Taylor's men more apt to attempt a takeover of the *Yorktown*, and for that reason the topside watch was armed with pistols. Thomas was noting this in his journal for the president when a light knock sounded on the door to the commander's cabin.

"It's open," came the curt response as he closed his journal and then quickly rolled up the map of eastern Turkey he had been studying. The door opened cautiously.

"Excuse me. I saw your lamps were still burning. May I have a word?" Claire Richelieu said as she poked her head into the opening.

John Henry didn't respond other than to nod his head. He started to stand but Madame Richelieu waved him down. "We don't need that while in transit, or no man would ever get any work done," she said seriously as she entered and closed the door.

John Henry remained standing. "Please leave the door ajar, Miss."

"Oh, yes, I guess we should show some propriety."

"Tongues wag even more on naval vessels, Madame."

"Yes, I suppose they would. May I have a word?" she said as she stepped farther into the large cabin. John Henry noticed she was absent the large hat she tended toward and her collar was unbuttoned above the tight bodice of her dress. For the first time in a trick of lighting Thomas could now see why Claire wore the large hats. Running along her cheek to her jawline was a thin scar that was usually hidden by a veil on her hat. In the light of the cabin she didn't seem to care if Thomas noticed the scar or not. She stood before him silently as he started to ease himself back into the chair. He quickly ran a hand through his dark hair and then studied Claire for the longest thirty seconds of the woman's life.

"Madame, I believe I gave explicit orders for you to be accompanied at all times by either a uniformed Union officer or any of the naval personnel. Never are you to roam belowdecks at any time. Is that now clear?" His blue eyes bore into her hazel ones and she didn't flinch.

"Colonel, I assure you I need no babysitter on this voyage."

"Nonetheless."

She half-bowed her head in compliance. "I acquiesce to the man's world we live in."

"Bow to whatever you would like, Madame. Stay clear of the prisoners." John Henry started to place the maps back into their proper order and then stood to unbutton his coat as he turned to Claire. "Now, what can I help you with?" He hung up the coat and then undid his loosened bow tie.

"Well, I'm afraid I came to see you about. well, *you*."

John Henry stopped all motion and then looked at the small woman with the blazing red hair, which now hung loose around her shoulders. She didn't look cowed at all and stood straight while keeping her eyes on him waiting for a reaction.

"Now you've seen me. What can I help with?"

She watched as he returned to the desk, frustrated at delaying his sleep.

"I believe you are going to get most of these men killed, Colonel."

"I suspect I may, Miss. But in the interest of clarity, in which context do you place your meaning?" He took the closed journal and placed it in the uppermost drawer of the desk and then he looked at her. His expression revealed he really wasn't pleased with the statement she had made.

"You, sir, are not taking this expedition seriously. Your behavior will spread to the members of this voyage and corrupt it. That will be very dangerous for you and for all of us."

John Henry did not respond in the least. His eyes remained on Claire.

Claire stepped farther into the room and the lamp from the desk clearly defined the woman's features. Thomas could see that she was quite beautiful in an academic way. She was a confident person and he immediately knew her to be a woman like his deceased wife. Headstrong and opinionated.

"While you may not believe in the tale, you must take this

curse seriously. The professor is not exaggerating the losses to previous attempts at Ararat. Many men have paid for not giving history credit. While you may think this is a Bible tale, I assure you, Colonel Thomas, it is much more than that."

"Madame, I take everything seriously when it comes to protecting my men under any circumstance. However, that being said, the only dangers I believe we face are human in nature. This little excursion into Turkey could cause problems that no one foresaw other than the president, and for the first time I cannot agree with his method of reaching out to the South after the war. It will take more than a biblical legend to heal this country. So you see, my attention in this matter is solely dedicated to getting all men home from this, North or South."

"I just need to ask, Colonel, if you hate this mission so badly, why did you ever accept it? From my understanding of the meetings held between Mr. Lincoln and Professor Ollafson, this was strictly voluntary. So why?"

"You are not militarily trained, Madame. You never ask an officer why he does something. I invoke that unwritten rule now, except to tell you that I would go to the ends of the earth for the president, and leave it at that."

"I was speaking with Colonel Taylor. He seems to be a very astute and intelligent man."

"Yes, he is. Very much so. And I may add he is one of the most dangerous men in the country. There was more than one reason why we brought the colonel along."

"And what was that?" she asked, watching John Henry's jaw clench, relax, and then clench again.

"He thinks faster in a saddle than any man I have ever known. He would be a detriment to the Northern cause if he were ever to escape and rejoin the fight. You may not have been briefed on this, but I will inform you anyway. Colonel Taylor was pegged early on by Robert E. Lee to become a commander in the western fight, which would have spelled disaster for General Grant in Tennessee. So I brought him along to stop that scenario from ever taking place. President

Lincoln thought so too, since he was picked for the mission not long after I was selected."

"I understand you two attended West Point together."

John Henry just looked at the woman from Harvard and didn't say anything.

"And that he is, or was, your brother-in-law."

"May I help you with some other . . . problem?"

Claire knew she would get no more from John Henry that night.

"Yes, you have answered everything, whether you wanted to or not. Just do not underestimate the dangers we face to the men, Colonel, because any carelessness on their part could turn this little fairy tale, as you call it, into a very real nightmare." Claire turned and left the cabin.

John Henry watched her go and then slumped down in his chair. He knew the scholar was right about one thing. He could not show his doubts in the presence of anyone ever again. That would make men sloppy in their duties. He just wanted to get there and convince the president there was absolutely nothing on that damned mountain other than the glacier they would have to climb. He shook his head and closed his eyes, and before he knew it he was fast asleep.

Claire stopped by amidships and saw the black mess steward was up early, or up late, she didn't know which. He was making coffee for the midnight watch when she tapped lightly on the small galley kitchen's door.

"Oh, goodness, Missy, you shouldn't be up roaming around at this time of the morning," he said as he moved quickly to the door, wiping his hands on a white apron.

"Couldn't sleep. I smelled that wonderful coffee of yours."

He immediately went to the enclosed stove and quickly poured her a tin cup full of the rich coffee. She took it with a smile and then sipped.

"Really, Missy, belowdecks on a warship is no place for a lady like yourself." The steward moved off to tend to a batch of biscuit dough and started kneading it.

"Yes, our intrepid Colonel Thomas has told me as much, time and time again."

The black man smiled as he worked. "His reputation is one that even we boys in the navy have heard about, yes, ma'am. He's a tough hickory nut to crack, almost as tough as Captain Jackson. Those two together can make for an explosive mix."

"I'm sure they are mixing up famously." Claire took one more sip of coffee and then reached out and handed the steward the cup. "Thank you for the coffee."

"Now, now, you hold up and I'll make sure you get back to your cabin."

"No, you have work to do. I assure you, I'll be fine," she said, smiling as she turned and made her way down the darkened passage. She could hear the prisoners one deck below snoring and coughing, but tried to pay the sounds no mind.

She eased around a barrel of flour and was almost to the door when a rough and smelly hand closed around her mouth. She was pulled into the darkness next to the hull and then forced down. Her eyes widened when she saw three men in civilian clothing. One was pawing at her bodice and ripping at her blouse while two others held her down to the damp deck. The man straddling her was bearded and his eyes were wild. She had seen him numerous times when the prisoners' exercise period had ended and they passed on the lower decks. She had noticed the way he had looked at her. That should have been warning enough to heed the colonel's words about putting desperately lonely men in a position where they reacted and didn't think before doing something stupid. The man was ripping her blouse and painfully grabbing her. The two other men holding her down looked to be frightened. She thought she could take advantage of that. Her eyes were pleading with the two men, who looked as if they would rather be somewhere else at that very moment.

Suddenly there was a roar from the darkness behind the three men. The next thing she knew, one of the men jerked wildly and then she saw his body being lifted straight up from where he had been, while the other two soldiers' eyes went wide. It was the black mess steward who had come to help. He brought a ham-sized fist down upon the top of the first man's head. He fell limp as a caught squirrel. Now the black man looked frightened at what he had done. The attacker, who was still squeezing and battering her upper chest, failed to help his companions because he was so intent on what he was doing.

The second man disappeared suddenly as a war whoop sounded against the hull. Gray Dog was there. He had a knife to the third man's throat, holding him in place by the sheer look of bloodlust in the Indian's eyes.

A gun was deliberately cocked right behind the ear of the man who straddling Claire, and his groping motions quickly stopped. Claire's eyes were wide as the man slowly turned his head and saw the cocked Colt pistol aimed right at him. John Henry Thomas was increasing the pressure on the trigger as his temper was close to boiling over. The mess steward and Gray Dog had the other two men well in hand. Claire felt the pressure leave her mouth and that was when she tasted the blood flowing from her cheeks where the man's fingers had dug in hard. She spit and then slapped the man across the face. He was attempting to smile at John Henry and knew immediately that the colonel was going to kill him right then and there. He felt the pistol waver minutely as the pressure on the trigger grew.

"John Henry!" came a voice from behind him, and then that was quickly followed by another.

"Colonel Thomas, stop!"

Claire saw the blue eyes of the colonel slowly start return to normal as he eased the hammer down on the Colt. He grimaced when he realized how close he had come to killing the man without a word being spoken.

Thomas finally stood and slapped the man out of his way with the barrel of the Colt. He helped Claire to her feet as she wiped blood from her mouth.

Soon Captain Jackson, resplendent in a dressing gown, had his pistol trained on the three men as Gray Dog pushed the second man forward roughly and the mess steward pulled the groggy third to his feet. Jessy Taylor was there also, having heard the commotion from where he had curled up for the night. The three assailants had passed him in the dark and had awakened him. He was furiously glaring at his three men. Jackson reassured the steward, who was afraid he would be in trouble for nearly killing one of the prisoners.

"Captain, take these men to the brig. They'll stand charges of assault," John Henry said as he looked from Claire to Taylor, expecting one or the other to protest.

Jackson, with the aid of five other sailors who had come belowdecks after hearing the commotion, moved the three men out. Before they could leave Taylor took the one man by the collar and stopped him. It was Corporal Loudermilk. Taylor should have known it would be him.

"You're lucky if they don't hang you tomorrow," he said, slamming his fist into the man's collarbone as he pushed him away. Loudermilk cursed as four navy crewmen led him roughly to the brig.

Jackson eased the hammer of his Colt down and then attended to Claire, who was leaning against the wet hull.

"Please, Captain, I'm fine." She looked up into the steward's eyes. "Thank you." She looked at Thomas, who seemed as if he were about to say something kind, but then his demeanor turned hard once more.

The steward didn't respond; he only looked at Jackson, who nodded that he could return to the kitchen. He nodded at Claire once and then sadly moved away.

"Colonel, I . . . I . . . ," she started, but was soon cut off by John Henry.

"I assume there will be no more timely points being made about you being unescorted belowdecks?"

Claire only nodded and then burst past the men in the companionway. She had expected a little more concern from the colonel. Instead she got nothing but a blast of iciness.

John Henry watched her go and then turned on Taylor.

"They *will* hang in the morning. I suggest you learn to control those men left in your command, Colonel."

"You are not hanging anyone. Those men will be brought

back to the States for trial. There will be no summary executions of any of my men. We will handle their discipline ourselves, the southern way."

John Henry smirked. He then looked at Jackson, who was watching the confrontation with trepidation. He didn't need this volatile mix of emotions on the high seas.

"Twelve hundred hours, Captain. I believe you navy men call it captain's mast?"

"Well, there is more to it than that, Colonel," Jackson said as he stared into John Henry's hard features.

"You are not hanging those men," Taylor repeated as he took a menacing step forward.

John Henry matched the move with his own forward step. Jackson saw what was coming and then he stepped between the two army officers, looking ridiculous in his nightcap and gown.

"Gentlemen, if I may remind you, we are on a warship full of angry men. May I suggest we take this up in the morning to allow heated tempers to cool?"

John Henry, with one last look at Taylor, moved away toward his cabin. "Twelve hundred hours, Captain. Every man aboard ship is to be present for the execution."

Taylor turned on Captain Jackson. "You know what will happen after that, don't you?" Taylor moved off past the stunned naval officer, who saw disaster approaching his ship's horizon.

The *Yorktown*'s company would not sleep well the rest of that long night.

At eleven thirty the next morning the marines were the first to gather. Lieutenant Parnell had placed four sharpshooters into the high rigging of the *Yorktown* as she made her way over the calm sea. The *Chesapeake* had been signaled from a mile off to come alongside to witness the punishment. The crews of both ships had never seen anything like what was happening on a United States ship of war. The *Carpenter* and her tow, the *Argo,* were too far back to participate in the execution of the Rebel accused. The crew of the *Chesapeake* had lined her railings and were high in the ship's rigging to witness the army colonel's stern mandate.

Captain Jackson had issued to John Henry his official protest in writing over the hastily tried prisoners. The trial had taken place early that morning with a panel consisting of Thomas, Jackson, Dugan, Parnell, and Taylor. Colonel Jessy Taylor was the only abstention on the panel. He had angrily stormed out after the trial's only witness was silenced when she tried to describe the assault as less than what it was, only for the sake of holding this motley crew together for as long as possible. They all knew it had been attempted rape, and one man had already paid for the indiscretion by having the top of his head crushed in by the mess steward's blow. When Claire Richelieu said that she was never actually frightened of the three men and that she was of the opinion the attempted rape could have been avoided, Colonel Thomas silenced her, and then excused her.

Taylor knew John Henry had already made up his mind to use his three men as a harsh example to the other men. After Taylor had stormed out of the proceedings and after Claire was excused, it was Jackson, this stiff-nosed naval commander who brooked no breach of regulations from anyone, who spoke in defense of the accused.

"As the naval representative in charge of seagoing operations, I must disapprove of your actions, Colonel. This event can only further separate the men even more than they are now. My crew has already been in several fights with the Confederate prisoners since this happened. The marines are walking around as if it had been their own mothers or wives that had been attacked. I implore you to keep these men in the brig until they can stand courts-martial when we return home."

Thomas was silent as he wrote the official verdict in his journal. He finally looked up when Jackson had completed his tirade.

"Sergeant Major Dugan, please be sure to enter the captain's statement into the record." He looked at Jackson and his eyes were cold. "Duly noted for the record, Captain."

Jackson grimaced but remained silent as he stood and left the cabin.

"Lieutenant Parnell, you haven't said much." Thomas said as he eyed the young marine officer.

The well-dressed marine stood and looked at Dugan and then Thomas. "I, sir, am a United States Marine. What those men did deserved summary execution. However, with that being said, sir, my opinion is in line with Captain Jackson's. Now is not the time, Colonel. I have the overall picture to look at, and frankly, sir, we are going into a semi-hostile empire with men that cannot be trusted as of now. Just think how loyal to our cause they will be after we hang three of their compatriots."

"These men are not compatriots, they are not even Confederates any longer, young lieutenant. They are members of a small regimental combat team that is extremely short handed. They are all under *my* command."

"I understand that, Colonel, but—"

"That is all, Lieutenant. You may return to your duties."

The marine was caught off guard as he'd been fully expecting this man to hear him out. His reputation as an even-keeled officer and one who always took care of his men was a distant memory now that he had seen the coldness of Thomas up close. He didn't salute as he left the cabin. John Henry watched him leave and then tossed his pencil down on the closed journal.

"Why didn't you tell them what you're up to, Colonel Darlin'? It would make for a lot less tension in the next few minutes."

"If I had to stop and explain to my officers every object lesson it would be no less than my explaining everything to *you* over and over again. These officers have to realize that I need them to pay attention to what we are about to do."

"Just sayin', Colonel, you're taking a risk. That Colonel Taylor, your friend, he's gonna bear watching. He won't take this lying down." Dugan gathered up the minutes of the panel and then saluted as he moved out of the cabin.

John Henry heard the naval drummer calling all hands to

stations to witness punishment. He closed his eyes and hoped
he could keep the Reb prisoners in line until his harsh point
was made. He lightly whistled and then he heard the noise
behind him.

Gray Dog appeared from the shadows and John Henry
spoke without turning.

"You know what to do," was all he said as the Comanche
vanished without speaking.

The crewmen of the *Yorktown* were all lined up in a square
surrounding the prisoners. The Rebs were all in an angry
mood. Their words to the navy men and marines were filled
with hatred. Thomas, in his short time standing on the quarterdeck, had seen several instances of marines pushing the
men a little too hard to stay in place. He hoped the situation
would be calmed after the festivities of the afternoon were
complete. The drums continued their sorrowful beat as the
three prisoners were led onto the main deck and then up a
makeshift platform to face their executioners.

Thomas's attention was drawn toward the back of the
gathered Rebel formation as men started pushing and
shouting. Thomas saw the mess steward as the big black man
made his way up from the kitchens. The man who had gained
the respect of the Confederates by supplying them with the
best meals they had had in more than two years had instantly
become the face of their imprisonment. Most of the southerners had never seen a black man raise a hand to a white man
in their lifetimes.

The last people to take to the upper deck were Claire,
McDonald, Ollafson, and the ever-silent Benton Cromwell.
Taylor was the very last to take his place at the head of his
formed men. His eyes bored into John Henry's. Thomas
didn't flinch as he saw Taylor looking at him as the accused
were led up the four steps to the wooden platform. Loudermilk's eyes pleaded with Taylor to stop this from happening,
but he knew the colonel would never stop the hanging. He
had seen that in Taylor's demeanor last night when Thomas
had threatened to shoot him before the hanging could even
take place. No, there would be no sympathy for him.

The drums stopped as Sergeant Major Dugan placed hoods over the three soldiers' bearded faces. This caused a stir inside the prisoner ranks. Taylor ordered them to calm down and to stand at attention.

"All hands present to witness punishment, Captain," the first officer said to Jackson, saluted, and then moved away, but not before eyeing John Henry and his stern visage.

Dugan took a step forward and faced the gathered prisoners and crew. He withdrew the verdict from his breast pocket.

"For the offense of assault on an unarmed civilian and for attempted rape of same, Harold J. Loudermilk, corporal; Parsons Whitney, private; and Philip S. Siegfried, corporal, Army of Northern Virginia, have been found guilty by United States courts-martial to be hung by the neck until they are dead. Execution to be carried out this day, the third day of October, in the year of our Lord, 1864." Dugan replaced the guilty verdict and then without hesitation, as if the act itself would be forgiven if done quickly, he placed the ropes around the necks of the three men.

"This has to stop, now!"

All eyes went to Jessy Taylor, who had taken a few steps toward the raised quarterdeck. Several marines headed him off with their bayonetted weapons at the ready.

"If Colonel Taylor takes one more step, he is to be shot," Thomas said as his eyes made contact with Taylor. Again John Henry nodded his head toward Dugan. Then he quickly looked above him and into the rigging. He wasn't looking at the marine sharpshooters there, but was hoping beyond hope that Gray Dog had made it into position in time.

Dugan was going to have to do this the old-fashioned way, like in the days back at County Cork in Ireland. He would have to push the three men off the front of the hastily built hanging scaffold. This he did quickly before Colonel Taylor got himself killed. The men dropped off the edge and the moan from the prisoners was audible and angry as the men started strangling to death, as the fall was not of adequate length to snap their necks. The men were kicking wildly.

The mass of prisoners tried to move forward through the

pointed marine bayonets. They were prodded back into position. Suddenly the three men dropped free and hit the deck with a thud. The three ropes had been cut at the last possible moment. Taylor was the first to see the three men, who had been only moments from death, struggling to gain their feet, the ropes still knotted around their necks.

John Henry and Captain Jackson looked up in time to see Gray Dog maneuver through the thick sail lines of the rigging until he easily slid down onto the upper quarterdeck. He nodded at John Henry. The prisoners slowly realized the three accused had been spared. They watched Taylor for their lead on what to do. As for the colonel, he only stared up at Thomas. He then moved to his fallen men and removed the ropes. He pulled them to a standing position and then snatched their hoods off. He angrily made them face the colonel, who was staring down at them. Jackson was there also with a look of amazement on his face.

"Sergeant Major Dugan, not for the record."

"Sir!" Dugan said loudly, turning and looking at the prisoners, who stood in stunned silence behind him.

"The sentence of the three prisoners is hereby suspended. The matter will be taken up again when we return home. Their cooperation and performance during this mission will determine if this matter will continue to its natural conclusion."

"I have to admit, your methods are a bit strange, Colonel, but effective," Jackson said as he took in a still-silent Thomas. Jessy was still fuming at not being let in on John Henry's ploy.

"I need every man I have under my command, Captain Jackson. Killing them piecemeal will only weaken us at a time when we need the strength of all. No, executions can wait. Let's see how the prisoners react."

"Yes, I—"

"Ship ahoy!"

Jackson froze. He looked up into the high rigging and shouted, "Where away?"

"Ten degrees off the starboard bow, closing fast!" came the loud call.

Jackson went to the railing and then raised his glass to the east.

"Who?" Thomas asked.

"Can't be good, coming from the wrong direction. The *Carpenter* and *Argo* are three miles astern. Whoever this is, is sailing at us from the east." Jackson looked at John Henry. "Europe." He again raised the glass to his eye. "Any identification?" he called up into the rigging.

Silence greeted his shouted call. He lowered the glass from his eye in frustration.

"French flag!" came the shouted return. "Man-o'-war."

"Damn, I had hoped we would have made it to Gibraltar before we picked up a tail," he hissed. He again lowered the glass and looked at Thomas.

"Orders, Colonel," he said.

"Do what you would normally do, Commander. We're only sailing to Constantinople."

"Normally, for a ship coming after us that fast, I would place a twenty-pounder into her main mast." Again Jackson raised his glass.

Thomas smiled and nodded that Gray Dog should come with him. It was now time to face Jessy Taylor and explain why he did what he did.

The French thirty-five-gun warship came to within a mile and then fell in line behind the Americans.

The supporting cast for this tragic comedy was almost complete.

10

Belowdecks of *Yorktown* the prisoners gathered for the evening meal five days later. The days since the Yank colonel had pulled off the fake executions had been filled with hate for the other side. The men felt they had been played with at the very least. Thomas had failed in bringing the men closer together. Still, the Rebel prisoners as a whole had nothing but loathing toward Loudermilk and his two accomplices in the rape attempt. They had been segregated from the rest of the Rebels and kept under lock and key. But the surprising thing was, it wasn't at the order of the blue-belly colonel, as the prisoners called Thomas, it was at the command of their own colonel, Jessy Taylor. The man had not spoken in the five days since the mock hangings. To either the Yankees or the Rebels.

The days and nights had been hectic, with most daylight hours being occupied by speculation as to why the French warship would be tailing them. It was rumored that their mission had been marked by the French as a mission to stop, or at the very least take advantage of. There was even a soldier's rumor that the French could possibly be tailing them to set the prisoners of war free from their bondage. Most experienced soldiers knew this to be flawed by the simple fact that the French had no true love for either side in the American conflict. Now, if it had been a British ship of war, the prisoners might have had hope of being freed.

The confines of the third deck were stifling. Most of the hundred men had their civilian clothing askew to attempt to allow cooler air to reach their sweaty skin. Keeping them belowdecks after the Loudermilk incident had been Thomas's idea to make sure the space between the navy, marines, and the prisoners was kept wide, curtailing their animosity toward each other. Jackson had ordered the gun ports opened so the men could breathe the air from one deck above them.

The men were talking when the mess steward, Grandee, came into the space with a cook pot filled with oxtail and potatoes. The looks he received were hostile at best, murderous at worst. Word had spread that one of the attackers had had his head caved in by the giant cook. Grandee kept silent as he set up his serving line. His two assistants, black men also, kept their faces neutral and their eyes down as they served the prisoners. This was the first time they had seen the steward since Colonel Thomas had ordered his exclusion from serving the Reb prisoners for the past five days.

As the men were served, they sat in various positions along the much-cooler hull and watched Grandee pack up his food and plates. Suddenly he was told to stop. He looked up to see the Rebel colonel enter the space with the marine lieutenant, Mr. Parnell, accompanied by the army sergeant major. Each had a tin plate in his hand as they waited for the steward to serve them. The men were silent as they watched the two officers fill their plates. The sergeant major only removed his blue cap and went to a far corner and sat facing the men. For the first time in the voyage they noticed the sergeant major was armed. Thomas had forbidden firearms belowdecks for obvious reasons, so to see the Colt holstered on Dugan's belt surprised them.

It was Corporal Jenks who had the first words of the evening. He sat with several other noncoms as they ate their evening meal.

"I always said marines are needed as much as ten teats for a five-piglet sow," Jenks said as laughter filled the darkened space.

Lieutenant Parnell hesitated before taking a seat next to Taylor. Dugan snickered in the far corner, but for the most part kept his silence. Parnell looked over at the ten noncoms as they each eyed him in turn. He adjusted the large spoon in his plate and then eased himself down next to the Confederate colonel.

"You have known a lot of marines, I take it?" Parnell asked as he raised a spoon to his lips and blew on a chunk of oxtail. He chewed as he looked up at Corporal Jenks.

"Well, maybe," Jenks said with a smile on his face as he stood, handed over his plate to a mate, and then confronted Parnell. His eyes went to Taylor, who was eating quietly and seemed not to be paying attention to the conversation. "Do ya mind standing up, Lieutenant?" Jenks asked as he watched the marine closely.

With a look toward Taylor, Parnell pursed his lips and then stood, plate in hand. His eyes roamed to the sergeant major, who was watching intently. Dugan kept his eyes neutral but his hand was ever closer to his Colt pistol. The holster flap was untied.

"Now, if you don't mind, sir, turn around."

Jenks and the others were watching the tall marine as he looked at Taylor, who only ate his meal. Parnell raised his brows but did as he was asked, expecting a large oxtail bone to slam into the back of his head. Instead he heard Jenks say, "Yep."

"Yep, what?" Parnell said as he turned back around and stood before the prisoners like a man on display.

"As soon as you showed your backside I knew you were a marine. Hell, I didn't recognize you as such until I saw your back," he said and then laughed along with the others.

Parnell stiffened. His eyes remained locked on the corporal as Taylor tried his best not to laugh with a mouth full of food. Dugan for the most part stopped trying not to laugh and soon joined the Rebel prisoners.

"Yes, sir, Lieutenant, I seem to remember a regiment of marines running away as fast as they could at the first battle of Manassas. Yeah, you boys hightailed it out of there that day as if old Patch himself was chasing, as I recall."

More laughter sounded at the young marine officer's expense. Even Taylor lowered his plate, stifling his laughter long enough to watch Parnell and his reaction.

"I take it you are referencing the battle of Bull Run?"

"If a battle is what you Yanks call it, so be it. We called it a rout," he added, to even more howling laughter.

"To correct your statement, we were under army command that day," was Parnell's only excuse. He had been a part of that disastrous opening battle of the war. They had expected the Rebel forces would scatter to the winds when the Army of the Potomac came at them. But that didn't happen. With most of the Washington elite watching from hillsides while picnicking, the Union forces had been routed by these very same men under the command of Stonewall Jackson.

"I would call that the blind leading the blind," Jenks said, and then joined in the laughter again. This time Dugan lost his smile as he remembered the battle as clearly as if it happened yesterday. The embarrassment would never end and would cause his and Thomas's eventual exile from the war. No, Dugan had no humor in his soul for remembering Bull Run. The marines were not the only soldiers to cut and run that day; the entire Union force would never be able to live those hours down. That day Stonewall Jackson announced in no uncertain terms that the war would be long and costly.

Parnell looked down at Taylor, who said nothing. The lieutenant sat back down and tried to eat, not understanding why Taylor had brought him down there to begin with.

"Hell, marines are about as helpful as this darkie here," Jenks said as the laughter quickly died down.

The large black mess steward stopped what he was doing and looked up at Jenks, who was waiting for him to respond. He had been pulled aside earlier and told by Taylor, with Colonel Thomas standing nearby, that he was needed to serve dinner to the prisoners that night. He didn't understand the Rebel colonel's orders but did what he was told after Colonel Thomas had nodded his approval. Now he was even more confused when Taylor did nothing to stem the foul words coming from the corporal's mouth.

"If he had been there, he would have knocked your ass right out of the saddle," Dugan said as he finally stood, took a tin plate, and allowed the confused mess steward to serve him. Dugan winked as he hoped the large man was ready for what was about to come his way. "Hell, I can't wait to get a million of these men of color to fight. That's when we'll see all of you Johnny Rebs start shitting yourselves." Dugan turned with his full plate and smiled. "And that time's a' comin', boyo."

Jenks was no longer laughing as he eyed the sergeant major.

"There's not a scrapper among you who can take this fella. He would pull you apart piece by piece." Dugan again smiled as he placed a bite of oxtail in his mouth and chewed.

"I don't know. Corporal Jenks was the wrasslin' champ of the regiment back in the day. He's mighty tough for a boy from Tennessee," Taylor said as he finally laid his plate down and stared at Dugan and his dark defendant.

"Why, that sounds an awful lot like a wagerin' proposition to me," Dugan said as he challenged the colonel. "Your big-mouth corporal here couldn't stand up to one blow from this man."

"It sure does," Lieutenant Parnell mumbled as he also placed his still-full plate down, feeling the sting of embarrassment.

"Boy's too damn big, too slow," one of the prisoners chimed in.

"Not your typical slave you can bully, huh?" Dugan said as he eyed the corporal and those men encouraging him to take the wager.

"I never owned no slave in my life. Me and my pa did all the work where I come from."

The same call was taken up by almost a hundred percent

of the prisoners. Dugan quickly saw the irony in their defense. Not one slave owner in the group of Reb prisoners. Yet here they were.

"What is the wager, gentlemen?" Taylor asked as he finally stood. Parnell watched and waited. He knew this was another attempt by either Dugan or Thomas to show the Reb prisoners that a man was a man no matter the color of his skin.

"Easy. You give the colonel every man's full cooperation until we enter American waters once again. Then and only then will you again become Confederate soldiers. Until that time, you fulfill the mission General Lee sent you on. Bet?" Dugan said as his eyes goaded Jenks from where he stood.

Jenks looked at Taylor for guidance. Taylor only shrugged.

"And if that big feller gets his ass whooped?" one of the men asked.

Parnell's head went up as he just realized what was happening. It was Colonel Thomas again and his very unorthodox way of making a point. He decided to play along.

"I imagine I could convince the colonel to allow you men free access to the weather decks and free you from this hell for the duration of the voyage," Parnell said as he saw Taylor smirk.

"It's a bet," Jenks said as he looked at his compatriots, who were nodding their heads in agreement.

"How about it, Grandee? Think you can take this Reb braggart?" Dugan asked as he turned and faced the large mess steward.

"I would rather not, sir," Grandee said as he lowered his head, hoping to blot out the hatred being thrown his way by the prisoners.

"As I say, the darkies don't have any idea what you Yanks are all riled up about. They's happy just to cook and tend fields. They're not fighters." The man who said the words slapped Jenks on the back. The corporal was seeing the size of the cook for the first time and was having serious second thoughts about what was going to happen. He looked at his fellow prisoners for encouragement and there was plenty of that.

Grandee slowly removed the filthy apron he was wearing and then stood rigid.

"Well, I think we have us a bet," Dugan said as he placed his plate of food down.

"Gentlemen, there will be no fighting belowdecks."

All eyes went to Taylor, who started for the stairs that led upward. Jenks grimaced and then closed his eyes only briefly as his heart sank at the lack of reprieve offered by the colonel.

"This will be done on the main deck," Taylor called back.

Jenks felt his heart sink to its lowest level as the men cheered, confident the black cook was about to receive his just punishment for denting the head of a white man.

Thirty minutes later Colonel Thomas walked out on deck with Captain Jackson as lamps were lit and lined the railing of the *Yorktown*. His eyes went to Dugan, who would referee the match that Thomas himself had orchestrated. Taylor had a good job convincing the colonel to allow this to happen, and had made a big show of it having been his idea. This was the payment Taylor owed John Henry for not executing Loudermilk and his two cohorts in crime.

"You are surely not going to allow this?" Professor Ollafson asked as he and Claire, with McDonald and Cromwell in tow, joined the officers on the quarterdeck. Ollafson was seeing whatever cooperation the two sides may have been showing go down the proverbial drain when he heard there would be an exhibition of fighting prowess among the northern and southern aspects of the mission. He saw his dream coming apart.

John Henry looked down at the professor and said nothing. Claire was just as surprised as Ollafson that Thomas was allowing this to happen. She suspected that John Henry was trying to make a point but she didn't yet know what.

"Foolishness! This is why we have little respect for the Americans," Cromwell whispered to Claire, out of hearing distance of the others. "This colonel is not an officer to be respected."

"Perhaps."

Below, the entire prisoner group was in a tight circle around wide-eyed Jenks, full of false bravado as he watched the large black man slowly remove his shirt. He swallowed when he saw the scars on the man's back. Claire winced when she saw how this man had been treated in the past.

"Mr. Grandee was a slave?" she asked Thomas, turning away. She did not want to see the horrible reminder of the pain this man and people like him had suffered over the years.

"Born into and escaped from, Madame," Captain Jackson said as he watched the proceedings below with disdain. He glanced at the older army officer and wondered what he planned to accomplish with this fiasco on his deck.

Colonel Taylor stepped into the center of the main deck. "Gentlemen, the wager has been accepted by the entire ship's company. The agreement will be respected. If my man loses, which he assuredly will not, we will cooperate fully in Mr. Lincoln's folly. However, if he wins, we will be accorded the open spaces of the ship and an opportunity to return to our army and our people when we return, and without the loss of honor. That's the agreement."

John Henry Thomas made eye contact with Jessy. The two men knew one another better than any two men in the military. Thomas knew Jessy would never wait until their return home. Thomas figured he would get his men out of this mission at any opportunity. That was the reasoning for him to sacrifice his man for a possible beating—to get his men above decks. Finally Taylor smiled and then caught the attention of Claire, who raised a brow underneath the dark veil of her sun hat before turning away from the Confederate officer.

"If you *gentlemen* will excuse us, the professor wants to meet with his team belowdecks," Claire said as she turned away from the barbaric spectacle readying itself on the deck below.

Thomas watched her, Ollafson, and the other two strange birds leave the quarterdeck. He had understood the emphasis she had placed on the word "gentlemen" as she departed. He smirked, as he had the same mocking opinion of not only

Taylor, but of himself. Perhaps he had been away from society too long and had forgotten how to do things the civilized way. Perhaps.

A loud cheer went up from the divergent group of men as the navy crew, marines, and prisoners started to gather around in a circle.

On the quarterdeck the men failed to see Captain Jackson nod his head. The marines on the main deck were all off duty and were in a light circle around the hundred Confederate soldiers. What everyone failed to notice was the fact that thirty marines were missing.

All voices went silent as the heavy sound of boot thumps sounded on the wood decking around the men. As the prisoners looked up, they saw the remaining marines file out on both the starboard and then port sides of the *Yorktown*. They came to a stop and then went to rigid attention. Each man was armed with a Henry repeating rifle.

Taylor angrily looked at Thomas once more. John Henry had sent his message and it was now being received loud and clear. The marines would not hesitate to shoot anyone who got out of hand. The Rebel prisoners gave the marines who had joined them on deck foul looks of distaste at the insult. There were more than a few choice words offered to the off-duty marines.

The mess crew was tending to Grandee and offering words of encouragement. The large man looked reluctant to take part in John Henry's little idea, and the colonel felt badly for having to pick the one man onboard who didn't deserve what was happening.

"I honestly hope you know what you are doing, Colonel Thomas."

John Henry smiled. "So do I, Captain Jackson." His eyes met those of his former friend below as he made his way to his man to offer encouragement. Taylor didn't look back at John Henry. "So do I."

"Insanity," Ollafson said as he spread out a large map on the table inside the captain's cabin. The sound of the men on deck gave the interior spaces of the *Yorktown* a vibrant feel. Ollafson was not impressed with the military's foolishness.

"Yes, this Colonel Thomas seems to work in mysterious ways. I believe he will have those prisoners at our throats before this voyage is at an end."

The old professor looked into the eyes of McDonald. He didn't know the man but he came off as far more than an amateur historian. However, if Claire vouched for him he had to tolerate his abruptness and arrogance. His eyes went to Cromwell, who seemed to be off in another world. He cleared his throat and then smiled.

"Gentlemen, and lady, I feel a closeness down here that is making me feel quite nauseated. If you'll excuse me, I think I am better suited to the air topside."

"Taking in the brutality above decks?" McDonald inquired with a wry smile.

"Not at all, old man. I have seen quite enough barbarity in my lifetime. Just air for me, thank you." Cromwell nodded and then left the overheated and stuffy cabin.

"Now," Ollafson said as he placed the oilskin-wrapped parcel on the tabletop over the displayed maps. The heat seemed to rise in the room as McDonald's and Claire's eyes fell on the mysterious artifacts ensconced in the oilskin wrapping. As soon as Ollafson started to untie the wrapping they all felt the change in temperature. Claire felt the cold air strike her neck and she shivered. Even McDonald looked around for the source of the sudden cold draft. He shook his head and then he too visibly shivered.

As the professor finally exposed the petrified wood to the cabin's weak lighting, they all saw the oil lamp flicker, sputter, and then dim. For a reason Claire would later try to dissect in her thoughts, she glanced into the far corner of the cabin where the captain's sea chest was sitting and she flinched when she saw the shadow between the trunk and the hull expand as if breathing. She closed and opened her eyes quickly only to see bright sunshine where there had been shadow a second before. The bobbing and swaying warship must be playing tricks on her eyes. She looked down at the Angelic script on the ancient wood. For a reason that seemed impossible, the specialist in ancient and dead languages had to turn away. The symbols made her increasingly uncomfortable, and for a woman in her profession, that was not good. She forced her eyes back to the artifact.

"For now, let us concentrate our efforts on these lesser symbols on the second piece." Ollafson removed the uppermost petrified artifact and set a smaller, less significant piece over the first.

Even McDonald felt far better having the Angelic curse out of view. He took a deep breath and was surprised at himself for acting like such a schoolboy with deep and hidden fears. He too glanced into the darker recesses of the cabin and noticed the black shadows had seemed to take on more defined shapes. He made eye contact with Claire as Ollafson's story came slipping into his thoughts. It was as if something were just awakening and taking its first few breaths of the day.

For reasons they could never explain, all three of them inside the cabin that day suddenly felt that death was near—very near.

Gray Dog slowly slid down the rope and landed lightly beside the form of Sergeant Major Dugan. The Irishman turned and looked over at the Comanche.

"Where have you been?"

"Why does John Henry allow this?" Gray Dog asked as he watched the foolishness happening in front of him.

"He has reasoning we barbarians don't see, I guess," Dugan said as he turned toward the smaller man and then winked. "The colonel thinks a little different than most. Differences I can't explain, Coyote Head."

"White men," Gray Dog mumbled, and then turned to face the sergeant major, "are touched by the crazed eye of the sick dog. They have the foaming sickness in their heads."

Gray Dog turned and left the scene. Sergeant Major Dugan spit a stream of tobacco juice over the side as he shook his head. "Damn Indian. 'Spose we do have a few cogs missing off the main assembly. But at least we don't go wearin' dogs as hats."

"Huh?" Jenks said, his eyes riveted on the sheer size of the black mess steward. He swallowed and then realized he had gulped his wad of tobacco and sent it burning its way down into his stomach where it coalesced with the stomach acid churning inside.

"Honor, son. This is for the honor of the regiment," Taylor said, smiling and then looking embarrassingly up at the quarterdeck where Thomas had his eyes glued on the events below.

"To tell you the truth, Colonel, I don't know how honorable it's going to be when I shit my pants in front of all these boys. That is by far the largest nigg—, hell, that boy is the largest anything I ever saw."

Taylor grimaced as he agreed and then gave Jenks a little shove forward. "Damn he is big," Taylor mumbled to himself as he watched the corporal enter the valley of death.

Grandee stood rooted to the spot as his ears heard the curses of the prisoners and the stunted encouragement of the marines who stood around them with hatred spewing from their mouths. Grandee's eyes were actually as wide as his opponent's but for the obvious differences.

Colonel Thomas nodded his head as he looked down at the man he had chosen for this most difficult of tasks: to make the Rebels learn the simple fact that there were no slaves, no South and no North. There was the company of men on the three ships. And he wanted these ships not to be flying any particular flag over the next few weeks and possibly months. He needed one unit of Americans and one only. He had chosen the object of all hatred and frustration to make his point. The large man stepped to the center of the deck to prove men were indeed equal—if not in size, then in honor and bravery.

Taylor stepped up and stood between the two men. He saw

the young marine lieutenant step through the crowd so he could see through the men. Jessy watched as the tall kid from Annapolis patted the mess steward on the back.

"Okay, gentlemen—and I use that term in loosest sense"— the men around him laughed—"let's get to it," Taylor finished as he snapped his hand at the deck and waved the two reluctant antagonists forward.

The war between North and South commenced once more as the three American warships approached Gibraltar.

Ollafson's eyes kept returning to the artifact. As he explained how the naval ordnance men would lay explosives to assist in digging out the Ark if they found it, he kept losing his train of thought. As he looked up at the others in embarrassment, he apologized. However, Ollafson could see that the piece of petrified wood was occupying their minds as well. The professor intentionally covered the piece with another map and immediately felt better for doing so. Claire noticed this.

"The artifact never had this effect on us while we were ensconced inside of a laboratory," she said as she stood from the table. A distant but loud cheer erupted from the main deck as Colonel Thomas continued to commit to the fiasco's possible disastrous ending.

"Yes, for some reason it feels as though the artifact is slowly awakening the closer to our destination we get."

"Come now, we're being a bit overly dramatic here, are we not? It sounds as though you are quoting a god-awful penny dreadful," McDonald said as his eyes were also on the map covering the ancient wood. "I think we had better concentrate on the possibility that if we do find what it is you are looking for, Professor, we may not have the ability to capitalize upon it. For instance, how in the world would we begin to get an artifact that size out of the Ottoman Empire without raising quite the fuss?"

"That particular job, my dear sir, has been delegated to our naval genius, Captain Jackson."

"By the high-handed way in which you speak of him you would think that this man has magical powers of engineering."

"Maybe not a magician, but a man who *is* known as a certified genius thinks he is something very special indeed. Mr. Ericsson believes in him, so therefore, we must have faith the man knows what he is talking about. According to Mr. Lincoln, we are being led by three very bright and distinctive men. Yes, they are having a hard time believing in what it is we seek, but they will seek it nonetheless because that was the order given them. Colonel Thomas, although not a believer in our cause, will do exactly as the president has asked, because that is what he does. Now, we have to discuss the route we must take to the glacier."

The three settled in to examine the route leading to the summit of Ararat. As they did a sea breeze came unbidden through the open hatchway and blew off the map covering the artifact. They felt the ship beneath their feet shake momentarily as if the keel had dragged along the bottom. They exchanged glances as the sun vanished behind a rain-laden cloud. As the shadows dimmed, something in the far corner moved. Three sets of eyes looked in that direction as the wind ceased. The artifact jumped underneath the partially covered wood. The map lifted and then settled, still covering a corner of the petrified wood. None of the Angelic writing was exposed. Then the map started smoldering. The written words seemed to be heating up, but before the three scholars turned back, the smoke had drifted away and the map had settled. The sun broke through the rain cloud once more and the shadows returned, only this time they seemed deeper and darker than before.

Corporal Jenks heard the cheers of the Confederate prisoners as they encouraged him forward. Grandee meekly took a tentative step toward the center of the main deck and waited. His eyes roamed toward the colonel, who was looking down upon them. He again nodded his head. Grandee took the final two steps toward the frightened fighter from the south.

"That is one big son of a bitch," Taylor said to the marine officer, Parnell.

"Yes, I would most assuredly say your man is quite over-matched," Parnell said, hoping beyond hope that the navy mess steward could do the job he was tasked to do. Grandee was not a marine, so Parnell had his doubts. He had volunteered his marines for this stunt, but Thomas had insisted it be Grandee.

Grandee faced down Jenks. The bearded Confederate was wide-eyed as he watched the giant black man raise his equally giant hand. He was shocked when he realized the black man was offering his hand in sportsmanship. With the whites of his eyes showing Jenks turned toward Taylor, who nodded that yes, he should shake the man's hand. When he nodded he raised his brows with a wry smile. Jenks knew his next step.

He took the offered hand and then suddenly pulled the large man forward. The steward's massive bulk leaned in at the same time Jenks hit the giant in the mouth with his left hand. The blow actually staggered Grandee momentarily as the surprise attack caught him unawares. He was shocked. Another blow came in and landed on his right cheek, stunning the mess steward. A loud cheer went up from the circling Confederate prisoners.

"That was rather unethical," Parnell said as he angrily looked over at Taylor, who was smiling as if he had been given the world's best Christmas gift.

"Ethical goes out the window when you're outnumbered, son, you know that," Taylor said, jabbing at the air with his closed fist as he watched another solid blow land on Grandee's nose, causing him to stagger once more.

"It's one against one!" Parnell shouted over the noise of the cheering prisoners, naval personnel, and Marines.

"Precisely," Taylor said, laughing aloud. "Outnumbered!"

Parnell turned back and had to admit that Grandee's size alone made the odds a little long for the Reb fighter.

Grandee stopped the next blow by grabbing Jenks's right fist and holding it in mid-throw. The large man shook his head to clear it, and then he became angry at the sneak attack by the corporal. Grandee brought up his right forearm and pounded Jenks on the back. Every centimeter of air expelled from the smaller man's body as he crumpled to the deck. Before Grandee could take advantage of his blow, Jenks knew he had to think of a better attack. He came up between the steward's legs and drilled him harshly in the testicles. The big man grunted and his hold on Jenks loosened. Jenks did it again, to the moans and groans of those men watching—even the southerners. After all, the man was hit in the true equalizer of all men, white or black.

On the quarterdeck Thomas worried Jenks's blows would take down his man for good. But he saw Grandee shake his head once more and then he roared like a caged animal and grabbed the kneeling man's fist in mid-strike with his massive paw.

"Uh-oh," Jessy said as he saw the demise of his man fast approaching.

Grandee pulled Jenks upright and then held him up by one arm with the frightened Rebel kicking and screaming. For a moment, the men watching thought the steward was going to just toss the Confederate overboard, but instead he slung the man like a paper doll into the crowd of cheering men. Jenks landed between four marines who laughed and called for his quick surrender. This infuriated Corporal Jenks, who was hefted to his feet by the very marines who were laughing at him. He quickly turned and hit the face closest to him. The marine went flying backward into several Rebel soldiers, who were now afraid of their man's eminent loss. They turned angrily toward the one man who had slammed into them. One of the angry Rebs then struck the fallen man in the nose. This action brought more marines forward as the Rebel prisoners simultaneously did the same.

Jenks was just about to throttle a second marine when a giant hand stopped him once more. Grandee was at him again as the marines and the prisoners started to exchange serious blows.

On the quarterdeck John Henry Thomas smiled.

Captain Jackson gestured for the marines in the rigging and the guards along the rail to be ready. "I knew this would happen." He looked over at the smiling John Henry and was confused by his utter lack of worry about what was taking place onboard his ship.

"When you are trying to make a sculpture, you start out by kneading your clay mercilessly."

"What in the hell does that mean?" Jackson said, astonished at Thomas's utter lack of concern.

Thomas just smiled wider as the brawl below was turning into a full-scale riot.

"This is enough! I'm going to stop this."

"You will do no such thing, Captain. You let this play out."

No one saw Gray Dog as he slipped from the high rigging, slid down an exposed rope, and then disappeared into the bowels of the *Yorktown*.

"You men, stop that!" Parnell yelled at his men as they were quickly losing control. They outnumbered the Rebel prisoners, but the worn and tired men were giving his fresh troops all the fight they could handle. He had to stop this before it got out of control. As he stepped forward, a tired-looking old man he recognized as one of the Confederate cooks from Taylor's division smiled up at him. As he was about to order the gray-bearded old fool out of his way, the old man reached up and clocked the lieutenant right in the mouth. He fell backward into Taylor's arms. His hat went flying free as Taylor pushed him forward.

"For right now, you better worry about your own front, Lieutenant!" Taylor said, trying to control his laughter.

Parnell quickly recovered and was about to turn on Taylor when he saw the small, old man approach with his fists raised.

"Now you halt right there, soldier! I am an officer in the United States—" *Boom*, he was struck again in the nose, and he staggered backward once more only to be caught again by a furiously laughing Colonel Taylor. The man and his men had lost all control at this point. He again pushed Parnell forward. This time the marine lieutenant turned quickly and before the roaring Taylor could react, Parnell punched him right in the nose. The lieutenant laughed himself and then put his fists up in a prize-fighter stance. Taylor held his bleeding nose and then broke out laughing as the old man had recovered and jumped on the lieutenant's back. The two twirled off into the melee taking place in the center of the main deck.

Thomas outwardly laughed as he watched the fights below. Men were taking out the frustrations of a war that had sapped all of their will power to ever laugh or be friendly to men different than themselves ever again. He watched the men actually smile as they were struck and struck hard by the marines, who were watching their hard-earned brawling reputation go down the drain pipe as the Rebel prisoners were more than holding their own.

The gunshot froze every man in place as they thought the marine guard had opened fire on them. Grandee, who had lifted Jenks over his head, turned and saw Colonel Thomas holster his smoking Colt revolver. Grandee let the beaten Jenks slip through his hands and land hard on the deck. When the large black man saw what he had done he quickly reached down and helped the stunned Rebel to his feet. He brushed at him as the other men, marines, sailors, and prisoners alike, started to return to their senses. There were some cuts, bruises, and missing teeth, but otherwise no serious injuries. Thomas looked at Taylor as he picked himself up from the deck. He wiped blood from his nose and then looked up at John Henry.

"At ease," Thomas said, as the naval officer Jackson watched this very confusing army officer and his strange methods. He slowly started to realize that Thomas had taken a shortcut as far as getting the men to become comrades rather than continuing enemies. He also realized that John Henry had taken a chance on his prank failing and seeing the prisoners cut down by the marine guard if the fight had gotten serious.

"Feel better?" John Henry asked as he watched the embarrassed marines starting to realize they'd had their hands full defending themselves. Respect for the weakened prisoners had sprouted in just the past three minutes—just as Thomas had hoped. "Okay, every man is to clean himself up and then get below. Prisoners are not to be shackled, and have the full privileges of the ship. Lieutenant Parnell?"

Parnell wiped the last of the blood from his nose, recovered his hat from underneath the boot of a Rebel, and then came to attention, expecting Thomas to ream him a new ass for fighting with the prisoners.

"Sir!" he said as his polished heels came together. Taylor smiled and then looked from the frightened marine officer to his old friend.

"I want new hammock assignments for all Confederate and marines. They are to be placed in together, and physical training is to commence in the A.M. with mixed troops. Is that clear?"

"No, sir, it is not," Parnell said, still at attention.

"Lieutenant, I want a mixed command. These men have now fought alongside each other, against each other, and I am here to tell you they are all lacking in the arena of defending themselves, even the marines. A new roster, Lieutenant. Now do you understand?"

Parnell finally relaxed and then looked at Thomas. "Not at all, Colonel."

Thomas looked frustrated. "Let me explain," he said as he stepped up to the set of stairs leading to the quarterdeck. "Colonel Taylor, join me please."

Jessy smiled, wiped his nose once again, swiped it on his civilian clothes, and then stepped forward, climbing the six steps slowly, watching John Henry the entire time.

"The object of this exercise, gentlemen, was to get out some of that animosity you have stored up for each other. Like this." Just as Taylor hit the top step, Colonel John Henry Thomas punched him right in the jaw, sending the colonel flying out and off the quarterdeck and into the arms of a stunned Parnell and several Rebel soldiers who were just as shocked as the marine lieutenant. Thomas shook his hand in pain. "You see, now my frustrations have been relieved and my animosity has magically vanished." Thomas took the steps quickly and then assisted Taylor from the arms of the men who had kept him from hitting the deck.

"That was for the night you broke your word to me, Jessy. Don't ever do it again," Thomas said so that Taylor was the only one to hear.

"Next time let me in on the plan," Taylor said and then stopped suddenly. "And by the way, John Henry, you're right about one thing—frustration, animosity, it does get to you." He turned and faced the colonel.

"Your point, Jessy?"

"This." The punch caught the colonel totally unaware. The blow sent Thomas spinning until he was finally caught by a smiling Sergeant Major Dugan and held in place as John Henry wiped his own nose free of the blood he had just spilled. "That was for my sister." Taylor tuned and walked away.

"Goes to show you, Colonel Darlin', never give a Reb an inch or he'll end up taking a mile."

"Oh, you're just full of great offerings, aren't you?"

Dugan straightened the colonel and made sure he was stable and then he smiled.

"I try to be, boyo, I try."

Gray Dog had been in the ship's high rigging watching what he considered even more white-man insanity as the fight was about to start below. Suddenly the Comanche looked from the scene below to the stern of the ship. He didn't know what had attracted his attention but a chill coursed through his bronzed skin as if a sudden cold snap had surrounded the *Yorktown*. The wind was strong enough that the nine enormous sails were full and billowing. Gray Dog knew the chill had not come from the weather. His eyes remained fixed on the stern of the ship. There was something either on deck or just below, he could not figure which.

Just as Taylor had stepped to the center of the mob below, Gray Dog silently slid down a rope and onto the ship's railing, startling a marine guard who gave the strangely dressed Indian a wary look. Gray Dog went below, hesitantly at first because he didn't like the confinement of the interior nor its varied navy smells, usually preferring clean air to breathe.

He never would understand how men could live like this. He slowly eased himself down the steps and into the semi-darkness as the fight erupted on deck. He didn't notice the shouts and the yells as his eyes adjusted to the blackness that accompanied his initial steps inside.

He looked to the stern and saw the passageway that led to the captain's quarters, and he even saw shadows of movement inside and suspected it was Ollafson and the woman, Claire. He heard a noise and the door opened and the small man, Cromwell, stepped from the cabin. Gray Dog stepped farther back into the shadows as he watched. Cromwell closed the door and then stood rooted to the spot for a moment, and then Gray Dog saw him lean over and listen at the door. The man then straightened and rummaged into his coat pocket and brought out what looked like a hand mirror. Gray Dog's eyes narrowed as he watched the man move toward the stern staircase heading for the aft quarterdeck. Gray Dog was curious if this was why his senses had told him to come below. He started to follow and then suddenly felt a change come over the companionway. He stepped back and watched as the shadows near the door to the cabin seemed to expand as if the sun—if there had been sunlight inside the bowels of the ship—had very quickly changed positions in the sky. It was like a deep breath was taken by the darker elements of the ship's construction.

Gray Dog heard the fight above and the cheers and jeers of the men watching. The thump of footsteps echoed through the teak decking of the warship. He saw something slip out from under the cabin door. He blinked as he thought he was seeing things, and then he froze as he felt deep, penetrating cold through his purple shirt and even through the bone-and-feather chest plate he wore at all times. He felt the sensation leave his body almost as if it had never been there at all. He closed his eyes, not knowing why he felt such relief in feeling the overheated interior of the ship once again. His eyes went to the bow of the vessel and knew that whatever force he had felt had gone in that direction. As his eyes probed the darkness ahead he saw another shadow expand, shrink, and then break free of the hull and vanish forward like a small dark thunderhead vanishing over the horizon. Gray Dog followed the strangest trail he had ever tracked.

Above deck, the two forces of men came together with a crash. Gray Dog came to the hatchway that led to the third deck, a section of the ship into which he had never ventured. He looked around one last time at the battle stations of the *Yorktown*, whose thirty-two cannon lay silent but still deadly looking. He decided he had to know what the movement of shadow meant. He started down the steps and into the total blackness below.

As he placed his moccasined feet on the third deck he felt the change come again. Suddenly the crowded warship was a menace, and for the life of him Gray Dog could not understand why. He sensed his answer was forward. He moved slowly until he saw a small porthole that allowed light to filter through to illuminate a certain area. He realized where he was as he stopped by a large barrel of flour that was strapped down to the decking. He watched as the weakened light slightly illuminated the small brig that was an even smaller joke on the *Yorktown*. The man inside, Gray Dog remembered, was the Rebel almost hanged four days before, Corporal Loudermilk. Even his own confederates had turned on him and the two men next to him in the small cell.

The two younger boys were sitting on two rolled-up blankets in the corner. One of them was rocking back and forth silently. Loudermilk was cursing at the boy to stop what he was doing, saying that if he had chosen better partners in crime they wouldn't be sitting there.

Gray Dog watched the three men and still saw nothing unusual. He was starting to think the ocean was beginning to affect his mind, so he shook his head and slowly started to back away from the brig and its very unhappy occupants.

Suddenly and without warning the shadow that was cast through the single, open porthole jumped and then spread until it entered the cell, where it seemed to blend in with the dark silhouette of the silently rocking private. Gray Dog watched as the boy stopped rocking back and forth and his head slowly rose from where it had lain on his knees. His eyes went to Loudermilk, who was occupying the only bunk in the brig. The man was still cursing his luck at his companionship in crime when the private slowly stood. The air became cold as the darkness enclosed the small space as if the shadows were sucking away the sunlight and its heat from the small porthole. Gray Dog took an involuntary step backward and was stopped by the flour barrels. He saw the strange way the boy was standing and just staring at the criminal Loudermilk. The second private saw this and stood and tried to get the boy to sit once more.

Gray Dog was confused as to what he was seeing, but he knew that a change had suddenly come over the boy as he stood with chin on chest as he stared at the man still cursing him. Suddenly Gray Dog was sure he saw a darker outline as if a shadow had attached itself to the boy. It was almost like a shimmering river at night with moonlight reflecting off its surface. The boy threw off the hands of the second private and then moved like a wild cat after its prey.

Gray Dog stumbled backward but the noise of him falling over the barrels and onto the deck went unnoticed. The boy flew through the small space between the two men and landed full force onto the reclining Loudermilk, who could only lose his breath at the impact. The Comanche was frightened for the first time since his family had been slaughtered by the Naches River many years before. He saw the boy's face descend onto the bearded Loudermilk's and the man's screams were suddenly muffled as the boy began to use his teeth. The pain the attempted rapist was suffering must have been unbelievable as the private dug his teeth deep into the man's face, lips, and mouth. His screams produced a fine spray of blood as the boy continued to chew at every exposed piece of skin his teeth could find. Loudermilk was kicking out with his stocking feet but the boy could not be shaken off. The third prisoner stood by in shock as blood started to splatter his face.

Gray Dog tried to stand and do something, but every time he moved it seemed his legs weakened and he slipped back down to the deck. Still the corporal screamed as he moved his head from side to side trying desperately to dislodge his attacker.

Then the screams stopped as the private finally found the throat. The teeth sunk deep and Loudermilk's legs went straight out from the cot as his carotid artery was severed by the private's canines. The boy tore at the corporal like a crazed dog that had finally gotten the upper hand on its prey. He shook the lifeless body of Corporal Loudermilk like a rag doll. Without notice the boy stopped. Gray Dog saw the deep breathing of the private as he spit out most of the Adam's apple of the Rebel rapist. Still heaving for breath, the boy's head slowly turned toward Gray Dog. The smile was terrifying and something that would haunt the Comanche for the rest of his days. The eyes were illuminated with an internal light as the grin widened and more of Loudermilk's skin fell free of the kid's mouth.

Gray Dog started to backpedal until he could back away no farther as the boy slowly rose from the cot and then made a lunge at the strap-metal bars of his cage. As he passed the third man he simply reached out and twisted the poor man's neck until the spine snapped. It all took place in less than three seconds. Gray Dog leaned as far back as he could as the boy finished by smashing his face and head into the eight-inch space between the bars. Blood flew from the severe gashes on the prisoner's face as his head actually broke through.

Gray Dog knew he was witnessing something that originated inside the captain's cabin. He had tracked it to this spot and now he was seeing what he was meant to see.

The boy backed away again with his forehead skin hanging free of his scalp. He smiled wider, exposing his teeth, which still held the remnants of Corporal Loudermilk's throat. He suddenly charged again, and this time the head went completely through the impossibly small space between the bars. The crazed boy screamed and then started twisting his head and neck. As the Comanche watched in horror he knew he wasn't trying to free his head; he was twisting it in an attempt to snap his own neck. The next sound Gray Dog heard was the boy's bones snapping like dry twigs. The severely injured private went rigid momentarily and then limp as the body started to sag, and then the neck completely separated from the rest of the boy's body. The skin seemed to separate like cloth being pulled apart. The head tore free and the body fell to the deck. The private's head remained wedged in the bars.

Gray Dog felt the warm blood on his face and then as he stared wide-eyed at the scene he felt the warmth come back into the confined space as the sun once more made an appearance in the porthole.

The only thing Gray Dog could do was run.

The men sat around the main deck tending to broken noses, missing teeth, and bruised egos when all eyes went to Corporal Jenks as he sat near the starboard railing. The man had acquitted himself admirably against the giant mess steward, but every man could see he was in no shape to feel superior about anything. He actually looked angry. Then all went silent as Jenks stood and walked over to the opposite railing where Grandee was tending to another cook's wounds. The black man stopped what he was doing as he saw the Rebel prisoner approach. He tensed for a continuation of the brawl. His eyes went to where the colonel had been but the space was empty. He was on his own.

Jenks stopped in front of the big man and the marine guard tensed. They slowly raised their rifles and watched. Jenks spit out a stream of blood and then glanced up and into the mess steward's face.

"I want you to know, boy, you broke my doze."

"What?" Grandee asked.

"You . . . broke . . . my . . . d . . . d . . . d'nose."

The hand came up so fast the men standing nearby actually flinched, thinking the two men were going to start a second round of fisticuffs. But the hand remained motionless in front of Grandee. The large black mess steward slowly raised his ham-sized fist and took the corporal's peace offering. The cheer was sudden and immediate from the prisoners and naval personnel watching.

Then a man yelled and then another. A path cleared through the men as Gray Dog shot up the companionway and without any word quickly scrambled up the rigging and vanished among billowing sails. All eyes went to the bloody footprints that Gray Dog had left behind.

"Murder! There's been murder done here!" came a shout.

The men on deck were stunned as one of the Confederate prisoners came on deck and shouted out the words that froze the hearts of every man.

"Loudermilk, Kindelay, and Segue have been butchered in their cell by Thomas's pet redskin!"

Suddenly the men on deck faced each other once more as blood started running just as high and hot as it had been before John Henry Thomas's wonderful unification plan.

Confederate, marine, and naval personnel faced each other and the hate that had vanished only moments before was back at full strength. Even Grandee and Jenks separated and angrily broke the friendly handshake.

The war was still present, but the real enemy was hidden in the shadows. As the angry men started shouting and cursing, the man posing as Cromwell stepped to the stern of the *Yorktown* and removed a small pocket mirror from his jacket. He looked up and found the sun and started flashing his message into the clear afternoon sky toward distant eyes.

11

John Henry had to physically push his way through the angry prisoners to get to the small brig. He made eye contact with the sergeant major and the unsaid words were unmistakable—clear this area.

"All right, lads, let's clear the area for the officers. Come on, we've all seen dead men before this," he said as he started to guide the shocked men out of the confined space.

"Yeah, we've seen dead men a' plenty, but not murder, and killin' this way ain't normal," a man said as Dugan shoved him from the crowded space.

Thomas walked up and looked at the torn face of the boy and then his eyes went to Corporal Loudermilk on his cot. The man looked as if he had been chewed to death. As for the boy, his injuries were almost as horrid. His ears were gone, having been scraped free of the scalp when the kid had shoved his head through the iron bars. His body hung limp as the bars kept the thin body from collapsing to the deck. The third lay with his back to the deck above, but his head was also looking in the same direction.

"It was that damn savage, we all seen it," a man said as he

finally pushed through the opening and into the next compartment. "Get that redskin and you'll have those boys' killers."

Dugan turned and looked at the colonel as Jessy Taylor finally entered the brig area. His eyes widened when he saw what had been done to his men. He angrily turned to Thomas.

"You saved them for this? Is this the example you wanted to make?"

John Henry didn't answer. He was looking at the way in which these three men had met their brutal fate.

"I'm afraid if you want answers as to who did this, you won't get them from the responsible party."

"What in the hell does that mean?" Taylor said turning on the colonel.

Thomas walked up and lightly raised the tow-headed hair of the boy and then he gently let it back down. "The meaning is, Colonel, your man Loudermilk was killed by this boy. You can see the corporal's blood around his mouth. It's clear to me that after he tore the corporal's throat out, he snapped the neck of this one and then he struck the bars until he killed himself."

"My God."

John Henry turned and saw they had been joined by Captain Jackson. He was visibly shaken at the gruesome scene before him. He removed a kerchief and covered his nose and mouth. The smell was atrocious as the dead men had voided themselves when they had died.

"The men say it was your Indian. They say he was covered in blood when he came from below. Where is he?"

John Henry turned on Taylor. "If you think Gray Dog is responsible for this, you are not as smart as I thought you were, Jessy. Comanche warriors don't kill like this. Blood obviously sprayed him from inside the cell. We won't know until I speak with the boy."

"I've seen what the Comanche or any other Indians are capable of firsthand. I saw what they did to my sister, so don't stand there and tell me they're not capable of it."

Thomas felt his blood start to rise. "You're missing one major point here."

Taylor didn't respond, his eyes on the seventeen-year-old boy he had barely known.

"The Comanche, hell, even the Kiowa need a reason for something like this, and Gray Dog has no reason to kill anyone—yet. And as far as the death of my wife is concerned, Colonel, I have told you a hundred times, it was Kiowa, not Comanche, and the same Kiowa responsible for Mary's death were responsible for Gray Dog's family being wiped out. The boy didn't do this."

"Well, if he didn't, he may know who did," Jackson said as he finally lowered the kerchief and managed a breath. "May I suggest we bring your man inside before he finds the same justice these men have found?" He nodded at the three dead men in the cell.

Thomas turned to Dugan. "Get Gray Dog. If anyone interferes before you find him, shoot them."

"Is he under arrest, Colonel?" Dugan asked. He was expecting to feel no sorrow for the Comanche, but like Thomas, he knew Gray Dog was not capable of killing this way. The Comanche were efficient killers, no doubt, but they needed reasons for being the barbaric savages the eastern press made them out to be. He knew they killed like this to make a point, but Gray Dog didn't have any points to make. Dugan headed out as he pulled the army Colt from its holster.

Dugan vanished just as Claire and Professor Ollafson half-stumbled into the room.

"Oh, my God," Claire said as she immediately turned away from the scene before her. It was Captain Jackson who took hold of the woman and started to guide her from the brig area.

"Get the hell out of here," Thomas said, his voice harsh. He angrily looked at Ollafson. "You too, out."

"My God, this is exactly the way my friends were killed on our last expedition," Ollafson said as he too was corralled by Jackson and pointed toward the exit.

"What's that?" Taylor asked, shelving his anger for the moment. Before Ollafson could answer they heard the men above shouting murderous epithets as Dugan must have been leading Gray Dog down from the rigging.

"My friends—they were torn apart in just this manner," Ollafson said as Jackson released him and he and Claire turned back to the murder scene.

John Henry was silent as he absorbed in the professor's words. He had heard them before, but had taken the story with the proverbial grain of salt. Ollafson had explained to him and the president that his team had been hunted down and killed over the four hundred miles of their return trek from Ararat. Thomas had seen how frightened witnesses were capable of misinterpreting the way in which men had died. Death in a situation such as that can be the most confusing thing in the world, so he figured that the professor's frightened mind missed the clues that would have told him just who their true killers were—he would miss no such sign.

As they turned and examined the cell once more, Claire shook her head as she realized these men had died only two hundred and fifty feet from where they had been examining the artifacts inside the captain's cabin. Her thoughts went to Cromwell.

"You may want to speak with our Mr. Cromwell, Colonel. He wasn't present at our meeting and could have seen something when he left. The time he left the cabin and the time these men died cannot be ignored," Claire said, not really knowing why. She despised the Frenchman so much for the callous way he did his job that she could not let him get away with this if he was responsible.

"Then we'll just have to have a little talk with Mr. Cromwell."

"You can talk now, gentlemen," said a voice from the stairs above. "As you can see, my clothing is rather pristine, with the exception of sweat, but I'm sure I can be forgiven for that. On the other hand"—he stepped aside as Sergeant Major Dugan led Gray Dog through the opening—"this man seems to be covered in what would be known as evidence."

Thomas eyed the man calling himself Cromwell and took his points to heart. "Thank you. We'll talk later." He turned to Gray Dog and Dugan. The Comanche was splattered with the blood of the murdered men.

"What happened?" John Henry asked as Gray Dog's eyes were on the three bodies illuminated in several oil lamps. They didn't waver even when John Henry stepped into his line of vision. "Gray Dog, report!"

The tone brought the eyes of the Comanche up. Thomas could see that the boy's facial features were nearly void of blood splatter. This meant that the Indian had not been the killer. John Henry could plainly see that Gray Dog had been hit by flying blood and not a soaking that would have occured if he had been inside the brig. Taylor was examining the boy as well as Thomas and was fast coming to the same conclusion. John Henry took Gray Dog's hands and looked them over. Other than calluses and dirt, they were clean.

Gray Dog finally moved his eyes to those of Thomas.

"Did you see who did this?" John Henry asked as Dugan placed the pistol back in its holster.

Gray Dog didn't answer, his eyes glancing from the colonel's to the staring faces of Claire and Ollafson. They both became uneasy when his dark eyes fell on them.

"They know," Gray Dog said as he shook off the hand of Dugan and then, with a look at Taylor and Thomas, Gray Dog moved away and into the shadows of the ship.

"What in the hell does that mean?" Taylor asked, but not before the Indian had vanished. "Is that it? That is all the questioning you're going to do?" Taylor was so angry his eyes were wide and his face red.

"As I said, Gray Dog didn't do this," Thomas said as he turned to face Ollafson. "Now, what do you suppose he meant by that?"

"I have no idea, Colonel. We did nothing but discuss our route to the mountain. That is all, I swear," Claire said.

"We examined the artifacts, I'm afraid." Ollafson was staring at the hull and his eyes didn't move. Claire got a cold chill when she realized Ollafson was right, they had been examining the Angelic Script on the petrified wood.

"Not the curse again?" Thomas said, getting angry that

these people could still advance outlandish speculation about what they were facing. In John Henry's experience they didn't need a curse to help with killing their fellow man; they could handle that aspect rather well. No, they didn't have a curse on their hands, but they did have someone who was pretty well motivated to throw a crimp in their mission plans.

Before Ollafson could once more try to defend his position, a signalman walked in and handed Jackson a message. "Gentlemen," he turned to face Claire, "and lady, we'll have to postpone this debate about murder and curses. I'm afraid our rendezvous point is upon us. The *Carpenter*, the *Chesapeake*, and the *Argo* are here."

"Does that mean—" Ollafson started to ask excitedly.

"Yes, Professor, we are five miles off Gibraltar. When the U.S. Navy says it will get you there, we get you there." Jackson turned to face Thomas. "Captain Abernathy has signaled that they have had quite a time keeping *Argo* afloat," he said in a low tone as the others made their way out of the blood-splattered brig area. "The crewmen have been working every hour to keep the damn thing from foundering. What we have hidden inside that barge is just too damn heavy."

"We may have to make other plans if *Argo* sinks before we need her," Thomas said worriedly.

"The plan is, we don't have a chance of escaping the European powers if they wanted to stop us, and they will when they find out why we are really here. Without the *Argo* we'll be blown clear out of the water, and not one witness will be alive to say what happened. We are far from home waters, Colonel."

"Where did all of that United States Navy bravado vanish to?" Taylor asked, breaking into the conversation.

"The confidence I have shown thus far only stems from my meticulous planning. If *Argo* is lost I am realist enough to know we don't stand a chance of getting out of these waters, much less a confined area like the Aegean or the Bosphorus Strait. I know my business, sir, and we need *Argo*."

"How is the crew of the *Chesapeake* taking the workload?"

"Well, I suspect that Captain Abernathy will request more men. He says the band is near exhaustion. It seems the boys with the drums and trumpets aren't used to physical labor all that much." Thomas saw Jackson smile for the first time since he had met the arrogant naval officer. "I will accede to his wishes when we meet in an hour. After all, now may be a good time to start separating the prisoners and dispersing them to the other ships."

"No. Transfer marine or naval personnel, but I want the prisoners kept together for the time being."

"All the rotten eggs in one basket?" Taylor asked without the wry smile this time.

John Henry paused as he reached the steps.

"Something like that. And keep this in mind—from this moment forward and until this mission is either complete or we are stopped, the captain here has orders to scuttle this ship with everyone on it if you don't keep your word."

Taylor watched the room empty and then he turned to the dead men inside the brig. His eyes wandered to the deck and then the lock on the door of the cell. It was still secured.

"Maybe it would be a good idea to sink this death ship right now."

Jessy Taylor looked one last time at his butchered men and in his mind he kept hearing the words of Ollafson about what had killed his friends. He wondered if John Henry Thomas knew exactly what they were in for.

Above decks and in the clear afternoon air, the three American warships and one tow barge were meeting for the last time on the high seas before entering the Mediterranean.

It took three hours for Captain Abernathy and the *Chesapeake*'s Captain Mize to be transferred over to the *Yorktown*. The commander of the *Argo* had begged off the meeting because they were still bailing water from the bilges of the supply barge. Any instruction from John Henry would be passed on to Captain Faraday, the commander of *Argo,* by the *Chesapeake*'s crew.

The captain's quarters filled to capacity as the team sat down for their first face-to-face meeting with all parties involved. Colonel Thomas was about to unveil his plans, with the exception of the exact role to played out by the *Argo*, the details of which would remain with Thomas and Captain Jackson.

The late lunch provided by the mess crew had been an exceptional meal. Captains Abernathy and Faraday had eaten with abandon as the cooks onboard their ships were nowhere near as good as the mess crew on the *Yorktown*. The large steward Grandee was complimented no less than four times by the visiting captains during the meal, with a wary eye toward the swelling on the large man's features. No questions were asked and no explanations were offered. The two captains had noticed that no one, with the exception of the army sergeant major, touched their food. As a matter of fact, most looked like they had just come off a bad bout of seasickness before the lunch had commenced. They also noticed the strange sight of the Indian as he sat in the far corner. Gray Dog had been cleaned up, and John Henry wanted to keep him close to either himself or Dugan for the duration of the voyage.

The plates were cleared and then John Henry nodded in the direction of Professor Ollafson. He rose and brought up his satchel and instead of bringing out the petrified artifacts, he removed three large drawings. He looked up at Commander Jackson.

"I had the engineering department at Harvard Yard make these up. They are drawn from memory, so please forgive any shortcomings." He spread the three large diagrams on the table as John Henry leaned over and used the candle on the table to light a cigar. His eyes met those of Claire Richelieu as she listened to Ollafson. For some reason the look from the ancient-languages woman made Thomas feel uncomfortable.

"Gentlemen, I give you the Ark."

Everyone at the table with the exception of Colonel Taylor leaned forward to see the drawing. Taylor, on the other hand, rose and moved to the credenza, removed a cigar from the humidor, struck a match, and puffed the cigar to life. He looked at the glowing end momentarily and then walked to the large windows at the stern and looked out upon the sea.

John Henry watched Taylor and then his eyes returned to the table. The drawing depicted what looked like the bow of a ship protruding from ice. From what he could see, the Ark had just about fifty or sixty feet of exposed timbers showing as the great vessel angled sharply from the frozen glazier it had rested in for what the Bible said was at least five thousand years. Ollafson claimed the ship to be very much older than even the Bible's estimate.

"The problem, as I see it—not that just climbing to the summit will be an easy feat—is freeing the Ark from the ice without destroying it." Ollafson looked up at Jackson. "I gave the captain estimates of size and weight before we left Baltimore. Captain?"

Jackson cleared his throat and then stood. He pointed to the glacier in which the Ark was buried. "If these are the correct dimensions of the . . . the . . . ship"—he looked embarrassed to call the object what Ollafson had—"the danger will be in placing the explosives in the right position to free the . . . boat without breaking its back. The forces involved have never been tested in freeing petrified wood. In this case we'll just call it stone, because stone, of course, is very fragile when subjected to explosives."

"Can you free it?" Thomas asked as he leaned forward and jabbed at the diagram.

"My naval engineer says yes, but he cannot guarantee that a salvage operation will be one hundred percent viable."

"Which means he believes the Ark will break if moved at all."

The young Jackson looked up at Thomas, who had already leaned back and was puffing on his cigar.

"To make the meeting as brief as possible, yes, Colonel, the Ark will break. There is no way we can stop that unless you have a way of melting an entire glacier to get at it."

"Understood. We simply bring back what we can; the rest we leave."

"Gentlemen, please, we have to return as much of the find back to American shores as we can. There is too much we can learn from this to leave anything behind."

Thomas ignored Ollafson's concern and then turned back to Jackson.

"Are Captains Faraday and Mize clear on the rendezvous plan after we have what we came for?"

"Yes, they have their orders. I must say I would prefer to have the barge and the *Argo* in the Mediterranean rather than the Black Sea; we will need her there. That is my opinion."

Thomas held the cigar and then slowly stood and paced to the same window where Taylor was looking out.

Jessy looked from the calm sea and faced Thomas, and then he turned with a sour look on his face and returned to the table.

"My fears do not lie in the Mediterranean, nor even the Bosphorus Strait, Captain. I believe any action by any power will be taken outside the line of vision of prying eyes. No, they'll ambush us before we reach the strait in the Black Sea. There are no witnesses there."

"As you wish," Jackson said with a resigned shake of his head.

"Now," John Henry turned back to the table and leaned on its surface. "Colonel Taylor will be issued a Union officer's uniform for our meeting with the sultan. Miss Richelieu will accompany us, along with Captain Jackson. Once the official greeting is concluded we will continue east from Constantinople to the final stop on the line. Is that clear?"

Most nodded.

"Captains, you will take the *Chesapeake* and the *Carpenter* through the Bosphorus Strait and then into the Black Sea with *Argo*. Then you will discharge your land element and railroad equipment at the coastal town of Trabzon. They will take the seacoast railroad line as far as it goes, where Lieutenant Parnell will be waiting to take overall command of land forces. From there my team will be less than fifty-six miles to the slopes of Ararat. Once we meet up we will begin the ascent to the summit with Parnell left behind to make ready for when we may need him and the . . . other elements."

"May I ask why I am to be included in this meeting with the Sultan of the Ottoman Empire?" Taylor asked as he smoked his cigar.

"It is for the simple reason that I can't trust you, Colonel Taylor. Any attempt to get word to the sultan or any other entity will result in the mission failing and your men trading one prison cell for another. Only this one is inside a country that is a little less forgiving than your own."

"You mean *your* country."

"Correct, mine. So I suggest you be on your best behavior, because from what I understand from the president, we will be dealing with a loose cannon in the sultan. I understand he is quite insane."

John Henry didn't respond. He turned and walked to the large windows at the bow, opened one, and then tossed the cigar out. He turned and faced the men and one woman in front of him.

"When do you plan to enter the Mediterranean, Captain?"

"We are expecting heavy fog tonight. They know we're here, but they don't have to know when we enter the Med. We should be in Constantinople before they can muster their trailing vessels, whether that be British or French. I suspect we have both hiding in our wakes."

"Very good. The more time you can give us, the more this little ruse is apt to work."

"Before we adjourn the meeting, Captain Faraday has something he wishes to share."

All eyes went to Faraday. The officer was even more youthful than his commander. The boy stood and faced Thomas.

"At 1310 hours this afternoon, our lookouts aboard the *Chesapeake* observed a signal light, most likely a mirror communication, emanating from the decks of *Yorktown*. The message sent was simple: *'Proceeding through Pillars, destination—Constantinople.'* Of course, this message was not flashed to us, or the *Carpenter*. It was flashed to the French warship a mile astern of us."

"What does this mean?" Ollafson asked as he realized they might have a person or persons onboard who meant to stop them from getting to their destination.

"It means that the security your great leader was hoping for has been compromised." Every face turned to Taylor, who was smirking and smoking his cigar.

"The message clearly stated that we would be moving through the Pillars of Hercules tonight. The Strait of Gibraltar is tight. If they want, all they have to do is string a line of ships across the strait and we won't be able to transit. Illegal, but at this point, who would care? We would have to wait and return home to even file an official protest," Jackson said as he looked worriedly at Thomas. "Unless, of course, you order us to open the strait by force, which would end the mission as assuredly as if we sank on the way here."

"No, but we can and will take care of the situation with our signalman. Sergeant Major Dugan, if you would, please."

They saw Dugan remove the Colt revolver from its holster once more and then he moved quickly to the side of the historian, Cromwell. He smiled as he reached into the man's inside coat pocket and removed a small mirror.

"You really should have chucked this into the sea after you used it," Dugan said as he threw the mirror onto the tabletop, where it broke into four pieces.

Cromwell looked ashen. When he spoke, the first traces of his true language shone through for the briefest of moments.

"I am to be condemned for carrying a mirror?"

Thomas smiled for the first time in hours. "Not at all, Mr. Renaud. You'll be convicted of being the French spy you are, not because of your small mirror."

Everyone at the table was flabbergasted. The man calling himself Cromwell stood suddenly and started to turn for the stairwell but was stopped by the pointed pistol of Dugan.

"You think very little of our own military intelligence, Mr. Renaud, or if you prefer, Mr. Cromwell. We knew who you were an hour after you reported to Professor Ollafson. The president's man, Mr. Allan Pinkerton, is quite aware of those men and women in Washington who intend us harm. Since you started to run from this cabin you must have had an escape plan. I will assist you in that. Sergeant Major, is the boat ready?"

"It is indeed, Colonel Darlin'."

"Escort our French friend here to the deck, please. Assist in his boarding."

"You barbarians cannot do this," Renaud said as Dugan took him by the arm.

Claire swallowed as she watched the French master spy being led by Dugan to the deck above. She then looked at Thomas who was staring straight at her. He finally broke eye contact and faced Jackson.

"Are you sure the French warship will pick him up?"

"Not at all sure," Jackson said with a wry smile.

"Good."

"Oh, that is precious. Can we all expect the same when and if we fail?" Taylor said as he smashed out the cigar in an ashtray.

"You bet, Colonel, because if we fail there will be no lifeboat to be placed into." Jackson thought a moment and then faced Taylor. "We can't execute him, sir. We are not at war. Although I admit that it would have been much simpler, it also would have spared my vessel a precious lifeboat."

The cabin fell silent as they heard the Frenchman scream a mighty stream of epithets from the main deck as Dugan rushed him over the side, to the astonishment of every sailor manning his station. As the sailors, marines, and Reb prisoners saw Dugan smiling at the spy's splashing as he swam toward the lone lifeboat awaiting him, they started doing their duties with a little more enthusiasm. If that was the way they were going to treat shirkers, they wanted no part in the disciplinary measures put forth by the crazed army colonel.

As the French spy pulled himself aboard the well-supplied whaleboat, he cursed the men watching him from the deck of the *Yorktown*. If he had his say, every one of them would be lying at the bottom of the sea very soon.

As he fumed, the three American warships, with the *Argo* in tow, made their way to the Strait of Gibraltar and the waiting Royal Navy of Her Royal Majesty, Victoria.

12

The fog had indeed closed in just as Captain Jackson had predicted. Thus far John Henry had to admit that the Swede John Ericsson's choice of wunderkind had been a good one. The man was just too silent and contemplative for Thomas's taste. Of course he also knew that his way of command was a far cry from the army's more tempered version of how to lead men. Yes, he was positive that Jackson and the others thought him particularly strange also.

"Three bells sounding from astern," came the call from the crow's nest high above the main deck.

"Damn," Jackson said as he turned to face the stern of the *Yorktown*. John Henry remained silent as he listened to the suddenly quiet night around them. The fog had deafened the night, and after the noise of the day it seemed eerily like a cemetery. "The frigates behind our formation weren't fooled. They're hot on our rudder. Three bells was the *Chesapeake*'s signal."

"I suspect either the British or the French have recovered Mr. Renaud."

Jackson spared John Henry a look that the colonel knew indicated his disapproval of John Henry's methods.

"Well, I admit we would not have delayed them long. It was worth a try. If you'll excuse me, I must keep a close eye out as we near the center of the strait." Jackson bowed and then left.

"I am to assume that the blame for the French spy falls upon Professor Cllafson and myself?"

John Henry turned away from the stern. The fog was not allowing any inspection of the tail they had at any rate.

"Your assumption is correct, Miss."

"Every time you call me Miss I turn in circles looking for my very much older sister. Would it be presumptuous of me to ask you to call me Claire? Why be so formal? After all, you are accusing us of planting a French spy onboard the *Yorktown*, are you not?"

"Well, he was in your company upon boarding." He half-heartedly smiled as he took in the striking redheaded historian. "I may be just an old and broken-down horse soldier in the United States Army, Miss Richelieu, but you don't have to kick me in the head like a stubborn mule to allow me to smell a rat hiding somewhere onboard this ship."

"Eloquently put, Colonel," she said as she suddenly turned away but stopped short of leaving the quarterdeck. "I don't know what has happened in your past to sour your way with people, Colonel Thomas, but I must say this: you are a horse's ass of the first order."

John Henry raised his brows and removed his hat as he watched Claire disappear into the fog-shrouded deck.

A dark form emerged from the fog near the very stern. It was Dugan, or his blurred image. He walked quickly past as if he were merely strolling in a park.

"Still have a way with the women, I see," he said as he placed his hands behind his back and continued toward his destination.

John Henry scowled as he lost sight of Dugan.

"You'll have to excuse the colonel. He's lost around women." Dugan removed his cap and looked at the woman before him. "The loss of his wife has played with his mind some." Dugan nodded as if Claire had spoken and then replaced his cap and started to move off.

"The trouble between Colonel Thomas and Colonel Taylor?"

Dugan stopped cold and then hesitated before turning to face her. He finally did and once more removed his cap.

"I don't go talkin' out of school, ma'am."

"I know the two are brothers-in-law, so tell me what happened to make them despise each other so."

"It's not Colonel Thomas who does the despising, ma'am, it's the Reb. He blames the colonel for the death of his sister, the colonel's wife."

"Tell me what happened," Claire asked. Despite the fact that the president placed all his confidence in his friend, she knew absolutely nothing about the man outside of his army file.

Dugan looked around and only saw crewmen going about their above-deck duties. He leaned in close to Claire.

"The one and only time the colonel was ever fooled by Indians was the day his wife was killed at their small ranch near the Brazos River. He was off chasing Kiowa. Her brother, Colonel Taylor—this was before I knew him—was also in the regiment. You see, back then we were spread so thin in Indian Territory that the regiment was broken up into troops." Dugan shook his head sadly as he remembered. "There just wasn't enough men. They were both off chasing Kiowa in differing directions. They had both been bamboozled and led away from the small settlements that were their responsibility. It was a cold-blooded murder raid. They got six ranches. Butchered families, killed all the livestock. They even raided into several Comanche villages. Gray Dog's family was lost on the same day. Yes indeed, ma'am, the Kiowa did a job that day."

"And each man is blaming the other?"

"While both men made the same mistake and were lured out chasing nothing, the Kiowa took what was the best of both men, and Colonel Taylor cannot begin to forgive John Henry for the loss of his sister." Dugan replaced his hat and took one step away and stopped. "The thing is, John Henry thinks the same way. He also cannot forgive *himself*."

Claire watched as the sergeant major moved away and knew he felt the colonel's pain. She just wished she could break through his hardened shell long enough to make him understand that they were facing far more than just legends on this voyage. They were facing what men and women used to believe the world over—that mankind was not calling the shots. This was God's domain and she believed as Ollafson did, that God would brook no interference in protecting what was his. She had most assuredly lost her scientific way of looking at the quest.

The *Yorktown, Chesapeake,* and *Carpenter* with the *Argo* in tow made their way past the British stronghold of Gibraltar.

The fog was still present as the sun rose over the Mediterranean. Gibraltar was now miles distant off their stern. An hour before, the gentle sound of the three signal bells of *Chesapeake* had chimed, so Captain Jackson knew that thus far they had transited the strait without landlocked eyes falling upon them. Now it was full sail toward the Aegean and then, for the *Yorktown,* Constantinople. It would be up to the *Chesapeake* to make landfall through the Bosphorus Strait and then the Black Sea. The land expedition would not fully form until Colonel Thomas's team made it to the slopes of Ararat.

Colonel Thomas soon joined Jackson on the quarterdeck and both watched as the Confederate prisoners slowly moved around the main deck. The mood was solemn, to say the least. Although they felt no love for the men that had been butchered in their cell, they still felt the loss of another three of their own. The mystery of their deaths had been placed on hold only because of the speculation and shipboard rumor that the French spy may have had something to do with it. Thus far neither Jackson, Thomas, nor even Colonel Taylor had denied the rumor. Murderous feelings had therefore been curtailed for the time being.

Fifteen minutes before, Sergeant Major Dugan had knocked

on John Henry's door to inform him of the makeshift burial at sea. He had been heavy into his journal that he kept for the president's eyes only and had not noticed the stillness of the ship. He was usually tuned into the happenings around him, but since the horrible murders his mind had been racing as to the real culprit in the savage attack. Thomas was more concerned at the moment for Gray Dog. The boy was refusing to sit with others. Avoided men of all affiliation, either north or south, with the same degree of mistrust. John Henry particularly noted Gray Dog's sudden fear of dark spaces. Both he and Jackson believed that Gray Dog had indeed seen who the killer was, and John Henry assured Jackson that his young Indian ward would come to him when he was ready to explain what he had seen in the brig.

John Henry watched as the three shrouded bodies were hoisted through the cargo hold at mid-deck. The bearers struggled as the marines and navy personnel watched. Thomas noticed that some men removed their hats while others watched with disinterest. Jessy was in the center and as John Henry watched, the Rebel colonel slowly removed something from his coat. It was a small Confederate flag. The stars and bars. It was only two feet by one and was hand-colored—with what, Thomas didn't know. Jackson cleared his throat when the small flag was placed on the sailcloth-covered bodies. The two officers strained to hear what was being said in prayer, but John Henry knew the faith of Jessy had been tested to the limits and he had walked away with the firm belief that God could not exist. After the loss of his sister, his only living family, Jessy had turned away from religion. John Henry knew he had helped his brother-in-law with that fateful decision by failing to protect Mary.

Soon Taylor lifted the small flag and then the platform was tilted and the bodies slowly slid into the sea. Jackson's brow furrowed as humming came to his ears through the thick fog. Then the tune was picked up by others and soon enough they were listening to "Dixie." Soft, mournful, and not at all directed toward the three men just committed to the deep. To Jackson and John Henry it was the sad refrain of lost men.

When the sound softly faded away he heard Taylor dismissing the men. The colonel walked to the quarterdeck and offered John Henry the refolded flag.

"I suppose this is contraband." he said, holding the flag out.

Thomas looked at the sad little remnant of these men's faith in a nation that had caved in on itself.

"I see an old and stained kerchief, Colonel, not contraband. You can keep that with the uniforms you had your men so meticulously repair."

Taylor smiled as he placed the flag back into his coat. He walked away without another word.

"I do not understand the bad blood between you two, especially when a blind man can see you are closer than what you portray. That hot-and-cold affection makes those of us in the dark rather uncomfortable." Jackson turned to face John Henry. "And that makes for mistrust. You have your mission at stake. I have three warships in that same position. May I suggest you sort this out immediately before we all wind up inside of a Turkish prison?" Jackson walked away. "We shall arrive at our destination in two days."

Thomas watched the back of Jackson until he vanished into the fog. He heard the anticollision bell sound four times and then the ship once more became silent, with the exception of the bow wake of the *Yorktown* as it cut through Mediterranean waters.

Thomas stood silent as he thought about what Jackson had said. He knew as well as the naval commander it had to be done. If they expected to get back home alive, he and Jessy would have to come to an understanding, and John Henry knew that one of them had the possibility of not walking away from the confrontation.

Gray Dog had been in the rigging for three full days. He had entered the interior of the ship only for food after the mess stewards had closed down for the night. It had been mess steward Grandee who had a suspicion that the small red man was making his clandestine forays after lights-out in the galley.

Gray Dog was moving cautiously in the dark all the time, staying away from the hull or anything that could cast a shadow by the lone oil lamp illuminating the galley. Suddenly he flinched when a wooden match was struck. Mess steward Grandee was sitting on a stool as he lifted the facing of an oil lamp and then stuck the match to the wick. He shook out the match and then looked up at an unmoving Gray Dog, who was standing rigid in the middle of the small galley.

"I must say, you're a real hard man to catch, yes, sir," Grandee said as he placed the lamp on the small table where a large plate of hot food was sitting untouched. He laughed. It was a deep belly laugh that sounded as though the voice was full of gravel. It immediately relaxed Gray Dog.

"I always wanted to say, I am sorely interested in that hat. What is it they call you?"

Gray Dog reached up and felt the coyote skin on his black hair. Then he realized that the large black-skinned man was not laughing at his hat but was complimenting it. Gray Dog slowly removed the headpiece and then offered it to Grandee. "Gray Dog."

"Looks more like a little fox hat," Grandee said as he slowly reached for the offered decoration.

"No, my name is Gray Dog."

"Oh, yeah, yeah, Gray Dog. Well, Gray Dog, this is a mighty fine hat," Grandee said as he returned the coyote head complete with tail after enough gushing over its beauty was accomplished. The mess steward smiled when he saw the Comanche's eyes roam to the steaming plate on the table. The eyes followed when the steward slowly pushed the plate toward Gray Dog.

"Go on, that's for you. Take it. You can eat it here or up there with the seagulls," Grandee said as his eyes rolled upward toward the deck and rigging.

Gray Dog looked at the roasted chicken thigh and the canned corn overflowing the plate. He immediately went to the table and scooped a handful of corn into his mouth. Grandee laughed that hearty laugh once more and then slid a spoon forward but Gray Dog ignored it.

"I didn't think you were getting enough eatin' done with you only taking stale bread out of here every night. You go on and eat up now. There will be a big plate for you right here when you're hungry. Nobody goes hungry on my watch."

"Maybe he gets a good appetite after murderin'."

Grandee looked up and Gray Dog jumped back from the table a step, suddenly leery of both Grandee and the man standing in the small opening to the galley holding the gray curtain aside.

Corporal Jenks walked in and with his eyes never leaving the two men he took a tin cup and poured himself a cup of coffee. The corporal's eye was still swollen and the knot on his jaw was finally receding into memory. Gray Dog watched the man, his hand on his knife's hilt.

"Scuttlebutt says it was the Frenchman spy fella that the colonel tossed overboard that did the killing."

"Maybe, maybe not," said another voice.

Colonel Taylor came in and repeated the pouring of coffee. He nodded at Jenks, who placed his cup on the table and then walked to the small curtain and stood there looking into the dark companionway. He would make sure Taylor had the time needed to get answers. Jessy slowly sat down with a nod of his head at the larger-than-life black man who was watching the Rebel colonel with more than just a wary eye. His fingers tickled the handle of a meat cleaver on the stool next to him.

"Why, I don't believe our Indian friend here has the prowess to tear to pieces three fully grown men. But I think he knows who did have that prowess." Taylor lifted the cup and took a drink of the thick, rich coffee.

"What is prowess?" Grandee asked as Gray Dog continued to watch Taylor. His eyes moved quickly to the doorway but then just as quickly back.

"The wherewithal to carry out the dastardly deed," he explained. "He knows the man that did this to my boys," he continued, "and I want to know who it is, now, tonight, or this mission comes to a stop right here."

"Now, you can't hold us here. The captain will—"

"No man."

The words caught both men off-guard. Grandee looked toward Gray Dog, who seemed to have shaken off his sudden fear of the two Rebels. He reached for the piece of chicken and then started to eat, paying no more attention to the men in the room than he did the rocking of the ship.

"What was that?" Jenks said, taking a step back inside the galley.

"Get back to your post," Taylor told Jenks as he turned his attention back to Gray Dog, who had finished the chicken and was now once more shoveling corn into his mouth.

"He says it weren't no man that did the killing," Grandee offered.

"Don't start with this Indian stuff. Tell me who did it," Taylor said, slapping the table with the palm of his hand.

"No man," Gray Dog said and then started to turn away when his corn was done. Taylor reached out and took the Comanche by the arm, stopping him from leaving. Grandee tensed as Gray Dog spun on the colonel and slammed his knife into the wooden table right next to Taylor's arm. Jessy slowly moved his hand away.

"You are John Henry's friend, so that is why I will not kill you. I did not kill those bad men. No one on this boat kill them." Gray Dog removed the embedded knife and then turned and left.

"Uh, Colonel?"

Taylor turned and saw Jenks being shoved into the galley at gunpoint. Sergeant Major Dugan once more had his pistol out and while still in a dressing gown that flowed to his ankles, he shoved the shocked Jenks inside. They were soon followed by John Henry. He was bare-chested and his suspenders were the only thing holding his blue pants aloft. He too was armed with a Colt.

"Colonel Taylor, would you join me in my cabin, please." John Henry uncocked the pistol and handed it over to Dugan, who was smiling at Jenks, who had been placed next to the man who had nearly beaten him to death four days before. They exchanged uneasy looks.

Jessy stood. He reached down and took his last sip of coffee and then half-bowed to the colonel. "By all means."

John Henry closed the door after leaving Dugan standing outside with pistol in hand. He walked to the small sideboard and then he shocked Taylor by pouring two glasses of whiskey. He turned and held one out toward the Rebel colonel.

"You're going to need this." Thomas nodded as Jessy took the glass, and then he raised it. "To the president," he said.

"Yes, President Jeff Davis," Taylor said with his own smile and then both men drank.

John Henry set his glass down, and then just as Jessy lowered his, Thomas punched him with a roundhouse blow to the side of his head. He staggered into the hull, which held him upright. Taylor shook his head and looked up at his brother-in-law. He smiled.

"'Bout goddamn time!" he said as he launched himself at Thomas. He struck the colonel right at belt level and drove him into the table still strewn with maps. The two men fell, and that was when the close-in fighting of the cavalry officers really commenced.

Captain Jackson was in a blue robe that had been a gift from his mother when he had been promoted at the early age of twenty-three to lieutenant commander. He was holding a carafe of water as he slowly moved back to the small makeshift cabin he had been in since offering his to Colonel Thomas. He was stopped and his sleepy eyes rose to the large man.

"They's fightin', Captain," Grandee said as his wide eyes went from a yawning Jackson to the smiling faces of Dugan and Jenks, who stood facing each other just outside the main cabin. The noise coming from inside his old cabin was like a hurricane ripping the place apart.

"Now, now, this has been coming on for some time. Don't get your knickers in a bunch," Dugan said.

Both Jenks and Grandee looked horrified, as they knew both men inside were in a killing mood for deeds done years before.

"What do we do?" Grandee pleaded with Jackson as the young officer yawned once more and then started to move away toward his bunk.

"This is an example of an army problem, cookie, not the navy's." He stopped only momentarily and said without turning back, "I am interested in the outcome, so see me in the morning and let me know who won," he said as he parted the curtain and entered his small space. "Good night, gentlemen."

Jenks and Grandee looked at each other, and then without a word both turned their heads to see Sergeant Major Dugan smiling like this was the most marvelous thing since P. T. Barnum's museum opened.

Dugan could not remember a fistfight lasting so long without someone calling for a doctor, or a mortician. The sounds of breaking furniture, glass, and the occasional "umph" ended only a few minutes later when the sergeant major was approached by Professor Ollafson, Claire Richelieu, and the ever-present Steven McDonald.

"I demand this foolishness be stopped immediately!" Ollafson said to a smiling Dugan when they approached. Claire looked absolutely horrified that not one man belowdecks had made an attempt at stopping the two madmen from this disgraceful act that surely was not the way an American military officer should comport himself.

"Sorry, Professor, orders were clear on this one. Until I hear a gunshot coming from that cabin, no one gets in."

"They could be killing themselves in there!" Claire said as her eyes went to the suddenly silent cabin door.

"That, ma'am, is highly probable," Dugan said, and then cocked his ear to the right. "Sounds as though they may be taking a small breather, or one of them is dead."

"Well, man, open the bloody door!" McDonald said.

"You all just go back to your studies or beds. If someone in that cabin needs attention, the ship's doc is standing by. Now go on, leave the two colonels alone to sort out their differences or this little fantasy mission will end before we reach Constantinople."

"This disgrace will be entered into the official report, I assure you," Ollafson said as he turned and left.

"Be sure you enter that little tidbit of information right alongside the entry about you allowing a French spy onboard."

Ollafson stopped, hunched his shoulders, and then continued on.

McDonald, with one last look at the sergeant major, quickly followed just to get those beady little rat's eyes off him. On the way he almost bumped into Gray Dog, who was waiting just underneath the stairs leading to the upper deck. Grandee was there also. Both were eating buttered bread from the galley.

"What is this, a prize fight?"

Both men looked at him. It was Grandee who summed it up the best.

"Soldiers fight."

"Oh, of course, that explains all." McDonald shook his head and then left the aft compartment.

Dugan faced Claire, who wasn't moving. She turned and pulled over a small stool and then sat.

"I'm not leaving until you allow me to enter that cabin."

"Then I suspect we'll be waiting together, Miss."

For a reason John Henry couldn't remember, he was staring at the polished tips of his boots. As he did, the left-side suspender attaching his pants to his body snapped. His head jerked as the elastic popped and stung his bare chest. Blood had coursed down from his left brow and dripped onto the floor. He managed to look to his right as Jessy was trying in vain to lift himself from the floor. The last time these two men had done battle with each other like this was back in their junior year after family day at West Point. That was the very first time that John Henry had seen Jessy's sister, Mary, visiting with their parents from Mobile. Thomas had never seen a girl like her before. Her confidence obviously had been earned after so many years with her brother, but it was her kind eyes that John Henry remembered first and foremost. That night when he had mentioned it, Jessy went crazy and they ended up in just about the same positions they were in now. The remembrance was short lived as Jessy gave up and then slid back down the damp hull to sit hard on the deck.

"You still hit like a flower-picking Yankee."

"Is that so? Well," John Henry swiped blood from his mouth and then spit a mouthful of it out onto the wooden deck. "This flower-picking Yankee just put you on the deck."

"Ha! And just where do you find yourself, Colonel?"

Thomas looked up at Jessy, who was also spitting out blood.

John Henry tried to rise, failed, stumbled backward, and then sat heavily on the floor. He let out a breath and then rolled over and lay down. He suddenly became inspired and rolled to a spot he saw upside down in his vision. Once where he wanted to go, he retrieved a bottle and then rolled back to his section of hull, where he finally managed to sit up. He uncorked the bottle of whiskey and took a long, double swallow of the amber-colored liquid. It burned but it was a good burn; it let him know his nervous system was functioning just fine. He held out the bottle toward Jessy, who was still cursing a loose tooth that John Henry had managed to dislodge from his cheek. He took the offered liquor and held it up. He wiped the lip of the bottle with a dirty sleeve and then took a drink.

"I loved your sister." John Henry took the bottle back and then looked at Taylor.

Jessy tried to stand again but this time he surrendered halfway up the hull and slid back. He closed his eyes and then reached out and snatched the bottle from Thomas's hand.

"The one man in the world I thought I could trust in protecting my sister failed me and her. Instead of leaving her in the east where most married men felt their families were safer, you brought her out to Texas. How did that work out, hero?" He took a drink while his eyes remained on his former brother-in-law.

Thomas remembered the day he and his troop were led away from the small settlement of six ranches. He never in his wildest imagination thought the Kiowa could mount a murder raid on so many ranches on the same day. He had been outsmarted, and that more than anything had driven him mad and led to him leaving his assigned patrol area to pursue Kiowa who weren't where they were supposed to be. Jessy had figured that out, and was the first of his troop to reach the ranch, only to discover he had been too late. The massacre had been complete. John Henry remembered riding up to the ranch after finding the small three-lodge camp of Gray Dog and his family. They had suffered the same cruelty as the settlements. Gray Dog had been shot in the shoulder with a Kiowa arrow and was riding behind John Henry when they came upon his home, the ranch that would allow him and his wife to live a life outside of the army. He had planned to resign his commission after 1859 and he and Mary would start raising children and cows on the Brazos River. But as he saw the smoldering house and barn, the outbuildings, and the covered bodies on the ground, he knew that his life for the most part was done. Until a few days ago he'd only seen Jessy one other time since he lost his wife. That was the day the regiment broke into two factions when President Lincoln had called for volunteers to fight the rebellious southern states.

"Tell me, John Henry, how many mistakes in judgment have you made? Or was it just the one?" Jessy spit again and then handed the whiskey back to Thomas. "The one that cost me my little sister?"

Thomas looked at the bottle in his hand. "Just the one." He took a drink.

"I don't care, it's been too quiet in there! Open the damn door!"

At that moment Sergeant Major Dugan opened the door

and backed in with a furious Claire Richelieu jabbing him with Dugan's own cocked pistol. The sergeant major's eyes were wide and his hands raised.

"Now, Missy, you put that gun down before we have us an accident."

"If this gun goes off, Sergeant Major, it will be no accident."

Suddenly Claire tossed him the cocked weapon and Dugan almost shat himself as the gun landed in his bumbling hands, where he finally managed to secure it.

"Goodness, we arrive at the capital of one of the largest and most unstable governments in the world and you two look like you just fought the battle of Bull Run all over again." Claire reached down and started to dab a white linen cloth to John Henry's eye. Then she heard Jessy start his slow descent to the floor once more from his sitting position. She grabbed the bottle of whiskey and before turning her attention to Taylor, took a long pull from the bottle. She placed it on the floor and then stopped Jessy from rolling completely over onto the deck. "Stupid son of a bitch," she mumbled as both Taylor and Thomas looked at the woman who cussed just as well as Dugan, who was also standing wide-eyed at the woman's harsh words.

"What are you standing there for? Go get the doctor!" she said as she looked back to Dugan, who finally broke the spell the woman had cast by the use of her foul language. Dugan had obviously come up with newfound respect for the ancient-languages expert.

"I hope it was worth it," she said as she grimaced at the nasty cut on Taylor's lower lip.

"The only good outcome would have been me shooting him," Taylor said as John Henry finally managed to get to his feet.

Before Claire could berate Taylor for being foolish, a drum started pounding the call to general quarters.

John Henry immediately broke for the door just as Commander Jackson came from his small space, placing a coat on. The man was completely dressed as if he had been waiting for the call to arms.

"I was afraid of this," Jackson said as he hit the stairs leading to the upper deck.

"The French?" John Henry asked as Dugan tossed him a shirt as he too made the stairs.

"I suspect the British aren't too happy with us sneaking by Gibraltar without paying our respects."

They made the quarterdeck as men ran to their battle stations. They were met by Jackson's first officer.

"Battle stations manned and ready, Captain."

"Very good," Jackson said as he took the long glass and scanned the horizon to their stern, and then his first officer pointed him in the right direction.

"Not there, sir. Over there."

As Jackson brought the scene to their front into focus he held his breath. Aligned three ships abreast was the Royal Navy. They were at half-sail and moving toward them slowly. He scanned the gun ports on the first ship in line. They were closed and the deck activity looked to be minimal. Jackson lowered the spyglass and faced Thomas.

"They're just trying to get our dander up a little. They know if they raise those gun ports I'll blow them out of the water. No, they're not looking to fight—just showing us they are the Royal Navy."

"But what if those cannons are ready to fire behind those closed gun ports?" John Henry asked as he felt someone step up beside him. It was Jessy. Thomas handed him the spyglass.

"Nah, those boys don't want a fight. Jackson's right, they're just wanting to see what we will do. No, there will be no first shot fired from these boys." Taylor lowered the glass and then handed it back to Jackson. "Now, if you'll excuse me, I think I'll let Miss Claire tend to my battle wounds."

Jackson raised the glass as he studied the three British warships in front of him. As he watched, the first started peeling off to the starboard, effectively making room for his two ships to pass. He lowered the glass and then looked at John Henry.

"From our secessionist friend's attitude, your little meeting of the minds didn't turn out the way you had hoped?"

John Henry finished buttoning the shirt and then started to turn away. He stopped and shook his head. "I was hoping to get the air cleared, but as in this entire war there's been too much blood spilled, too much talk. No, Jessy won't come back. He hates not only me, but himself."

"I don't follow your logic," Jackson said as he watched his men at their stations.

"Colonel Taylor fails to realize that the area of responsibility for my wife's death resides not only in my camp, but his also. He ignored my order to keep his troop in the vicinity and went after the Kiowa raiding party that killed the first family near where his troop was quartered."

"In essence he is as much responsible for his sister's death as yourself?"

"Yes," John Henry said as he started to walk away. "No," he quickly corrected. "I own that."

Jackson watched the army colonel walk away and kept his next question unasked. He knew why John Henry didn't use that against Taylor; it was simply because one man accusing the other never solved anything. He could not imagine having that thrown in his face—that the death of his sister was his responsibility also. Maybe that's why the hate was so deeply imbedded in the Confederate.

Jackson watched as the British warship slipped past the *Yorktown*. He eyed the English captain standing at his station on the quarterdeck. He watched the man raise a hand toward him and he could swear he saw the smile from that great distance.

"I'm sure we'll meet again, Captain. I have no doubt." He smiled and saluted also.

One hundred and thirty miles astern, the French navy, with a very angry Paul Renaud ensconced on the first warship, entered the Mediterranean. The entire world was now focusing its attention on the Aegean Sea as they entered the azure waters of the once-mighty Greek nation. In a day and a half they would reach the departure point for their meeting within the Ottoman Empire.

Ararat was growing ever closer.

13

CONSTANTINOPLE, CAPITAL OF THE OTTOMAN
EMPIRE

The *Yorktown* was being tied up to the crowded dock. Many
citizens of the empire's capital had spilled out to see the
American warship as she entered the harbor. The sailors and
marines were surprised to hear the "Star-Spangled Banner"
playing. A thirty-piece band had been secured to welcome
the Americans and their kind but surprising gift of a railroad
to the empire.

As John Henry came topside he felt embarrassingly uncomfortable in his dress uniform. The bright red sash highlighted the saber in its polished sheath, and his boots had
been cleaned and polished by the crew of the *Yorktown*. The
one accoutrement that he despised was the helmet with its
gold trappings. The braided plume that rose from the centerline spike made him feel more like a flamingo than an officer in the United States Cavalry. John Henry pursed his lips
and then placed his white gloved hands behind his back as
he awaited the others by the gangway.

He was soon joined by Jessy, dressed the exact same way
as Thomas, and he was feeling equally awkward in the Union
colors. He hated the fact that his men down below had gotten

a very good look at their commander as he quickly walked past them a few minutes earlier. Both men still carried the battle scars of their fight three days before. Claire and the doctor had done an admirable job of stitching and making the bruising look far less than it really was. As Captain Jackson joined them he had to smile at the uncomfortable way the two army officers waited for the others. Unlike the two men who stood before him, Jackson felt no discomfort whatsoever in his dress blues. The two-corner hat was a bit much, but he was still proud to wear the gold braid and tails of a U.S. naval officer. He'd had many more chances to become comfortable in his uniform than the other two frontiersmen.

"Well, I must say, you two cleaned up nicely," Claire said as she stepped around the two for a quick inspection.

"I know to you this may be a ridiculous question, but why is she is coming along, again?" Taylor asked without turning his eyes away from the overflowing dock area.

"Because the planners of this so-called mission neglected to include an interpreter that speaks the language of the empire," Jackson said as he saw his second-in-command approach.

"I'm being brought along for purely aesthetic reasons, I assure you. You know as well as I that according to Secretary of State Seward's report, the sultan is an unapologetic womanizer, and that I very well could be an asset for keeping his mind on something other than your railroad ruse."

"I can't believe she said that all in one breath," Taylor mumbled. In their silence the others secretly agreed.

They heard Sergeant Major Dugan long before they saw him.

"Why do I have to stay aboard and watch Gray Dog and these Rebs?"

"Because we don't need you popping off at the wrong time and creating an international incident. Now, you watch things and we'll rendezvous with you across the strait to catch that train east."

Dugan frowned and glared at Thomas and then saluted and moved off.

"All lines secure. Deck watch has been set, Captain," said the young lieutenant junior grade.

"Very good, Daniel. Now, as soon as we leave, and when this crowd finally gets tired and moves off, cast off and get to the eastern side of the strait. Keep the professor off the main deck, Lieutenant. He is not to show his face. No telling how many eyes are on us. Once tied up, get our supplies off-loaded and leave them with Sergeant Major Dugan and his team. The prisoners will be guarded and then placed aboard the train as soon as it arrives. The train's passenger cars are to be quarantined for the duration of the trip east. Once that is done, your orders are to set sail through the strait and rendezvous with *Chesapeake* and *Carpenter* in the Black Sea. Clear?"

"Yes, sir. Good luck." The boy saluted and then returned to his duties.

Jackson turned to face the others in the official party of Americans. "Lady and gentlemen, our carriages await."

The trip through the city streets was an uneasy one, especially when they passed the berthing area for a British warship that had docked not long after the *Yorktown*. Her name was emblazoned in gold script across her stern. H.M.S. *Westfield* was a forty-two-gun battle cruiser.

"Damn," Jackson mumbled under his breath, drawing the attention of Taylor.

"What is it?" he asked as his eyes examined the giant cruiser. Her sails looked brand-new and her cannon were on full display as she tied up and opened her gun ports, to the thrill of the gathered onlookers. The British flag flew proudly at her stern.

"The *Westfield* is the newest ship of the line in the Royal Navy. Forty-two rifled guns. She could punch holes in us all day if we aren't careful."

"She looks like a handful, all right," Taylor agreed.

"Don't worry, Colonel Taylor. I'm a very careful man myself. I don't give ships all day to do anything."

Taylor saw Jackson's arrogant smirk and wondered if

Lincoln and Ericsson's wunderkind was up to the task or if
his bravado was the act of a scared young man. Time would
tell, as their escape was purely in the captain's hands.

In the second carriage John Henry had also noticed the
newest arrival in the harbor of Constantinople. He wasn't as
worried about the giant battle cruiser, as he was paying attention to the way their guest, Mr. McDonald, took note. He
saw the way he looked at the ship and then quickly looked
away. He observed that Claire Richelieu had noticed also, but
for the life of him he didn't know why he felt she knew something about McDonald that he didn't. She had claimed never
to have met the man from Harvard before, but knew him by
reputation, and that reputation was a good one. He regretted
not having a full investigative report generated for both of the
men that had accompanied them from Baltimore. One had
already proven to be a spy, and now this one wasn't making
any good impressions either. John Henry might have to consider finding out this man's real credentials, or as he thought
about it, McDonald's real profession.

Thomas had finally confided in both Taylor and Jackson
his suspicions about McDonald and Claire as far as the subject of trust was concerned. He explained that while he had
his suspicions, McDonald could be who he said he was. Plus,
Thomas would be a fool to leave the man onboard the *Yorktown* if he was indeed in the service of Queen Victoria.

Claire was looking at him and he relaxed. Her eyes
watched him underneath the dark veil that covered her face.
Her gown was as gorgeous as John Henry had ever seen, and
her smell was like roses after a cool summer rain. Her eyes
remained on him and didn't turn away as they approached
the new palace of the sultan. To Thomas it looked as if she
were getting ready to decide on something—a course of action, maybe?

Colonel John Henry Thomas closed his eyes and when he
opened them again saw that they were entering the gates of
a large palace that gleamed in the late afternoon light.

Dolmabahçe Palace was surrounded by the most magnificent gardens any of them outside of McDonald had ever

seen. Secretary Seward had briefed them as much as he could on the palace and its principal occupant. The structure sat upon eleven acres of reclaimed naval land and boasted two hundred and eighty-five rooms. As the garishly dressed guards allowed them through the gate, Taylor commented on the new Martini-Henry rifles that had been sold to the empire to replace the old breechloaders they'd had but eight months before. Yes, the European powers were having a field day selling arms to the sultan.

As their drivers approached the large and ornate portico of the palace, they saw a carriage ahead of them as several brightly uniformed men were escorted inside. John Henry pursed his lips when he recognized the two differing designs of uniforms.

"Our friends, the Germans and English, have also been invited."

Claire closed her eyes and wondered if they would fail before they even started.

The two carriages pulled up and the Americans were led into a magnificent parlor. It was a parlor in the loosest sense of the word, since it was larger than what the Americans knew as the Hippodrome in New York City. The large arena was small compared to this structure, which was massive and filled with men and women.

Every ambassador to the empire was present, and the Americans soon learned that the sultan had bragged openly to the other powers what a magnificent gift the people of the United States had given his empire. A play on their hatred of the Americans, John Henry felt, probably to garner more gifts from his European neighbors. The five were stopped before entering. The American contingent was wondering what the protocol was when they heard an announcer.

"May I present to the Caliph of Islam, his Majestic Deliverer of the Ottoman Empire, Son of Mahmud II, Sultan Abdülaziz I, these delegates from the United States of America, Colonel John Henry Thomas."

Thomas stepped forward and with one leg almost in front

of the other, bowed to the heavy man sitting on the large throne surrounded by fifty guards.

"Colonel Jessup E. Taylor."

Jessy repeated the bow and then stepped aside.

"Mr. Steven McDonald, of Harvard University, and Captain Steven Jackson, United States Navy."

Jackson stepped forward, clicked his heels, and bowed. His two-cornered hat came off his head with a flourish before he straightened.

"And Madame Claire Richelieu, Harvard University, special assistant to the president of the United States."

John Henry was surprised that Seward and Lincoln had wanted Claire announced like that. He didn't know what her pretense was, but he kept silent.

The men and women in all their finery started to applaud the Americans as they were led to the ornate throne. They were soon standing before the sultan of the Ottoman Empire.

The man was heavy, so heavy that the pillows on which he sat squished out from his behind like too much cream filling stuffed into a morning roll. His beard was impeccably curled and oiled. His clothes were a rich mix of shiny material, obviously silk, and his jewelry was on display. The fingernails were polished and his facial makeup evident. The man's eyes never left Claire's cleavage and she was feeling as much on display as the heavy man's jewelry. She shot a sideways glance at John Henry after her short but courteous bow to the sultan.

Thomas stepped up, took the hilt of his sword, and then with one foot in front of the other, bowed and flourished his tasseled helmet just as Jackson had with his two-corner hat. The navy didn't have all the etiquette—the army also shone sometimes. When he straightened Jackson was at his side and in a very briefly rehearsed bit of theater, he handed John Henry a small and ornate wooden box. Thomas took a step forward and saw that his movement caused the six bodyguards to tense momentarily until the sultan smiled and held up a hand.

Thomas noted that the sultan wasn't interested in the box as much as Claire's cleavage. John Henry didn't exactly know how he felt about that. Maybe it was just a foreigner ogling an American that made him a touch angered, but then again maybe the woman had affected him in a different way since their voyage began. Thomas shook off the thought and held the box out to the sultan, who finally noticed he was being offered something.

"On behalf of the president of the United States, Abraham Lincoln, we ask our most gracious host to accept this small token of the American people's desire for good relations between your great empire and the United States of America." John Henry waited but the sultan made no move to take the gift. Finally one of the red velveteen–clad bodyguards stepped forward and relieved the American of the gift. He turned and opened the lid and only then did he show the contents to the sultan. The robust leader of the largest empire in the world smiled and then reached out and lifted a small golden locomotive from the polished wooden box. He laughed heartily and then nodded his round, turbaned head at Thomas.

"We would have expected your gift of a railroad line a far larger matter than what your beautiful box could contain." He laughed again and then everyone joined in, foreign diplomats and military attachés included—only their laughter was more on the spiteful side.

John Henry turned and saw that even Claire had smiled. He felt lost and uncomfortable. Jackson saw this and, with his hat still tucked neatly under his arm, stepped forward and bowed his impeccable greeting once more.

"Great Sultan, as we speak and talk of good relations, the gift of the American people is even now entering your Bosphorus Strait and should be sailing the Black Sea within the next few hours. Everything from railroad ties cut from the magnificent forests of the state of Maine, to steel rails manufactured in Pennsylvania, and even to the locomotive and six cars manufactured in Illinois, the home of the president, is ready to serve the great sultan of the Ottoman Empire. The gift of this and the labor force to construct the most modern railroad for your most barren provinces, are all for your great empire on the anniversary of your birth."

The sultan handed the golden locomotive to the bodyguard and then stepped down from his marble pedestal and embraced John Henry. His head was first turned right and then left and in the wake of both actions a wet kiss was planted on his cheeks. He raised his brow as the process was completed, with Captain Jackson taking the assault far better than his army counterpart. Then the sultan came to McDonald, who stiffly accepted the greeting. Claire was actually looking to John Henry for help, but there was nothing he could do as the sultan took Claire by the shoulders and kissed both cheeks. Then he moved his hands toward her chest which made her react. Instead of screaming and running, as she surely wanted to do, she curtsied and bowed her head, effectively cutting off the sultan's advance.

This time the applause was started by the Turks in the crowded room, and soon, out of necessity, the European contingent slowly joined in. To John Henry's relief the sultan bowed and then returned to his overly large and very ornate throne. A small string band started playing and the mood shifted as the guests started milling about as they were served with all manner of delicacies.

"That was a brilliant tactical maneuver, Miss Claire," Jackson said with true admiration. She smiled and curtsied again. She turned to face Thomas, who was intentionally looking in another direction.

"And what did you think of my miraculous escape, Colonel?"

Thomas turned and acted as if he had not heard what she said.

"I asked what you thought about—"

"Yes, your performance, I heard." He smiled only half-heartedly and then looked at her veiled eyes. "I wish I would have thought of it, but I would have butted heads bowing instead of curtsying. I'm afraid you think far faster than I,

Madame. I'm just an old soldier, not a woman of the world such as yourself."

"Valid point, Colonel Thomas, I'm sure," she said and then suddenly took McDonald by the arm and moved off toward the magnificent buffet table that stretched a hundred feet.

"What did I say?" John Henry asked as he watched Claire leave in her recently purchased turquoise dress.

"Perhaps it was not what you said, Colonel. Maybe it was how you said it."

"You make as much sense as she does," Thomas said as he watched Jackson smile and then head in the same direction as the other two.

"Still have that touch of class, huh, John Henry?" Jessy said as he strolled by in his new Union dress blues.

A baffled Thomas watched as Jessy nodded at a fair-looking British woman with a rather large rear guard and then smile again and move once more to the next lady he saw. John Henry mumbled and then smiled and bowed his head as the sultan started making his way toward him with his bodyguard and the English ambassador in tow.

"This is not a good time." He looked around and saw the others had no intention of rejoining him, so he smiled his best disarming grin and then greeted the sultan once more.

Claire turned from McDonald as he removed delicacies from a tray and filled two plates. She saw John Henry talking with the sultan and then a strange thing happened. They both looked up at the same time and they locked eyes. At least she thought they did, and it gave her the queerest feeling in the pit of her stomach. She quickly turned away when McDonald joined her.

She failed to see not only that she had John Henry's attention, but also the contingent from the French Embassy. And they both failed to notice that the German and Spanish representatives were also paying close attention to the Americans.

The most powerful nations of the world wondered how they could blow this ruse of the backward Americans out of the water without causing damage to their own nations' relationships with the empire.

They all had a plan.

The stringed instruments lent an air of unreal quality to the proceedings due to the fact that almost every set of eyes was on the Americans. It was Claire who noticed that Steven McDonald had wandered over to the side of the banquet table where the military attaché of Great Britain was eating and was in quiet discussion with his counterpart from the German Embassy. She saw the British colonel nod his head and then excuse himself from his company and make his way down the line of rotund eaters. She saw the simple way he stopped and greeted McDonald as if they had never met before. McDonald, unlike Renaud, was an unskilled spy. Why Colonel Thomas had caught the Frenchman first and not this bumbling fool was well beyond her comprehension. McDonald was a soldier and was good for little else. The two men smiled and nodded, uttering the quiet musings of two men who had just met. Claire's attention went to John Henry, who was speaking to the sultan, his interpreter, and none other than the British and French ambassadors to the Ottoman Empire.

"Careful, Colonel," she said under her breath.

"The only thing he should be careful of is eating this food," Jessy said, stepping up next to her as he stared at the offering the sultan's cooks had plopped on his plate. That item was a red-shelled bug. His look was one of horror.

"You've never seen lobster before?" Claire asked as she smiled for the first time in days at the naiveté of Taylor.

"If lobster means the biggest damn bug I've ever seen, no, I have not." Jessy was still staring at the steaming shell and the massive claws of the lobster. "Kind of reminds me of the bedbugs in the hotel rooms just south of Wichita. They were about this big."

Claire actually laughed as her daintily gloved hand slowly removed the china plate from his hand. She set it down on the buffet line and handed the colonel a replacement plate with roasted chicken on it.

"I think I'll steer my little ship away from the lobster also," she said after hearing Jessy's description of bedbugs in the west.

"Well, before you do, maybe you'd better ask if this is roasted chicken . . . or . . . something else," Taylor said as he leaned over his plate and sniffed.

"The sultan was informed by Mr. Wigand here that you not only had a Frenchman thrown from your vessel, but that you also incurred murder onboard. The sultan asks if American sea crossings are always so eventful," the Turkish interpreter said as the four men strolled along the magnificent full-length wall portraits of Ottoman sultans long dead.

"I must say, Your Highness, that the French ambassador is very well informed, but wrongly so, I'm afraid." John Henry nodded his head once at the fat ambassador from Paris and then looked at Britain's representative as though he were looking at the real danger.

"The ambassador has also informed our naval arm that you have only brought one of your four vessels into the empire's home harbor. The sultan would like to know the reason for this." The interpreter looked uneasy as John Henry realized that the French ambassador was indeed intriguing the sultan about his real mission to the empire.

"That aspect of the ambassador's briefing to members of your court is true." Again he nodded toward the Frenchman, who did not return the gesture this time. He just walked beside the sultan silently as the British ambassador listened closely. "Since the shorter route for the railroad supplied is from north to south, the heavy equipment will be off-loaded in your coastal port of Trabzon. The men and equipment will be transported from there to the termination point where my engineers will join them."

"Of course you will allow for inspection as soon as your vessels dock?" The sultan did not need his interpreter for the question.

"Of course. We fully expect the sultan himself to take

possession of the locomotive and bless its commissioning on behalf of his people."

This time it was the Frenchman who bowed in John Henry's direction for his successful deflection of the questions.

"Gentlemen, if you will excuse the sultan he has a wonderful surprise for his guests." The sultan and interpreter abruptly returned to the throne. The Frenchman turned and faced Thomas and the warm smile vanished. The representative of Victoria listened in with curiosity.

"I have been informed of your true intentions in the East, Colonel Thomas, and so has my colleague from London. I must say it is a marvelous double ruse put on by your President Lincoln. To use the lie of presenting the brutish sultan with a new railroad line was brilliant. But to have the double-edged falsehood of covering up an attempt at bringing back a legend from a desolate mountaintop is magnifique," he said as he kissed the fingers of his right hand as if he had just tasted a fine wine. "It makes me think your president has at least a small amount of French blood flowing through those veins of his. Now, what are you Americans really after, Colonel Thomas? It cannot be the Ark. No one would be as foolish as that."

"Addressing your first concern, Mr. Ambassador, I'm afraid Mr. Lincoln has no blood in his veins other than American, which is why he is fighting so hard to keep it whole. To address the second concern, I don't believe in most legends, and as to your third, what in the world could possibly lie on a mountaintop in eastern Turkey that would concern Americans in the least?"

A perplexed look crossed the representative's features and he became angry. He looked at his British colleague and then again faced the American.

"Your American wit notwithstanding, Colonel Thomas, we will discover what it is you have really come for. If it be gold, minerals, or just the start of an invasion of the Ottoman Empire, sir, we will learn the truth, and then you will see how responsible nations react to piracy. It's about time the United States is brought under control and restrained before the stain of your backward war spreads." The ambassador clicked his polished heels together and then moved off. The British ambassador smiled, bowed, and then followed suit.

"Don't be shy, Froggy. Tell me your true thoughts," John Henry mumbled.

"I see you are playing well with others," Claire said as she, Jessy, and Jackson all stepped up to him.

"For the moment," he said as he watched the Frenchman turn to his British counterpart and, to his surprise, Steven McDonald, who graciously excused himself from the conversation he had been having and then made his way toward the group of Americans.

"I see your Mr. McDonald is also playing well with others," Thomas said as he watched the man approach.

"If he is, why should that concern me, Colonel? After all, you know the man about as well as I," she said with a tinge of anger in her voice. She didn't wait for John Henry to answer, she simply curtsied and then moved away.

"Yes, sir, you still have a way with the opposite species," Taylor said as he slipped a piece of chicken into his mouth and then followed Claire.

The pounding drums startled most with the exception of the military personnel on hand. The Americans watched as the main floor was cleared and the guests were asked to step aside. Then as the drums continued, ten men came in line abreast, wielding the largest swords Jessy, Jackson, or John Henry had ever seen. The ten men wore flowing balloon pants made of pure white satin. They were all bare-chested and had bright red sashes around their midsections. Each had a large ponytail of dark hair bundled at his scalp. Each swordsman had to weigh in excess of three hundred pounds and was no less than six and a half feet tall. They lined up five to a side. As they did, an eleventh man walked out with a Saracen sword almost double the size of any of the weapons the others had. This man stood at the head of the two lines.

"Ladies, gentlemen, and special guests, His Royal Majesty would like to present to you the entertainment for this evening. Almost three thousand years ago, the Persian Empire ruled most of the known world. To achieve this feat the great kings of the past had a special unit of soldiers who would die upon command, the fiercest, most loyal soldiers of the empire. Ladies, gentlemen, special guests—the sultan gives to you a demonstration of the most elite unit of soldiers in history, the Immortals!"

The drums began blasting and the two sides came together with a clanging of Saracen swords. The demonstration was magnificent as each choreographed move was met with *oohs* and *ahhs* from the gathered luminaries. Their leader stood with sword crossed over his bare chest. He watched each pair as they demonstrated their prowess with blade and maneuver. Finally, with a last exchange of clanging swords the two sides separated with one last flourished backward spin and each man was in his original position with sword at the ready.

The guests applauded. Even the Americans were impressed. Jessy was chewing on his chicken as he saw the conspiracy long before John Henry. The man always thought officers in any military would act accordingly, but Jessy knew the ulterior motives of men with a plan. And he knew the Europeans were getting a plan together. He didn't know what or how, but he knew they would make one, maybe more, attempt at either embarrassing the American contingent or stopping it completely. He glanced at Thomas, who was also watching not the swordsmen, but the Europeans, who watched with quiet intent.

"The sultan would like to ask if there are any volunteers to challenge the mighty Immortal commander to see if their name holds true."

"Surely he can't mean a fight to the death?" Claire asked nervously.

"Even here I think that would be a bit barbaric," Jackson said. All could see in his eyes that he was very interested in the Immortals and the possibility of one-on-one combat.

"I may be wrong, Colonel Thomas, and I often am, but I

believe this challenge is directed solely at you," McDonald said, looking pleased that he had been the first one to point this obvious conclusion out to the others.

Suddenly the leader of the Immortals stepped to the center of the two lines and started twirling his sword to a slow but powerful drumbeat. The man was a giant. He swung the large curved sword in a circle and all present could hear the sharp blade slicing through the air. Finally the man slowly started to approach their side of the hall. He continued to twirl the Saracen sword in a wide arc that made most of the women in the room come close to swooning as his sweat-soaked body moved past them. Still the drums beat.

John Henry turned slightly and saw the French, the German, and English delegates all very interested in what was happening. Thomas figured they had made a suggestion to the sultan to put on this little show of his. As he looked, the French ambassador smiled, and not only due to the situation that was fast developing. The ambassador pointed out the man who had just joined him. It was the French spy he had put overboard, the man they had known as Cromwell— Renaud actually smiled at the American. He turned and saw that Claire was also staring at the group of men, Renaud in particular. To his astonishment Claire turned and angrily strolled toward the men in black tie and sashes. John Henry and the others all raised their eyebrows at the same moment when Claire walked straight up to Renaud and the French ambassador.

"This needs to stop now."

Renaud only stared at her. Then without warning he stepped up to her and grabbed her shoulders, and this caused all to tense up. Jessy almost dropped his plate of pomegranate-roasted chicken when he instinctively reached for his absent Colt in its holster. John Henry grabbed his arm and then slowly shook his head no.

"You return to your duties, or I will make you my next special project. Is that clear, Madame? We need more information than you are sending to us. You have not signaled any progress reports from the *Yorktown*. I am beginning to think you may have another, or maybe two more employers, other than us. You send me regular reports or the Americans may learn the identity of your real employers."

Claire angrily shook off the Frenchman's hand and then turned and went back to the others.

"I would ask what that was about, but it looked a little personal, so I'll let it go until we get back to the ship. Then I think you'd better start coming to the side of the Lord, Miss Richelieu." Thomas turned his attention back to the swordsman, who was getting ever closer to the group of Americans.

The giant of a man finally stopped in front of John Henry and Jessy. Both men watched as the Immortal bowed all the way to the polished tile of the great hall as the drumbeat came to a halt. The man lowered his head and splayed out the arms that were the size of tree trunks. Soon a smaller Immortal emerged from the crowd and approached Thomas and Taylor. He held a Saracen sword and offered it to John Henry. Thomas looked from the shiny blade to the beast of a man bowing before him.

"The great Sula-Man-Khan of the sultan's famous Immortals offers you this sword of honor. He wishes to show the American honored guests the battle prowess of the great leader and his men."

Thomas looked from the smaller Immortal, who still held the large sword out with both hands with head bowed, to the sultan sitting on his throne. He saw the French and British ambassadors were both near but not actually speaking with the leader of the Ottoman Empire. The smile on the sultan's face was a clear indication of the challenge. John Henry knew they were setting up the Americans as fools, and this led the colonel to believe that the French or the English had passed on to the sultan the real meaning of their fabulous gift to the empire. John Henry half-bowed toward the throne and the fat man sitting upon it. He straightened and started to reach for the sword.

"You're not thinking of really accepting this challenge, are you?" Jessy asked as he blindly handed Claire his plate.

Thomas looked at Jessy and then tilted his head. "If you have an alternative plan, now would be a good time to voice it."

Taylor took a step closer to John Henry. "Look, if I recall, you were the third from the bottom in fencing and swordsmanship at the Point."

"Your point?" John Henry asked, smiling at the sultan as he spoke through the side of his mouth.

"That is my point." Jessy looked from Thomas to the enormous sword in the Immortal's hands. "I was first in both disciplines." He stepped in front of John Henry. "Maybe you should sit this one out, Colonel, or you may receive a point you can't outthink." He nodded toward the very lethal-looking Saracen sword.

The giant of a man slowly stood as Taylor stepped forward in front of Thomas and then moved the smaller man aside, disdaining the large sword. He immediately drew his saber from its shiny sheath. It was a bad time to think about it, but Jessy was just hoping that Thomas hadn't supplied him with a ceremonial sword instead of the honored Wilkinson he was used to. Taylor smiled again and then brought the saber up to his face and saluted the large Immortal, who was now facing the American with admiration. The giant looked back at the sultan, who leaned over and conferred with his interpreter. He then nodded his head at the ceremonial guard. The huge beast of a man turned back and the smile was now a smirk.

"Look, you're not defending the honor of the Confederacy here, but the country you have forsaken. This isn't your style, Jessy."

Taylor turned and the smile was still there. "Honor is honor, and this fella here, he looks like the type that likes to pick on smaller people."

"Jessy, you can't kill him," John Henry said as he noticed the guests and the sultan were growing impatient.

"Perhaps our American friends would prefer a smaller opponent?" came a voice that emanated from the area around the French and British contingents, which elicited another laugh from onlookers, albeit an uneasy one.

"No, sir, we like 'em big in the States," Jessy said as he

swished his saber through the air and then stepped forward just as the first beat of the drum sounded. The giant twirled his blade and grinned as he stepped forward.

"This is insane!" Claire said as she squeezed past Jackson to get to John Henry.

"This is coming from our French and British friends, not the sultan. If we don't do this then we lose face—we lose face and the mission is over."

"How do you know all of this?" she asked, astonished.

"That's the way the world works, Madame. This part of the world anyway."

The drums pounded as the two men, one a giant, the other a tall, thin American, circled each other. Suddenly the Immortal lunged while spinning his curved blade as he came on. Jessy held his ground. Just as the beast's sword started down Jessy stepped to the left and the blade whistled through empty air. John Henry tensed when he noticed that the Immortal had swung through and had not intentionally missed. The Saracen steel slammed into the stone tile, sending shrapnel into the air. As he flew past, Taylor slapped his sword into the man's behind with the flat edge. The giant was goosed and he immediately jumped and spun on the American to the laughter of more than just a few of the guests. The British and the French were not among them. Jessy smiled and then dropped into a stance with sword at the ready. He figured old Professor Courtney at the Point would have been proud of his stance. He flourished the sword and then lowered it, inviting the giant in.

He didn't have to wait long as the Immortal swung his sword with a mighty bellow and once more Jessy easily sidestepped the blow. The large man overcompensated and went flying past Taylor, who once more swiped his blade around and slapped the man's ass once more. This time Jessy drew the smallest amount of blood.

The Immortal was now beyond furious as he turned and swung the sword and missed Jessy by mere inches. The blade cut through the air and all who saw the blow coming cringed as they waited for the head of the American to roll free of his shoulders. Claire came close to screaming as she took a hold of John Henry's coat sleeve.

"Colonel, I must say that this may have been a bad decision on your part," Jackson said as he too saw that this was not going to end well.

"Now, now, we do not want any bloodshed," the sultan said, but all could see his smiling, excited eyes as Jessy came within inches of being decapitated.

Taylor felt the wind rush past his face and he figured this had gone on for far too long. He waited for the giant to recover and then stepped to the middle of the hall once more. Again the drums started beating and everyone knew this was no demonstration—the Europeans were making a point. This time there was no smile or polite nod of the head. Jessy opened up with sword at his side, inviting the bear-sized man to attack. He did. With sword raised high he came on. Women screamed, men readied themselves, and John Henry smiled.

The giant felt the American's much smaller sword glance off his large Saracen blade. The *ting* was loud as Jessy countered once again. The noise was tremendous, and most wondered why the American's blade didn't break. But Jessy countered again and again. He stepped lightly around the large man, slapping him again and again on his backside. The Immortal was becoming furious at his embarrassment and that was just what Jessy wanted. Again a lunge, again another quick move to the right, and then the sword slap. Once more the lunge, once more the dodge and slap. The crowd was now beginning to laugh as if this had all been choreographed. Taylor was like a matador from Spain dodging a furiously charging bull in the ring. Finally the giant of a man lost it and charged with sword held high again. One final time Jessy let him come on. He was now tired of the game and as the blade started down once more, Taylor fell to the floor, kicked out, and caught the Turk in the left shin. The man tripped and went flying into the large buffet table, knocking more than a few British and French delegates over.

The crowd went wild with laughter. That was until Jessy approached the struggling man. He turned, bowed to the sultan, who was still smiling, and then quickly raised his sword before anyone could say anything.

"Jessy, no!" John Henry yelled as the others gasped just as the sword came down.

The guests saw the blade descend and the legs of the Immortal go stiff. Several of the gentler women swooned and fell into the arms of their escorts while the rest just stared wide-eyed. Thomas felt his shoulders slump as he did not have to picture what the Wilkinson sword had just done to the Immortal. He had seen Confederate handiwork with a blade before and he knew it not to be a pretty sight.

Then he heard the gathered guests laughing and applauding as Jessy slowly brought the sword up. On the very tip was a melon that Taylor tossed high into the air, and then before it completed its arc he sliced it in two before both halves landed on either side of the head of the prone and embarrassed, but alive, Immortal.

John Henry took a deep breath as the crowd continued to applaud Taylor for his chivalry in the face of an out-of-control opponent. Taylor turned and faced the throne and a cowed sultan. Finally the monarch looked around and saw all eyes were on him. He half-smiled and then stood and also started to add his congratulations to the American. Jessy bowed, leaned over, and wiped off the blade of his sword on the Immortal's backside, and then slammed the sword into its sheath. He turned and made his way back to the group of pleased Americans. Jackson was smiling and nodding his head. Claire was aghast and McDonald shocked at what had just transpired. John Henry only raised his brows at a smiling Jessy.

"A truly gifted swordsman," the sultan said loudly as he waved men and women to silence. "You have my deepest apologies for the overzealous nature of my guard. Immortals are taught to control their attacks. He will be punished, I assure you."

Taylor watched as the giant was led away by two of his compatriots. Taylor looked at the sultan with as much distaste as he could muster. He nodded and then stepped away before he said something that would make the giant's attack seem feeble by comparison.

"I think that's just about enough entertainment for this evening," John Henry said.

"You know that wasn't the sultan's little idea," Jessy said as he removed a half-full glass of wine from an undamaged table and drank deeply.

"No, but it was his way of letting us know that he is watching our little group." John Henry looked up and smiled at the sultan, who seemed to have regained most of his color after the humiliation of his Immortal.

"Surely you cannot still insist this mission go forward?" McDonald asked, as he had been shocked beyond measure at how easily the American had disposed of the Turk.

"What has changed?" John Henry asked, watching the French contingent as they made their way toward the front of the hall. The French spy Renaud was with them, and every few seconds he would look behind him at the Americans with hatred etching his features.

Thomas nodded at the retreating contingent of Europe's finest. "They're who we have to worry about for the time being. The sultan may eventually catch on, but by then hopefully we will have accomplished what it is we came here to do. It will take a while for our European friends to convince him to expose himself to embarrassment again. But yes, Mr. McDonald, they will eventually come to stop us." John Henry turned to the false instructor of antiquity. "So I hope you are good at what you do, sir, because we have far less time than I had anticipated."

"Perhaps we can make our apologies and get the hell out of here. I doubt if the rest of those Immortals are too much pleased at having Colonel Taylor make their man look like an amateur," Jackson said.

"I made up that little bit right at the end there. Did you like it?" Taylor asked as a way of teasing both Claire and John Henry.

"Just as much as those angry Immortals who can't seem

to look away from you," Claire retorted as Taylor noticed for the first time the number of enemies he had just made.

"I agree. Maybe now is a good time to catch that ferry to the eastern shores."

As the Americans started to move off to offer their thanks and good-byes, Thomas shook his head as he looked over at Jessy.

"Why do you look so pleased?" Taylor asked.

"Nothing in particular, Colonel. It was just nice to see a Reb humiliate someone not in a blue uniform for a change."

Taylor couldn't help it. He smiled for the first time in days.

14

Lieutenant Parnell looked at the small pocketwatch once more. He saw the time was ten minutes after eleven before closing the cover and replacing it in his uniform jacket. He turned to face the *Yorktown*'s first officer.

"What time was the last departure of the ferry from the capital?"

"If they are not on the next boat, they won't be here tonight," the first officer said as he turned back to continue the off-loading of the expedition's supplies.

"Great," the marine officer mumbled under his breath.

"Any word yet?"

Parnell turned and saw Professor Ollafson as he too was looking at a pocketwatch.

"Professor, why don't you go and wait inside the station? It may be a while until the supplies are off-loaded to the train."

"Sitting drives me insane," the old man said as he again looked at his watch. He glanced up at the spit-polished Parnell and knew he would get no sympathy from a boy like him. "I wish I had the patience of that Indian boy. Look at him," he said as he brought Parnell's attention to the last railcar in line before the caboose. Perched on the roof of the car was none other than Gray Dog, who had been there since they had off-loaded from the *Yorktown*, which was quickly preparing to head back to open water where she would wait to transit the Bosphorus Strait into the Black Sea to join the *Chesapeake*.

"Well, can't say as I blame him much," Parnell answered before yelling an order at a sailor for mishandling a box of concealed weapons disguised at surveying equipment. "After all, all the Rebel prisoners and not just a few of the naval and marine personnel think he's responsible for the three murders. I think he feels comfortable by himself until the colonel returns."

"What do you think?" Ollafson asked as he continued to look up at Gray Dog, who sat silently and watched the night.

Parnell looked down at the much-smaller professor. "Well, for me it's simple power of deduction, the same deduction and conclusions that both Colonel Thomas and Captain Jackson came up with."

"And that deduction is?" the small man born in Scandia asked as he once more removed his eyes from the strange Comanche only to pull his pocketwatch out of his vest once more to check the time.

"I find it a little difficult to believe that anyone, much less a savage, even one as resourceful as Mr. Dog up there, could enter a locked cell without the key and slaughter three men who outweighed him by two hundred and fifty pounds combined."

"Then it's someone with a key to the ship's brig, then?"

"The obvious answer, yes." Parnell smiled and then before returning to his duties of cargo master looked down to take in the bearded professor's face in the lamplight of the train station. "However, the only man onboard the *Yorktown* with a key to the brig is Captain Jackson."

"I see the conundrum."

"That's the problem, Professor. Anyone with a brain can see that particular conundrum and that's what has everyone on edge." Parnell walked away with his hands placed behind his back.

With one last look at Gray Dog, Ollafson shook his head as he wondered if the Comanche had seen belowdecks what he himself had witnessed on the slopes of Ararat.

Twenty minutes later, a signalman approached Lieutenant Parnell.

"Sir, Privates Cochran and Peavey report that a French warship from Constantinople has just tied up."

"No ferry?" Parnell asked.

"No, sir, not yet."

"Very well. Thank you, Corporal. Is the off-loading complete?" he asked as his eyes started to watch a thick blanket of fog roll in from the Bosphorus Strait. Fog always made the marine officer uneasy, something he could never get used to not only because of its blinding effects but because sound was mixed up inside the veil of white, which he found very disorienting.

He failed to see four men as they watched the *Yorktown* from their vantage point on the long, narrow dock.

"I suspect it would be inside the captain's cabin. That's all I can tell you. When you enter, be mindful of the marines onboard. Since the three murders let's just say they will have a heightened sense of awareness and will not be too tolerant of more French invading their territory. So my advice is, don't get caught. You may find the mood onboard quite unfriendly."

The three men looked at the master spy who had transited the strait ahead of the Constantinople ferry. Renaud disarmed each man in turn and they looked none too happy about it.

"You send us in with nothing?"

"You are Frenchmen and out of uniform. If you get caught on a United States ship of war you could legally be shot. It may go easier on you if you are unarmed. That may sway that bunch of pirates into not hanging you on the spot. Now, you may take your weapons if you wish, or you can just try not to get caught."

The men had to agree with the French spy. After all, he had suffered the humiliation of getting caught and they had not hung him. They just threw him overboard. One man nodded his head but knew if he drew the comparison Renaud would simply reach out and slice his throat before the man knew he had a blade. The rumor was Renaud was hated among even his own colleagues.

"And one other thing: Watch out for that American colonel's pet Indian. He can be a pest."

"Indians now?" one man said, glancing at the others.

"Yes, a savage one also."

The three men felt helpless as they started off into the fog.

It seemed too simple for the three men to board the *Yorktown* without being noticed. The marines and deck personnel were busy finishing the off-loading of supplies, most of them mumbling that it would have been better to sail with the *Chesapeake* and the marching band already sailing on the Black Sea. They would rather pretend to be laying track than hauling freight across the Ottoman Empire.

The three French spies easily slipped in belowdecks. They immediately saw that most personnel were above deck and some had already transferred to the train. The leader placed one of the men at the companionway as he and his partner slowly slipped down the dark passage toward the captain's cabin at the fantail of the ship.

They all froze when the door suddenly opened and an old man stepped out into the dimly lit companionway. The man looked at his watch and then turned the lock with a key and went above deck. The two men waiting in the shadows took a deep breath after almost having their mission end in such a short time had the old man looked up. He hadn't, and the men thought they stood a good chance of getting what they had come for. The first left the shadows along the hull and approached the door and then removed a small pick from his coat. He had the government-issued lock off in seconds and then he simply stepped over the threshold of the cabin. The second man joined him.

The cabin was illuminated by a small candle. The oil lamps were doused, and thus the men had to feel with their hands to find what it was they sought. The first spied the small bundle of tightly wrapped cloth. It sat upon the large table alongside rolled-up maps.

"This is it. He said it would be inside waterproofed sailcloth." The thin Frenchman picked up the bundle and then he immediately dropped it with a loud thud. The sound frightened the other man, who looked at the first as if he had lost his mind.

"What in the hell is in there, rocks?"

"It felt, felt—"

"Hot?" the second man asked when the first stammered as he took in the wrapped cloth on the table.

"No, it was freezing cold," the man said as he touched a finger to the package. He withdrew the touch quickly, but then he extended his finger once more and then placed his palm on its top near the string that tied the bundle together. It was cool, but not freezing. He must have imagined it. He snatched up the bundle, feeling embarrassed. "Take the maps also."

The second man reached out and snatched up four rolled maps and started for the door. It slammed shut for no apparent reason.

"What in the hell are you doing?" the first asked as he stood in the center of the room with the heavy bundle in his hands as the second stared at the closed door to his front.

"I didn't do it," the man said as he placed the maps underneath his arm and tried the door. It seemed to be either locked or had closed so hard that it had jammed in its frame, which cabin doors often did on sailing ships due to warping. "Damn, Philippe, open this door!" the man hissed through clenched teeth.

"Damn," the first said as he placed the bundle of artifacts on the table. He struck a match and lifted the chimney on an oil lamp. He placed the flame to the wick and it caught. He held the light up and looked around the cabin. They were alone and none of the portholes or large windows was open, so there could not have been an inadvertent breeze that closed the door. The man pulled out a small six-inch blade from his coat and continued to examine the interior.

"Look," the second man said as he backed into the same door he had being trying to open.

The tall, fresh candle that had been left alight on the credenza started to lose its brightness. The flame was still there and glowing brightly, but the light cast by the beeswax candle dimmed. Then the lamp being held by the first man started to die. He brought the lamp up and watched as the flame remained the same but the light in the room was slowly drained of color first, and then brightness. The cabin went dark with the exception of two pinpoint dots of light that had been the candle and the lamp.

"What is this?" the second man asked as the maps slid out from under his arm. They fell to the floor with a hollow thump, and then they both heard the decking creak as something moved around them.

Before either man could react, the door suddenly opened and the third man stepped through and then quickly closed it.

"What are you doing and how did you get that door opened?" the first man asked as he tried desperately to see the faces of his two men.

"It's too dark out there. Something ate the light, even from the open hatchways."

"We could not get that door opened," the second man said as he reached around the frightened man and tried the latch. It moved but the door failed to open. He pulled, and then pulled again.

The first man placed the dead lamp on the table and as he did he noticed that the wrapping covering the artifacts had mysteriously opened. He leaned in closer and saw that he could discern some form of lettering. The carved images looked as if they had an inner glow to the etching. He started to reach out and touch the symbols but remembered the intense cold when he had picked up the bundle. He quickly moved his hand back.

"Listen," the second man said as he abruptly ceased trying to open the cabin's door. "Do you hear that?"

The other two men cocked their heads. Yes, there was something coming from the darkness. It sounded like several people chanting in a language they had never heard before. The sounds came and went, intensified and then calmed. Deep and childlike. Booming and then almost-silent sobbing. The cabin became intensely cold. Condensation came from the three Frenchmen's noses and mouths.

"That's enough. Get that door opened."

The two men nearest the cabin door started pounding and then slamming their shoulders against the wood. The door held firm and didn't budge. It was as if the two men were battering a stone wall. The fog outside of the large windows on the stern started to vanish as if even the internal light of fog was being extinguished. Still the two men pounded and charged the door to no avail.

"Damn it, get the attention of the Americans! We have to leave this place and I don't care if they hang us or not, I don't wish to die in here!"

All three men started screaming and pounding on anything they could.

Still, the cabin became even blacker than before as the shadows along the hull started to grow and then move in.

Then it was there. The dark shape was silhouetted in front of the large stern windows of the captain's cabin. It was large and the way it was highlighted against the swirling, white fog beyond the leaded glass made it that much more terrifying to the three French invaders.

The leader of the three tried to move away from the center of the cabin with all thought of scooping up the canvas-covered parcel now gone from his mind. As he slowly tried to slip closer to the door and the two men fighting to get out, he saw the entity that had sprung from the darkest areas of the cabin move toward him. Suddenly some unseen force thrust him down to his knees. The man felt the pressure of a hand, but he knew in his heart there was no hand actually on his shoulder pushing him to the cabin's floor.

One of the two men fighting at the closed and unmovable door turned and saw their compatriot as his arms splayed out

behind him while upon his knees. It was if the man was being tortured by an unseen taskmaster. That was when the
man's eyes took in what was doing it. The shape was that of
a man that stood well over eight feet tall. The facial features
were a swirl of dark colors ranging from green to dark purple. The features were a jumble of movement like the swirling fog beyond the windows. The face slowly turned toward
the two men at the door as the shape held the first man in
place. The man screamed as he watched the first man's head
twist in his direction. The two men could see the first pleading with them to help him. Then suddenly the head had turned
too far and snapped. The men screamed as the head kept
turning even as the spine was severed. The entity allowed the
first man to fall to the deck. His chest hit the floor first followed by his head. The face was still staring up at the dark
ceiling in its twisted shape.

"God help us," one of the men said as he continued trying
to twist the door latch open. The entity seemed to stand until
the topmost portion vanished into the wooden beams that
made up the ceiling of the cabin. Both men froze as a large
black hand stretched out. The long fingers were like a trail
of India ink released inside a water bucket. The fingers caressed the first man as his eyes bulged out. Then the ethereal
digits tightened around the Frenchman's face. The first man
turned in time to see the fingers of the entity scrape down-
ward. The second man started to relieve his stomach of its
evening meal when he saw the skin first stretch, and then tear.
It was like the sound of a piece of paper ripping in two. The
face came off as the man screamed. As the skin was lifted
free of the skull the head turned toward the frightened man
at the door. The look was horrifying as the blood spurted
from the man's open blood vessels. The jaw worked and the
tongue moved but no scream could come from the shocked
man as he slid to the floor.

The man at the door had lost his mind. It was if a string
had been pulled too hard and the twine snapped with a twang.
The mind of the third departed this world just as his body
joined it. The apparition twisted the head of the crying man

until the neck separated from the shoulders. The body didn't fall to the floor, it slowly slid into a sitting position.

The sudden absence of screaming allowed the faint echo of a chant to reverberate throughout the cabin's interior. The sounds were foreign and the words ancient. The cloth wrapping the artifacts started to smolder and then as smoke started to rise from the burning wrapping, the chant finally ceased and the bundle of artifacts stopped sizzling in its cloth. The entity came forward and stood over the table for the longest time. The image of the intruder widened, expanded, and then started swirling like an inner tornado.

The entity started to disperse as soon as the beating heart of the last man stopped thumping.

The screams of pain and fear had reverberated off the thick wooden hull for more than ten full minutes and not one sound had been heard outside the cabin.

The Angel of Death had come and gone and not one person had seen or heard anything.

The mess steward, Grandee, and several other crewmen had been organizing carefully packed canned goods and dried meats for the expedition and had wandered quite close to the captain's cabin. The men went about their work silently and efficiently and not one of them heard a sound coming from the darkened cabin. Six hundred feet away on the train siding where the chartered train awaited its American passengers, Gray Dog stood on the roof of the second-to-last car and looked around through the now-swirling fog. It was the same as before the three prisoners had been murdered. The night had become still and preternaturally silent. Gray Dog heard the men loading the supplies and the Comanche even heard several marines cursing their luck at dice by the tracks, but nothing coming from the distant *Yorktown*. Gray Dog sat back and knew that darkness had raised its presence once more, and he also knew men had already died this night.

As the small paddle-wheeled ferry tied up next to the large French warship, *Dumas*, John Henry led the procession from the boat. The colonel was only slightly put out that Taylor had went gone of his way to embarrass the sultan's Immortal, but deep down was secretly pleased.

As they made their way down the gangplank it was Jackson who summed the evening up.

"Not to belabor the point, Colonel, but I think the sultan has had his large ears bent about what our true intent may be and has had a slight change of mind in his welcoming pageantry."

"I concur," Claire said as they gained the fog-enshrouded dock. "He fully expected one or the other of the combatants to die a horrible death. He fully expected either you or Colonel Taylor to be the example."

"Sorry I couldn't have been of more assistance to the sultan," Taylor said, and even Claire had to stifle her chuckle behind a gloved hand.

"If that's the case, our return trip may get a little dicey," John Henry said as he started to put on his helmet but then scoffed at placing the thing on his head. He shoved it under his arm instead.

"The *Yorktown* will have to make a speed run for the Black Sea, but I think she can make the rendezvous on time. If you're still allowing only five days for any recovery efforts."

"Yes, I figure it will take the Turks or anyone else at least that long to get any substantial force to the area before we either have what we came for, or have failed miserably."

"You have yet to inform Professor Ollafson of your restricted time frame, Colonel. He will not be pleased."

John Henry slowed his pace and waited long enough for Claire to catch up. "Madame, we did not inform Professor Ollafson because he does not need to know. You know because I refuse to excuse ourselves and locate to a more discreet area for speaking purposes. Now you know. Just as I must know how you know that Frenchman. You and he seem to be familiar at the very least." Thomas stopped to make sure that Claire understood the seriousness of his accusation. Jessy, Jackson, and McDonald had stopped also and wondered what it was that the colonel had seen to prompt him to throw so much mistrust at Claire.

"I . . . I just wanted to know why he did what he did. This mission is not warlike in nature, so why spy? The mountain range has been there for eons and has never been thought of as a significant place by any government, so why now? Is it because the Americans are interested, or is it something else?"

John Henry didn't respond to her explanation. He simply continued looking at her beautiful face before turning and making his way down the dock toward the *Yorktown* and the waiting train.

They were stopped by a man running their way. It was a marine corporal who slid to a halt in the fog and then saluted Captain Jackson.

"What's happened?" Jackson said immediately.

"Sir, we've had murder onboard, and Professor Ollafson may be very ill; his heart, maybe, we don't know."

"When?" John Henry asked as he saw that the boy was terrified.

"Twenty minutes ago, sir. But that's not all. We found pieces of men strewn about the captain's cabin. We don't know how many, or who, but they have been slaughtered like cattle, sir."

"Our men?" Jackson asked as he started heading for his ship. The others hustled to catch up.

"No, sir, our personnel are all accounted for. Lieutenant Parnell took a count after Professor Ollafson collapsed."

"The Indian?" Jackson asked without a guilty look back at Thomas.

"On the train the entire night. He never went close to the *Yorktown*, Captain."

As they approached the ship they failed to see a single man slip away into the fog. Renaud had heard all he needed to on the failure of his men and their mission to recover the artifacts. He knew the Americans had caught and killed them. The stakes had just been raised.

"Let's get that train fired up and get the hell out of here,"

John Henry said as they arrived to see the men all standing around on the dock. The talk was rampant about what had happened not once, but twice inside of closed areas of the *Yorktown*. Thomas knew if they didn't get moving he would lose the men before they ever started this fanciful flight of hide and seek.

"Lieutenant Parnell!"

The marine officer appeared out of the thick fog and saluted the captain. "Sir," he said.

"Instruct the men to board the train. We depart immediately. Keep the Confederate prisoners separated from their brethren, not as much as fifteen men per car. I want armed marines at each exit at all times. Inform Lieutenant Anderson to see me for departure orders for *Yorktown*. I have an addendum to his mission parameters. After that he must get to the Black Sea rendezvous as quickly as possible. The men of the first section will be arriving in the east in about two days and they will start making their way south soon."

"Yes, sir," Parnell said enthusiastically, excited to be on the move and not stuck on the slaughterhouse that the *Yorktown* had become.

"And this is the reward we get after I upheld the honor of the nation?" Taylor said with a smirk. "You treat my men as a very untrustworthy lot."

"Trust has yet to be earned. Almost, but no cigar for the moment," John Henry said as he spied the figure of Gray Dog on top of the second-to-last car. He turned and saw his old friend and brother-in-law staring at him. "It may not be just mistrust, Jessy. It seems something may be traveling with us who doesn't want this mission to succeed."

"You mean *someone*, don't you, Colonel?" Claire asked as she slowly removed her large hat and veil.

John Henry looked at each expectant face in turn. He settled on Claire as he explained.

"I really don't know what it is I mean, but I believe you may, Miss Richelieu, and when we get aboard that train I want to know everything you do about what that Angelic Script means—and I do mean everything."

Claire watched as the others made their way to the ship and train that awaited them. They vanished inside the thick veil of fog and she was alone.

The woman who sided with both the French and the British in this matter knew that she could no longer hide the truth from Colonel Thomas and the others. She would have to explain just what darkness they were really heading for in the east. There a mountain awaited, and her experience at both spying and world history told her they were headed to a spot on the map that had been forsaken to mankind. The curse she had made them aware of was something that frightened her far more than the specter of getting caught spying for foreign nations.

Claire knew the Angel of Death watched over that black mountain known as Ararat in the east.

As the last of the supplies were loaded and the prisoners and marines were onboard the train, John Henry was informed by the navy watch commander that a carriage was coming down the dock in a hurry. Thomas turned to Jackson with a wishful thought. Captain Jackson popped open his pocketwatch and looked at the time. He shook his head negatively.

"We still have the last of the mess equipment to load, unless you want to start this little foray into the wilds without adequate food?"

Thomas pursed his lips, almost tempted to say, "To hell with it. Move the train before whoever this is stops us." He peered into the dense fog surrounding the train and the dock six hundred feet away. He heard the carriage come to a stop and a voice filled with authority order several things unloaded. Then he heard an American-accented voice call out.

"Permission to come aboard?"

Before Jackson could answer, a young midshipman raced to the quarterdeck with a piece of paper. He handed it to Jackson, who read the note. He whistled and then passed it to John Henry.

"You're going to absolutely adore this one," Jackson said

as he nodded at the young sailor. "Permission granted, sir!" Jackson called into the fog and the boarding ramp below.

"Damn, what now?" John Henry asked as he crumpled up the hastily written note.

Two men came up the boarding ramp followed by Jackson's dock watchmen carrying several large trunks. The larger of the two men advanced to the quarterdeck. He was heavily mustachioed and had sideburns extending to his jawline. The man looked as stern of visage as Secretary Stanton himself. He removed a black top hat and used a handkerchief to wipe the sweat from the band.

"Mr. Ambassador, we're sorry to have missed you at our welcoming ceremony." Jackson held out a gloved hand. It was ignored.

"If I'd been there, I assure you the diplomatic ruckus you stirred up never would have happened." The large man turned to face the questioning look on Thomas's face. "You have made a hell of a mess for me to clean up, Colonel."

"Apologies, Mr. Ambassador."

"Yes, I have had quite enough apologizing for the time being, thank you. Gentlemen, I received a communiqué from President Lincoln this morning, and thus I was sent on an errand and thus I missed your entrance at the palace. This is Mr. Daniel Perlmutter, an assistant to Mr. Mathew Brady. The president has sent Mr. Perlmutter here to document anything you find," the ambassador said as he reached into his pocket and brought out a sealed envelope. He handed it over to John Henry.

Thomas looked at the large man from Pennsylvania and then raised his brows.

"Your orders have been changed, Colonel, which is why they sent a ship after your small fleet to get Mr. Perlmutter here in time. You are not to bring back any artifact recovered on Ottoman Empire soil."

"What in the hell are we even here for?" Jackson protested.

Thomas opened the letter from his friend. He leaned into

the nearest lamp to read the tight scrawl of Lincoln's hand-writing.

"Document only. It seems we are to discover, document, and then claim American provenance to the world."

"I'm an educated man, but just what in the hell does that mean?" Jackson asked as he turned and saw the last of the mess kitchen being lowered to the dock for its transfer to the train.

"It means we find it, take a few photographs, and then get the hell out of here." Thomas looked relieved to a point. "Which suits me to the ground."

"What about recovery?" the naval officer asked, incredulous.

"There will be no recovery of the vessel. The engineering alone would be too difficult for the time frame involved. The president now knows that the European powers have discovered your true intent in the eastern mountain range." The ambassador had one more item for Thomas. He pulled two smaller pieces of paper from his coat pocket. "These are two receipts. This one"—he handed it to John Henry—"is for the purchase of one hundred and sixteen horses from the Black Sea Trading Company. They will have the animals waiting for your men once they arrive at the end of the line. This one is for one hundred and sixty-one horses and saddles from the same company that will meet you at the town of Talise, fifty-six miles from Ararat as the crow flies. And I must say, these two purchases nearly broke the embassy petty-cash box. There you have it."

"Why so many mounts when we are no longer to recover the artifact?"

"Perhaps the president still thinks you may have to leave this place posthaste. I am afraid your guess is as good as mine on that front, Colonel."

John Henry looked from the receipts in his hand to Jackson, who was slowly shaking his head. Thomas decided to let the matter drop for now. Instead he turned to the newest addition to his mission of fools.

"Welcome, Mr. Perlmutter," Thomas said as he gestured

for his equipment to be loaded onto the train. The men turned and with his trunks in hand made their way back to the dock and the hidden train beyond.

"Thank you, sir," the young man with wire-rimmed glasses said as he held out his hand to the colonel. John Henry ignored it and the boy lowered his soft fingers.

"What am I supposed to be photographing?"

The ambassador tilted his head and then laughed as he placed an old newspaper in John Henry's hand. He then turned away and laughed heartily all the way down the loading ramp.

"Good luck, gentlemen, especially since you'll have half of the European powers out to either stop you, or steal what it is you find." The ambassador stopped halfway down and then turned and through the swirling fog he had his last say. "Out there, gentlemen, the rules of conduct may be a little lacking in civility, so may I suggest you play the same way. After all, what could happen? War?" He placed his top hat on his head as he started to laugh once more and then vanished.

"What in the hell has changed since we left home?" Jackson wondered aloud.

John Henry opened the newspaper and scanned the week-old headline of the *New York Herald*.

Sherman Burns Atlanta to the Ground! Pbt. E. Lee
Surrounded at Richmond, Military Campaigns
in West Winding Down.

"The war is almost over and our European friends are a little worried about a growing power in the west."

"Who?" Perlmutter asked as he was given a foul look by Jackson.

"The United States, and they figure to stop us. Put us in back in our place, so to speak."

Both men looked at John Henry, who handed the *Herald* over to the captain.

"Well, since we don't have to dig anything out of solid ice, we may stand a chance of getting out of this alive," Jackson said as he perused the headlines. "Can't say that I want to be the one to inform Professor Ollafson his mission has been curtailed." He handed the paper to Jessy, who looked at the type and frowned as he read. He turned away and John Henry saw his shoulders slump in sorrow over his drowning nation.

John Henry walked to the ship's railing and stared out at the fog. He watched the last of the marines disappearing into the swirling mist as they moved operations to the train.

"Now all we have to do is find out what it is that's killing people right in front of us without being seen," Thomas said.

"Excuse me, killing?" the twenty-year-old Perlmutter asked a little nervously. "And what are we digging in around in ice for?"

Jackson saw that John Henry was going to remain silent, so he took the boy in the brand-new suit, obviously purchased through the Sears and Roebuck catalogue, and guided him to the boarding ramp just like a father explaining the facts of life to a confused son.

"I take it you have not been briefed on our mission here?"

"No, Mr. Brady just threw me this suit, gave me some old equipment, and sent me to the New York docks. The next thing I know I'm here, and I don't even know where here is."

"Well, let me ask you a question instead, my boy," Jackson started. "Do you read your Bible?"

"Not in a few years, no."

"I think maybe you'd better brush up on it a little in the next two days."

"What parts?" Perlmutter asked nervously.

"Genesis would be good for openers; the story of Noah, to be more precise."

John Henry heard them speaking but his mind was on just how he would gather evidence of a mysterious ship on a mountaintop, and then his only duty would be to get these men home alive. The news of the war made him more determined to do just that.

The Civil War was winding down. Now they would have

to survive the peace, but would the rest of the world allow them to do that?

Thomas knew he had a lot of questions he needed answered, and he knew whom to go to for those answers.

Claire Richelieu.

15

The train departed for the east an hour later. The wind of the passing cars had just settled when four men came running up the dock from the shore side of the city. It was Renaud, and he had three Turkish policemen with him.

The American warship was empty of supplies and passengers. The first mate of the *Yorktown* had been afraid something like this would happen, so he wanted to greet the visitors off of American territory, which the *Yorktown* was, just in case there was some unpleasantness.

The young lieutenant waited patiently for the men to approach. The three Turks looked as if they had been awakened from a nap and were irritated at the Frenchman. The lieutenant heard the last few words and with his limited French understood. The small man who had been tossed from the *Yorktown* three days before was giving a description of his three men and was pointing at the ship.

"May I be of assistance to you gentlemen?" the naval officer asked as he stood ramrod straight by the foot of the boarding ramp.

The first policeman, dressed in a black uniform complete

with a bright red fez with golden tassel, stepped up to confront the American.

"This man reports that his friends went aboard your ship and have yet to return. We would like you to produce them, please."

The young American looked at the three officers and then at the French spy, Renaud.

"Three men. Are these men Americans?" the lieutenant asked innocently. As he spoke, the gangway was lifted and then slowly swung over to the boarding side of *Yorktown*. They all heard her heavy lines being cast off.

The colonel had inspected the cabin where they had discovered the bodies of the three men. There had been no time to make the dead men vanish, nor to clean the cabin thoroughly, so Colonel Thomas had ordered it closed off until the ship made open sea.

"You know they were not American. They are French citizens and our embassy would like them returned."

The lieutenant turned fully to face the man the colonel had uncovered as a spy.

"I assure you, sir, there are no other personnel other than crew onboard *Yorktown*. If they're not American, they're against navy regulations."

"My men are inside that ship and I want them back!"

The American turned and tilted his head at the three confused policemen. "Gentlemen, I would love to stay and chat, but we have to make a rendezvous in the Black Sea in just four days. I hope you find your men."

The agile lieutenant simply turned and jumped onto the low gunnel of the warship as she slowly drifted away from the giant dock. The lieutenant turned as his hand took a firm hold of the rigging and waved at the stunned men on the dock.

The Frenchman cursed as the massive visage of the *Yorktown* slid into the fog as it drifted with the outgoing current. It was like the men were watching a spectral ghost slide into a white veil of nothing. The only sound heard was three bells as they chimed in the night.

"Thank you, gentlemen. On behalf of the United States Navy, I bid you good night."

The voice had a light lift to it as it came from the dense fog. They could hear the rigging as it came taut against the light southerly wind. The bells chimed again and the American warship slipped into silence.

On the dock the Frenchman turned angrily toward the three Turkish policemen.

"You fools! You let them leave!"

The three men exchanged amused looks. The man in charge stepped up to the Frenchman, whom he had decided early on was a cad of the first order. He smiled down at the smaller man.

"And how do you suppose we should have gone about arresting a thirty-two-gun warship? Handcuffs, perhaps. Maybe my men should have shot at the fleeing ship to disable her sails?" The man smiled again as his two men laughed. "No, perhaps you'd better file a protest with the American Embassy, but from what I hear, the Americans are little preoccupied with a small civil war at the moment. I wish you good luck, sir," the policeman said, and then said something in Turkish to the other two, who burst out laughing.

Renaud turned toward the fog and the strait beyond as the last of the warning bells from *Yorktown* chimed.

"You may think you are clever, Colonel Thomas, but I assure you my sense of humor has its limits."

The last sound heard that night on the fog-enshrouded Bosphorus Strait was the music of a harmonica as the tune "Dixie" was played by the northern navy men. The southerners had learned that the catchy tune was almost as popular in the North as in the South. It was a small tribute to the men who were now headed east toward a bleak mountain range that clung to the very edges of the ancient Persian Empire—Ararat.

Claire was still in the car's only water closet. She was sick to her stomach after viewing the cabin onboard *Yorktown*. The clickity-clack sound and swaying movement of the train cars did nothing to alleviate the situation. Nor did the accusing eyes of John Henry Thomas after he had ordered her not to view the death scene inside his cabin. She had insisted on getting the artifacts into her own hands after Professor Ollafson had been removed to the train after discovering the massacre. She had paid dearly for her venture into the bloodbath.

She started to use the pitcher of water to wash her face but then saw that the old and chipped pitcher had seen far better days, and the water within smelled as if it had not been changed. She took a deep breath, opened the door, and entered the private car that was attached to the train as a special office offered by the sultan. That was the last favor John Henry expected from the Ottoman government. Very soon their ruse would be uncovered and the pressure from the Europeans would come to bear on the sultan for his kindness to the lying Americans.

John Henry had summoned all of the principal players for their discussion of the mission and what was left of it. Professor Ollafson was white as a sheet as he sat down at the long table. The mess steward, Grandee, came in with fresh coffee. Sitting next to Ollafson was McDonald, who was still a concern after he'd been noticed spending an inordinate amount of time with a few of the British Embassy staff at the ceremony earlier that night. Every once in a while McDonald would turn to look out of the train's window as the fog-enshrouded night flew past outside. To Thomas, the man was starting to look frightened after the discovery of the three murders onboard *Yorktown*. John Henry had to make a decision sooner rather than later. If he were truly a spy, the man was a terrible one.

Jessy had managed to change out of his dress uniform and was comfortably dressed in a white shirt with black work pants. His hair was askew and his beard was growing longer each day. After the Rebel colonel's clean-up two weeks earlier, he was slowly starting to revert back to his guerrilla appearance. He was sipping coffee and waiting for John Henry to explain the situation that had developed in his cabin onboard ship. They were all interested.

The door opened and through the steam and the noise entered Captain Jackson, followed by the newest member of the expedition, Daniel Perlmutter. The young man was looking quite uncomfortable, as a moment before he had run into a few of the Rebel prisoners and marines in the accompanying cars who had teased the boy about his dress and his lack of a manly demeanor. Then the strangest thing happened when they learned he was a photographer. It was like someone had turned on a switch and the men stopped teasing and started staring at the boy as though he were a plague carrier. Not one man, North or South, wanted the photographer anywhere near them. They were all having thoughts of the battlefield photographs emerging from the death zone that had become the American landscape. The boy clearly was confused, as he was used to working with willing subjects like Union officers wanting their glory depicted in image for all time. These men cared nothing for glory. They just didn't want to be the subject of a death photo.

Finally Gray Dog came in through the back door of the car where he had been found by Lieutenant Parnell, who was with him as they both sat, the marine officer at the table, Gray Dog on the floor by the cold wood stove. Grandee smiled down at his friend as he finished pouring the last of the coffee. He quickly reached into his overly large apron and tossed Gray Dog a biscuit and a small chunk of bacon. He winked at the Comanche, who dipped his head once in acknowledgment. So far the cook Grandee was the only person outside of Dugan and Thomas that Gray Dog conversed with. The former slave was most interesting to the young brave because of the scars he had seen on the man's back during his fight with the Reb corporal, Jenks. He found that a man can suffer for what he dreams, and he could see the large black man had done that.

"How are the men, Lieutenant Parnell?" Thomas asked as he pushed his tin cup away and spread the latest map delivered by the Ambassador.

"Restless at the least, mutinous at the most."

"So, things haven't changed?" Captain Jackson asked as

he removed his hat and sat down at the opposite end of the table.

"I do believe that you northern folk conveniently expect us to kowtow to your demands without memory of what we have tried to do to each other since 1861. While I gave you my word that we would see this through, do not expect us to embrace you for the chance to die on some other barren and lonely spot in the world. Dying is dying, and these men would rather that event take place a little closer to home. So if you expect singing and rejoicing that we are working alongside our northern brothers again, well, I'll have to inform Mr. Lincoln that it may take a little bit more than just a fairy tale to draw us back into the fold. Maybe if the killing of our families had stopped first, we would be a little more cooperative, but alas, the war goes on and so does our disdain for all humanity north of the Mason-Dixon Line."

"That's rich coming from you," John Henry said as he slid the weeks-old newspaper toward Jessy, who stopped it and allowed the paper to open to the headlines. His eyes scanned it momentarily and then he returned the glare of Thomas. "The war will be over soon, Colonel. The country will have to find a way to work together once more. This mission may help in that goal, or it may not, I don't know. But if the president thinks it can, the least I can do is try. I owe the man that." He looked around the table at each face. "A few years after this insanity is concluded, you will all see what this was about. Lincoln expects this nation to take its rightful place on the world stage, and now that we have close to two hundred years of hatred coming to a close, we can achieve that."

They all heard the mess steward, Grandee, cough as though he had choked on something as he was about to leave.

"What is it, steward?" Jackson asked as Grandee opened the door allowing in the train noises from outside.

"T'was nothin', sir." He started to exit.

"I asked you a question, sailor," Jackson insisted.

Grandee stood silent with the empty coffeepot in his hands as the door closed, effectively silencing the night. Gray Dog was chewing his biscuit as he glanced up at his friend. He then looked at John Henry and hoped the colonel would open his ears to the black man.

"Well, with all due respect to Colonel Thomas and the president, this war will never be over, sir."

"What do you mean by that?" Claire asked as she fanned herself with a bare hand.

"You all have forgot what this war was about. No, sir, Colonel Thomas, it will take much more killing and hate before the last shots are fired, and I suspect that it won't happen for a hundred years. America will be punished by God, for he did not mean this to be for the country."

All eyes and ears were open to what the former slave was saying and they all had to admit that it was a question none of them wanted to contemplate.

"The way I figure it, the Lord allowed the founding of this nation for the purpose of freeing the world from bad men. Instead the Lord has watched as the nation committed suicide for something that should have ended in the time of Moses. So sad. Slavery is the darkest evil to ever infect men." The mess steward lowered his head when he realized there was no comment from the people around the table. "May I be excused now, Captain?"

"Return to your duties," Jackson said as he could not look the black man in the eyes. "And thank you for your insight. We all pray that you are wrong."

Grandee shook his head and then exited the car without comment.

"That opinion should not startle you, but it does. Freeing the slaves is only the start of the harsh feelings. It will take two hundred years to end the hatred between the races, maybe even more between North and South."

Thomas stared at Taylor and shook his head.

"His opinion is valid, but one of the reasons we are fighting this war, Jessy, is the fact that you and your people in the South don't give two tinkers' damn for what his or any Negro's opinion is. They had no say."

Jessy popped out of his chair so fast that it tipped and tumbled to the floor. Thomas remained staring at his old friend.

"Gentlemen, this line of inquiry will only hasten our downfall on this mission. May I suggest we table that discussion for a later date when we can sit with brandy and cigars and discuss this with a little dignity?" Jackson said as he looked from John Henry to Taylor.

"That is exactly how we wound up in a war. Gentlemen, all with brandy and cigars, discussing what to do about the abysmal mess we had gotten ourselves into. But I agree. Jessy, when the time comes we can settle this between you and me, but for now we have other enemies at our throats. I don't expect they will differentiate between blue and gray if we are caught."

Jessy looked from Thomas to the others as he returned his chair to the upright position and then sat down. He looked again at the expectant faces around the table.

"You have my apologies."

"Accepted," Thomas said as his eyes locked with Jessy's. The two came to an understanding at that exact moment. They would decide the right and wrong of their personal dilemma when and if they arrived back in Washington. They both knew they had far more than just hatred between them. They had blood, a history, and they once had love of one another.

There came a soft knock on the door and once more Dugan rose to answer it. He saw a very young officer in dress blues standing in front of him, twisting his cap into an unrecognizable wad of cloth. Dugan smiled at the young officer and then allowed him inside.

"We have company, Colonel," he said as he returned to his chair beside the door.

"Lieutenant Parmentier, reporting as ordered."

All eyes took in the youthful appearance and the sparkling blue class-A uniform of the second lieutenant. The handlebar mustache was one that impressed even Dugan, who had shaved for the greeting ceremony at the palace he wasn't allowed to attend.

Thomas smiled when he saw the terror on the face of the boy. He had been taken from the decks of the *Chesapeake* as she sailed past Constantinople for her run into the Black Sea. He was the leader of the band, so to speak, and John Henry Thomas's unit commander for the forces arriving on the Black Sea side of the operation.

"The lieutenant joins us from the new 316th Drum and Bugle Corps of the Army of the Potomac. Sit down, Lieutenant, please."

The young man looked around and then quickly moved to an empty chair next to Claire. The woman glanced over the boy's features and thought to herself that he could not be more than seventeen years of age. She looked from him to Thomas and shook her head.

"Lieutenant Parmentier will hear his final orders before rejoining the Black Sea expedition at rail's end. A horse and escort will be waiting at our destination, and from there you will bring in the support if needed. Are you up to the task?" John Henry asked the stunned officer.

"No, sir, not at all. I am in command of one hundred and twenty-two band members. We haven't fired a weapon since they gave us basic instruction back in Ohio."

"Well, right now you and your men have been penciled in as window dressing. Hopefully just your mounted presence will scare someone off."

"Mounted, sir?"

"Don't tell me you've never ridden a horse before?" Taylor asked, smiling as he anticipated the boy's answer.

"No, I mean, yes, but most of those men in the band have never seen a cavalryman outside of a parade."

"Yep, you can tell this was planned by the U.S. War Department," Taylor said.

Even Dugan had to snicker at the obvious observation by Jessy.

"Nonetheless, you were what was offered, Lieutenant. I will have the sergeant major show you the basics."

The young officer started to say something but a shake of

the head from Sergeant Major Dugan stopped him. The lieutenant sat stunned and silent.

Ollafson reached down and brought up the satchel and then started to remove the artifacts. It was Claire who stood so suddenly that McDonald next to her thought a snake had bit her.

"Excuse me, but I would prefer it if that thing was taken from here while we discuss this mission."

"What?" Thomas asked as his eyes went from Claire to the satchel Ollafson was holding.

"I want those items taken from this car."

"I understand that part of your request, but I need the reasoning behind it."

"There have been six unexplained murders revolving around those artifacts. Seven if you count the professor's student in New York."

"From my understanding, the boy was mugged and stabbed by hooligans," Ollafson said.

"In the presence of those," she said pointing at the artifacts as calmly as she could.

John Henry remained silent as he took in a very clearly upset Claire Richelieu. His eyes went to a startled Ollafson.

"Do we need the artifacts in our discussions here, Professor?"

Ollafson slowly lowered the satchel containing the petrified wood to the floor of the private car.

"Well, no, I guess we don't—"

"I mean out of the car entirely," Claire said, still staring at the satchel.

"Now, now, let's not be foolish," Ollafson started to say.

"I agree. I hate those damned things and would feel better if they were not present."

John Henry looked at Jessy and could see the colonel was not in a jesting mood. He was also looking at the satchel and Thomas could see his uneasiness. The room was so quiet that most jumped when Dugan spit heavily into a spittoon. The *ting* sound reverberated in the sudden silence.

"Sorry," he said as he wiped spittle from his chin.

"Sergeant Major, place the professor's valise in his car, please. Post a marine and then return."

"Sir!" Dugan said as he stood and almost had to pry the satchel from Ollafson's hands. He finally managed and then left the private car. During this exchange, Gray Dog never allowed his eyes to leave the satchel.

"I find this most disturbing, Miss Claire. I fully expected of all my associates you would be too professional to believe in such nonsense away from the mountain. The curse could never extend this far from the summit."

"But yet you still believe in the curse, just not now. When we arrive you will learn to respect its power. Well, I think its power is massive and can reach out wherever it needs to," Claire said as she finally saw Dugan leave with the artifacts. She took in a relieved breath and then sat once more, feeling far better than a moment before.

Ollafson knew she was right. You couldn't believe in the curse as a matter of convenience when trying to convince people of your cause and then put it away until you needed the power of persuasion once again. No, the curse was real and he would have to start respecting that part of the legend.

"All right, the curse can be discussed between you educated folk at a later time. For now, we've got to discuss the new directives from the president."

"New directives?" Ollafson asked as he sat back in his chair with a questioning look on his bearded face.

John Henry hated the fact that it was he who was going to deliver a death blow to the old man's dreams of glory.

"The president believes that establishing provenance in regard to any vessel we may find on that summit will be enough to not only prove your theory, Professor, but give you the lead on any legal expedition to the mountain. The world would have to acknowledge your rights in that regard."

Ollafson looked as if he had been poleaxed with an ax handle. His eyes went blank as he took in what the colonel was saying.

"What of the artifact?" Ollafson asked as even Taylor saw the hurt and sorrow in the old man's face.

"The president explains that since it would take a massive engineering effort to remove your Ark from the mountain, he has given you permission to bring back any viable evidence that is easily recovered. Like the smaller petrified items you recovered on your previous expedition."

"In other words, we are allowed to bring back any trash we find up there and leave the real find where it sits?"

"That's the way I read it, Professor. I'm sorry. The realized threat from other nations and their interest in this expedition is forcing the president's hand on this. We just don't have the available engineers to do it. Most importantly, we also don't have the time it would take to accomplish what you want most, full recovery. That will take peace and a whole lot of money this nation does not currently have."

Ollafson started to say something, then he saw Taylor look at him and lightly shake his head. He patted the professor on the leg in sympathy.

"Don't worry, Doc. If I find the Ark and if it's viable, I'll bring her back for you."

John Henry knew that Jessy was just trying to placate the old man, and for the first time since their reunion Thomas saw a little of the old Taylor inside the burned-out colonel.

The deflation of Ollafson was complete. He knew he was backed into a corner and there was no way out. He would have to do what he could once on Ararat.

"This talk of curses has to end here, in this car, right now." John Henry surprised them all with this short comment. "If word of this reaches the men, and I don't care what uniform they wear, it will frighten them, and there is nothing worse than a soldier frightened of something he can't see to fight. So"—he looked right at Claire—"this stops now."

They could all see the logic in the argument so no one reacted. The door then opened and Dugan returned and nodded at Thomas.

"Done, sir."

"We suspect that *Chesapeake* is now docking at the Black

Sea village of Trabzon. From there they will board the Black Sea Line to our debarkation point, Talise. From there, Lieutenant"—he looked at the young band leader who was still wide-eyed with all the talk about presidents and curses— "if you and your cavalry are needed, you will be sent instructions. It's fifty-six miles to Ararat from Talise. It should take you a hard day of riding to get to us. Hopefully you won't be needed."

"Hopefully," Taylor laughed and then winked at the frightened lieutenant. "If you are called on, this could very well be another battle of the Crimea."

The lieutenant really lost his color as again Dugan had to snicker at the boy's discomfort.

John Henry nodded. "Which is the point I would like to make. The Crimean War could be this mission's salvation. You see, Russia, one of our only friends in the world, lost their war to a combined allied force of British, French, and Turkish troops. The Russians are still a little put out, to put it mildly. We can exploit that little European disagreement between the Czar and his cousins if the need arises, for escape purposes, or maybe a little sea interference. The Russians really do not care for the Ottoman Empire or her fair-weather friends."

"Okay, we may have Russians on our side. Is there anyone else crazy enough to see this mission as anything other than what it really is? A way to show the world that we can throw away lives without conscious thought like Europe. Will that make us a legitimate nation?" Jessy asked with interest.

"We can discuss the shortcomings of the world powers, both ours and theirs, at a later time, Colonel."

"Of course. Excuse my little observation." Taylor's eyes were serious.

"Lieutenant Parnell."

"Sir," the marine lieutenant started to rise but was stopped when John Henry made a sitting gesture with his hand. The lieutenant relaxed.

"You, sir, are our main defense. You and Colonel Taylor

will run defensive and offensive operations if the need arises. You will be in overall command, with Colonel Taylor as the field commander and tactician. Is that clear?"

Parnell looked from John Henry to the smiling face of the Rebel colonel. He frowned. "Sir, I'm not so sure this man can be trusted."

"Neither am I, Lieutenant, believe me. But I am sure of one thing, if the colonel has a preference between a Turkish prisoner-of-war camp and a Union prison, he has not mentioned it yet. I'll let you know if he does."

Taylor lost his smile.

"Yes, sir. What are our rules of engagement?"

"Right now they are simple. If fired upon, don't shoot back."

"Sir?"

Dugan spit into the brass spittoon once more as he too was shocked.

"Although we are willing to bluff, the president is not willing to go into a world war if this thing goes to hell. We are to avoid all contact if possible. If they shoot first I will determine the cause and effect of any possible reaction by us. And yes, Colonel Taylor, a war with all of Europe, while assisting the cause of the Southern states in rebellion, will undoubtedly destroy what's left of your Confederacy, and also all of the United States, and thus would defeat your very purpose, so I expect full cooperation. After all, you are under orders from Robert E. Lee himself."

Taylor remained silent with not so much as a snappy return salvo at Thomas.

"It should take us two days to Ararat and another two to the summit. Foul-weather gear will be issued to all personnel. The weather at the base of Ararat will be no problem, but at the higher elevations we could come across moderate to severe weather patterns."

"My duties, sir?" asked the small, girlish man in the middle of the table.

"Well Mr. Perlmutter, you have what I believe you call a

camera. You will use it as much as possible, sir. And you will
start with a command picture of this car when we arrive. I
want our presence well documented."

"Yes, photographs may come in handy at our courts-
martial."

"That we can agree on, Colonel."

John Henry remained looking at Taylor and then turned
to the rest. "After our arrival I want the men and equipment
on the trail in no more than two hours. The train will not be
returning to the capital. We may need it to get out, and I'm
not a trusting-enough soul to think that the sultan won't
change his mind about our so-called gift. He may make a run
for us. As far as the other European powers are concerned,
the only force available to them is what they have at sea. As
formidable as that is, they can't travel overland. So, the only
opposition we may face is the empire's, and that's only if they
have a change of heart. They can only do that if the British
and the French gain the sultan's ear."

"Which I suspect they will by the time we make the summit of Ararat," Jessy said as a serious point.

"Understood."

"Now, the questions you undoubtedly have can be covered
in the next two days, so we'll adjourn. Would Captain
Jackson, Colonel Taylor, and Miss Richelieu stay behind,
please?"

The group got up to leave with McDonald paying particular attention to Claire. All noticed the silence of Ollafson
as his dream of Ararat had come crashing down. Everyone
gave him a clear path out of the car.

Claire sat silently, wondering why she'd been asked to stay
behind. She suspected that her recent hysteria over the artifacts was the main cause. She apprehensively looked over at
a smiling Colonel Taylor. The handsome officer had no concern whatsoever about facing Thomas. Jackson remained at
the opposite end of the long table. He was also curious about
what Thomas wanted to say.

"I've noticed how uncomfortable you are around Professor's Ollafson's artifacts of late."

Claire looked up. She noticed that John Henry's question was directed at her. She looked from him to the others, who watched and waited.

"I think the murders have me thrown off a bit. They do make me uncomfortable."

"Yes, I've noticed." John Henry stood and saw that Gray Dog was still sitting by the door and hadn't moved, even after Dugan had tried to boot him from the car a moment before. He took a small bite of biscuit and watched. John Henry winked at the boy and then made his way around the table. "So, you're telling me after a full year of study you have just now become a believer in ancient biblical curses?" John Henry asked as he poured four glasses of whiskey from the decanter on the sideboard. He placed glasses in front of each, Claire, Taylor, and Jackson. Then he returned to his chair and sat. "For a lecturer in Angelic Script and ancient languages, you seem to be very vulnerable to the foolishness of myths and legends—not very comforting for us novice biblical followers, would you say?"

"Colonel, I have noticed that instead of coming directly to a point you skirt the tactful way of asking and go with an approach that will allow a subject to say more than they were willing to say. That may work on some, but not all."

Taylor raised his brow at the quick way Claire defended herself.

"If you have a question, sir, by all means ask it."

John Henry smiled. "All right, Madame, I will." Thomas leaned forward, smiling. "How long did you know that your Mr. Cromwell was none other than Paul Renaud, French Intelligence?"

Claire's breath caught in her throat.

"And what makes you think I knew he wasn't who he said he was?"

"For the same reason you're not telling us why you and Professor Ollafson have a British spy on your academic team as well."

Jackson slowly stood and walked around, nudging past Gray Dog, and silently locked the door. They were now isolated. He returned to his seat and faced a stunned and silent Claire Richelieu.

Claire refused to say anything at first, at least until she found out how much the colonel knew, or guessed. Thus far, if he were guessing, she figured him to be at the very least clairvoyant.

"Now, this is at least interesting," Jessy said as he placed his hands behind his head and waited on Claire to answer John Henry.

"And your sudden fear of something that you claim to be knowledgeable about, well, it's a little too unbelievable. How long did it take you to learn Angelic Script?" Thomas asked as he stood and then poured himself a drink. That was when he noticed that Jackson had a Colt revolver placed in his lap as he courteously waited for the woman to speak.

Finally Claire stood suddenly and this brought Jackson's Colt into the open.

"Whoa, take it easy there," Taylor said as he came fully awake as Claire didn't even look at the weapon as she moved past John Henry, and as she did she drained the small glass of whiskey and then she lifted the decanter and poured another. As she did she eyed Captain Jackson.

"Don't be so melodramatic, Captain, really." She swallowed the second drink and then poured another and then returned to her seat with the glass and the decanter. She sat and then watched as John Henry returned to his seat. Captain Jackson lowered the Colt as Thomas sat down.

"McDonald is not to be touched or molested in any way. Is this clear to all of you?" she asked as she toyed with the top of the glass. She then looked at each face one at a time.

"Clear? Yes, that's clear, but who in the hell are you to be giving orders?" Jackson asked as he smirked and looked from Claire to the colonel. "Especially as you are about to be thrown off this train."

"No, I am not," she said as she downed her third glass of whiskey. She hid a small burp behind her elegant hand and then smiled as she poured a fourth.

"You're not?" Jackson enquired.

"No."

Thomas smiled as he sat back and relaxed. "I'll ask again, Miss Richelieu, how long did it take you to study a crash course in Angelic Script?"

Claire smiled sadly at Thomas. "A full year of the most boring lectures you could ever imagine."

"After hearing Professor Ollafson's oratory abilities, I cannot imagine that particular hell," John Henry said as he saw the confused looks on the faces of Taylor and Jackson. The latter finally lowered the hammer on the Colt pistol and then placed it fully exposed on the tabletop.

"What in the hell is this?" Jackson asked as even Taylor was showing a great amount of curiosity.

Thomas ignored the question from Jackson.

"Why should we not chuck Mr. McDonald into the night air?" John Henry asked instead.

"Because he may know how the Crown will act if we discover the provenance of anything we find up there. I believe he and the British may overreact."

"What makes you believe that?" Jackson asked.

"Because, gentlemen, they are terrified of what our nation can become in later years. It's that simple."

"I noticed you said *our* nation," Jessy stated flatly as his eyes caught Thomas's.

"Relax, Miss Richelieu, if that is your name. The president does not believe wholeheartedly in sending men off totally blindfolded."

Claire looked at John Henry and knew then that this army officer had known all along who her employer was.

"It is Claire, but not Richelieu. In Paris and London, yes, but my real name is Anderson. Claire Anderson."

"How long have you worked for Mr. Lincoln?" Thomas asked as Taylor and Jackson sat stunned.

Claire slowly sipped her whiskey this time. She heard the clickity-clack of the train wheels striking steel as she realized that the hard thumping was her heart, because for the first time in her professional career she had been found out and she didn't know how to take that.

"For the president, one, almost two years, or ever since this plan of Ollafson's started to come together after Gettysburg. For Mr. Allan Pinkerton, I have worked for four years. I started training under him in 1859 in preparation for the war he saw coming. Later I was transferred from the war department to this . . . this mission."

"A woman spy. What a marvelous and advanced age we live in," Jessy said as he reached for the crystal decanter and poured himself a drink.

"I gather information from men who are a little weak in the area of security."

"Meaning your talents were learned for operations against the South," Jessy said as a statement, not a question.

Claire drank her whiskey and smiled. "Exactly, Colonel."

"As I said, what an age." He drank his drink and stared at the woman with a newfound respect and dislike.

"Now, why the fear behind this so-called curse? Was that a play, or are you concerned?" John Henry asked as he now got to the point of his questioning. He knew before Lincoln had explained things that Claire was not the person she said she was. Her reactions and her eyes betrayed her.

"Renaud is not just any French agent; he was and is their best. The man never takes a life without the need for it. The killing of the student was not like him. Why kill the boy when he was just a ruse and not carrying the artifacts with him? No, that is not his style," she said as she finally slid her empty glass away. "After his attempt to get the petrified items from the professor he became like a man possessed."

"So, you are what we call a double agent?" Jackson asked as he finally shied away completely from drinking his glass of fiery whiskey. This was not unfolding the way he had expected.

"A triple agent is more accurate," she said as her hand reached slowly into her bodice. The eyes of every man went wide for a moment as she sent her small fingers into the area of her breasts. She pulled out a small envelope. "My official orders from the War Department."

John Henry reached for the envelope but didn't read it.

"Miss Anderson, I knew about your credentials long before we left the docks in Baltimore." He gave the envelope back to her. "I don't care what this says. From this point onward you are working directly for me and me alone. Is this in anyway unclear?"

She looked at John Henry as she replaced her orders into her bodice. "Yes, Colonel Thomas, it is very clear. But if you don't heed my warning about those artifacts we will run into trouble. The kind of trouble you read about in the book of Genesis. Is *this* clear?"

John Henry saw the determination in the woman's face but kept his skepticism to a minimum for the time being.

"I will give you your way when it comes to McDonald for now. But if he does anything to corrupt our mission he will be left in the wilderness. The last I heard, you cannot be blamed for a man falling off a train."

"Understood. He will be valuable when the time comes in figuring out what the British will do if and when we come up with the evidence."

"Gray Dog," Thomas said, turning to face the seated Comanche. "What was it you saw in the brig onboard *Yorktown*?"

Gray Dog finally stood, much to the surprise of Claire who never knew the Indian was even in the same car.

The Comanche looked at the woman and then at the men. "Great Spirit does not wish for men to travel to his black mountain. His mystery *is* mystery and the dark ones watch and wait. The black one is here now and has awakened since we travel. Black medicine is working in this place."

"What did you see, boy?" Taylor asked as he lost patience with one of the race of men who murdered his sister, regardless of what John Henry said. His prejudice he kept close to his heart, and he lashed out at anything related to it.

"The dark ones live in the shadows of this world and they grow strong once again. It will protect the mountain and what lies buried there."

"Women spies and Indian superstition. This is a wonderful combination, John Henry. All of this combined should make for excellent planning." Taylor had lost all of his humor.

Thomas looked from his young friend to Claire.

"Report anything unusual from our British army friend immediately or you may find yourself off this train also."

"I will," was her curt and angry reply.

"Good, dismissed." John Henry watched them leave and then turned to Gray Dog. "You're reverting back to old ways. I need you to speak in terms I can understand."

"There is no understanding of this, John Henry. Men will die if we continue."

"Ask Sergeant Major Dugan to bring in the artifacts before he beds down."

"John Henry, we must not go to this black place."

Thomas watched Gray Dog leave and wondered if every person he knew had gone off the proverbial cliff as far as reality was concerned. With the country killing itself in a war that should have been fought a hundred years before, he didn't need fairy tales to keep him busy.

He would discover the truth behind those ancient petrified wooden relics.

16

Jessy sat at the wood-burning stove, allowing his feet to feel the warmth they had been seeking since the winter of 1862. The second year of the war had seen one of the coldest winters on record and his feet did not come out of the conflict well at all. Taylor was well aware of a soldier's right to complain about his feet, and he utilized that right by making his men keep constant vigil on the stove. He sat in his stocking feet as he propped them as close as possible to the stove without actually setting them on fire.

Mess steward Grandee was moving through the car with a tray of coffee and his version of a sweet bun most of the men had never eaten before. Both marine guard and Rebel soldier had been pleased to get the treat from the giant black man. Even Taylor accepted the coffee.

Inside the car there were twenty-two prisoners and ten marines. Thus far they had kept separate company with only an occasional glance that relayed the men's distrust of one another. Most of the Rebels were gathered near the back of the car around a single table, leaving their wooden bunk areas for the marines. The accommodations supplied by the Turks had surprised both Union and Confederate soldiers.

The soft melody of "Bonnie Blue Flag" permeated the train car. The harmonica was slow and bold. The song was normally an upbeat and rollicking tune sung by the troops in the South. The chorus would usually be a blaring *Hurrah, hurrah, the boys are home, hurrah*, but instead it was just the harmonica playing a sad refrain instead of the patriotic, inspired verse. Taylor was hearing the sadness as the tune came home to roost.

As the car moved along into the night, a single note sounded from the area where the marines sat. Then another was sent into the sad refrain of the Rebel contingent. It was a slow start to the tune "Battle Hymn of the Republic." It was another harmonica, only this was used by a marine corporal. The music got louder, interfering with the Rebel tune. In turn the Confederates became louder. Soon a few words to both songs sounded and Taylor grimaced as he foresaw what was coming.

"Shit," he said as he sat up and started pulling on his boots as the harmonicas gave way to pounding and louder lyrics from both sides.

Suddenly Taylor was saved the bad experience of breaking up a fight between factions when a louder tune started filtering through the other two. It was loud and played with spirit. It was another harmonica, and as the men all stood their words and rhetoric started to dwindle down to nothing. They saw the man who had come into the middle of their songs with one of his own. It was Grandee and the steward was playing the old tune that all American men knew—"Yankee Doodle."

Taylor had to smile as the men, both marines and Rebels, didn't know what to do or say. It was Corporal Jenks who started singing the words to the old American folk tune. Soon others joined. Both marine and Reb started caterwauling to the song as loudly as they could.

The door opened at the back of the car and Taylor turned and saw John Henry with a drawn Colt as he stood in the

doorway after hearing the loud voices erupt. Jessy smiled as
he once more kicked off his boots. He looked at Thomas and
then his smile grew and he shook his head. John Henry
holstered his weapon and then nodded, leaving the car as it
erupted with both sides singing the same song.

For both Taylor and Thomas, that was a start—again.

John Henry closed the door with a mild sigh of relief. The
men were not brawling as he'd suspected they would.
He smiled and shook his head as he started back to the private car at the back of the train.

"Is everything all right?" came the voice from behind him.

John Henry turned and saw that Claire had left her sleeping berth, the only occupied one in this car, to see what the
shouting and singing were about. She was in a white dressing gown and her long, flowing red hair cascaded around her
shoulders. Thomas looked down and the dressing gown was
not the only item to catch his eye. Claire was holding a small
Derringer in her right hand. John Henry looked from it to the
woman's green eyes.

"Expect to bring down many a Rebel with just that?"

"No, just you for exposing my cover story. We could have
discussed my orders in private."

"Well, you can put that away for now. I'll answer your
challenge after this is all said and done." He started to turn
and then thought better of it. He smiled. "If you really want
satisfaction, of course?"

Claire grimaced and then she lowered the Derringer. She
half-smiled and then looked at the colonel in his long-
underwear top and blue pants.

"Are you going to tell me what that is all about?" she asked
as she nodded toward the forward train cars.

"Just a few men remembering who they are." He shook his
head and turned away. "Or were."

Claire listened to the rousing tune coming from the men
who had been joined by others, both naval personnel and Confederate, as they came together to remember something from
their shared past. She understood why that was significant.

"Sometimes it's the simplest solutions that stump you, isn't it?"

"Sometimes," John Henry said as he opened the door and without looking back he stepped inside the private car.

Claire stood and watched the closed door for the longest time. Then she jumped as she felt someone behind her. When she turned she saw it was the Comanche, Gray Dog. He nodded and stepped past her to Thomas's closed door, where he sat. He watched her until she turned back to her berthing area.

When she climbed inside and pulled the thin curtain, her thoughts turned to Thomas and she wondered what made a man so resentful of being alive. She got a strange sensation that the colonel would rather be laid low in a grave than be among the living. She suspected she knew why, but for some reason could not understand why it was she cared.

Her thoughts were still on John Henry as she closed her eyes for sleep.

In the dim lamplight Thomas once more unfolded the waterproof cloth covering the two artifacts. The strange symbols were highlighted as darker etchings as the lamp did not fully expose them to light. He ran his fingers over the deep-cut etchings and then he felt the coldness of the petrified wood. He removed his fingers and rubbed them together. He could almost feel the frost as he wanted nothing more than for the feel of the wood to leave his skin.

John Henry reached out and swallowed the last of his whiskey, and then as he reached for the decanter found that it was empty. He pushed both the decanter and empty glass away from him as he felt his eyes growing heavy. His attention was again drawn to the two pieces of artifact and the strange symbols on the one. His fingers almost touched it again and then he pulled them back. His eyelids drooped as he again rubbed the tips of his fingers together. It was as if the cold was extending outward now and he could feel it without actually touching the stone. Finally his eyes closed and he felt the gentle touch of sleep as it claimed his conscious mind.

Outside the door, Gray Dog's eyes also closed, but not before he pulled the blanket given him by Grandee up around his shoulders as subconsciously he felt the cold as it claimed the car.

Claire was deep asleep in her berth but still managed to pull her quilts and blankets more securely around her.

The two small lamps inside the railcar started to dim as John Henry embraced the sounds of the train as even they fell distant inside his sleeping mind. The soft tinkling of the whiskey glasses and decanter settled to a mournful tune that only added to his deepness of sleep.

Just before the lamps expired to nothing, a large shadow detached itself from the rear section of the car. As the light died it took a giant's form as its wings spread wide and engulfed John Henry Thomas. The entity spread and then after feeling the thoughts of the American, the shadow slowly dispersed.

Jessy opened his eyes at the same moment John Henry started screaming in his dreams. He hurried from his car and made it through the windblown opening between. As he approached Thomas's car he saw Gray Dog as he had never seen him before—asleep and not moving. It was as though the boy had been drugged. He pushed aside the sitting Comanche and tried to open the door, but it refused to budge.

"What is it?"

Jessy turned and saw Claire standing behind him. His eyes told her everything. Their gaze was punctuated by a scream inside the darkened railcar. As Claire pulled her dressing gown tighter around her, she realized that it was freezing inside the car. As she passed between the cars she'd felt the night was brisk, but not as cold as it was inside once she entered the second-to-last car. She heard John Henry yell something incoherent.

"Break it down!" she cried as she feared what was happening inside.

Taylor battered the door. Then another body slammed into it from the side as Gray Dog had finally awakened from his unnatural sleep. Both men pushed with their shoulders and the door cracked. Again they pushed as the air rushed by in between cars. The door finally gave, but both men came to a startled stop. Even Claire could see the entity as it stood over John Henry. It was large and it was blacker than the darkness of the car. The giant shadow turned toward them and they saw its mouth widen. They were struck by the sounds of thousands of dying and distressed voices. They were mixed women, children, and men as the maw widened farther. The sounds of slaughter—ten thousand years of man's crimes against men sounded in all of those terrified and pain-filled voices coming from the blackness.

"Oh, God!" Claire screamed as the entity turned fully. The blackness was complete, but they could all swear they saw things moving in that blackness. It was like a shadow covered with millions of moving insects.

Suddenly with a last scream from John Henry the shadowlike darkness closed and then opened the massive mouth wide and out came a roar of an animal the likes of which had not roamed the world in its existence. Then the shadow vanished and the two oil lamps slowly came up in intensity.

"What in the hell was that?" Taylor said as Claire rushed past him and into the railcar.

"Death," Gray Dog said as finally he too went in to see about Thomas.

Jessy watched as they slowly coaxed John Henry to come around. As for Taylor, he stepped back into the cold night air and closed the door as he realized what it must have been that made John Henry scream the way he had. They were the same screams he had heard the day he had come upon John Henry cradling his sister's headless body on a burning porch. John Henry was reliving the past.

He moved his head into the slipstream of the moving train and looked eastward. In the moonlight he saw the range of mountains for the first time. He shivered in the night as he spied the snowcapped summit.

"Gray Dog is putting him to bed. He says the colonel has

never been this drunk. I suspect that had something to do with his vivid dreams," came the raised voice as it reached him through all of the train's noise.

Taylor turned and saw Claire standing outside in the cold air.

"For a spy, you don't seem to be very observant, Miss Anderson, or Madame Richelieu, whatever you prefer," Jessy said as he turned fully to face her. "I'll tell you what I saw. I saw a large shadow standing over John Henry with an outstretched hand touching his head as he slept—that's what I saw."

Claire didn't respond as she started to turn away. Jessy took her arm and spun her back around.

"Now, tell me you saw different."

"I told all of you, something is attached to that artifact that's not natural. I can't explain it, and the colonel doesn't want to hear any theories about it, so I suggest you leave it be." She angrily shrugged out of Taylor's grip.

Taylor reached out and took hold of her arm again and pulled her to the opening of the section between cars. The wind caught her hair and it flew back. She saw the mountain range and she froze.

"I think you'd better explain it to us before we reach that!" he screamed against the noise of the tracks.

She saw the mountain range and she wanted to turn away but her head wouldn't move.

"Because, my dear, we are fast arriving at our destination."

Claire finally managed to turn back to face the Rebel colonel.

"That," he pointed harshly, "is Mount Ararat!"

The blackness of the mountain range became visible long before the dawn light of morning illuminated the barren landscape.

Only the peak of Ararat looked down upon the approaching Americans with silent scorn. For this was not the first incursion the mountain had faced.

History would never record the truth that the summit of Ararat had claimed more lives than were lost at the American Battle of Gettysburg.

It had been more than twenty-four hours since the incident in the private car with John Henry. Most had noticed the dark circles under his eyes as he moved past them inside their berthing cars. The Rebel prisoners raised their brows when they saw the silent way he moved about. It was Claire who cornered John Henry as the train pulled into their last water stop before they hit Talise. The sun was bright but the morning had grown cold as the weather took a turn for the worse. Claire bundled herself as best she could without breaking into the cold weather gear. She saw the men milling around as the colonel had ordered most off the train to stretch their legs. She waited at the bottom step of the private car until John Henry and Jessy made an appearance.

"Colonel Thomas, do you have a moment?" she asked as John Henry pulled on a pair of leather gloves. He nodded his head and then looked at Taylor.

"Would you excuse us?"

Jessy took his time lighting a cigar and then looked up as the tobacco caught. He smiled and then looked at Claire. "Careful now. I just glued him back together." He smiled even wider and then tipped his hat and moved away, humming a tune she couldn't place.

"He is one complicated man," she said as she followed the easy gait of the Confederate officer.

"Not exactly the word I would use to describe him," John Henry said as a little of his old self shone through for the first time in a full day.

"Colonel, about the other night, I just wanted to say—"

"Look, I don't know what happened. I only have what you people say. I had a nightmare about the death of my wife. It happens quite often, I assure you," he said and then started walking toward the edge of a small road as the train took on water. He turned and saw the men, even their guards, relaxing on the wild grass that grew on the Turkish plains. The area somewhat reminded Thomas of the Llano Estacada in North Texas in its bareness.

"Colonel, I assure you, there was a presence in that car with you. It was touching you as you slept."

"That is what Colonel Taylor has been saying. All I can say is that I was dreaming." He turned away in his stubbornness.

"Listen, I understand that you dream, but I was informed that you never act out in your nightmares. You were screaming. It was if you were watching the event right in front of your eyes. It was terrifying."

"And you came upon this information how?" he asked as his attention was brought back to the beautiful woman questioning him.

She stood silent, knowing she had betrayed a trust.

"I'll be having a talk with Sergeant Major Dugan, I can assure you."

"He's as concerned as myself, so I'm sure the sergeant major will bear up. I have a feeling he does it quite often anyway. I understand you are plagued by nightmares."

"You have me there. Yes, and Dugan needs to keep quiet."

For the first time in what seemed like days they both laughed.

They saw Gray Dog approach. The boy was eating an apple. It was something the Comanche could not get enough of. Grandee had also introduced him to the banana and he found it to be a magical fruit of wondrous taste. John Henry had felt bad for depriving the boy of such simple pleasures in their time in the west. He knew he had been lost for the past five years and how badly it had affected those around him.

Gray Dog chewed on his apple.

He watched the two stop laughing and then John Henry looked at him, waiting to see what Gray Dog had to say.

"We are being watched, John Henry."

The two of them became still as the colonel slowly turned and looked at the low-slung hills surrounding the train line. He failed to see anything.

"Where?" he asked.

"A mile south of us. Four mounted men. They sit upright in their saddles. Soldiers."

John Henry looked at the spot Gray Dog had indicated. He was surprised when he saw how far off the Comanche had spotted their guests. He could barely make out the shapes of men sitting upon horses.

"Perhaps they are just Turkish drovers. They're quite abundant in this region," Claire said, failing miserably at spotting what the men described.

"Maybe we ought to mount up and go see who they are," Thomas said as he started to turn back toward the train.

"No," Gray Dog said as he tossed his apple core away into the tall, dry grass.

"Why?" Thomas asked as he stopped next to the Comanche.

"Because they come," Gray Dog pointed south.

John Henry turned and saw that the riders were indeed headed toward the stopped train.

"I guess we better put on the tea," Claire said as she finally saw the four men riding hard toward them.

There was no comment from John Henry as he clearly made out the shining sabers as they flashed in the sun. Whoever they were, they were indeed as Gray Dog had described—soldiers.

The only uniformed officers on the train siding that day were Thomas, Jackson, Taylor, Dugan, and Lieutenant Parnell. The prisoners and the U.S. Marine guard were attired in rugged civilian work clothes. The men idly milled about as normal men would after a long and tiring ride on rough rail. As the military men were posing as army and naval engineers, it stood to reason that they would wear their corresponding uniforms. As for Claire, Ollafson, and McDonald, John Henry had ordered that they stay aboard and away from prying eyes.

As the four riders fast approached, Jessy stepped up to John Henry as he finished his cigar.

"See what color those fancy uniforms are?" he asked as he made a show of not looking in that direction.

"Good old blood red. Rather startling after such a bleak landscape."

"Why would the British be so brazen as to approach our little band of fools?" Taylor asked as he watched his men for any sign of them not following orders. Word had spread among his men that if any escape attempt was made without his knowledge he would charge the perpetrators with treason.

"I suspect they will have reason. If not, they expect us to be terrified at the sight of royal red." John Henry smiled as he faced Taylor. "I am not one to frighten easily at mere colors. You boys in gray should know that."

"Yes, but then again I guess those gray uniforms were kind of hard to distinguish way out there in Nebraska and Kansas counting Indians."

Thomas kept the smile on his face as he faced Jessy. "You have an innate ability to get my dander up right when I don't need the aggravation, you know that?"

Taylor puffed on the cigar as he smiled broadly and waved at the four riders as they entered the water-station area.

"Hell, John Henry, that's what in-laws are for. You know that." He waved more vigorously as the men stopped and watched the activity around them. Taylor saw a captain and two lieutenants. The fourth was a bearded sergeant who looked as tough and gruff as Dugan. Each wore the shortened versions of the white pith helmet made famous in Britain's India campaigns. Taylor thought they looked silly and doffed his fedora just for show.

John Henry reached into his tunic and brought out a cigar and slowly lit it, cupping his hands against the freshening wind. His eyes never left the British officers.

"Gentlemen, welcome to the wilds of the Ottoman Empire. Strange to see more lost souls out here."

"We are most assuredly not lost. We are in the service of Her Royal Majesty, sent to survey a possible new trade route into Iran and points east."

Taylor made a show of looking around and then he settled on the mountains not that far distant.

"Mercy, now that would be a task getting men and equipment through those passes up there. Sure you're up to it?"

"I assure you, sir, those small mountains are no hindrance to Her Royal Majesty's Engineering Corps. Now, may I have your name, sir?" the blond captain asked as he located the rank on Jessy's uniform jacket. Spying the small shoulderboards with the silver eagles, the captain waited.

"Name's Jessup Taylor, colonel, United States Army." He smiled and bowed with a flair of hat swinging wide and low. He half-turned and smiled at John Henry who watched silently while smoking his cigar. His blue eyes went from a bowing and graceful Taylor to the ruddy face of the English captain.

"Now that the matter of who's lost and who's not is settled," John Henry said as he kept the cigar firmly in front of his face as he smoked, "and you see the rank of the officer in front of you, I believe in our army as well as yours, that the eagles on his shoulders rate a salute, sir." He stepped forward with one hand in his pants pocket and the other holding his cigar. His size compared to the mounted British was still imposing.

The captain cleared his throat and then noticed the eagles on John Henry's uniform coat also. He immediately stepped down, but not before lightly slapping the knee of the lieutenant next to him to follow suit. All four men dismounted. The captain approached John Henry but he held a hand up and gestured toward Jessy, who was smiling and smoking. The captain turned and faced the wrongly attired Rebel officer.

"You have my apologies, sir. I am normally not discourteous, no matter what the uniform or situation."

Taylor smiled as his eyes roamed to John Henry, who had also caught the slight as the captain made a show of examining the Union blue uniform.

"Relax, Captain." Jessy returned the openhanded salute from the officer. He did it quick and not exactly the way he had been taught to do it at West Point. "We are all friends out here." Jessy walked up to the captain's mount and patted the animal on the front leg as if admiring it.

"Captain Jeremy Satterfield, Her Majesty's Black Watch, on assignment to the Ottoman Empire to assist our ally in road construction." He turned and this time his salute was directed at Thomas, who merely dipped his head without returning the officer's courtesy.

"So, you, like ourselves, are engineers?" Taylor asked, turning away from the horse and then approaching the silent lieutenants as they stood ramrod straight. Only the gruff color sergeant had the courage to eye the American as he examined them like a species of insect.

"Us? Oh, no, Colonel. We are selecting a safe route for our engineers. The British armed services like to have our boys protected. We are just the vanguard of an entire British regiment. We have been granted permission by the empire to deploy for security reasons."

"All of that security for an allied army in a friendly state?" Thomas finally broke his silence. "Must be nice to have such friendly relations."

"We try to do our best, sir," Captain Satterfield said as he moved away toward the resting and playful prisoners as they were preparing to board the train once more. The train's whistle sounded as the first man Satterfield approached just happened to be Corporal Jenks.

Taylor turned away from the three remaining soldiers and looked at John Henry, who tried his best not to pay attention to what Satterfield was doing.

"Good day, young man," Satterfield said with a smile as he placed his hands behind his back as if he were attempting a normal greeting and conversation.

Jenks only nodded his head and tried to step past the tall and very thin red-jacketed officer.

"I would have thought strapping men such as yourselves would be in the armed services of your country?"

Jenks looked at Taylor, who was watching silently. He turned and faced Satterfield. He removed the dirty hat from his head and scrunched it up in front of him as if he were frightened of the British officer.

"Fight for men like you? I think I would rather break rocks in the desert," Jenks said in a rough imitation of an Irishman. He was trying to conform to Colonel Taylor's orders as best he could. "First we are driven from our island by the likes of you and then when we get to America we're treated no better than dirt and they ask us to fight for them?" Jenks spit into the dust at Satterfield's feet. The officer just looked at the bearded Jenks and said nothing.

John Henry watched what amounted to a British interrogation of his men. He saw that Jenks held up well as Satterfield turned his nose up at him. Somehow the redcoat had been informed about the men being something other than what they represented. Jenks did well to hide his southern accent, but Thomas figured the officer wouldn't know the differing dialects of the people of the United States. Hell, even he himself had a hard time distinguishing regional tongues.

"These men, as you may have heard from rumor and innuendo, are in fact draft evaders. Their sentence is to work this railroad. Any other questions can be directed to my second-in-command." John Henry turned on his polished heels and boarded the train.

Satterfield watched the large American colonel vanish into the train's second-to-last car. He turned and approached Taylor, who was gesturing for the men to board. He was pleased to see the marine guard mingling with their charges in an attempt to maintain the deception. Jessy turned and nodded at the captain.

"May I offer the services of the United States Army for your transport east? I assure you we can accommodate your mounts and find space among the Irish workers for bedding purposes."

"That will not be necessary, Colonel, although the offer is most assuredly taken for what it was meant for." The eyes were the only part of the smile that failed miserably.

"I suspected it would be, Captain." Jessy did have the eyes for the smile that was present on his face after the offered insult as he picked at the shoddy relationship between the English and their Irish brothers.

"Colonel, the empires, both Ottoman and British, know exactly why you are here. I suspect that the sultan is at this very moment regretting his decision to allow you Americans access to the eastern mountain ranges. Your attempt at gaining access to this abominable myth will cause irreparable damage to America's international future."

"Now, you see, you lost me there, Captain. We Americans have the irritating ability not to see things the European way. We stumble along the best we can and try to do what we think is right. Now, we're here to build a rail line that connects north and south all the way to the Mediterranean. To what myth are you referring?"

Satterfield remained silent as Taylor held the man's eyes with his own.

"Suffice it to say, Colonel Taylor, you will not be allowed to succeed in stealing what most assuredly is not yours." Satterfield turned and made for his horse. The jangling sword at his side made for a dramatic effect as he mounted. "You are a long way from your home, Colonel. Stop this madness and return there before you cause a stir America can ill afford at this time."

"I think you'll find we don't think that far ahead, Captain. Good day, sir."

Satterfield did not wait for Taylor to finish before he wheeled his horse around and started whipping it back to the south.

The only man to remain was the sergeant, and he was staring at the three up and three down stripes of Dugan, who had taken an interest in the exchange between nations. The two gruff sergeants held their gazes upon each other and then the British color sergeant winked, as if he and Dugan shared a link that only they had. Then the sergeant turned his mount and rode after the officers.

Jenks stood next to Dugan.

"I don't think my acting convinced them of nothin'," he said.

Dugan watched the riders as they shrank in the distance.

"Those boyos know exactly why we're here, Corporal, make no mistake about that."

"If that's the case, I would feel much better with a gun in my hand."

Dugan laughed hard and loud. "Yep, right after I give you command of a regiment."

Jenks spit again and then shook his head.

"What do you think?" Taylor asked when he joined John Henry and Jackson as they watched the British ride off from the darkness of the rail car.

"You know what I think. The whole damn world knows why we're out here and if we're not careful this could turn into a real shooting war."

Taylor laughed and then surprised John Henry by slapping him on the back.

"Maybe that's what old Abe wanted all along, ya think?"

Thomas watched Taylor walk away as the train whistle sounded and the first charge of the steel wheels started them forward once more.

"I sure hope he's wrong," Jackson said as he stepped up. "Because all we have as a backup plan is the *Argo*, and that, Colonel, will not be enough."

Jackson walked away and left Thomas alone. Once more John Henry stepped outside and then leaned outward between cars. The mountain was growing larger. It seemed he could see a weather front on its summit and wondered if the risk was worth the reward. As he thought about this, Ararat stared back at the approaching Americans with a silent face. Her peaks and valleys awaited the incursion by an unbelieving species that knew no bounds in their arrogance born of success.

As he watched, it seemed the shadows that grew onto the plains in front of the mountain range lengthened, as if reaching out to embrace the newcomers.

John Henry knew Ararat's embrace would be a cold one.

PART FOUR

THE GOLDEN FLEECE

The gods are best served by those who need their help
the least. . . . as to why I leave temptation and traps for
mortals? It is so the gods can come to know them, and
men may come to know themselves.

—**The Greek god Zeus, from**
Jason and the Argonauts
(1963)

17

The end of the Ankara line was just as the words described—
the end. The bleak landscape gave credence to the rumored
ghostly aspects of the region. The station at Talise was nothing more than two ramshackle huts and a water tower. There
was a siding for the locomotive to be turned back west, but
that was all. The onetime village of Talise had been wiped
out by smallpox nearly four years before and the remaining
homes had collapsed under the onslaught of the severe winters in eastern Turkey.

As John Henry scanned the work going on around him he
felt as if he had started to regain the strength he had before
his assault at the hands of Claire's supposed curse. Thomas
had refused all questions from the officers around him about
what had frightened him so. How could he explain to them
the reliving of the day he'd found the mutilated body of Mary?
They would never understand the horror of what he had seen.
War in the east could not compare to the compassionless way
in which men survived in the west.

He was approached by Lieutenant Parnell, who saluted as
he made his report.

"Lieutenant," John Henry said as he returned the salute.

"Sir, I have dispatched the two couriers north along with our bandleader to meet up with the Black Sea contingent to escort them here if needed. The telegraph is up and running, but we have a break in the line somewhere between here and the town of Iziz, the hamlet where the northern line ends a hundred miles from here."

"Very good, Lieutenant. Are you clear on your own orders?"

"Yes, sir. I am to remain here with half of the men, one hundred and three charges. We are to slowly work our way eastward toward Ararat for obvious reasons. We'll make a grand show of laying ties, as per our mission. I will await any orders from you from the summit."

"Remember your rules of engagement, Lieutenant Parnell. You are not to open fire unless fired upon by any outside force, and then it is only to buy time to disengage. If approached by representatives of the sultan, you must not, under any circumstances, engage Turkish forces."

"And other forces?" the young and straight marine asked worriedly.

"I'll leave that to your good judgment, Lieutenant." John Henry smiled at the eager officer. "French, German, or British, if they so much as frown at you I would show them how tired you are from all this traveling and stomp their asses if the opportunity arises. Other than that, keep the men ready and their horses inside the train. No one is to know our capabilities. Are your rules of engagement clear?"

"Not at all, Colonel," Parnell said facetiously as he watched the long line of horses and pack mules as they were made ready by the one hundred and twenty men that would accompany Thomas and Taylor to the summit. "I'll try and do my best, Colonel."

"That's all any of us can do, son."

Sergeant Major Dugan came toward the two men as Thomas turned and instead of returning the final salute of Parnell's, he nodded and shook the boy's hand.

"Let's hope we don't have too much explaining to do to

our grandchildren when they ask what we did in the great rebellion, huh, Lieutenant?"

"I must admit the thought of making it out of here and having grandkids thrills me to no end at the moment, sir."

"I knew you were a levelheaded young man. Good luck, Lieutenant." John Henry buttoned the top of his fur-lined greatcoat and accepted the reins of his horse from Dugan. He saw Gray Dog ride up and wait for him. Even the Comanche had a long fur-trimmed coat on over his leather skins. Dugan mounted with a nod to Parnell.

"Lieutenant," Dugan said with a tap to the brim of his cap.

Parnell watched as John Henry spurred his large mount forward. The golden piping lining his saddle blanket was clearly visible with its two crossed sabers in the corner. Parnell could see that John Henry Thomas was now in his element.

As the colonel rode along the long line of men, horses, and wagons, he saw Claire at the front of the column. He reined in his mount and sidled up next to her horse. A few snow-flakes fell from the bleak sky and settled on her thick coat. Thomas had to smile at the bulky and very unfeminine clothing Claire was forced to wear. The fur hat was the topper, and John Henry had a hard time keeping his face straight. McDonald had settled in next to Claire and looked far more miserable than the Pinkerton agent. Thomas was enjoying this to no end.

"I can see you two are as snug as bugs in a rug."

Claire looked his way. Her nose was starting to tint red but her eyes were clear. They told John Henry his ill-suited humor was not going over well at all.

"Don't fear, we only have fifty-odd miles of barren terrain to cover." He smiled but turned away before Claire could focus her angry eyes on him. "Isn't it nice to be on a horse again?" he said loudly as he, Gray Dog, and Dugan spurred their horses forward to take up station next to Taylor at the front of the civilian column.

Thomas smiled at Jessy, and the Rebel colonel returned it

with an uneasy one of his own. He glanced over at Dugan and Gray Dog and the sergeant major just shrugged his shoulders as he was used to the exuberance of John Henry when it came to his chosen profession—cavalry officer. Both Dugan and Taylor knew the man to be the most gifted cavalry tactician West Point had ever turned out this side of Robert E. Lee himself.

"Column, forward!" he called out loudly as he waved his gauntleted right hand in the air and then extended his fingers toward their dark destination—Ararat.

The American expeditionary force moved onto the Plain of Mount Ararat. The summit now rose seventeen thousand feet above them. As the column advanced to its ultimate goal, a tune was started by none other than the naval mess crew. As they moved east men started picking up the old favorite, and soon the words were clear to John Henry at the front of the column. Why that particular old tune, Thomas would never know.

As snowflakes started to accumulate on man, animal, and wagon, the first horses and riders crossed the shallow Murat River as the soft refrain of the old hymnal "The Old Rugged Cross" reverberated from man to man, from Rebel to marine. The scene was surreal as every man knew what they were being drawn toward and the old hymn was the only thing the men of both North and South could think of to sing. To Thomas and Taylor it was a most appropriate choice.

The American raiders grew closer to God's mountain, and every man knew the owner to be rather pricklish at times and one who never hesitated to make an example out of foolish mortals.

Seventeen thousand feet above them, buried in thirteen-thousand-year-old ice, the Ark waited.

Since the men had ample rest and food for the past two weeks, John Henry knew he could push them. The weather had held off on the first day, sputtering snow from time to time, but the sun was being held back by some of the more ominous clouds Thomas had ever been witness to. The thunderheads that developed on the vast reaches of the American southwest were this way also, but in his experience they moved fast in their destruction, while these just seemed to hover around the summit of Ararat and extend to the lower elevations as if the weather was reaching down for them. He could see that the expedition members were indeed wary of the signs.

He rode up and down the line extolling Dugan to keep his wagon train up to speed. The Reb drivers were cautious on the uneven terrain in front of the steeps of Ararat.

He spurred his horse forward when he saw that McDonald and Ollafson had decided to take a break from the cold by vanishing into one of the mess wagons where the men had a hot stove going. Claire had not accompanied them.

"Not joining your friends?" he asked as his horse settled in beside her own. Thomas's animal nudged hers and then the two bumped heads.

"Whoa," Claire said softly to make her mount calm in the presence of the large roan. "I can only take so much belly-aching about how miserable the weather is. McDonald is not your everyday field officer. I think he's used to getting what he wants from the sitting side of a desk planted inside a well-warmed room."

"It's a soldier's right to complain, even in Her Royal Majesty's Black Watch, I guess," John Henry said as he took in the reddened features that blotted Claire's face. "Miss Anderson, go to the mess wagon and warm up. Take some time to thaw out. We've been riding for fourteen hours and won't settle in until sunrise when I can post less of a guard detail."

"I'm fine, Colonel. Unlike Captain McDonald, I have been field trained and rather excel at it."

"I can see that, Miss Anderson, I just—"

"My name is Claire, Colonel. Every time you say Miss Anderson I look around for my mother, who wouldn't have appreciated it either."

"Fair enough. My meaning was not intended to insult, but rather to inform, Miss . . . Claire," he corrected himself quickly and received a small dose of a smile from the spy.

"You see, although the temperature is a balmy thirty-one degrees, the wind is the real danger here. If you could see your face right now you would agree."

Sudden panic filled her eyes as she pulled down the thick scarf from her mouth and face.

"What do you mean?" she asked pointedly.

John Henry almost smiled but held off. She was a stubborn woman, but like every woman the world over she was vain to a point. And that was the way he attacked this formidable woman. Thomas knew he was thinking like a caveman.

"Frostbite, Madame. The splotches on your cheeks are just the onset of a not-so-severe case of frostbite."

Claire cleared her throat as she turned in her saddle for a look back a quarter mile to the mess wagon, whose small stove pipe was bellowing smoke, and she could imagine the enticing heat as well as Grandee's cooking aromas.

"A cup of coffee would be welcome, I suppose," she said as she quickly raised the scarf to her face so John Henry could not see her rough skin. This time Thomas did smile as she abruptly turned her horse and galloped off.

John Henry laughed as he heard the quick beat of hooves after Claire realized she might lose part of that gorgeous skin to the weather. Before he realized it Gray Dog was riding beside him. The Comanche turned and saw that Claire had almost made it to the chuck wagon at cavalry-charge speed. He turned back and faced John Henry with a strange look on his face.

"All right, what is it?" Thomas asked.

"Is the red-haired woman your friend, John Henry?" Gray Dog asked as they rode.

"First Dugan and now you?" He turned to look at his youthful friend. "She's brave, but no, not a friend."

"No, she is a friend. She trusts John Henry."

"Hell, there's a lot you have to learn about women, Gray Dog. She's the one that's a little short of trustworthy characteristics."

By the look on Gray Dog's face he could see that he did

not understand what Thomas was saying. He decided to leave it for another time.

"We are being watched again."

"I suspected as much. Who?"

"Uniforms, black and red."

"Damn," he said as he turned and looked around at the vast terrain. "That could be anyone. German or Turk. The Germans we could bluff, but if it's representatives of the empire we may have some hard questions to answer for being so far out of line of the supposed track extension. I was hoping they would be observing Parnell and his men. Damn it. How many?"

"Five, maybe six riders," Gray Dog said as he moved his horse away and then galloped toward the front where he was scouting ahead.

Taylor saw the exchange and rode up beside Thomas. "Bad news?" he asked with that irritating and ever-present smile.

"We have more company," Thomas said in exasperation.

"Kind of wastes your forced march from the station, doesn't it?"

"It was a judgment call, Jessy." Thomas turned angrily in his saddle. "You do remember the variables of command, don't you?"

"I seem to remember the course at the Point. I also seem to remember I failed and you were at the head of the class."

"I know there's a point in there somewhere, Colonel."

"The point, Colonel Thomas, is the fact that if that is a reactionary force and not a scouting element, you have a handful of tired and sleepy men. They may not have the quickness you hoped for if confronted."

"What makes you think I would order a defense? Maybe we talk our way out of any situation."

"Listen," Taylor reined in his horse, forcing John Henry to do the same. "You can say these dumbass things to some shavetail lieutenant, but it's me you're talking to. The first shot at these men, marine or southerner, these boys will shoot back. Maybe you forget what all of these men have been doing for the past four years, John Henry. They're killers of the first order and I don't think whoever is out there has taken that into account. So you better wrap your arms around it—if we're confronted these men will not surrender to the likes of them."

John Henry saw Taylor's point but chose to remain quiet. He did turn to Sergeant Major Dugan.

"There's a small rise ahead and we only have two hours until sunup. We make camp there. Make sure every man is fed well. We pull out in twenty-four hours."

"Yes, sir," Dugan said as he turned his horse and sped to the front to terminate the forced march.

"I see my powers of persuasion are still viable," Taylor smirked. "Must be that ol' southern charm."

"That's it, Jessy, that old charm. Now see to your men."

John Henry watched Jessy ride off knowing that he had been right. Expecting men who had been fighting a merciless war against their own kin to be able to hold off defending themselves against a European foe was rather naive of himself. He had to think things through better or they would fail at every aspect of their mission. He decided that Claire had been right after all—he had been affected by his dream. He knew now that the episode was not just memory, it was a warning about the power they were possibly facing. He had to start owning up to the fact that this mission might have more mystery than he first believed.

John Henry Thomas watched as the column ahead slowed and then started to circle as they made the rise in the land. As he watched, his eyes were drawn to the dark shape of the mountain range with its bright sheeting of white snow.

Up there the shadows would be dense and impenetrable.

THE BOSPHORUS STRAIT, CONSTANTINOPLE

Lieutenant J.G. Riley Montague Abernathy stood on the bow sail of the U.S.S. *Carpenter* as she slowly slid past the eastern shore of the capital. The fog was so thick it seemed it was pressing down on the young naval officer. He tilted his head as he heard the shallow-draft warning bells as they sounded across the strait. It was hard to discern the distance and he hoped he didn't run aground with the *Carpenter* or the vessel the large thirty-two-gun warship was towing into the Black Sea, the U.S.S. *Argo*.

Abernathy turned and shouted out behind him. "Give me distance to *Argo*!"

"Towline is taut, warning chime still at safe distance," came the reply from the aft section of the *Carpenter*.

The lieutenant was one of the brightest up-and-coming young officers in the United States Navy. He had been hand-picked by Captain Jackson for the task of getting *Argo* into position.

"Ten degrees right rudder," he called out.

"Ten degrees right rudder, aye," came the reply.

"Depth?" he called again as he tried again to penetrate the dense fog with nothing more than faint hope working for him.

"Back to forty fathoms!"

"All right, Mr. Harvey, straighten her out."

His second-in-command watched the lieutenant, who was now a ship's captain for the first time in his life, hop down from the rigging and onto the darkened deck.

"Aye, Captain," he said. "Helm, rudder amidships, steady as she goes."

"Rudder is amidships, steady as she goes, aye," came the relieved reply.

The two vessels had just crossed the narrowest point of the strait. They were only a few miles away from entering the Black Sea where they would hide for as long as Colonel Thomas needed. But the way the *Argo* had performed thus far, Abernathy was worried she would founder long before she was called upon. Twice the *Carpenter* had to stop to save the large *Argo* from foundering in calm seas. It had taken long hours to shore up the flotation balloons inside her hull to keep *Argo* above the waves. He had almost lost the one-hundred-man crew of the *Argo* long before they had arrived in the Mediterranean. Twice she had rubbed her keel on the bottom of the strait since the fog had set in, but she had made it through with much sweat lost in the process.

"I thought for sure we would have torn out *Argo*'s keel when we hit that twenty-fathom mark back there, Mr. Harvey."

"Aye, the hairs were standing straight up on my neck on that one." The young naval officer chuckled in relief. "Odds are we still left some Maine oak back there on the rocks. *Argo* draws ten more feet of draft than does the *Carpenter*."

"If Ericsson hadn't come up with the idea of transferring *Argo*'s ordnance over to *Carpenter* we might indeed have lost her. The extra tonnage would have weighted her right to the bottom of the Bosphorus."

Lieutenant Harvey looked at his pocketwatch in the weak lighting of the bow. "Well, in a little while the *Yorktown* will make a daylight show of entering the strait for all the prying eyes to see. Meanwhile, we'll be cruising the Black Sea where no one expected us to be."

Abernathy raised his brows at the comment.

"Let us just hope we can get back out when the need arises. As I recall, that part of the plan was rather vague."

"You mention that now?" Harvey asked, incredulous.

"Need-to-know basis, Mr. Harvey, and you—"

"Didn't need to know," they both said simultaneously.

Abernathy nodded and then watched the swirling fog as it started to thin the closer the two vessels got to the Black Sea.

"The only real thing we have to worry about is one item, I guess," Harvey said.

"And that is?"

"If they brought the *Argo* along for the ride, hiding her inside a barge, someone was expecting big trouble."

"Indeed, Mr. Harvey, indeed."

At 0510 hours on the morning of October first, the United States Navy entered the Black Sea in undeniable force for the first time in American history.

Three hours later, and while ordinary Ottoman citizens on the western shore cheered, the U.S.S. *Yorktown* entered the strait.

It was but five hours after that the French warships *Especial* and *Osiris*, two thirty-six-gun frigates, slipped past the lighthouse at the mouth of the Bosphorus and into the Black Sea.

18

THE PLAIN OF ARARAT

Most of the men had collapsed immediately into their tents. Each four-man cover held three Rebel prisoners and one marine. You could no longer call the marines a guard; they were just as tired and apprehensive as their charges, and the cause was the summit that was looming ever larger.

John Henry was surprised to see Claire up and about two hours before he wanted the column to reassemble for the final leg onto Ararat. He would have thought she would have taken more advantage of the singularly large tent with which he had supplied her. Thomas had also made sure that Grandee and his mess crew made hot water available for her use. He continued walking as Claire accepted a cup of coffee from a mess steward. She nodded her thanks and then noticed John Henry. She nodded but did not approach. She looked again and then vanished back into her tent. Thomas pulled his pocketwatch from his coat and saw that it was 1620 hours. Two hours until the sun set.

Sergeant Major Dugan stepped up, rubbing his hands together. To John Henry's surprise Dugan had trimmed and cut his beard to a manageable jumble. His boots were polished and his brass shined in the dreary late-afternoon sunlight that filtered through the black clouds overhead. Thomas did a double take when he noticed the change in the gruff Irishman.

"Is that a hair treatment I smell?" Thomas asked as he took a tentative step away from the sergeant major.

"Might be a touch. Had a hard time getting my cowlick to settle in."

"Uh-huh. And instead of sleeping you polished boots and brass and curtailed that jumble of baling wire you call a beard."

"I slept plenty on the train." He sniffed the air and then slapped his hands together. "Well, I think I'll go see what the navy has rustled up for mess call." He started to turn away.

John Henry kept his gaze on the east as he scanned the plain for a sign of Gray Dog, whom he had sent ahead to scout.

"I suppose this sudden change has nothing to do with that spit-and-polished first sergeant of Her Majesty's Black Watch making you feel somewhat"—he turned to Dugan with a smirk—"lacking?"

"Me, lacking decorum to a bloody damn Brit? Not likely Colonel boyo. Why I would—" His words trailed off when he saw Gray Dog riding hard and fast for the camp. Dugan nodded his head. "Gray Dog's back and it looks like he might have something to say."

The Comanche rode hard directly into the center of the large encampment. The noise of beating hooves woke many, including Captain Jackson and Colonel Taylor. Others stepped out into the cold to see what the excitement was about.

Gray Dog remained seated on his saddle blanket. His horse was winded.

"Riders, over fifty men."

"Same uniforms?" Thomas asked as he made sure Jessy was awake and listening. Grandee assisted in this by handing both officers a steaming tin cup of thick and rich coffee.

"No, dress in black, flowing robes. Headdress. Swords, and are well mounted."

"Who in the hell is this now?" Jessy asked as he stepped closer and took hold of the reins of Gray Dog's horse. "How far?"

"They wait in a draw two miles up."

"For a barren wasteland it sure is getting crowded out here," Taylor said as he took a sip of the coffee and then made a face and dumped the cup into the fire.

"Report," John Henry said to Gray Dog as his eyes scanned the horizon in the east.

"They not come from west of us, but east. I backtrack and pick up sign coming from a pass next to Black Mountain."

"Again, I didn't fare too well in geography. What's over those mountains?" Jessy asked.

"That is Persia. Not a real friendly place. However, they have no love for the Ottoman Empire either," Jackson said as he too nervously watched the horizon.

"Good report. Get some hot food in you. I need you back out there," John Henry slapped Gray Dog's horse on the hindquarters and sent it toward the smell of cooking food.

"Odds on hostility?" Claire asked, walking up from behind, surprising them all. She was dressed and bundled and looked as if she were ready to travel. She was joined by McDonald and Ollafson, the latter looking like death warmed over, as if he had gotten no sleep at all.

"Transitioning state, that's about all the briefing I received on Persia. After all, we didn't plan to gain the summit of Ararat from the eastern side," Jackson said as he nodded a greeting at Claire, who was impressing the young naval officer more each day.

"Inform the mess to slap some bacon on a biscuit and drown the men in coffee. I want to break camp in fifteen minutes. Get the tents struck and the wagons hitched." The officers and sergeants stood rooted to the spot for only a moment at the sudden change of orders. "Move, gentlemen."

The men broke and started rousing the camp. The men grumbled, but soon enough word spread that there might be a hostile force nearby and they started moving more lively. John Henry gave the Rebel cavalrymen their due, they were fast and efficient after years following the zigzag command tactics in hit-and-run employed by Robert E. Lee. They were silent and precise as they hitched and reloaded wagons.

It was Claire who noticed the rumblings first. Corporal Jenks and five other prisoners were speaking with Taylor and the talk looked animated. Claire turned to John Henry and pointed this out.

"We may have a situation here, Colonel," she said, getting his attention.

Thomas turned and saw the confrontation developing between Jessy and his men. He watched as the colonel looked their way and then said something to the six men who also looked toward them. Taylor nodded and then turned away and made for John Henry. He rubbed his beard and then looked up into the expectant face of his former brother-in-law.

"The men are scared. Besides that goddamn mountain spooking the hell out of them." He turned toward Claire and dipped his head. "No offense." She shook her head, indicating that his words did not make her blush in the slightest. "But that ugly mountain combined with our wandering friends out there is having a most undesirable effect on the boys."

"They want arms." It was a statement from Thomas, not a question. "No."

Taylor didn't say anything but looked over at Claire. "Does he realize that frightened men fail to do what's expected of them?"

Claire remained silent as she glanced at Thomas, who stood steadfast.

"The marines are armed. If we move fast enough, we can—"

The first gunshots caught John Henry in midsentence. He turned in time to see at least twenty-five riders top the small rise and charge into the head of the camp. Several were swinging large Saracen swords at the men as they raced past. Many more were firing old-fashioned powder-and-ball rifles. Thomas saw one and then a second man fall. One marine and one Rebel. The marine tried in vain to grab the reins of a passing horse and failed, being cut almost in half by the large, curved sword. The Rebel cavalryman was shot as he tried to get to the fallen lance corporal. Taylor and John Henry both pulled their Colts and immediately started to return fire. Slowly the marines started to respond. Several of the black-clad riders fell off their mounts and were beaten half to death by the unarmed men who descended on them like a pack of wolves.

"My tent!" Ollafson screamed loudly, startling a frightened McDonald next to him.

Thomas turned and saw several of the flowing headdresses as they entered the professor's tent. The four men had sneaked into the camp from the side opposite the attack. Now John Henry could guess why.

"The artifacts!" Ollafson called out as he blindly ran for the tent.

"Dugan, bring that shelter down!" John Henry yelled.

Sergeant Major Dugan saw what was happening and hurriedly ordered ten marines into a firing line and in seconds had them rapid-firing with their Spencer carbines into the large tent. Bullet holes appeared and the white canvas looked as though it were being buffeted by an internal windstorm as the large rounds tore it to pieces.

"My things!" McDonald screamed in horror as the tent started to collapse.

"The last of them are running, Colonel," Jackson reported as he holstered his smoking navy Colt.

The marine line ceased their torrid fire into the now-flattened tent. The only thing still standing was the shelter's center pole, and even that strong member was tilted and shattered. Dugan approached cautiously and just as he got to the tent he was charged on from the inside. A large Persian with a gold band holding his headdress in place slammed into the sergeant major as he jumped from the wreckage of the tent. The man swiped at Dugan with his sword and the Irishman dodged backward and fell into the grass. Taylor raised his pistol to shoot but John Henry stayed his hand. Thomas shook his head as he saw the Persian had the satchel, which contained the two artifacts. As they watched, the man grabbed a set of reins and jumped aboard the horse. With a twirl of his sword he sped out of camp.

John Henry looked quickly around. He saw who he wanted. It was Gray Dog, who had yet to leave camp. He was wiping blood from his knife, and that was when most noticed the dead Persian at his moccasined feet. Thomas whistled and when Gray Dog looked up he gestured at the fast-retreating rider. He pointed and then made a fist. Gray Dog jumped upon his horse and then sped as fast as a bolt of lightning toward the running Persian thief.

"I need him alive!" Thomas said as the Comanche rode past at breakneck speed.

The officers looked around the shattered camp. Men were assisting others who had taken sword wounds to their bodies.

"Damn!" John Henry said as he took in the destruction that had occurred during the short and very one-sided battle.

"I want my men armed," Jessy said as he helped a wounded Rebel soldier to his feet.

John Henry eyed Jessy and it told him that was now was not a good time. "Report, Captain," he said instead, turning to Jackson.

"Very lucky, for being caught off-guard, I would say. One dead and sixteen wounded. Two severely." He turned to Taylor. "Both of them your men."

"Correction. From this point forward, they're *my* men, Captain."

"Are they?" Jessy asked angrily.

"Sergeant Major Dugan!"

"Sir!" The sergeant major was a little embarrassed but no worse for the wear after his encounter with the sword-wielding Persian.

"Break out the crates of arms. I want every man armed with one of the new Henry repeating rifles. Marines also. I want each trooper issued a sidearm with fifty rounds of ammunition for revolving pistol. Each is to get a full field pack. Is that clear, Sergeant Major?"

"Sir!" Dugan started to turn away with a cautious look at Colonel Taylor. "Giving guns to those hooligans is like giving dynamite to a group of drunk Irishmen, I swear . . ."

They watched the grumbling sergeant major inform the marines what to do.

"I am happy to see you listening to the voice of reason," Jessy said as he faced John Henry.

"Hell, Jessy, I probably just signed the death warrant of every man in this expedition."

As Taylor walked away Thomas saw Claire as she tried to console Professor Ollafson. McDonald was using the toe of his boot to see if any of his personal property was still intact. But it was Claire he was thinking about. Issuing weapons to a band of Confederate prisoners who were over six thousand miles away from home seemed a good way to start either a war or a rebellious mutiny. As he watched Claire and her ministrations toward the old man, he wondered if he had also condemned her to a short trip and a brutal death, because the last he heard the Persians did not hold their women in high regard. He was terrified how they would treat the emancipated Claire Anderson, the former Madame Claire Richelieu.

But even more confusing was the concern he was feeling for someone he hardly knew.

He turned away from the image of the woman and saw the mountain ahead. What lay in store for them at the summit was constantly on his mind and the subject had him wishing his friend the president had just left him alone on the American plains counting savages.

The Plains Indians were tame compared to the foreboding peaks of Ararat.

The marine medical corpsman had to sedate Ollafson. The young marine didn't like doing it for the simple reason he suspected the old professor had a bad heart. The man's color was faded and the rumors were quickly spreading, as rumors always do in camp, that Ollafson was being affected by the mountain. The corpsman had tried to put the kibosh on the ridiculous talk but it spread nonetheless. Having lost the only two artifacts to come from the summit of Ararat was just too much for the enduring Swede to recover from.

The men and wagons had been loaded and John Henry ordered the column forward just before the sun set in the western sky. For the first time that day the sun had actually peeked out from the ominous clouds, but only after the burning orb had been chased into the west and had lowered in the sky. Still, after the humiliation of the day at the hands of the Persians, Thomas observed that seeing the sun, no matter how brief in duration, assisted in putting the men in a better mood. That and being armed once more.

"Your mount is saddled, Colonel," Dugan said as he turned quickly and looked ahead to see if there was any sign of that troublesome Indian, Gray Dog. Thomas could see that even the heartless sergeant major was worried for the young Comanche, as this land was not exactly his element.

"Don't fret, Sergeant Major. I'm beginning to think Gray Dog understands more of what's going on here than we do." Thomas pulled on his leather gauntlets and then accepted the reins from a marine corporal with a nod of thanks. He saw Jackson and Jessy waiting. A wagon rolled past and he saw Claire in the back on the second in line tending to Ollafson. Even with John Henry's assurances Ollafson had lost hope of ever seeing those cursed artifacts again John Henry saw the gentle way Claire had about her. She looked up and gave Thomas the barest hint of a smile.

"Rider!" one of the Rebels cried from atop his wagon.

It was Gray Dog, and it looked as if he was dragging something behind the small pony he was riding. Many of the wagons and most of the riders slowed their march to see just what the Comanche was up to now. They were shocked, but pleased, to see that Gray Dog hadn't failed in his mission. But by the looks of his captive, he might not have. Gray Dog pulled up on the reins and hopped from the pony just as it skidded to a stop in front of John Henry. He immediately drew his bone-handled knife and cut the rope he had used to tie up the battered Persian. Taylor was smiling and shaking his head as the Persian sat upright and cursed the young warrior. The bearded Persian spat as Gray Dog sheathed his knife. He turned and looked at John Henry and then went to his pony. He untied the satchel and tossed it to Dugan. Then he silently mounted and sped off to the east once more to start his scout.

Two marines, with a helping hand from Corporal Jenks, slapped and kicked the Persian to his feet. Jenks reached out and pulled off his headdress to reveal the black hair underneath.

"Take that to Professor Ollafson. Maybe it will cheer the old boy up," John Henry told Dugan as he slapped one gauntleted hand into the other. Jessy saw the determined look in Thomas's face and then decided he should be in on this before John Henry lost their source of intelligence.

As Dugan rode off, Corporal Jenks pushed the tall Persian forward to face the officers.

"That's enough, Jenks," Captain Jackson said from the back of his horse. The Persian turned and spit toward Jenks, who immediately made a move to throttle the thief.

"At ease, Corporal!" Jessy called out.

Jenks finally shot the Persian one last hateful look and then quickly mounted his horse and rode to hard catch up with the column, angry that he couldn't question the thief.

"Allow me the honor of questioning this man," Jessy said as he also pulled on his gauntlets and eyed the large man, who was held on either side by two marines.

John Henry was thinking the same thing as Taylor had thought just a brief moment before. He reached out and took Jessy by the arm and stopped him.

"Maybe we'd better have someone a little more even-tempered do the questioning, Colonel," John Henry said.

Taylor gave Thomas a sly look. "And I suppose that's you?"

John Henry knew Jessy had a point. He was even more capable of losing control than the Confederate colonel. He hated losing men, and to lose them to brigands was something that irritated him to no end. Thomas looked from a smirking Jessy to the solid form of a perfectly dressed and comported officer, Captain Jackson.

"Captain, have you ever had the duty of questioning a prisoner of war before?"

Steven Jackson looked taken aback. He tilted his head as he looked from Thomas to the man Gray Dog had just chased down. The arrogant Persian looked hatefully upon the mounted naval officer.

"No, I have not," Jackson said as he calmly stepped from the saddle.

"Careful, he's a spitting sort of snake," Jessy joked as Jackson approached the large man. The captain tilted his head as he stood in front of him. The brown eyes were calm and his face kindly.

"I don't know if you understand me, but it would be to your benefit to explain why you tried to steal something that wasn't yours. What are you doing in this country?"

The Persian looked at the strange two-corner naval hat Jackson was wearing and again the man spit into the grass at Jackson's feet.

"Told you," Jessy said as he was finding Jackson's interrogation method amusing.

The cool and calm Jackson smiled and nodded his head. "Barbaric," he mumbled as he faced the man.

"You, you American, you dare to call the children of God barbaric. You, the unbeliever? I spit on you and your godless kind. You come to God's mountain and you steal what is not yours."

"Damn, he speaks better English than I do," Taylor said.

The prisoner turned and saw the wagons as they moved east. "That old man is a blasphemer. He steals what is not his. He desecrates our most holy place and then returns as if this land is his. I spit on America!"

"Your name, who are you working for? The French, British, the Germans?" Jackson asked, trying to get the true believer to talk rationally.

"I am not in the employ of other dogs and their masters.

I am Aliheem Akbar Mohamed Sutari, follower of Nasser al-Din Shah Qajar, the true King of Persia, not that pig of a man that sits on the Ottoman throne—the sultan of swine."

"You represent the Shah of Persia?"

"The true Shahanshah of Persia."

"Whatever the hell that is, the title sounds made up," Jessy said, eager for Jackson to finish with his interrogation so he could commence, but he wouldn't be exchanging pleasantries with the man the way the captain was.

"God's messengers will not allow this desecration of his mountain to go unchallenged."

The Americans exchanged looks. The Persian only smiled.

"I see the Angel of Death has already touched you. The curse of the mountain is upon you."

"I'm beginning to think this fella had that speech ready to go before he was even caught," Taylor said as he looked at John Henry.

"Our ancestors sprouted and grew from the spring of Ararat. Our great peoples are the family of man, the descendants of Noah, God's messenger. We will not allow you to do what it is you are attempting." The Persian smiled, showing blood on his teeth. "Either the faithful of God will stop you"—he looked around at the swiftly darkening skies—"or the darkness will claim you."

"You do know that if the sultan finds your people inside the borders of his nation he will kill every one of you."

"The heretic sultan has not long to rule. Soon the faithful will be on Ararat in force. If the curse of Azrael fails, I assure you, we will not."

Jackson turned and looked at John Henry and shook his head negatively. The captain removed one glove and then slapped it into the other as he turned and took in the Persian. The man wasn't smiling, but just staring.

"Get him a horse. Cut him loose."

"What?" Jessy was startled that Thomas was letting one of the killers of his men go free. It was Jackson who answered for the colonel.

'He's told us everything. Believe me, he held nothing back,

as you heard. We don't need him and we don't kill prisoners, despite what you southerners think."

"Wait a minute. I've had firsthand experience at the subtleties of prisoner treatment by your northern standards, and believe me when I say you are full of goose crap, young captain."

John Henry saw that Taylor was about to lose that famous temper of his, so he stepped between him and Jackson, who looked stunned that the Confederate colonel was ready to kill him just for voicing his opinion.

"I want him to take a message back to his people."

Taylor turned on Thomas and waited. Fogged air billowed from the mouth of the Rebel colonel as he waited.

John Henry approached the Persian and then everyone saw his black eyes go wide as Thomas pulled a large bowie knife from his belt. He shocked the prisoner by reaching around and cutting the ropes binding his hands together. The two marines were as shocked as everyone else when Thomas gestured for them to let the man go. Another marine brought an unsaddled horse forward.

"Tell your master if he comes for us he better bring that vengeful angel with him, because we will chew his ass as well as yours. You took the lives of two men and wounded others. We don't bow to people who commit murder, haven't for many years. Now get the hell out of here."

The Persian, with his eyes wide in suspicion, looked from angry face to angry face. He quickly jumped upon the horse's back and shot out of the camp.

"I must say, Colonel, that your method of keeping our intentions secret fell by the wayside somewhat. I agree with letting him go, but letting him go after explaining that yes, indeed, we are climbing to the summit, well, let's just say I'm a bit confused."

It was Jessy who angrily had to agree with what John Henry had done. It took him a moment but the thought struck him as John Henry smirked in his direction.

"Would you like to explain it to the Captain, Colonel Taylor?"

"If we crowd the field it will confuse all parties involved, muddy the water, make the situation unpredictable. The Persians are the wild card in the game."

"Why?" Jackson asked turning to John Henry.

"Because they despise everyone, from the sultan of the empire, to the French, Germans, Russians, and the British."

"In other words, Captain Jackson, they may just come in handy," Jessy answered for Thomas.

"I think they're too unpredictable to count on."

"Then there's that." Jessy smiled for the first time in a while. "Ah, the vagaries of command, what a wonderful thing." Taylor mounted his horse and then spurred him forward. "Come, gentlemen, let us face the great unknown!"

Jackson shook his head but mounted his own horse and rode away. John Henry Thomas just kicked at the rapidly hardening ground and then looked up. For the briefest of moments he could swear he spied stars peeking through the dark clouds. Then his gaze went to the white phosphorescent summit of Ararat just as thunder rumbled over the mountain range.

They would arrive at the base of God's mountain by dawn the next morning.

19

DOLMABAHÇE PALACE, CONSTANTINOPLE

The French spy Paul Renaud waited for the minister of foreign affairs to answer yes or no. The letter he had presented placed the empire on notice of a French arms embargo against the sultan if the French government's request was not granted. The small Turk was a close relative of the sultan and owed his career to the man, but to see twenty million francs in arms just vanish from the empire's books would be too much for even the sultan, or in the case his cousin, to endure. It was either a friendship with the backward Americans and that baboon sitting in their White House, or remain friends with a country that had bailed them out during the Crimea campaign. Renaud suspected he knew which way the minister would go. Especially when he saw the man slip the large bank folder into his top drawer. After all, another personal guarantee made up of one hundred thousand dollars in French notes had been given directly to the minister to smooth out any entanglements.

"And we have your guarantee the sultan will not recall the support you have just agreed to?" Renaud asked while eyeing the small man with the pencil-thin moustache and dark, weasely eyes.

"The sultan only knows what I tell him. I and a few learned men in office have his complete trust. The Seventh Guards Regiment will move out within the next three days. That should be adequate force to convince the Americans of their folly."

"We need the troops sooner than that."

"My French friend, if I recall a scattered regiment overnight, that will attract attention and surely the sultan would hear that one of his most elite cavalry regiments was currently moving on one of his own provinces. They are spread out in many regions. I will have them here in two days and on their way east in three. The Americans cannot stand up to that size of force so far away from home."

Renaud cursed under his breath as he turned to the naval attaché from the French embassy.

"How soon will our warships be in place in the Black Sea?"

"Within the next day and a half." The navy captain pulled Renaud aside and then whispered, "Does Paris know how far this has gone? The orders thus far have been for observation of American activities only."

"Yes, and our naval forces will observe American naval activity in the Black Sea. Have the landing force, once they have docked, find the Americans that started from there. I will remain here and travel with the Guards regiment. We should meet up in seven days."

"Should I inform Paris of the change?" the captain asked hopefully.

"No, I will take care of that."

The captain clicked his heels together and then left the office. Renaud approached the minister, who was locking the desk drawer with the French bribe contained inside.

"The man commanding this American incursion in your land is very cunning. I understand that the buffoon Lincoln thinks highly of him. And I must say from personal experience that he's not a fool."

The minister laughed and then stood to walk the Frenchman to the door.

"My friend, once the Seventh Guards Regiment sweeps into a land, the people of that land cease to exist. The Americans will soon learn the profit in bearing false gifts."

The two men shook hands and Renaud left.

The minister watched him go and then turned to his secretary before reentering his office.

"Send a message to Shidehara Barracks. I want to see General Isriam as soon as possible. From this moment on, tell him his regiment is on alert for movement east."

An hour later messages went out across the empire, and one of the most elite regiments of cavalry in Asia Minor started to gather.

Destination—Ararat.

Commodore Wesley Hildebrand read the dispatch and then handed it back to the captain of H.M.S. *Westfield*.

"Is the message from our man, Captain McDonald?" he asked the twenty-five-year veteran who had spent most of ten years in and around the Mediterranean and the Aegean.

"No, London. It seems our intelligence boys have learned that the two American vessels, *Carpenter* and *Argo*, made it into the strait and entered the Black Sea two days ago. Now we know why the two French frigates entered the strait not long after."

"The two American supply ships?" the captain asked.

"Yes, but London says the Americans have no intention of building a rail line for the sultan. It seems they have another goal in mind."

"Our orders?"

"Pursue into the Black Sea and observe the movements of both American and French naval assets."

"Observe? Rather ambiguous, wouldn't you say, Commodore?"

"Quite."

"If the Americans are not gifting the sultan with a rail line, just what are our wayward cousins up to this far from home?"

The commodore stepped to the railing of the newest battle cruiser in Her Majesty's service. He pursed his lips and then looked up into her tall rigging and saw the flags. They were blowing to the north. He made his decision.

"Prepare for sea, Captain. Get word to men ashore, especially our marines. Leave is cancelled and I want to make sail by 1600 hours."

"Very good. Once we enter the Black Sea I want a fifty percent alert status and I want battle stations set."

"You really think the Americans would dare fire upon the Royal Navy?"

His thoughts turned to the Americans and the man who was leading this foolish quest. He wondered and hoped that the soldier had a good head on his shoulders and would realize in time that anything hidden on that mountaintop was not worth the entire world going to war.

But then again, what cause ever was?

TALISE STATION, THE OTTOMAN EMPIRE

Lieutenant Parnell watched the last of the railroad ties being unloaded. For a rail line that would cover in square mileage more area than New York to Illinois, the amount of wood ties was far short of the number required. Luckily, they had no intention of building any such rail line. The few ties and steel rail they had on hand were for show only, and he had the men spread them out to look as if they had far more material than they did. He was following Colonel Thomas's orders to the letter and hoped the army officer had a sixth sense when it came to running a bluff.

The snow had started falling at dawn and it looked as if the bad weather was there to stay. It was starting to accumulate on the ground and on the shoulders of the fifty-seven men in his command. He opened his pocketwatch and saw that it was just past four in the afternoon, and that meant if the Black Sea section had not arrived before the sun set they would not make it to Talise before sunrise tomorrow. He closed the watch as a navy signalman walked up and saluted the marine lieutenant.

"Pickets report that those Britishers are at it again. They circle the camp and then stop and then circle the camp again."

"They're trying to get under our skin, like Stonewall Jackson did the second day at Bull Run. They want us to do something stupid." He smiled and looked at the navy man. "But we only make the same mistakes two and three times, and not one of those boys out there is Stonewall Jackson, are they?"

"No, sir." The boy saluted and then went back to his duties.

"Ensign Dwyer?"

A naval officer turned away from the warm fire and reported to the marine.

"Yes, sir?"

With caution Parnell turned toward the smoking engine of the train, which was due to return to the coast in less than an hour.

"Did your special ordnance team plant our surprise for the Turkish rail system?"

"Yes, sir. I must admit that the Reb explosives man looked as if he had done this sort of work before."

"Yes, Colonel Taylor said that his regiment was responsible for the Rock Island and the Ohio Limited sabotage in '61 and '62. He said his man was the best."

"Well, he placed the charges right beneath the main boiler. We will have Lance Corporal Killeen in place at the halfway water stop. By the time the train makes its return trip, if it has unexpected guests onboard, he'll blow the charges as per Colonel Thomas's order."

"Very good. Let us hope that won't be necessary. After all, that train is another escape route we may need to get the hell out of here."

"Damn, there they are again," the naval officer said as his eyes went to the ridge a mile away. The four British soldiers sat atop their horses. They made no move or signal. They just watched the activity below. Suddenly the riders turned their horses and were gone as fast as they had arrived.

"Thank God. They were beginning to make the boys a little jumpy."

Parnell was about to reply when he heard something in the distance. He cocked his ear to the north and decided that the sound was coming from there. Soon the naval ensign heard it also. Suddenly a cheering rose at the far northern end of the camp. Parnell smiled when he finally digested what it was they were hearing. It was loud music. A marshalling song they all knew well and it was coming through the air with power. More cheers from his small command as Parnell finally spied the cause.

"The Battle Hymn of the Republic" blared across the Plain of Ararat as the one hundred and twenty-two member Army of the Potomac Band marched into the far end of the camp to rousing cheers. The applause soon dwindled as the full scope of what they were seeing registered in every man's mind. Here was the band—where was the army to go with it? The cheering soon dwindled to nothing as they realized the band was the only unit arriving. Still, the boys in bright blue parade dress played with all the enthusiasm of a victory celebration.

"Uh, sir, where are the support troops? The cavalry we were expecting from the Black Sea sector?"

Parnell turned away from the spectacle of the precision marching band and he smiled at the young ensign.

"You are looking at it, sir. Our salvation, our cavalry."

"Shit."

"Yes, Ensign, I believe that is an accurate description of what it is we have just stepped into."

The band members smiled after their long march from the end of the northern rail spur and then their forced night march, but were confused as the men watching them stopped cheering. Several of the gruff soldiers had their mouths ajar. Most of the young musicians believed the troops were in awe of their musical prowess.

"Colonel Thomas, I sure hope the president's faith in you is justified, because right now it seems you are one mad son of a bitch."

MOUNT ARARAT, OTTOMAN EMPIRE

The line of one hundred and sixty-five men stretched for almost a mile up the goat trail that led from the base of Ararat. The mountain itself was unlike most large peaks of the world as it stood almost alone and not inside a typical range. The plains stopped and the mountain began; it was that simple.

They had ridden in three miles before they had to dismount. Another full day was lost as they loaded supplies into packs and, with the fifty mules at hand, started early on the second day. All the while they were observed by the local goatherds. They had seen incursions before, but they were always led by academia and not men such as these. Although they wore civilian clothing, most looked as if they were trained in drill. John Henry had allowed Professor Ollafson to speak to a few of them to allay their fears about their presence. He explained that they were only there to map the summit. Thomas knew the locals didn't believe Ollafson. It was as if they knew exactly why the foreigners had come to Ararat.

Thus far the Confederate prisoners had responded well to the march up the mountain. Most had been shocked at the cold-weather gear that had been supplied them. For the most part the Rebel cavalrymen had not seen new shoes since the times before the Battle of Bull Run. The fur-lined jackets were something most southerners had never seen before, as well as the strange tinted glasses that strapped to their hoods. To John Henry it looked as though the new clothing and the issuing of arms to the men had had a most beneficial effect on the southern contingent. Even Jessy was more talkative since they started the ascent.

John Henry dropped back from the front of the line after he made sure that Gray Dog, who was a mile or so in front of the column scouting the dangerous trail, had not reported back as of yet. They were at eleven thousand feet and wanted to see how Professor Ollafson was holding up. He was maneuvering around several snow sleds being pulled up the mountainside by the men when he spied Claire a few feet away. He smiled when he saw the thick fur-lined hood covering her features. She used a large walking stick, as did most. Her wool skirt was thick and covered heavy cotton pantaloons underneath. Her boots were also top-of-the-line trail wear. She looked as if the weather and climb had no effect on her at all.

"It looks like you were born for the infantry, Miss Anderson."

"What did I say in regards to calling me Miss Anderson? For crying out loud, Colonel, we may never leave this mountain, so give yourself a new order and leave off with the formality." She raised the thick, dark goggles and looked at John Henry. "It's Claire."

"All right, Claire," he said as he turned and started to pace her. "How is the old fella holding up?"

Claire looked over at the colonel and his heavy winter coat and decided that he really was concerned about Ollafson and wasn't just trying to say, "I told you so" about the professor's ability to climb the mountain again in his old age.

"Better, since Gray Dog returned the artifacts. But there's something that's affecting him. He's been acting a little strange since we started getting close to the mountain, and that started long before the Persians attempted to steal his property. He goes out of his way to move around shadows that are cast along the trail."

"With the absence of the sun, it's a wonder there are any shadows at all."

Claire looked at the colonel again. "That's another thing, why are the shadows so prevalent since we started the climb? I mean, you're correct, there shouldn't be, but there are. Deep and dark as though the sun was directly casting them. But no sun."

"I hope you and I are the only ones that have noticed."

"Well, Gray Dog avoids the shadows for the most part also. As for the men, I think they're just happy to be moving."

"That and their new clothing."

"Sad isn't it?"

"Sad?" John Henry asked as he adjusted the Henry rifle strapped to his shoulder.

"Yes, that men can be as excited as schoolchildren over those ugly spiked boots and a new jacket. It says something about how sad this war has become."

John Henry looked at Claire and said nothing. He just dipped his head and then allowed her to move forward as he slowed down. The woman was far deeper of thought than he'd realized, and he knew at that very moment that this spy interested him to no end.

As they climbed, the summit vanished behind thick, dark snow clouds and the wind picked up as if in warning they were trespassing.

The Americans drew closer to one of the greatest mysteries in the history of the world.

Colonel Taylor was in the extreme front of the column. John Henry had placed him in charge of the scouts, Gray Dog among them. Neither he nor the Comanche had much to say about it. Gray Dog could not fathom the deep hatred Jessy had toward all Indians, not just the Kiowa, the tribe responsible for killing his sister. Thomas figured he was the cause of that confusion for the simple fact that Gray Dog saw that Mary's actual husband had no ill will toward any Indian, while her brother could not get over the fact. Thomas knew Jessy respected the ability of the Plains Indian, he just didn't like them.

Taylor slowed the advance as they came to a sheer rock wall covered in winter run-off ice that never melted in the summer months at this elevation. Taylor took out his hand-drawn map that had been supplied by Professor Ollafson and examined his route. He was sure that this was the proper trail as depicted in Ollafson's tight but fluid scrawl. He raised the large goggles and then looked about. With absolutely no sun he wasn't even sure which way they were truly headed.

"Colonel, the Indian," Corporal Jenks said as he too lowered his goggles and fur-lined hood.

Gray Dog was there. He was standing atop a rock wall and

looking down upon them. He looked up into the falling snow and shook his head.

"Dumb savage, if he climbed that it must be straight up. He knows we can't take that route. Does he know what wet dynamite will do if impacted hard enough?" Jessy cupped his gloved hands and called up. "You have to find another way! Too steep!"

Gray Dog tilted his head. He was dressed in a long-sleeved leather jacket with fringe and thick leather breeches. His head was still covered in the coyote-skin hat and his hair was bundled against the cold, which strangely enough did not affect the Indian much at all. Before Taylor could blink Gray Dog vanished.

"What's the holdup?" John Henry said as he came to the front with Claire, Ollafson, and McDonald in tow.

"That little spider monkey needs to learn what ledges *he* can traverse and what ledges an army bogged down with equipment cannot."

"Where is he?" Thomas asked as he lowered his hood and goggles.

"He was up there a moment ago. Probably fell off for all I know," Jessy answered as two of the advance point men came up to report.

"This is not the same. There must have been heavy avalanches in the recent years to block the trail like this," Ollafson said as he braced himself against Claire and McDonald.

"We wasted a full day!" Taylor said angrily. "We're going to lose what little light we have soon."

Before he could finish speaking a loud whistle sounded and echoed off of the stone and ice walls of the small valley in which they traveled.

John Henry smiled as did Claire.

"Well, looks like the Injun can fly," Corporal Jenks commented as he spit a stream of tobacco juice from his bearded face.

Before them stood Gray Dog. He was waiting for Taylor

to move the column. He stood just at the base of the rise and then he simply stepped back and vanished.

"What in the hell?" Jessy mumbled as Claire and John Henry stepped around him and followed Gray Dog.

Once they rounded the small bend that was hidden by a large crevice, they saw a slim tunnel that had been left clear of avalanche debris by a fluke of Mother Nature. It was as if engineers had carved this especially for them. John Henry stood in awe at the size of the upward-sloping tube that had inexplicably covered the old goat trail. The falling ice was once a waterfall during the hotter months, and then it froze in mid-fall and formed this natural arch that was invisible from farther down the trail. It was a miracle that Gray Dog had found the opening because of its hidden location. Right in plain sight.

"This is amazing!" Claire said as she removed her hood and glasses and stared at the beauty of the natural ice cave. "Hello!" she said loudly and John Henry cringed at the amplified echoes that returned. Even Gray Dog stepped into the middle of the ice tunnel to see what all the noise was about. The echoes finally died away and Claire giggled like a schoolgirl.

"I am glad to see all of that educational training paid off," Thomas said, smiling widely.

"Maybe not, but its fun, Colonel." She had said *Colonel* like it was a sour-tasting fruit in her mouth.

"Well, in your education did you learn anything about sound amplification and its destructive nature in unstable environments?"

"No, but I have learned something of late," she said with the most radiant smile.

"And that is?"

"That you, Colonel, can be a total ass." She smiled wider and then turned back to the tunnel. "Ass!" she shouted again creating an echo that seemed to be endless.

"What was that? I don't think they heard you in Spain," Jessy said as he eyed both John Henry and Claire as he entered the cave. He stepped past and caught up with Gray Dog.

"Miss Anderson . . . excuse me, Claire, was just clearing her throat."

"Uh-huh," Jessy said, ignoring the two as they tried to stare each other down and joined the Comanche.

"Go another way," Gray Dog said.

Taylor stopped and turned as John Henry and Claire finally made peace and joined him and Gray Dog.

"What did you say?" Taylor asked as he stopped and turned. "You just saved us a full day of backtracking to another trail, and now you want us not to take a God-given route?"

"What's the matter?" Thomas asked as he and Claire saw what was going on.

"Your Indian boy wants to take another route."

"Why, is this one blocked farther ahead?" John Henry asked.

Gray Dog didn't answer, he only turned and beckoned the three to follow. They did, exchanging looks that lent credence to their confusion. As they followed they noticed the ice walls seemed to become more transparent and Claire was still in wonder at what she was seeing. To her it was like being inside of a giant diamond of magnificent brilliance. They saw Gray Dog ahead as he waited. He was barely discernable in the weak light that filtered through the ice.

"Well, I don't see any block in the road," Taylor said as Gray Dog looked at him. Without speaking he waited for John Henry and Claire. He struck alight a match and put the flame to a torch. As the flame grew in strength Gray Dog held up the torch and placed it near the wall of ice. Claire saw what he had seen earlier and then she screamed, and this time the echo never died, it went on to the ends of the earth.

The men awaiting an order outside heard the scream and it was powerful enough that several large rocks were dislodged from the cliffs above them. All men, Rebel to marine to naval personnel, exchanged worried looks. They had been silent and apprehensive after stepping foot onto Ararat and now this. The column waited as the echo finally died away.

Inside the tunnel John Henry had taken Claire into his

arms as they saw the horrific sight. There were six men in the ice. The face of each was frozen in a grimace of horror as they had obviously drowned. The sheer shock of how they died locked into a mountain was startling to Taylor and Thomas. It was Ollafson who entered the tunnel and was not shocked but saddened at what he saw. He stepped up to Gray Dog and pried the torch from his hand. He held it to the ice wall and examined each face as best as he could.

"I do not know him." He shifted the torch as McDonald entered the area and gasped as he saw the frozen bodies suspended in an animated fight for their lives. "I do not know this man either." Again he shifted the torch to another body. This one was situated about four feet over the professor's head, so he reached up to place the torch as close to the tortured features of the well-dressed European man as he could. "Professor Antanov." He moved the torch to the next frozen body. This one had severe damage to his skull as if he had been hit in the head by a large stone during the avalanche and flood that killed him. "Professor Ali Kasseem. I know both of these men. They disappeared three years ago. Both men are tenured professors at Oxford University."

"Well, it looks like they may have lost that tenure," Jessy said as he removed the torch from Ollafson's hand and then handed it to Gray Dog. "Continue. We will still go this way."

Gray Dog looked from Taylor to John Henry, who only nodded his head.

"All these men are old soldiers. The colonel is right; we move forward through here."

Gray Dog didn't reply. He simply turned and vanished once more.

"Still, it may help to forewarn those that follow us," Claire said as she eased herself out of Thomas's embrace. She looked embarrassed as she replaced her hood. "I apologize for my womanly hysterics. I have seen dead men before, I assure you."

"Should I start moving the men in, Colonel—Jesus Christ, the saints be with us!" Sergeant Major Dugan said loudly and started crossing himself when he saw what it was that had held up everyone and the reason for that lingering scream. Even Dugan's exclamation was still echoing. John Henry turned to Claire with a smile.

"Yes, you may have seen dead men, but it looks like the rough and tough Irishman before you may have màde wee-wee in his pantaloons."

As Dugan turned away from the frozen bodies staring back at him he failed to see what everyone was snickering about.

The incident with Sergeant Major Dugan made the passage past the frozen explorers a little easier for the men to take with a brave front, thanks to the rumor spread by Colonel John Henry Thomas, a man Dugan would never, ever forgive for spreading it—after all, he only lost control of his bladder a little.

The laughter made everyone forget where they were, if only momentarily.

The column was a day and a half from the summit.

20

ONE HUNDRED MILES NORTH OF TRABZON
HARBOR, THE BLACK SEA

The crew of the U.S.S. *Carpenter* knew the late-arriving *Yorktown* could do her no good in her fight to keep the tow barge, *Argo*, afloat. The *Chesapeake* was docked at Trabzon, where she was off-loading her contingent of marines for transport to the rail link at Talise for their rendezvous with Lieutenant Parnell, so she could not come to the aid of the battling *Carpenter.*

The problem was the same as they'd had in the Atlantic: The swells were nearly swamping the large barge, so much so that the captain of the *Carpenter* was close to ordering the *Argo*'s crew off the ship. The barge sailors were already tired from bailing, pumping, and keeping the flotation bags filled, and that meant constant use of the man-powered billows that supplied the air bags with the necessary air to keep the *Argo* afloat.

The captain, a young lieutenant j.g., kept his eyes glued to the binoculars as he scanned the *Argo*'s high-water mark. It looked as though the hard work of not only *Argo*'s crew, but of the barge's navy riggers was finally paying off. He took a deep breath and lowered his glasses.

"The damn cargo is just too heavy, Captain. That barge was designed for calmer seas than we have shown her. Ericsson didn't figure on the winter swells in the Black Sea."

The captain nodded his agreement and then smiled.

"I'll let you mention that little bit of information to Ericsson upon our return."

"No thank you, I value my head too much."

"There, *Carpenter* is signaling," the captain said as he once more raised his glasses. The signal lamp blinked off and on several times, lasting a full five minutes. He soon lowered the glasses feeling far better than he had a moment before when he thought they were about to lose Colonel Thomas's prized possession.

"What does she say?" the first officer asked.

"They've controlled the flooding in the inner hull area and have added the last four flotation bags to her hull. She's stable for the moment, but they're fearful of any gale that may spring up. They say they cannot reinforce the hull again. She will founder."

The first officer raised his own glasses and scanned the towline, and from there his eyes traveled to the barge. She was riding extremely low in the water.

"Damn dangerous," he said.

"The *Argo*'s crew will not come above decks. They refuse to allow the sea to take a hold of their vessel."

"Ericsson's boys. They would rather die and go down to Davy Jones's locker than to face Ericsson after failing to keep his baby afloat."

"Can't say as I blame them," the captain said as he moved his glasses around to make sure their end of the towline was taut.

"Ship ahoy!" came the call from the *Carpenter*'s crow's nest and her two-man lookout.

"Where away?" he called out.

"Two points off our stern!"

The captain swung his glasses around and fought to clear the mist behind the towed *Argo*.

"Thank God, it must be either the *Yorktown* or the

Chesapeake," the first officer said as he too raised his binoculars.

The captain finally spied a tall mast through the haze of the late afternoon. He smiled. It was a frigate, more than likely the *Chesapeake* on her way to meet them after discharging the marines ashore.

"Ah, there she—"

"Second vessel ahoy, a thousand yards behind the first!"

The captain lowered the glasses for the briefest of moments when his heart skipped a beat. One American ship he could believe, but both arriving at the same moment in the middle of the Black Sea was a little too convenient. He raised the field glasses again.

"Two French frigates, can't make out their class!"

"Damn," the captain said as both he and the first mate saw the battle flags of the two French warships simultaneously. The captain zeroed in on the bow of the fast-moving frigate in the lead. "That's the frigate *Especial*. Thirty-two guns and an oaken hull." He now concentrated on the second, even larger frigate. "This is not good, Lieutenant. It's the *Osiris*. The two newest class of warships in the French navy." He lowered the glasses and shook his head. "It seems someone is out to impress us with their firepower."

"Yeah, all we need now is for the British to show."

"Now would be a good time for *Chesapeake* and *Yorktown* to arrive. I'm feeling a little naked out here with just our guns and a floating weapon that will sink if one of those French sailors even sneezes against her hull hard enough."

"Tell me, why are we here again?" the first officer asked jokingly.

"Yes, it does make boring blockade duty seem more attractive, doesn't it?"

In just a few hours their worry would be multiplied when the British warship, *Westfield*, slowly pulled into the eastern Black Sea. As it stood, the Americans were outgunned ninety-six guns to thirty-two. Even the American navy couldn't pull a battle like that out of the fire. They needed help and they needed it fast before someone realized they could call their bluff and blow the American ship and her tow barge of equipment to pieces.

Colonel John Henry Thomas's expedition was fast running out of time.

MOUNT ARARAT, THE OTTOMAN EMPIRE

The storm hit the expedition moments after they had started erecting the shelters for the night's camp. They would settle in for the snowy, windy night with hot food in their bellies thanks to the United States Navy and their foresight to include coal in their supplies. They had enough coal for five days of cooking and heat, after that they would have to rely on the sparse trees of Ararat. Grandee handed out plates of hot beans and corn bread. How he managed to bake corn bread no one dared ask. They accepted the hot meal gratefully after the strenuous march up the mountain.

John Henry Thomas stood on a small incline and watched as the men ate and erected their shelters. He'd called this halt not only for sleep but to also confront Ollafson about the route they were taking. After certifying that this was the fastest route, Gray Dog had reported that they could cut their time in half by changing direction. He wanted the column to veer to the left and take the glacier route. It was smoother and had far fewer crevasses for men to fall into. They had nearly lost four men already when the ice they were walking on gave way. That was when Gray Dog reported the alternate route.

Grandee walked up to John Henry and held out a plate of food. The colonel nodded and accepted it. He immediately spooned beans into his mouth and was pleased with the rich taste.

"My wife couldn't boil the water to cook the beans," John Henry said to Grandee with no preamble. The large black man listened politely as John Henry chewed. "She had to learn how to cook like most soldiers have to learn how to fight." He lowered the spoon and looked at Grandee. "Only they learned far faster than she did. Many a night when I was close to home while on patrol I would stop in and she would fix me dinner. You could imagine how good an actor I had to be when she fed me chicken that had looked as if it had got caught in the P. T. Barnum museum fire. It was horrible." He scooped another spoonful of beans into his mouth, chewed, and then a sad look came to his face. He handed the plate back to Grandee, who accepted it without comment. He turned away, figuring the colonel had lost his appetite while thinking about his dead wife.

"Thank you, Mr. Grandee."

By the time Grandee stopped and turned, John Henry had vanished into the falling snow. The mess steward turned away and saw Claire looking at him.

"The colonel not hungry?" she asked.

"Well, Miss, he is and he isn't."

"I don't understand."

"Well, a man has certain appetites, and the colonel's just not hungry for what old Grandee's cookin', is all. That's one lonely man. I figure that's what he's hungerin' for." He laughed lightly. "Yes, sir, that's what I figure."

She watched Grandee turn away with the plate of food. She saw the activity around her and she pulled her thick coat tighter. With the absence of light the mountain took on a far more ominous tone. The men were in a jovial mood, but every now and again she would see them looking at the crevices and cracks as if there were some beast ready to spring at them from the mountain.

"I see our intrepid leader has no appetite this lovely evening."

Claire turned and saw Steven McDonald standing next to her. She made no attempt to answer his observation.

"I have noticed your recent proclivity for avoiding my company since our French friend was asked to leave us a few days back."

Claire turned and faced the Englishman. "Since Colonel Thomas is no man's fool and since he shook out Renaud so easily, I thought it best we keep our distance before he suspects the French fool wasn't the only one he had to worry about."

McDonald smiled as he leaned into her shoulder. "Such high praise for a man that you clearly despise. Imagine that, Madame Claire Richelieu, cowed by a man." He laughed lightly and then started to turn away. "Do not get too close, my love, unless you would like to take up permanent residence here with him when this idiocy is concluded."

Claire watched the British officer vanish into the tent he shared with Ollafson. When she turned back she felt that deep-seated chill once more. She decided to take a brief walk to shake out the cramping in her legs. She knew she wasn't fooling herself about John Henry; it seemed he hated her and her chosen profession so much that he could not see her as anything other than an underhanded woman playing men for information. She didn't know why his opinion of her meant so much. But it did.

As she slowly walked around the large camp she heard the soft sounds of a harmonica and then the strings of a violin start up as the men settled in for some much-needed sleep. The light mood of the men actually made the camp seem less cold than it had when they first arrived. She started humming the tune the Rebel soldiers were playing. It made her think of home and how much she would miss it if this expedition failed. She hummed and walked as the tune "Oh Susanna" bounced from ice to rock and then back again.

She was humming so loudly that she failed to realize that she could not hear the sounds of the camp any longer. She stopped walking and suddenly saw that she had strayed so far from the men that she could not see the camp at all. The darkness was almost complete as she found herself inside a small cutout in the stone and ice. It was like a small box canyon. She turned and hastily started back. Before she could get clear of the boxed-in area, she saw a dark mass block her path. It was huge. The blackness towered over her and looked as if the blur of deep darkness had spread its arms wide to block out the terrain beyond. It was only her and the dark shape. She froze, as did the entity.

"Help!" she called out, but soon realized that no word

escaped her mouth. There was only the empty hiss of air as she became so frightened that she lost her voice. She stumbled backward when she saw the dark shape move. It came on slowly, and as it did Claire had a blurred vision of men, women, and children screaming as if from a great distance. She heard the crashing of waves against a solid object, more screams, and the cries of animals.

Claire fell as the dark shape seemed to spread out wider at the top, as if wings were stretched as a giant bird of prey sought its dinner for the night. This time she managed to force out a scream. As she lay in the snow-covered revetment, she heard what she thought were shouts. The dark shape vanished as she was pulled to her feet and the next thing she knew she was being forced to run.

When she finally realized she had been pulled from her predicament, she saw John Henry holding onto her. Gray Dog came running from the small canyon, pointing a Henry rifle back into it. He finally turned to face Claire and John Henry. He nodded and then left.

"It's a good thing I told Gray Dog to keep an eye on you."

"I . . . I . . . Did you see that thing?"

"I don't know what it is I saw. I did see you trying to fend off something only you could see."

"There was something in there with me, damn it!" she said a little too loudly as men started to pay attention. John Henry took her by the elbow and led her away.

"Look, I believe you." He looked around and made sure there were no ears to hear him. "Right now I don't need those men out there to believe you. It wouldn't take much to send frightened men over the edge, and believe me, we are asking a lot of these men, the mysteries and old wives' tales of this area notwithstanding."

Claire felt embarrassed. John Henry pulled her hood up and then he smiled as best he could.

"I apologize, once again, Colonel. I am not prone to hysterics." Her eyes narrowed and she used a gloved hand to punch little Morse-code taps into the colonel's chest. "But I know what I saw in there. That curse is real and I believe every word that Professor Ollafson has said about the entity on this mountain."

John Henry watched Claire as she started to turn. She stopped and angrily confronted him. She stepped up and repeated the tapping on his chest. This time it was much harder.

"And what do you mean you had Gray Dog watching out for me?"

"Look, since you are the only woman, I thought—"

Again the finger jabs. "That's your problem, Colonel Thomas, you think far too much, and sometimes not enough!" She turned and stormed away.

"Yes, ma'am, I've been told that," he said under his breath as he watched her leave.

"I can see you two are growing closer."

John Henry turned and saw Jessy as he walked past on his way to eat chow.

"Jessy, you can kiss my—"

"Yes, sir, ever closer." Taylor whistled the tune of "Dixie" as he strolled away nonchalantly.

John Henry was actually tempted to pull his Colt and at least shoot Jessy in the back of the leg to shut him up, but he chuckled instead.

"God help me."

Thomas didn't know it, but God was going to sit this one out.

21

Jessy was the first man to make it to the ledge and was shocked to see Gray Dog sitting on a large boulder that was covered in a fine sheet of ice. The Comanche was eating an apple obviously supplied by his new best friend, mess steward Grandee. The colonel bent at the waist to recover his strength and breath.

"No good," Gray Dog said as he took a bite of apple.

Taylor took another three deep breaths, feeling the burn in his lungs not only from the cold, but from the lack of oxygen that was now starting to take a toll on the men. That was why he'd gone ahead to see if Gray Dog's assessment of Ollafson old route was viable. He was quickly learning it was not. The route had suffered avalanches since the professor was last on Ararat in 1859. In some places it made transiting the glacier easier, but in others the landslides had created massive voids in the ice, which had already claimed several of the supply sleds and nearly their handlers. The men were growing increasingly frustrated over the slow progress up to the summit. Each knew that time was as valuable a commodity as the sparse air they were breathing.

"Damn," Taylor finally managed to say. "If we go your route we could lose a full two days."

Gray Dog tossed the apple core into a deep crevasse as if to illustrate his point. "It is a straight climb up the ice face. It will take us directly to top. Rope lines will help the men make the climb. We will save a full day."

Gray Dog didn't wait for Taylor to reply. The Comanche scout figured the Confederate cavalryman simply had no choice. Jessy started to say something when his feet gave out underneath him. He immediately reached out and grabbed the edge of the void and managed to keep from falling. He struggled with his own weight as gravity insisted on taking command. He felt his fingers through the thick gloves start to slip. He looked down and as he did his tinted goggles fell from his head into the endless void over which his feet dangled. He knew he wasn't going to make it.

That was when he felt something take a hold of his foot from below. He fought to see what it was that was pulling him to his death. As he struggled to see far below, all that was visible was darkness and the occasional free-falling ice from the crevasse. Then he saw it. The dark shape of a large hand was actually trying to take him down to a crushing death some hundreds of feet below. He kicked out, trying to dislodge the grip of his unseen assailant, but only managed to loosen his grip on the ice above him.

Suddenly hands were grasping his wrists and pulling. He felt the thing that held tightly to his boot grow in intensity as it fought the resistance from above. Finally Jessy felt the weight on his left boot fall away and he could have sworn he heard a faded and mournful cry as the entity lost an opportunity. After some struggle with Jessy using his other foot for leverage, he was pulled from the void. He fell over onto his back and then when he opened his eyes he saw Gray Dog standing over him with his ridiculous coyote hat also staring at him.

"I suppose I have an 'I told you so' coming," he said as he allowed Gray Dog to pull him into a standing position. Taylor caught himself after a brief dizzy spell and then looked at the Comanche. Gray Dog didn't understand what he was trying to say. "All right, Indian, you got the better of me on this one. Show me your route."

Gray Dog nodded as he started to turn away but was stopped by the strong hand of Taylor.

"Look, I'm glad you came back. That would have been a long fall."

Gray Dog nodded, not understanding the way in which the white man chose to say thanks. In his world there was no such word.

"Evil spirit lives in the mountain, wants all men dead."

The words caught Taylor off guard. "Then you did see it?"

Gray Dog only looked at Jessy and said nothing. The Comanche merely leaned over and took a hold of two large coils of thick rope and then turned away and left.

"Damn, it seems Miss Claire's not imagining things after all."

Dugan was pacing in front of John Henry as a navy chief petty officer reported to Captain Jackson.

"The trail ends a quarter mile up. We followed their footprints until they vanished before a large crevasse."

"Oh, Jesus, don't tell me we lost the Indian and the colonel?" Dugan said as he knew immediately that he'd overstepped his bounds with John Henry. But the colonel remained silent as he listened to the report to Jackson. Thomas figured Dugan was secretly as worried about Gray Dog as himself. His eye movement told Dugan to be silent.

"We called down into the void, but there was no answer, Captain."

"Very well. Go warm yourselves up by the mess area."

Jackson turned to face John Henry with a questioning look on his face—an expression that asked, "What do we do now?"

"I'll go check it out myself. Can't trust the goddamn navy to do anything right," Dugan said as he started to return to the route they were taking before the halt.

Before the sergeant major could take two steps a thick

rope dropped from above and whacked him squarely in the head. He cursed as it knocked from his head the Union cap that he wore underneath his hood.

"What the hell?" he said as he grabbed the rope. He looked up and standing on the ledge high above them was Gray Dog, who was smiling at his targeting prowess. The sergeant major started to curse in anger, or was it relief at seeing the Comanche still alive? Thomas smiled as he saw Jessy standing next to Gray Dog.

"Ollafson's passage is blocked. Your Injun boy found another route. Should get us to the summit by dawn tomorrow."

The words echoed and the men, who had taken to lying down for rest and to regain the oxygen levels in their lungs, all heard the report as it bounced from one ice wall to the next.

"And how do we get up there?" Captain Jackson asked, very afraid of the answer.

"Well, you better tell Miss Anderson to tie down that skirt of hers because we have to haul everyone up four and five at a time. It would take too long to backtrack and then go around. Apologies to the miss."

"Tell Colonel Taylor I climb just as well as any man," she said as she took the rope from Dugan and then deftly spit into her gloves and rubbed her hands together. She shrugged out of the small pack that Dugan had bogged her down with and then looked up.

"Anytime," she called up.

Thomas looked from the one who was scaling the rope like a professional circus performer, to the face of Captain Jackson, who looked around nervously.

"You know, Colonel, besides a complete failure in our mission, I find myself more terrified of failing to match that woman's prowess at climbing."

"I've got news for you, Captain Jackson. You're not alone in your fears."

"Oh, goodness and saints be praised, I think I better go the long way," Dugan said just as another heavy rope struck him in the head.

"Oops, apologies, Sergeant Major," Taylor called from above. As Dugan looked up he saw a smiling Gray Dog, who had obviously just thrown the rope because Taylor was too busy assisting Claire to the top.

"I guess that settles it, you Irish rogue, now get to climbing. We have a lot of men and equipment to get up there."

Dugan looked at Thomas, horrified. "But . . . but . . ."

"Yes, you could fall, but then you would have to listen to Claire's bragging all the way home. For six thousand miles she will never let you live it down," John Henry said, smiling.

Dugan dropped his pack and then did as Claire had and spit into his gloved hands. He took hold of the rope and then with a dirty look at the naval personnel watching him, started up the wall. As soon as his feet came off the ground a rather large chunk of snow hit the sergeant major square in the bearded face. He lost his grip and fell the four feet to the snow-covered ground.

"Sorry, that was my fault," Claire yelled down as Dugan looked up. All he saw was Claire holding her gloves to her mouth as she had watched the snowball fall. But it was the smiling face of Gray Dog standing next to her that irritated Dugan to no end.

"That does it, I'm going to kill him."

This time it was Taylor, three of his men including Corporal Jenks, and the mess crew that were left below to secure the last of the supply sleds. As the last ten-by-seven sled was hoisted up the side of the ice face, Jenks faced Jessy. He made sure that the big man Grandee and his navy boys didn't hear what he had to say.

Taylor had steadied the last sled and then slapped Grandee on the back. He nodded that he was appreciative of the man's size and strength. Grandee saw Jenks approach and nodded a greeting, which Jenks still didn't know how to react to, so he just stared at him until he moved off to get ready for their own climb.

"Colonel, the boys sorta elected me to talk for 'em."

Taylor lowered his hood and then pulled his goggles down. He looked around and saw the other two men outside the circle of mess cooks and noticed they were intently watching the conversation. Jessy slowly pulled off his gloves. He waited without inviting Jenks to continue.

"Colonel, sir, we figure it's time for us southern boys to skedaddle outta here."

"Just us four, just up and get, is that it?" Jessy said as his eyes became cold.

"No, sir, not at all. But once we've climbed this mountain, we figure we've kept our side of the bargain. It's time for us to go and find a way to get back home and into our own fight. That's where we belong, Colonel. Not here where we can be kilt and no one will ever know. I mean, at least at home we can die for what we believe, not"—he waved upward toward the rest of the expedition—"what those Yankees think they want."

Taylor took a deep breath and then looked at Grandee, who was slipping on a rope so he could take his turn to ride the mountain. Jessy reached up and brushed away some of the ice that had built up in his mustache and beard.

"We go when I say we go, not one moment before, Corporal." He looked toward the expectant faces of the other two. "You make sure every man in my command understands that. I wouldn't care if it was Old Abe himself up there, I wouldn't leave him in a place like this. Whether they be Yank or Johnny Reb, no one deserves to be left here, and until we come down from this mountain we stay together."

Jenks looked taken aback as if he had been slapped by Taylor.

"And once that's done, Colonel, do we head back nice and easy and all them people with guns out there will just let us walk right on outta here? Sir, you know as soon as we put to sea those Frenchies and Brits are liable to blow us right out of the water."

"Once down from this mountain, who is to say how we get back?"

"Colonel, sir?"

"I figure once we've proven that Swedish fool's little boat exists or doesn't exist, we've fulfilled our oath, or at least my oath to Colonel Thomas, and then we're on our own as far as I'm concerned. After all, Corporal, the navy is not the only way to get home."

Finally the light of understanding dawned in the Tennessean's eyes.

"Now, not one more word about mutiny." Taylor smirked. "At least until I say to mutiny."

"Yes, sir, Colonel," Jenks said and then moved off.

Jessy still had the smirk on his face when he turned and saw Grandee staring right at him. Taylor watched as the black man slowly shook his head just as they started hauling the man up the rope. Jessy watched a moment and then replaced his goggles and hood.

He didn't know how long he could keep his now-armed men in check.

The line of men and equipment stretched out for a full quarter of a mile as they made slow progress up the ice shelf. They could see the gleam, even in the overcast skies, of the glacier a mile or so up. The Indian had been right, the new routes had shaved at least a day off their journey and not one man had died because he fell through a void.

John Henry and Jackson walked in front, digging their climbing staffs into the ice with every step. Claire was right behind them with Olafson and McDonald. Each person was roped together as per Captain Jackson's orders.

"I don't know about you, Colonel, but I am truly wondering what sort of spy our Mr. McDonald is. I mean, he has made no overt moves even to slow our progress. No messages sent, none received. What do you make of it?"

John Henry lowered the woolen scarf from his bearded face. "I thought by keeping him close I could figure out his game, but as you say I don't know if he has one. Maybe he's just to observe and report."

"I believe he could accomplish that merely by cornering

a drunken sailor or marine and bribing him to talk once we return."

"Perhaps McDonald doesn't see us making it out alive."

"I see your point, sir."

"Point?" Claire asked as she joined them.

"We were just wondering when our Victorian spy was going to act like one," Thomas said.

"Yes, I suspect we're pretty safe until we either return with the proof, or we fail. Then he will report and then London will have to make a decision. Until then, I'm pretty sure Mr. McDonald does not want to remain up here for eternity, and without us that is surely what would happen. I mean, the man threw a fit because he lost his toiletries in the Persian attack on our camp."

"Colonel, Gray Dog is signaling," Dugan said as he slowed his pace to allow them to catch up.

It took several minutes for the column to reach the point where Gray Dog waited. John Henry stepped up to the Comanche, who simply turned and pointed. Thomas raised his goggles and looked into the blowing wind. The glacier.

"My God, it stretches on forever," Claire said as she also lowered her hood and goggles.

"A great expanse of nothing," Taylor said as he caught up to the rest.

"Yes, it is," Thomas commented.

"And do you notice what's missing?" Taylor asked.

Thomas and Claire turned to face him.

"The Ark. Where is it?"

Ollafson finally arrived, looking like a young child on Christmas morning. He let his staff fall to the ice and he slapped his gloved hands together once.

"The summit!"

"And where is your biblical rowboat, Mr. Ollafson?" Taylor asked as he removed his hood and glared at the old man.

The professor laughed. "Do you think it sits upon the glacier, my young friend?" He laughed with such glee that even Steven McDonald took a step away from him as he thought him suddenly insane. "This glacier had to have been formed a hundred, maybe even a thousand years after the Ark came to rest."

"Biblical scholars place the flood at roughly four thousand years ago. Geologists claim the glacier on this mountain range is more than ten thousand years old," Claire said as she was also looking at the professor like he had fallen off the trolley car.

"Simple. The biblical scholars are wrong in their estimates. The Ark was on the flooded seas twelve to thirteen thousand years ago."

The comment was met with silence. As for John Henry, he felt his heart fall through to the bottom of his stomach. The man *was* insane. Most believed civilization was only five thousand years old, and now here was Ollafson saying everyone was wrong. He lowered his head and felt Claire's hand on his shoulder as she realized the same thing.

"Did you mention this to President Lincoln?" Thomas asked as he raised his head.

"Mention what?"

"Your time frame for these events, you old fool!" Taylor said, suddenly frustrated just listening to the old man. His men could possibly die on the assumptions of an insane professor who had been fired from his teaching post at Harvard for these very same beliefs.

No one ventured to go further with the conversation. Claire hung her head and then stepped over to a large rock and leaned heavily against it.

Ollafson didn't seem to notice the distance everyone was putting between themselves and him. He just smiled and stared out onto the expansive glacier.

"The Ark has to be right down—" He reached down and retrieved his walking staff and then jabbed the ice with its spiked tip. "Here!"

Thomas looked up and saw the staff sticking in the ice. He looked at Jessy, who was insane with rage at having dragged his men six thousand miles away from home to please an old fool with dreams, or was it delusions, of grandeur.

Snow started to blow in from across the Persian border. The winds were cold and the snow stung their exposed skin. Still, Ollafson looked from face to face in anticipation of their excitement at arriving.

Gray Dog and Dugan watched from a distance away.

"Well, my guess is that it's time we go home," Dugan said as he spit a stream of tobacco juice into the snow and ice. Gray Dog grimaced at the disgusting habit of the sergeant major and looked down at the brown stain on the snow. He cocked his head to the right when he saw not only the stain, but the ice it was upon, vanish. Gray Dog knew what was about to happen and could do nothing to warn anyone. He grabbed Dugan and pushed him away and they both fell into the snow.

"Professor, we have no way of digging down through what is possibly a mile of ice to find your fantasy. This is a fool's errand and always has been," Jessy said as he threw his gloves into the snow. The wind had picked up by at least thirty miles per hour in the past two minutes and the snow was of a much thicker volume than any time before.

"Look, the petrified wood was found only feet from where we are standing. The Ark is here." Ollafson was pleading after he read the faces of those around him and he finally started to understand. They did not believe him.

"You have the rest of the day and tomorrow. Then we leave this place," John Henry said as he started to move off. The realization struck him that for the first time in his military life he had failed to complete a mission.

"You can't mean that!" Ollafson cried as he tried to catch Thomas.

"Get down!" came the distant call.

All heads turned and they saw Gray Dog waving frantically toward the line of soldiers.

"What in the hell is he—" Jessy started to say.

The crack sounded like a large-bore cannon exploding only inches from them. The tear in the ice was so sudden and so loud that it hurt the ears of every man who heard it.

Without further warning the entire ice shelf gave way. The

first one pulled in was Thomas. He scrambled frantically to remove the rope from his waist before he was pulled in. Claire and the others started doing the same but it was far too late. John Henry vanished into the dark void that formed in the few feet of stone before the actual glacier.

One by one the expedition was pulled down into the darkness. Finally the sixth man in line managed to cut his rope and saved the bulk of the men from being pulled in. The shock was palpable as they saw the entire command team being pulled into the hole.

John Henry struck his head on the edge of the hole as he was pulled in, and still he tried to get the rope off to save those he could. He landed hard on his back and then he started to slide. The darkness of the void slipped by with only the notice of a rough grade and the flow of rushing air to attest to the speed of his slide. Above him he heard the screams and shouts of others as they too tumbled down deep into the beginnings of the glacier. He bounced off a curve in the strangely made tunnel of the void. He heard a woman shout and then cry out in pain above him in the darkness. Then the voices of others as they started their free fall to whatever death awaited them. Finally he slid to a stop and was absolutely shocked that he was still alive. Bruised and battered, but he was breathing. Then he heard another thud next to him and Claire, with Jessy atop her, landed at his feet. He quickly pulled them back as the rest of them, McDonald, Jackson, and then finally Ollafson, came sliding and crashing to a stop.

John Henry could not speak for the briefest of moments. He felt Claire take hold of him in a death grip and hug him as hard as he had ever been hugged. It was Jessy who managed to extricate himself from the pile of humanity and then strike a match. He raised his brows when he saw the tight hold Claire had on John Henry, then moved the match around.

"My God!" Ollafson said.

They were inside a giant void. It had been formed more than ten thousand years ago by volcanic activity that produced bubbles the size of Manhattan Island and created what it was they had landed in—a giant geode of water and ice. There was a waterfall. That much they could hear in the distance, and they all wondered just how far they had slid.

Claire finally regained some composure and released John Henry.

"Sorry. I thought we would slide off into oblivion at any moment."

"As far as that goes, I'm pretty sure we just did," John Henry said, as he rubbed at his hurt and aching muscles. He felt the back of his head and the hand came away with a patch of blood. Claire saw this and made him bend over.

The match soon burned out and before Jessy could light another McDonald stayed his hand.

"Look," he said in wonder.

As they glanced around the immense ice cave, they saw that the sun, as weak a light as it was, was showing through the thickness of the ice from above. It was though the cave was brushed with soft moonlight.

"Amazing. It's as though the ice is amplifying the weak sunlight into an incandescent state," Ollafson said as Jessy looked at him as though he still thought him insane.

"Is anyone alive down there?" came the voice of Sergeant Major Dugan as if from heaven. The question echoed for a brief moment and then John Henry called up.

"We need ropes, block and tackle!" he called.

"Yes, sir. Glad to hear you're still sucking breath," Dugan said, going on faith alone as he could not see past a few feet into the giant void.

"Colonel, we must explore this magnificent structure before we evacuate," Ollafson said.

"Professor, this has gone on long enough. Wasn't that fall convincing enough for you? This is a dangerous place."

"Yes, but we must—"

"We must do nothing but end this charade, old man. There is nothing up here for us but death." Taylor's eyes were wide in anger and he was very tired of beating circles around the proverbial bush. He faced John Henry, whom he could now see clearly in the strange and diffused light. "Now, you know we tried, John Henry, but not one life is worth proving this maniac's dream." He turned and looked at Ollafson. "Now, I appreciate the fact that this is your life's work, but this will end up costing men their lives. Men who want to survive not only this fool's errand, but the war also." Jessy looked down in sadness. "They want to go home to their families. Not just my men, but every man who wears a uniform."

Claire heard the honest words and felt for not only Ollafson, but the men on this venture. For the first time she realized every one of these men was someone's father, husband, or brother. What right did Ollafson have to send them to their death just to prove a point of theory? She walked until the darkness became more complete and she was surprised when she walked right into a wall. She was startled but stepped back.

That was when her world changed forever.

Ollafson was despondent. He slowly slid down the wall when he realized Thomas was calling an end to the mission. There was just too much area to search and they were fast running out of time. John Henry stepped over and assisted the old man to his feet.

"In better times, Professor, I have no doubt you'll come back for the Ark and actually find it," Thomas said as he looked around and noticed that Claire wasn't with them. He had just started to search when she stepped into the soft light filtering through the ice. She walked to her pack and removed a small lamp and lit it.

"Why wait to come back?"

"What are you talking about?" McDonald asked as Claire held the small lamp up high.

"We may as well do something with it right now. I mean, we are here, are we not?"

She turned and held the lamp higher. Everyone, including John Henry Thomas, the man whom nothing surprised, felt his eyes go wide.

There, buried in many thousands of years of ice, was the

curved bow of a ship. It rose sixty feet above their heads and vanished into blue-tinted ice. John Henry could make out the wood of its beams, but then again he knew it wasn't wood, because after all of this time it looked as if the giant bow had been carved from black stone. It was the Confederate colonel who summed it up for the rest of them in an articulate way that only Taylor could accomplish.

"I'll be a son of a bitch!"

22

John Henry stood atop the glacier after he and the others had
been pulled out by Dugan and the men. Word of the find sent
a shock wave through the tired troops, North and South. After most had figured the headquarters staff had been killed,
they learned the news that made all of those days in Sunday
school class as children come into their thoughts.

The large hole had been widened and a sling system was
built by the navy riggers. Men and equipment were now below shoring up the large system of caves. After the initial discovery had been made it was learned that the cave had many
duplicates, and sections of the great Ark could be seen
through many thin or bare spots. The size of the vessel was
enormous. Ollafson noted that the Ark was heavily damaged
not only by the passage of time, but by the elements that had
combined to crush large sections of the ancient ship.

More than a hundred oil lamps assisted the weak and fad-
ing light of day to illuminate the most amazing sight the
men had ever seen. Even McDonald was in awe of what the
Americans had found. His mission had changed somewhat
since their thrill ride through hell. The bloody Yanks had

proven the myth. Now they would have to get the proof back to civilization, and that was what McDonald had to stop or claim as England's own. He would have to move fast. He would not tell Madame Claire about his plans. For some reason he could not fathom, she had become distant and she was constantly observing him, and to be frank about it, it made him uneasy.

Jessy was leading the men who were busy shoring up the tighter and more fragile areas of the cave system. They had sacrificed ten of the valuable sleds for the wood needed and they would still be dangerously short if the ceiling of the void came crashing down. For the most part the men had settled into an uneasy silence since their initial viewing of the Ark. Now their eyes were constantly moving to the ice around them, waiting to hear the sound of cracking, indicating they were about to be buried alive.

The latest man down was Daniel Perlmutter. The equipment inside the wooden boxes was handled by him alone as he used the rope sling to carefully maneuver the camera equipment down.

Ollafson, who was walking around the exposed section of the Ark taking notes and making diagrams, saw the young photographer and smiled. He approached him as the boy was unloading the first of his equipment.

"I see you are about to do your magic with that box, eh?" the old man asked as he saw the rope sling heading back to the surface.

Perlmutter looked up and smiled. The young man pushed his wire-rimmed glasses back up his nose and then lowered the hood of his jacket.

"Oh, hello, Professor. Yes," he said as he looked around at his scattered camera equipment. "I figured I better get my things down here before the navy starts lowering the explosives."

"Sensible," Ollafson said.

"Now, Professor, don't go wandering off. We want to immortalize you and your find," Perlmutter said with a wink.

"Oh, my. No, there will be plenty of time for that. We have other work we need to do."

"So I understand. The colonel is getting ready to send down the men who will disassemble some of the Ark after I take my images."

Ollafson froze with pencil and notebook in hand. He was looking at Perlmutter as if he were deranged. "Excuse me, disassemble?"

"Yes, the colonel said they need a few sections for your proof—well, that and the photographs I take, that is."

"No, no, no, young man, you must have heard wrong. We must stay and excavate this site properly. There will be no disassembly for samples."

Perlmutter could see that the news had unhinged the professor somewhat.

"I'm sure I heard right, but you can double-check the orders."

The notebook and pencil fell from Ollafson's hand and his eyes went wide just before he lunged at the young man. Perlmutter yelped when the professor grabbed him by the throat and both men went down over the scattered equipment. Ollafson had lost control and was trying his best to kill the messenger.

Taylor heard the boy call out and he turned to see two men rolling on the ice floor of the cave. He thought for sure it must have been one of his men and one of John Henry's. He ran over and was surprised when he pulled Professor Ollafson off the learned student of Mathew Brady. He had to shake Ollafson to get him to stop trying to claw his way back to Perlmutter.

"What in the hell has gotten into you, Doc?" Jessy said as he shook the man, trying to shock some sense back into those crazed eyes. Taylor shook him so hard that Ollafson's glasses went flying. Then the man went semi-limp in Jessy's hands. He looked down at Daniel Perlmutter, who was rubbing his neck and trying to stand up. A few of the marines and Rebs gathered around to see what the ruckus was about. "What did you do?" he asked the still-shaken Perlmutter.

"Nothing. I just told him that the colonel had ordered samples of the Ark and its images recorded."

"We can't just leave it here," Ollafson said as his eyes stared off into the distance as though Taylor was not even there.

"Professor, the find is yours. You have proven that it exists. No one can ever take that away from you. You'll be back. Lincoln will surely support a more legal expedition now."

The Rebs who had gathered around exchanged looks when Taylor mentioned Lincoln. It was if he was conceding Lincoln would always be there, meaning the war was lost in his opinion.

Ollafson continued to stare at nothing.

"All right, you men get the professor hooked into that harness and get him out of here. I don't want him anywhere near that dynamite when it gets down here."

The men didn't move at first, and then the professor lowered his head in defeat. The men moved to follow the command of Taylor.

It had taken Claire two full hours to get Ollafson to sleep, and it also took several sleeping aids prescribed by the marine corpsman at that. The sun had set and the snow was falling at a brisk pace, the winds were picking up, and it looked as though the camp was in for rough night. The rest of the late afternoon had been taken up by Captain Jackson and John Henry as they pondered the communication problems that had arisen along with the bad weather. They needed to signal Lieutenant Parnell on the plain below by rocket fire that they had made their goal of the summit. The cloud cover was so thick they couldn't see the slope of the mountain, much less the plain below. They would have to await a clearing of the skies before contact could be established.

"I think that part of our plan could have been thought out better," Jackson said as he scanned the skies above.

"Well, we didn't have the time to lay a telegraph line from Talise all the way up here. We'll have to make do. Maybe in a day or two we can send a messenger back." The two men knew that without the signal rockets they would be blind as to what was approaching them from the west.

Four hours later John Henry stared up at the raked and curved bow of the Ark and shook his head. Jessy and Claire stood next to him as they examined the giant's bow under lamp-light for the first time. The men were above trying to bed down as best they could with the storm intensifying.

"It kind of makes you wonder what else you've been mistaken about all your life, doesn't it?" Thomas said as he saw the tool markings that had been carved in the wood more than thirteen thousand years before. He saw the wooden pegs that held the massive vessel together, all turned to stone.

"I don't take well to reflection," Jessy said as he gave John Henry a sorrowful look. "Hell, I've been wrong so much it's become a career objective."

For the first time since the mission began all three of them laughed at the same time. They stopped when they heard the men who were assigned the task of shoring up a small cave that extended halfway to the middle of the Ark. Jenks, several Confederate prisoners, a few marines, and Grandee and his off-duty mess crew were assisting.

The laughter died and then John Henry handed Claire the lamp and shocked her by starting to climb the rope ladder that had been placed on the large bow for work crews to enter in the morning when the Ark was examined.

"Hey, your own orders were to await the naval engineers in the morning," Claire called up.

"I have a history of not following orders. That's why I'm here," he said as he made the top of the curving prow of the Ark and then vanished over the ancient gunwale.

Claire looked at Taylor. He just half-bowed and then gestured toward the rope. "You're the one that climbs like a ring-tailed lemur. After you," he said, smiling.

Claire lowered the hood of her coat, gave Taylor a smug look, and then smiled and took hold of the rope. Jessy had to grin as Claire shot up the rope ladder almost as fast as Thomas had done. When she made it over the top, a small piece of ice was thrown over and struck Jessy on the head. He looked back up and saw Claire smiling down on him.

"I think you've been spending too much time with that Indian boy," he joked and then blew out the lamp and attached it to his coat before he started climbing—intentionally faster than Claire.

McDonald watched Taylor vanish over the side wall of the Ark. His eyes remained watching for the time being. Then his gaze shifted to Captain Jackson as he stood and supervised the unloading of the dynamite. He wanted to make sure his navy demolition team handled it right because Thomas had men working not far from them inside a small cave where they were using the last of their wood to shore up that area.

The British agent watched as a tarpaulin was placed over the six cases of dynamite and tied down. They made sure the area was well roped off before they started the climb back to the surface.

McDonald watched the great cavern empty. All was quiet except for the distant sound of hammering and talking from the men in the smaller cave. He heard the voices of Thomas, Taylor, and Claire as they moved about on the deck of the Ark.

Then he went over to the stored dynamite and started to remove the tarpaulin.

When John Henry hit the frozen-over deck, the bow was curved to such an extreme rake that he slipped and fell onto his back. It seemed he slid for a hundred feet before his boot heels hit a higher object that arrested his sliding fall.

Then he heard a cry for help and before he knew it Claire smashed into him. She had done the same thing as he had just done.

"That first step is kind of tricky," Thomas said as he gained his feet and then assisted Claire to hers. She brushed off her backside with as much dignity as she could and then was about to say something when an accursed shout came to her

ears. Before she knew it she was back down on her butt and
John Henry was sprawled on top of her. Taylor was laughing
as he tried to pick himself up, fell on top of Thomas, and then
was laughing so hard he was close to losing control. Meanwhile, John Henry and Claire were nose to nose.

"Now you know why I hate him."

"Understandable, Colonel. Now, if you don't wish rumors
to start swirling about, may I suggest you move that pistol
from my pelvic region and get the hell off of me?"

John Henry smiled widely and his old self emerged, a man
he hadn't seen or heard from in more than five years.

"Who said I was armed?"

With that, Claire pushed him off and he went flying backward into a laughing Taylor and they both fell once again.

Claire stood and started brushing the ice from herself once
more, and then she stopped and saw the open doorway. It was
partially covered by a thin sheet of ice, but there was a hole
in that ice about as wide as a barrel.

Taylor and Thomas finally gained a little control and saw
that Claire was standing rigid. They walked up and saw the
portal into blackness. Taylor unhooked the oil lamp and then
struck a match. The lamp flared to life and they saw what
looked like a way to enter the Ark. All of a sudden the humor
they felt a moment before had vanished as if it had never been.

John Henry moved Claire aside and struck out with his
boot and caught the ice center mass. The thin sheet shattered
like fine crystal and they were left staring into a darkness that
none of them had ever experienced before. He reached over
and took the lamp from Jessy and held it just inside the well
of blackness.

"Any lions, tigers, or elephants in there, maybe a lost uni-
corn?" Taylor joked and both Thomas and Claire turned and
looked at him in silence, finding the humor a little droll.

John Henry came back to reality and stepped inside the
interior of the Ark.

Ollafson awoke from a nightmare that had shaken him to the
core. He sat up from his bedroll and saw that he had been

placed there after being drugged. He rubbed his eyes and thought about what had awakened him. He didn't know and couldn't remember anything other than the cold, icy hands of death as it caressed him and the others.

He shoved the thick blankets off him and in a panic he rummaged through the tent, tossing the last of McDonald's personal property about. He finally found the satchel and hugged it to his chest. He fell back with the artifacts and took a deep breath as he felt inside for the strangely warm petrified wood of the planks. He started to doze off again after he knew his artifacts were secure, the drugs still affecting him.

After the professor's eyes closed, the satchel started to smolder in his gloved hands. Soon it died down and then the tent's front flap blew outward. A dark shadow shot from the tent and made for the excavation site.

"I'm just saying, my accounting would have been better, but that ship was moving so much I could hardly stand," Jenks said in defense of his performance aboard the *Yorktown* when he and Grandee had put on their little show. Now it was his own brothers-in-arms giving him a hard time about the whooping he'd taken at the hands of the mess steward. Grandee heard the joking way in which they teased Jenks but continued to place the last of the wood over the small cave opening. When a particularly harsh barb was landed by another Reb, Grandee turned and confronted the men. The other mess stewards stopped working to watch, as did the six marines.

"I've been on ships like the *Yorktown* for more than six years. My footing is used to the rocking of a large vessel. Your friend there, he did all right in my book."

The men listened to the deep, throaty voice of Grandee as he turned away and went back to work. He started to sing "Swing Low, Sweet Chariot" as Jenks looked his way. He stood from where he had been sitting and moved to the opposite end of the cave. He didn't know what to think about the large black man coming to his defense.

Corporal Jenks turned away and saw that he was near an exposed section of the Ark. He reached out and felt the ancient petrified wood and then he pulled his gloved hand back quickly. The black stone was so cold the gloves had zero effect at stopping it. His eyes traveled upward and he noticed large holes in the hull before it vanished into the ice far above. Then he noticed what looked like long claw marks dug deep into the wood. It looked like thousands of fingers had tried desperately to hold onto the sides of the hull as the world around them flooded. He didn't know why that thought struck him when he saw the scratches in the ancient wood, but it did. He shook his head and then returned to the company of real men, not the blank stare of an object he never would have believed was real.

As he moved away, a dark shape reached out from a large crack in the petrified wood and barely missed Jenks's head as he turned to leave. There was a hiss of anger and then the hand-like shadow backed into the crack.

After thirteen thousand years, the Ark was waking up from an ancient sleep.

· The inside was dark and smelled like old vegetation. John Henry held the lamp high as he examined what he could. The area was small, and he could see that anything beyond was buried in a solid wall of ice.

"What are these, do you suppose?" Claire said at his side.

John Henry held the lamp close to the nearest object and saw the cage-like pen. It looked as if it had been hand-crafted from extremely thick vines.

"Cages?" Taylor ventured. "Looks like a mess of them. But I'm not buying that story about animals boarding two by two and all of that. This vessel, though large, could never fit that many beasts inside."

"Well, Colonel, maybe you are taking the Bible a little too literally when it comes to the descriptions. After all, the Bible was written by men. Men such as yourselves, and as I have had recent dealings with the male species, I believe the stories were embellished somewhat."

John Henry and Jessy exchanged a look. They had just been insulted in the strangest way, and they knew it.

"Now wait a minute, I think—"

That was as far as John Henry got when the world shook and knocked them from their feet.

The cave started to fall in beneath the Ark where the men were struggling to shore up that area.

Thomas and Taylor both knew that men had just died.

Grandee heard the men talking behind him as the mess crew started packing up their tools. The last of the wooden planks had been laid and now the small cave was as secure as they could make it with the limited amount of wood they had to work with.

Jenks and the others watched as first the marines and then Grandee's mess crew started to leave the cave. The corporal still pictured the images of the humanlike scratch marks on the side of the Ark's hull. The image, he knew, would stay with him for the rest of his life.

Grandee saw the shadow first as he turned to retrieve the last of the tools. His eyes widened when the large manifestation spread what looked like massively strong arms. The entity knocked down the nearest soldier and fell upon him. Jenks screamed in horror as he fought to help the man. He was flailing and fighting with something they could not see. As Jenks reached him the shadow turned on him and then struck out, and the blow sent Jenks into the wall of ice. Other men yelled and screamed as the shadow rose to the cave's ceiling and then the boards they had just placed started to shatter as if they had been hit by a sledgehammer. They all heard the horrid noise at once as the wooden bracing gave way and the wood went flying. At that same moment each man would swear later that he heard the cries of a thousand voices as they shouted out in terror. The men would also say they heard the roar of a great beast as the shadow shot free of the cave.

Suddenly large chunks of ice started to fall from the ceiling. Grandee was the first to react. He started to pull and push the Rebel soldiers from the cave. All the while he was screaming at Jenks to get cut. More ice fell and Grandee knew that Jenks and two others would never make it. He ran as fast as he could, stooping over in the low-hung cave. He reached up and braced the main beam they had used for the centermost reinforcement. He pushed with everything he had, bending the cracked and broken wood upward.

"Get out while you can!" he screamed as his muscles bulged and sweat poured from his face.

Jenks pushed the last two men outside the cave opening and then turned back to help Grandee.

"Come on, let it go! You can make it!"

"Go, I can't hold it any longer!"

The cave started to come down, but still Jenks was fighting his way through the falling ice to reach Grandee. Suddenly the big man kicked out with his size-fifteen boot and hit Jenks, who went flying backward until assisting hands caught him and pulled him free of the collapsing cave.

"Get out of there!" Jenks cried in frustration as he angrily slapped the helping hands away from him. He locked eyes with the man he had fought only a week before and saw in his eyes what he himself already knew.

"Go!" was all Grandee said as the entire world fell upon him from above.

The horrified Jenks shouted and yelled and cried that Grandee could have gotten out.

The men picked up Jenks and started dragging him away. The corporal shook them off and then turned back to see the closed space that was once the small cave. He looked around at the exposed hull of the ancient Ark. He spit and then cursed it with the last ounce of faith he had.

The hard-luck night was just beginning for Americans everywhere.

ONE HUNDRED MILES NORTH OF TRABZON HARBOR, THE BLACK SEA

The captain of the U.S.S. *Carpenter* relieved his first officer at 0400 hours. The seas were finally calm and the winds had died down. He received the report from the *Argo* that her flooding was now under control and they were stable for the time being. The first officer saluted and made the announcement that the captain had command of the deck watch.

The young captain went aft and checked on the towline and spoke with the men manning it. He saw that the men were awake and the towline was tight. He went to the quarterdeck, where he took a bearing from the stars that were finally visible in the night sky.

Suddenly the crow's nest warning bell started chiming at an alarming rate. The captain strained to look up into the tall rigging.

"Ship on a collision course, bearing two-three-two degrees to starboard!"

Captain Abernathy ran to the starboard side and his eyes widened until he felt they would pop free of his head. The French frigate *Osiris* was bearing down upon *Carpenter* at a speed that said this was an intentional act—an impossible mistake on a cloudless night such as this.

"Warning rockets, fire!"

The captain swore that if he had been at battle stations he would have laid waste to the French ship with every cannon he had, but then he realized that was exactly what the French captain wanted. He was daring the Americans to open fire.

From the stern the officer of the deck was ready. Soon three signal rockets of bright red and green fired into the sky and exploded in a shower of sparks, but still the *Osiris* came on.

"All hands brace for collision!" the captain called out and hung onto the starboard railing.

The *Osiris* started to veer off at the last second. It was too late. The bow of the new warship struck the *Carpenter* a glancing blow along her starboard side. She scraped along, tearing rigging from both ships as their main masts and sails came into contact. The captain heard his rigging being torn away as the huge warship shuddered as *Osiris* finally broke contact and turned away.

The captain regained his feet after the collision had sent him flying to the deck. He stood and saw the crew of the French ship watching the spectacle as though it were a Parisian

Burlesque show. He saw the officers standing on the quarterdeck as she slid past. The men only stared at him. The captain swore he would have planted many a cannonball into her if he could have.

"Damage report!"

The first officer was there. He had come running from his quarters when the collision warning was sounded. He was buttoning his shirt as he shouted down, "Get the carpenter to sound the ship!" He turned back angrily to face the captain. "Bastards! We should have fired on her!"

"That's exactly what they wanted, Jim. Us to fire the first shot. Right now it was all just a horrible accident."

"My ass!"

"The formal apology letter from their embassy is probably already on its way to President Lincoln. A letter that was more than likely drafted weeks ago."

"Scheming sons of bitches."

The ship's master carpenter reported a few moments later.

"We're up to six feet of water in frames ten through sixteen. We've cracked some ribs for sure, Captain."

"Is my ship in danger of foundering?"

"Too soon to tell, Captain. We have to get the pumps ahead while we shore up. Until then we have a job on our hands for sure." The captain only nodded, sending the carpenter back to his duties.

"Jim, cut the towline. Signal the *Argo,* inform her of the situation, and let them know they are on their own for now. We will send *Chesapeake* and *Yorktown* her last coordinates as soon as we are able."

"Captain?" the first officer said, astounded that they were going to cut loose the barge and its complement of men.

"If we go down, we'll take that unstable platform to the bottom with us. Cut the towline, now!"

Several men started hacking at the thick ropes as the first officer started to signal *Argo* by message lamp.

A moment later the tow barge *Argo* and her crew were cut adrift. She was now on her own as the U.S.S. *Carpenter* fought for her life.

23

It had taken six men to hold Corporal Jenks back from reentering the cave system below and beside the unstable Ark. The corporal was convinced that the large black man was still alive. It had been four hours since the expedition held its second funeral service since the mission began, and John Henry suspected it would not be the last.

The mood after the gathered soldiers had broken up was somber even before the colonel had laid out the orders of the day. They would clear a few tons of ice from the Ark and her bow so Daniel Perlmutter could get evidentiary photographs and then they could end this mission and go home. Still, the death of Grandee not only affected the naval and marine personnel, but strangely enough all of the Confederate prisoners as well. Captain Jackson pointed out to John Henry that the southerners were taking it far harder than he would ever have believed. Even Jessy was not in a talkative mood. Breakfast that morning had consisted of hot coffee and bacon. The mess crew missed their leader and the men missed Grandee's food.

The colonel, Dugan, and Gray Dog watched as the men

slowly returned to their work. There was none of the usual joking or glad-handing, nor was there the hard talk of northerner against southerner. Today it was a fellow American they were mourning, not a naval mess steward.

Thomas looked down the steep slope of Ararat and saw that the cloud cover was still blanketing the region. The snow had stopped just before dawn and the winds had calmed. It was as if the mountain were taking a restorative breath before its next performance. He opened his pocketwatch and saw that they had wasted half a day with the futile recovery effort to remove Grandee and the Rebel soldier from the cave-in. He examined the sky and then looked at the navy petty officer who was standing by the signal rockets and he shook his head. There would be no signals to the plain far below that day.

"This non-communication is getting a little dicey, Colonel Darlin'."

Dugan was right. Soon they would have to send a messenger down to give and receive information from Lieutenant Parnell.

Captain Jackson and Taylor came to report. John Henry returned salutes without much enthusiasm.

"Ordnance is ready to lay the charges and clear the bow," Jackson said.

"And we're sure that the rest of the cave will not collapse when those charges are detonated?"

"We're only using quarter sticks at fifteen-foot intervals. Two charges at a time, we should get a delayed collapse of ice and then the bow section should be cleared," Taylor said, knowing it would be two of his experts with the two navy ordnance men doing the work. In Jeb Stuart's cavalry Taylor was known as a guerrilla fighter who was prone to blowing things Union straight to hell.

John Henry spoke low so the rest of the men did not hear. "Will there be any chance to recover the two bodies?"

Jackson looked hurt and Taylor just looked away. Jackson just shook his head that no, they could not be recovered.

"Look, we can ignore this all we want, but the word has

spread to every set of ears Union or Confederate that something was in that cave with those boys. That it was the curse
that brought that cave down. They claim they saw it. Not just
my men." Taylor looked at Jackson. "But yours also."

John Henry wanted badly to tell both Jackson and Taylor
to stop acting like shavetail second lieutenants—that it was
an unstable cave and it came down, nothing mysterious at all.
Not even Thomas was buying all of this bad luck as random.
He decided not to comment at all until he could meet with
Claire so she could explain things to the men and stop this
talk of angelic curses—even if he had to force her to lie.

"How long will it take to remove the ice from the top of
the Ark so we can get some needed light for our Mr. Perlmutter?"

"The ice sheet covering the top is only ten feet thick. A
small charge in the direct center should break open the cave's
top and we should be able to see the Ark from here."

"Proceed, gentlemen."

Jackson saluted and then went to his ordnance men and
told them to start laying the charges on top of the ice above
the vessel.

John Henry didn't comment when Jessy stayed behind.
Gray Dog saw the seriousness on the colonel's face and decided to leave the two old classmates alone.

"You know and I know what those men saw down there.
Get your photography done and let's get the hell off of this
mountain."

"Colonel Taylor, may I remind you we haven't received or
sent word to Lieutenant Parnell since our arrival. When we
finish here, if we haven't yet established contact, we could
be walking into an entire army of angered Turks down there.
We may as well do the job we were sent here to do until that
can be established. Are we clear on that?"

Taylor slapped his gloves against the side of his leg and
then angrily moved off to assist in laying the charges.

John Henry knew that Jessy was right, but he felt trapped
as he did not know the disposition of the rest of his men.

TALISE STATION, PLAIN OF ARARAT

Lieutenant Parnell had a difficult time convincing the Army of the Potomac band that they were in serious trouble. The men were silently working at laying the rail ties for a rail line that would never be completed, just as the Americans had known all along. It had been a full day since he had sent a marine corporal off to the halfway point to await any response from Constantinople, or any other government that came looking.

"That summit is still blanketed in weather, Lieutenant. There's no way we can see any signal with this system closing in around us."

"Keep an eye out. A break may appear instantaneously and we must see the signal when we get a break. Clear?"

"Aye, Lieutenant." The naval ensign pointed to the hill to the south. "Have you noticed the number of our audience has grown?"

Parnell looked to the rise and saw that the British officers had been joined by ten more men.

"Things are apt to get interesting around here soon enough," he said as he turned away from their constant watchers. Parnell looked at the remaining marines and the hundred-and-twenty-member Army of the Potomac band. He shook his head.

"What am I supposed to do, serenade them when they come charging at us?"

The situation was getting desperate.

WATER STATION, CONSTANTINOPLE LINE

Lance Corporal Walter Campbell watched the five-hundred-member Seventh Guards Regiment board the train after the locomotive took on water. He had almost been caught getting to the charges he had planted four days before at Talise Station. When he managed to reach the dynamite charges, he was relieved to find them still in place and undiscovered. He had lit the fuse and hoped the length was long enough not to blow up the water tank and surrounding buildings. He saw that the last of the Ottoman Empire's most elite troops had boarded and the locomotive sounded its whistle. A blast of steam powered the steel wheels into a spin as the train slowly started to move.

The explosion ripped open the huge boiler and sent shards of iron into the air. The locomotive hissed and then slowed as the boiling water and steam were blown free of the boiler. He saw men scramble off the train's cars and start to fan out, expecting the Americans had opened up on them with cannon fire. There were even a few stray shots fired as the Turks didn't know from which direction the attack was coming.

"Stupid bastards," the marine corporal chuckled, and then turned to his horse.

The commanding general of the Turkish regiment ducked his head for cover and then straightened and turned angrily to the Frenchman Renaud and raised his brow.

"It seems the Americans may be a mite more aggressive than you thought."

"Well, what are you going to do?" Renaud asked angrily as he hopped down from the private car that had been the home of John Henry just a few days before. "Damn," he said when he saw the horse and rider burst from the shadows of the dilapidated station. The rider was hell-bent on getting to the east.

"I am going to do what I was ordered to do, my French friend. I am going to pursue." He turned and found his second-in-command. "Captain, unload the horses. We ride east within the hour."

The Seventh Guards Regiment had been stopped—but only momentarily.

ONE HUNDRED FIFTY MILES NORTH OF TRABZON HARBOR, THE BLACK SEA

It had been almost eighteen hours since the *Argo* and her towline were cut loose from the *Carpenter*. The crew of the barge roamed from station to station checking the pressure valves on the sixteen flotation bags inside the hull of the awkward-looking barge. Each of the bags was the size of an observation balloon used by both sides during the war. The designer was, of course, John Ericsson. The men on deck kept a sharp eye out on the horizon for either the damaged *Carpenter,* the *Chesapeake,* or *Yorktown.* Thus far, with the exception of the French frigate *Especial,* the seas had been clear. The French observers were surely wondering why such a strangely designed vessel was of such importance to the French admiralty. She was ungainly and extremely wide of girth. She was thirty-five feet longer than the massive *Yorktown* and was almost double her tonnage.

A hatch that was situated at the stern opened and the real commander of the *Argo* stepped onto the barge's wooden decking. The captain, actually another navy lieutenant j.g., took a deep breath and then unbuttoned the top few buttons of his tunic. He removed his hat and allowed the cool sea breeze to wash through his sweat-soaked uniform.

"Sir, the French frigate keeps signaling and asking if we could use their assistance," a young helmsman reported.

Lieutenant Giles Ferguson straightened and then, remembering his position within the two crews of the *Argo,* rebuttoned his tunic after the brief respite. He placed the hat back on his head.

"The bastards are damn well lucky we have other priorities at the moment, because to tell you the truth I'm in the mood to sink every damn foreign-flagged naval vessel in the Black Sea after what they did last night."

"Yes, sir, it would surely be pleasing to the boys down there in that hellhole."

Ferguson glanced back at the hatch, which remained open, as were the other twelve on the barge's main deck for the men below to get some fresh air. As long as they were being spied upon by the French frigate, he couldn't allow the full complement of crew up from the *Argo.* As it was, he had to bring them up no more than ten men at a time to mix in cleanly with the barge crew. If the French knew they had a complement of two crews onboard, their little deception might end real soon.

"Captain, the *Especial* is making another run at us," said the helmsman at the wheel of an unmaneuverable ship.

"Damn it!" Ferguson cursed as he ran to the port railing and watched helplessly as the harassment continued. He saw the French crew lining her gunwales and laughing at the sailless and mastless barge.

The *Especial* finally made her turn close enough that her bow wave struck the *Argo* and rocked her. Captain Ferguson watched as an old veteran sailor waited until the faces of the French were close at hand, and then the old bearded sailor turned and lowered his pants and showed the French crew and their command his bone-white butt. The men of the *Argo* cheered as the *Especial* slid past. The French sailors looked on as the rest of the American crew did the same as the first.

Ferguson, a stickler for military protocol, saw this and had to smile as close to a hundred American sailors lined the railing with their breeches down around their knees showing the French exactly how the United States Navy felt about the French actions.

The captain paced to the railing toward the sailor who had started the avalanche of emotion by sending his pants to half-staff. The sailor was just pulling up his pantaloons when he noticed the captain standing next to him.

"Apologies, Captain. Major pants malfunction," the chief petty officer said as he secured his pants to full staff.

Ferguson had to smile, though he hid it well.

Every crewman below or above decks knew that soon their good humor would wear thin and the surface of the Black Sea would possibly roil in violence.

Argo and her crew were itching to break free of their wooden cocoon.

MOUNT ARARAT, THE OTTOMAN EMPIRE

John Henry looked at his watch and knew they only had an hour before they attempted to blow the cave's ceiling free of ice, so they did not have long to conduct the meeting. He closed the watch and looked around the interior of the space they had viewed two days before when it had been covered in ice. Now that it was illuminated he could see why the subject of a curse was running rampant throughout the camp.

The deaths of the Rebel soldier and Grandee were still weighing heavily on all of their minds.

Claire and McDonald arrived first and they had Professor Ollafson between them. The old man was looking pale as he clutched his satchel to his chest. Claire eased him onto the folding camp chair in front of the small table. The light cast eerie shadows on the petrified wood making up the familial enclosure of the Ark. Taylor and Captain Jackson soon followed. Gray Dog and Dugan watched from the opening and looked equally uncomfortable inside the ancient wreck.

John Henry cleared his throat. "Professor, first off I want to say that the decision to only take photographs and recover provenance of the Ark's existence was not mine to make. The president is receiving very disturbing reports from Europe that the powers that be will not allow any American prestige to exit this mountain. He suspects that they will attempt to stop us, legally or illegally."

Ollafson continued to clutch the relics to his chest. That was when Taylor and John Henry both noticed the scorch marks on the cloth of the large satchel. It was if the case had been singed in a fire. Thomas looked at Claire, who in turn reached over and tried to pry the artifacts from his strong grip. Without acknowledging Claire's efforts, Ollafson continued to hold the satchel. Finally Jessy stood and wrenched the bag from the professor's grip. He looked up at Taylor and his face was a blank mask of hate and confusion. Taylor tossed the heavy sailcloth case onto the table where it made a sickening, wet sound as it struck the table.

Thomas looked at Claire. She remained standing and cautiously opened the case and revealed the artifacts inside. She stepped back for only an instant and then felt embarrassed by her childish reaction. She shook her head and then pulled the petrified wood free of the case. She used her gloves but could still feel the coldness through the leather.

"As I've explained before, this Angelic symbol here is for the Archangel Azrael. These others are of other lesser angels sent by God for the protection of Noah and his kin. The way

the Bible explains it, Azrael was also known as the Angel of
Death."

"You mean this curse revolves around a hood-wearing,
scythe-wielding skeletal specter?" Jessy asked.

"That, Colonel, is the modern interpretation of the entity,
yes. But in ancient times it was somewhat different. According to legend, Azrael was involved with Lucifer and it was
suspected by the other Archangels, most notably Gabriel and
Michael, that Lucifer and Azrael conspired to overthrow
heaven and the throne of God."

"It sounds as if you're referring to when God tossed Lucifer's ass out of heaven. If so, why not this Azrael?" Taylor
asked as John Henry sat silently and listened. Ollafson and
McDonald were wearing unreadable blank faces. As for Gray
Dog and Dugan standing by the opening, it was if they were
mere children listening to a spooky bedtime story. Their eyes
were wide and kept roaming the interior of the Ark and its
long-dead petrified wood. As for Captain Jackson, he was fast
becoming a believer.

"That has been debated by Angelic scholars for centuries.
None of this is ever mentioned in the Bible. I believe it would
have scared most true believers to death if they heard it."

"Why is that?" John Henry asked, for the first time breaking his silence.

"Because it is argued inside of Christian and Jewish circles that Azrael was the only archangel that God ever feared,
because Azrael was the only angel given the power of death
over mankind."

"And thus the Lord sent Lucifer into exile to rule over
hell, and Azrael's punishment was to be placed on earth for
eternity in the company of man for the protection of the first
family of God."

All eyes turned to face a now-silent Ollafson after he had
managed to frighten them all when he spoke. In the corner
Gray Dog listened and Dugan accidentally swallowed his
chewing tobacco.

"Noah and his family?" John Henry asked, still looking

at a grinning Ollafson, sure the man had lost all thought of reality.

"Yes, that's the conclusion of the league of biblical scholars." Claire saw that Thomas was still skeptical to say the least.

"And this Azrael is still here after thirteen thousand years? I hate to break it to you but Noah and his family have been dead a very long time," Thomas countered.

Ollafson suddenly stood and paced the room. It was though he was recently awakened from a long slumber and knew it was time for class. He placed a gloved hand against the petrified hull of the Ark and lovingly caressed it.

"The Bible is incorrect in regards to the tale of the flood." Ollafson turned to face Claire and his eyes were clear. Claire sat down, shocked at the professor's sudden wakefulness. "Noah's family is most assuredly not dead, Colonel. Would you care to explain? Miss Claire?" Ollafson stood over them like he was a lecturing professor tutoring ignorant students. Claire cleared her throat trying to ignore the strange way Ollafson was looking at her.

"Transcendentalist scholars have come to the conclusion, as we have discussed before, that the entire world was not flooded five thousand years ago as the Bible says. Thirteen thousand years ago the entire Middle East region was destroyed by what some believe to have been a natural disaster that God allowed to happen. Thus, all of mankind did not perish in the great flood, only those in the Middle East. After the Ark settled into a new land, Noah and his family went about repopulating the Earth, well, as best as they could of course. But modern thought is that a third of the world's population is directly related to Noah and his descendants. Thus, the family of man is still here"—she cautiously smiled—"in a sense. Azrael's job was never completed and is he still working. Far weaker than in ancient times, but his punishment from God still intact."

Thomas stood and took the lamp from the table and walked to a far wall where a few of the ancient animal pens had been. He held the lamp high. They all saw the symbols at the same time. It looked as if the ancient writing had been placed on every square inch of hull from deck to ceiling. John Henry placed the oil lamp next to a missing section of hull. Claire saw what he wanted and then brought the two artifacts over and held them up to the missing planks. They fit exactly.

"This is where our missing pieces of the puzzle originated. Miss Claire has had a chance to decipher the symbols and that is why I called us together." He nodded at Claire, who returned the artifacts to the table and was happy to do so. She relieved John Henry of the lamp as he returned to his seat.

"We know that the symbols carved into the wood of the Ark were done by Noah himself. After all"—she smiled rather sheepishly—"he signed his work."

"What does the rest of this say?" Jessy asked, not liking at all the feeling he was getting.

Claire cleared her throat. Since this afternoon when she had transcribed the symbols she had realized that Noah might have had a falling out of sorts with the decision-makers of the time—meaning God himself.

"Gentlemen, all of this"—she moved the lamp from floor to ceiling, revealing an entire hull section covered in the Angelic symbols—"is a curse, not on men, but on Azrael himself. Noah hated God's angel of death. Noah despised the creature so much that after the Ark had settled, he cursed Azrael to remain on this mountain for eternity. Which was what happened until the professor brought back pieces of the Ark."

"So this is not a curse keeping men out of here, it's a curse trapping the angel of death?" Jessy asked.

"You must admit that there hasn't been any mass kill-off of humankind the way the Bible describes it for thousands of years. Maybe that's because the Lord's mass murderer is trapped here."

"That is the most ridiculous theory I have ever heard uttered," McDonald said as Claire shot him a sour look. "For one thing, there is no Azrael or whatever you call it. There is no curse and most definitely there is no angel of death."

McDonald reached out and took hold of the two artifacts and exposed them to the bright lamplight. Sergeant Major Dugan looked from the haughty British spy to a very interested Gray Dog. The Englishman picked up the largest piece with the symbols emblazoned upon it and held it high. "I believe this is nothing more than an elaborate hoax!"

Before anyone could react McDonald was thrown backward as if he had been smashed in the chest by a runaway train. His grip on the artifact was lost and the ancient wood clacked to the tabletop as McDonald was thrown hard into the arms of Dugan fifteen feet away.

This time they all saw the shadow as it rose from the deck of the Ark. It stood over them momentarily and then it dissipated to nothing. Dugan and Gray Dog picked up the startled but uninjured McDonald. Both men saw it at the same moment. There were two handprints etched in ice on the man's fur-lined coat. The size of the hands was the most terrifying thing—they were four times the size of a regular man's prints. Dugan looked at John Henry as McDonald started to cough from having the air knocked from his lungs. Claire immediately reached for the two fallen artifacts and jammed them deep inside the satchel. Then she sat hard into her chair.

John Henry watched as the Englishman shook off the helping hands of Dugan and Gray Dog and then he bolted from the interior of the Ark without a look back.

"I guess old Azrael dislikes spies," Taylor said, and then realized just how flat his sudden bout of humor had fallen. Jessy had become angry when Thomas had voiced his suspicions with him.

"For the time being, that satchel stays where it was intended," Thomas said as he stood.

"So you are now a believer?" Claire asked as she looked up at John Henry.

Thomas didn't answer as he quickly left the Ark.

As for Ollafson, he sat smugly down and then stared at the satchel in front of him.

"Maybe we should just blow the whole thing straight to

hell," Taylor said as he placed a gloved hand on the outside of the satchel.

"The angel of death is weak. This is the time to take the Ark while it can only frighten. Any longer and there is no telling how Azrael's power could grow."

"Professor, even if we didn't have some spook running around here killing men, we could never in a lifetime get this hunk of petrified stone off of this mountain. No engineer in the world could accomplish the feat," Jackson said as he raised his hood and then followed John Henry out. Dugan and Gray Dog followed, leaving Ollafson, Claire, and Taylor behind.

"The most dangerous thing is for an intelligent man to ignore the supernatural," Claire said as she reached out and pushed the satchel farther away from her. "John Henry is still a nonbeliever and that could cost him."

Taylor stood and then helped Ollafson to his feet.

"He believes, Miss Anderson, he believes. He just doesn't know what to do about it. The Point didn't prepare their soldiers to fight this kind of war. We don't belong here."

Claire had to agree. They needed to leave Ararat as soon as possible before Azrael truly awoke and showed them why God was fearful of his own archangel.

24

An hour before the detonations were scheduled to bring down the ice covering the forward section of the prehistoric Ark, Claire had Gray Dog find McDonald. The Comanche took her to where the British intelligence officer was huddled on the far side of the encampment. She thanked Gray Dog for finding him and the young brave looked from her to a cowering McDonald and shook his head.

"His mind runs away; soon it will be gone." With that said Gray Dog turned and walked away.

Claire hesitated before approaching the captain. He was sitting on a ration case looking into the ice at his feet. What caught her eye was the British-made Webley revolver he had clutched in his hand. The hood covered his facial features and the falling snow covered the fur. John Henry had tasked her to keep a close watch on McDonald. The spy hadn't uttered a word since the incident and had vanished from the rest of the company. As she watched he cocked the hammer of the Webley back and then uncocked the pistol. Once, twice, three times.

"Steven, they are about to detonate the ice cap."

The pistol in his gloved hand stopped moving and his head slowly came up.

"You need to leave now," was all he said. McDonald's eyes seemed to be blank as he looked past her as if she weren't there.

"I think you need to talk about what happened."

"What happened? What happened is that my insides are stone cold. When I was touched I saw all of the countless deaths that have happened on these very slopes." His head lowered as did his voice. "I am so cold."

Claire saw that McDonald was close to going insane. The event had affected him so much that he had mentally checked out of the present.

"London will need a full report on what has been uncovered. You need to witness what is about to happen." She saw that he once more started playing with the gun.

"You file the report for me, Madame Claire." He smiled creepily and looked straight at her. "It should be quite a read."

Claire watched McDonald as he lowered his gaze and scary smile and then continued staring at the ice at his feet.

"Where are the artifacts?" he asked, catching her off guard.

"Colonel Thomas is keeping them inside the Ark for the time being, but has plans to get the cursed wood far away from us. He is going to send a marine courier to catch the first civilian transport out of here and get the artifacts back to Washington for safekeeping. Since the satchel has been inside and away from men, there have been no further incidents. Even the weather looks to be clearing somewhat and the mood of the men is far higher than just this morning. I think it's because the artifacts are not near any men."

"Do you think Azrael can be contained by the Ark?" He chuckled and that just about did it for Claire. "He only toys with us for now. Soon the killing will begin. But I will stop him, you'll see."

As Claire backed away she quickly came to the conclusion

that Steven McDonald had slipped into a realm designed by madmen.

The chief petty officer reported to Captain Jackson that the light charges had been placed at the various pressure points of ice covering the find. It should be just enough to crack the roof of the ancient bubble and expose a large section of bow for photography. They just needed the confirmation by the Rebel colonel.

Taylor inspected the charges and declared them good. The navy had done a fine job of making sure they didn't blow off half the mountaintop—pretty good even for Yankees. He conferred with Corporal Jenks, who was an expert at explosives, having blown many a Union train vault to seize gold meant for Union payroll.

"Are the charges adequate in your humble opinion, Corporal?" Jessy asked as he made his way back to the safe zone well above the blast area.

Jenks had not spoken kindly ever since the death of the mess steward. Taylor figured the man was confused as to how he was supposed to feel. Grandee had saved the lives of every southern man inside that cave. What was bothering the corporal, in Taylor's opinion, was the question every man has to ask himself—would I have done the same for him? Jessy figured the corporal felt his answer to that particular question was somewhat lacking in the area of honor and it was affecting him.

"Yes, sir, them navy boys did a fine job. Should be no problems that I can figure." Jenks nodded his hooded head and then started to leave with Taylor to the safety area.

"Jenks, I believe you would have done the same thing as Grandee."

The tired corporal stopped and looked at his colonel.

"How do you figure, sir?" he asked with hope etched in his eyes.

"Because you're one of my boys, and my boys do the right thing. That's why we ended up in a prisoner-of-war camp and old Jeb rode off to glory."

"I don't see it, sir." The mournful words showed Taylor how deflated the corporal was.

"Every man asks himself if he would give his life for his fellows. When the thought strikes me I find myself saying I would, but inside I think I may fold up at the wrong time."

"That's the way of it, sir."

"I was told you tried to go back for Grandee. Is this true?" Jenks lowered his head and said nothing.

"I think I would have to base my opinion on that act, not the failings of a good soldier suffering from survivor's guilt."

"I truly wanted to save him, sir. I guess my failure is that I didn't treat Grandee as a man would treat another. My failure is there, sir. And I think in the end that is why we have already lost this war, Colonel."

Taylor watched as Jenks walked away and then followed as he realized the backwoods corporal was right. The South had no right to win the war and Grandee's death proved it.

"Did you find him?" John Henry asked Claire upon her return.

"Yes. I believe he is a danger to himself. Perhaps you'd better come clean about his identity and arrest him."

"That means exposing you as a triple agent. Your career would effectively be over." John Henry looked down at her and saw that she was possibly not sad at the prospect. Her smile was out of place for the subject matter.

"That was decided when I heard the professor's student was murdered"—she gestured at the spot where the Ark lay beneath—"over this."

"Decided?" Thomas asked as she finally looked away from him.

"Yes, my letter of resignation was delivered in triplicate to the war department, Allan Pinkerton, and the president before we sailed. It's effective upon my return."

John Henry responded in a way that would confuse him forever. "Good."

Claire's brows rose underneath her hood, which she quickly pulled down. She looked at Thomas with a questioning face.

Thomas cleared his throat and then nodded his head and walked away so suddenly she was left staring at the spot where he had been standing.

"Uh, why is that good?" she asked his retreating backside and slightly under her breath, but she knew he hadn't heard her question.

"Fire in the hole!" came the warning from the navy.

Claire shook herself out of her short trance as she thought about John Henry's strange response. She moved to a spot where Sergeant Major Dugan and Gray Dog were hunkered down behind several upturned sleds.

"Do you find that the colonel can be a little odd at certain moments?" she asked as she leaned in close to Gray Dog.

Sergeant Major Dugan gave her a queer look and then stuck his gloved fingers into his ears, as did Gray Dog.

"Missy, I find the colonel odd at all times, now you better—"

The explosion shook the ice they stood upon. The quartered sticks of dynamite detonated and sent a long crack line extending a hundred feet downhill and then shooting back up the mountain, almost a perfect oval in shape. Then the world gave way.

Claire heard a tremendous crash as if every chandelier in Washington fell and broke at once. She cringed when she and the others were inundated with ice and snow as the earth settled back down. Dugan smiled and looked at Claire and Gray Dog.

"Well, let's see if we just blew thirteen thousand years of history to hell, shall we?"

He assisted Claire to her feet and then frowned at Gray Dog, who held his hand up for Dugan to help him up also. The sergeant major shook his head and walked away.

By the time Claire and the others arrived they saw all one hundred-plus members of the expedition standing at the edge of the crater that the dynamite created over the remains of the Ark. Not a word was said as the snow and ice settled around them.

Claire stumbled as she saw the precise way the ice had cracked. It opened up the area directly over the petrified vessel. There was also an opening extending three hundred feet, making the effort of lowering men down into the cave system moot. Now they could walk a little ways downhill and then take a slick ramp right up to the old cave. She finally made it to the edge, where Gray Dog held out an arm and arrested her forward momentum before she went into the void in front of her.

"Thank you. Clumsy of me."

Gray Dog only nodded and then turned to see just what they had uncovered.

The circle of men waited until they could see through the falling ice crystals still floating in the air, giving the scene a surreal look.

John Henry saw it first. The curved bow of the Ark was visible clearly for the first time and it was a shocking sight. Thomas took a deep breath as he realized for the first time what he was really looking at. Myth, legend, and children's tales of wonder were all there before them.

The men were silent as they viewed the thing they had come to see. All thoughts of the war, of the hardship in getting here, even the deaths that had occurred at the hands of an angered God, vanished as they beheld the greatest sight any man in the history of the world could ever have imagined.

Most men, either from the North of the South, marine, sailor, or soldier, could see for the first time what Lincoln's train of thought had been at approving such a risky mission. The Ark was capable of immense power. Perhaps even the power to heal, if the world could see that this was the very beginning for all men regardless of race or birthplace.

"Wow!" was all the articulate Jackson could say.

At that moment the snow stopped and the sun actually showed itself for the first time in days. It spotlighted like the foot lamps of a theater one of God's greatest gifts to man— the Ark.

Only the bow had been exposed to the modern world. Just

two hundred feet of the petrified fossil could be seen as the rest vanished into the now blue-colored glacier. The sunlight made the ancient wood sparkle as if God was highlighting his gift of life to man.

One of the more amazing sights was the fact that everyone could see the beginnings of the raised section of housing on the deck of the Ark. It was even shingled in a rough sort of way. All assumed it was the living quarters for the family of man—Noah and his offspring. The deck from their vantage point looked to be far more sloped than previously thought. Even the wooden pegs used to adhere one plank to the next could be made out in the petrified wood. It was clearly an engineer's dream of ancient wood carving and building. Jackson knew that John Ericsson would have had a stroke upon seeing God's design for a vessel. For once Ericsson was outdone.

"It a shame we're not taking it out of here. If we only had the time."

"How do you figure?" John Henry turned and asked Jessy, who was looking at the destroyed cave.

"At the opening of the excavation there is only a small wall of ice remaining to impede us from removing the bow section from the glacier and just sliding it right out of the grave it's trapped in. The way it looks"—Jessy squinted his eyes against the sudden brightness—"we would have almost a straight run to the base of the mountain. Maybe two or three days to transit back down with our prize."

"Don't let Professor Ollafson hear you say that. It will get him wound up tighter than a five-dollar Ingersoll watch."

Both Jessy and John Henry turned to see a smirking Captain Jackson, who was proud of his simple, witty remark.

"Well, I think the world will have to be healed by the knowledge that it was Americans"—he looked at Taylor directly—"*all* Americans that found this. And it will be heavily documented." He turned away from Jessy after making his point and then faced an astonished Daniel Perlmutter.

"Think you can capture the scope of the discovery now, kid?"

"Oh, yes! Before the darkness would have affected the quality, but now! Boy, oh boy. The sun will be directly overhead in two hours. It will expose the Ark and give the images true depth, and you know you can always use good lighting, why this is—"

Perlmutter failed to notice that he was standing there alone as the others had quickly walked away once he had started harping on his favorite subject—his work.

An hour later the men had begun clearing off the one-hundred-and-fifty-foot exposed section of the Ark. The mood was far better now that they had something meaningful to do. Even Corporal Jenks was far more festive than he'd been before the detonations. Perlmutter had decided to photograph the Ark and the men that had found her first. He would position the shot from the edge of the void down onto the deck with the Ark's new crew standing onboard. He could see the many awards he would receive for the documentation of the greatest archeological find in history.

Many of the men still working above on the ice shelf saw Gray Dog running toward them. He found John Henry and pointed down the mountain.

"Signal from Parnell," he said.

This got the attention of Claire, Jessy, and Jackson. Dugan was late reporting the same thing and gave Gray Dog a dirty look for beating him to the punch.

John Henry quickly raised his field glasses. Three rockets were just starting to fall after they had reached their highest arc. Parnell was signaling imminent danger from the plain below. As he watched another three shot up into the clear blue sky.

"Answer Lieutenant Parnell, Sergeant Major," Thomas said as he scanned the expansive lands beneath Ararat.

Dugan ran to get the naval ordnance crew to signal with rocket fire that Parnell's message had been received. All knew that if the night sky was as clear as the daylight hours they would be able to signal Parnell with the large Morse lamps they had hauled to the summit with them. Then they would learn the particulars of the danger signal.

"What do you think it is?" Jessy asked as he removed the field glasses from John Henry's grip and scanned the world below for himself.

"My guess would be that we will have company soon. Either up here or down there in ambush." He smiled at Taylor.

"And your thinking is never wrong?" Jessy asked as he slowly lowered the glasses but still stared at the lands beneath Ararat.

John Henry knew the point Jessy was making and he decided that it was time for truth.

"Only once." He faced Jessy. "Only one time, and that killed me inside."

Taylor slowly looked at his brother-in-law. He only nodded.

John Henry saw the understanding and then started to walk away. He stopped though when he saw Claire in the distance talking with Jackson. She glanced his way and there was just a hint of a smile. Thomas nodded his head and then a smile slowly broke out. For once it didn't feel manufactured in any way. Jessy saw this but raised the binoculars back to his eyes.

"Let's try and not make another mistake, because you may have just as much riding on this if you're wrong.' He lowered the glasses and then smirked at John Henry.

"I may have at that." Taylor saw that the colonel's eyes never left the face of Claire.

John Henry was inside the Ark where headquarters had been established now that there was bright sunlight available and shelter was now abundant—a little old and musty, but still better than spending the night wondering if your tent was going to blow away. He decided that he would catch up on his journal entries that he had let slide since they started to traverse the mountain. He was using the lamp to see with. He was having a hard time concentrating because the decision he had just made was weighing heavily on his mind.

Thus far Jackson had some men start removing the ice that

was blocking access into the house-like structure atop the Ark. So far they had uncovered nothing much other than unrecognizable objects from a time long past. A few petrified animal remains that could be as old as the mausoleum that sheltered their corpses. One area that made every man who saw it take pause was what looked as if it were the familial quarters of the Ark's passengers. It had been a revived Ollafson who had recognized the bedding pallets that may have been used by Noah and his kin. There were frozen hides of some long-dead animals that looked as if they were some ancient form of mattress. Oil lamp bowls that had been dead for thirteen thousand years. Lamps that may have illuminated a frightened family as they were tossed about in a flood-induced terror. There was a large cooking pit that had an exhaust that ran high and vanished through the battered and torn roof of the living quarters.

John Henry had been furiously working since late last night when they received the Morse signal from Lieutenant Parnell and his command on the Plain of Ararat. The situation, he had learned, was fast becoming untenable and now he had to send instructions to the marine telling him what to do.

Since yesterday the most disturbing thing discovered since they opened up the cave's ceiling was the Angelic symbols found along the main bulkhead of the familial quarters. There were six lines of characters and five characters per line. Claire and Ollafson were doing their best trying to interpret the symbols. John Henry could hear their muted mumbling in the room next to the starboard animal pens of the Ark. The voices gave John Henry pause as they talked. It was as if he were hearing ghostly voices from a long ago past. Eerie, some would call it.

Thomas stopped writing and flexed his hand. His eyes roamed to the oilcloth satchel. Claire had wanted to take it into the room with her and Ollafson to compare to the newly discovered symbols, but John Henry had refused. The satchel with its contents would not be handled any longer by anyone on the expedition. That was what his conundrum was. He had to kill two birds with one stone, and one of those birds he had grown rather fond of over the weeks.

"Here it is," said a voice from the ragged opening. Jessy was there and he was silhouetted in bright sunshine before stepping into the darkened interior. Taylor held up a large cloth-covered package he had retrieved from John Henry's tent. "What is this?" he asked as he placed the parcel on the table next to the satchel. Taylor pulled up a camp chair and sat. He removed his hood and then reached into his tunic for a cigar and lit it with the aid of the oil lamp. He sat back down as John Henry finished his journal entry.

"What's in here?" he asked again as he toyed with the twine that held the bundle together.

"You should know. You found it many years ago."

Taylor raised both brows as he looked from John Henry to the filthy white cloth bundle he held. John Henry slowly slid the bundle away and then waited.

"Sir!" Dugan said from the opening. "Private Willard and Gray Dog. Took some doin' to get the Indian to report, but here he is."

"Show them both in," Thomas said.

The first in was one of Jessy's men. A nineteen-year-old private from Alexandria. A boy bred in a fine family and well educated for the time. John Henry had noted that the kid spent a full two years at the Virginia Military Institute. The real draw to the boy was Taylor's statement that he was also the best damn rider he had ever seen. Willard spoke to horses and they did his every bidding. It seemed his father was a fine horse breeder and Private Willard, or Sam, as Jessy called the boy, was most knowledgeable about the equine species. The private stepped in and lowered the hood to his parka. The boy looked frightened as he removed a woolen cap also and twisted it in his hands. Gray Dog squeezed past Dugan, giving him a strange look as he did.

"Is that how you report, Sam?" Jessy said as he leaned back in his chair and puffed on his cigar.

"Uh, no, Colonel." The boy stood ramrod straight and then snapped a salute, first toward Taylor, and then thinking better of it directed the respect toward John Henry, who immediately returned the salute. Gray Dog watched this as he stood next to the boy and he was non-plussed at the respect shown to the two officers. Gray Dog just stood there looking at Private Willard, who was keenly aware the Indian had his eyes on him and was feeling a bit nervous about it.

"At ease, Private," John Henry said.

Willard did not place himself at ease at all. He continued to twist his stocking cap in his hands.

"The colonel informs me you're one hell of a horseman," John Henry stated.

"Yes, sir, some say that's a fact."

"You have also had some international travel before the war started, is that correct?"

"Yes, sir, my pa and me had to travel to Europe for horse flesh, Colonel, sir. For breeding purposes."

John Henry saw that the boy was barely able to shave. The chin whiskers on his fresh face were sparse and his cheeks as red as a schoolchild. But John Henry knew he had no choice. Besides, it would take the youngest person on this mission out of here. That was the least he could do. He only wished he could send Claire out with him.

"Good," Thomas said as he exchanged looks with Jessy, who was silently smoking his cigar and watching. John Henry then held up a letter. The boy's eyes widened when he saw it was addressed to the president of the United States and was sealed closed. John Henry reached out and took a hold of the satchel's handle and then opened it. He felt the air in the room grow far colder than it had been a moment before. He quickly placed the white envelope inside and then hurriedly closed the satchel. Jessy and Dugan saw how fast John Henry had done this. It was if the colonel were afraid if he left the satchel open for too long Azrael would escape like a crazed genie in a bottle. "You are going home, Master Willard." John Henry slid the satchel toward the boy.

"Sir?" Willard said, confused. His look went from the Yankee colonel to a stunned Jessy, who said nothing, but he did remove the cigar from his mouth and then looked at Thomas waiting for the explanation.

"You are ordered to immediately descend the mountain with Gray Dog, my scout, and then once at the base return to camp there and select five good horses. I hear you can do that, at least, from what your colonel has informed me?"

"Yes, sir, I know horse flesh well enough."

"You are to take this satchel and guard it with your life. You are to return to the coast near Constantinople and board the first transport out of this country. Get back to Washington as fast as you can travel. Ride hard, ride fast." John Henry slid a large leather sack toward the private. "Travel in civilian attire and speak to no one until you're home again. You are to deliver this to the White House. That letter inside the satchel will get you access to the president personally. Deliver this into his hand with the letter. Is this clear?"

"Not at all, sir."

"Excuse me?" Thomas said as he shot Jessy a look.

"I don't wish to go, sir."

"And we don't want to lose such a good trouper, but you go on and do what Colonel Thomas says. He chose you special."

The boy straightened and then nodded his head. "Make my way home the best and fastest way possible, yes, sir, Colonel," he said sadly.

John Henry nodded his head at Jessy for assisting in convincing the young Rebel. Thomas could see why Taylor was so close to his men. He knew them and they were loyal to a fault.

John Henry retrieved a smaller leather bag and tossed it to Willard. "There are six thousand dollars' worth of gold double-eagles inside. That should be enough to get whatever transport you see fit to travel on."

"Choose the best, Sammy boy, this one's on old Honest Abe. Perhaps board the liner *The City of Paris*, go first class."

Willard smiled for the first time. "Yes, sir."

John Henry stood from his chair and approached the boy.

He held his hand out to Sergeant Major Dugan, who placed something there.

"It took the sergeant major here all day to dig these up. I think you should have them." He handed Willard the items. They were a set of gold corporal's stripes. The boy looked up at the Yankee officer. "We couldn't very well send a mere private to meet with the president of the United States, now could we?"

"No, sir," Willard exclaimed with excitement as he looked at the two stripes of a corporal that sat in his gloved hand. He looked over at Jessy to confirm that he had actually been promoted. Taylor smiled and nodded his head.

"You go on now, Sammy boy, do the regiment proud, and be sure to insult the Yankee president as much as you can while you are his guest."

"Sir?"

"Good luck, Willard," John Henry said as he saluted the boy who immediately returned it. With one last salute to Taylor, John Henry's messenger boy left.

"I guess lives can be sold for the cost of two cloth stripes, huh?" Jessy said as he tossed the cigar aside and looked at Thomas, who said nothing.

"Gray Dog, it's time for you to go also."

The Comanche said nothing. He looked at Dugan, who spit a stream of tobacco juice that landed outside of the opening.

John Henry held out the second letter to the scout. "Get this to Lieutenant Parnell. Ride fast and get it to him before tomorrow morning. He's expecting company and I hope these orders will help him. If not we'll have a nice little surprise waiting for us when we leave this mountain."

Gray Dog slowly reached out and took the letter. He raised it to his face and then sniffed the envelope.

"You'll stay with Lieutenant Parnell, understand?"

Gray Dog looked up and then shook his head in the negative.

Thomas knew he wasn't saying he did not understand.

Gray Dog was flat-out telling John Henry he wasn't leaving him.

"This is important, and you must go or many a boy may very well die down there."

Gray Dog turned and looked at Dugan. The sergeant major was about to say something and then stopped. He thought about it and then faced the boy he found he had come not only to admire, but actually like, and for Dugan to say he liked another human being was astounding.

"You go on, boyo, do like the colonel says. We will try and get along without you."

Gray Dog lowered his head and started to turn.

"You may as well take this with you. I was waiting to give it to you on our return." Thomas actually looked embarrassed. "I figured you would be of age by then." John Henry swallowed as he looked at his adopted son. "But it seems time has run out on me." He slid the cloth-covered package toward Gray Dog.

The Comanche touched the package but made no move to pick it up. He only looked from it to the colonel.

"Colonel Taylor, well, back then he was Lieutenant Taylor, found this in your village the day . . . the day your family was killed. He took it and delivered it to me because he knew I was close to your father, No Water. Its time you have it. It may come in handy when you meet with Lieutenant Parnell and if things get bad."

Gray Dog finally reached for the parcel and slowly undid the twine. He let the cloth fall to the petrified decking as he saw what Taylor and John Henry had delivered into his hands. It was his father's headdress, a war bonnet with more than seventy-five eagle feathers arranged along the train. From headband to tail feather the war bonnet was more than six feet long. Gray Dog's father had been one of the legendary Comanche warriors of that time. Gray Dog held it up and let the feathers unroll to their full length. He smiled like John Henry had never seen before. The Comanche turned and showed Dugan.

"Now ain't that somethin?" the sergeant major said as he started to spit again, but instead held it in check. "Your pa would be real proud right about now."

Taylor saw the grudging respect the sergeant major was showing the young brave.

John Henry reached out and took Gray Dog's hand. He wanted to hug him but knew that would only embarrass him. He shook the hand and then turned away.

"Good luck, son," was all he said.

Gray Dog looked confused and then made up his mind that he would do as he was told. He straightened and with the war bonnet in hand stepped up to Taylor, who had saved this magnificent gift for him, and held out his hand, and Jessy took it and stood at the same time. The handshake was exaggerated with wide up-and-down shakes. Taylor smiled and nodded.

"Godspeed, Gray Dog."

The Comanche turned away and left.

John Henry looked up and his thoughts turned sad as he expected not to see the boy again. He faced Taylor.

"Yes, Jessy, you're right. Some things can be bought pretty cheaply."

25

It had taken Captain Jackson's reorganized work crews thirteen hours to clear the lowest level of the raised living quarters of the Ark. It was a small percentage because the rest of the five-story structure was in thick and unyielding ice. Jackson and his ordnance men claimed if they had the time and the right equipment, such as phosphorous charges, they could clear most of the communal living area that saw its last use more than thirteen thousand years before.

Thus far Ollafson, who had recovered from his initial shock at not being able to remove much in the way of artifacts, was as excited as a schoolboy as he moved the oil lamp from one location to the other. Raised areas for bedding, the petrified remains of fire pits, and huge lumps of frozen and prehistoric vegetation. All of this could have kept botanists busy for a hundred years identifying strange and extinct plant life. In one corner of a small alcove on the highest mark of the living quarters, in a place where a child would retreat to play alone, Claire came across what looked like a child's rag doll embedded in the ice. It had taken her with the assistance of Sergeant Major Dugan over five hours to remove it.

The doll was now sitting upon a table on a piece of sail-cloth for examination and return to American soil. When holding the sodden mess in her hands it was far more un-recognizable than it had been when it was embedded in the ice. The ancient materials were not reacting to the air all that well and the huge discovery was quickly turning into a pile of mush. Claire cursed herself for not having sample jars available.

The sun had set more than six hours before, and everyone in camp felt the loss of light and a gloom settled over every-one, especially since the thrill from this afternoon had worn off. As for Steven McDonald, Claire had been shocked to see the British captain standing in line for chow at dusk. She had stepped up to him and he had actually smiled and greeted her as if nothing strange had happened that afternoon. She had informed John Henry of the spy master's reversal of attitude and she could see in Thomas's eyes that his concern was great, maybe even as great, to order the elimination, or ex-pulsion, of the British intelligence officer. Claire didn't know if John Henry had it in him to order Steven eliminated, but the strain and guilt of sending Gray Dog off to an un-known fate was weighing heavily on the colonel's mind.

"You know, for a master spy you seem to be taking this academia thing to the extreme," said a voice behind her, which startled her so much it made her drop the large brush she had been using to search the walls of the Ark for any more Angelic Script. Personally she hoped she would never see any of the symbols ever again.

"If there is one place on this planet you do not sneak up on somebody, this is it, Colonel," she said with her hand try-ing to still her heavily beating heart through the thick coat.

Dugan snickered and spit his tobacco and then decided to get out of there and get some coffee. John Henry watched him go and then faced Claire again.

"Tomorrow I am going to have our British friend escorted from the mountain and delivered back to his people." He paused and then looked into her eyes. "Unharmed."

Thomas could see the relief in her eyes.

"Thank you. Call it professional courtesy, or a favor to me. He doesn't need to be killed, at least not as much as our French friend Renaud."

Thomas lowered the hood of his coat, intentionally not answering her relief with a comment. After all, he did not want her to think he had grown too barbaric over the years. But if the career military man had his druthers he would hang any person caught spying for any nation, including his own; he despised them that much. It bothered him that Claire was a spy, and he knew he would have to come to terms with that.

"As to your question, I feel I have a certain obligation to Professor Ollafson," she said with a nod toward the busy professor in the far corner where he was examining the remains of the large, communal fire pit in the center of the large room. "He needs me more than the nation does at the moment and I figure I can spare him at least that little bit of dignity."

John Henry paced to the gallery and then looked down upon the areas the naval engineers had cleared of ice. It was expansive and he imagined most articles that made up the Ark's interior had been stripped by the survivors for use in home building and for heat. He could imagine just a portion of the Ark would have provided wood for enough housing for several large families, and as he looked around at the many giant holes in the structure he could see that was exactly what had happened.

"You have to hand it to the old bastard, though, he surely did what he told the president he could do. I never would have believed it." Thomas's eyes scanned the area beneath that used to be alive with every animal the family of Noah could save. It must have been a horrid and fearful voyage for the family of man.

"You know, Colonel—"

"John Henry. It's about time we drop the formalities, especially since we may end up here for eternity."

Claire smiled like she had been complimented by the school's most eligible boy.

"Finally, some common sense has been displayed by our fearless leader. John Henry, then. You need to remember something. There are many historians, even those adamantly refusing to believe the tales of the Bible as based on reality, that are coming around to believe that the Bible, though flawed, is the greatest historical text in history. There are men"—she smiled at Thomas—"and women who are making new discoveries every day in the field of archaeology that are being taken as serious revisions to the atheist point of view. In other words, John Henry, it is becoming very evident that every story in the Bible, no matter how outlandish or strange, has a basis in fact. Each tale has an origin, no matter how much that tale has changed as it was handed down, generation by generation."

Thomas turned from his high vantage point. "You have placed some deep thought into this, haven't you?" he asked as she reached down to pick up her brush.

"I guess the professor has rubbed off on me a bit."

"More than a bit, I would say."

"Oh, my dear. Allow me to assist in transcribing these symbols."

John Henry saw Ollafson in the doorway watching them.

"Well, on that cheerful note, I'll be turning in."

"I have to get these symbols interpreted."

Ollafson returned to the bent and broken doorway and made to get his materials.

"Not without at least two soldiers in here with you at all times," Thomas said, capturing Claire with his eyes as he raised his fur-lined hood.

"I'm not going to argue with that. I wish Gray Dog were here. That boy has a sixth sense when it comes to seeing our angelic host." She saw the sadness in John Henry's eyes at the mention of Gray Dog and Claire wished she had not brought it up.

Thomas took a last look around the room and tried his best to keep his face straight as he thought about the boy and his descent down Ararat with the young Rebel soldier, Private Willard.

"I wish he were here also," he said and then looked closely at Claire. "Good night, Miss Claire."

"Good night, John Henry."

She watched the large man leave and wondered if the colonel would ever be capable of letting go of the vivid memories of his wife. Claire didn't know if it was deep-seated love, or the fact that he blamed himself for her loss. Perhaps both emotions ruled what the colonel did in life. She sighed and then smiled as the professor came back in full with his former enthusiasm.

"Shall we get started, my dear?"

Claire finally tore her eyes away from the spot John Henry had occupied only a moment before and felt that the night was now lacking in some uncertain manner. It was if the man left a vacuum behind him. She shook her head in total confusion about the subject of John Henry Thomas.

"Yes, let's see what Noah had to say to God. It could be interesting."

It took Clair and Ollafson more than two hours of hard searching even to find the starting point of the Angelic text that stretched from deck to ceiling in symbols. Thus far they had deciphered only five percent of the symbols on the hull. Claire could easily see that their earlier assumption about Noah hating the archangel Azrael was spelled out right in front of her and Ollafson. The curse was not on the site, but on the angel of death himself.

McDonald was there before Claire and Ollafson heard a sound. How long had he been in the dark listening? She didn't know and was afraid to inquire.

"I see you are feeling better. It must have been the excellent meal that Captain Jackson ordered for the men. I'm glad that you finally ate."

McDonald just smiled at Claire as he entered the room fully and as he did he lowered the hood of his coat and then removed his gloves. He lovingly ran his hand along the carved script that looked as if it had been etched in pure, black stone. His eyes ran along the prayer walls and the smile remained. Claire exchanged worried looks with Ollafson, who also watched McDonald very closely.

"Yes, who could pass up the chance of hot beans and fat-back?" He turned and with that creepy smile still on his face took in both of the people in the darkened room.

Claire didn't know where to go from there. McDonald's eyes were flicking between herself and Ollafson. She cursed under her breath for not having her pistol with her. She wondered where the two soldiers were that John Henry had stationed outside. Her eyes went in that direction.

"Looking for your Rebel guardian angels?" Steven asked as he continued to smile.

Claire didn't respond, but she did notice the blood on the sleeve of McDonald's coat. Her eyes went briefly to the gloves he held in his hands and she saw they were soaked in red. He moved them to his coat pocket when he saw her eyes.

Claire waited until Steven sat down and then she slowly removed the ten-inch hairpin from her coiled-up red hair. The long tresses fell around her shoulders and she prayed that McDonald wouldn't notice. She briefly raised the long pin to show Ollafson. He showed her what he had. She rolled her eyes when all he showed was his tobacco pipe. He looked deflated as he sat down. No use in making a break for the door. Steven was younger and far faster, and if he could murder two soldiers, what chance did they have?

"As you can see, I've been out of sorts somewhat since I was touched by your angel of death." Steven made as if he were reaching for something under the table.

"I can see that," Claire said, realizing that she was facing something other than a British spy, or a human being for that matter.

Claire's heart froze when she saw the Webley pistol rise from underneath the table. She reacted by slamming the hairpin deeply into Steven's right shoulder, making the gun fall from his hand as he screamed in pain. She and Ollafson were moving in a split second. For a man approaching his seventies, Ollafson's speed was surprising as he shot out of the room after Claire, actually pushing her before him.

"Run, children, run!" McDonald cried out as he yanked

the pin from his shoulder and smiled at the simple weapon the woman had used against him. He quickly retrieved the Webley and started after them.

Claire stumbled over the bodies of the two young soldiers McDonald had murdered. She held her hand over her mouth to keep from screaming as she ran up the sloped deck. The snow was falling harder and the ice was returning to sheet the slippery slope. She fell and Ollafson was there trying to help her up in the bulky cold-weather clothing.

A shot rang out and Ollafson grabbed his left shoulder as he released Claire's hand and allowed her to fall to the ice-covered deck once again. Another shot rang out and she saw the sparks as the bullet ricocheted away harmlessly. Then she saw Steven as he approached. The gun was still smoking as he walked up to a wounded Ollafson.

"I neglected to thank you for bringing these men to my Ark, Professor." McDonald was no longer there. It was if she were facing Azrael himself.

"No!" Claire shouted as McDonald brought the English-made weapon up and pointed it at Ollafson, who bravely stared down its barrel.

Suddenly McDonald reeled away as a bullet struck the same shoulder the hatpin had damaged. He fell and the gun went flying out of his hand.

Claire reacted as her training dictated. She stood and even on the slippery ice managed to get Ollafson moving. She practically threw him off the Ark's upper deck onto the rope ladder. She was about to climb on when she saw the image of John Henry, Jessy Taylor, and Sergeant Major Dugan, still with a smoking Henry rifle clutched in his hands, climbing over the opposite gunwale. She pointed behind her at the spot Steven had been. He had vanished.

John Henry quickly holstered his pistol and ran to assist Claire and the professor. Jessy and Dugan continued on into the vast interior of the Ark to track down McDonald.

"I knew I should have hung that bastard!" he said as he helped get the wounded Ollafson to his feet. Then he held out a hand for Claire. John Henry only had on uniform pants and a long-sleeved white underwear top. The suspenders were flapping at his sides.

"I agree," Claire said. "That son of a bitch has completely gone over the cliff of sanity."

"He thinks he's the angel of death!" Ollafson yelled.

"Well, he will think something else when Jessy catches him," John Henry said as he started to help Ollafson down the rope ladder.

"What orders does the colonel have?" Claire asked as she swung one impressively shaped leg over the gunwale. John Henry took notice.

"Two of my men dead; McDonald is to be . . . eliminated."

"About damned time you made that call, Colonel."

"But you said—"

Claire was already over the side.

John Henry shook his head at the exasperating woman and then made for the rope ladder. Before going over the side he stopped and looked back down the sloping deck. He needed to know about Taylor and Dugan.

Since the engineers had cleared a great deal of the ice from the confusing passageways of the interior, Jessy quickly decided that an armed and crazed McDonald could be hiding anywhere. He could see by Dugan's overly cautious way that they were bound to make a mistake they wouldn't walk away from. The darkness was more complete the lower they went and Jessy hadn't thought to bring one of the lamps strewn about the deck of the Ark.

"This is no good, Colonel. That bastard could be hidin' in any of a thousand places."

"There's nowhere for him to run," Taylor said as he nodded for Dugan to back out of the tight space they found themselves in. Just as the sergeant major took his first backward step, he was knocked from his feet. Before he hit the petrified deck he felt a tremendous pressure descend onto his chest. It felt as though a large foot was pinning him down. He struggled for breath and flailed with the Henry rifle at the unseen force.

Jessy could barely make out Dugan as he had been flung backward into the hull and then onto the floor. He saw the flash of brass as the Henry rifle was flung in all directions as Dugan flailed on the deck. Jessy immediately broke the spell he was under and ran toward the struggling sergeant major. Just before reaching him he was stopped dead in his tracks by something that wrapped around his throat. The pressure was great as his body was lifted free of the deck. His boots were kicking out at whatever had him by the throat. It was if some entity were holding down Dugan with a foot and Taylor by the throat with its free hand. They heard the growl as something in the dark seemed to be satisfied. Jessy felt the invisible force shake him like a wayward child. He felt the navy Colt slide from his hand as he felt his larynx start to give way. He brought both hands up and tried to pull the hands off, but when he did his heart froze as he felt the scaly skin of the thing that held him.

"Jesus," Jessy managed to say as his breath was fast being depleted by the horrendous pressure being exerted.

Dugan was having no better success with his situation. As he beat at the foot holding him down, he had the distinct impression that it was not a foot, but a cloven hoof. His eyes widened as he imagined just what it was that was holding him down. He beat harder, bringing the butt plate of the Henry down again and again.

Taylor's eyes started to roll into the back of his head as he was quickly losing his battle with consciousness. His gloved hands beat on what felt like large claws that strangled him with what seemed very little effort.

Dugan felt the first of his ribs snap and he expelled what little breath he had in his lungs. The darkness was growing more complete.

The growl of pleasure that sounded in the closed room was the one of a being that had never seen the graces of heaven.

Both men knew that this was the angel of death.

Just as John Henry entered the new areas that had been cleared he heard the struggle coming from somewhere ahead.

The blackness was complete as he moved forward. He saw a brief hint of movement ahead and instinctually knew it wasn't Jessy or Dugan. The shot from the Colt came without thought. He heard a yelp of pain as the man ran farther into the darkness. More movement. Thomas fired again.

Suddenly and without warning the roar of a wounded animal sounded inside the darkened room. Jessy felt the pressure increase, but it was only momentary as the claws dug in, and then they were gone. He fell to the rough deck grasping his throat.

Dugan also felt the pressure fall away to nothing as whatever was holding him seemed to lose strength and then fade to nothing. The sergeant major rolled over in pain as the broken rib pushed against his lungs as they refilled with air. Then strong hands were helping him up and with a scream he settled onto his feet.

"You hurt?" asked John Henry.

Dugan couldn't make out his face but nodded that he was all right.

Thomas helped Jessy up and saw that he was having a hard time drawing breath. Once he knew he would be all right, John Henry exited and then came back a moment later with a lantern. He held it up just outside the entrance to the new excavation. He leaned down and felt the deck with his gloved hand. When it came back into the light it was wet with blood. John Henry knew that he had hit his target at least once, but more than likely both shots had found their mark. The amount of blood spread on the deck told him that McDonald was mortally hit from his two shots and Dugan's one. Thomas knew this wasn't over. Something was happening that was well out of his expertise to battle.

It was time to leave the mountain.

THE PLAIN OF ARARAT, THE OTTOMAN EMPIRE

Lieutenant Parnell lay in his bunk and counted the minutes. He knew sleep wouldn't come anymore that night. He had been awakened by the cry of an animal in his dreams. He didn't even know what the dream was about but it had scared him to wakefulness.

The lieutenant sat up and started to dress. He knew it was just before dawn and he also knew that with the camp at fifty percent alert status, he had no right to be sleeping while his inexperienced command watched and waited for the Turks to arrive. Until he received instructions from Colonel Thomas he was on his own, and for the first time in his marine career he didn't know what to expect or what he was to do. He buttoned his thick coat and stepped out into the falling snow. He shook his head as he raised his hood against the falling temperature.

He saw that the eager band members of the 315th were on guard along with a marine watch commander guiding them and making sure they didn't shoot at snowflakes. Farnell had never seen troops so anxious to fight, but not one had any idea how to do it.

"Lieutenant?" said the camp's mess cook who handed him a tin cup of coffee.

"Been quiet?" he asked the navy cook as he gratefully sipped the rich brew.

"I never seen so many nervous boys with guns before in my life, Lieutenant. Every time a rabbit runs from his hole you can hear them musician boys about crap themselves. Yes, sir, mighty tense out there."

Parnell knew just how the men were feeling. Ever since his rider arrived with news that the Turks were heading their way, the men had been at the very least antsy, and at the worst comically afraid.

"Well, these boys are new to being scared. The worst thing they have ever had to deal with was missing music or a wayward instrument. Facing Turkish cavalry is something they hadn't really signed on for."

"Yes, sir, but by the looks they're eager."

Parnell chuckled. "That they are."

"Riders approaching from the east!" came the shout from the outer pickets.

Parnell tossed the coffee from the cup and threw it to the mess cook as he ran to the perimeter.

"Hold your fire!" he called.

"Two men, riding hard, Lieutenant!"

"Stand down, all pickets, stand down!" came the order as Parnell paced and waited.

The two men rode in hard. It had taken Gray Dog and Private Willard thirty-one hours to reach the base of Ararat and another ten to get here, going through six sets of horses to do so.

Gray Dog rode in first just as the dreary sun made its crest of Ararat. Willard was right behind. Both dismounted as if the ride in had been a contest.

"Whoooee, but that boy can ride now!" Willard said, slapping Gray Dog on his back. His eyes widened as he realized he had just hit the savage Indian.

Parnell approached quickly.

"Dispatches?" he hurriedly asked.

Willard stepped away from Gray Dog, who was confused by Willard's slap on the back. Instead of taking offense, when the private turned, Gray Dog slapped him on the back, which almost sent the Rebel flying into Parnell. Willard turned and Gray Dog nodded.

"Report," Parnell said, eyeing Gray Dog before focusing on Willard.

"Lieutenant, sir," the Confederate said as he saluted in the dim dawn light. Parnell could see both he and the Comanche were about rode out. Their thick coats were mud-covered and their horses were spent. "Private Willard, cavalry corps, Army of Northern Virginia, reporting."

Parnell returned the salute from the enthusiastic private.

Willard reached into his coat and brought out the first of the sealed orders. Parnell asked for a lantern as he tore the wax away and read. His brow furrowed as he did.

"Well, it seems you have one hell of a journey ahead of you, trooper," he said as he replaced the note and moved it to his own coat pocket.

"Yes, sir. I would rather stay with the colonel, both colonels, but they said I had to deliver these to Washington," he said as he moved to his saddle and untied the leather satchel.

Parnell started to reach for it and Willard turned away. "No, sir. Colonel Thomas said the only other person to touch this bag is President Lincoln, sir. I have a sealed message also."

Parnell nodded his head. "Very well, trooper, you have your orders. Now, go get issued new cold-weather gear and two civilian changes of clothing. No uniform; the colonel's orders say you are to leave it. We don't need you getting shot when you enter Washington, I guess," Parnell said in mock disappointment. "Now, go get some breakfast. Eat well."

"Yes, sir," he said as he nervously looked at the Comanche. "Sir, Gray Dog has your orders from Colonel Thomas." Willard saluted and then started to walk toward the wonderful smell of cooking food.

"Trooper?" Parnell said.

Willard stopped and turned. "Sir?"

"Was it there, really?"

Willard actually walked back to face the lieutenant.

"A sight to behold, sir. A real sight, just like the Bible said. Yes, sir, it was there."

"Imagine," Parnell said.

"No, sir, we don't have to do that no more. It's been proven as fact, Lieutenant, sir." Willard saluted once more and then left.

Parnell watched him go, wishing he'd had the opportunity to see the Ark, but he knew his duty was here. He held out his hand toward Gray Dog, who approached and placed the sealed orders into his hand and then immediately turned to get some food. After the hardtack and dried bacon eaten in the saddle for the past forty-plus hours, he was ready for some navy coffee and biscuits. He undid his pack from his exhausted mount, patted the horse several times and spoke softly to it, and then joined Private Willard.

Parnell broke the red wax seal and read. Again his brows rose as he looked up from the orders. His eyes saw the sleepy-eyed band members as they rose from sleep and stumbled from tents. They joked about having to rough it and the scary sounds they heard at night. Parnell reread the last section of the orders and then looked at the bandmates, all younger than the average soldier. They laughed and joked on their way to the chow line. Parnell closed his eyes before reading the last of his orders.

When done he placed the orders into his pocket with the first. He might need them for his court-martial at a later date, if he survived that is, which he now had serious doubts about.

"Sergeant Killeen," he called out, startling many of the army band men as they strolled past.

"Sir!"

"Make ready to break camp. Leave the railroad equipment. That farce is now dead. We move east and set up in this draw here." Parnell had pulled out his map and pointed at the spot into which John Henry had ordered his one hundred and fifty-six men.

"Yes, sir."

"Sergeant Killeen?"

"Sir?" the old marine said he turned back.

"The 316th is to bring their instruments, and also issue them Henry repeaters. Every man. Unload the horses." He slowly shook his head at the purely government way this was being handled.

"Excuse me, Lieutenant, but has some brass-hatted bastard lost his ever-lovin' mind? Uh, sir?"

"It seems the nation is a little short of qualified cavalrymen and we surely do not have enough marines, so I guess it's time these men stop playing war, and join one. We have orders to set up in between the mountain and the station in a cut that will hide our . . . force," he said with tongue in cheek. "I guess we'll see now why Washington has such faith in Colonel Thomas. We move out in three hours, Sergeant."

"Three hours, yes, sir."

Marine Lieutenant Parnell turned toward the snow-covered summit of Ararat and frowned.

At that moment lightning struck somewhere on the plain between the camp and Ararat, and for a reason he couldn't fathom, Parnell was chilled at the sight.

A sudden cheer went up from the center of the camp and Parnell saw the Rebel cavalryman, Willard, obviously bypassing breakfast as he shot from camp on a fresh mount. He had four other relief horses strung together behind. The entire camp again erupted in cheers as every man watched as he gave the Rebel yell leaving camp, twirling his hat in the air. It was a stirring sight and even the old-time marines were chilled as Willard broke for the west and his journey home.

"Good luck," Parnell said as if in prayer for the young Confederate.

MOUNT ARARAT, THE OTTOMAN EMPIRE

The snow began falling harder and the winds remained steady, just enough to shake the tent sides and flaps as Claire made sure the professor was all right. The old man seemed as if his narrow escape from death had started his heart rather than stopped it. He paced the tent with his coat unbuttoned and excitedly explained what Claire had missed.

"The diagrams of the artifacts, do you still have them?"

Claire rummaged through her own bag until she produced the reproductions of the symbols. She handed them to Ollafson just as the tent flap opened and in came John Henry with two very frightened men, Dugan and Taylor. Both men immediately went to the far corner of the tent and John Henry tossed over a small bottle of whiskey. They shared the bottle until their hearts started beating at a normal rate. It was Jessy who began.

"All right, tell me what's happening here. That was not God or heaven sent. If it was, we're worshipping on the wrong side of the church aisle." He took another drink and then passed it to Dugan. "Sergeant Major, I know you're hurting, but get out there and organize a proper search party and bring that son of a bitch back here. He's wounded and far more insane than we ever figured. Kill him if you have to, but get that man under submission."

"Sir," Dugan said as he held a gloved hand to his ribs. He took one last drink of the warming liquid and then excused himself.

"Now, Jessy's right, that thing was not sent by God. You could feel it."

Ollafson was looking at the symbols Claire had recorded on the sheets of paper. He found the one he was looking for.

"Azrael, Colonel, is not of heaven. I remind you that the archangel was an ally of Lucifer. A powerful ally, enough so that even the archangels Gabriel, Michael, Simon, and the others were afraid of him. For God, Azrael was the perfect, unconscious killing machine. He was despised by all, even his own God. I guess that would make for a touch of insanity, even for an archangel."

"Do you believe all of this?" Taylor asked, looking from Claire to John Henry, who listened silently.

"I don't know what to believe. But one thing is for sure, something is trying to kill us, and by the looks of our friend McDonald, it's getting more powerful. I was hoping that getting the artifacts away from here would help, but it seems I may have exacerbated the situation by keeping this prayer incomplete. It doesn't matter at this point. We leave the mountain today and place as much distance between us and the Ark as we can."

"Agreed," Claire said, looking at Ollafson. "It is time to go."

"Yes, I think I've had all of the Ark history I can take for the time being." Ollafson looked like he'd had a revelation, such as, he didn't want to meet Azrael face-to-face at all. He looked at Taylor and rubbed his bruised neck.

"Colonel, we have a problem," came a voice from outside of the tent.

"Come," he said as he rebuttoned his coat. "Jessy, tell our camera boy, Perlmutter, he has three hours to get his pictorial documentation done. We move out in three."

Jessy nodded just as Dugan came in.

"Colonel," Dugan said, trying to keep his hard breathing under control because of the pain of his broken rib. "The navy ordnance boys, well, they say they're missing a case of dynamite."

"What?"

"Yes, sir, missing."

That was all that needed to be said as John Henry and Taylor burst from the tent.

"Get every available man into the Ark. Find that madman before he blows half of this mountaintop off!"

John Henry and Taylor ran to the edge of the camp and looked down upon the Ark. The men were all over the decking and were searching every exposed nook and cranny of the ancient wreck. Soon they too joined the search. Claire had also come onto the snow-covered deck and assisted the men. Rebel, sailor, or marine, all wanted McDonald found, especially after word spread that he'd killed two men in his attempt on the lives of Claire and Ollafson.

Dugan reported to John Henry at the bow of the Ark where he and Jessy started making plans for hastily breaking camp.

"Half of the camp's complement is on the Ark searching, Colonel Darlin', nothing to report."

Claire and Ollafson joined them on the deck as men hustled around going in and out of the exposed areas of the ship.

"You didn't think you could stop Azrael that easily did you?"

The voice echoed inside the once-covered cave. The words bounced off the ice wall, making it nearly impossible to see where they had originated from.

"He's been waiting thirteen thousand years for you, Colonel Thomas!"

"Look!" Dugan said as he hastily raised his Henry rifle and took aim. John Henry quickly reached out and lowered the barrel of the rifle.

"I've got a bead on him, Colonel. He's right there by the original excavation opening, and he's just got a pistol!"

"That's not all he's got."

Claire saw the slowly burning fuse in McDonald's hand.

"Jesus!" Taylor said, wanting to scream for the men to vacate the petrified wreck. "That son of a bitch is going to blow the Ark!"

Thomas and the others all saw McDonald in his crazed

state. He stood leaning on the cave wall and he was bleeding heavily. He was weak from being shot twice by Thomas the night before. The crystalline ice was streaked with a transparent bloodstain as it ran down the ice. Still he held tightly to the burning fuse. Where the dynamite was, they could only guess.

"No, God has passed judgment on you. And you arrogant Americans will be responsible for releasing the old world into the new. All things that have been forgotten will be reborn!"

They watched as McDonald grew weaker by the moment. He slumped as blood poured from his wounds. Several of the Rebel and marine sharpshooters had him in their front sights. Taylor waved them off for fear McDonald would simply drop the burning fuse.

"Steven, don't do this," Claire called out. "We can fix—"

Every heart on or in the Ark froze as they all saw the giant shadow on the ice wall behind McDonald. It was a dark mass that was so black it looked obsidian. As their eyes widened, great wings of inky darkness spread behind McDonald and that was when he smiled and slowly started sliding down the wall in death. The shadow spread out wide as McDonald's body slid to the ice floor, the fuse slipping from his hand. The fuse burned down to the first of the one hundred and eighty sticks of dynamite McDonald had placed under the exposed section of bow.

The explosion rocked the world under them. The Ark lurched inside her grave of ice. The walls tumbled in and inundated the deck. John Henry and Taylor both knocked Claire and Ollafson off their feet and covered them. Dugan was thrown forward, breaking another two ribs. The exposed men on the deck all fell down and covered their heads. Thomas knew he was about to lose a lot of his command in this suicidal act by the insane spy.

The area of prehistoric ice directly beneath the bow was blown free and the tremendous explosion cracked the Ark along the line in which it vanished into the glacier, from the top of the living quarters through the hull to the keel. The mountain shook. The Ark remained intact as every man realized that the explosion did not have the effect McDonald had been expecting. It mostly blew ice from under the wreck where he had planted the charges and dug a huge crater under the exposed bow of the Ark.

The ancient vessel held together. John Henry slowly started to rise. He heard men cheering from the deck that sloped away from them. They had survived. He assisted Claire to her feet as Ollafson was thanking Taylor. Dugan was cursing his luck, but every man involved in the search felt that he had been saved by McDonald's poor placement of the dynamite.

John Henry looked at the spot where McDonald had been. The body would never be recovered, as thirty tons of ice had smashed out the remaining life of the British Army officer. The shadow of Azrael was nowhere to be seen, if it had ever been there at all.

"Okay, we found McDonald. Now can we leave this miserable mountain?" Taylor asked as he took in the frightened men around him.

"My thoughts exactly, let's—"

The crack sounded like a bolt of lightning had rent the mountain. John Henry was knocked from his feet and the rest of the men were thrown into the Ark's gunwales. Another loud crack was heard and all felt the giant Ark lurch in her tomb of ice. Then the sound became unbearable as timbers hewn thousands of years before started to crack and separate like shattering glass. Every man who was on the deck felt himself fly into the air as the bow section of the massive Ark broke and fell to the floor of the once-buried cave. The tension and power of the breaking keel was so loud that many of the men inside were crushed by the enormous pressure wave created when the petrified wood released its stored energy. The sheer weight of the bow slammed its remains into the ice so hard that all fifteen men inside the cave were crushed when the bow fell.

John Henry tried to pick himself up, that was when he felt the first forward movement of the Ark. He managed to gain his feet in time to see the bow swing away from the rest of the entombed ship. The raised prow started to roll to the right and Thomas grabbed a firm hold of the roughened petrified wood and held on as the centrifugal force started reading its laws to every person fighting for a handhold. John Henry dug in his gloved fingers and hugged the large prow as it swung so fast that he was fearful of the force slinging him from the deck. As it was, he was horrified when one Rebel and two marines were swept off only to be smashed against the ice wall as the ship swung around crazily, hitting the wall and straightening out, finally stopping its manic spin. John Henry saw what was happening and his heart froze.

"Oh, shit!"

The Ark's broken bow section started to slide down the exposed cave system toward the open air of the world that hadn't seen its like in more than thirteen thousand years.

"Hang on!"

The ancient artifact started to slide down the side of Mount Ararat with more than seventy-five men clutching onto anything they could grab.

Two hundred feet of Noah's Ark were moving in open air once again.

26

The speed at which the Ark accelerated seemed far faster than it was, but the sheer weight of the ancient and petrified wood directly translated into a force that smashed any obstacle in its way.

John Henry had a high view of the scene. He saw the camp above the cave system fly past as his hood was torn from his head. He felt the rush of air and knew the Ark was picking up speed.

On the deck Jessy reached for Claire's hand as she slid past him. His grip was strong and arrested her fall toward the torn and jagged stern. Ollafson was not so lucky. The Ark reached the rise of the berm that had survived the initial detonation two days before. That was the only gate that would have a chance at stopping the terrifying slide. The bow hit and John Henry was inundated with large and small chunks of ice. He felt one strike his head and he momentarily blacked out but maintained his grip. The wall exploded as if a cannon shell had struck it, and then the Ark was free. The giant hit the remains of the berm and flew skyward. The weight was so great that it only spent a split second airborne, and then it

came down with a bowel-wrenching *boom* as it crushed some
of the men on the ground who hadn't made it out of the way.
When airborne for that short period, Ollafson was bounced
high and then he was just gone. The professor went over the
gunwale and vanished into the cyclone storm of ice as the Ark
continued to pick up speed.

Thomas saw the photographer Perlmutter as he was
thrown off the deck, hitting the large rise of the damaged
familial quarters. The body smashed into the stone-like wood
and then the wind caught him and he was gone. Thomas
screamed in anger as he hung on for dear life. The box camera and other equipment went soon after. Men were screaming and were starting to lose their grips on handholds as the
great vessel continued down.

Men in camp started running after the giant object. Ropes
were tossed to reaching hands but missed. Other ropes were
lassoed around broken spots on the deck. The lines quickly
became taut but the momentum was too great. The men
holding the ropes were pulled through the air only to smash
into the ice in the Ark's wake. Other men started throwing
crates and any other piece of equipment they could into the
path of the runaway behemoth but the Ark merely crushed
anything in its path.

Again and again the Ark bounced over rocks, rises in the
mountainside, and huge cliffs, and again and again it would
smash into the snow and ice and continue on its way down
the mountain as if it were on a train track.

Jessy was losing his grip on Claire's hand. Her glove gave
way and he yelled as she vanished. Dugan was hanging on
by his fingers as the Ark dug into the snow and ice for the
fifth time. He heard the scream and then he saw Claire sliding toward him. He knew that just beyond him there was
nothing but a jagged edge of the stern as she was fast running out of deck. With a last-ditch effort he released one hand
and grabbed her as she sped past. He pulled with all he had
and then she was able to get a handhold just as Sergeant
Major Dugan's grip failed him.

She was nearly blind without her goggles, which had been

the first thing to fly free of her, so she barely saw the sergeant major. His fingers were tearing loose from the broken gunwale. Claire managed to see the strain in Dugan's face as he tried but failed to hang on.

"Tell the colonel—"

Dugan was gone.

The sliding brick house was now traveling at thirty-five miles per hour, nearly matching the speed of the train they'd ridden during their trip to Ararat. The Ark looked as if it would keep going until it flew off the wrong cliff and then all would be smashed in a thousand-foot plunge.

John Henry felt the impact as the ship slammed into a large ice wall and then the Ark started to spin. It hit another wall and the spin slowed, then another and it was nearly tipped over. Again it struck and spun, the centrifugal force shooting men free of the crazily suicidal vessel.

Then it all stopped at once as Noah's Ark struck the snowfield at the six-thousand-foot level, which meant that the great ship had traveled more than eleven thousand feet. Before anyone knew what was happening the two hundred tons of petrified wood buried its broken bow into the snow and earth. The Ark stopped so hard and fast that John Henry was thrown forward through the cold air and then he felt his body go numb as he slammed into the snow.

The world finally stopped moving and then went silent.

THIRTY-FIVE MILES NORTH OF TRABZON HARBOR, THE BLACK SEA

The captain of the *Carpenter* was still fighting a losing battle. As soon as the pumps seemed to be catching up, another oaken plank would separate from its kin and they would have to start shoring up all over again. They were down a total of eight feet and were now in imminent danger of foundering. As for *Argo*, the *Carpenter* had not seen her since cutting her towline four days before. As it was, the captain figured they may be right in the middle of a major conflict, even going as far as believing that it was now a possibility that *Chesapeake* was lost, and also the long-overdue *Yorktown*. If the French had the gall to disable them, why not both of the other American frigates as well?

"Captain, if we don't receive assistance soon, we'll lose her," said his first officer, who was standing on deck soaked from leading the efforts of the crew to save his ship.

"It seems the Russians are sitting this one out." The captain lowered his head as he paced the quarterdeck. "I had hoped that they would at least make an appearance seeing as we're in their backyard with foreign warships in the Black Sea."

"It does look like they'll just sit back and watch how this plays out, sir."

The captain saw the calm sea and the clearing skies. He had not made sail for three days as he needed every man available to battle the flooding from the collision with the French.

"Warship, dead on, one mile!" came the call from above. "French flagged!"

"Damn," the captain said as he raised his spyglass toward the eastern horizon. There she was. The *Especial* was making a run at them again.

The last time they had come on like this was the day before, and that time she had come so close that her bow wake nearly swamped the *Carpenter.*

"Damn them, this time we are going to at least make a show for the bastards!"

"Captain?" the first officer said, confused.

"Battle stations. Have the gun crews ready both starboard and port guns. Don't run them out, but raise the gun ports. We'll at least make them sweat a little."

"Aye, Captain."

Moments later the tired crew of the *Carpenter* broke from the bowels of the large ship and made ready battle stations as the *Especial* sped toward them.

"She's lowering her battle flag, Captain!"

"Why would the *Especial* do that?" the first officer asked as he too raised a set of binoculars.

"I can only think of one reason. She's going to finish the

job this time, and they refuse to fly their colors while committing the despicable act."

"Or," the first officer said as he lowered his glasses, "they want to surrender."

The captain could not help but admire his first officer for his false bravado.

"Here she comes!" a lookout called from the bow. Men lined the railing as the *Especial* was only three hundred feet from the *Carpenter*. The open gun ports didn't seem to have the desired effect. The captain could see that this time the Frenchman was going to contact them, and that would just about shake the last of the *Carpenter*'s life from her. How sailors of any nation could stand by and watch as another warship was in danger of foundering was beyond the American's comprehension. The *Especial* would be a special guest in the maritime center of hell.

"Sound collision warning!"

"God, give us strength!" the first officer said as he started looking for a handhold.

The ship's bell started clanging and every man tensed up, awaiting the final "accidental" blow that would send the proud *Carpenter* to the bottom of the Black Sea.

The *Especial* was only sixty yards away as she started a slow turn to port to "avoid" the damaged American warship, but all knew they would come so close that the mere passing of the French frigate would send a pressure wave into her hull that would undo every repair they had made.

Suddenly five splashes erupted in front of the *Especial* as she began her turn. The five shots from the American-made Cumberland cannon came so close to the *Carpenter* that one of the shells struck her topmost rigging.

The captain turned and saw that help was finally there. The *Chesapeake* with her massive twenty-pounders had fired her warning shots and any sailor in any navy knew that the next shots would be right down *Especial*'s gullet.

Suddenly the French frigate veered away sharply, cutting it close but deciding that egress was better than calling the crazed Americans' bluff. The French battle flag started rising at her stern as she cut away.

The crew of the American warship erupted in cheers as the *Chesapeake* became a wall of firepower between the *Carpenter* and the *Especial*.

"Thank God," the captain said as he raised his hand toward the *Chesapeake*. The crew of their savior all lined the rails of their ship as they waved, saluted, and shouted.

An hour later crewmen were transferred along with more pumps to the *Carpenter*. The captain of *Chesapeake* joined them for a meeting with his opposite number. The mood aboard the seemingly doomed ship was upbeat. But the rumor was about that *Chesapeake* had come alone because the *Yorktown* may have been lost. That dampened the mood quickly as the two officers met on deck and shook hands.

"Jimmy, I see you're having some trouble here?" the captain of *Chesapeake* joked as the men shook hands.

"It seems someone has differing ideas about the rules of the road."

The captains stood apart and were happy to see three large portable pumps being lowered into *Carpenter*'s hold.

"I'll have my ship's carpenter meet with yours and we'll see if we can get this old girl patched up without dry-docking her."

"You know, you took a chance firing on the *Especial* like that."

"We honor them with a five-gun salute for assisting our sister ship, and you misinterpret that as opening fire? I resent that, sir!"

Both men nodded and laughed.

"Any word from the *Yorktown*?"

"Not a word. I am therefore assuming we are on our own. We'll get *Carpenter* to where she's not leaking like a sieve and then you'll continue on to Trabzon Harbor and hope that Colonel Thomas and the others are there to meet us in a few days. In the meantime the *Chesapeake* will begin a search for the *Argo*. God, I hope we haven't lost her also."

"Tom, you know this isn't going to turn out so good, don't you?"

The captain of the *Chesapeake* only smiled. "What, would you rather be back in home waters where the war is winding down and we're stuck with blockade duty for the duration?"

The captain of *Carpenter* smiled and shook his head as he watched the distant *Especial* holding station at a mile with her tail firmly planted between her legs. She had linked with her sister ship, *Osiris,* and both were now standing off watching the two American warships from a safe distance.

"Yeah, why not stay out here and stir up another war?"

Both men laughed, but deep inside where men can show fear, they knew the European powers would soon stop playing at war, and start one.

MOUNT ARARAT, THE OTTOMAN EMPIRE

John Henry could hear the voices around him but it seemed they came from miles away. The words would echo and then go silent. Finally he forced his eyes to open. It was as if every bone in his body was broken. He blinked in the semi-dark. He heard the wind as it rustled the tent he now knew he was in. He closed his eyes and was in danger of losing consciousness again when he felt the coolness of the cloth as it was applied to his forehead. His eyes shot open and his hand went to his head, where he took hold of someone's fingers. Another hand soon covered his.

"Easy, easy, John Henry. You took quite a shock to your system."

Thomas focused on the voice and willed himself to concentrate. He remained holding the hand and cold compress.

"What . . . what happened?" he said as his eyes came to rest on Claire's beautiful green ones. She tried to smile but failed miserably. This made John Henry attempt to sit up.

He heard men cry out in pain somewhere and that was when he remembered seeing men flying through the air. Falling to an unknown fate and him holding on for dear life as he was sped to a crushing death. He shook his head, causing the pain to flare, and the colonel concentrated on that.

"We couldn't find you for two hours. We thought . . . thought—" Claire stumbled as she lowered her eyes.

John Henry opened his eyes and looked around. They were inside the large mess tent that was now filled with men writhing in pain or speaking about the horrid event that had befallen the cursed mission. The vaguest memories started to flood back into Thomas's injured mind.

"When we finally found you, you were nearly frozen to death in a snowdrift, which luckily broke your fall."

"I need a report. Where's Dugan?" he asked as he again tried to sit up but Claire restrained him.

"You're not getting up until the corpsman says you can," she said as she applied the cold compress onto his head. John Henry slowly pushed her hand away.

"Get me the sergeant major," he said, and this time he did manage to rise from the cot.

"Sergeant Major Dugan is dead."

John Henry turned his head and saw that Claire was looking right at him. He stumbled and Claire stood quickly to steady him.

"Who else?" he asked when he felt stable.

"Too goddamn many to name," came a voice out of view. John Henry knew it was Jessy, who finally came into the tent.

"You should have let me cut that bastard's throat when we had the chance."

"That's not fair, Colonel. We can't be faulted for being civilized," Claire said, speaking up in Thomas's defense.

Jessy cursed and then pulled the hood from his head. He sat on the end of the cot and then ran a gloved hand through his black hair.

"How many?" John Henry asked.

"Twenty-six dead, fourteen injured."

Thomas was stunned as he tried to remember who was standing on the deck of the Ark and who was below when that crazed son of a bitch McDonald blew it up.

"Ollafson?" he remembered.

Nothing was said. Claire lowered her eyes and Jessy was silent as he stood and pulled his gloves free.

"Captain Jackson?" Thomas asked, expecting the worst.

"We were lucky there. He rode the Ark down the mountain while inside the family spaces. He's been stuttering ever since, but other than that, he's fine." Taylor paced over to the next cot and spoke softly with one of the injured Rebels. He returned and then made his report.

"We also lost our official documentarian and all of his photographs and equipment. Things are a real mess. The detonation took out half the damn camp above the Ark."

"Where is the Ark?"

"Right outside. Well, what's left of her anyway. We managed to move the camp away from the glacier and relocated here at the six-thousand-foot level."

"I'm sorry about Sergeant Major Dugan," Claire said as she watched John Henry waver and then straighten up just as Jessy tried to help. The colonel shook Taylor's hands from him and straightened his coat and then tried to focus.

"You've had a pretty serious blow on the head. You need to rest for a while longer," Claire said.

John Henry slowly made his way to the tent's flap and pulled it open. He saw that the snow had stopped and the weather had cleared. The sun was close to setting as he took in the men setting up and repairing what was left of the camp's equipment. His eyes soon fell on the giant bow of the Ark. It was dug deeply into the snow that had forced it to slow and then eventually come to rest. It was tilted at an angle so severe that Thomas could see onto her sloping deck. The jagged scar where the bow had been separated from the bulk of the vessel ran from keel to the raised housing of the family quarters. Only twenty percent of the Ark stood before them. The remains were a shambles. Broken and cracked petrified wood was proving to John Henry that as tough as Noah's creation was, it would never stay intact. Spiderweb cracking dominated the great prow of the Ark. Lanterns had been placed on her deck and around her broken hull as the men still searched for anyone caught inside during the treachery of the Englishman. It was a surreal scene of destruction.

Claire watched as the colonel lowered his head and

allowed the tent flap to close. He turned and saw the same Rebel trooper to whom Jessy had spoken a moment before. Thomas stepped up to the bunk, expecting words of venom from the boy about getting a lot of men killed. He would never get used to seeing men under his command dying in front of him.

"Trooper, we're going to need you soon. Will you be ready when we do?" John Henry thought the boy wasn't going to answer. It looked like he was thinking something over and then his eyes flicked over to Jessy before returning his attention back to the Yankee.

"Yes, sir, Colonel. It's only a broken arm and wrist."

Thomas patted the young Reb's leg and then started to turn away.

"I just asked the colonel what this was all for, sir. He couldn't rightly say."

John Henry froze as he turned to face the boy. He had no words; he just grimaced and then smiled and patted the leg again. He returned to Claire and Jessy and sat on the edge of the cot.

"The sergeant major had a wife and eight children."

Claire and Jessy were caught off guard as John Henry sat and talked like he was in a confessional.

"He always said that he despised his wife so much he satisfied her with a passel of kids and stayed away at the furthest outposts he could volunteer for."

Both Claire and Taylor were silent.

"He never knew he talked in his sleep. Sometimes in English, and then the Irish would take over. But one thing I know, that man loved his wife and kids."

Claire wanted to swipe at the tears she felt forming. The colonel truly admired Dugan, and this made her think of the deceit she had shown to Professor Ollafson before his death and feel that much lower. John Henry had a simple way about him, and Claire knew she was a long way from the integrity of one soldier mourning another.

Taylor cleared his throat when all was quiet except for the

soft moaning of the injured. These sounds were clearly heard by John Henry, who looked up at the many occupied cots.

"I say we take as many samples from the Ark as we can and then get the hell out of here."

Thomas looked from Jessy to the boy lying on the cot. He suddenly stood and walked to the tent's flap again and then pulled it back. He started thinking. He let the tent's opening close and then he turned and walked to the young Rebel's cot and smiled.

"We're about to show you what this was all about, son."

Claire exchanged looks with Jessy, who was worried Thomas was still out of it. John Henry turned and faced his second-in-command.

"Get Captain Jackson in here." John Henry started to slip on his heavy fur-lined coat over his uniform jacket. Taylor didn't move for a second as he tried to fathom John Henry's intent. "How far away are the railroad ties that we were using for our little ruse?"

Taylor was caught totally off guard by the question, but started to think anyway.

"We have more than a thousand wooden ties and rail at Talise Station that Parnell was using."

John Henry finished buttoning his coat and turned to face Jessy.

"That won't do. That station will soon be back in the empire's hands."

"Then the only option is the railroad supplies at the Black Sea line north where our intrepid band abandoned them. We have more than two thousand railroad ties there. Why?"

"We need platforms and we need crating. We'll have to strip the wagons of their wheels, but we can do it."

"Do what?" Claire asked.

John Henry smiled and Taylor's heart froze.

"The last time I saw that look you charged into a Kiowa encampment with five men and scattered their horses, and as Sergeant Major Dugan told me a few weeks ago, you had this same look when you accused General McClellan of cowardice in the face of the enemy at Antietam. And you had the same look when you were a kid at the Point when you stuffed goose feathers in Professor Jenkins's boots. That's not a good look."

Thomas actually laughed when he thought about Dugan forewarning Jessy about his impending future with the Yankee colonel.

"Do what?" John Henry repeated Claire's question.

"Yes," Claire said hesitantly.

"We're going to bring back the provenance." He looked at the wounded boy. "We're going to bring back the proof Mr. Lincoln wanted that the Ark exists and that Americans were the first to find her." Thomas walked to the tent opening and pulled the flap back, revealing the illuminated and heavily damaged bow section of the grounded Ark.

"Oh, shit," Jessy said as he lowered his head.

"Precisely, Colonel," he said as he left the tent.

"I've truly hated that man since we were freshmen at the Point."

27

John Henry watched as the men started the last of the crating. It had taken two weeks to build the new wagons from the old with the addition of more than two thousand railroad ties to assist in the new configuration of the large twelve-wheeled conveyances. The apprentice carpenter's mates supplied by Jackson had done a job beyond the normal call of duty.

The communication with Lieutenant Parnell had been sparse but effective the past two weeks. The six hundred strong Seventh Guards Regiment looked as if they had taken up permanent residence at the Talise railway yard. They had taken what equipment Parnell and the men left behind in their haste to follow Thomas's orders. The force under the command of Parnell was now encamped five miles away waiting for word to unleash the plan that John Henry, with the reluctant help of Colonel Taylor and Captain Jackson, had concocted.

As John Henry walked the perimeter of camp he glanced at the spot that had been reserved for the burial of the dead. Almost half the men he had started with on the Ararat mission had been killed. Now he was down to fifty-five men, and this time the Confederate prisoners were the most abundant and the strongest. The marines had lost a lot of men in and around the Ark when McDonald had blown it. He saw the makeshift crosses the men had made from the scrap railroad ties. That task had been their first priority even ahead of securing their proof of the Ark's existence.

In many ways he knew he had failed these men because he had not taken this mission as seriously as he should have from the outset. He had even tricked himself into thinking that he could do this mission for the sake of his friend, the president, but knew all along that it was a fool's errand. Now he was facing his image in the mirror every morning and knew that his disbelief had cost the lives of all of these men.

Gray Dog had received word that John Henry wanted him to sneak back into the eastern camp as soon as he was able to traverse the four miles safely in between the Turkish patrols, but as yet he had not shown up. John Henry believed that the news of Dugan's death might have affected the Comanche far more than the boy was willing to let on. As much as they had fought and argued over the years, Gray Dog had learned most everything from the gruff sergeant major. Thomas looked for his adopted son every evening and night, but he never came.

"John Henry, Chief Petty Officer Pettit is ready."

Thomas turned from the sight of the makeshift graveyard and faced Jessy. He nodded and then followed him back to camp.

"Gray Dog is probably absorbing what he's heard. I know I still am, and I was here to witness the events," Taylor said as they walked through the thickening snow. He saw that John Henry wasn't going to respond.

"As far as sending a navy CPO with half of your command in the opposite direction, may I say that cutting your force while the Turks are still out there is cutting it quite close?"

"Jessy, you've been fighting battles for almost four years

and have never once outnumbered your enemy. Don't tell me now that after all of this leisure time you're growing overly cautious?"

"Back then all I had to fear was getting shot in the gut by one of you Yankees. Now if we fail we get . . . hell, I don't even know what the Turks do to their captured enemies, especially those who come bearing false gifts."

"They chop their heads off with a rather ugly sword, I would imagine."

Jessy looked at John Henry and knew he wasn't joking.

"You know, you can fudge the truth once in a while."

Captain Jackson approached them as they walked past the posted pickets. John Henry saw the two long lines of newly rebuilt wagons. One line of twenty-three would head south toward the Mediterranean, the other to the north. Thomas saw the last of the crates being sealed and placed onto the last wagon going with the chief petty officer and his men.

"They're ready, Colonel," Jackson said as he exchanged looks with Taylor, who lightly shook his head in the negative.

"Very good," John Henry said as he walked to the head of the first wagon string. The wagons themselves were something to behold. The carpenters and riggers had done a nice job increasing the size of the wagon beds for the extra weight, and reinforcing the many wheels for support of the giant load. He approached the man standing by his leading wagon of twenty-three. The short, stocky CPO saluted Thomas. His men were mostly the remnants of the mess crew and several of the wounded who had healed enough to take part in the plan.

Instead of returning the navy man's salute, John Henry just removed his thick glove and held out his hand. The chief looked startled but then lowered his hand and then he too removed his glove and shook the colonel's hand. When done Thomas reached into his coat and brought out another sealed envelope.

"Your orders for the navy, countersigned by Captain Jackson. Let's just hope there's a ship there to meet you when you arrive. This was thought up months ago, but with a different cargo in mind. We hoped to be taking men out of that port in an emergency, and not . . . not . . ." John Henry waved at the twenty-three wagons under the chief's command. "This."

The older chief laughed. "We'll get her through, sir, don't you worry. Let's just hope you don't get food poisoning with me taking all the mess cooks with me."

"We don't have enough food left to worry about that, Chief. Good luck and Godspeed."

This time the salute was returned by Thomas and Jessy, and then Jackson escorted the chief to his wagon and spoke softly to him. Then the two men shook hands and then the chief mounted his wagon with its enormous load.

The heavily loaded wagons started moving and John Henry silently watched them leave. He turned and then saw the eighteen wagons that would depart the base of the mountain with him.

"And just how do you think old Abe is going to react when we show up with only part of the Ark cut into pieces? Not only that, we have all disobeyed orders and instead of bringing back the provenance we were ordered to get, we end up bringing back twenty percent of the damn ship."

John Henry placed a hand on the first wagon going north. He patted it and then turned and faced Taylor.

"Years they'll have."

"I never understand what your mind is thinking, haven't since the Point, haven't since our days in Texas."

Jackson walked up at that moment. He too wanted to hear this; they had all been so busy the past two weeks that no one had even bothered to ask outside of Claire, and she wasn't speaking. She had seemed satisfied with Thomas's answer. Now they would see if they agreed.

"Gentlemen." He turned and looked at the forlorn graveyard a quarter mile away. "I'm doing it for those boys"— he gestured at the men sitting around the campfires they were allowed to have since they had plenty of wood—"and those boys. They deserve the recognition for what it is they have done. Blue or gray, these boys did what was expected and I'm not going to allow these European bastards to deny them that right."

"We're going to fight?" Jessy asked as his opinion and hopes rose.

"About damned time," said the prim and proper Jackson.

"Let's just say the Turks will have some decision-making to do and a short time to do it in."

"May we be let in on this?" the navy captain asked.

"Well, let me say this, Captain Jackson," John Henry said and smiled. "There has been a theory advanced at West Point, and I believe Annapolis if I'm not mistaken, that just about made every man in the classroom laugh hysterically."

"Oh, God, not the shock factor?" Jessy said with slumping shoulders.

"Exactly."

"I guess I missed that class," Jackson said.

"It was good in theory, when men's lives aren't at stake, but those are real crazy-ass Turkish cavalrymen out there, and they gained their experience in the Crimean War. Does that give you pause?" Taylor argued.

"I'm banking on that very Turkish fearlessness. I am also banking on the fact that this regiment has not been reinforced by Constantinople either."

"You think this is a play between their foreign office and the French, possibly even the British?" Jackson added.

"Yes. What the sultan doesn't know won't hurt him."

"Behind Constantinople's back, you mean?" Taylor said as he just caught on.

"That's an awful big gamble, Colonel," Jackson offered.

"Or bluff," Taylor added, again trying to sway John Henry from what he was planning to do.

"Who says it's either?" He walked away toward camp and the men he wanted to be around tonight. Before he got too far distant he stopped and turned. "Please send a message to Lieutenant Parnell and his command, operations against any opposing force will commence at approximately noon tomorrow. Tell him to watch and wait for the signal." He slowly walked away and joined several Confederates by a fire where a harmonica was softly playing.

"Has he always been this way?" Jackson asked as he watched John Henry sit and accept the offered whiskey from one of the men. He drank deeply and then passed the bottle over to three marines who had come over to join them. The Confederate soldiers made room for the Yankees. Soon John Henry started telling the Rebel soldiers a story and they seemed to be paying close attention. "And what's he doing now?"

"Haven't you ever seen a man say good-bye before?"

"I didn't realize."

"Now, as far as your first question, Mr. Jackson, if things had gone somewhat differently at the outset of the war, you're looking at the officer that would more than likely be the commanding general of the entire Union army. Even General Lee knew that." He faced Jackson. "The man is just that brilliant. So for now I'll bite my tongue and find out tomorrow what fantastic death he has arranged for us." He smiled at the shocked face of the naval captain. "It should be eventful at the very least."

Taylor with one last wink at Captain Jackson moved off to join John Henry.

Jackson was left standing where the torches and lamps still illuminated the spot where the giant Ark had come to rest.

The gouged and scarred earth of the snowfield where the ancient vessel had come to rest was empty—the Ark was gone.

John Henry was of the old school in regard to command. He needed to know his men, and with no army personnel and just navy, marines, and soldiers of the Confederate army in his charge, he was lost as far as their abilities were concerned. He knew on the Plain of Ararat Lieutenant Parnell, a young, brash, and very excitable officer, was in command of one hundred and seventeen band members and a scattering of marines to fill out their ranks. The plan had been laid and their return to American shores fully depended on the young officer to do what was expected of him and his truncated command tomorrow.

As he made his way through camp he looked up and saw, or was it that he noticed for the first time in weeks, the stars. They were brilliant in the night sky and seemed to add warmth to the otherwise cold evening.

The mood in camp on this last night was reserved to say the least. But one thing John Henry took note of was the fact the men were mixed among their campfires. Some marines and sailors sat with Rebel soldiers and they all seemed to have the same stories of home and family, the only difference being that some families were north and some south of the Mason-Dixon Line. There was laughter, but again it was subdued as one man would joke about another's sister or vice-versa. Harmonica and a soft slide of bow against fiddle strings told of home and loved ones and the music seemed to pull a caul over the men as they waited for the day to dawn that would either see them home, or see their deaths in a place none of them had ever heard of before—the Plain of Ararat.

Thomas noticed Jessy was speaking with Captain Jackson, who seemed to be nervously wading in among the men of his naval command. Jackson had not taken kindly to the repeated reminder that he would be the first marine to lead a United States Cavalry charge. The rumor had spread that the strait-laced officer had been ill for quite some time after he was informed. John Henry could see that Jessy was going over some of the fine points of cavalry showmanship. He had a sword in hand and was in the process of twirling it well over his head. As he watched, Thomas saw a pained expression on Jackson's face and then he trotted off to the outskirts of camp where he became ill once more. Taylor happened to glance his way and even from that distance Thomas could see the Rebel's wry wink. Jessy spun the sword again, sheathed it, and tossed it to one of his men as he moved to join John Henry.

"How's the head?"

Thomas looked sideways at Taylor. "You hoping for some late effects that would render me unsuitable for command?"

"Something like that. I do have both of our navy corpsmen available to testify to that very fact, Colonel Thomas."

"So, now I know how you became Jeb Stuart's right-hand boy." Thomas lowered his hood and smiled at Jessy.

"I rose in rank despite old Jeb. I swear, that man never met a newspaper headline he didn't like."

"Yes, we have a few of those also. More than our share, come to think of it."

They walked in silence for a while, only stopping from fire to fire to warm their hands and say something to the solemn men.

"Listen, about Mary. I want you to know—"

"No more, John Henry," Jessy said as they moved away from the fires and the hushed sounds of songs of home. "I have seen how you are with that Indian boy. I know this may have nothing to do about nothin', but when you sent him off I saw in your eyes what it must have been like for you to leave Mary at that ranch. And I see how deeply you care. I know it was her death that drove you mad and made you act against that fool McClellan. The sergeant major told me two weeks ago when you were still unconscious that you had a suicidal streak in you when the war started. That you didn't really care if the general had you shot or not after you called him out for cowardice. I know why now. So no more about Mary." Jessy stopped walking and faced John Henry. He smiled. "Besides, we may get our chance to see her again tomorrow with this cockamamie scheme you've thought up."

Thomas nodded his head in thanks for the thought of Mary. "And that scheme you seem to hate so much was actually advanced by Napoleon. You should know that from the advanced tactics course at the Point. After all, Bobby Lee's been using the same theories for the past four years."

"Maneuver and deception are a general's best aids."

"You do remember. So that high-class education did pay off." He smiled again at his old friend. "Somewhat."

"Well," Jessy turned and started to walk away throwing his hood over his head. "At least when we do go out, we go out with a flourish. But this is going to be something that will never be taught at the academy alongside the Stand of the Three Hundred at Thermopylae."

"Why not?" John Henry called after him. "They died for a cause."

Taylor stopped walking and didn't turn, but just pointed to the wagons lined up for departure the next morning.

"This, John Henry Thomas, is no cause for which to send men to die."

As he left, Claire passed him with a pot of coffee and three cups. She saw Taylor and was confused when he pointed at her and then faced a distant Thomas who was watching.

"This, Colonel, sir," Jessy said, still indicating Claire, "is a cause, not that." His gloved finger moved from Claire to the wagons.

Thomas watched as Jessy shook his head and then slowly walked back into the soft glow of the camp.

"What was that about?" Claire asked as she stepped up to the colonel holding a cup.

"Nothing, just philosophical differences."

"I can imagine for you two that could be a rather wide gap."

John Henry took the offered cup and she poured him coffee. He gratefully sipped it and then nodded his thanks.

"John Henry, why are you doing this? I mean, we could have left here with nothing and the Turks would have allowed us to leave, but here you are doing the exact opposite of what your orders demand. Why?"

"You're the intelligence expert; you tell me." He sipped the coffee and then turned and strolled away. She picked up her step over the rocky terrain and caught up to his long-legged stride.

"I have been trying to figure you out since we met in Washington, and I still haven't a clue as to who in the hell you are."

"Look. See that spot over there?" He nodded toward the crooked crosses marking the men who had died at the hands of McDonald.

Claire looked and saw the soft outline of the markers in the soft moonlight.

"That's why I'm doing this. It's for them. Ollafson, Dugan, Grandee, all of them."

"It's not that you think you are the only man capable of pulling this off, an act of arrogance?"

"Absolutely," he said with a large grin.

Claire shook her head and followed John Henry until he came to a fire with only a boy from the south sitting near it. The boy was deep in thought and then he noticed the colonel and Claire and suddenly stood and froze at attention.

"Sit back down, trooper." Thomas watched as he did and he followed suit. He gestured for Claire to sit on an old biscuit box.

Thomas saw the boy pick something up—the Stars and Bars battle flag of the Confederate Army. John Henry sipped his coffee as Claire poured herself some. Next to the young Rebel private was his gray tunic. He knew the men had kept their old uniforms and had actually repaired them the best way they could.

"You carried that old flag all the way here from prison?" Thomas asked as he handed over his hot cup of coffee to the boy, who placed a needle in the flag and then accepted the cup.

"Thank you, Colonel, sir," he said as he gratefully drank the hot liquid. "Uh, yes, sir, I saved it from the fire pit at the camp. I took a few licks on the backside for that, but it was worth it. As I see it, too many boys have died for it to see it go up in flames."

John Henry exchanged a sad look with Claire. The private laid his coffee cup down and then picked up the battered Stars and Bars and then his repaired tunic of gray cloth.

"I'll be a'thankin' the colonel for the coffee." He dipped his head at Claire. "Ma'am," he said and then he slowly walked away.

Claire let her coffee cup slip to the ground as she buried her face in her hands and shook her head vigorously, fighting back the rise of tears.

John Henry watched a moment and then turned his face away.

Finally Claire looked up and swiped angrily at her eyes.

"Apologies, Colonel. I just pictured that boy out there tomorrow."

John Henry remained silent.

"Maybe the Turks will allow us to just leave?" she asked hopefully.

Thomas looked from Claire to the wagons and the strapped-down crates upon them.

"I'm afraid I've seen to it that they don't." He stood and tossed the remains of his coffee out of his cup and then walked over and sat next to the Pinkerton woman. "Claire, you'll just have to trust me when I say that Americans have been fighting for close to five years. Hell, we've been fighting for our existence since 1757, and it hasn't let up. The Europeans don't understand us, the way we think, and the way we act. They truly know nothing about us other than that we are crazed beyond belief. I'm banking on that very limited perception tomorrow," he said as his hand covered hers. There wasn't much warmth in the touch because of the gloves, but Claire covered his with her own and she squeezed.

"That's the first time you have called me Claire without my haranguing you to do so." She smiled up at him.

John Henry felt a fluttering in his stomach as he looked into Claire's green eyes. He seemed to know that he could get lost inside those pools of green and so he moved his gaze to her face in general and studied her.

"I hate to break the mood here, but there's movement down on the plain," Jessy said as he and Captain Jackson approached.

John Henry stood after releasing Claire's hand. The funny thing to Thomas was that he wasn't in the least embarrassed at being caught off guard.

"What is it?" he asked.

Captain Jackson handed over his spyglass and pointed to the west. "There, just outside of the station where Parnell had been. See?"

John Henry looked through the glass but could only see tents and campfires.

"Lieutenant Parnell alerted us by signal lamp. Look just to the left of the station's water tower; you see the empire's flag. Now look next to it. They rode in about an hour ago from the west."

Thomas finally saw it. He removed the glass from his eye and handed it over to Claire, who also looked down onto the Plain of Ararat. He pointed and that was when her heart froze. It was the British Union Jack flying next to the Turkish flag.

"Damn," she hissed as she too lowered the glass.

"Three hundred cavalry. Can't see the unit flags, so your guess is as good as mine," Jessy said.

"With the Turkish regiment at six hundred, it seems we are now facing close to a thousand crack cavalrymen."

Taylor smiled at John Henry.

"Now's a fine time to start learning how to count. We're outnumbered three to one. But then again I forget that more than half of our force can attack while playing 'The Battle Hymn of the Republic.' That's gotta count for something."

"I must say, Colonel, your gallows humor is a little unnerving," Jackson quipped.

"Colonel Taylor, there you go again being impressed by numbers," Thomas said as he moved back to the fire. "I expected more from a man who prides himself on being outnumbered."

"It's not being outnumbered, Colonel, sir, it's the off chance of being embarrassed that has my heart skipping beats."

The colonel turned to Jackson. "Captain, that wooden box we carried all the way from Baltimore. I think it's time we gave it to Colonel Taylor."

Jackson frowned, but then moved off.

"Follow me, Colonel, I think I have something that will not allow you to be embarrassed."

Intrigued, both Claire and Taylor followed. As they approached a lone wagon where the camp's mess equipment had been placed for the move in the morning, Jackson reached up and placed his gloved hand on a lone crate. Several marines and Rebels gathered around.

John Henry turned to Jessy. "Now, if you fail it won't be the Union blue you embarrass, my old friend." He nodded at Jackson, who simply pulled the crate from the back of the wagon. The wooden box struck the rocky ground and broke open. Jessy felt his heart beat a little faster. Thomas looked around and he saw the boy he and Claire had sat with earlier. He walked over and removed the old tunic from his hands and then tossed it to Jessy. Then he reached over and took the repaired Stars and Bars from the boy, and also tossed that to the Confederate colonel, who caught it as John Henry walked over to the broken crate. He reached down and retrieved one of the items from the ground and then threw that to the wide-eyed private. The marines were shocked at what the boy was now holding.

"Compliments of President Lincoln."

Every man saw the bright, brand-new gray tunic of the Confederate army. Then John Henry tossed the boy a new butternut cap with "CSA" emblazoned just above the black bill.

Thomas paced over to Taylor, who unfurled the large Stars and Bars battle flag. He smiled as his eyes found John Henry.

"Now," Thomas said as he turned his head to speak to all of the gathered Rebels. "You won't be embarrassing my uniform, but yours."

The men cheered and even the marines and sailors joined them. They felt the pride that the new uniforms delivered to their fellows and were happy for them. Now if they died, they would die wearing their own clothing. Taylor walked up to John Henry as he started to turn away with Claire and Captain Jackson.

"You son of a bitch, you did that on purpose!"

"Maneuver and deception, Colonel, maneuver and deception. Next time instead of cheating off of someone else's paper, actually study the course." Thomas smiled and walked away with Jackson. Claire stayed behind.

"What's maneuver and deception?" she asked.

Jessy smiled as he watched his friend. He started folding the flag and then placed it under his arm.

"It's just something that I forgot about, but should have seen coming."

"I do not understand either of you two," she said as she started to turn away.

"Let's just hope that after tomorrow we have plenty of time to get to know each other's little quirks far better. And from the looks of the hand-holding earlier, I would say you may have the art of maneuver and deception down far better than I." Jessy half-bowed. "On that note, I bid you good evening, Madame."

Claire watched Jessy go, only just realizing what he meant by the strange comment.

"Hey," she started to say but stopped when she realized that Taylor was right.

She was maneuvering for the heart of a man who had regained some of the passion for life that had been missing—John Henry Thomas.

28

The day had dawned as bright as the young marine lieutenant could ever remember. It reminded him of a Maine morning when he was but a child. All of that seemed far distant and foreign as he looked toward the mountain, knowing that soon he would get the signal that Colonel Thomas and the Ararat team were starting their run for the Port of Trabzon, where all hoped they still had ships waiting to take them home—a far and distant hope, he feared.

As he stepped from his tent and into the unseasonably warm morning, he placed his gloved hand on the hilt of his sword and then looked up to see his command already standing to. He looked up as he made his way forward. Gunnery Sergeant Miles Kendrick, a rough and grizzled old sea dog from Massachusetts, stood at rigid attention.

"Report, Gunnery Sergeant," Parnell said, trying not to let the fear show in his words or his hesitant actions

"Sir, all personnel are present or accounted for."

Parnell returned the salute of the old marine and the two of them locked eyes. The gunnery sergeant nodded that all was right and that Parnell could do the easiest thing in the world according to any top sergeant—command.

"Perhaps a word for our . . . our . . . cavalry detachment, sir?"

Parnell looked to his right at the one-hundred-and-eighteen-member Army of the Potomac band. The 317th Drum and Bugle Corps stood at rigid attention. The sun shone brightly off their brass and their swords that had been issued the night before, much to their astonishment. Most had been ill the entire night and frightened like never before after hearing what the colonel's plan was. There was not one word of fear voiced from the young men and not one question asked, but most felt the fear that entangled itself in their stomach and intestines. For the first time since the bloody war started, the band was now asked to put up.

"It's hard to face men in the morning that you know may not be there in the afternoon," Parnell told his old gunnery sergeant, who only smiled at the young officer.

"A task that's been done since the time of Julius Caesar, sir. You *and* they will do fine. Just think of it as a carnival sideshow, sir. Our task is to ask the other side, what are you willing to do? We're here to force them to ask themselves that question, and Colonel Thomas is just hoping the answer is that they won't do anything. That's what we are doing. Let's just hope our young men are as convincing enough actors to pull it off."

Parnell nodded, took a deep breath, and then stepped forward. He saw the young lieutenant in command of the 317th. He stood at rigid attention and Parnell could see that the boy's legs shook, only slightly, but the tremor was there.

"Lieutenant, good morning to you, sir. Are you and your men ready to pull off the miracle command says you're ready for?"

"Sir, we . . ." The officer lowered his eyes. "We're scared sir."

Parnell remained quiet as if he was hearing his own fears voiced by the soft tone of the army officer.

"I'll let you in on something, Lieutenant. There isn't a man who awakened within a hundred square miles this morning who wasn't frightened. Anyone who says they're not, stay away from him. He's an idiot, a fool, avoid him at all costs. Our fear is what makes us perform."

"Sir, it's not just that we're afraid to die. All of us have hated the ridicule of our opposites in infantry and cavalry units. We know what they say about us, that we're shirkers, boys that were so afraid to fight they would sit out the war playing music. We hated that. What we're afraid of is failing the colonel and the others."

Parnell, not much older than the lieutenant, placed a gloved hand on the boy's shoulder and then smiled and leaned in close.

"We all have something to prove here today. We all have our demons and this morning we'll see if we can slay some of those, huh?"

"Yes, sir, we're ready."

"Good. Now, are you clear on the band's placement behind the rise of the gulley?"

"Yes, sir. The drum and bugle men have been placed. The rest will be mounted and ready to move upon your command."

Parnell patted his shoulder one last time and then looked over his command. Arrayed at attention to his front were the one hundred and eighteen members of 317th, the fifty-seven United States Marines, and twenty-six U.S. Navy sailors assigned to him. Two hundred and one men. A small unit expected to face more than nine hundred cavalry. He nodded at his men.

The sun broke free of the summit of Ararat and beat down on the frozen earth that guarded the mountain.

His men were as ready as they ever would be.

TALISE RAILWAY STATION, THE PLAIN OF ARARAT

Renaud stepped into the cold morning air and stretched his aching body. He looked over and saw that the recent additions to their force, the 25th Palace Fusiliers, a unit scraped together by Her Majesty's government from her embassy and consulate staffs, were already fed and were going about their morning duties, while the Turks were just crawling from bed. He shook his head as he started to turn away.

Suddenly bugles sounded and men started to run. Renaud grabbed a passing Turkish soldier and tried to make himself understood.

"What is it?" he tried to ask, but the harried soldier only looked at him strangely and pulled free.

"Damn it," the Frenchman cursed as he looked around.

"I suppose he was in a hurry to report to his unit. It seems the Americans are coming."

Renaud turned to see a British officer. He wore a red coat trimmed in green piping and his helmet had a flourish upon the top. He was sipping a cup of hot tea and looking to the east.

"They must know they'll never be allowed to pass. Why would they challenge a force this size?"

The British officer placed his china cup in its saucer and then looked over the French spy as if he were at a bug.

"Perhaps because they are bloody Americans who despise being told what they can and cannot do," the man said as he smiled. "We had to adjust to that very attitude. Can you imagine the arrogance?"

Renaud thought the officer was taking this situation a bit less than seriously.

"I avoided asking this question upon your arrival last evening, sir, but just what are your orders for this engagement?"

The officer again sipped his tea and then looked to the eastern region where the Americans would come out of the morning sun on their approach, a tactic he had expected, but obviously the Turkish commander hadn't, as he comically struggled to get out of his dressing gown and into a semblance of a uniform.

"Our orders?" He chuckled. "Our orders are to avoid engagement, sir. We're here for show and show alone. For all we know, the Americans could be here to start a war, and at the present time it would be a war Her Majesty's government would be ill prepared to fight."

"You're admitting—"

"I am admitting nothing, sir. However, I must explain"—he looked down at the small Frenchman and smirked—"there is a certain and special place we hold for all Americans. They are like a wayward son that has struck out on his own and has thus far out-achieved his overbearing parents. From a distance we howl and scream about the lack of respect they have for those nurturing parents, but deep down, they are still our relations. While there may be less love than before, the respect we have is true to the mark. We will not fire on the Americans." He smiled and saw that the Frenchman was aghast. "Who knows, maybe you and your wayward Turkish regiment can frighten them into surrendering their plunder." He saw the shocked look on the spy's face, about whom he had been briefed earlier that week. "Yes, we know all about the Empire's foreign minister and his maneuvering behind the sultan's back." He sipped the almost-empty tea cup and then handed it and the saucer to an aide as he placed the cavalry gauntlets on his hands. "If your mission fails here today, perhaps you'd better find another route home other than through Constantinople. From what I understand the sultan may be a bit of a clown, but understandably harsh when it comes to influencing treason."

Renaud watched as the British officer tipped his hat and then accepted the reins of his white mount.

"Well, shall we congratulate the Americans on their archeological discovery, and then ask them ever so nicely to leave it behind for the glory of the Ottoman Empire?"

The Frenchman watched him lead his horse away to join the three hundred men of his command.

Around him, the Seventh Guards Regiment was called to colors.

The flying standards of the American line were now visible coming out of the morning sun.

The Seventh Guards Regiment formed within fifteen minutes. Men were mounted and officers present. The captain of the 25th Palace Fusiliers ordered his three hundred cavalry to the far left of the Turkish regiment. He remained with the Turkish command unit and was soon joined by the French-man Renaud, who looked anything but comfortable on the large mount on which the Turks had placed him.

"What a spirited mount you have there, sir. He should serve you well in the upcoming . . . well, whatever this is go-ing to be," said the captain without even the benefit of a smirk.

"I should think even these backward Americans would be hesitant to shoot a man in such a splendid uniform as yours." The Frenchman looked toward the gathering Otto-man troops. "While they may not have the same respect for other uniforms."

"As I may have alluded to in our earlier conversation, the Americans, my uninformed sir, respect very little of our world."

"You sound as if you admire them," Renaud said with a hint of concern in his voice.

"Admire? Well, maybe that's a bit strong. However, let us say that mutual respect is not out of the debate."

Before the Frenchman could voice an opinion, the bugle announced officers' call and the British captain smiled, tapped his white-gloved fingers to his helmet, and then rode off toward the Turkish cavalry. His regimental colors went with him. Renaud watched the two riders' backs and then wondered just what the sneaky English were up to. He soon spurred his horse, almost slipped from the saddle, and then awkwardly followed.

John Henry Thomas was in the lead column of fifteen ma-rine riders. They escorted the line of eighteen heavily laden wagons driven by the naval crews, including the cooks and the engineers. The outriders on each side of the line were twenty more marines on horseback.

Stretching out before John Henry's eyes was the expan-sive Plain of Ararat. He saw the four squared positions taken up by the Turkish regiment. To the regiment's left were the detached British light brigade. He took note of the fact that

Her Majesty's cavalry had not committed to any course of action, which told John Henry that his hunch about the legality of this confrontation was dubious at best. He hoped.

Claire watched Thomas from the seat of the front wagon. She had insisted on being able to see what their fate would be, mostly wanting to make sure a certain colonel wasn't shot from his saddle. Claire saw John Henry raise his gloved hand and the men and wagons came to a slow stop. The wind had picked up and blew the Stars and Stripes outward, blocking her view of the approaching forces.

John Henry turned in his saddle to make sure that the wagons had stopped. Once he had Claire in sight he turned away and saw eight men riding toward his column. One rider carried the standard of the empire, a pure white flag with an elongated blue cross sectioning the banner. He noted once more that the two representatives of Great Britain carried only a regimental flag, two facing lions with crossed swords. No Union Jack, at least for the time being. The riders stopped a hundred yards to the front of the American line.

Thomas hoped his freshly pressed uniform was good enough to die in. The gold-yellow stripe that coursed down his pant legs to the top of his knee-high boots made him feel whole again, that he was once more a cavalryman. He only wished Sergeant Major Dugan was at his side. The colonel spurred his mount forward to meet the men who had come a long way to meet him.

John Henry rode his horse with authority, reining in the large roan only feet from the eight men, making their mounts shy away. Thomas backed his horse away, showing the Europeans his horsemanship. Deep down, Thomas was hopeful the horse didn't step in a groundhog burrow—so much for the dramatic entrance. He stopped the horse four feet from the men, bringing his right gauntlet to the brim of his white hat and then saluting the men before him.

"Colonel John Henry—"

"Thomas. Yes, we are aware of who you are, Colonel," said the large Turkish officer in the abundantly decorated green uniform. The fez upon his head was bright red and would have caused Sergeant Major Dugan to lose all self-control if he had been there. Thomas actually smiled at the thought and the men in front of him noticed that smile. "You, sir, are to be escorted to our border, or the nearest seaport, for expulsion from the empire."

"A rather harsh punishment for merely being delayed in the railroad's construction." John Henry half-turned in his saddle and gestured at the wagons. "We now have our soil and core samples from the survey and are escorting them to the Port of Trabzon."

"Colonel Thomas, we are well aware of your mission's parameters and are here to assure the sultan that no empire property leaves the country. Therefore we must confiscate your wagons."

"Very well, sir. I assume you can provide the written order from the sultan?" John Henry held the large Turk's eyes. The man blinked and it was not just from the rays of the rising sun behind the American column.

"Colonel, we are here to confiscate the cargo of those wagons. Any interference from you or your men will result in a situation that I guarantee you cannot handle."

"Not without a signed order. I have my duty also. You will have to physically take my cargo." Thomas moved the large roan forward a few steps so the men before him could see his eyes and judge if he were bluffing or not.

"Hhm, hhmm," the prim British captain cleared his throat. "Colonel, I see your point, but I'm afraid my Turkish ally does not. I am not even sure if he knows what a bluff is, in military terms that is."

"And you are, sir?"

"Who I am makes little difference at this point. Suffice it to say that Her Majesty would prefer the contents of those crates stay where it was that you found them."

John Henry only looked at the captain, trying to judge what his orders were. He thought the captain played his hand well in not saying anything at all.

"Enough of this. Will you surrender your wagons, Colonel Thomas?"

"No, sir. We worked very hard building those."

John Henry watched as the Englishmen slowly turned and rode back to their own unit. He also turned and rode back to his column, where a marine corporal was awaiting his orders.

"As soon as the Turkish regiment starts its advance, do not wait on me. Fire the red signal."

"Yes, sir, Colonel," the boy said and then tore off toward the rear of the column. Thomas turned to his fourteen men. "Form a skirmish line. Bring the remaining men up."

The fourteen marines sent their mounts in a straight line for a hundred yards in front of the wagons and then turned sharply left. The men from the wagon escort arrived and broke right. A skirmish line of thirty-four mounted United States Marines stood in between the greatest prize in the world and nine hundred men determined to stop them. The American flag was placed next to the bright red Marine Corps flag and they both marked the center of the line as John Henry took his place in front and then waited.

He was soon joined by the lance corporal commanding his right flank.

John Henry nodded and looked around him. His eyes momentarily went to the front wagon and the woman sitting on the bench next to her driver. He smiled when he saw the Spencer carbine in her hands.

As the British captain reined in his horse, he turned to the general.

"Your plan of action, General?" he asked the puffed-out marionette attached to the main puppeteer, the empire's foreign office.

"I figure the straight-on approach. Should not take more than a few moments to take such a weak adversary; it's almost unsporting."

The captain smirked as he turned back to the front and saw the American colonel sitting atop his horse, just waiting.

"Yes, almost," he said as he wondered if the Turk felt as uneasy as himself. He looked over at the heavily mustachioed general. No, he was oblivious as he proudly scanned his line of march. His men and mounts were perfectly aligned and the general pushed out his chest even farther as the initial three hundred cavalrymen inched ever closer to the Americans.

A bright red rocket suddenly burst and spread its fiery trail across the sky to the east at the rear of the wagons.

"Ah, a signal perhaps?" the captain said as if merely commenting on an unusual sight.

"Does it matter, my friend? No one can stand up to my regiment on open ground. We are the greatest light cavalry in the—"

The drums drowned out all noise from the plain. The sound of more than three hundred sets of hooves was nothing compared to the heavy beating of the bass drums as they tattooed a rhythm that was reminiscent of the long-ago Roman legions.

The general held his right hand high in the air, bringing the forward progress of the Seventh Guards Regiment to a halt.

"Bad idea, sir. Keep your regiment moving forward."

The general didn't answer as he was looking to a far-off knoll that blocked his view of the canyons beyond. The sound of the many drums banged and echoed off the rock facade of the canyon. And still the drums seemed to increase in volume.

"What is this?" the general asked loudly so he could be heard over the infernal beat of the drums.

"I would say it is at least a regimental-sized band coming your way."

"Regimental?"

Trumpets started sounding and the British captain looked to see several of the front-line cavalrymen had to stay their horses to keep them from bolting. The situation was loud and very frightening to anyone who had never seen a battlefield before. And still the heavy beat of the drums grew ever louder.

"Look, sir!" an aide pointed to the first series of canyons and from the mouth of the far left came riders. Their mounts were trotting. The leading officer was wearing a nontraditional cavalry helmet; as a matter of fact, it was no helmet at all. It was a naval department two-cornered hat. The double line of cavalrymen flowed out of the canyon behind him. The American flag waved in the breeze as the large unit of blue-clad cavalrymen came on. The drum beat made the waiting Turks wary of what might come from the canyon next.

The Turkish captain turned and watched his own men in the near distance as they in turn watched the unknown American unit come on. They were still but watchful.

The uniforms were immaculate. They all wore brightly colored blue tunics and their brass buttons shined in the early morning sunlight. Still, the infernal drums from hell boomed on and the trumpets played as though Julius Caesar himself was leading the procession. The line of Turks started to seriously hold their frightened mounts in check.

"Steady, men, steady!" the general shouted as he turned toward the faltering line of Ottoman troops. "It's all for show! Steady on!"

The British officer raised his brows at the general's pronouncement. He turned to the lieutenant who was acting as his second-in-command.

"If this is for show, I don't know if I want to stay around for the curtain call."

The drums actually increased in volume as if whoever was striking them were attempting to smash them to oblivion. The trumpets echoed off the canyon's walls and made them sound as if a hundred trumpeters announced the American movement.

Finally the double column of more than a hundred and thirty-five men took up station to the far left of the American line. A lone officer sat atop a horse, placed his sword in front of his face, and then gave it a flourish in acknowledgement of Colonel John Henry Thomas, who only nodded and smiled at the proud marine officer. Parnell had led his men out as if they had been on parade in front of the president, which most of the young band members had done.

Suddenly the trumpets stopped as suddenly as they had begun. The drums gave one final flourish as the last line of men came to a stop, sitting straight and deadly looking to the common observer. The flag of the American nation proudly flew side by side with the flag of the United States Army and next to that the solid red flag of the Marine Corps.

"What the bloody hell is this? Where did these soldiers come from? My intelligence reports said nothing of a cavalry unit traveling with these supposed engineers!"

The British colonel rolled his eyes.

"Perhaps these men are not what you believe them to be, General? Maybe you were actually sent here to face an enemy that will shoot back?"

The general watched as the two British officers turned their horses opposite the line of Americans.

"Where do you go, sir?" asked the Turkish officer.

"I was ordered to observe, sir. I have done so, and now will report to my superiors what it was I observed." The captain dug his spurs into his horse's sides and both Englishmen sprinted toward their own men. "Good luck to you, sir!"

"Cowards!" the general bravely said, trying to impress his subordinates with his bravado. They were not.

"Orders, General?"

"The order is to advance and take those wagons. Our reserve will attend to these men, who still find themselves sorely outnumbered."

His officers exchanged doubting looks.

"Sir, we don't even know what units we face," said his second-in-command.

The general turned on him. "It does not matter. This unit can outfight any American cavalry unit!"

The men in the HQ command had heard the newspaper stories of the American cavalry regiments and their bravery. They had read about the glamorous charges of men like General John Buford and the young General Custer at Gettysburg, and romantic newspaper accounts of the maniacal maneuvering of the Confederates Jeb Stuart and the far more famous General Stonewall Jackson. No, they had their doubts about the ineptitude of American cavalry units according to the general's opinion.

"All units advance on my command! Bring up the reserve. We go in as one mighty regiment."

The men in his command turned and saw the three hundred British cavalrymen ride off to the west toward Constantinople. Finally the men broke and rode to their individual units.

"Forward!" the general called out loudly.

A bugle sounded and the Turkish advance commenced.

John Henry cursed as the first bluff failed to send the Turks running. He turned in his saddle and saw the sun as it crested the summit of Ararat.

"Anytime, Jessy," he said under his breath.

As the Turkish Seventh Guards Regiment advanced at a conservative pace, they received the order to take up arms. They each withdrew a shortened version of the venerable Enfield breech-loaded single-shot carbine.

The sound of the American bugle call brought all eyes in the advance forward. They saw a lone rider sitting atop a brown horse as the animal reared up on its hind legs. The bugler called again; this time John Henry and the other Americans knew it to be the assembly call

Without being ordered to do so, the line of three hundred Turks stopped cold in their advance as they studied this new, unexpected move by the Americans.

"Forward, do not stop!" the general called out angrily.

Suddenly the ground shook as the bugle call was returned. As the frightened men watched a new column of men broke free of the canyon. They were in a ragged but swift-moving line as they broke into the open. The bugle call was frightening, but the screams and yells, yips and yahoos of these newest troops scared the Turks far more than the sound of the heavy drums had.

"What in the name of Allah?" the general said as he saw a mixture of blue and gray uniforms with both battle flags flying as they rode forward. The Confederate Stars and Bars flashed by the mounted armies and it was a chilling sight to the Turks, and a surreal sight to the waiting Americans.

The two lines of Rebel and marine cavalry formed up to John Henry's right. Now the full complement of three hundred and thirty-six Americans faced a force almost two times its size. Thomas, Taylor, Parnell, and Captain Jackson, all with swords notched to their shoulders, waited in front of their men so they could play out their little theatrical number to the close of curtain.

"Ooh," the Turkish army seemed to exhale at once as the last rider broke from the canyon. John Henry had to shake his head at this last little bit of theater.

Gray Dog, complete with the flowing six-foot-long headdress of his fathers and wearing nothing but a loin cloth and his chest plate of eagles' bones and beads, held a battle lance on high as he fronted the combined commands of John Henry, Parnell, and Colonel Taylor. The white horse of the Comanche came to a skidding halt and Gray Dog brought the magnificent animal to rear up as his headdress flowed back with the wind.

"My God, Confederates, Union cavalrymen, *and* savage Indians. Are we to fight all of America here today?" asked his subordinate with little or no respect lacing his words to the general.

"Look!" said one of the men.

The bugler started blowing the charge and John Henry's bluff was beginning to look as if it were no bluff at all. The charge sounded and the Confederates and the marines were the first to charge with Jessy and Gray Dog leading the headlong plunge into danger. John Henry called out, "Charge!" and then his unit started forward at breakneck speed. Then it was Parnell's turn. The 317th marching band, sounding like banshees from the gates of hell, also charged. All were waving the new swords they had been issued with the warning from Parnell not to slice each other to pieces.

The first to move was the front line of Turkish cavalrymen. They watched wide-eyed as the savage Indian came at them, and that was all they needed to see. The lance was pumping up and down and Gray Dog was screaming at the top of his lungs. The rest of the men followed. Jessy was out front with Gray Dog waving his men forward, twirling the bright flash of his saber. For the colonel, it was old times all over again.

That was it; the rear ranks of the Seventh stayed in place as the forward three hundred smashed into them. The entire unit was now in free flight. Even the general, with his eyes on the crazed Gray Dog, turned and spurred his mount brutally.

"They'll kill us all!" one of the men shouted.

Renaud, who had stayed as far away from the action as he could, saw the insane charge of the Americans. A charge that would never see the inside of any war college textbook, but one that would be immortalized by any solder who witnessed it that day.

The Frenchman cursed the cowardice of the Ottoman Turks and then wheeled his horse around and clumsily made his way north. He would now have to meet up with the French squadron at Trabzon Harbor.

The French navy would correct any embarrassment suffered that day. He would make sure the Americans never escaped the Black Sea.

He would personally destroy the army of Ararat.

The men celebrated as if they were all one American unit. No war to step between them, no politics other than American bravado against European arrogance. Even the proud but frightened 317th started playing "Dixie" loud and hard as every man belted out the words to the southern classic adored by none other than Abraham Lincoln himself. The men danced and exchanged hugs and slaps on the back between army, navy, and Confederate comrades who only knew that Americans couldn't be beat in any arena.

John Henry was not of the same sentiment as he dismounted. He almost stumbled as his left foot freed itself from the stirrup. He laid his head against the saddle to steady the nerves that had come on after he realized the Turks had broken and run. It was nearly reminiscent of the break the

Union Army made at the first battle of Bull Run. His breath came in ragged gasps as he found breathing was hard. He was startled when a sharp slap on the back made him jump.

"I'm afraid those boys won't stop running until their horses give out," Jessy said as he turned and watched the dust rise in the west as the Seventh Guards Regiment made a bid for the overland record for speed of horse. He turned back and saw John Henry was having a hard time focusing on him. "Hey, you all right, Napoleon?"

Thomas bent over and placed his hands on his knees. His sword was still clutched in his right hand. He finally managed a deep breath and faced Jessy as Parnell, Jackson, and Gray Dog joined them. The sound of revelry was loud.

"I had a fleeting moment there when I thought you and Gray Dog were going to actually attack."

Jessy laughed. "We were. The damn Turks just ran too fast. I didn't want to run out our own mounts. We still have to get the hell out of here, you know?"

"I think I wet myself," Claire said as she turned Jessy around and hugged him. She then did the same to an embarrassed but happy Lieutenant Parnell and a startled Captain Jackson. "That was amazing," she finished as she faced John Henry and suddenly didn't know what to do. He instead hugged her just to make sure he was still feeling after the shock at what almost happened. Jessy exchanged looks with Gray Dog, Parnell, and Jackson. They all watched as they were witnessing the first emotions they had ever seen from the legendary cavalry officer. John Henry finally let go and then straightened his tunic as he sheathed his sword.

"Gentlemen, that was played out well. You had me a little concerned at the end, but we managed to bluff our way out of this mess for the moment without starting a shooting war with the Ottoman Empire."

"Yes, but what a moment it was!" Parnell said loudly. "Now that's something to tell the grandchildren about, by God!"

Thomas finally saw Gray Dog as Claire gave him a blanket

to cover his bare skin. The colonel placed a hand on the boy's shoulder and squeezed.

"Your pa would have been proud today. So would the sergeant major."

"I think that was the one element that pushed the Turks over the edge," Jessy said. "This boy"—he grabbed Gray Dog and shook him—"insisted he lead the charge, and by God he did."

"What now, John Henry?" Claire asked as she watched the revelry around her. She smiled as she saw the men of one nation once again.

John Henry Thomas paced away from the men and looked north along the track that would take them to Trabzon Harbor. He removed his hat, wiped the sweat from the band, and then held it at his side as the warmth of the sun hit his face. He finally turned and faced Claire and the others.

"Let's go home."

29

It had been a full week since the *Carpenter* had limped into port. She was still leaking heavily but the carpenters from both ships, including the *Chesapeake*, promised command that she would be good as new when the time came to sail.

The *Carpenter*'s captain watched his crew as they lounged on the deck. He had forbidden any shore leave in the port town simply because he knew the French frigate *Osiris* was berthed only two docks down. He could imagine the French crew lying in wait for the Americans to make an appearance in town.

"Captain, we have a courier from Colonel Thomas," his first officer said as he saw the young marine corporal from Thomas's unit. The boy was worn and tired.

"See the corporal gets a good meal." He tore open the envelope and read. "Wait, how far out is the colonel?"

"The column is a day back, sir. I'm afraid we have company also. The British are a distance away."

"Very well. Dismissed. Get some food and rest."

"What does the colonel say?" the first officer asked.

"He says for us to be prepared to take on ten and half tons

of cargo." The captain turned and looked out to the calm surface of the Black Sea.

"Cargo? What sort of cargo, Captain?" The first officer looked perplexed and then looked at his commanding officer. "You don't suppose—"

"We're going be sailing heavier than normal, it looks like. So, make ready the loading teams and let's get the last of that water out of our bilges. And we still don't know the fate of *Argo*. It's been two weeks and the *Chesapeake* hasn't found her. God, if she foundered we could be in a whole new situation we did not count on. Go on, get the crew moving. We're going to have company."

"Yes, Captain." The first officer moved off to inform the crew.

"Just what in the hell are you bringing to my ship, Colonel Thomas?"

It was late at night when the lone rider abandoned his played-out mount on the outskirts of town. He made his way through the silent village of Trabzon until he could smell the sea. He saw the high masts of several large ships and he was cautious as he made his way to the harbor.

The French spy Renaud had been lost for the last three days and barely made it to Trabzon before the column of Americans. He was exhausted and worn to a frazzle. He spied the American ship before he made it too far. He saw the activity onboard at this late hour and assumed they had been informed of Thomas's expected arrival. He grimaced, cursed the American, and then saw the French-flagged warship berthed close by, but not too close to the American. Now he would see who ran from what field of battle.

He had to convince the French navy that it was now a shooting war.

The next morning dawned cloudy and rainy. The water mixed with the snow and the world became a clogged mess of snow, mud, and rain.

John Henry and his mixed cavalry escorted the wagons

through town and even at that early-morning hour the citizens of the backwater harbor came out to see the Americans. Most eyes fell on the heavily laden wagons as they progressed through the cobbled streets. Thomas was nearly asleep in his saddle when Claire reached out and touched his leg.

"John Henry, we've arrived," she said softly until his eyes fluttered open.

"Apologies; must have dozed off."

"You're exhausted. It's time you get aboard and let Captain Jackson do what he was trained for."

"I will never be happier to relinquish command than I am this fine blustery morning."

The men were greeted by sailors of the *Carpenter*, who were quickly amazed at what they had achieved. They saw wagon after wagon wheeled onto the dock and wondered just what the army colonel had dug out of Ararat's summit.

The captain of the *Carpenter* bolted down the gangway and greeted a slowly dismounting Thomas and Taylor. He saluted Captain Jackson and then he saw how worn the men were and observed the mixed uniforms of the combined command. His face fell when he saw the new Confederate clothing.

"Well, while you were digging away on Ararat, I see Congress authorized the raising of a new cavalry regiment. Not sure they'll approve of the new uniforms, though," he joked, but could see none of the officers were in a very jovial mood.

"Report, Captain?" a weary Jackson said, returning the man's salute.

He filled in Jackson on the developments and saw that the news of *Argo*'s possible loss hit him and Colonel Thomas rather hard. The Rebel officer only shook his head and then looked at Claire with a frown. The news was not good.

"That, and we have not seen a trace of the *Yorktown* since we parted at Constantinople."

Jackson looked at John Henry, who only nodded his head that the captain could inform the commander of *Carpenter* the truth.

"*Yorktown* will not be joining the squadron. She has been assigned other, more pressing duties. She is currently at the emergency egress point on the Mediterranean Sea. Beyond that, I cannot explain further. So, Captain, we are conceivably on our own with just the *Chesapeake* to run interference for us from the Black Sea through the Bosphorus and then the Aegean Sea. Then we have to slip past Gibraltar without getting our tails shot off. Simple, really."

The captain watched the tired men of the combined excavation team slowly dismount to allow the sailors access to the wagons and their precious cargo.

The captain repeated and looked over at the tall main mast of the French warship, *Osiris,* and then shook his head.

"What are you thinking, Captain?" his first officer asked after rousing the crew to offload the wagons.

"I'm thinking I missed that particular lecture at Annapolis on how the described scenario could possibly be construed as simple. Suicidal maybe, but simple?"

The captain turned away and saw the lamps of the French frigate burning brightly as the French crew of the *Osiris* awoke to the Americans making ready for sea.

Claire found John Henry on deck as he leaned against the ship's railing and watched the Black Sea slide along the hull of the heavily loaded *Carpenter.* From time to time she watched Thomas turn his face to the stars looking deep in thought. She pulled her shawl more tightly around herself and was happy for the warmth, and for the fact that she had been able to salvage at least some of her more womanly clothing from the destroyed camp at Ararat. John Henry had forsaken his coat and hat on the blustery night that found the bulk of the crew fast asleep. Only the deck-side watch was on duty, and among the men awake was Gray Dog, who had found a new home in the highest point on the ship—the crow's nest, which by now the lookouts were happy to share after they learned about the Comanche's exploits on the Plain of Ararat.

"After all we have been through, you still can't get any

sleep?" Claire asked before Thomas could turn to see who had approached. John Henry had become very aware of shadows in the night since his days on the mountain's summit.

"Captain Jackson has informed me that if the French make a move it will be in the dark of night. Now I can only relax in the daylight hours."

"Is that all it is?"

"And you're referencing what?" he asked as he looked down upon her slight frame. He could clearly see she had not recouped any of her lost sleep either.

"It's just that I've heard most of the men that spent those dark nights on that damnable mountain are having a hard time sleeping as well. I know Colonel Taylor has been pacing every night until he can no longer stand upright and he collapses. The joy that the men felt after the Turks ran has long since dissipated and now the men have had time to think. And the curse of Azrael is on their minds."

"I can't help them. Each man has to evaluate what he saw up there and face his own demons, Azrael notwithstanding."

"What do you believe?"

"I believe that we made up what we needed to believe. I don't have any idea what it is we ran into up there and on the voyage over. Okay, let's just say it is Azrael. If that's the case, the one thing I am sure of is the fact that whoever placed that curse was trying desperately to save what he loved."

"Noah and his family?"

"No, not just his kinfolk. I believe the love he felt for all humanity dictated that he go against God and his killer angel."

"Why can't you say that to the men?" she asked as she watched his blue eyes against the glow of the moonlight.

"Because I'm sure they will eventually take what happened and either live with it, or find a rational explanation in their own way." He smiled as he looked at Claire closely. "As I have done."

"So, Colonel Thomas, you are now an official believer of fairy tales."

"I guess I am," he said, and they both looked at each other for the longest time. They were interrupted by the officer of the deck.

"Colonel, Captain Jackson would like to know if you'll join him on the quarterdeck."

With one a last look into Claire's eyes, John Henry walked away leaving Claire longing for him to stay.

Thomas found Jackson as he looked through his single-lens glass to the aft seas.

"We have our full complement of onlockers," he said as he handed over the glass to John Henry, who looked where Jackson was pointing.

Barely visible in the moonlight were the silhouettes of not one, but both of the French warships.

"Now, three points to the north," Jackson said as John Henry adjusted his view.

Thomas sighed as he saw the tall masts of two more ships that were frigate-sized. He lowered the glass and returned it to Jackson.

"The newcomers, French?"

"Unable to say at the moment. However, I don't think the Royal Navy would dare meet us in closed seas. They would wait until we make our way past Gibraltar. No, my suspicions are that they are also French."

"What do you think, Captain Jackson?" Thomas asked with a small smile.

"Officer of the deck?"

"Sir!" the first officer called from his station at the helm.

"Beat to general quarters. Let's get the crew to battle stations, shall we?"

"Sir!"

"Gentlemen, signal the *Chesapeake*. We are going on the attack. Let's see if these boys can dodge us for a change. Inform *Chesapeake* we break formation at first light."

The four French warships heard the drumbeats of the two American frigates as they brought crews to battle stations. The French were confused until their own lookouts called out that the Americans were reversing course and headed right for them.

Three hours later the men onboard all six warships were ready and at stations. Captain Jackson had placed Thomas's men high in the rigging of the *Carpenter* in case they were boarded.

"Four against two, now those are odds I can relate to," Jessy said as he joined Thomas on the foredeck.

"We're about to see how serious the Frenchies are about stopping us," John Henry said as Claire joined them. He whispered something to Gray Dog, who nodded and then headed the woman off and roughly lifted her from her feet and, as she protested, moved her belowdecks.

"Chivalrous, I must say," Taylor quipped.

"My ass. The last thing I need is to find out she's also a better shot than me."

Jessy laughed as he saw the French frigates growing larger in his view.

"Tell me again what happens if they don't interpret our ramming them as an accident and they open fire on us?"

"Well, Colonel Taylor, as long as the first cannon shot isn't fired by us, let the war begin. Off official records, of course."

"Oh, but of course," he said with a roll of his eyes. "But tell me, do you think governments will wonder what became of their frontline ships when they don't return home, even old honest Abe?" Jessy asked with a smirk.

"Accidental sinkings happen all the time, I imagine. It will be marked up as acceptable wartime losses for us. As for them, I don't care how they explain it to their citizens, but I imagine the truth may be fudged a little in that particular arena."

"Well, we'll soon see."

As they watched, the *Chesapeake* broke her side-by-side formation with the *Carpenter*. The larger frigate made a run at the lead ship, the *Especial*, the very ship that had rammed them north of Trabzon.

"Go, go," Captain Jackson called out as he watched the

Chesapeake charge forward. Without the heavy cargo weighing her down the sleek warship sped past *Carpenter* and made her run for *Especial*.

Suddenly the forward-facing twin mounts on the *Especial* erupted in smoke and flame as she let loose two twenty-pound shells toward *Chesapeake*. All eyes widened as the intent of the French navy was made abundantly clear.

"Forward mounts, fire!" Jackson called out, trying to give the *Chesapeake* some covering fire. He cursed as he ordered *Carpenter* to turn so she could bring her main starboard guns to bear.

The shells struck the *Chesapeake* as she returned fire from her own forward mount. The forward prow erupted in splintering wood and burning sailcloth as the two warheads blew apart the two forward cannons and their gun crews.

Four exploding shells found the mark against the forward superstructure of the *Especial*.

"I think our bluff has been called," Taylor shouted as he struck the deck as wood and men flew past him as two shells from the *Osiris* hit the *Carpenter*.

Before their turn was made *Carpenter* was struck three times by the advancing French ships. The companions of the *Especial* and *Osiris* had joined their fire with the two damaged ships.

"Damn, I really didn't think they would have the gall," Jackson sang out as he ordered the full complement of the starboard battery to return fire. Just as he did several shells struck the *Carpenter* and one penetrated her deck and slammed into the cargo hold, killing fifteen band members of the 317th.

"Bring her guns to bear on the turn!" Jackson called out just as a tremendous explosion erupted from the forecastle of the *Chesapeake*. "All guns fire at the turn!"

The starboard side of *Carpenter* seemed to blow outward as all twenty-three gun crews opened fire one after the other in rapid succession.

John Henry was helped to his feet by Taylor as the *Carpenter* heeled to port after discharging her starboard battery. Before they knew what was happening they were again thrown from their feet and men fell screaming from the rigging above them. The third and fourth frigates of the French navy fired all forty-four guns on their port sides in as rapid a discharge as anyone had ever witnessed. Captain Jackson fell to the deck as grapeshot shattered the wooden railing and masts around him. Men again started screaming as the steel balls ripped mercilessly through their bodies. Rigging and sail fell to the decks.

The French navy had become serious in their attempts to stop the Americans.

John Henry heard the whistle of flying iron balls as they passed overhead and through the wooden hull of the large frigate. Taylor screamed in frustration as the *Osiris* passed close aboard and let loose with her port batteries.

The main mast of the *Carpenter* was struck and the thick wood splintered but held firm against the onslaught of wind and fire.

A quarter of a mile away the *Chesapeake* was circling aimlessly as her rudder was blown away. The Americans were now fish in a barrel.

The noise was tremendous as the six ships exchanged gunfire. Thus far the combined guns of the *Carpenter* and the *Chesapeake* had only managed to damage *Especial*, but the men came on deck to cheers as the *Especial*'s main mast came crashing down into the sea.

John Henry knew he had led them into disaster by pushing their luck a little too far in his recommendation to turn on their pursuers. The bluff had been called in no uncertain terms by the French.

The passing winds did nothing to clear the thick, acrid smell of gunpowder and burning wood from her decks. John Henry cursed as small hands helped him up. When he looked he saw it was Claire who had somehow shaken free of Gray Dog, who was still trying to physically coax her belowdecks. He was bloody from several large splinters of wood that had pierced his back and arms.

"Get below!" he screamed as more grapeshot tore into the *Carpenter*.

"Most are dead down there. I want to stay here!" she screamed and Gray Dog ceased pulling on her as *Carpenter* was rocked as one of her exposed deck guns exploded from a direct hit from *Osiris*.

As suddenly as the violence had erupted, it all ceased at once. The four French vessels circled the two heavily damaged American frigates. It was if they were viewing a wounded wild animal and were judging its lethality through cautious observation.

"They've stopped," Claire said as she leaned over to assist Jessy to his feet. He looked at John Henry and all of the mirth from days gone by had vanished. For the first time Thomas saw real worry in the Confederate colonel's eyes.

"They have to come in close now," said Jackson as he moved over to the railing with his spyglass to his eye. They could see a man trying to tend to Jackson's exposed wounds. He had been peppered by flying splinters from the helmsman's station. The ship's wheel was half torn away. Jackson ignored the corpsman and the wounds. The captain lowered the glass and blood dripped to the decking at his feet. John Henry saw the deep wounds and knew the captain was running on adrenaline alone. "They have to come close and destroy the evidence that we were ever here. They have to sink all trace of us." Jackson finally acceded to the corpsman who was attempting to remove his shredded coat. "Colonel, get ready to get your men off. These bastards are not going to board my ships!"

"What is your plan?" Thomas asked as he tended to the wounds on Gray Dog's back and arms. Claire was dabbing a dirty piece of cloth to Jessy's forehead, which had taken a flying nail rather handily. Jackson held eye contact with the colonel for the briefest of moments and in that short time Thomas knew exactly what the captain was going to do. "Chief, inform the gun crew captains to spike their cannon. We'll draw the enemy in and then take at least one or two of them with us. Colonel, get your men off my ship."

John Henry shook his head. He was not about to give that order. The navy men under his command did not run under fire, so he would have to be thrown overboard before he ordered his men off.

"If we're staying, I think I want my sword," Taylor said as he smiled and then removed Claire's soft hand from his head. He dipped his chin and kissed her hand. "You, on the other hand, must evacuate the ship my dear, dear lady."

"Yes, lower a whaleboat. Gray Dog, get Miss Anderson off the ship and as many of the wounded from below that you can."

Gray Dog stood his ground and shook his head. He was refusing the first order from his adopted father. He would die with the rest. From Claire's angry face he could see he would have to physically remove her from the battle.

"*Osiris* is signaling, Captain!"

Once more Jackson raised the glass to his eye. Lowered it once more and swiped at the blood that coursed down from the head wound. He again raised the glass and watched the bright flashes of light from the forecastle of the *Osiris*. He lowered the glass and took a deep breath and then he faced John Henry.

"They're ordering us to lower sail and battle flags. They intend to board us."

Jessy was handed his sword by one of his men. He smiled as he rebuttoned his tunic. "Well, we didn't get all fancied up for nothing. John Henry, shall we accept our guests' invitation to board us?"

"Smoke on the horizon!"

The captain felt his heart go cold as he realized that the French must have a steam-driven reinforcement coming to their aid. "This is a tad bit of overkill, I must say," he said as he raised his glass once more. Thomas joined him.

"It's the *Argo*!" came the joyful yell from the lookout. 'She's under her own power!"

Jessy gave the smiling John Henry a funny look. "How can a sail barge full of railroad equipment be steaming to our aid?"

"Well, it's not exactly a sail barge," Thomas answered as he took in the confused faces of Claire, Taylor, and Gray

Dog. "This is our little gift from the president and Mr. John Ericsson."

"Thank God for Lieutenants Ferguson and Faraday!" Jackson said loudly as the first of the French warships turned to meet the new threat that did not seem much of a threat at all.

The slow-moving *Argo* billowed smoke from the center of her decking. The stack had risen in the days she had been absent and presumed sunk.

It came on like an aged locomotive spewing its blackened anger across the blue morning sky.

Renaud joined the captain of the *Osiris* on the quarterdeck of the frigate. He smiled when he saw the two smoldering American vessels in the near distance as the signal for surrender was sent.

"Ship ahoy!" came the call from *Osiris*'s crow's nest.

"Where away?" called the French captain. Renaud turned in a circle to see if the newcomer was a threat. He saw the thin trace of smoke on the horizon and then as he watched the *Argo* came into view.

"It's only the cargo barge, *Argo*. She poses no threat, Captain, I can assure you."

The captain looked from his binoculars to the French spy. "I've seen a lot of barges before, my good man, but I have never seen one under coal power."

"What?" Renaud asked as he took the binoculars from the captain and then sighted the line of smoke and the large barge producing it.

"Now, sir, explain this."

"The barge is in no way a threat. I've seen it. I've also seen her cargo of rail ties, track, and a locomotive."

"Well, it seems she has a brave crew, because they are coming on as if attacking!" The last few words to the spy were yelled by the French captain.

"Starboard batteries, stop that ship!"

"Starboard batteries, open fire, fire as your guns come to bear!"

As the *Especial* and the other two frigates turned toward the approaching threat, the eruption of gunfire shook the *Osiris* as she let fly all twenty-three guns of her starboard gun crews.

John Henry, Taylor, Jackson, Claire, and Gray Dog watched in the distance as twenty-three exploding rounds impacted the sea around *Argo.* They saw the water geyser up and over the slim platform and still the *Argo* kept steaming toward them. Claire saw both Thomas and Jackson saying the same words. "Wait for it, wait for it."

A second burst of rifled cannon flamed their charges toward the approaching *Argo.* This time several warheads detonated on her massive wooden decks. The topmost portion of the barge seemed to go up in flaming wreckage as the crew on *Osiris* cheered loudly.

Claire gasped as she realized that their savior had lasted only moments into the engagement. Jessy felt the heat from the flaming wreckage as it cascaded into the Black Sea.

As they watched, only John Henry and Captain Jackson knew what would emerge from the smoke and flames.

"My God!" Claire yelled as she grabbed Gray Dog by the shoulder and shook the small Comanche.

The *Argo* came free of the churned water and smoke. The black soot still rose from her flaming superstructure but it looked as if the barge were still intact. Her decks were smashed and her crew was nowhere to be seen on the deck that was now awash in flames.

"Why does she keep coming?" Taylor asked just as the four French vessels turned in full force to meet this strange but seemingly inept threat by the Americans. *Argo* maneuvered herself in between the heavily damaged *Carpenter* and the flaming *Chesapeake.* She slowly turned to face the enemy.

"She's doing what she has been designed to do," Jackson said proudly as he watched the smoking ruin of the *Argo* wedge itself between them and a cruel fate. Just as the lead warship, *Osiris,* fired her front gun mount, Jackson jumped

and shook a fist and then just before the shell struck the barge
the young and enthusiastic captain turned and faced Taylor
and Claire. "Finally, Miss Anderson, Colonel Taylor, I give
you the real U.S.S. *Argo!*"

The captain of *Osiris* watched as the strange vessel ignored
her battle damage and still managed to maneuver inside their
blockade of the two American warships. He raised his field
glasses and watched as the large barge swung around and
faced the oncoming threat.

"Foolish people, will they never learn?" he said as he
handed the glasses to Renaud, who was amazed at the American audacity. It was the most shockingly brave act he had
ever seen, but as the captain said, very foolish. "Forward
number one mount, fire!"

Renaud instinctually ducked his head as the twenty-five-
pounder cut loose her shot. They actually saw the abbrevi-
ated arc of the warhead as it traveled the quarter mile to its
intended target—*Argo.*

The warhead detonated on the forecastle of the barge. The
explosion sent debris flying high and the crews of the four
French vessels cheered as if they had just seen a marvelous
sporting event. It was all in good sport, as the Europeans
would say.

They were about to learn it was no longer a European cen-
tury, though.

The captain took the glasses from a very happy Renaud
and scanned the seas ahead, expecting to see the bow of
the *Argo* shot away and possibly sinking. As the smoke cleared
and the seas settled, the crews cheered once more as they saw
the *Argo* was splitting into two distinct pieces. The starboard
side exploded outward and then that was followed by her port
side from the railing to the keel, both halves slowly sliding
away. As the two halves parted and split, the French sailors
were amazed to see the railroad equipment that had been
loaded into *Argo*'s hull start to fall into the Black Sea. Another
cheer erupted as the prized locomotive, the supposed gift to
the sultan of the Ottoman Empire, slowly rolled over and fell

into the sea. Water cascaded into the air as the heavy locomotive, actually a refurbished and very much retired coal burner from Chicago, sent a large wave over the wreckage.

"That was not a well-thought-out tactic by the Americans. I don't see what all the fuss over American ability is about. All we needed was—"

The explosion struck so close to the *Osiris* that the cascading water threw Renaud from his feet just as another explosion rocked the nearby *Especial.* The captain raised his glass once again and saw a sight that froze the blood in his veins. There, driving through the smoke and flames and shedding the last of her camouflaged hull, was the U.S.S. *Argo,* the latest creation of that Swedish madman and engineer, John Ericsson, the man who made the Battle of Hampton Roads the turning point in naval warfare in the recent history of the world. That night when Ericsson's folly, the U.S.S. *Monitor,* battled the Confederate ironclad, *Merrimack,* the navies of the world had instantaneously become obsolete overnight.

The ironclad broke free of her own debris and the captain of *Osiris* gasped at the low-slung, black smoke–spewing Monitor-class warship as she started belching fire from her main battery, the revolving turret housing the fifty-five-pound Columbiad cannon.

The shells started firing in rapid succession as the French captains opened fire on the amazing ship and its hearty crew. The *Argo* started to return fire just as the first of the French shells exploded against her iron decking and turret. The tall smokestack took a direct hit and bent somewhat, but still the *Argo* came on, the American flag waving proudly at her indestructible stern. Everyone could see her as her crew braved the exploding rounds striking the thick armor plate as they cut away the last of the flotation balloons that had kept her afloat during her long and arduous voyage.

The detonations of her armored shells started to smash into the wooden hulls of the French frigates. It didn't matter where they were in line; large pieces of wood, flame, and men arched into the sky from the seemingly invulnerable American warship.

Renaud screamed in anger at the obvious American deception. He stood only to be knocked down again by the explosions sent their way by the *Argo*, which continued to fire round after exploding round into the French squadron.

Acting as a shield, *Argo* fronted the two damaged American frigates and kept the wolves at bay.

A cheer erupted on the decks of the *Chesapeake* and the *Carpenter* so loud that the French sailors could hear the joy of the Americans even over the shelling and the orders for them to turn about.

"We must not run. We have what we want right there!" Renaud shook a shaking finger toward the two disabled ships in front of them.

"Are you mad?" the captain said as he angrily pushed the French spy's hand down. "That is French war shot bouncing harmlessly into the air! We cannot sustain an attack against this . . . this . . . pestilence of the sea!"

The mighty warship started to swing about as did the other three. The *Especial* looked as if she wouldn't last the day and the *Osiris* was listing heavily to port as she made her turn to the east, away from the trap set by the cursed Americans.

"That did it!" Jackson called out as he spied the French retreat. "They're making a run back to Trabzon to lick their wounds!" The crew of *Carpenter* erupted again as most stopped for the briefest of moments of battling her flaming decks and rigging to witness the most inglorious end to French dominance in the Black Sea.

John Henry watched as the gift from President Lincoln sat between them and the retreating squadron of heavily damaged warships. Jackson joined Thomas and a stunned-to-silence Taylor and a mortified Claire. Gray Dog could only smile at the audaciousness of the plan. Thomas nodded at Jackson, the wunderkind of the U.S. Navy and a favorite of John Ericsson, the inventor of the new ironclad warship, the U.S.S. *Argo*.

"Signal *Argo*, and say to Captains Ferguson and Faraday, well done indeed," Jackson said proudly.

The flashes of light from the now-visible crew on the top deck of the ironclad answered *Carpenter*'s praise.

"Captain Ferguson signals, sorry he was late; had a little problem asking directions from the locals. The Russians found them adrift and were most helpful in towing them here."

John Henry and Jackson laughed. Claire and Taylor on the other hand did not.

"Ah, you can always count on our friend the czar. He likes no one. He interfered just enough to embarrass the French and English!" Jackson said as he replaced the hat upon his head and then straightened his filthy tunic.

"When were you going to let us in on the big ruse?" Taylor asked as his brows and hackles rose.

"I figured the great Confederate tactician would have figured it out," John Henry said as he also turned to Claire. "And as for the master spy of Mr. Pinkerton, are you saying all of this construction and deception took place right under your nose? Imagine that!"

"Can you imagine my thoughts at this very moment, Colonel Thomas?" Claire said as she nonchalantly brushed grime from her dress.

"About the same as mine," Taylor said as he watched the two smug men before them.

"Captain, the *Argo* is flashing," said the wounded first officer standing at the damaged helm. "She's asking if we need a tow into Constantinople."

"Signal Captain Ferguson, not at this time. We will sail with full colors into the capital."

"The capital?" Claire asked, astounded at the bold statement. "With every Turkish officer in the country looking for us, you wish to go to the capital? Have you lost your minds?"

Thomas and Jackson exchanged looks and then looked back to Claire and Taylor.

"Yes," they both said simultaneously.

30

CONSTANTINOPLE, CAPITAL OF THE
OTTOMAN EMPIRE

As the three American warships tied up at the docks on the western side of the strait, the British battle cruiser *Westfield* sat anchored in the middle of the Bosphorus. All eyes were on the long procession of carriages as the Americans were greeted. They watched as the sultan himself was escorted to the dock as John Henry, Captain Jackson, and Colonel Taylor walked calmly down the boarding ramp to greet the sultan. Captains Ferguson and Faraday came over from the ironclad, *Argo*, to meet the three men face-to-face for the first time. Hearty handshakes and slaps on the back were made as the sultan was cheered heavily by the capital's faithful. He raised a hand in greeting to his subjects as he confronted the four Americans. Claire and Gray Dog watched with the rest of the three crews who lined the railings of all three ships.

It was Claire who noticed the crew of the *Argo* was leaving the ironclad with their seabags slung over their shoulders, saluting the naval ensign at the stern of *Argo* as they stepped onto the dock. Her brows rose as she thought about what was really taking place below on the dock.

The sultan greeted Thomas with a bear hug just as John Henry bent low at the waist in greeting the monarch. The burly man in his splendid green uniform with the bright red fez reached for Thomas and hugged him like a large bear.

"It was reported to me that you faced serious threats to our planned activities upon the mountain. Is this true?"

"We encountered"—John Henry looked at Jessy and a ramrod-straight Ferguson and Jackson—"some resistance from not very imaginative officials of your government, sir."

"Yes," the sultan laughed heartily. "The idiots only think of me as the jovial fool that sits upon the throne of all Islam, but we know the truth, do we not, Colonel Thomas?"

"Yes, sir, we do."

"Good." He gestured to the rear of his procession and snapped his fingers. A man was led forward in chains. It was the commanding general of the Seventh Guards Regiment who was looking none too pleased with his current situation. "Because several of my trusted advisors seem to have been listening to the rumors of my early abdication." He turned and faced the rotund general and then used his manicured fingers to send him away to a fate awaiting him that John Henry wished upon no man.

"So, have you gentlemen retrieved what it was you came for?" the sultan asked, exposing his gold-capped front teeth.

"Yes, sir, we have our samples and will be returning them to the States with thanks from our nation." He looked at Jessy and smirked. "The entire nation."

"Very well, I guess that concludes our business."

A shocked Jessy leaned into Captain Jackson and whispered, "But we didn't deliver the railroad as promised. The sultan seems to be taking this rather nonchalantly."

Jackson smiled and then nodded his head in the direction of the dock behind him. Men with green uniforms were marching up the gangway of the *Argo*. They took up guard stations around and upon the American ironclad.

"The railroad was never the gift promised to the sultan, but *Argo* was." Jackson looked sad and forlorn as he placed a hand on the shoulder of Lieutenant Ferguson and his subordinate, Lieutenant Faraday, feeling for the men as they were currently losing their first command. "The sultan of the Ottoman Empire now has the single most powerful navy in the Black Sea region. The *Argo* is now his."

The sultan laughed as he dipped his head to the Americans. "Please inform your President Lincoln, the Ottoman Empire's fondest wish is for American prosperity at such a difficult time."

"We will, Your Majesty," John Henry said and then all four officers came to attention as the sultan turned and waved at his citizens and they cheered him as he made his way to his newest, and proudest warship—U.S.S. *Argo*.

The officers watched the sultan leave and then Jackson turned to the crew that lined the decks of *Chesapeake* and *Carpenter*. "Three cheers for the sultan!"

"Hip, hip, hooray," sounded three times from the American vessels as the 317th marching band erupted spontaneously in a rousing chorus of "Yankee Doodle," even enticing the Rebel contingent, what was left of them, to sing along. The sultan continued to wave at the crowds as he boarded his new ironclad.

"Before you say anything, I must remind you, Colonel Taylor, that you never in your life could keep a secret," John Henry said as he headed off the anger of the Confederate colonel.

"Who was I going to tell? The fish on the way over here?" he argued.

"For all I know you were going to desert me and take your men with you. Then where would I be with my secrets out in the open, huh?"

"I gave you my word, John Henry!" Jessy argued as he followed close behind Thomas.

"Your word? Please!"

Claire watched them leave as the crews of the two frigates began the tedious repairs needed for their voyage home. She wondered if John Henry's distrust still included her. Claire smiled as she extended her purple parasol and spun it lazily and then she slowly fell in line as the officers argued onto the gangway. *Maybe, maybe not*, she thought, but she had plenty of time to work on that trust. She hummed "Yankee Doodle" as she strolled onto the deck of the *Carpenter*.

"You trust Gray Dog!"

"Gray Dog doesn't go around drinking and bragging about his exploits as you do, Colonel."

"I have never bragged about anything that didn't deserve to be bragged about, Colonel Yankee, sir!"

Claire continued to hum as she thought about the way the argument would continue all the way home. That was when she knew her future.

"Yes, I have plenty of time to work on Colonel John Henry Thomas."

WASHINGTON D.C.,
APRIL 14, 1865

Private Willard, resplendent in his recently bought suit, made his way down a crowded Pennsylvania Avenue. The men and women he passed seemed jovial and ignored the shy boy from the south. The private held a satchel tight to his chest as he made his way past the gate of the White House. He presented the guards there with the sealed envelope and the satchel sent from Colonel Thomas. The guards eyed the boy and then told him to wait while they delivered the letter and package to the president.

Willard cautiously looked around him. His eyes fell on the fluttering American flags draping the windows of the White House. Before the guard could return to escort him in to see the president, an overwhelming sense of loss filled the boy's mind. The three-month journey home had aged the nineteen-year-old by at least five years. He once more looked at the flags and then sadly turned away, wanting nothing more than to return home to a father who waited for him and the horses he so loved. He sadly turned away and went into an unknown future.

When the guard returned he faced his fellow soldier. "Where did he go?"

"Your guess is as good as mine."

The first guard shrugged and then took up station at the family entrance to the White House.

President Lincoln sat at his large desk. Secretary of State Seward smoked his cigar and then faced his longtime adversary and friend. He flicked his long cigar ash into the cold fireplace.

"All I am saying is that those . . . those things should be thrown into the sea," Seward said as he stared at Lincoln.

"And would you have me do the same when Colonel Thomas arrives? Throw his hard-won prize into the sea?"

"Things have changed since Colonel Thomas and his men left Baltimore and you know it. The war is over. We won. We now have all the time in the world to gain the trust and respect of the southern states. We need not announce to the world what it is that our arrogance has wrought."

"That is not the problem you foresee, old friend. What is it?"

"This thing could backfire into our faces. If the public had an inkling of what we exposed the nation to on the high seas and at Ararat, the gains we have made since Appomattox would be moot. Trust would be lost when they learn we exposed them to a possible shooting war with the two most powerful nations in Europe." Seward lowered his head and once more faced the cold fireplace.

"There's something else bothering you, Mr. Secretary. Tell me what it is," Lincoln said as he unclasped the satchel containing Ollafson's original artifacts—the cursed petrified wood of the Ark. He saw the wrapped cloth and slowly opened it. "The *Carpenter* and her crew will arrive any day now. I'm sure they wish this ordeal over also. Being interned at Gibraltar by the British had to try their patience. Now tell me, after so long at sea what do my intrepid explorers and discoverers of myth and legend have to fear?"

"I have received word from a reliable source that a United States marshal will be awaiting the *Carpenter*'s arrival. He plans to arrest Colonel Taylor for murder. The warrant was sworn out while the *Carpenter* was interned for the months of February and March on the bogus plague rumor spread by Her Majesty's government. But the warrant is very real, Mr. President."

"Murder, you say?" the president asked.

"Yes, it seems the gentleman bringing the charges is the same disgraced commandant at Lafayette prison that our intrepid Colonel Thomas had arrested. The former officer is highly placed in the abolitionist movement and it seems his father is well connected to both parties."

The president shook his head slowly as his fingers ran along the cloth that covered the artifacts. "That will not happen, Mr. Seward. Am I clear on this point?" The blaze in the president's eyes was unmistakable. He was angry.

"Yes, Mr. President, but that, sir, is my concern. The bastard will obviously bring Colonel Taylor kicking and screaming into the forefront right when we don't need it. I mean, who could ever blame the colonel for mounting a defense against murder? The parameters of your mission to Turkey will come full circle and be out in the open. What then?"

"I see your point, Mr. Secretary. I'm sure we can manage to whisk away our Confederate accomplice before the evil abolitionists make their arrest. See to it."

Lincoln held Seward's stare. They both missed the shadow as it slipped from the cloth wrapping and slid off the large desk and then vanished into the wall of the president's office.

"I'll do my best," Seward said as he reached for his hat and coat and slipped them on. A light knock sounded at the door and Seward pulled it open. It was the president's personal secretary, John Hay.

"Sir, the First Lady is waiting in the carriage. And she stresses beyond reason that you will be late if you don't hurry."

"On that note, I'm off to save the world, at least a certain Confederate colonel's world." Seward tipped his top hat toward the president, who only smiled that soft smile of his as the secretary of state left the office.

"What was that, John?" the president asked as his fingers

undid the twine and then he ran his long fingers over the engraved Angelic symbols. He shivered.

"Mrs. Lincoln, the theater?"

"Oh, Nelly, just about incurred the wrath of the real boss, didn't I?" the president said as he placed the cloth back over the relics and then placed them inside his desk. He smiled and then accepted Hay's help in getting into his coat.

"And what horrible miscarriage of theater are we witnessing this evening?" he asked.

"*Our American Cousin*, a comedy, I believe."

The president buttoned his coat and then smiled at John Hay.

"Well, I guess I'd better skedaddle out of here," he said as he placed a fatherly hand on his secretary's shoulder. "You keep your ear to the pavement, John. You get me out of that theater if Colonel Thomas sends word that he's arrived while I'm at the play, clear?"

"Immediately, Mr. President."

John Hay watched as the tall, lean president walked toward the doorway. He thought he saw something strange as the president ducked his head to exit. It looked like his shadow, but it was not opposite the lamps in the office.

"Curious," he said, and then shrugged it off.

The president of the United States would never meet his old friend again and see his wonderful prize. He had a date with the man known as John Wilkes Booth, who for the past five months had been plagued by dreams of dark shadows coming at him in the dark. The nightmares had nearly driven the actor insane.

BALTIMORE HARBOR
APRIL 17, 1865

The harbor was eerily silent as the *Carpenter* slid in on the night's tide. It was an hour later that her tired crew tied up at the U.S. Navy berth at pier sixteen. The sailors were silent as they went about securing the ragged bulk of the damaged warship. The men kept looking around at the emptiness of the pier. The only sound was the soft whisper of the water as it lapped against the tired old hull.

A knock sounded on the door and Jessy stepped into the captain's cabin, once more occupied by John Henry. The colonel looked from Taylor to Claire, who slipped easily into her shawl. She smiled at Taylor as she moved by him to the companionway. She stopped and faced Jessy. She held out her small hand.

"Colonel, I did not know if I would ever have the opportunity of saying this since the first moment we met, especially after barely overcoming your brashness and your true southern charm, but despite first impressions, it has truly been an honor," she said as she looked straight into his dark eyes.

Taylor, dressed as a civilian once more, twisted his hat in his hand and then took Claire's into his own and instead of shaking it he bent over and once more kissed it.

"The honor, Madame, has been this officer's, I assure you."

Claire gave him a small curtsy and then left the two men alone.

John Henry took the colonel in. He looked forlorn without his proud gray tunic. Now Jessy looked like an ordinary man. They had not spoken much, and for that matter the entire contingent of remaining Rebel soldiers, all twenty-eight of them, had remained to themselves after showing such camaraderie with the rest of the Union marines and sailors after the damnable British had gotten word to them while they were quarantined at Gibraltar that General Lee had surrendered to Ulysses Grant that very day in Virginia.

The shock had been hard on the men. While the Union men silently celebrated the end to the bloody affair, the Confederate prisoners became silent and reflective. As for Taylor he withdrew with the question every soldier had to answer for himself—what was it all for?

"What now, Jessy?" John Henry asked as he buttoned his tunic.

Taylor entered the cabin and then walked to the large windows at the stern and saw the calm waters of the harbor. Thomas watched him.

"Mary's death wasn't your fault, John Henry," Jessy said without turning to face him. "But I needed to blame you. I had to make sense out of things and I did blame you for allowing my sister to talk you into her joining you in Texas. I can't blame two people for loving each other. But when we lost her, I couldn't see the truth of things, even though I tried. Every time I thought of her, I saw you, my best friend. Love turned to hate so fast"—he turned and faced John Henry—"so hard, that I saw you differently. I resented the fact that you lived and she died. You see, we're expected to take the risks, fight the good fight, but never are we prepared to lose those who are innocent of that life."

Thomas pulled at the hem of his coat and then cleared his throat. "You heading west?"

Jessy smiled and John Henry saw his old friend for the first time in years.

"I was always more comfortable west of the Mississippi. You know that." Taylor placed his boot on a chair and then looked at his brother-in-law. "What about you? Going to let Uncle Abe talk you into staying?"

"I think I've given about all I can to my country. Time to take a shot at living."

"And I thought you still wanted to be King of the Army," Taylor said as he straightened and walked toward Thomas.

"Being king isn't all it's cracked up to be. Look at the sultan."

Both men laughed as they shook hands.

Gray Dog, resplendent in a brand-new purple shirt and his ever-present coyote-head hat, poked his head through the open doorway.

"Fat men with cigars are here."

"I see Gray Dog's power of description is getting better," Taylor said as he gestured for John Henry to precede him out of the cabin.

* * *

Captain Jackson met the three men at the top of the companionway. He smiled and for the first time in recorded history Jackson seemed pleased with life.

"There's been some snafu. The navy has no assigned men to offload the cargo, so it will have to stay aboard until tomorrow."

"Then what for the navy?" Jessy asked the young officer he had come to respect.

"I think I'm going to accept the research-and-development position open with Mr. Ericsson."

"Leave the navy?" Thomas asked, astounded that the career officer would even consider resigning his commission.

"There is a new science rising from the depths of the sea, gentlemen, called submarines, and I want in."

"What in the hell is that?" Jessy asked.

"Why it's the most exciting thing to come along in—"

"What it is, is beyond us," John Henry said, cutting off Jackson's enthusiastic answer.

The men were all on deck as the three officers and Gray Dog came up from below. The men all stood on the main deck and looked up at the men who had gotten them home. Many had been lost, but these men, from both sides of the war, had become used to the empty chair at the table when a comrade had fallen. This time there were quite a few empty chairs, but for the men who made it back that spring day in April, the smells of home were enough.

As one the men—all sailors, 317th band members, marines, and all civilian-dressed Confederate prisoners—stood to attention and then as one saluted the three men.

John Henry was the first to react. He did not return the salute, which shocked both Jessy and Jackson. Even Gray Dog raised a brow at the possible snub in courtesy. Claire came up, aware of what was happening.

"Gentlemen, lower your hands, please."

The men didn't know what to do at first as hands started

down, then went back into salute, but then they all slowly lowered their right hands as they watched the army colonel.

"It is not we who deserve the respect you give us, but it is we who owe you everything. We had the honor of commanding the bravest men in any army in the world. It doesn't matter how we started out, it is where we ended up—as friends and men we respect. Gentlemen, it has been our great honor."

The men watched as Jackson and Taylor stepped up beside John Henry and all three saluted the men down below.

The men all saluted and then watched as John Henry, Jackson, Claire, and Jessy made for the gangway to greet the fat men with cigars.

The three men and one lady waited for the five men to transit from an ornate carriage to the long dock. Gray Dog had left, and where he was John Henry could not say.

The men stepped from shadow into light and the three officers froze and Claire actually gasped.

These weren't representatives of the president. Three of the men had large stars pinned to their lapels and were carrying papers. The other three wore refined suits and flashed signs of wealth the men noticed immediately. It was the man in the middle who had their attention. He was no longer in uniform and looked quite smug.

"Colonel Jessop Taylor?" the large man in front asked. He had a large handlebar moustache and was armed, as his open coat clearly demonstrated.

"What is the meaning of this?" John Henry asked, cursing himself for not putting his holster onto his belt. All he had was his worthless sword. He looked at Jackson and he was in the same state of unreadiness.

"This is a signed warrant for the arrest of Colonel Jessup Taylor, prisoner number 59503476, Camp Lafayette. Charges are murder while attempting escape from federal custody."

"This is ridiculous," Jackson said as he reached for the warrant quickly enough that the two deputies beside the marshal drew their revolvers. The captain immediately shot a look of hatred at the men. John Henry lowered the captain's hand and eased him back.

"I'm Colonel Taylor," Jessy said as he stepped forward.

"Did you think I would brush this under the rug? Did you think I would allow a backwoods Rebel officer to ruin my military career without doing something about it? I told you that day I would get to you, Colonel, and now I have."

Taylor didn't flinch as he took in the small-framed man he had so embarrassed. The former major, Nelson Freeman, stood between two of his father's expensive attorneys and smirked.

"We'll see what the president has to say to your federal warrant."

Nelson Freeman honestly looked taken aback. He looked from his companions to the lone woman in the group, Claire. He wondered what her story was in all of this.

"You don't know, do you?" Freeman asked as he placed his hands on his hips as if he were lecturing.

"Know what?" Claire asked anxiously, not liking the smug look on the former prisoner-of-war-camp commandant.

"President Lincoln. He was assassinated three days ago in Washington."

Taylor reached out and steadied John Henry as the news sank into the deepest part of his soul.

"Oh, my God," Claire said as she brought her hands up to cover her mouth.

The federal marshal stepped forward and turned Jessy around and placed manacles on his wrists. He turned him around to face his accuser. Angered shouts rose from the deck of the *Carpenter* as the men watched one of their own being detained. Several curses were flung onto the dock.

"My lawyers have done some investigating of our own. It seems we may have uncovered a web of illegal activity. There will be a warrant issued in the morning, confiscating your cargo. Yes, we know all about the Ollafson expedition and know what it was you were after. Your cargo will be public knowledge by tomorrow, along with a full accounting of certain indiscretions when it comes to war department funds being funneled illegally through the Department of the Navy. Yes, I'm afraid there's to be an accounting, gentlemen. And the proof we need to scar the president and hang you is currently in your hold. Your friends in office will run for cover on this one. I mean, with a new administration and all, what's a few worthless old soldiers?"

The second deputy stepped forward and presented a large sealed paper.

"Captain Jackson?"

Jackson didn't respond; he only looked at the pistol the deputy never holstered. The man simply held out the paper.

"This is to inform you of your cargo's confiscation. It is to be locked up until federal marshals arrive to secure it."

Jackson finally accepted the warrant.

Suddenly several men jumped onto the dock from the rigging. They all had rifles. John Henry quickly noted that it wasn't only Rebel soldiers, but U.S. Marines in full uniform confronting the marshals.

"We expected something like this. Brothers in arms and all of that," Freeman said just as a hundred federal officers swarmed the dock from a warehouse nearby.

John Henry, recovering too slowly from the shock at hearing of his friend's murder, waved the men to lower their weapons. He returned his gaze not to the officers, but to Freeman and held it there. The man smiled, felt it fail, and then smiled again, this time giving up on it. The stare from the colonel had totally unnerved him.

The marshal started walking Jessy down the dock toward the waiting carriage. It was John Henry who made the first move, just as a hundred crewmen and soldiers on the deck of *Carpenter* sprang into action by raising a hundred Henry rifles over the gunwale of the ship. Their aim was at the hundred deputized men of the marshal's service.

"This is madness," one of the high-priced attorneys said loudly as his hands flew into the air.

"As our own history says, sir, if there is to be war, let it begin here," John Henry said to the U.S. marshals with a glint in his eye. Even Claire had her small Derringer out and at her side.

"You will not dodge this, Colonel," Freeman said as he took a menacing step forward.

He jumped back in terror when an arrow struck the wooden dock only inches from his polished shoes.

John Henry didn't have to look up to know that Gray Dog was above them in the rigging.

"Everyone, at ease and lower those weapons!" came a booming voice from the shadows.

Every man froze but no one lowered anything. The stand-off was real and no one was about to back away from this.

"I said lower those weapons!"

Freeman smirked. "I would do as they say, Colonel, or you'll be responsible for more of your command's deaths."

"The marshals' also. Lower them damn weapons or suffer the wrath of the Lord!"

Freeman's eyes widened as he turned and saw United States Army soldiers break from the very same warehouse his men had come from.

As they watched, a large, rotund man emerged. His cigar was glowing and he wore a giant bowler hat. The three-piece suit was rumpled, but expensive.

"Do you want to force me to kill every one of you sons of bitches?"

John Henry looked to his men aboard ship and on the docks. He nodded and they all followed orders.

Claire smiled as she recognized the heavyset man. He looked at her and quickly shook his head for her to stay in place.

"I have a signed warrant for the release of this man."

"We also have a warrant," the marshal said as he finally holstered his weapon.

"That right?" the man said as he clamped down hard on his cigar. "Well, my warrant is signed by the chief justice of the United States Supreme Court," the man said as he leaned in to look at the warrant in the marshal's hand. "You have a signature like that?" He saw the marshal's face drop. "Yeah, I thought not." He reached out and took Colonel Taylor by the arm and pulled him back. He reached into his pocket and brought out a duplicate key and unlocked the manacles.

Jessy rubbed his wrists and then as he approached John Henry he pursed his lips and raised his dark brows as if saying, *That was too close.*

"Now, gentlemen, run along. I'll take it from here."

"This cannot be legal!" Freeman cried as his hatred flowed through his eyes as he watched Taylor walk free. The man was pulled away by the marshals as they and their men backed away in the direction they had come. The crazed eyes of a very insane Freeman never left Jessy's face as the colonel blew the abolitionist a kiss, which infuriated the man even further as he struggled to shake free of the hands that held him.

"Uncle Allan, I didn't think you cared!" Claire said as she ran to the large man and swung her arms around his neck while still holding the Derringer pistol, forcing all the officers to duck as the man swung his niece in a circle.

"Uncle Allan?" Jessy said as John Henry realized just who this man was.

"He's your uncle?" Thomas asked when the man set her down.

The man sniffed and then tossed his cigar into the stagnant waters of the harbor. He held out his bear-claw hand.

"Allan Pinkerton," he said as John Henry shook his hand.

"What happened to Mr. Lincoln?" he asked, not caring about anything else until he learned the truth. and all that entered his mind was the fact that he had forwarded the artifacts to the White House, and possibly the curse of Noah along with it.

Pinkerton released the colonel's hand and then removed his hat as he explained.

"Yes, I understand from certain circles that you and the president were extremely close. I'm sorry I wasn't there to prevent that madman from shooting him."

"What madman?" Jackson asked.

"Name was John Wilkes Booth. He murdered the president while he watched a play at Ford's Theatre, against my advice, I may add." Pinkerton saw that the men before him weren't asking to place blame. They actually needed to know about the man who had sent them to a world of mystery and death. "Troops cornered the coward in a barn not far from here, killed him."

"So what does that mean for us?" Claire asked.

Pinkerton shook his head. "Well, that's the real wrench in the old cog, isn't it?"

"What do you mean?" Jackson asked.

"What Mr. Pinkerton means, gentlemen, and lady, is that you cannot exist. Your cargo cannot exist; therefore, you must vanish."

They all turned and saw an aged, drawn face they immediately recognized as Secretary of State William Seward. The man was literally being held up by three burly men. The secretary stepped into the light to show the returning officers the results of the night the president was murdered. The cuts were evident on his facial features. The hands were covered in cotton gloves and it looked as if the secretary had risen from his deathbed to meet them. John Henry and Jackson walked forward and assisted in getting the secretary to a piling, where he gratefully sat down. The blanket was pulled tight around his gaunt frame.

"I told him he shouldn't come, but he insisted," Pinkerton said as he reached into his pocket and retrieved a small bottle of laudanum. Claire recognized the strong painkiller the moment she saw it. "The same bastards that conspired to kill the president also targeted Mr. Seward and Vice President Johnson." He held the bottle to the secretary's lips and he swallowed the pain-killing dose. "They took a knife to the secretary and his wife."

"Has the world gone totally mad?" Claire asked.

Seward waved everyone to silence. He gestured to Allan Pinkerton and waved for a package. The spy removed a large envelope from his coat and then passed it to Jessy Taylor.

"What is this?" he asked, expecting more bad news.

"A new start. Since you are now wanted for murder, and since we cannot very well allow you to take the witness stand to defend yourself, we are therefore creating a new you, Colonel." Pinkerton slapped the envelope. "Use it well."

Jessy looked at John Henry, who nodded that it was his only option.

"What of my men?" he asked.

"Their discharge papers are awaiting them. Back pay based on our Union scale for each man below the rank of sergeant will be allotted—the sum of fifty-six dollars and forty-two cents."

"So, that's the going rate for what we did?" John Henry asked angrily.

"Yes, that and the fact you completed the mission as ordered should serve you well when it comes to the question, " 'What did you do in the great uprising of 1861, Granddad?' "

The angry eyes turned to Pinkerton, who didn't make any excuses for his harsh words. Thomas knew he had a point. Why would he expect any consideration from people who just didn't care?

Seward coughed. "I was never in favor of this stunt, but you men . . . actually pulled it off. Now I'm sorry to say the Ark and all of its records must be destroyed."

"What?"

"Why?"

The questions were venomous as they were spoken.

"Since we lost Mr. Lincoln, we lost all credibility on what is right and what is wrong. The order of the day is punishment." He coughed again and then pushed one of the large men's hands away as he continued. "If it now became public knowledge, we would lose the legacy of the man who led us through this disaster, and as his friend, I cannot allow that." He looked directly at John Henry. "As I'm sure you will agree. History is never fact until it's written down."

"Captain Jackson, your last set of orders, sir," Pinkerton said as he sadly handed over a thin sheet of paper. "From Secretary of the Navy Welles."

Jackson read the order and then he exhaled as he found he couldn't catch his breath.

"Accident?" he asked, directing his question at the sickly Seward.

"Yes, you are to set the *Carpenter* adrift and she will succumb to an onboard explosion of her powder magazine. The accident will remain a mystery. Is that clear?" Seward asked with his gray eyes boring in on the young naval officer. "The portion of the Ark you have gallantly returned to our shores is to be sent to the bottom of Chesapeake Bay."

The three men gathered Secretary Seward into their arms and lifted him free of the dock. He paused and turned to face the men he had hurt beyond measure.

"I am truly sorry. Colonel, your reputation will be tarnished. You will be held responsible for the damage to two American warships and thus far, the disappearance of another, the *Yorktown*. That we cannot cover up, sir. I'm sorry. That little weasel Freeman will see to it you are embroiled in controversy the rest of your life. And we couldn't very well kill off the entire abolitionist front, now could we?"

Pinkerton leaned over and kissed his niece on the cheek and then faced a stunned John Henry. He slapped a large envelope into Jessy's hands.

"There are two complete sets of identification papers inside. Use them, Colonel. You owe the nation nothing."

The three officers and Claire watched the men vanish into the darkness along with their futures.

The *New York Herald* reported the bizarre accident that happened inside the Chesapeake Bay area of Baltimore. It seemed an old and damaged warship, the *Carpenter*, exploded with no hands aboard killed. It was said by the Navy Department that an unsecured storage locker and an unattended lamp were the cause. The ship and its cargo of newly designed uniforms gifted to the United States Army from the sultan of the Ottoman Empire sank in deep water and recovery of the cargo was ruled out. When asked to comment on the accident, Secretary of the Navy Gideon Welles was quoted as saying, "They were godawful uniforms anyway." Congress was not so quick to laugh.

NEW YORK CITY
APRIL 30, 1865

The rowboat eased out into the harbor. At the oars was a large man with black hair and a recently purchased suit. The man pulled as he looked at the woman and the two men sitting against the transom of the boat as they easily made their way through the fog. One of the men was dressed as always in his bright, stiff naval uniform, the other in a new suit like himself.

Bertram T. Bartles eased up the oars when he heard the soft chime of the ship's bell.

"I hope you didn't take us to the wrong ship, Bertram?"

Jessy looked at John Henry and made a sour face.

"I want to meet the man who came up with that alias, let me tell you. At least you have a name that people won't laugh at behind your back."

"Yes, I do like his new name," Claire said as she placed her arm through the stiff-looking former colonel's.

"Okay Mr.—"

"Don't say it until I get used to the name," John Henry said as they came through the dense fog and rounded the stern of a large ship. Claire looked up and smiled.

Rising above them, the fog had parted to show the name emblazoned across the stern—U.S.S. *Yorktown*.

Jessy laid to near the gangway and they were met by an officer who assisted the four aboard. As they stepped upon the deck they hadn't seen since they'd parted ways in Constantinople, they saw the activity aboard as men went from station to station silently performing their last duties aboard *Yorktown*. The first face Jessy saw once on the main deck was Gray Dog, who had been hidden since the night in Baltimore when they tragically lost the *Carpenter*.

They were greeted by none other than Lieutenant Ferguson, the man who had saved them in the unreported and highly secretive Battle of the Black Sea, as the men had dubbed it. He saluted Jackson as he was the only man in uniform.

"Report?" Jackson said as he returned the salute.

"We're off-loading the last of the crates now."

John Henry, Jessy, and Claire, with a Comanche Indian at their side, watched the last of the crates being raised above the ship's railing toward the open water.

"The Ark was sent to rendezvous with the *Yorktown* in the Mediterranean along with the wagons you sent south, the long route, you sneaky bastard. We had nothing but rocks the whole time," Taylor said as he watched the last of the giant crates as it teetered on the end of the long cables of the crane that held it in place. "You really didn't trust me, did you?"

John Henry smiled. "Not on your life. Besides, it wasn't my fault you failed to notice what was going on which wagon."

"I say again: sneaky bastard."

All eyes watched as the last of the crates containing Noah's magnificent vessel eased into the waters of New York Harbor where they would remain forever.

"Think we'll regret depriving the world of this knowledge?" Claire asked.

"Why, so more people can kill each other over their religious beliefs instead of riches?" John Henry faced Claire and held her eyes. "They really don't deserve to know the truth, because we haven't changed all that much, nor was the lesson of what happened more than thirteen thousand years ago ever learned. No, the world doesn't deserve to know."

"Only those we left on that godforsaken mountaintop," Jessy said as he watched the top of the crate vanish beneath the soft swell of the harbor. He decided at that moment the misery of the past few months needed to be laid to rest.

"That, as they say, is that," Captain Jackson said. "I feel pretty splendid after our little act of treason. How about you folks? Mr. Bertram T. Bartles?"

"Very funny . . . Steven," Jessy said, but smiled anyway.

"You know, there is a rumor going around about an agency tasked to go after antiquities, like the Ark," Jackson said.

"I'm sure. Besides curses, what in the hell could we ever learn from the past?"

They all looked at Jessy and thought he was right. A government department such as that could never work.

"Could you imagine the headaches involved?" Claire said.

"It would take some extraordinary men to run something like that, and I believe we may not have the patience for it. So, if an agency ever does appear that travels the world looking for history, count me out," Jessy said as he turned away to return to the small rowboat. He turned and faced John Henry.

"Colonel?" Thomas said as he placed his arm around Claire. This elicited another rise of the brows of Gray Dog, who took a step back from the white woman.

"We really did rattle the gates of heaven, though, didn't we?"

Jackson, Ferguson, and John Henry exchanged looks and then Thomas's eyes and smile settled back on his old friend.

"That we did, Mr. Bartles. We surely did."

EPILOGUE

A FAMILY AFFAIR

The gods want their entertainment.

—Zeus, King of All the Gods

31

Major Jack Collins lowered the journal and placed it on the chair next to him. He stood and paced to the vault's prized exhibit—the Ark. He examined the damaged bow of the colossal ship and then made his way up the stairs of the permanent scaffolding to the top and looked down upon the reconstructed ship. The crisscross cracks that permeated the wreck had been meticulously rebuilt and aligned as they'd been before the sabotage of the British spy, Captain McDonald, more than a hundred and fifty years ago.

He walked along the theater-style seating as he looked at the large Ark, actually seeing it for the first time. He had seen it before on his initial tour but now he looked more closely at the object that had cost many men their lives. Jack didn't think about the curse mentioned in the colonel's journal, but he realized that if Thomas had actually penned it in the journal, it must have been very real to the men on that voyage.

Jack heard someone coming up the stairs and he turned to see Niles Compton. He was holding the journal Jack had left below. Niles was silent as he joined Collins by the railing.

He leaned upon it and stared down into the cavity of the greatest archeological find in history.

"Who raised the Ark from the harbor?" Jack asked as he saw the living quarters of the family of Noah and thought about Colonel Thomas, Claire, Jessy, Captain Jackson, and Gray Dog, as they sat inside many, many years ago.

"Ah, 1961, a brash ex-senator from Maine decided to close the original Event File 00001."

"The Ark?"

"Yes, the Ark. Senator Garrison Lee brought her up and she found her way home to the desert."

"No curses?" Jack asked, wondering what kind of answer he would receive, and if he received one at all, just how polished it would be since Niles was trying to convince him to stay.

Compton smiled. "No, no curses. But that doesn't mean that there was not one." Niles faced Jack and then removed his glasses and started cleaning them with a handkerchief. "Major, we have run into some very difficult situations where we have to throw out all of the known sciences and natural phenomena and have to settle into a gray area. For instance, other than those"—he pointed down to a small display case that held the original petrified wood pieces with the Angelic symbols emblazoned upon them—"we have no absolute proof this is the Ark that Noah built. Although we have his name inscribed, along with the symbol for Azrael, the angel of death, it's all just speculation. That's what we do here, Jack. We try to discover where it is we have been on this small planet, and for God's sake, where it is we are going. We've learned that the Ark, such as it is, is only a piece of the grand puzzle that we someday hope to solve."

"Why me, Dr. Compton?"

"That's the real point, isn't it? Why you, why any of us? Because we were all meant to be here. From Gunnery Sergeant Campos, whom we buried yesterday, to the men we lost in that desert valley in Arizona, even to the small green man we have downstairs, we all belong to the history we uncover.

But you?" Niles chuckled and moved to the set of stairs and started down past the ancient Ark that rose six stories above the vault floor. He gained the bottom steps and then paced to the nearest chair and sat. He closed his eyes momentarily and waited for the major.

"Vague at best, Doctor," Jack said as he sat next to the director of Department 5656.

"This whole complex can be that way, Major."

"Tell me. Is the file on the Ararat mission closed, or was there follow-up done?"

"Major, you've been here a few weeks. You've seen our completed files. What do you think?"

"Okay, I'll bite. What happened to the colonel and the others?"

"Ah, the human side of the tale. Very good, Major. Let's see. Colonel Jessup Taylor, alias Mr. Bertram Bartles. A rather famous attorney in Denver, Colorado, I believe. Represented as a civilian jurist Major Marcus Reno, Custer's adjutant in the Seventh Cavalry in 1876, at the army's hearing into the Little Big Horn disaster. Got him acquitted, I believe, but with the admonishment in open court that Major Reno failed his commander in the field against hostile Indian tribes, although there was no dire deed that required a court-martial. Mr. Bartles died in 1927 at the age of eighty-seven years."

It seemed Collins had come to know the men he had read about and felt sad about learning the colonel's fate.

"Gray Dog, now that's a story. He eventually became the largest cattle breeder in the state of Oklahoma. He was funded by a private citizen who remained anonymous throughout the years until we discovered the source."

"I can imagine," Jack said, realizing that Colonel Thomas would never have abandoned his adoptive son.

"Gray Dog was accidentally killed in 1936 chasing down a band of rustlers. He fell from his horse at the ripe old age of seventy. He's buried with honors at the soldier's cemetery at Fort Sill, Oklahoma."

"The navy boys?"

"Steven Jackson committed suicide in 1919 after the accidental sinking of his latest test platform, the submarine S-23, off the coast of Maine, killing all twenty-eight men onboard. He couldn't live with himself after that. I guess he didn't take on all of his mentor's traits. Ericsson would have laughed it off and kept right on designing. But as you've read, young Captain Jackson wasn't built that way."

Jack reached out and picked up the battered old journal.

"We recovered it from the National Archives where Secretary of State Seward had hidden it those many years ago."

"The colonel and Madame Claire?"

"There is the big mystery. We never uncovered the alias as given to him by the Pinkerton Agency. But you may have noticed how tenacious Senator Lee can become when he is faced with a puzzle. He finds the answers, just as he did in the case of the mysterious Colonel John Henry Thomas, for whom we could find no records from the Department of the Army after his service in the department and territory of Oklahoma, in 1863."

"What became of him?" Jack actually needed to know.

Niles smiled as he faced the army major. "Jack, let me ask you this. Your family is steeped in military history, is it not?"

"Yes, mostly on my father's side."

"Yes, it's all in your file, with the exception of your mother's side of the family."

"That's because the last person to serve in the military was my mother's father in World War II. My mother was a hippie." Jack smiled. "My father, the polar opposite."

Niles smiled as he learned a little more about the man to whom he wished to turn over the Group's security. He waited for Collins to continue.

"There has always been a one-sidedness to our shared military history. On my mom's side we have virtually all pacifists, not a soldier mentality among them."

"Say, their priorities lie in other areas of endeavor?"

"To say the least, yes."

"What is your mother's maiden name, Major?"

Collins laughed as he turned away from Compton. "My mother always says she was teased about her last name and was happy when she took the married name of Collins." He turned back to face Niles. "It was Pennypacker."

Niles smiled as he saw Jack relax.

"Strange how genetics works its miracles, isn't it?"

"I'm not following you, Mr. Director."

"Your talent at soldiering. You assume it came from your father's side, when it actually stemmed from your mother's family."

"Excuse me?" Collins said, getting that special feeling when you know a punch to the chin is headed your way.

Niles opened the file he had carried into the vault and then smiled again.

"Here is the birth certificate for one Harold R. Pennypacker, born in 1871 to a Mr. and Mrs. John H. Pennypacker of San Bernardino County, California. Mr. Pennypacker's wife's name was Claire."

Jack felt his jaw drop open. "John Henry Pennypacker?"

"He's your great-great-grandfather, Jack." Niles cleared his throat. "The name he hated, just as your own mother did a hundred years later. John Henry, you see, ended up bringing water to the desert with his official office of county engineer. He was never recognized for who he really was. What he actually did for the nation."

Collins was stunned. He had heard of the engineer who brought water to the desert of San Bernardino and Riverside counties, but that was all he thought the man was.

"John Henry Thomas died in 1919 of a heart attack. He was preceded in death by Claire three years earlier. Both never spoke about their mission to Ararat or the men who had accompanied them to that mountain." Niles watched as the dawning of understanding wove its way across Jack's face. "We have known about you for years, Major, and have spent a lot of time following your career just out of pure curiosity. The subject of John Henry Thomas has occupied Garrison Lee's thoughts for sixty-plus years. When he heard you were to face the Senate hearings on mission failures in

Afghanistan, the senator moved heaven and earth to save you. That's why you're here, Major. We need you, just as Lincoln needed John Henry many, many years ago."

"I don't know what to say," Jack said as he turned away from Niles.

"Say you'll stay, Major. My people need protection, and according to your records, you're that man. Hell, according to your family history, you're that man. The Event Group needs Jack Collins, the great-great-grandson of John Henry Thomas. It's perfect and it's deserved. Come home, Jack."

Niles stood from his chair and then slapped Collins lightly on the arm with the Event Group numbered file. He smiled sadly and then left the vault.

Jack looked at the file and then to the journal meticulously kept by his distant relative. Then his gaze rose to the massive presence of the Ark and for the first time he felt he was a part of something. He slapped the folder into the palm of his hand and then retrieved the journal. He stepped up to the damaged and broken bow of Noah's creation and placed a hand upon the petrified surface. He closed his eyes as if he could speak to it, or maybe it was John Henry he wanted to feel. He looked up and smiled at the prize that had been delivered to the nation, only to fall prey to vicious politics.

Major Jack Collins smiled one last time as he removed his hand from the cursed and ancient Ark. He backed out of the vault and then made his way to his quarters on level seven.

The next morning, Jack had risen to eat and was on his way to report to Niles Compton when he was stopped by the diminutive geologist, specialist fifth class, Sarah McIntire, who greeted him with her ever-present smile. The young specialist seemed to be putting the mission to Chato's Crawl, Arizona behind her, as well as the loss of her best friend, Lisa Willing, or she was trouper enough to allow it safe storage as soldiers usually do.

"And why are you so spry this morning, Specialist?" Jack asked as she skipped for a moment and then realized Jack was still an officer. She settled in to walk beside him.

"Oh, Pete Golding asked if I wanted to observe our KH-11 satellite, Boris and Natasha, as they refuel and start her back up again."

"That's where I'm headed."

"Later I am getting on a plane with Mr. Everett for our little foray to Okinawa. It seems we have a date with a possible Chinese junk from the Khan Dynasty."

"Sounds thrilling," Jack said as he relaxed for the first time inside of Department 5656.

"So, tell me, Major, are you accepting Senator Lee and Director Compton's offer of gainful employment? I mean, if the scenario in Chato's Crawl bored you, I'm sure we can come up with something that won't. Possibly when you least expect it," Sarah said as she held the computer center's door open for him. He nodded his thanks and then before entering the center leaned over.

"I'll stay as long as you promise me one thing."

"Name it, Major."

"Never die on me, Specialist. I don't take that very well."

"Ah, we never die here, Major, we only join the collection."

Jack Collins, descendant of the man who brought back Noah's Ark, had made his decision to accept the position offered him by Lee and Compton.

The major figured it would be far safer than a front-line military unit. After all, how dangerous could looking for ancient artifacts truly be? He entered the computer center to the cheers of the technicians as the satellite known as Boris and Natasha flared to life a hundred and seventy-five miles above the Earth.

As Jack vanished behind the electronically tinted glass center, the dark shadows inside the deep corridors of the Event Group complex underneath the desert sands of Nellis Air Force Base were constantly held at bay by the bright fluorescent lighting that was always aglow inside Department 5656.

Some silly curses you just couldn't ignore.

Read on for an excerpt from the next book
by David L. Golemon

THE TRAVELER

Coming soon in hardcover from Thomas Dunne Books

THE WELLSIAN DOORWAY

"Expand the doorway, please gentlemen," Thompsen said as an assistant started passing out ear plugs. It was Himmler who raised a brow. "The sonic wave that assaults the inner ear can be rather uncomfortable without protection, Herr Reich-fuher." He nervously watched as the leader of the SS nodded his head only once.

Below the technicians were moving about excitedly as the doorway started to expand by hydraulic lines that allowed the stainless steel frame that was lined with ceramic tiles, designed to hold back the generated heat that would in turn protect the Traveler from being fried alive inside. The Wellsian Doorway was now six times the size it had been when the hydraulics expansion had started. A loud clang was heard as fifty technicians came through an expanded tunnel with an electric car pulling a long train of what looked like chain link. The entirety of the chain was one hundred feet in length and looked as if it went from one conductive coil to the next. Once the electric car was in place a remotely controlled arm started pulling the secured end of the chain up until the entire length was only a few feet from the concrete floor.

"All nonessential personnel clear the test area," came an announcement from below as the room was totally cleared with the exception of ten technicians who remained fixated on their consoles. "Connect the light accelerator."

Himmler stood from his seat and went to the window as he watched the most expensive piece of hardware ever developed by German science as it dangled off the floor. The chain itself was constructed out of a hard plastic material that had been 'weaved' together, forming a composite of nylon, copper and plastic to form a new element called Rylar, a composite manufacturing system originally regarded as years ahead of the curve in composite technology and would eventually fill the need in the aircraft industry for lightweight materials.

In this experiment the material would be used to control the tremendous amount of heat generated by the doorway. Interspaced at equal intervals along this chain was what made the proposition of displacement possible—industrial blue diamonds. Hard to come by diamonds that Himmler and his SS had spent two years collecting the world over. Stolen from museums that had been ransacked by the German army to raids on South African mining facilities. All together there were fifty-six five-ounce diamonds ensconced in the ceramic cocoon which resembled large, oblong pearls.

As the observers watched, the chain was moved to the very top of the expanded rectangle of the doorway. The robotic arm held it there by the manipulations of a trained technician. They heard loud humming as a bracket was lowered from the top of the doorway and the arm hooked the chain to it. Then the arm released that end and connected the opposite end. Now the large diamond ensconced chain was loosely hanging from the hook as the manipulating arm was moved away. The mood was silent as the robotic arm was moved and stored.

"Standby for charging of the system," Thompsen said into the intercom as a protective wall was raised below to protect the technicians at their controls. They would be shielded by the charging of the Doorway when a flood a neutrinos and charged particles of ion were introduced to the conductive chain. Thompsen could see that Himmler was wide-eyed as he watched. Even though he had seen film of the previous tests and its success he was still fascinated as he watched it live. For the success, or was it just the chance to watch one of his precious subjects lose their lives, Thompsen wasn't sure. "Herr Reichfuher, when the Doorway is fully charged, do not be alarmed when you feel a disorientation as it comes to full power. It acts as if it is an hallucinogen for some."

"Is it dangerous to us?" he asked as he once again took a seat to watch.

"Frankly Herr Reichfuher, we just don't know what any long term effects will be."

Himmler nodded. He really didn't care since the damnable technology would only be used once and for a singular purpose—his escape from the Russians and or the allies.

The lights throughout the complex dimmed as power was brought online. Five miles down the line, buried deeply underground was the three large rubber-encased conduit electrical lines that ran in from the Mohne Dam twenty-five miles away were heating up so much the rubber casing started sizzling.

"Preparing to charge," came the confident announcement from below. Thompsen, with a final look and nod from Himmler opened the intercom to the laboratory below. "Charge the Doorway!"

A piercing scream filled the airways around every man watching the test. Himmler forced his hands to his ears and then he quickly inserted the ear plugs that he had forgotten about. As the audio assault continued, one of the SS guards bent over and then went to his knees as he became violently ill. Himmler angrily nodded that the man should be removed and punished later for showing his weakness. "Pulse!" Thompsen said, hoping that the final charging of the doorway would also double Himmler over. But the small man held firm and only gritted his teeth at the onslaught of inner-ear sound.

Below, the charge of electricity burst into the chain and it stiffened to a straight line of two rows as electricity flowed through it.

Thompsen paced to the side of the Reichsführer and leaned down. "The magnets inside the door's frame will be charged and the chain, or what we call it the 'particle accelerator,' will conform to its designed structure.

Below, the final charge was sent through the accelerator and suddenly there was a bright explosion of light as the circular chain rounded and became taught as the force of the magnets inside the doorway distributed magnetism to equal parts of the chain which brought the expensive links to attention forming a perfect circle inside the rectangular doorway. As Himmler watched, the interior of the man-made circle started to shimmer. It was if an invisible wave moved the very air around inside the accelerator.

"We are forming a man-made current, just as if we have shot an arrow underwater, the particle accelerator has now forced ions into the doorway. We are seeing this shimmering simply because as of this moment the current and flow has no place to go or to lock onto, so to say, so the entire assault of our time and space remains contained in this laboratory. Start the revolution please."

Below, the magnets started to rotate and then faster and faster until there was nothing but a trail of blue light forming the brightest flare of light any of the men had ever been witnessed to. The RPM's increased as even more power from the Mohne Dam was used. The sheer power was pulsing energy into the surrounding air.

"We are now going to send our signal into the doorway." Thompsen again spoke into the intercom. "Go to full revolutions on the particle accelerator!"

Below, the circular chain of composite material, steel, plastic and ceramic was spinning at the speed of sound, which was bringing men to their knees. Himmler grimaced and took hold of the arms of his chairs to fight the nausea filling his throat.

A blue haze started to fill the interior of the accelerator as the RPM's continued to multiply. For three hundred kilometers around the Mohne Dam, lights dimmed and transformers blew in almost every town and city. Light bulbs and fixtures exploded inside the laboratory, making men duck and technicians smile as they felt the power of the very universe strike deep inside the landscape of Germany.

"Now we are near to the power we need," Thompsen said excitedly.

"For what, Herr Professor?"

"To make the connection to the dismantled gate of two years ago, Herr Reichführer."

God, Himmler thought to himself, this maniac may have actually produced a viable plan for the second most powerful man in Germany. "You may proceed as soon as you are ready."

"Bring in the Traveler," Thompsen said as his eyes went to a small doorway in the far wall as it opened and two white coated lab technicians escorted a frightened girl into the lab. She was emaciated to a point Himmler thought she would collapse.

"Our subject for the test is 12-year-old Moira Mendelsohn, she is from—,"

"I do not wish to know the Jew's name, or anything else about her for that matter, Professor."

"Yes, yes, of course. You have my apologies. Needless to say the Traveler tested at a one hundred forty-seven IQ. Her brother tested only a few points less. Thus far the Traveler has performed magnificently. Now with the guarantee of her return by her brother's very presence."

Himmler watched below as the thin and sickly girl was led to the front of the Doorway. They had already placed earphones on her small head to protect her from the audio assault element of the test. Her clothing was not anything special as Thompsen wanted the Reichsführer to see that nothing special outside of headphone protection was needed.

Her clothing was the same gray rags she had on when she

had been transferred from Bergen-Belsen a month before. All the observers could see the yellow Star of David badly stitched to her dress. The small scabs on her head from lice infestation from the camps were hidden as well as possible so as not to offend the sensitivities of Himmler, who was known for his weakened stomach when it came to observing the men, women and children he had so ruthlessly rounded up. He could talk a good game, but when it came to facing the things he did he was more on the shy side, according to British and American intelligence sources. The girl was shaking and crying. The task she was to perform had been explained to her and would be no different than the last test, which she performed flawlessly. To ensure the girl's cooperation, a small boy was also escorted into the room and placed in a chair. The doe-eyed male was no more than eight years of age.

"I was led to believe that there would only be one test subject," Himmler inquired as he saw the tears in both the boy's and the girl's eyes as they saw each other. It looked as if the girl tried to shrug the hand of the technician away in an attempt to see the small boy.

"The boy is not a test subject, Herr Reichsführer, he is what we would describe as insurance."

The dawning of understanding illuminated Himmler's features.

"After all, we do want certain guarantees that our wayward Traveler steps back into the first Doorway and returns, she does know this is the final test with her involvement. Soon after her usefulness is at an end she will be returned to Bergen-Belsen for . . . . ," he looked briefly at Himmler, "Whatever her fate will be."

No more needed to be said. Thompsen was proving he was as brutal as Himmler himself.

"Start the signal!" Thompsen cried excitedly.

The Doorway was acting like a centrifuge, so powerful in its rotation that the frightened girl shied away from the forces assaulting her. The technician patted the young girl on the shoulder and then stepped away. Suddenly a burst of sound penetrated the noise from below and held steady.

"Tone is sounding and is now in active search mode."

Himmler grimaced as the piercing sound of the signal assaulted his ears even through the earplugs. The girl went to her knees as the pain of the signal coupled with the spinning accelerator knocked the senses from her small body.

"We have signal bounce-back!"

Thompsen smiled as he knew the Doorways were talking to each other. The space between times had been breached.

"The Jew Einstein was right all along."

Thompsen smiled down at Himmler. That Jew, as he called him, was the most brilliant theorist Thompsen had ever studied. Himmler was a fool for chasing these people off like they had, science would not benefit from the action. He went to the intercom.

"Stand!" he said loudly. The girl looked up from her sitting position and looked back into the glass at the face of the man ordering her to stand. She started to rise but fell back.

"Perhaps you are not strong enough? Your brother perhaps is a better candidate?"

The girl shot a defiant look up at Thompsen. She angrily raised herself from the floor of the lab. With hatred still burning in her green eyes she finally turned and stared into the swirling bands of color that whirl pooled inside the Wellsian Doorway.

"Displacement Event 007 commencing at 0410 and fifteen seconds. Commence test."

With a last defiant look back at the observers, she looked over at her frightened brother and mouthed the words, I'll come back for you, and with that Moira Mendelsohn stepped into the hurricane force of the Doorway.